All the Son

By El(

The bodies that occupy the celestial vault,

These give rise to wise men's uncertainties;

Take care not to lose your grip on the thread of wisdom,

Since the Powers That Be themselves are in a spin.

The cycle which includes our coming and going

Has no discernible beginning nor end;

Nobody has got this matter straight-

Where we come from and where we go to.

The Ruba'iyat of Omar Khayyam

Dedication

To Cheryl, James, Abby and Georgia, for all their love, understanding and support, without which this could never have been done.

1. The Interview

"Fair point, so how have you found Paris?" Alex Bell looked up from his overpriced plate of fish and chips and figured that the easy part of the interview was pretty much finished.

"Well..." he paused as he replaced his carefully nursed gin and tonic back on the table. "I can say now that it's been worth the struggle as we've all really adapted to the Parisian lifestyle, but the first few months were a bit of a nightmare really."

"Is that right?" Barma paused before adding, "Well the French are pretty stuck up themselves aren't they?"

Alex considered this for a moment. "Well the 'Baysaybayjay' can get on your nerves." The French pronunciation was exaggerated.

"Baysaybayjay?" Barma had already admitted to Alex that he didn't speak a word of French. Dressed in a sombre dark suit, pristine white shirt and silk Hermes tie, he was the complete item for life in the City.

"Sorry, BCBG. It stands for *bon chic, bon genre*, French Sloane's basically."

"Yes, I can imagine, it's quite different from here isn't it?" The reply came in his now familiar deep mid-Atlantic tones and Alex still couldn't quite figure out if he was American or British. Several years at various US investment banks had given Chris Barma the stereotypical banking executive's accent. The slow emphasis on the first word of his reply suggested to Alex, that Barma was the recent victim of some sort of management course on listening.

Alex's head sympathetically bobbed in agreement.

Barma continued, "And you know, the weather here in London is always pretty grim", he grinned with a pitch of his head in the direction of the grey shaft of light, watery through the window. "I'm looking forward to getting back to the warmth."

Alex picked up his glass and drained the remainder of his drink. "Yeah, it's pretty bad here. I guess that nobody talks much about the weather there." Alex's face brightened, "I guess the easiest job of all out there must be being the TV weather man, `Sun again folks!'", he waited for Barma to acknowledge his humour.

Barma looked a little confused but then he politely obliged and broke into a wide smile, "Yeah…" he growled out in a low drawn out laugh. "You know, it's in the mid twenties right now, just about perfect." He kept on smiling, his big frame shaking as he chuckled. He examined Alex up and down for a moment, "Say, do you play tennis Alex?"

"Yes, but not that well, I prefer squash." His answer was calculatedly off-hand but Alex quite fancied himself as a sportsman, he had been quite useful in his youth but at 34 he was now past his prime, hair thinning and a little heftier than he would have liked but, even so, he was still in reasonably good shape.

"Want another drink?" Barma enquired, as the waiter removed the plates from the table. Alex looked down and saw that the other man hadn't even finished his Evian. The waiter hesitated for a moment and looked on with studied disinterest.

"No, I'm fine thanks", he lied. He could easily have had a beer or a glass of wine but as the other man hadn't joined him with his gin and tonic, he didn't want to look like some inebriate. This caution was well placed. In his own words, Alex would describe himself as an enthusiastic social drinker. He could quite happily down a bottle of wine by himself with the right company. He rightly judged that now, Barma was not such company, much less such a formal setting as this. It was after all, a job interview. In the hanging silence that now followed the waiter, who had been politely adjusting the table settings delicately broke in and enquired, "Gentlemen, Would you like to see the menu for some dessert?"

There was a brief pause as Barma looked at the waiter and replied. "Yeah, that'll be great", he smiled at the willowy waiter who discreetly nodded and turned to fetch the menus. "You know that was a great idea of yours to come here."

"I'm glad you like it. I've always enjoyed Langan's, though it can get a bit rowdy in here sometimes."

Alex suddenly heartily regretted saying this as it drew attention to the fact that they were one of only four tables occupied out of around thirty or more in the restaurant. The place had slowly emptied during the course of their meal and he inwardly winced now that Barma was peering around the room. "Mind you I haven't been here for a couple of years" he added suddenly in perplexed after thought, not entirely sure it had been his idea in the first place.

The waiter came back with the menus, placed them in front of the two men and left them to continue their conversation. They carried on their discussion, their talk only discernable as a low counter-pointed drone to anyone just a few meters away. The waiter discreetly watched them, but aside of their conspiratorial whispers, there was nothing remarkable in the two of them. He had observed many such conversations in his time at the restaurant, these business types bored him. He much preferred the famous footballers or actors that periodically showed up, they at least might exchange a few words or offer a glimpse of the next tabloid headline. Much more interesting than these two expense account jockeys. The waiter looked at his wristwatch, still the evening shift and a Thursday too, to get through he thought. His features darkened for an instant as he looked over towards where his manager was seated. The boss was sitting hunched over a table, his thick fingers flicking expertly through invoices. A sixth sense guided him into practised activity just as the seated man started to look up. The waiter hurriedly proceeded to tidy up a place setting nearby, maintaining the sense of quiet busy efficiency so essential to the restaurant manager.

Barma gave Alex an intense look, "So if you had to describe yourself in one word Alex, what would that be?"

Alex' features clouded, how he hated these stupid types of questions. His mind raced ahead, what should he say; ambitious, hardworking, intelligent, professional, funny, complex, thoughtful, aggressive, loving, passionate, athletic, driven, son, father? None worked, for each confined him and excluded the other. It was an idiotic question. "Alive" he blurted out.

Barma broke into a big grin, he had good teeth. "Alive, not exactly a unique quality is it?"

"It's a tricky question."

Barma thought for a moment and then leant forward in his seat, "So Alex, tell me, what are your thoughts?"

Alex looked Chris Barma straight back and returned the gaze as steadily as the big man. It was almost too good to be true. This was a great opportunity no doubt at all. He, like most people, had been somewhat taken aback when he had first met this imposing man. After all, there weren't many six foot four inch tall, black men running trading desks in the City, but then again, he reassured himself, there was nothing like, "Prop Trading" to expose incompetence.

Proprietary or "Prop" trading is when a Bank takes positions in the market on for its own account. It is considered the most risky activity that a bank can take on. Only the most competent and trusted individuals are let loose on the Banks own account. This guy had worked for some of the premier names on Wall Street before IAB. Alex figured he had to be pretty damn good to have worked for some of the best of them on the 'Street'.

Alex paused but there was no hesitation in his voice. "It sounds like a great opportunity. I'd love to be part of it"

Barma smiled and reset himself back in his chair.

"Great, you're gonna love it I'm sure." Picking up the menu, he glanced at it and dropped it back on the table. His tone was now much lighter, "Fancy some dessert?"

Alex hesitated and considered his waistline. "No thanks, just some coffee will be fine." He suddenly felt elated.

As the tension subsided, his mind started gently tip-toeing into in a sea of dollar signs. It lasted only a moment as he caught himself before being carried away in its satisfied current. Rousing himself from this reverie, the deal now safely settled, he decided to lighten the conversation and give himself the time to collect himself. "So Chris, how do you find living in Jeddah?"

It wasn't his best conversational gambit, but it was enough to tide the two men over.

The big man, his bald pate shining like a bowling ball, leant back in his chair and folded his arms. Barma clearly spent a lot of time working out; his biceps bulged under his shirt. Just at that moment he reminded Alex of some kind of James Bond villain, all he needed was one of those mechanical hands or a set of metal teeth. He drove the thought from his mind before an inopportune chuckle could emerge.

"I enjoy it, it's peaceful and I can just kick back and relax, chill out you know?" He smiled broadly and continued speaking. "It's a great place to raise a family you know?" His mixture of Yank expressions with English accent was still just ever so slightly disarming. "You have how many kids?"

Alex smiled and finally rid himself from the Bond imagery, "Err, three boys."

"Great! Kids really love all the sunshine and everything. What age are they?"

He had to think for a second before answering, "Seven, five and just three."

Barma gave one of his smiling nods that Bell was starting to recognize as a particular characteristic of his potential future boss. "Sounds good"

The two men drank their coffee and the last details of the job offer were dealt with. There were no surprises in store. It was the usual ex-pat package and pretty much what he'd been expecting after several previous phone interviews with Barma. Chris Barma unobtrusively glanced at his watch. It had been another successful lunch. He let out a silent sigh of relief, four final interviews in the last four days and they had all gone as planned, though he was getting tired of eating at Langan's. Alex Bell hadn't been Barma's first choice but he'd thoroughly checked him out, technically strong and clearly ambitious the only doubt was how he was going to fit in with the others. This interview had settled that concern for him, Bell was an open book to him and there were no serious flaws he couldn't deal with. Admittedly the pretentious dropping in of French words was a bit annoying, but still, he seemed manageable. Above all, Barma didn't want any big egos on his team and this man's was about the right size. Barma knew exactly what he was looking for and wanted in the team he was carefully building. Bell would be fine, an obvious team player but with his own unique skill set, it should be a nice fit. He leant back into his seat, assured that his cardinal rule was not threatened, it was not. He remained the undisputed captain of his team.

Satisfied, he turned towards the waiter and made a little gesture of writing in the air. The sacerdotal server acknowledged the movement and went to make out the final bill.

"Of course there's an interview you need to do with the management back in Jeddah, but it's pretty much a formality". He smiled, "They could say no, but I'd be pretty pissed off". He laughed a little half ironic noise and his intense look now suggested that nobody would ever dare to piss him off. "I'll have my secretary organize it all."

Barma signed the bill and the two men moved to the coat check, he towered over the five ten of Alex. They then took their overcoats from the pretty blonde behind the counter and each dropped a couple of pound coins into the saucer that held tips. The waiter stepped up opened the door for them. Barma put on a hat, a dark Fedora which he pulled firmly onto his shining head.

Alex looked a little quizzically at him.

"Can't stand being cold." He stated as a matter of fact.

"Thank you very much sir, see you again?" To Alex, the warm smile of the portly manager indicated that Barma's tip had been more than generous.

"I'm sure you will." said Barma with a quick conspiratorial wink.

The two men stepped into the dank London air. The December drizzle was still spitting in ill tempered squalls. It was a typical winter afternoon and the reflections of the two black London taxi's that were waiting for fares, shimmered on the wet flagstones along with the glowing yellow light from the warm restaurant they had just stepped out from.

Barma adjusted his thick dark overcoat over his beautifully tailored suit before opening the cab door. "So, when are you back in Paris then?"

"The week after New Year."

"Want a lift anywhere?"

"No thanks, I think I need to do some shopping, my wife wants some stuff." Bell did need to do some last minute shopping, but it also seemed a nice way of making his exit. It had been a taxing exercise and he felt he was almost visibly wilting. Besides, he wanted to be alone for a moment to do a few laps in that pool of dollars that was now sloshing around his head.

"Fine," Barma got into the taxi, he pulled at the window, it was slightly jammed and he struggled to move it. For an instant Bell thought he might pull the door off and the cab appeared to be ever so slightly rocking. The Bond baddie imagery returned for an instant. The cab driver turned round, alarmed at Barma's efforts.

"Oi it's locked mate! Push the latch on the side."

Barma looked and saw the offending mechanism, he pushed it just as the driver had suggested and then eased the window down. The cabby's face was visibly relieved as he realized that his door was now safe. "See you in Jeddah Alex and a Merry Christmas."

"Bye Chris, same to you and a Happy New Year."

Chris Barma waved back at Alex as the taxi pulled away.

"Yup here's to great 1997." Alex thought to himself as he returned the gesture to the departing cab.

The taxi pulled away down Stratton Street and turned left into Piccadilly. He hesitated as he considered taking a taxi as well but decided against it and slowly ambled down the street towards the busy traffic running along Piccadilly. The rain was falling quite heavily now and blew horizontally into his face, reddening it with the vigour of sandpaper. The light had almost entirely faded and he wrapped his overcoat tighter around himself by pushing his hands deeper into his pockets. Despite the falling temperature he wasn't really feeling the cold. He was warmed, by the cosy blanket of dollar bills that had slowly materialized around him and was now insulating him against the icy gusts that were blowing onto all the other windswept shoppers as they hurried along beside him.

2. Paris Profit and Loss

Three weeks later and Alex was back in Paris. Despite attempts at restraint, he was a few pounds heavier after the usual Christmas and New Year excesses. The winter morning light was just breaking through the curtains into his bedroom on the third floor of his apartment block. He was washed and nearly fully dressed because his son had been playing noisily since six o'clock and his boisterous activity had made his alarm redundant for some months. Today he had been awoken by train and car noises from the youngster. Alex was just fixing his tie in the mirror as the phone by the bedside rang out. He stepped a little clumsily between his sons scattered toys.

"Daddy, get off Annie and Clarabelle!" the boy squealed.

"Mr Bell?" The line was really terrible, the voice sounded faint and crackly on the line.

"Yes, speaking."

"This is Saleem from the office of Mister Chris in Jeddah."

"Get off Annie." David Bell, aged three was not happy that his Dad was apparently making no effort whatsoever to get off his wooden train track.

"I need to send..." The line was heavy with static noise and David was now repeating his cry.

"David!" Alex's voice was harsh and the little boy blinked animatedly and looked wide eyed at his father, "can't you see I'm on the phone". Tears started to well up in the boy's eyes. Alex rarely raised his voice to his kids. He sat down on the bed and hunched himself up over the handset and tried to listen.

"I'm sorry Mr. Saleem, I can't quite hear you. Please could you repeat what you just said"

The handset crackled. "I ..." inaudible, "... a fax"

"You want to send me a fax?" he best guessed through the static.

"Yes, from Mr. Chris, do you..." the line again broke up into an electric haze and David was now crying loudly with all the righteousness of a wronged toddler.

He covered the phone with his hand and bellowed. "Claire..." he waited for the reply from the kitchen and put the receiver back to his ear, he could just make out the scratchy voice was now calling his name.

"Can you hear me Mr. Bell?"

"Yes, just about, the line is very bad." Alex replied slowly and loudly. Years of talking on atrocious phone lines to remote parts of the globe had taught him to speak, when needed, like a language course tape. He had found that it was easier than repeating himself every ten seconds.

He covered the mouthpiece a second time and called his wife's name out even louder than before.

Claire Bell was already peering round the bedroom door. Her normally sleek, shoulder length chestnut brown hair was unruly with the morning's chores.

"Yes, what is it?" She spoke the words sharply then checked herself as she recognized the scene. She knelt, down picked up Thomas the Tank Engine and the toy carriages which were now beside Bell's feet and reached out for her son's hand.

"C'mon David, your Dad's on the phone and your breakfast is ready. It's your favourite." Her face brightened and the words were spoken in coddling enthusiasm, like a kids' TV presenter.

The boy stopped crying just as soon as he had started, stood up, bleary eyed and left the room to the sound of diminishing little hurtful breaths.

Alex smiled wanly at his wife and made a facial expression to express gratefulness, all the while listening intently to the crackling phone line. At last he understood what the voice on the line was saying.

"Yes, you can use the same number as this to send a fax."

Mother and son left the bedroom together and he was able to finish his phone call in relative peace.

Ten minutes later he stepped into the bright light of the kitchen; in his hand was a scroll of shiny paper. He held it up to show his wife, he had been waiting more than a fortnight for this fax and now it was here at last. He was both relieved and excited, though since half the document was written in Arabic, a large part of it was meaningless to him. The front page informed that the fax was 8 pages long. He looked at the missive and realized it was missing the last two pages. They'd probably have to resend the whole thing.

Claire looked at her husband and her heart sank a little further, she looked back down at the table and feverishly buttered a slice of toast. "Saudi bound?" Her voice was strained.

Ever since he had first mentioned the possibility of working in the Middle-East, Claire had been on a slow but downward spiral. She had not liked Paris when they had first arrived but after three years, she had again tirelessly rebuilt their social circle. Despite her earlier doubts, some of this ever widening social whirl had now become very close friends. She looked at the children who sat in their pyjamas happily munching jam covered toast. The thought of having to go through the whole process of packing up home and making new friends, not to mention settling the boys back into new schools was not one that she relished.

The phone rang again and she moved with practised ease across the room to pick up the handset. The high pitched warbling signalled an incoming fax and she hung up the line as their fax machine cut in.

"Another fax is coming" her tone was flat. She studied her husband with her grey blue eyes, waiting for him to respond.

"Yes it looks like the first was a bit messed up. Look darling, I still haven't made up my mind, you know." He gave her a reassuring look. "I really will check out what it's like there. You know that don't you?" Alex was trying to sound as convincing as possible, but deep inside both of them knew that the decision had probably been made. Nothing had been signed, he kept reminding her, yet.

"I know." She smiled and tried to look pleased, but her eyes told another story. "So Alex, when are you going?"

He looked through the pages and found an itinerary.

"I'll leave Friday, they work Saturday and Sunday so I'll be back by Tuesday morning latest."

"You will be here for Anthony's birthday won't you?" Her voice turned a little accusatory.

"Of course, I will." And he gave her a rueful look. "I'd never miss a birthday" he looked at his wristwatch. "Look I've got to go, I'm late. I'll call you from work, OK?" he moved forward and kissed his wife on the forehead. Then he kissed each of his sons, stepped out of the kitchen and picked up his briefcase that was sitting in the hallway.

Claire called out from the cheerful clattering din of the kitchen, "Aren't you going to wait for the fax?"

19

Alex was still fiddling with his thick overcoat and sports bag, paused. "Err...Oh yes I nearly forgot about that." His feigned casual tone fooled neither of them.

"Don't forget we've dinner with Pat and Eileen this evening"

"I haven't, I'm playing Pat at the club tonight and we'll meet you at the restaurant, OK?"

A few minutes later, eight shiny pages of fax paper were neatly folded in his pocket. Covered in official stamps and signatures, they confirmed visa requirements, an invitation to visit Jeddah with contact address for the Saudi consulate in Neuilly to the west of Paris, and details for where he could pick up the plane tickets at the airport.

As he stepped out of his apartment Claire called out again, her head craning round into the hallway. "Don't forget, 8 o'clock at Lucas Carton and don't be late!"

"I won't" he hollered back and he pushed close the heavy front door of their apartment behind him.

Alex re-read the faxes more thoroughly on the Metro to work. Three of the pages were written in Arabic and he had no idea what they said though they were all intended for the consulate. There was a map and two short letters written on IAB headed paper. The first was from Chris Barma, with a list of people he was to see in the bank. The second letter was a more formal invitation. This was illegibly signed by someone named Ed Moore, with the title of Treasurer.

As he sat on the train and it pulled through Harve-Caumartin and onwards towards his offices in the 9th arrondissement he wondered how much he would miss this life he had in Paris. There were parts that were good and he mentally checked them off. The apartment he lived in was lovely. The restaurants were great. His daily commute was mercifully short. There were easy weekend breaks to places like Deauville and Giverny which were both diverting and pleasant. Then there were the bad things. He shut his mind to the worst of them and thought of work. His move from London to Paris had been a bit of a misfire. Despite its plans, Banque Paris was not as aggressive or ambitious as he had been led to think when he had been coaxed to join them from Salomons, a huge US investment bank. His boss, Alain Bicholot, aged 46, had collapsed with a minor but devastating heart attack eight months earlier and was now simply one of the walking wounded of the corporate battlefield. Bicholot's position, and by implication so now too Alex' team, was being increasingly marginalized by further Machiavellian corporate wrangling. In short the big payout promised him had not materialized and as he kept telling himself, it was high time to make up for lost time. Saudi Arabia promised much, its tax free earnings, stress free ex-pat lifestyle and the balance sheet of the largest bank in the Middle-East, was a quick and easy way to make up for the three lost years.

After bouncing up the steps to street level at Metro Cadet he stopped, exchanged his habitual pleasantries with the ruddy cheeked newsvendor and bought his usual copy of the International Herald Tribune. He quickly scanned the front page and then strode purposely over to the small café where he would take his morning coffee. As he sipped his Double Espresso he checked his phone, which mutely indicated that he had missed a call whilst riding the Metro. He dialled and listened intently to the message whilst simultaneously scanning and turning the pages of the newspaper. It was Osama Mounima, an old friend and former boss from his Saloman days. He had asked for and been given some impartial advice and Osama had also obligingly made a few discreet enquiries into the IAB setup. Osama was Lebanese, though he had lived most of his life in Europe or the US. He was as at home in Princeton, where he'd been a grad student as he was in London, Lugano or back in the Levant. Presently he was based in Switzerland and was the epitome of the discreet Private Banker. Charming, suave, erudite and with a passion for good Bordeaux and *Habanos*, he remained one of the few men that Alex still really admired and more importantly, trusted. As Alex' first boss he had been helpful and had always offered colourful pithy one-liners, hilarious mixed metaphors and anecdotes. He remembered them all, like when Alex had lost money on a trade on the back of a recommendation of a broker.

"Bears make money, Bulls make money, but sheep get slaughtered. Never follow the herd" and another time when a price offered by a counterparty was particularly bad. "That's slatherass garbage, your bid is lower than the belly of a snake" and he would put the phone down and grin and wink to the others on the desk.

Given Osama's contacts in the region, he had asked him for a background check on both Barma and IAB itself. Osama had done this for him and everything had come back as advertised. There was not much to say about Barma, but he had checked out the bank pretty closely. It was definitely the largest in the region, though still privately owned by a secretive Saudi family, the Bin Bafaz', who had increasingly moved into the background, leaving day to day management to imported professionals.

He carefully listened to the recorded message a second time, his old friend's voice, familiar though metallic sounding on the playback of his handset, again informed him that all was seemingly well with their offer. It was reassuring to hear. Osama also asked him if to look up a friend of his in Jeddah once he was there and wished him a safe trip. Alex took a mental note of the name and saved the message on his voicemail before wandering into his office.

He pushed past through the glass doors and took the lift up to his floor. He walked briskly and with a purposeful vigour through the office, giving the requisite polite salutations to the three beady eyed receptionists, who returned to their chirruping conspiratorial chatter. Ordinarily their arched brows and would you believe it looks would not have bothered him, today it did and this concern was not misplaced. As he walked in he thought he could hear something break in the men's washroom. He hoped that it was simply the grumpy Algerian cleaner having another bad day as he strode over to his desk.

The room was half empty, 7:30 in Paris was still very early and none of the analysts or support staff was yet in. Unlike London with its huge trading floors and one hour handicap, Banque Paris had a number of cramped floors in the renovated and modernised Haussmann building that was home to its Investment Banking group. His group, FX and Debt Capital Markets was located on the third floor, Equities were on the fourth and fifth. Management was at the top both figuratively and literally.

Alex sat down and removed the yellow Post-It note from his screen informing him that Sandrine Giraud had called for him last evening at 6 pm.

"Check out your email Alex"

Jean-Marc spoke with rising bitterness and eyed Alex unswervingly as he sat down next to him.

"Why, what's happened now?"

"Just read it, its fucking crazy"

Alex flicked on his computer and browsed through his inbox, scanning quickly through emails until his eyes stopped on the rarely seen name of the head of Capital Markets, Christophe Blanc. He opened the email and read the electronic missive. Twice.

"You know what this means Alex?" Alex turned towards Jean-Marc and rolled his eyes upward in tired frustration, his mouth clamped shut over his gritted teeth.

Jean-Marc muttered foul curses under his breath in French.

Alex understood immediately what the email meant. The message was simple and banal, but utterly devastating.

"How much have they dropped?" asked Alex.

"Does it matter?"

"Fuck me!" Alex looked at the computer screen numbly. He spoke softly with his head slowly shaking in disbelief. "Shit... and now Alain's reporting to Altenburg, that's us totally screwed."

"It just means our bonuses are fucked." He was watching the door to the men's bathroom to see when Willi might come out.

Alex took the news badly but not like Willi Spethmen their options trader who had left to collect himself from his incandescent rage. Spethmen had amassed the biggest profits and his personal loss was going to be much the greatest.

The huge German, over six foot six, ranged into the room with eyes that were blazing with anger. He stood behind his seat on the opposite side of the dealing desk to Alex; his voice was breaking with emotion.

"The wrong side in Crude, Gas, and something called Heating Fucking Oil" he laughed mirthlessly before continuing reading from a piece of paper he held out in front of him.

"All against something called Enron" he threw the paper down onto his desk with furious disgust. "What the fuck does a bank know about energy markets? Can anyone please tell me?" he looked around the small dealing room, but all eyes averted his gaze. He kicked his chair which spun out into the room. "Why are we even involved in this shit?"

"Look calm down Willi." Jean-Marc stretched out his arms, palms up in an almost religious act of supplication.

"Are you fucking crazy? It's OK for you to say that. You guys were only up for a couple of hundred each. This was my big fucking payday. Remember?" He banged his forefinger repeatedly into the side of his head.

"Look maybe Alain will be able to swing it for us." Even Jean-Marc knew this was remote in the extreme. The

German's eyes lit up even further at the mention of Alain Bicholot's name.

"Are you kidding me? The Arse hates fucking Alain and he's all washed up now anyway. The Equity boys will take what's left after our P&L has been used to offset some of these fucker's losses in New York and we'll get fuck all. No, I'm totally fucked.

Willi starting to pick up pieces of paper from his desk and shoved them roughly into his shoulder bag. "Tell you what I'm going to fucking do, I'm going to join this fucking Enron, maybe they need somebody who can trade FX." He then picked up the remainder of his belongings and walked out of the dealing room.

Jean-Marc and Alex looked at each other with expressions of bafflement giving way slowly to dawning realisation of their situation. Their bonuses now would be arbitrarily doled out by Herve "The Arse" Altenburg. He and Bicholot's rivalry was legendary in the corridors of Banque Paris, now it had been resolved.

Jean-Marc Sevres eyed Alex coldly with a quizzical squint. "Well Alex, you seem remarkably cool about this news, did you know about it before?"

Surprised at the accusation he replied a little too defensively, "No. Not at all", but the truth was that Alex was indeed much less concerned than he had shown.

Naturally none of them, even the distraught Willi, resigned on the spot that day. Despite the fact that their bonuses were now most likely only going to be nominal, they would all wait for the actual day, which was slated for the first week in February and see what would happen. However, each had in turn decided to make a move. Some, like Alex, were already well on the way to new pastures and most likely, though he had no way of knowing, so were the rest of Bicholot's trading group.

3. L'Affaire Ordinaire

Of course for Alex the decision to move from Paris was not just a question of wanting to coin a small fortune as fast as possible. Admittedly the money was a powerful incentive but there were other factors to weigh. Firstly there was the reality of his job in Paris. It was not remotely what he had hoped it would be when he took it on nearly three years previously. The fact was that being French in a French bank counted big time. It wasn't like the Germans, Deutsche Bank now held their board meetings in English and had a multitude of nationalities as directors. As far as Alex could see, this was a completely inconceivable event in the case of Banque Paris, despite their well publicized global ambitions. The fact was that there was not a single non-Frenchman on the board of the bank, furthermore being Anglo-Saxon with a dash of American influence as Alex was, almost certainly counted as an even greater handicap to his future career progression within the mighty French institution. Subsequently his career was slowly descending to what the French disparagingly call *Metro-Boulot-Dodo*. This Gallic daily grind and the fact that the years in Paris had been much less lucrative than London were however not the only reasons for his wanting to leave the City of Lights. His personal life was not uncomplicated.

For the most part, married life had been good to Alex and like most couples who'd known each other for more than a fair few years they had had their share of ups and downs. The arrival in neat planned stages of the three boys had kept them both busy with the hiatus of a young family. But Alex' decision to move to Paris at the insistence of his dynamic French boss, who wanted to move his entire trading team to his old student stomping grounds, had put additional stress on their relationship. Initially Claire had slowly simmered with resentment at the upheaval of their move to Paris from London. It was predicated by the usual modern woman's dilemma. Having given up work as a marketing executive in a drugs company to have the kids, she still, not unreasonably, periodically hankered for her independence. Bright, articulate and good looking, her own sense of self worth, that earning her own money gave, as well as the social structure and her peer's respect had been removed. It was difficult and whilst she absolutely loved being a mother, Alex's move to Paris had only focused and magnified her dependent status. It was this that she really resented.

Nevertheless the decision that Claire should become a full-time Mum had been one they had both emphatically agreed to. Both were committed to the idea that their children should be raised by themselves rather than by a stranger. Both the expensive Norland Nanny stand-in and the cheaper Eastern European language student option were looked into, considered and rejected. The first promised a dim-witted Sloane with an overbearing coercive nature, the other required qualifications in psychological counselling and ex-boyfriend management. They had witnesses both first hand amongst their friends.

Alex had promised Claire that she would not lack for creature comforts and for the most part he had held to his side of the bargain, his earnings increasing the next few years to well beyond the loss of Claire's salary. However they had not anticipated that in order for him to continue to keep his side of the agreement that he would end up having to follow his boss to wherever he should want to go. Presciently and increasingly irritatingly as far as Alex was concerned, her forecast that his move would not turn out to be a good one for his career ran from concept to reality. At the time Alex was equally convinced that the crossing of the *Manche,* was hardly the Rubicon and would represent no major hindrance to his rising career. As the months had rolled by he had been proved wrong and Claire had not been backward in reminding him of her foresight. Frustratingly, his resolute stubbornness to recognize her accurate prognosis had in turn increasingly irked her. Consequently Claire had decided that the best strategy to push him to return to London would be to live life to the fullest, to entertain lavishly and to take as many expensive holidays as possible. The diminishing bank balance would force her husband to go back to London.

So it was that during the previous summer, what had started as a drunken liaison in a nightclub four months earlier was quickly spiralling out of his control. He'd read Bonfire of the Vanities and seen Fatal Attraction and had promised himself he would never end up in the same position as either Sherman McCoy of the former or the hapless Michael Douglas character of the latter. However this was proving to be easier said than done. Sandrine had seemed a harmless and exciting diversion, now she was rapidly turning into his potential nemesis.

He remembered the Wednesday night in August that they met. Josie's was a bit of a dive as far as he knew but the seedy nightclub had the main advantage of being quite near to his work. It was hard to recall the exact series of events that led to their meeting. He had stayed out later than normal after meeting up with a couple of his friends, unlike when they had been in London, the team now virtually never went out together anymore. More kids and fewer dollars in bonuses made the group he had come over from London less fun and more divided. Feeling quite drunk he had decided to go home but since his wife and family had gone to England for the month of August, it being a particularly torrid summer in the city that year, he asked the cab driver to drop him at the nearest bar for yet another quite unnecessary beer.

Claire had deserted the sweltering city much as most of its inhabitants did each year, for less airless and more parochial surroundings. Parisians vacate the city to make their annual pilgrimage South via the *Autoroute du Soleil*, their beautiful city is then filled with hapless tourists who sweat and push each other around the *Musees* and *Places* until the *R'entrée* commences in the first week of September. Lunch with her determinedly expanding circle of friends in the Hotel Costes or Cafe Marly had taught Clair that to be in Paris over the summer was not something to be caught safely doing. They had spent July down on the Riviera, renting a villa near Cap D'Ail consuming meaningful chunks of next year's bonus and topped up with chilled Bandol and Veuve Clicquot. They visited friends, some of whom had rich parents that had retired to the warmth of the Cote D'Azur and who sat and drank gin and tonics in the shade of the Monaco high rises, the notorious sunny place for shady people. She and the kids then spent the remainder of the summer back in England renting a house on the Isle of Wight keeping up friendships with their old circle of London based friends. So Alex found himself sitting at a bar with no pressing need to get home, when Sandrine stepped up and ordered a vodka and orange. He couldn't remember the opening line, whether it was him or her that spoke first and it was something they would tease each other with, claiming the other had started their affair and disturbed each their own happy domesticity. However it happened, the conversation kicked off and jogged along quite easily. Alex spoke in his heavily accented, idiosyncratic and tipsy French, she periodically bent laughing at the weird turns of phrase he would contrive and he struggling with her slang as the music blared out white noise in the background. Surreptitious little glances at rings on fingers and subtle questioning established that they were both married, and as the warm fuggy night turned to early summer dawn their conversation idled from the flirtatious to the teasingly desultory and back again. She had lived in Paris but was now living in the somewhere in the *Banlieu*. She told him that she was married to a policeman. Her occasional swearing and earthiness suggested to Alex a little risqué roughness to her well shaped edges. Not conventionally pretty, her eyes were set just a little too close together for that, Sandrine had bleached blonde hair, a generous full mouth and a free and easy smile. However what anyone, including Alex even in his myopic beer goggles, could see was that she had an absolutely stunning figure, which her black clingy low cut dress emphasized beautifully. She was part of a group of office workers who were celebrating somebody's birthday. It seemed that they had all departed.

They talked in the night club, knees consciously touching, until throwing out time, which was around four in the morning. Stumbling out into cool night air they were drawn like moths into the bright lights of an all night cafe that beckoned to them further down the street. Hunched at the counter, Alex chatted animatedly to her, whilst the man behind the counter cleaned glasses in a scene reminiscent of Hopper's Nighthawks. By the time Alex invited Sandrine back to his apartment it was past seven in the morning. He remembered kissing her in the tiny two man lift that took them up to third floor and being taken aback by the force with which she responded to him. Her arms pulled at him and her breath broke into short excited snorts and he felt the unmistakable thrust of her hips into him which confirmed her knowledge of his desire for her. As they reached the third floor and Alex opened the lift doors, he was sufficiently sober to be concerned that the *Gardienne* or one of his neighbours might see him, whilst sufficiently drunk not to care. He was lucky, nobody was about and he quickly opened the door to his spacious apartment and they entered it unobserved.

Once inside, they were again self conscious and briefly embarrassed by their illicit meeting and quietly excited by their shared guilt. Sandrine walked around the reception rooms and acquainted herself with the layout of the apartment. Alex could hear the sharp deliberate tap of her stiletto heels on the wooden parquet flooring and the occasional murmuring of complementary noises at various bibelots and small objet d'art that his soon to be wronged wife had gathered. Whilst she sashayed through the rooms Alex moved into the kitchen and hastily boiled up some water and called out to ask how she would like her coffee.

"Belle appartement"

She stood at the doorway and was looking at Alex with the smokiest look she could impart, a Venerean glint in her eyes, lips half pouting, half smiling and slightly bent forward with her shoulders thrown back and showing off her ample cleavage. She was teasing him and he responded. Alex stepped forward and pulled her gently towards him and he kissed her lightly, she gave him the merest of smiles and then pulled him forward with his half undone tie and kissed him with sudden passionate intensity. Still slightly overawed he reached tentatively around her drawing her more tightly and ran his fingers down her back, down towards the base of her spine. She responded eagerly to his touch, tilting neck and grinding herself against him, inviting him to explore her and cup her taunt rear in his firm grasp. He grabbed her right cheek roughly, forcing her towards him and her body answered as she swayed her hips, grinding her mound into his now rampant manhood. Their breathing had turned to short breathless snorts and he could feel her rising heat, which intoxicated his already drunken mind with a raging carnal desire that overtook all his senses.

He started clumsily to reach for the zip of her dress and suddenly pulled back, her voice now soft and breathy. She gave him deliciously wicked smile "You want me Alex?"

"Yes, yes" His French now reduced to breathless monosyllabics.

In an instant she had twisted her shoulders and the tight black dress that she had been wearing now began to slide down her thighs to the floor. He drank her in, the lush full breasts now only barely restrained by the Eau-de-Nil balconette brassiere. She waited and watched as his gaze moved over the soft curve of her womanly belly, gracefully underlined by matching briefs and suspenders. He felt himself ache with intensity at the long strong thighs clothed in sheer black lace top stockings. She was irresistible.

These were almost the only words that were spoken that morning. Two hours later Alex was clinically disposing of the evidence, the used *preservatifs* were carefully removed and binned in the outside trash and the dishevelled bed linen was stripped off the bed and put in the washing basket for Alice, their Filipino au-pair, to deal with. Alex eventually made it into work that day, claiming a problem with the washing machine which had flooded and needed the help of an engineer. His colleagues jeered and ribbed him about his hapless domestic disaster when he eventually rolled into work around midday.

As far as he was concerned that was probably, in fact not probably, definitely supposed to be the end of the matter. He wasn't racked with guilt because he simply put it out of his mind besides both US Treasuries and the Dollar were now moving. He grabbed a trade blotter and checked expertly over his voluminous computer generated pages of positions and P&Ls and tried to focus on the numbers. The afternoon had moved quickly on and now that the markets started to quieten down, tiredness was just starting to creep into him. He mulled over what he was going to eat that evening. Perhaps he would go and get a video and call in a pizza, or maybe he would just flake out as soon as he got home.

"Alex…Alex, there's a Sandrine Giraud for you on line five."

Alex looked up from his screens of blinking digits. For a moment the name meant nothing to him and then recognition came unwelcomingly flooding back you him. He lunged at the handset and picked up the flashing line on his iridescent dealer phone-board.

Suddenly he was business like again, "Alex Bell speaking"

"Hi Alex, it's me, how are you?"

The tone of familiarity was completely unfazed by his stoned faced opener. In an instant he remembered how he had given her his business card.

"Oh hi Sandrine, err how are you?"

"I'm fine. I'd just thought I'd call to say what a wonderful night last night was."

He looked around and dropped his voice to a studied politeness checking that no-one was clicked in on his line and hitting the private button to stop his colleagues eavesdropping his conversation.

"Yes it was very nice."

"I'm in Paris tonight, would you like to meet up?"

"That would be very nice but unfortunately I have a business meeting" he lied with quiet firmness.

"Then tomorrow perhaps?" her voice trailed off a little.

"Look could I call you tomorrow, I'm a little busy right now?"

"Of course, I understand."

"OK, bye then" Alex was just about to put the phone down.

"You haven't got my number though".

"Oh no I haven't err", he picked up a pen "OK, what is it?"

She carefully gave him her phone number, it was a mobile. Alex didn't even bother to write it down. "OK speak to you later"

"Goodbye Alex"

He clicked out the line with a long drawn out sigh, relieved to be rid of the conversation and the risk of being overheard in a busy dealing room that now seemed painfully quiet. Surveying his colleagues around him they all appeared reasonably busy and preoccupied enough to have missed his discomfort.

Of course he was still mightily flattered that this hugely sexy woman should be so keen on him but at the same time he knew that this relationship was not going anywhere. So whilst he and Claire were going through a rough patch he still felt that in the cold light of day he could not have swapped her and his boys for any wild lover no matter how good the sex was. It was just a one night stand.

When he got home that evening he fixed himself an iced drink, flopped into a sofa and called his wife as soon as he'd kicked of his shoes and got himself comfortable.

She told him in a conversation peppered with "No David" and "Wait David", that Anthony was showing signs of middle child syndrome and that their eldest boy Christopher had hurt his ankle playing football in the garden. Her friend Nessa Simmonds was staying with them with her two children and all the kids were getting on fine. She added that the Simmonds might stay on over the Saturday night if the weather stayed good. She reminded Alex that he needed to get some items she needed from the delicatessen. Claire then asked how work was going and which Eurostar Alex was catching on the Friday. All the time Alex listened intently to her he sipped his orange juice. She talked at her usual tumultuous pace and he made the mandatory grunts of agreement and acknowledgement unprompted. The one sided nature of the conversation was even slightly palliative, he was able to just relax and listen to the tale of their cosy domesticity and put the guilty thoughts of last night out of his mind.

"Look I'll have to go. David's exhausted and needs to go to bed."

"OK love, I'll call you tomorrow."

"See you tomorrow then. Oh just one thing darling."

"Yes?" A momentary panic filled him.

"Can you bring Christopher's Gameboy? He's driving me mad for it."

 Alex let out a silent sigh of relief. "Yes, yes of course!"

"OK, love you, bye."

"You too, bye"

He hung up the walkabout phone and sank back into the comfy depths of the sofa, suddenly aware that his body was aching with tension from the phone call. He finished off his drink, his thirst was quenched but his mind was still whirling over the previous night. He needed a proper drink. Restless, he got up quickly despite his tiredness and went out to the kitchen. He peered about the bright white room with its spotless gleaming black work surfaces and for a moment he checked himself as he thought he recognized the last feint traces of the perfume that Sandrine had been wearing. Everything had been cleaned and put away. He walked over and opened up a bottle of cheap burgundy. Pouring out a big glass for himself he turned and went into the bedroom. Alice had cleaned and made up the bedroom in her usual meticulous manner. He looked at her simple and elegant, dark oak dressing table in the corner. Claire's scent bottles and her assortment of expensive crèmes and carefully chosen lipsticks, her little china curios, and photos of their kids were all neatly in their places. He suddenly felt awful and swigged a large draught from his glass and slunk back into the living room, his bare feet accompanied by the occasional creak from the ageing parquet.

Back in the lounge, slumped listlessly on the sofa, he channel surfed for a while trying to find something of interest. Finding nothing that he wanted to watch he got up slowly, put on a CD and then refilled his glass. REM's "Automatic for the People" filled the room and he looked morosely at the half empty bottle that sat on the coffee table. Gradually becoming aware of his maudlin state of mind he sat himself up and tried to make sense of what had happened.

What should he do? Confess his stupidity to Claire? It seemed so meaningless and what was the point of bringing hurt into her life? He lay back and closed his eyes and dredged his memory for something so salve his conscience. Some many years previously, they had both once drunkenly discussed what they would do if either had an affair. They had both agreed that they would rather not know about it if it should ever happen. At the time they had been living together for only a year or so and the conversation seemed such an artifice, the concept of a betrayal so alien that the whole idea of there being someone else that could be between them had seemed wholly ridiculous. Alex shook his head and grimaced to himself at the innocence of that time. Now that period in a Greek taverna, on a package holiday they had gone on, just a few years out of college seemed a small lifetime ago. He roused himself from his torpor. Thoughts and conversations rolled around in his mind. There was no reason to dump his stupid guilt onto her. He was a big boy, he could live with it. He refilled his glass. The alcohol was having the desired effect and his Dutch courage was on the rise. He was decided. He would just put it down to experience. It had been, after all, a pretty amazing one. He finished off the last few drops of the bottle. Unsatisfied, he went to the drinks cabinet and poured himself out a whisky, sat down and lit up a cigarette. He drew heavily on it, the first since last night and wandered over to the hi-fi. He pushed a button to eject the doleful sounds of REM and flicked through the CD cases distractedly. Nothing appealed. He returned to the coffee table, dropped the glowing butt into the empty wine bottle which let out a little hiss as the stub expired, and then flicked the TV on. Nearly an hour and several fingers of neat whisky later he went heavy headed and gratifyingly numbed to bed. That night he drunkenly dreamt about a beach in Greece and didn't stir despite the vivid dream of Claire telling him she would cut his balls off if he ever slept with another woman.

The alarm clock assaulted him early the next morning and he was greeted with the sour taste of whisky and the stale reek of tobacco coating his tongue. He stumbled groggily out of bed and took his usual shower, dressed, skipped breakfast and got into work on time carrying his copy of the IHT and an uncomplaining hangover.

He walked past the chattering receptionists, who sang in three tone counterpoint their habitual dawn chorus, and sank slowly into his seat. Several more cups of coffee and a litre of water were downed before senses were partly restored. It was around eleven, his hangover was at last starting to go, when his outside line flashed.

"Banque Paris, Trading"

"Can I speak to Monsieur Bell"

"Speaking", Alex was straight back into panic mode. Hangover expunged. He looked furtively around the desk to check that he was not being overheard.

"Hi Alex, It's me Sandrine, how are you?"

Clandestinely, "I'm fine Sandrine."

"So you are off this weekend back to England?"

He had forgotten how much they had chatted, or more pertinently, how much he had said.

"Yes, I'm on the train this evening."

"Well have a nice time. I'm staying here at home. It'll be another quiet weekend for me." She broke into a nervous little laugh. Cautiously, "Do you think you'll have time next week to meet up?"

Alex hesitated before answering, "Well I might"

"Only might?"

The image of her draped across his bed flashed before his eyes. Alex pulled himself together. "No, I'm sure we can meet up. Is Tuesday OK for you?" A Pavlovian tumescence was already stirring in his loins.

"Tuesday will be great."

So there he was, in twenty seconds he'd resolved to see Sandrine again despite all the alcoholic self flagellation and promises to himself of the night before.

He was back in Paris by Eurostar on the Monday morning and the following Tuesday evening he met up with Sandrine at the *Café de la Paix*. She was already sitting there, reading a book, waiting for him when he stepped into the glass fronted terrace of the café. The café, situated just beside the Opera, in the heart of the tourist stomping grounds was not the most discreet place to meet. They were in plain view to anyone passing by so Alex had a couple of beers which steadied his timidity. They had dinner and then went on to his place in the 16ᵗʰ arrondissement for the night. This pattern intermittently repeated itself for the next few weeks until the first few days of September, when Claire and the boys returned.

At this point there was no doubting that Alex found the whole thing deliciously exciting. He even took a perverse pride in the sense of living the quintessential existence of the French businessman. After all, a mistress was mandatory to a serious *homme d'affair*. It was just, he would shrug to himself, an ordinary affair. So it was goodbye to boring old *Metro-Boulot-Dodo* and hello and welcome to the illicit and invigorating *Cinq à Sept*. When Claire returned, they then started to meet at a small hotel, twice sometime three times a week. It was during this time that Sandrine would gradually tell him about herself. She had lived an unenviable life.

Originally she came from near Chambery, high amongst the breath taking beauty of the French Alps. She joked that her long legs and athletic figure were due to the healthy rigours of a mountain life. She certainly had energy particularly in bed where she was a riotous noisy lover, who would whisper delicious obscenities in his ear as they fucked. Sandrine told him how she had left home to study after her baccalaureate and had not completed her course at Grenoble having become pregnant by another student. Her parents had insisted on her keeping the baby but she said she didn't want it, so she had an abortion. This was the only time she mentioned her parents as she hadn't spoken to them in over eight years, their relationship having broken down over the termination. She had then moved to Paris where she had worked in a logistics company and had an affair with a married policeman. After a year or so the cop's wife did her own sleuthing and had found out about them. She then predictably threw him and his errant truncheon out. Gerard the gendarme then moved in with her and they eventually moved to Louveciennes to the west of Paris. She had fallen pregnant again and had given birth to a little girl. She loved the girl dearly, she was called Yvette after her mother, but she was severely handicapped and was in specialist care. Sandrine wasn't actually married to Gerard but he was the father of their daughter and that was her life. She deliberately wore a wedding ring so that other women's husbands would keep away from her, and other husbands wives would come to her. Though she never expressly said it, Alex suspected that her policeman boyfriend was violent as she seemed genuinely scared of him when she mentioned him, which was infrequently.

Of course this pitiful existence was not relayed to him at once. If it had been, he would have run back to London barefoot faster than the Eurostar, scared witless by the rawness and misery of her life story. It was only as they lay entwined in the hotel room that she would tell him little horrific cameos of her impossibly difficult life. So it was with mock horror that she would berate him about the life of simple happy domesticity that he had taken her away from.

And take her away from it he guiltily did. As each little page of her tale was turned and painfully revealed to him, he was drawn ever more into the complicity of her woes. He was ever more racked with remorse, how was he to extricate himself? Each week saw the phone calls become more emotive, the need to see him more pressing and their rendezvous more necessary. When they met, her endearments rapidly became more direct and more passionate and then the litany of personal losses and tragic events would follow. Before long she was telling him that her life was now only bearable because of him and then she told him that she loved him, loved him desperately. Alex's own stubbornly determined omissions of any declarations of love made no difference. Perversely this only served to increase her ardour for him.

"Don't you love me?"

"Sandrine, I told you before. No. I cannot love you."

Then she would smile and say, "You English are so reserved. I know you do really. It's OK, you don't have to say it."

In the cold light of day he endlessly resolved to end it, but each time he turned the conversation to the impossibility of them ever being more than lovers, he was met first with truculence, then threats and finally pleading.

"I'll call your wife and tell her what a bastard you are" she threatened.

"She doesn't speak French", he lied.

"Then I'll come round and see her and show her what we do." Then the tears would start and another heart rending tale would unfold before finally settling with the status quo. She would then say that what she had now was enough to keep her going, but to end their relationship was impossible for her.

His sense of impending doom was finally made palpable the day, it was an afternoon in December, when she revealed that she'd twice attempted suicide, once as a student and then again a few years ago after the doctor's diagnosis of her baby's disability. This was said about five minutes after she'd declared that life was only worth living, thanks to him. Dumbstruck he was barely able to think straight. It was a nightmare. Suddenly he was really terrified of her. Petrified of the responsibility he had arrogantly and stupidly taken on. Crushingly the understanding of his position became apparent to him. The calls, the threats, the pleading, he was trapped and if Claire ever found out his home life was finished. This was why he was so compliant, so unable to extract himself from the nightmare. He was afraid of losing Claire, the boys, everything. He knew it was cowardice but only a fool would not fear such a loss.

Disentangling himself from the paralysing web of deceit that he had spun was going to require a dramatic and determined piece of escapology. All he knew was that he needed to get out of Paris as soon as possible, so when at last the call from the head-hunter from London came with the chance of a move, if it had been to Timbuktu all the better. From that moment on his plan was hatched and he schemed and honed his exit with cold hearted precision.

4. Battered Cabs and Voltaire

It took another three days from the day the faxes arrived for the visa's to be processed and for Alex to square away the holiday required for his trip to Saudi Arabia. His boss, Bicholot, had been fine and had even encouraged him. The Frenchman's cardiac driven close encounter with the Styx had left him determined that he and all about him should take life at a more conventional Parisian pace.

"Enough of this Anglo-Saxon lunacy" he had joked to Alex.

Alex smiled, and asked after his boss' health.

"So-so" he replied. "Are you doing anything interesting for the weekend?"

"Skiing, actually."

"Excellent, where are you going?"

"Meribel" Alex could feel his cheeks flushing.

Bicholot looked at Alex and half smiled, "Well take care my friend and regards to Claire."

In hindsight, the process had been so frighteningly fast that now as he sat in the departure lounge of Charles de Gaulle waiting for his flight to be called it had only seemed a few hours since his chat with Chris Barma in London had happened. It was, however, a month since that first meeting had taken place. He looked out the window of the lounge towards the planes and could see the blustery

January weather pounding the baggage handlers on the tarmac below. They were wrapped in layers of clothing against the sharp cold that he had only just shaken off with his third Americano, inside the warmth of the terminal building. As he sat waiting at the gate to board the plane he looked around. He had expected and was not disappointed, to see various dark haired men sitting in groups, smoking feverishly as they nattered to one another. The visual cliché of a thousand films and images he'd seen were fulfilled at this sight and it comforted him with its familiarity. He listened to the strange guttural sounds of what he safely assumed was Arabic. In his imagination he could almost smell the Turkish coffee. Nearby he noticed a couple of young women. In their mid twenties, festooned in designer clothing and carrying several bags emblazoned with exclusive logos, they were chatting quite animatedly but were aware of their surroundings enough to be throwing occasional glances all about the departure lounge. For a moment he caught a rather coquettish look from one of them and what for an instant, he thought passed for a smile. In another corner a group of North Africans, Algerians or perhaps Moroccans were sitting in quiet contemplative mood. Several of them appeared to be reading out inaudibly, just their lips moving soundlessly, from little green books. More familiar to him was the sight of several businessmen. They sat mostly alone, reading papers or making last minute calls from their mobiles. In one corner an increasingly rowdy group of Western men were good naturedly messing around. They numbered just over a dozen and were aged from twenty five to what looked like late fifties. They all carried large canvas bags with "Saudi Aramco" written down the sides. Oil workers thought Alex. They were the loudest group of travellers and they all looked like they'd already had a few drinks. Alex subconsciously sniffed at them, he never drank before a flight, in his experience it was always a bad idea. Nevertheless despite this snobbery, he couldn't help feeling a small pang of jealousy, they, safe in their group, pals together, he on the other hand was feeling quite solitary.

During the seven hour flight from CDG to Jeddah, Alex had slept or attempted to sleep most of the way. Briefly he flicked through the Arabic phrasebook he had recently purchased and tried to memorise some words; please, thank you, good morning, goodbye. Tiring of his attempt to learn another language, he watched a Jeanne Moreau film and then drifted off before he finally awoke, with the Airbus on its final descent into Jeddah. The same two designer clad women he had noticed in the departure lounge were behind him. They were still talking as busily as when he had first boarded the plane, Alex found that their chatter was mildly reassuring, even slightly soporific. He started to doze off again but then was roused by the harsh squawking sound of the flight stewardess's voice over the PA system. He half listened whilst peering intently out of his window. The stewardess informed the passengers, firstly in French and then in English that all miniatures, empty or otherwise, were to be returned to the bar, that alcohol was strictly banned in the Kingdom of Saudi Arabia, that all magazines were to be returned to the flight crew, that ownership of Israeli currency was forbidden and that the local time was 5:45 pm. He started to stare out of the window and he began to feel more nervous and a strange sense of foreboding was eating away at him. He realized that he sensed this unease because it was the first time since leaving school that he had heard such a litany of do's and don'ts and an unpleasant sense of not being wholly in control.

"Israeli currency, what are these people on?" he said under his breath.

These doubts flashed through his mind but he countered them with the thought of how bold he was, how he was taking such a mighty leap into the unknown, the challenge and of course, the money. "A life of new and strange rules", he rationalized to himself. He was slowly starting to reassure himself that he was doing the right thing when his train of thought was interrupted.

"Please, move the seat back to the upright position", said the stewardess. Her face was rather too heavily made up and Alex starred at her flashing lips with their freshly applied lipstick. The foxy gaudiness of her mouth made more absurd by the lack of even the merest sign of a smile. Alex could sense her tenseness, the way her uniform was tightly buttoned up and her unnatural stiffness all added to her general look of unease. Her nametag announced her as Angelique, though to Alex right now, that seemed almost laughably inappropriate. She certainly did not look like she was looking forward to arrival.

He smiled weakly and pushed the button to move the seatback to the correct position for landing as she had requested, but by the time he looked back up, she had already moved on.

The sun was starting to drift below the horizon and the ground below that he could just about see looked like a vast old dusty brown carpet. He looked harder, but there really was not even the slightest trace of green anywhere to be seen. As the plane started its final descent, everything below looked amazingly flat, the land was almost featureless, the reddish brown ground every now and then threaded with the occasional black vein of a road. The plane banked heavily and at the same time the pilot's voice sounded overhead told the cabin staff to take to their seats. The plane turned and the great red semi-orb of the sun moved to momentarily obliterate Alex' view, the plane continued to bank and once again he could now see the low rise buildings grow larger as they raced by below. A few minutes later the wheels touched down and the aircraft taxied on and eventually came to a halt. Alex strained in his seat to look forward and saw the unsmiling stewardess sitting rigidly on a jump seat just ahead of him. She looked quite the prim school mistress, bolt upright and unsmiling, whilst in the background another voice announced that the passengers had arrived at King Abdul Aziz International airport in Jeddah and that they looked forward to seeing the passengers again on Air France.

In the darkening dusk, the airport terminal could be seen some distance away. Through the window, Alex could see some yellow flashing lights; the dark shapes behind them slowly coalesced into the arrival of several of those wide-bodied articulated buses that can only be found in airports.

He silently cursed to himself as the realization dawned that it was going to be another delay filing into and then out of the bus.

As he undid his seat belt and stood up he was slightly unnerved by what he now saw. Like a weird conjurors act, where before there had been women wearing smart Armani and Dior designer outfits, now he was surrounded by a sea of black robes. Some had veils drawn across their faces so they were almost completely covered up. The two women behind him, whose chatter had seemed so endless, were now silent and Alex could not tell which one was which as they were both now covered head to toe in black. As they shuffled forward down the aisle he noticed some women were wearing glasses on the outside of their veils. He smiled inwardly at the scene, which reminded him of some creepy old black and white movie.

"The Revenge of the Myopic Mummies," yes that would be a great comic title he thought to himself. Warming to this train of thought, he again noticed the North Africans. They were all now wearing white towelling robes. He hadn't seen them change, but they all seemed in holiday mood. Alex wondered what they were up to as he shuffled to the doorway.

The light had now completely gone, but not the cloying heat and the fearsome humidity. As he stepped out into the open air, the first since boarding at Paris, he felt warmth radiating from every object. The heat was coming at him from all directions. The steps that led down to the runway tarmac felt hot through the leather soles of his shoes and the handrail was like a car radiator. Dressed in a business suit, his clothes, which had come from a European winter, were not helping him at all. As he stepped onto the black tarmac, heat belted out like the blast of an open oven. However the real surprise was the humidity, the small walk to the waiting bus suddenly seemed hugely energy sapping. The First and Business class passengers were loaded onto the bus but this did not help much as they waited for the bus to fill to capacity. As the passengers piled onto the bus he was squeezed towards two big obese men, who like Alex, were also wearing suits. They were perspiring profusely whilst talking in guttural German to each other. Outside, a couple of gleaming silver Mercedes limos were waiting and he made out the two women he had been sitting behind on the flight, disappear into one of them, which then smoothly pulled away and moved out of sight.

After what seemed like an age, but was no more than ten minutes, the bus started to move towards the terminal. It trundled along for a couple of minutes then drew up beside a ramp leading into the airport building and the doors squealed open to allow the tightly packed passengers to spill out. It seemed that in one moment everyone had decided that they wanted to be inside the terminal and a mighty scrum formed. He clung to his hand baggage as it was being carried along in the powerful undercurrent of the passengers as they surged forward. The pushing came from all directions, the most vigorous from the most diminutive of the passengers. Alex found himself first carried along then quite forcefully pushed to one side by one of the older men dressed in what seemed to him to be an oversized white towel. Behind the towelled men came the marauding mummies, followed by children of all sizes wearing T-shirts with DKNY or GAP scrawled across them.

Like the others he waited patiently in line to pass though passport control and then picked his way through the stationary masses that looked glumly towards the frozen baggage carriers. Years of business travel had taught him that it was smart to travel light. Mercifully the customs check was much shorter than passport control. He couldn't fail to notice that where all the immigration control staff ranged from thin to emaciated, the customs men on the other hand were positively rotund. There were obviously fringe benefits for customs men.

By prior arrangement Alex was to be greeted by a driver from the hotel he was staying at. As he passed into the tumultuous arrivals area, all he could see was as another flock of white clothed, dark haired men, bodies so closely crushed together it felt like a furious white walled wave was about to come sweeping up to carry him away. As he stepped out through the railings into the hall, those immediately in front of him ebbed away before surging back around him, clamouring for his attention. Boards with the names of the hotels they were going to: the Hilton, the Intercontinental; the Sheraton and many others he had never heard of all vied for the newly arrived passengers' attention. According to the fax he had, Alex was looking out for one named the Red Sea Palace but he was unable to see his hotel's name amongst the chaos that now swelled around him.

Directly in front of him several men thrust closer towards him. Hirsute faces pressed eagerly forward and the smell of stale sweat started to give a short vision of hell. For an instant it was a scene from Brueghel, as limbs strained at him for salvation. Looking in all directions and without a word of Arabic he suddenly felt quite hopelessly lost and craned his neck to see a familiar or friendly smile amongst all those bearded faces that pressed in on him from all directions. The plaintively, questioning cry of, "Taxi?" being repeated to him over and over again.

He turned to the nearest, "Do you know the Red Sea Palace hotel?" he asked the man.

The man he asked looked quite blankly back at him while another just behind him pushed through and replied, "Red Sea... no problem, please Red Sea ...Yes you come please."

Alex didn't hesitate but followed the small and somewhat wizened man, he seemed the least threatening of all those about him. The driver offered to carry his bags but Alex declined it. He still wasn't sure at all if the man might not just run off with his baggage into the crowded masses. He almost ran out and followed the man out of the arrivals hall and into the car park immediately facing the airport. In the half lit gloom, the fetid smells of poorly functioning drains rose up around him and he quickened his pace to get away from the stench. The thin, wiry man was now walking faster and faster and Alex was having trouble keeping up with him. After two or so minutes like this the driver came to a halt and opened the boot of a car, which as Alex approached it more closely, he recognized as a very old GM sedan. Painted a bilious yellow, it looked like it had failed to finish in a stock car race. He momentarily hesitated, but the time, the heat, the awesome humidity and his mounting fatigue meant that he was ready to take the risk. He climbed into the back and lodged himself in the corner opposite the driver. Gathering his wits he remembered a piece of advice he had read in his guide book on Saudi Arabia. Haggle before buying anything. He leant forward and asked the driver how much the ride was going to be to the hotel.

"Three hundred riyals!"

At a fixed exchange rate of 3.75 to a US dollar, he quickly calculated this was around eighty dollars. "Outrageous!" he said under his breath. Still, knowing that this was just the driver's opening gambit he decided to show the little fellow that he wasn't about to accept this first offering and immediately bid half this, "One hundred and fifty" he said with feigned forcefulness.

"Two hundred fifty", the driver countered almost immediately.

"No way", Alex paused for effect, "two hundred riyals."

The driver, who was scrutinizing Alex very closely in the mirror while all this haggling went on, turned round and switched the key to the ignition on. "OK, two hundred Riyals" he said as he gunned the engine. Alex sat back and tried to wedge himself in his seat. Secure in the corner, his baggage sitting primly on his lap, he felt quite satisfied that he had successfully completed his first haggle; he figured he would quite enjoy that aspect of life here. He smiled to himself and gave himself a mental pat on the back that he was no pushover in the haggling stakes. He might be new to this part of the world, but he was no Candide, being taken for a ride by this old rickety toothed man.

The journey into Jeddah was mercifully uneventful despite the initial alarm he suffered when he noticed the speedometer of the taxi was broken. Whilst the needle remained stubbornly fixed at zero, the hurtling roadside vista eventually prompted Alex to ask the driver to slow down, which the driver had obligingly done. As he was driven through to the centre of the city along the six lane highway that runs from the airport to the city, he recognized the usual billboards and flashing neon lights that advertised familiar brands from Pepsi to Sony. It was strange but in a weird way these totems to western consumerism had an oddly reassuring feel to them, like seeing an old friend in a room of strangers. However unlike home, whilst the billboards peddled their well known products and global brands there were no smiling faces or retouched unattainable bodies in suggestive poses. In fact as the cab jerked and bounced along the increasingly congested roads, this actually became more and more disturbing to him. The complete absence of the human form became ever more self evident as he bumped along in the back of the cab and was as perplexing as a face without eyes.

As they drove into the city centre the buildings grew thicker and taller as the journey progressed. By the time he arrived at the grandly named Red Sea Palace Hotel, it was half past ten at night and he was feeling quite exhausted from the whole journey from Paris. The beaten up taxi pulled up in the hotel entrance and a hotel doorman opened the cab door and took his two small bags from him as Alex paid the driver the 200 riyals previously agreed. The driver took the money and waved his hand at him with a mild natured grunt and then grinned. The smile revealed a rickety set of broken and stained teeth, the sight of which added a little impetus to Alex's stiff legged departure from the back seat. He ungracefully levered himself out of the fetid taxi and into the welcoming cool of the air conditioned hotel lobby.

Walking across the large open area that led to the hotel reception desk, the noise of his footsteps rang out sharply on the hard tiled floor. The lighting was quite bright and harsh and he was forced to squint a little as his eyes started to adapt from the dark outside. He paused for a moment, taking in the room. To the right he saw a sign pointing to a restaurant, obliquely to the left he could see the sign for the reception and the concierge. Moving slowly towards the reception desk, he noticed several groups that were sat around the large lobby, one group of men, dressed in traditional long white *dishdashahs* and with full headdresses, were sitting around a table drinking what looked like tea. One man talked with quiet restraint whilst the others, all bent slightly forward, were listening intently to him. At another low table sat a large group of aircrew who chatted noisily in huddled twos and threes amongst themselves. Several of the faces were still glowing with sunburn; they were all in uniform and waiting for their transfer to the airport. Also dotted around were a couple of solitary men either, reading papers, smoking cigarettes or both. He noted with the exception of the stewardesses, there was a distinct lack of any women in sight.

When he reached the hotel reception, Ahmed the receptionist, seemed surprised that the driver assigned to meet him at the airport had missed Alex and he apologized profusely for the mistake. "So you will be with us for just one night?" he asked as he tapped expertly into the keyboard.

"Yes, that's right"

"IAB have also requested a late check out for you tomorrow."

He then took Alex's passport and made photocopies of all the details he needed and then once all these formalities of the hotel registration were done, gave him his room key with an efficient looking smile. After checking the room, Alex gave a tip to the pockmarked bellhop who had shown him to his room on the fourth floor and who had waited patiently whilst he checked in.

Once in the room, the first thing he did was open the mini bar. He was feeling quite dehydrated and he swigged down a small bottle of mineral water. Having slaked his immediate thirst he then had a poke around the fridge to see what was on offer. His initial pleasant surprise at seeing a couple of cans of beer was dampened by the heavy bold type on the side of the can, which read, "Alcohol Free Malt Beverage". Intrigued by this, he poured himself one and fell back onto the big double bed whilst automatically reaching for the remote on the bedside table and switching on the TV. Vacantly surfing through the channels he eventually settled on the familiar and anodyne CNN. After slowly finishing his beer, which he reckoned tasted pretty foul, he quickly phoned his wife to let her know that he had arrived safely from his mobile phone. The conversation was short and functional, Claire was in the middle of putting the kids to bed, he said he would call back later on to speak to them all, probably in the morning his time. Jeddah was only a couple of hours ahead of Paris so after a quick shower and some room service he was not particularly tired and so decided to have a nose around the hotel.

He was on the fourth floor, which was labelled "Executive Floor" of the hotel. Taking the lift down to the ground floor lobby he became aware of a peculiar scent. It was a strange mixture of the over recycled air conditioning and the strange pot-pourris, which littered the large lobby on small but heavily ornamented tables. The lobby itself was now much less busy, Ahmed was still behind the reception desk and he gave Alex a friendly wave as he passed by him, but the flight crews had gone, as had the large party in the corner. With less people to observe he now could see that the décor of the hotel was a heavy mix of middle-eastern influences with western kitsch. Many dark ornate wooden tables were sprinkled around and the walls had gold and mirrored effects around deep red geometric shapes mixed with Islamic motifs. The decoration gave the hotel an ambiance between a rather seedy night club and a Turkish bath - a sort of aggressive anti-minimalism.

Oppressive, Alex felt relief as he stepped outside and found that the evening had brought a welcome respite from the heat of his arrival. Now that he was more practically dressed in a polo shirt and chino's it was not anything like as unbearable as it had been at the airport. In fact, it was rather pleasant.

The headquarters of IAB where he was going the next day was on the next block, not more than two hundred meters from the hotel. He walked around for about half an hour, careful to keep his orientation. He hadn't a map on him, so getting lost was the last thing he needed. To his genuine surprise, the streets were bustling with activity. His watch, still on Paris time read 9 o'clock, which made it 11 pm there. Strolling down into the old city, fairy lights adorned nearly all of the shops and arcades, which ran in all directions as far as the eye could see. Roaming these shopaholic delights were large families of Saudi's, the men always dressed in their traditional white, the women in opaque black *burqa*, invariably surrounded by a gaggle of riotous children, four, five sometimes even more. On this survey, Alex figured that the average Saudi family was considerably more than the two and a bit, or whatever it was, for the UK. The mood in the streets seemed quite frivolous and light, people were clearly enjoying themselves. He looked at his watch, it was nearly midnight. "Didn't these kids go to school and what about sleep?" he thought to himself. When he got back to the hotel, Ahmed was still looking bright eyed and watchful behind the desk.

"It's very busy tonight", said Alex.

"Yes sir, it's always like this during *Ramadan*", replied Ahmed.

"Oh yes I'd forgotten about that, when does *Ramadan* finish?"

"It's one month exactly, so it will finish in two weeks." He added with a good natured look.

Alex thanked the receptionist for the information and bade him goodnight. He then went up to his room and dug into his briefcase to find his guidebook. He looked under the section for religious festivals and holidays and sure enough, there it was. *Ramadan* was the holy month of the Muslim year during it people should fast and only break the fast once the sun had set. You couldn't eat or drink anything apparently. He read on but the guidebook didn't say anything about partying through the night, so he closed it a little non-plussed. He lay on the bed and fitfully tried to get some sleep, the only sound he could hear was the low-pitched drone of the air conditioning.

5. The Essential Ed

The wakeup call he had set up came at seven thirty and woke Alex from a very deep slumber. His mouth felt dry from the air-conditioning, its purring sound now quite unnoticed by him. Despite his tiredness from the previous day, he had only managed to get to sleep at around two thirty in the morning. His sleeplessness was caused partly because he had been running through what he would say during the forthcoming interviews, and partly due to the slight time-zone difference of two hours. He had ordered breakfast in the room, which he finished off hungrily, he then showered, shaved and prepared himself for the day ahead. He checked himself, sideways on, in the long mirror of the wardrobe. The suit he put on had just been bought during the New Year sales in London and was sombre and businesslike. He picked up the shiny paper of the fax machine and scrutinised it again. The schedule he had received a few days earlier showed he was going to meet around eight people that day and the first meeting was planned for nine o'clock. The bank itself was only a few minutes walk away but Chris Barma was going to meet him in the lobby at 8:45 am.

Alex was still in his room when the phone rang.

"Mr. Bell, we have a Mr. Chris Barma waiting for you in reception"

"I'll be right down", he said as he looked at his watch, which told him it was still only 8:30 am.

Alex slugged down the last of his coffee, clicked off CNN and before taking the lift down made a quick call on his mobile to Claire. They were all up and she wished him good luck for the day ahead, though he probably wouldn't need it. She seemed fine and he hung up as the lift doors opened on the ground floor.

In daylight the hotel lobby was a little less Turkish bath, but not much. He paused and was looking around the lobby for the obvious sight of an imposing Armani suited man of six foot four, the image of him in the London rain outside the restaurant still fresh in his mind. He scanned the faces all around but there was still no sign of him then a voice called out behind him.

"Alex, how are you, how was the flight?"

He turned around, to the familiar trans-Atlantic intonation but then was almost struck dumb by the sight that met his eyes. Chris Barma was wearing the full white Saudi outfit, including the head-dress and sandals. He grinned as he offered his hand, clearly pleased by the effect his appearance had provoked.

"Well…, Hi Chris, err, I wasn't expecting to see you like this!" he stuttered, clearly somewhat shocked.

"Well, when in Rome do as the Romans" said Barma with a smile as they shook hands. "You know it's actually quite practical in this weather"

Still unnerved by the sight of Barma in traditional Arab clothing, Alex could only nod his head in agreement as Barma released Alex from his resolute grip.

"You ready for the interviews then?"

At last gathering himself together he replied more steadily.

"Sure, as ready as ever. Shall we?"

Alex made for the door, but Barma halted him.

"I brought my car, it's just outside."

The two men then walked out of the lobby towards the car park. Alex kept glancing sideways at the strange apparition that was Barma, hardly able to withhold staring open mouthed. As they passed through the hotel's glass revolving doors a big navy blue Ford Explorer pulled up beside them. Barma opened the rear door and climbed in, Alex followed him. The driver, dressed in a simple short sleeve white shirt and dark trousers, gunned the engine and eased the four wheel drive out of the hotel driveway without a word. The two men sat in the back of the car in a slightly awkward silence as they were driven the embarrassingly short distance to the bank.

The building they entered was easily the tallest in the city, twenty-five stories high, its imposing structure sat next to the waterfront and dominated the cityscape, a succinct statement of potent intent for the organization it housed. Once in the cool of the cavernous banking hall, Barma signed Alex in and then they rode a lift up to the trading floor on the seventeenth. As the doors opened Barma stepped out of the lift and spoke to Alex for the first time since the car ride.

"This is the Treasury", he announced with a small flourish. They passed through another set of glass door with a security pass and entered. "Take a seat here for a moment and I'll go and find Asif, he's the first one you're to meet."

Alex sat down and took in his new surroundings. The décor of the floor had a calming effect. Large square white pots were dotted around and housed luxuriant plants and the whole floor was carpeted in dark green. He took a breath suddenly aware of something odd. He looked around himself and then it struck him. There was a complete absence of any women. Everywhere it was men.

Edgy, he watched Barma walk over to a small dark man who was dressed in a long sleeved white shirt. The other man had already risen to his feet as he'd been approached and was nodding his head and looking towards Alex as he listened to Barma. The two men then walked over to Alex, who stood up to meet them. Barma turned to the diminutive man and introduced him.

"Alex, this is Saleem, my secretary."

He shook the man's hand "Hello Saleem"

"Hello Mr. Alex," he replied with a winning smile, "so nice to see you here in Jeddah"

"Thank you and thanks also for all the help you gave me with the consulate in Paris"

"You are most welcome Mr. Alex", the smile accompanied with a little self-deprecating head nodding.

Barma broke into this exchange of pleasantries, "Saleem has been with IAB for over twenty years, haven't you?"

"*Inshallah*, Yes Mr. Chris, twenty two" he replied with gentle but firm precision.

Just then another man across the room called out to Chris that he had a phone call on hold. Barma walked off in the direction of the man leaving Alex and Saleem together. "So where are you from Saleem?"

"I come from Java, Sir"

"And do you have any family here?"

"Here, oh no Sir," he said with a slight shake of the head and a little half laugh that mocked the suggestion. He smiled and added, "No, my family are all at home in Java." Alex thought about this for a moment before continuing, "How many children do you have then?"

"I have five Sir"

Just before the conversation could continue any further, Barma returned.

"Asif is free to see you Alex" and he led him through into one of the small offices behind them.

"When you're finished, go back over to Saleem and he'll sort your next meeting, which is with Abdullah."

Alex was duly introduced and the interview with the man named Asif went ahead as exactly scheduled in Alex's tightly packed itinerary. It began in a friendly manner and the discussion proceeded along familiar lines to someone as experienced as Bell. Asif Shastaq was the financial controller of the Treasury, broadly speaking a purely administrative function. To men like Alex, in the hierarchy of a trading room, the guy was nothing more than a glorified pen pusher. Shastaq introduced himself as "Chief of Staff", in Alex's eyes yet another ridiculous title, which left one with no better idea of what he actually did in the bank. For ten minutes or so the interview meandered along like a man in a darkened room, bumping into familiar points of reference, but always threatening to trip him up.

Alex was therefore visibly irritated when the interview took off in a wholly unexpected direction. Shastaq paused for a moment and then lent back in his chair before speaking whilst clasping his hands across his chest in an almost reverential manner.

"Tell me Mr. Bell, How, do you people, justify such large salaries?"

Bell was taken aback by this statement. "I'm sorry Mr. Shastaq, I'm not sure I understand your question completely."

The man pointed to a copy of the Financial Times, it was a couple of days old but it covered the breaking story of a female fund manager who had flown to Frankfurt to demand payment from her employers. It looked very much like an act of singular desperation to Alex, a very risky gambit. It was only on this account that he gave the woman a begrudging credit.

"Traders, Fund managers, people who manage other people's money, whatever you may call them, morally do you think that you can justify these millions that they demand?"

Alex couldn't remember when he'd been asked such a naïve question and worked hard to stifle an outright guffaw. "Well", he paused to consider how he might answer the question. "Let me put it this way. There are two issues to consider. Firstly when you say morally, then I think that there is no justification whatever. Pay and morality are not related". As Alex spoke Asif Shastaq studied him carefully whilst tapping his fingertips silently together.

Alex continued, "As for the question of too much, well that is simply what the market is. Employers seek to pay the minimum and as an employee, we should seek the maximum."

Alex paused for a moment; he was quite enjoying this patronizing line of argument. He studied Shastaq's face before continuing.

"I'm sure that you yourself seek to be paid as much as you think you deserve, but most of us tend to get less than what we think we should", he added with a wry smile. "Anyway, the equilibrium point is payment...it's simply where the two parties agree to do business. In this case it's to manage other people's money."

Shastaq was wholly unimpressed by this answer and showed it with a slight murmur and a quizzical expression that he hoped conveyed his deep dissatisfaction. Is that it, the self-serving logic of a two rupee prostitute? He thought the answer he'd just heard was a typical piece of arrogance. This Englishman hadn't answered the question; he'd simply avoided it by these trite little simplifications. It was just another example of the moral bankruptcy of these men that Barma had selected and brought to the bank. Bell, in his tailored suit and his cocky attitude was as bad as all the others he had seen, maybe even the worst of the lot.

Still what did it matter what he thought? Barma had been given carte blanche. It was totally ridiculous but that was the situation. Shastaq disliked Barma more intensely each day.

He picked up Alex's C.V. and took one last look. It was like all the others in this team that Barma was bringing to the IAB, Western educated and privileged, his working life littered with blue chip American and European Investment banks, nothing but enviable opportunities. He folded the paper and put it onto his desk.

"Well, thank you for your time, it was nice to meet, I'm sure you'll enjoy your time with us."

"Thank you."

The men stood up, shook hands and Alex walked out of his office back into the reception to find Saleem.

Shastaq watched the Englishman as he walked and closed the door behind him. He made a short muffled snort as he considered the man. Why would someone like this man come to a place like this? It was just greed, pure and simple.

He, on the other hand, was there because he had to be. Cruel necessity was his master and despite this he performed his job diligently and with pride. He had worked his way from miserable beginnings in northern Pakistan, to getting to a good university and then into a good job. He had done it with nothing but hard work. It rankled with him how easy it all was for men like Bell. More than that, he loathed the way they would look down their smug noses at him and he was even angrier with himself for letting them make him feel inferior. He wasn't.

He knew he has better than these men with no morals, no loyalty, and no honour. For the last fifteen years at IAB, Shastaq an honest and hardworking man, had seen many of these Western ex-pats join the bank, each was paid a small fortune, to do what exactly? Risk the banks money and for what good? When these men made money they wanted their cut, when they lost it they just disappeared with their fat salaries. Anyone could do that. Bell would be just like all the others and he smiled to himself at his foolishness in getting so bothered about them. They'd soon be whingeing for his help and then we'll see how grand they really were. They always did.

Barma came over to where Alex was now waiting.

"OK, now for Omar. He's the head of risk management. He's a really nice fellow."

Barma was right. As far as Alex was concerned, Omar Al-Hamra did indeed seem a very nice enough fellow and the man's avuncular manner was most welcome after the first somewhat tetchy and taxing interview. The Arab enquired about Alex's background, where and what he had studied at university and then talked of the importance of education and training. Towards the end the two men fell into a short and uneasy dialogue over English football. Uneasy that is, for Alex, who knew next to nothing about soccer. He was much more of a rugby fan.

Taken aback by the man's sudden enthusiasm, Alex tried to keep up his end of the conversation. "Manchester United look quite useful this season", he added hopefully. He was aware of the fact that they had a huge overseas following, some poorly remembered article in the FT on replica shirt sales dawned on him. He figured that Omar Al-Hamra must be one of them.

"Manchester United?" replied the Arab with undisguised shock before shaking his head. "No, no, I think Newcastle will do it this season. That Shearer is fantastic, just like SuperMac"

"Superman?" Alex was totally flummoxed.

Now it was the Arab's turn to look confused. "No. I said, SuperMac. You know, Malcolm McDonald? He was really great." Al-Hamra's face had lit up with boyish enthusiasm. Alex tried hard not to look completely flummoxed. The name, sort of rang a bell, but he nodded as if he was on first name terms with the man.

"Ah yes, of course, SuperMac."

The talk with the head of the Back-Office, Ali Bakra, was interminable. Alex convincingly assured the little bearded man that his greatest motivation in life was writing out trade blotters and tickets correctly. It seemed to do the trick.

By the end of this last interview, Alex was now starting to feel decidedly jaded. As far as he was concerned they had gone much as expected. He sat, shoulders a little hunched, his crisp shirt collar starting to feel uncomfortable, waiting for the last interview and realized he was feeling parched. He'd had nothing since the coffee he gulped down in his room earlier that morning. Alex walked over to where Saleem was sitting typing in a slow deliberate way at his workstation. His speed wasn't much faster than that of the immigration clerk who had so riled Alex the previous night at the airport.

"Err Saleem, sorry to interrupt you, but could I get a glass of water somewhere please?"

Saleem looked up slowly with a pained expression spreading across his good-natured features.

"I'm so sorry Mr. Alex, but it is *Ramadan* and we are not allowed any food or drink until the sun has set." As he looked up at Alex from his workstation, his whole defeated body language suggested it would have been easier to fly straight out of the window than to get something to eat or drink over *Ramadan*.

Alex immediately felt sorry for the little Javanese man and tried immediately to put him at ease.

"Oh, I'm sorry, I had completely forgotten." He made a little conciliatory smile and retired back to the sofa.

Saleem smiled weakly and said *"Inshallah*, evening is nearly here."

Alex sat waiting until Chris Barma came back into view.

"OK Alex, now you're to meet the Treasurer, Ed Moore." Barma could see that his new hire was starting to wilt a little. He looked like he needed a little pepping up.

"Not long to go now Alex. Ed's the Treasurer and essentially he's behind this whole idea of the Prop group." He looked at Alex and continued. "Once more into the breach eh?" and he gave Alex a little encouraging wink.

Moore's office was much larger than all the others, a large conference table sat at one end and a desk sat in a recessed area at the far end of the room. The interview was short and sweet.

Showing Alex a seat he sat down and picked up Alex's details.

"So you're our new derivatives guy?"

"Yes, that's my area of expertise." Alex looked around the room and noticed a framed photograph of a younger Moore, smiling and shaking hands with one the Reagan administration's Secretary of State. It was George Shultz.

Ruminating for a moment, Moore then put down Alex's C.V. "British."

It was not intoned as a question, just as simple statement of fact but Alex still smiled and nodded his acknowledgement.

"Why here?" Moore's eyes narrowed slightly though his tone still seemed only passingly interested in Alex's answers, perhaps even in the whole interview process.

"Money and opportunity" he paused for a moment, "but mostly it's the money." Alex had decided that directness was the only course of action. It was ludicrous to suggest he was looking to further his career or save the world.

This seemed to momentarily grab his attention and Moore looked over his half rim glasses and nodded his head.

"How long do you reckon you'll need?"

Alex looked at the American, "Two years." It was the length of the contract on offer.

Moore smiled. "I think you'll need longer, give yourself longer."

The American then stood up and Alex offered his hand.

"Good luck, see you soon then."

Alex reached and grasped Moore's hand which had all the force of a week old lettuce.

"I look forward to it" and he let go quickly, glad to be rid of the American's insipid handshake.

He stepped out of Ed Moore's office and there was Chris Barma standing waiting for him.

"Well that was quick"

"It always is with Ed when he gets the right answers." Barma said with a wide smile.

His bright eyed expression of happiness conveyed that the day's proceedings were now drawing to a satisfactory close.

"Can you hang here for just a few moments? I've got a couple of things for you to read and then sign and then we can get back to my place and have something to eat. You must be famished."

Another ten minutes and he was back with the contracts which he gave to Alex in a large Manila envelope. He looked at his watch; it was just past 4:30pm in the afternoon and he was amazed to discover that he had gone the whole day without anything passing his lips. Only his groaning stomach gave lie to his stoic performance.

"So you eat nothing for lunch during *Ramadan* Chris?"

"Well I'm Muslim, so no, I don't, but you can get lunch over in the Italian Consulate restaurant."

"Is that so", said Alex with some relief.

"Yeah, obviously all the restaurants in Jeddah are closed during the day during *Ramadan*, but that one is allowed to remain open as it's on a diplomatic compound"

Alex knew where he'd be spending *Ramadan* lunchtimes next year.

They made their way out of the bank and exactly where they had left it this morning, the big blue Ford Explorer, engine running, was waiting for them outside.

"Home please Ali," said Chris and turning to Alex he added with a chuckle, "I couldn't get a driver called James!"

Alex grinned at Chris Barma's joke. The car's cool air-conditioned interior was spotless and it had the familiar smell of newness about it.

"My cook has prepared something for us and I thought I'd show you the compound so you can see the kind of place you will live in. I think you'll find it quite", he paused for a moment thinking of the right word before settling for, "pleasant."

The drive up the Medina Road took about twenty minutes during which Alex silently surveyed the battle scarred central reservation of the highway and tried not to flinch as cars weaved drunkenly by.

"So this road runs all the way to Medina?"

"Yes, well sort of." Barma made a funny little hollow laugh.

"What do you mean sort of?" Alex asked with a quizzical tone.

"Well this six lane highway comes to an end shortly outside the city limits, then it becomes pretty rough all the way to Medina."

"Have you been there, is it worth a visit?"

Barma looked at Alex and smiled grimly "I have, though that might be a bit difficult for you."

Alex asked why this was the case and Barma explained that, one needed specific authority to travel out of Jeddah and that this had to be requested by your employer. Besides that, Medina and Mecca were both holy cities and strictly forbidden to non-Muslims.

"Well I guess I won't be going there then."

During the entire journey Ali had driven with notable, and to Alex's eyes, well deserved caution. Every now and then a car would come hurtling past them, the yellow coloured city taxis being by far the most recklessly driven.

Barma registered the rising alarm in his potential new recruit and thought he'd try and put him more at his ease. He had suffered an accident shortly after his own arrival in Jeddah and was consequently highly attuned to the hazards of the highways of Saudi Arabia.

"To be honest, the driving is a nightmare here, particularly during *Ramadan,* as everyone is driving home to break their fast." A car veered wildly across the road just as he spoke. "It's not normally this bad", he added unconvincingly.

At last they turned right off the Medina road and headed towards the glare of the setting sun, along ever more pot holed roads. Now the route was hemmed in all around by high-sided walls, and almost entirely deserted except for feral looking cats and some hideously emaciated dogs. The car came to a halt.

"Here we are, Mura Bustan, this is where I live."

Ahead a blue shirted security guard peered into the car and smiled in recognition as he caught Chris Barma's eye. Seeing the familiar face he happily waved them on through before signalling another security man. Another thin faced guard started to raise the yellow and black striped barrier that had barred their entry, the task causing him to briefly contort his face in effort. As they drove slowly past him Alex saw him tiredly smile and wave, revealing the dark sweat stained rings of his shirt.

Outside the compound there had been very little greenery or signs of life; inside it was quite different. A verdant mix of well watered lawns, luxuriant palms and smooth roads greeted them. Signposts pointed in various directions; restaurant, office, supermarket, swimming pool.

The houses were mostly painted in a cream or beige on the outside, with doors frequently half open and only thin mosquito netted doors keeping the interior of the houses free from an outsiders prying view. As they drew into Barma's driveway, as if on cue, the sound of the call to prayer ran through the heavy, scented air of the compound. All across the city the call was relayed from the multitude of minarets that peppered the city in all directions.

"Perfect timing"

"What's that?" asked Alex.

"Well the sun is setting and you can hear the *Maghrib* call to prayer, so I can now break the fast" said Barma. Alex considered that he was quite a stickler for the details. Maybe he was a recent convert to Islam or something.

He followed Barma into the cool interior of the house. Looking around it seemed to be very lightly furnished inside. A few personal effects were dotted around, a couple of photographs here and there and music stand with a classical guitar standing next to it.

"You play the guitar?"

"Yeah, I do indeed. I love it actually."

Just then a young woman came out of the kitchen. Dark with delicate features, she looked like she was Somali or Ethiopian though Alex was not exactly expert on the subject. She said nothing as she noiselessly started to lay out the table for the two men. Alex couldn't help but notice that she was really quite attractive. For the first time he became aware that he hadn't even asked Chris if he was married. He had always assumed that he was single, but now he suddenly considered other options. Having said that, she was the first woman he had seen all day. The woman discreetly busied herself preparing the meal but she studiously avoided any eye contact with Alex.

"What would you like to drink Alex?"

"What have you got?"

"Anything you like, just no alcohol." He replied with a smile.

"I'll have an orange juice, if you have it."

He turned towards the young woman and spoke. "Elsa, one orange juice and one Iced Tea and a big jug of water with lots of ice please."

Barma then wandered over to the other side of the room. "Any particular music you'd like?"

"Anything, I'm not fussy."

"OK", Barma, picked up a CD, briefly examined the case, took out the disc and loaded it into a gleaming hi-fi.

"Violin Concerto OK with you?"

Alex nodded his agreement and waited for the music to play whilst Elsa served the drinks. This is all very civilized, thought Alex; he's quite the Renaissance Man.

After a few minutes, Alex had a shot at trying to redress the balance. "It's Mozart isn't it?" he said as nonchalantly as possible, though he wasn't a hundred percent sure at all.

Barma grinned. "Yup sure is, beautiful isn't it?"

Elsa now stood at the kitchen entrance looking at the two men. This was the signal that their meal was ready and they sat down to eat. Elsa may have been pretty but she couldn't cook to save her life. It was simply horrific. Despite not having eaten all day and nursing a gargantuan hunger, the food that was served was almost inedible. Barma wolfed his meal down and was well into his second serving whilst Alex struggled to make any headway. It had been announced as lamb and couscous but Michelin starred it was not. Alex vainly tried to compare the delicious *Tagine* Moroccan dish he was so familiar with from one of his favourite restaurants, the 404 in Paris, but it was quite futile. He chewed as slowly as he dared, not seeking to draw attention to himself.

"Are you OK, you're not eating much?"

"I'm fine thanks, just suffering a little from the heat I expect." He lied.

Barma finished up the last morsels on his plate with relish and put down his knife and fork with a satisfied clink. He peered at Bell who looked to be struggling with his fork and kept constantly wiping his mouth with his napkin. Still, he seemed a nice enough guy, perhaps a little on the pompous side, probably all that high living in Paris he reasoned to himself. He wondered too, if he wasn't a little hen pecked as well.

"So you see it's a great place for kids. It's safe, the weather's great and the kids will just love the outdoor life I'm quite sure. They all do."

Alex made a slight non-committal noise, but nodded agreement anyway. Barma noted some concern had crept into his new hire's eyes.

"C'mon, let me show you quickly around the compound."

Alex followed Barma, taking in pools, tennis courts and all the red faced enthusiasm of the compound. They passed by a restaurant, where bikini clad women, sitting under brightly coloured parasols, chatted and shrieked. Alex relaxed, perhaps it would not be so bad here, after all. Here, at least, there were some signs of normality.

They approached a doorway, marked 'Resident's Office'

Barma turned to Alex. "Hang here a sec, I need to get something for you."

Alex stood and peered at a glass covered notice board. The patchwork of notices conveyed a slightly disorientating mixture of after school club chirpiness and ear bursting market stall. Sewing and needlepoint lessons, visits to souks, tribute bands and cars for sale all screamed for attention.

"Are you alright there?"

Alex turned towards the questioner and there was Chris smiling broadly back at him.

"Here, I wanted you to have a look at this" Alex took the Manila envelope and peered inside it. "It's a number of brochures for different compounds, take them back and have a look at them on the plane."

Alex thanked Barma and then the two men continued their way around the compound. Barma added, "It's incredibly safe for kids here." Alex looked ahead and saw a number of children on bikes and roller blades racing towards them.

They stepped to the side of the road to let them hurtle past in a full throated convoy.

After only a day of solely men's company, Alex was already starting to feel a little divorced from reality. He re-gathered himself, reasoning that this was a major culture shock compared to where he'd just flown in from.

They rounded another corner and they were now back where they had started from. Ali was sitting cross legged on the driveway beside the Ford enthusiastically tucking into the remains of Elsa's culinary efforts.

The two men stepped back into the house and the familiar strains of Mozart greeted them. Barma picked up Alex's drink and passed it to him.

"So when do you think you'll be able to start?"

"End of March I'd have thought." He took another long draught from his iced water.

"Great, that's good to know. You know it's a great opportunity Alex?"

Alex gave a nod of understanding.

"I've met the owners you know?"

"Really? Alex was not sure what this actually meant, other than that Chris was trying to impress him with his networking skills.

"Yup, Khalid Bin Bafaz, he's a very private man, but he likes what we're going to do." Barma's tone had suddenly become very serious and he paused to let Alex take in the implications of this last statement before giving a knowing shake of the head. Alex noted this and responded with a suitably impressed nod of his own. "That's very good news for us", added Barma as he then beamed his confident big toothed smile at Alex.

"Bin Bafaz…" Alex slowly repeated, now recalling that this was the family name that his old boss Osama had mentioned to him when he was back in Paris, that or something very much like it. He gave another nod of understanding and instinctively looked at his wristwatch; he didn't want to miss his plane. "I have a flight at 11:30 pm, how long do you think it will take me to pick up my stuff from the hotel and get out to the airport?"

"I should give it an hour minimum". Barma also looked at his watch before adding in a slightly defensive way, "I have to go and meet some friends this evening so I'll need the car, but I can get Ali to drop you at the Red Sea Palace. You can then get the hotel limo to the airport."

"That sounds fine."

Barma then gave Alex a quick rundown on the other people he had hired. There were to be a total of six traders and they'd all be starting at about the same time give or take a month or so. Two came from London, one from the Middle-East and another from New York. He couldn't tell Alex their names because, they like him, were all in the process of resigning and he didn't want any problems with anyone. Alex understood perfectly, he was acutely aware that this was a delicate stage of the process of changing jobs.

Brightening, "What I can tell you is that they're all first rate" he said with a grin followed by good natured slap on Alex's back.

A few minutes later the Mozart concerto finished playing and the renewed silence neatly signalled the time for Alex's departure. Chris Barma shook Alex's hand warmly.

"See you in a couple of months then Alex."

"Sure thing, I'll keep you posted on developments as they occur. See you soon"

As at Langhan's, back in the cold of London, only now with the roles and temperature reversed, Alex waved his goodbye as he was driven off by Ali.

During the drive back to his hotel Alex was in a contemplative mood. Mura Bustan was a sort of sub tropical Trumpton, it might easily become quite unbearable. This was starting to concern him. Certainly he couldn't live like Chris Barma for any length of time, he'd simply go mad. And as for Claire, he shuddered at the thought. Also he couldn't quite put the images of Barma and his girl Friday, Elsa out of his mind. She wasn't such a great cook, but maybe she offered other delights to Barma. He shook his head; he certainly didn't want to end up like something out of a Conrad novel either. His thoughts drifted in the smooth rocking of the car, he closed his eyes and suddenly imagined himself drinking iced tea and then fucking Elsa through the night, who suddenly transformed into Sandrine, tits jiggling astride him, *"Ce se sent si bon."* "Oh my God!" he checked himself, "Stop this stupidity" and suddenly realized he had just spoken his thoughts out aloud.

He jolted forward in his seat as the car came to a grinding halt. "Sorry Sir." The driver's hurt response was as if he'd been violently sanctioned. Alex immediately apologized and tried to explain that he'd been talking to himself. His explanation didn't help the poor driver who slowly and cautiously resumed driving. Perplexed, he looked straight ahead and now and then dared cast furtive glances in the rear view mirror at his seemingly agitated passenger.

Alex looked out of the window at the streetlights as they flashed past. His mind darted back to his wife and tried to reason with himself, Cooks, Drivers, Gardeners, Cleaners, hot and cold help running on tap, surely Claire would manage, even quite like that for a couple of years he thought. Would it be sufficient compensation for all the other more obvious hardships of living here, he asked himself? Claire would not be able to drive, the potential claustrophobia of expat existence and the Stepford Wives effect of living in another country. France had been difficult to adapt to but this was an altogether more challenging environment. These mental points and counterpoints ebbed and flowed through his mind and left him feeling restless and fraught. "I'm just over tired." he soothed himself. Steadying himself, he automatically pulled out his phone from his jacket pocket looked to see if he'd missed any calls. He called into his voicemail and listened, the most recent was from Sandrine, another from his wife and the old one from Ossama that he had, saved some days back. He noted the number and then dutifully called the number that Ossama had given him. It would have rude, given how helpful his old friend had been, not to have called and made his excuses for not being able to speak to Ossama's friend. The phone rang a few times before switching to an answer phone. Relieved, he quickly left a short message.

Meanwhile they pulled into the hotel driveway and Alex climbed out of the car.

"Thanks very much Ali, sorry about that mix up earlier." he said.

Ali smiled nervously back. "No problem Sir." He was relieved to get his strange nervous passenger out of the car. Ali eyed him and wondered what Mr Chris saw in this weird man, in his heavy suit, that talked out aloud and then phoned people who weren't about and left odd messages for them.

Alex slammed the door shut and turned and walked back into the hotel. The lobby was again sparsely populated and Alex momentarily looked hopefully towards the reception desk but could not see the friendly face of Ahmed. In a few minutes he was back in the room and after a quick shower and change of clothes he packed up his few belongings in to his suit carrier. Before leaving, he made one last visual check of the hotel room for anything he may have left behind, then closed the door and took the lift down to the lobby.

At the checkout he was asked if he'd had anything from the mini-bar.

Alex smiled ruefully and remembered the revolting non-alcohol malt beverage. The clerk behind the counter noisily tapped the items into the computer and printed out an   invoice.

"IAB will be paying for this, but they require you to confirm that everything is in order Mr. Bell."

He cursorily ran his eye over the listing, it seemed fine and he started to write out his signature with his usual concentrated flourish when his eye caught one item.

"Airport Limousine" he read it out aloud on a rising note.

"Actually your car didn't pick me up." His tone was now a little peeved as the image of the bearded rabble that greeted him on his arrival came flooding back him.

The clerk checked the computer.

"Ah yes Sir, we are sorry about that, but actually it's for the ride to the airport. Our manager assumed you would be taking it this evening."

"Ah yes, quite right" Alex spoke the words as he read the amount. "So the limousine is thirty Riyals?"

"Normally it is thirty five each way Sir, but the manager insisted we give you a discount and we are only charging for this evening. Again, please accept our apologies for last night." The cashiers face darkened for an instant as he added, "It was a new driver and he has been warned."

Alex looked suitably chastened by this and his voice trailed off slightly as he replied, "Well it was no problem really…"

"Thank you Sir, Your car is now waiting for you outside" The clerk then signalled to the doorman who quickly came and picked up Alex's suit carrier with his heavy winter overcoat draped over it. He followed the fleet footed doorman out through the thick glass plate doors and into the sultry evening air. Parked in front of him sat a gleaming white limousine with its door opened waiting for him. The doorman closed the spotless car door with a satisfyingly chunky clunk and Alex fell back into the soft air conditioned comfort of the back seat.

Driving back towards the airport on a road that now seemed as smooth and flat as a billiard table he imagined how the previous night's driver must have been laughing through his broken tobacco stained teeth all the way back home and he winced at his own smug faced stupidity. He remembered his sense of pride for having successfully haggled with the old Arab. Apparently it had been a great bargain at two hundred riyals and he visibly smarted with the knowledge of how easily he'd been duped. Voltaire's Candide or Conrad's Lord Jim, he was going to have to sharpen up either way.

6. Take the Metro

Willi Spethmen walked into the office wearing a brand new suit and carrying a pristine black calf skin briefcase. It was the first time he had not brought in his beaten up shoulder bag with his habitual crushed copy of the *Frankfurther Algemeine Zeitung* stuffed into it along with his voluminous gym kit.

"Let the games begin". It was likely to be an interesting day. Bonuses were to be announced.

"Well look at Willi! Nice suit my man." announced Jean-Marc with a mock theatrical flourish from his seat.

Willi just grunted and sat down. Everyone had made an effort to smarten up themselves. Jean-Marc, who was almost always the most well-dressed of the lot anyway, had invested in a new dark blue and very expensive Hermes tie. Alex was wearing the same suit, crisply dry cleaned, that he had worn for his clandestine trip to Jeddah. Earlier that morning he had needed extra effort to polish up his black brogue Church's. He had found that the fine dust of the Arabian Peninsula had been quite difficult to buff away, and had seemed to get everywhere. The remaining two members of Bicholot's team, George Tatsakis and Eric Sonnerman were equally spruced up. They had good reason to be. Herve Altenburg was calling people into his office from ten o'clock onwards.

"Has anyone seen Alain about?" George Tatsakis asked looking anxiously around the desk.

Bicholot's office, which was located in a glass fronted room that was directly behind their trading desk, was eerily quiet and dark that morning. A year ago it would have normally have been brightly lit, filled with the heavy set Frenchman, phone welded to his ear, nursing a steaming cup of coffee and his ash tray half filled with spent Camel Lights. Now of course, as a result of his heart condition, he had given up smoking, was about 10 kilos lighter and drank only Camomile Tea. It was a regimen that he loathed and would joke bitterly about his transformation from Camel Light Man to Camomile Man in one easy step.

"He's not coming in today," said Alex.

"You spoke to him?" Jean-Marc immediately asked.

"No", he lied, "his secretary told me."

In fact he had spoken to Bicholot at some length on the phone that previous evening. Alain had told him that he was being forced out of Prop Trading and was going to be given a role pushing pens around at head office. "New Technology and Electronic Wanking" he said with tiredness.

"I suggested to Herve that they should appoint you to my role, but I doubt they will Alex." He said it with a brutal honesty that pricked at Alex's ego and make him swallow hard. As Alain's number two, he had hoped he would get the nod if his boss ever went. It was not to be.

"Still don't worry about it too much and remember, *Qui terre a, guerre a.*"

So Alex had ridden in on the Metro that day with some knowledge of what to expect but still wondering what Alain had meant with his little aphorism, "He who has land, has war."

With bonuses, the earlier you are called in the better and for obvious reasons. Bankers maintain grim faces particularly when they receive huge cheques. After all, nobody is ever overpaid in a bank. Just ask a banker at bonus time. However this dilemma was not one that Alain Bicholot's team was facing. Willi's earlier foul mouthed assessment was spot on. The group's profits disappeared into the disastrous Energy trading groups' black hole losses. Hopeful rumours circulated that they were not as great as feared, but Altenburg did little to clarify this for them and was keen to keep the picture as cloudy as possible. It's called managing expectations. Bicholot's team had another, more succinct term for it; getting fucked.

Altenburg was now in his late forties and had first worked for the French Treasury and then for Banque Paris. His educational pedigree was *impeccable*. Graduating first from one of the *Grandes Écoles* and later the *L'Ecole Nationale d'Administration* or ENA as it is known, he was destined for great things. Alex knew that right now, Altenburg's stock was riding high on the crest of a wave within the institution and that, equally as Spethmen had cruelly remarked, poor Bicholot's was floundering and washed up.

Spethman, as expected, was called in first and returned with an absolutely thunderous expression. He sat down with a weary thump, his massive frame folding over his desk. The others sat waiting.

Softly he spoke under heavy breath.

Alex didn't speak German, but it really did not need translation. Before Willi could say anything more the dealer boards were chiming an incoming internal line. Different phone lines had different sounds, internal calls had a high pitched evenly spaced ring, external lines had a long lower pitched ring and direct lines to brokers and other banks buzzed. They all looked at Alex as he picked up the flashing line.

The answer was his automatic response to any incoming phone call. "Banque Paris, Trading"

It was the less familiar squeaky tones of Altenburg's secretary. "Can I speak to Jean-Marc Sevres please?"

Puzzled, Alex paused for a moment, before calling out his colleague's name.

"It's for you Jean-Marc" he said putting the call on hold.

Sevres picked up the line and spoke. He then got up and said in a slightly embarrassed way. "He wants to see me next?"

Willi looked up from his desk and stared hard at Jean-Marc, his head cocked sideways and his chin jutted out aggressively. He watched the Frenchman rancorously as he got up and made his way to the lifts.

Alex just looked ahead at this screen, deep in thought.

In fact, once Jean-Marc came back it was then the turn of Eric and then of George. Alex was now thinking the worst. Silently he cursed to himself and tried to think what the hell was going on. Had Sandrine's existence become known, had she phoned up the bank and asked to speak to his boss? His mind was feverish with paranoid thoughts as he walked into Altenburg's office.

Altenburg spoke to him in English.

"Sit down please Alex." He took in the seat offered to him. It was still unpleasantly warm from its previous occupant. George must have had a hard time, he thought. Altenburg watched him closely as he settled himself down. The large dark wooden desk's surface between them was littered with papers.

"Well let's get down to business." He picked up an envelope, checked the name on it and handed it across to Alex.

Alex opened it, unfolded the letter and read the contents, his eyes quickly finding the all important numbers. It was exactly one half of what he would have expected to have received if the Energy trading losses hadn't occurred. He folded the letter in half and put it into his jacket inside pocket. His worst fears were misplaced. Altenburg smiled inwardly to himself as he saw the Englishman's tense shoulders relax. He knew how traders worked and his intention had been to bring down this fellow a little bit. He had a reputation for being a bit of a stickler for detail. Making him wait seemed to have worked. No great histrionics yet. That German had been a nightmare.

"You understand that we've been put in a difficult position?"

Alex nodded his understanding as the French technocrat made his introductory preamble. Alex wondered when the Frenchman was going to get to the point. He did not have to wait long; Altenburg was also a busy man.

"Co-heads?" Alex's experience of the Co-Head condition was that it was the prelude to confusion and destructive jockeying between the Co-Heads. It was always a temporary arrangement. So, this was the palliative on offer, a new title and a divisive working arrangement. His earlier paranoid mood had completely evaporated and his face could not hide that this news was less than satisfactory. His feigning now turned to the real McCoy.

"Yes, Alain has given me a glowing report on both of you and it was his recommendation to me." Altenburg smiled with a face that suggested the matter was no longer up for discussion and pointedly looked at his watch. "Well I'm sure you have much to do, I know I have."

Alex got up from the seat and Altenburg stepped around his desk and offered his hand, "Let's arrange to meet next week."

Alex gave a short nod of assent and shook the proffered hand. "Sure." He said in a determinedly measured tone.

Before going back to his desk he took the lift right down to the ground floor and made a quick call on his mobile from the small café opposite the bank's building. Chris Barma picked up the line.

"Chris? It's Alex Bell speaking."

"Hi Alex how are you?"

"Fine thanks Chris, and you?"

"Just great thanks. How're things going?"

"Good thanks. I'll be faxing through those contracts this evening."

"That's great news Alex. I'll tell Saleem to look out for them. "Make sure you send the originals by mail too please."

Next he phoned Claire. She immediately picked up the phone line. "How did it go?"

He quickly gave her a broad brushed picture of his talk with Altenburg and more importantly the numbers.

"What bastards!" Alex then told her that he was going to fax the signed contracts back to Jeddah.

"OK." Her enthusiasm was underwhelming. They agreed that they would discuss it all that evening over dinner. Stepping back into the nearly empty dealing room, he strode over to his desk and removed an A4 sized envelope from one of the locked drawers. He took out the signed contracts from IAB and walked over to the fax machine and plugged the phone number that Chris Barma had just given him into it. He waited the five minutes or so it took for the papers to be sent warbling on their way through and then picked up the print out from the machine which confirmed that all the pages had been sent correctly. He carefully tore up the fax confirmation and chucked the bits of paper into his bin.

The phone line started to ring out, it was the long lower pitched drone that signified an external line. He turned to the desk and saw it was one of his lines that was flashing menacingly in the darken gloom of the room. He reached over and picked up the call.

He knew, before he had even heard the voice on the end of the line, that it was her. "Banque Paris, Trading."

"Alex! It's me Sandrine. How are you my darling?"

It had been a tense day and he really did not need another one of these harrowing calls. He collected himself and replied. "I'm fine. How are you?"

"I'm OK, but missing you so much." She paused for waiting for him to respond.

"Look Sandrine, I'm a bit tied up at the moment." He looked around the empty room with only a few support people left, tapping away expertly at their workstations. "Can we talk tomorrow? It's a bit busy here…"

"Yes of course my love. So I'll see you at five tomorrow?"

"That might be a bit difficult." His mind was working slowly, he was tired and he struggled to remember what he had said to her last.

"Why?"

"I've got a business meeting tomorrow." He said hesitantly.

"Well Wednesday then." She sounded frustrated. "Then I'll come to your office shall I?"

Rising panic acted to blow away the tiredness from him. "No, no, I'll meet you at the usual place."

"OK, good, that's settled then." Then more sweetly, "I'm really looking forward to it. Speak later my love. Kisses"

"Bye Sandrine."

He hung the phone up and shook his head. The woman was impossible but he had to keep his nerve, keep her sweet and stick to his plan. He steadied himself while he quickly tidied his desk. As long as he kept his cool everything would be fine he said to himself. He finished up and walked over to the lift and pushed the button to descend. When the doors opened three salesmen from the Equity floors above were in riotous mood, their laughter spilled out of the opened doors, their faces already as red as they were about to paint the city.

After looking in on the boys, who were getting ready for bed, he and Claire went out to dinner to discuss what the next practical steps that they would be taking would be. Before leaving, Claire gave details of where they were going to Alice who was babysitting that night. Alice was normally fine about babysitting. She would have her 'sister' or 'cousin' come around and help keep her company. It never ceased to amaze both of them how many relations Alice had living in Paris. Most of the Filipino maids like her were illegal migrant workers. You could see then by the dozen, pushing immaculately dressed toddlers around the well kept sandy parks of the 8th and 16th *arrondissements*. Alice had previously been working for a French couple who had moved to Brussels and she had been recommended to them by mutual friends. That was how the system operated within the blessed triangulation of NAP; Neuilly, Auteuil and Passy. Rich folk with cheap labour.

When he had moved to the area on the advice of a snooty American, "relocation expert", Jean-Marc had teased him and had sung a little ditty.

Auteuil-Neuilly-Passy, c'est pas du gâteau;

Auteuil-Neuilly-Passy, tel est notre ghetto

Alex later learnt that the words came from a song by Les Inconnus and viciously satirized BCBG brats. It was, he had to admit, very apt.

His sons, Christopher and Anthony would be breaking up for half term soon anyway and David was still only in the Montessori nursery. They were all young enough that the move shouldn't be too disruptive to their schooling. They had already given notice to their tenants, an American couple with a clutch of children, that they would need their house in Fulham back by the second week of March. They had agreed in late November that Alex would most likely be leaving Banque Paris and though Claire had initially been excited to be going back to England, the disappointment that this was only going to be for a few months, was not one that she bore easily. The prospect of the Middle-East was not worth thinking about. They settled on a date, the first week in March, when they would go skiing and then return to London after the holiday. She and the kids would then move in to the Fulham house and Alex would see to the arrangements for the packing up of their life in Paris. Alex would be in Jeddah by the first week of April at latest.

"You know I'll miss Paris, it's been good after all," she said with a tired yawn as they walked up Avenue Mozart back towards their apartment. Alex would miss it too, he thought, but not just yet.

Not yet indeed. That following Wednesday Alex met Sandrine at their usual place and as they were dressing gently let drop the fact that he might be going on a business trip to the US. Sandrine stopped buttoning up her blouse and turned towards him.

"How long will you be away?"

"I'm not quite sure, could be almost three weeks."

"Three weeks. God! Why so long?" Her face had suddenly darkened with deep concern.

"It's a work thing, you know, couple of weeks in New York and then Chicago."

Sandrine looked down and tears were starting to well in her green blue eyes. "Three weeks will be unbearable without you." She looked up at him blinking away the hurt. Alex was feeling dreadful too, but it just had to be done. There was no alternative and he knew that he could not avoid this. He replayed the words in his mind he had rehearsed but the mental tape was blank.

Instinctively he spoke. "I know. It will be hard Sandrine."
Actually it was hard. He was genuinely concerned for her
welfare, indeed he could not fail to be so, because she was
so desperately needy, but he knew also that to hesitate now
or deviate from his carefully woven plan would just bring
further distress on all around him.

"I'm sure you'll be fine. Perhaps you'll find another
lover?" He gave her a little encouraging smile.

Sandrine pouted her lips downwards and uttered miserably,
"*Jamais.*"

Never. Alex looked at her and his eyes flashed anger like a
caged animal for a spine tingling moment. The word
instantaneously brought back to him all the fear and resolve
and he felt the hairs on the back of his neck rising.

He smiled reassuringly. "I'll be back in no time, you'll
see."

Within the next few days the slimmer than hoped for
cheques were paid and cleared into accounts and it was
then that the roll call of resignations began. Willi
Spethmen was the first to announce his departure and
needless to say the least unexpected. Jean-Marc had
already bet Alex that he would be gone by payday, the
wager now rested on the time. They agreed on one hundred
francs an hour, Jean-Marc thought it would be done by
eleven am, Alex said by three pm. The news that they were

to be jointly running the trading group had not changed the relationship between the two men. Alex knew it was a short term one and Jean-Marc had guessed as much too, having taken a similar bet on Alex's departure with Willi.

The giant German stepped purposefully into the office around ten o'clock that day. He called his girlfriend to make some dinner arrangements and generally sorted out his personal life at leisure before striding up to the sixth floor. It was 11.05 according to the clocks on the wall, when he re-emerged and started shaking the hands of Eric and George who sat either side of him.

He stepped round the desk to the side where Alex and Jean-Marc sat. "Looks like you owe me some money" Willi said to Jean-Marc as he offered his hand to the Frenchman. Jean-Marc smiled and shook his hand.

"We'll see. Good luck Willi."

Alex looked at the two men and a lopsided grin spread across his face. He fished into his jacket, pulled out his wallet and handed over two hundred francs in crisp hundred franc notes to Jean-Marc. Now it was the turn of Willi to look a little confused and his big boned features darkened for a moment.

Dawning realization spread across his features and Spethmen shook his head knowingly. "Ever the market maker, eh Jean-Marc?" Sevres shrugged and smiled sheepishly back at the German.

Willi stepped gawkily around the Frenchman and now shook Alex's hand vigorously.

"See you around Alex", and he gave Alex a sly look. Alex felt his hand almost vanish in the oversized grip of the towering Teuton.

"Pleasure knowing you Willi, keep in touch." Trading floors were not the place for heartfelt goodbyes.

"You too Tommy"

A security guard had just walked onto the trading floor. Willi walked back round to his desk for the last time and looked up around the desk.

"Why don't we have a farewell dinner?"

"Good idea", said George.

Alex gave a vigorous nod. "Sure thing, I'm sure we'll all be up for that."

A few grins and backslaps later, Spethmen wandered good naturedly off the floor. Jean-Marc looked expectantly at Alex, waiting for him to make the same move, but the Englishman just smiled and sat down.

Two hours later and Alain came into the room. He slipped quietly into his office hardly noticed by anyone except for the watchful gaze of Alex who had been waiting patiently for his arrival. He had been playing Solitaire on his computer and was now heartily sick of it. He gave his old boss a few minutes to settle before he went up to the glass fronted office. Bicholot signaled him in with a friendly wave.

Camomile Man was not surprised. In fact he would have been a little disappointed if Alex hadn't tended his resignation. It was, of course, one of the outcomes that he had warned his superiors was very likely to happen should he be removed from the Prop Group. It was proof of his leadership and he was damned if his departure should not cause them distress and inconvenience. Bicholot agreed immediately to the idea of a dinner and was insistent that he should host it. He stepped around his desk and came up to Alex to shake his hand.

"Where are you going then?" curiosity had got the better of him.

"I'll tell you at the dinner."

Bicholot smiled and slowly nodded his head. "Well thanks for letting me know. I appreciate it and I'm sorry things didn't work out as planned."

"I've no regrets." Alex proffered his hand.

Bicholot clasped Alex's. "I hope so."

Alex turned and was on his way with a friendly parting pat on the arm from his old boss. He stepped quickly over to his desk and called up Altenburg's squeaky voiced secretary and requested a meeting with him. He could almost feel Jean-Marc's gaze on him as he spoke.

"I'm afraid he's very busy." She intoned in the textbook manner of a well oiled PA. It was the only part of her that wasn't squeaky.

"It won't take a minute. I really need to see him"

She put him on hold and then came back onto the line. "Is it very important?"

"Urgent"

He could hear her muffled voice, she had put her hand over the receiver, before she spoke again. "OK if you come now he'll see you."

It was a short interview. Altenburg expressed surprise, but his strength was in statistics and differential calculus, not Emmy awards for scenes playing emotive shock. He was sorry to see him go, difficult situation, understandable, all the usual mumble. Details would be dealt with later. He would have an exit interview with Personnel in a week. It was very sad but these things happen. Good luck. Security would need his pass shortly. Five minutes was all it took.

He stepped out of Altenburg's office and walked past the mousey woman, glancing at his watch as he entered the lift. It was 3:30 pm and he had about 30 minutes before the heavyset security guard would come panting up to his desk and chaperone him out of the building. When he got to the desk only George and Eric were about. He needed to make

just one more call. There was just one last detail to deal
with, he dialed.

"Hi! Sandrine?"

"Yes?"

"It's me, Alex…"

"I know it is." She paused before continuing, "Hi, my
darling how great to hear from you." She was caught a
little off her guard as Alex rarely phoned her. "Is something
wrong?"

"Well nothing serious. But I'm afraid that business trip has
been brought forward. I'll be leaving in the next few days."

"When?"

"Well I have a couple of day's holiday first and then it
starts from next week."

"Next week? But I didn't think it was for ages the way you
spoke about it last time." Her voice was accusatory and
just ever so slightly panicky.

"I know I can't help it. I'll call you later OK"

He hung up the phone as quickly as he could. He was fine
from now on as far as Banque Paris was concerned. Any
calls from Sandrine to his office would be handled by the
routine declaration that he was not available for his notice
period. That was one month. Alex was now effectively on
'gardening leave' which he would use to wind up his life in
Paris.

The evening they had planned, kicked off in fine style. Bicholot had organized the restaurant and insisted on paying for the dinner for his old team. It was to be a grand farewell and he chose a grand setting for their eponymous last supper, a table at *La Tour d'Argent*. Beside the Seine and overlooking the Ile de la Cité, the spectacular views of Notre-Dame. Alain Bicholot sat centrally, Alex to one side and Jean-Marc on the other, Sonnerman, Tatsakis and Spethmen sat on the opposite, subconsciously aligned in their old order of their trading desk, disciples arrayed around their leader like the Leonardo. Then they broke bread and talked bread; bread, lucre, dinari, *fric* and *kohle.*

"So where are you going then?" asked George impatiently.

"Enron" replied the German with a huge grin.

"Enron? C'mon, you're kidding surely?" George was astounded.

"Nien my friend, Enron…in London."

"Unbelievable." George shook his head and turned to Eric.

"How about you?"

"I'm staying in Paris, Martha likes it here", he replied primly.

George flashed a knowing look in the direction of Willi. "Not telling then?"

"Not finalized yet," replied Eric with polite firmness and taking another sip of his mineral water. They all looked at Alex.

"So Monsieur Bell, are you moving into interior design?" Sevres was grinning luridly and speaking in a particularly camp voice.

"Not yet?" he was not quite attuned to what the Breton was saying.

Sevres was looking around the table as he spoke. "Just asking, we thought you were going into business with Sandrine Giraud." Spethmen and Tatsakis laughed out aloud and Jean-Marc was grinning mischievously at him.

Alex felt his face flush. After the third or so message he had off handedly explained that she was an interior designer who was trying to colour co-ordinate his kid's bedrooms. It was the first thing that had come into his head at the time. He joined in the laughter and quickly changed the subject.

"I'm off to the Middle-East."

Sonnerman was the first to look surprised at this announcement. He had barely touched his wine and was watching everything with his usual hypnotic strabismus.

Willi stopped laughing and immediately became serious. "Abu Dhabi?"

"No not ADIA."

"C'mon then, where exactly and with whom?" Spethmen was insistent.

"Jeddah, Saudi Arabia, with IAB."

"IAB?" George looked confused and was looking at Jean-Marc.

"International Arab Bank" said Jean-Marc flatly "Biggest bank in the region, big punters."

Bicholot looked at Alex. "So it wasn't Meribel then, more Mecca." He dropped his voice to a whisper and added conspiratorially, "I hope they're paying you enough."

"Just," said Alex demurely.

By the final course the conversation had turned to an unending train of nostalgia, shared jokes and foolish anecdotes. The times they had in London loomed large in their collective memory. The time George had sent his steak *tartare* back, requesting it to be cooked 'medium to well done', Willi's frequent run ins with London's cab drivers, who refused to take him south of the river, Eric's constant fear of being blown up by an IRA bomb. For the first time in many months they fell back into the friendly personas they had once all been. Willi and Alex did their clichéd Fritz and Tommy routine, Jean-Marc did his effete designer bit, George threatened the china and was having a "smashing time" and finally Eric was an unwittingly hilarious Wise-guy, half Woody Allen, half Joe Pesci, "Whadya lookin at?"

Bicholot laughed but gradually become less talkative as the evening wore on. For him, this really was a farewell dinner and he was drifting into maudlin thoughts despite his best efforts. Sonnerman sat primly, increasingly po-faced and periodically taking illicit looks at his handheld pager, his original glass of Sauternes barely half empty. Spethmen was holding forth on the merits of Latvians and in particular his girlfriend Svetlana. She came from the unfortunately named Ogre, which was near Riga apparently, or so he informed them. Actually they had all met her shortly after he started going out with her a year or more ago and whilst she came from Ogre, never was such a contradiction more acute. She looked like a supermodel. They all agreed that Willi was wholly undeserving of her.

When at last the coffees and Armagnacs arrived they were all ready to bid their goodbyes. Alex proposed a toast to their host.

"To Camomile Man, great boss, great friend. Good luck and our best wishes."

Bicholot raised his cup of herbal tea in acknowledgement and thanked them all for their kind thoughts. His valedictory tones were sobering. After he had finished, the men talked quietly amongst themselves as the bill was paid and taxis were ordered. With the formalities done they made their way down to ground floor where they then packed Alain into the first cab that arrived and all waved him goodbye.

Alex felt great sadness as he watched the taxi disappear into the red tailed blur of the Parisian traffic. Jean-Marc shrugged and turned to his colleagues.

"OK, who's up for a drink then?" Jean-Marc's facial expression and workman like tone suggested he had had enough of the funereal mood that had descended on the group.

Willi hesitated for a moment before reaching into his jacket pocket. "Let me make a quick call."

George immediately agreed, but Eric was not in the mood to continue. "You guys go ahead. I'm all done" and with a few perfunctory handshakes he was into a cab and on his way.

As Sonnerman's cab pulled into *Quai de la Tournelle* George remarked. "Martha wants him back I expect, it's well past his bedtime." Spethmen was busy talking to his Latvian love.

"So it's the old crew" said Alex. The four men looked at each other and were suddenly reminded of their days back in London. It was the first time they had been out together as a group for well over a year.

The big German hung up his call. "No Eric? There's a surprise." He looked at his colleague before speaking with

'B' movie comedic excess, "*Achtung* Tommy! We to the bar are then going?"

"You'll never take me alive Fritz," the laughter started, it was a familiar old routine they had, rarely used over the last year but now back in full flow after its dinner table resurrection. The mood was once again up-beat and irreverent.

"So where shall we go?" George was stamping his feet to keep warm.

"How about *Les Bains-Douches*?" Jean-Marc suggested with a mischievous grin.

They had been there a few times when they had first arrived in Paris. Alex had since been there twice with brokers and a couple or so times taking visiting friends out for a night on the tiles. It was probably the best nightclub around at the time.

"Well let's get going its bloody freezing", said Alex. So the four men squeezed into the waiting cab, the driver's vociferous bellyaching to carrying four passengers having been cured with a palliative banknote. Willi gently prized himself into the front seat like a piece of awkward origami and they drove the short distance to the trendy *boîte de nuit* on rue Bourg l'Abbé. Spethmen's bulk, slowly unfolded out of the front seat of the car, still wedded to his mobile and in they went. It was a Tuesday evening so fortunately it wasn't crushingly busy, besides few people would have tolerated standing in a queue in the bitter cold. Once in they peered around the dimly lit smoky interior and after wandering around eventually found a table on one of the upper floors and sat themselves down around it. The music was thumping out with wall shaking intensity and the lights on the dance floor flashed and caught the well heeled denizens of Paris. George, who had momentarily disappeared, was last to sit after, the others all assumed, strutting around the murky nightclub checking out the talent. Finally recognizing the others in the gloom he came and sat down next to where Jean-Marc was sitting.

"Christ George, what is that stink?" Jean-Marc demanded.

"What?" George cupped his hand to his ear.

"I said, what the fuck is that stink?"

George had just come back from the washrooms and replied a little wounded. "They've got some samples of aftershave for testing in the men's." He had obviously tried more than a few. He stank like an overactive polecat.

Alex lit up a cigarette, the first of the evening as a pretty red-haired waitress carefully placed four '1664' bottles of beer on their table. Alex paid and gave her a generous tip. She smiled at the group and then turned on her heel and stepped gracefully back to the bar.

"Nice ass." George's eyes followed the woman as she disappeared from sight.

"You should give that up Alex," said Willi before grimacing and adding as he rubbed his stomach, "Nice restaurant but that food has given me wind", he slugged his beer and belched, "or more likely being bent double in that fucking cab."

Jean-Marc lifted his beer raised it in a toast and said in mocking mimicry of Alex's earlier valediction. "You know, there is a little kid's rhyme I know which is just perfect for you lot."

"*Mon grand-pere a trois cochons, un qui pue, un qui pete, un qui fume la cigarette.*"

"Oh yes, very funny, hysterical. One that smells, one that farts" said George sarcastically, still pricking from Jean-Marc's earlier comment. He took a big draught from his beer and stared out into the room. Having Jean-Marc as a boss was proving to be a bit of a pain in the ass, the Greek thought to himself.

"Well we certainly pigged out. I'm feeling stuffed" said Alex.

"Not as stuffed as you will be by those camel racers" said George with a leer.

"Yes they like a nice bit of pert English arse," Jean-Marc agreed, his use of the long 'a' in arse, testament to his years spent in London.

Willi was watching the entrance to the floor they were on when he next spoke. "So Jean-Marc, I believe there is some money owed around this table."

"What did you say?" The DJ was playing 'London Calling' by the 'Clash', very loud.

Louder, "You owe me some money Jayem!"

"Money?"

"Yes money. Alex?" Willi turned to Alex. "What time was it when you resigned?"

Alex thought for a moment, it was already becoming ancient history in his mind. His mind raced back to the day and rewound through to the moment he stepped out 'The Arse's' office. "Four o'clock."

"Ha! There you have it. Hand it over Jean-Marc." Willi flipped his huge hand out for payment.

"Are you quite sure?" Jean-Marc had money riding on it.

Alex concentrated through the Sauternes, Lynch Bages, Armagnac and the '1664' that was clouding his memory. In the background they had put on the Macarena and some of the trendy crowd on the dance floor below them, were joining in despite the irony that the DJ had intended. "No wait it was about three thirty, err, yeah half past three."

"What did you say?" His answer had been drowned out by "Oh! Macarena's"

"I said half past three." Alex was shouting.

"OK. So three thirty then Mr. Sevres" Willi was looking pleased.

Jean-Marc pulled out his wallet and the Frenchman paused for a moment and made a quick calculation. "OK so it was mid market 1:30 I owe you two hours which is exactly one hundred …" Sevres already had the hundred franc note in his hand and slapped it down on the table with relish, "Enjoy!"

Alex smiled. "You went long at 4 o'clock Willi?"

"Yup" Willi eagerly pocketed the note.

"Very nice doing business with you gentlemen" Jean-Marc was grinning. "And just to show what a good guy I am, I'll buy the next round."

George was still looking a little confused. "What was that about?" he asked Alex.

"It was a little bet we had running. Smart Arse here hedged himself up quite well it sounds. Fifty francs an hour right?" Sevres nodded enthusiastically. Alex continued, "Except he had bet with both Willi and with me, though neither of us knew it at the time."

"Well I figured that at least one of you was going to go in the morning and one would be forced to wait. I was only pissed off that Camomile Man came in so late. Both of you had pretty much told me that you were going so it was a bit of fun."

Willi had just stood up and his face had taken on a look of bright eyed happiness whilst he waved his arms above his head. The men all turned to look in the direction he was waving and from across the room appeared the siren from Ogre. Svetlana Pavliva floated across to the assembled group.

"Hi" she said to them all after she emerged from the enveloping hug of her German amour. She had straight dark hard hair and a flawless complexion. About 23, her oval blue eyes, their long lashes fluttering, danced over the four men who had by now all taken to their feet. Her smile revealed a perfect set of white teeth, which flashed in the reflected light of the dance floor. She was wearing just a simple T-shirt and hipster jeans, which revealed an impossibly flat mid-rift. Paris suited her.

"You remember George, Alex and Jean-Marc" Willi helpfully pointed to each of them as he spoke. The music was still pumping out at a tinnitus inducing level so that the introductions were unheard by the men themselves. Nonetheless each of them nodded their acknowledgements and a seat was offered to her beside her beau.

"So how did Willi persuade you to come out at this time of night?" George was almost dribbling as he spoke.

She laughed pleasantly at the question before answering. "Vell Willi vanted me to give him a lift hoom, zho here I am?"

"mein Liebling sind du zu mir so gut." He placed a hand proprietarily on her lap and gave her thigh a gentle squeeze.

"I could have got a cab you know?"

"She leant forward and kissed him lightly on the nose. "I vanted to. It vas no problem."

"Can I get you a drink?" Jean-Marc was waving to get the attention of the red-haired waitress.

"A Badoit vood be great, thanks."

The round was ordered and another four beers and a bottle of mineral water duly arrived. The slavering Tatsakis was no longer interested in the shapely waitress and she smilingly eyed the competition as she poured out the mineral water. Seeing the Latvian she realized that there was no competition and she offered the bill to the Frenchman with a perfunctory smile. Sevres paid the waitress as he talked and left, as the flame haired server had correctly predicted, a small tip. That was the end of the big tips from this table she thought and she turned and snake hipped her way back off back to the bar. They sat there making small conversation for a while but the music below made conversation increasingly redundant. Willi and Svetlana were more and more engaged in their own little conversation. George sat watching out for women as they cruised past the table, Jean-Marc was starting to look tired. Alex looked at his watch, it was nearing one.

"I think I'm going to head for base."

"Do you guys want a lift home?" Willi enquired.

"No it's OK I'll take a cab or the Metro" said Jean-Marc, not wanting to be a gooseberry.

"No. No, pleezhe it vood be a pleazhure", insisted Svetlana and so Alex and Jean-Marc begrudgingly agreed. It would be a pain to get a taxi now.

George declined the offer saying that he was hoping to get lucky, but both Jean-Marc and Alex accepted and before long they were in the car, pleased to be out of the falling sleet. Jean-Marc and Alex, whose knees were up by his ears to accommodate the German in the front, sat in the back seat whilst Willi gave Svetlana directions. She started the car and crunched the gears and off they went. Jean-Marc rolled his eyes and put on his seat belt. Alex followed suit. Reaching Rue de Rivoli, they then drove into Place de la Concorde. The traffic was quite light, but that which there was, moved cautiously over the slippery sleet covered streets.

"Svetlana passed her test two months ago" said Willi proudly. After the initial poor start, she was now driving with increasing confidence and the two rear seat passengers were now much more relaxed about their impromptu chauffeur. Svetlana caught Alex looking at her in the rear view mirror.

"Vhere dyo live Alex?"

"Rue Henri Heine" Alex replied automatically with the 'H's dropped as if speaking to a Parisian cab driver.

"Vhere?"

"Heinrich Heine Strasse", said Willi helpfully.

Her blue eyes sparkled in recognition. "Reely? He is very vel known in Latvia."

"Is he?" In the whole time he had lived in Paris, he had never thought of who Henri Heine was. Avenue Mozart, Avenue Winston Churchill or Place Georges Clemenceau were all pretty obvious. He had always assumed that Heine was some French revolutionary or writer.

"Oh yerzh, His poetry is vel known ezhpezially in Ogre. His verks were all banned by zhe Nazis."

"That's interesting Svetlana, why is that?" The copious amounts of alcohol he had consumed that night were starting to make him feel decidedly queasy thanks to the unpleasant swaying of the car. He leant forward to try to quell his rising nausea. Jean-Marc was starting to fall asleep his head was lolling about as the car, a powerful BMW, turned right onto the Quai heading west.

She shifted into a lower gear and accelerated into the traffic before continuing. "Yerzh in Ogre ve have a famous factory zhat makes clothz and Heine vas a great supporter of ze vorkers in clothz. Ve studied his poetry in zchool."

Alex was feeling like he was going to be sick and he was just about to undo his seat belt so he could sit right forward when she put her foot down and Alex felt himself lurch back into the seat and the car charged down Cours Albert Premier with the spectacularly lit Eiffel Tower majestically rising to meet them on the left hand side. She slowed the car as they passed a stationary vehicle parked on the nearside.

"What else did they teach you in school?" Svetlana was laughing at Willi's attempts to squeeze her legs just as they drove into the tunnel at Pont D'Alma, she shrieked with laughter and just clipped the central reservation. The car veered towards the other side of the road and she hit the brakes, frantically spun the steering wheel just as the car passed over black ice.

"Fuck" was all that Willi uttered as the BMW's tires screeched as the car spun like a top on its axis, rotating through 360 degrees before colliding with the nearside of the tunnel and scrapping along it with ear bursting noise to a halt. They all sat in perfect silence in shock for a few moments before Svetlana started sobbing.

"Svety are you OK?"

"Yerzh" was all she could say though heaving gasps of air.

"Fuck me. Fuck me we were lucky." He undid his seatbelt and leant over to console her.

"I'm zhorry, zho zhorry", was all that she kept repeating over and over but Willi just hugged her.

Jean-Marc who had awoken at the point where they had hit the curb was now shaking and trying to undo his seat belt.

"Jayem, let me out I'm gonna be sick." The right hand side of the car was jammed up against the tunnel wall so they could only get out on the drivers side. Alex just made it and stood bent double, hands on knees, in the beam of the car's left hand headlight, the right was shattered, and immediately began violently throwing up.

Svetlana gingerly got out of the car and Willi quickly followed her. She let the German pass and then sat back down in the driver's seat. Willi came around to where Alex was.

"Fuck me. Are you OK Alex?"

Alex wiped his mouth with the back of his hand and signaled with the other that he was alright with a shaky wave of his hand.

"I'm fine mate." Sleepiness and alcohol had been driven out of his system by the sudden rush of adrenalin that was now still coursing through all of their veins. He turned and looked back towards the car squinting through the harsh beam of the single headlight but he could not make out anything other than her dark silhouette still sitting at the driver's seat.

"How is she?"

"She'll be OK."

"I'm fine Willi honest, go help her."

132

By now several other cars had come to a halt and one of the drivers had stepped out and was on a mobile phone calling for help. Others drove slowly past by them, rubbernecking their way through the tunnel. Within a few minutes the tunnel had come to a virtual standstill. Jean-Marc was the first to notice the reflected blue flashing light on the white tunnel walls of the police car as it weaved through the stationary traffic and in the distance another tell tale siren was also wailing towards them.

Spethmen was once again correct in his curse strewn way, they had been incredibly fortunate. The paramedics arrived shortly after the police who had insisted on breathalysing the shocked Svetlana, despite Willi's increasingly vociferous protestations with them. Then there came the witness statements, both Jean-Marc and Alex said they had seen nothing from the back seat, just squealing tires and the horrible sound of the car being skinned alive by the tunnel. Some officers went back up to the tunnel entrance but the black ice which had caused the crash was enough evidence to absolve them of any charges of reckless driving. They were indeed very lucky, if they had hit the wall front on, rather than slantingly on the side of the BMW 5 series, it would have been another story. The policeman shook his head in tired recognition of how close they had been to a fatal accident and Alex was quietly sick again.

By the time the Englishman got home in a taxi shared with Jean-Marc it was past four in the morning. They traveled in absolute silence each wrapped uncomfortably in their own thoughts. Alex thought of Claire. She would be waiting for him, worried sick after being told on the phone by Alex of their remarkably narrow escape. The taxi pulled up Alex's apartment building. Alex turned and looked at his friend and colleague.

"Well that was quite an evening."

Jean-Marc shook his head and made a hollow laugh. "It certainly was..."

"Perhaps we should have taken the Metro after all?"

"What, and miss all that excitement?" He looked exhausted.

"Well I'll be seeing you", he pushed his hand forward and Jean-Marc grabbed it warmly. His hands felt cold, he was still slightly in shock.

"Good luck mate and say hello to Chris Barma when you get there."

Alex was taken aback by the Frenchman's announcement.

"You never said you knew him."

"You never asked", he replied simply with a weary smile.

Alex looked expectantly for the Breton to continue. "Well are you going to tell me then?"

"I met him a couple of times, you know..." he said enigmatically.

"Right" said Alex, head nodding slowly and with dawning realization. "It's a small world isn't?" Jean-Marc shook his head tiredly in agreement. Alex opened the cab door, "See you around."

"Sure. Keep in touch Alex", replied Sevres.

Alex got out of the cab, a regulation white Renault, and watched it drive up the slight incline of rue Henri Heine and disappear from view over the brow of the hill. He smiled to himself, whilst deep in rumination, before concluding with a weary sigh. Sevres really was a funny chap. Alex automatically tapped in the four digit code on the ground floor entry-phone security system and entered the building completely unaware that Chris Barma's first choice was now speeding off to Neuilly.

7. The Fountain of Youth

Alex was sitting in the reception of the 17th floor of the IAB building amidst the restful green and was quickly filling out some forms which would give him various passes; security, canteen, parking. Chris Barma had told him to take his time coming in that morning, having arrived late on BA 133 from Heathrow, but Alex was keen to get going. He knew that it would be a couple of days to sort out all the necessary admin but he was eager to get stuck into the real work as soon as he could. His intention had been to hit the road running and, whilst in this respect Sandrine Giraud might loudly contest such a claim, he considered himself both a man of his word and an impatient one too.

His first surprise was the requirement to sign a whole load of new contracts which were all in Arabic.

"What was wrong with the ones I signed earlier?" he asked Barma.

"Nothing as such Alex, except this one's actually legal in the Kingdom."

Alex felt a sharp sense of unease. "Well, I still don't understand why I need to sign these papers?"

"Relax Alex. These papers need to be signed to allow you to be paid, look here." Barma pointed to the third page that showed a table but all the details were in Arabic.

Alex looked at Barma with a look of quizzical anxiety, his brow deeply furrowed.

"It's pretty simple really, the country works on the Moslem calendar, and this form just converts the pay from a Moslem to a Christian one and also opens a bank account for you, the rest is just standard terms and conditions." Alex looked perturbed he was not yet familiar with the lunar based calendar of Islam.

"That's it?" Alex looked at his boss with the same questioning look. "But there's about eight pages of stuff here. What does all the rest say?"

Barma smiled reassuringly and placed his big hand on Alex's shoulder. "Working hours, entitlements, housing allowances. Honestly, it's nothing more than a formality. Trust me it'll be fine."

Alex paused for a moment and then signed the papers with a quick movement and handed the completed paperwork to his boss.

Barma took the papers. "Right, let's go and meet the others."

As they walked through the reception they came up to Saleem who had been typing painfully slowly, with his index fingers at his workstation, but who had also been casting furtive little glances in Alex's direction since he had entered the room.

"*Alhamdulilah* Mr. Alex.   So nice to see you again, welcome to Jeddah."

"Thank you Saleem", replied Alex with a smile.

"Saleem, could you process these for me as soon as possible?"

The small Javanese took the papers from Chris Barma with both hands like a devout communicant. Saleem looked at them as if he'd never seen their like before then replied, "*Inshallah bokra* Mr. Chris." The little fellow spoke in a distinctly simpering fashion and his eye contact was minimal with his boss.   Alex turned to look at the bigger man and noticed Barma's face which had taken on a furrowed look for an brief instant at this reply.

"Well, do your best Saleem, will you please?" The Indonesian smiled with a little self deprecating shake of his head and put the papers on his desk.

They quickly passed on by the secretary and on through the glass doors and entered the busy dealing room.   Alex lengthened his stride to keep up with the purposeful long legged gait of Barma.   They entered the dealing room, walking past the rows of desks, as heads turned and eyes watched the new recruit pass by.   Alex followed Barma who was dressed in his localized mufti, a brilliant white *dishdashah* and sandals.   Alex was dressed in a lighter summer suit, the heavy worsted one of his interview back in January, was safely packed away in his Fulham wardrobe.

The far desk was manned with three traders, each sitting with an empty place next to them, one of whom had turned and been watching them approaching.

"Guys, I'd like to introduce Alex Bell." Barma introduced each of the team to the Englishman; Andy, Joe, Pete and Eamon. The first three were on one side of the desk; Eamon was not visible, hidden behind a series of large monitors, on the other side. Andy and Joe each in turn shook hands with the new boy on the desk and introduced themselves. Pete was engaged on a phone call and nodded his acknowledgement of Alex's arrival. Andrew Whiteman was first, he spoke with the long vowels of a Lancastrian, or more particularly a Mancunian. His northern accent was immediately redolent of a hundred comic impersonations, flat, brusque, matter of fact. Alex almost expected him to say, "where's there's muck, there's brass!" Sitting next to him was Joe. He had been the one who had turned to watch the two men's approach. Unlike the shortish Northerner, Joe had brown hair, was slim and tall and spoke with extraordinary pluminess. "Jozef Karpolinski, pleasure to meet you Alex." His tones dripped dreaming spires, surely Oxbridge, definitely Home Counties and he shook Alex's hand with a firm shake and a keen smiling face that was slightly pock marked by adolescent acne. Only the name was awry from the quintessential Englishman.

"That's an interesting name, Russian perhaps?"

"No, though quite possibly if you go back far enough", Karpolinski laughed before adding with an open faced smile. "It's Polish actually." At this point Andy Whiteman sat down and was already back concentrating on his screens, though still clearly aware of what was going on around him.

They stepped around to the other side of the desk. Eamon, despite Alex's first assumption was clearly not Irish. He now stood up and in doing so, what had been just a white shirt, was now revealed as long white *dishdashah*. He offered his hand which Alex duly shook and from which a heavy gold watch conspicuously flashed. "Ayman ibn Seyf", Ayman explained that he had just come from the Saudi American Bank and was formerly based in Riyadh. "Welcome to Saudi Arabia", he said. The thin dark moustache was complemented with a wispy goatee beard that partly masked a sallow complexion. Lastly there was Pete who had just finished off a phone call.

He stood up and shook Alex's hand with a firm grip. "Hi mate, nice to meet you." He had apparently been the first of Chris' new team to arrive and had previously been based in London. His languid delivery, complemented with a big floppy mop of long blonde hair and a suntanned face gave him the healthy look a surfer. His accent was a strange mixture of the clipped diction of South Africa and somewhere, for the moment unrecognisable.

Chris Barma stood beaming over each of the little encounters and once completed then spoke across the desk to the little band of bankers. His deep trans-Atlantic drawl reverberated in his heavy chest. "As you know fellows, Alex will be doing our interest rate derivatives. He's been working with the French for a while so watch your step!" He laughed to signal his light humour and the team all obligingly grinned for the boss' benefit. All of them, except Andrew Whiteman, joined in the convivial mood. For his part, the Mancunian just stared unblinkingly at this computer screen with a face that looked as if he was about to announce the death of a close relative.

Alex took his seat as directed by Barma who parted with the words that he should try to get as much of the Admin that he could, done straight away.

"Don't worry about trading until you get all this sorted out". Alex nodded his understanding. Taking his chair he sat forward and started reading the little booklet he had been given by his boss. He figured it was simply a case of getting various documents together to get his resident papers or *Iquama* as he found out it was called. By all accounts this was a quite vital step because without this piece of identification, nothing else could be done.

Housing, getting his family over to Jeddah, even leaving the Kingdom required the possession of a valid *Iquama*. Before arriving in Saudi the bank had required he have a full medical and according to the book he was going to have to have another one. The whole thing seemed absurd since, if the roads and general infrastructure of Jeddah were anything to go by, the hospitals promised to be pretty dire. Besides being a complete waste of time he was absolutely sure that the French medical system was head and shoulders better than anything Saudi Arabia could offer. Nevertheless, the bank had given him the little primer on the process of getting his *Iquama* so he set himself down and dutifully started reading though it. It didn't seem too difficult. He quickly called his wife and then had an hour or so familiarisation of his workplace with an efficient Filipino from IT, who gave him various passwords and checked his market vendor screens and systems were all in order. He was about to send an email to Jean-Marc when he was quietly interrupted by a small but firm tap on his shoulder.

"Hi Alex, Glad to see you made it to Jeddah in one piece."

Abdullah El-Khoury was standing behind him, the square shouldered Egyptian had a huge grin plastered across his face. He was dressed in a grey green sports jacket and wore a loud silk tie with little jugglers hopping around on his barrel chest. Alex got up and shook his hand enthusiastically. "Good to see you Abdullah."

"Flight was OK then?"

"British Airways were fine, I haven't flown with them for a while."

"I always try to", said Abdullah with an affirmative nod, then with more seriousness.

"Look if you need anything, don't hesitate to ask, OK?"

"Thanks very much, I'm sure I'll be fine, but if I do I'll definitely take you up on that." El-Khoury then gave Alex a friendly nod and strode off into the middle of the room.

It was not long after this that Pete suggested lunch, so the team descended in a lift down to the seventh floor where the canteen was located. Alex followed the others as they lined up and made their choices. There was a fish dish in a thick sauce, a lamb dish in a thick sauce, and vegetables in a thick sauce. Several types of rice were on offer, simple boiled white or saffron, heavily garnished with currants and emitting the strong aroma of cardamom. There were a couple of burgers frying noisily on the grill behind the counter. Alex asked the man serving what type of fish it was.

He smiled and revealed a set of gnarled and yellowed teeth. "Feesh" he answered simply.

"No, erm what type of fish?" he enquired with a friendly face.

The smile was returned with more enthusiasm by the Chef and he repeated sweetly, "Feesh"

Alex took the burger and some chips and the other men cast knowing looks with smiling eyes watching his moves with repressed humour. They sat down by a window which looked out over the undulating sea of low rise buildings that fanned out eastwards below them. The canteen had about twenty or so tables, most of had groups of three or four men sitting eating and chatting. They were the only Westerners in the room.

"A few days!" Andrew Whiteman laughed mirthlessly as they were all seated around a table eating lunch. Noo, ya most joking", he continued in his distinctive way. "Mine was five weeks at least. Bloody eye bee em!"

"IBM?" Asked Alex and was immediately starting to fume at the thought of being held up by some stupid computer failure. The other men watched Alex's reaction to this and Joe was the first to respond, recognizing that the new boy needed some assistance.

"*Inshallah Bokra, Malesh*", said Joe helpfully before adding, "It basically means, 'bugger off I can't be bothered.'" Alex's face clouded for a short instant.

Andy Whiteman shook his head vigorously, "Noo it doesn't. It means 'Fuck you, *mañana.*'"

"Well everything in Saudi is *mañana* to the power of ten", said Joe in a carefully measured tone.

"Actually what it literally translates to is 'God willing, tomorrow, don't worry'", said the South African with gentle authority and looking around the canteen. "But what it really means is, 'I don't care, don't bother me'" Alex listened to the blonde man's words, was it a slightly West Country burr that was occasionally threaded through the South African's speech? Alex suddenly had a quick recollection of the words that Saleem had said to Chris Barma earlier that morning. He was sure he had said, '*Inshallah*', but then the little Indonesian seemed to bring God into conversation quite freely.

He brightened "Which compounds are you living on?" Alex still had the envelope with the brochures of the many different compounds Chris had given him. It was buried in his suitcase somewhere back in the hotel.

"I'm on Mura Bustan." said Pete.

Alex smiled in recognition "That's where Chris is, isn't?"

"Not any more, he's just moved off. Got himself a villa somewhere just off the Corniche."

Alex considered this before turning to Andy. "Andalusia Village", his tone was flatter than the immobile sea of rooftops that were scattered below them.

It didn't mean anything to Alex and he turned to Joe expectantly. Joe's jaw visibly tensed. "I'm still in the Red Sea Palace."

Alex looked at Karpolinski who had taken a big mouthful of his lunch and was now chewing animatedly. "How long have you been here then?"

He looked at his watch before answering and swallowed hard. "Eight weeks on Sunday." He forked up another piece of stewed lamb. "Still no bloody *Iquama*."

"Shit, why has it taken so long?" Alex who had been eating his chips while listening took a first bite into his meaty patty. The burger was brim full of garlic and was pretty spicy too. Andy was watching him as he chewed.

Joe Karpolinski put his fork pinioned with the lump of lamb back onto his plate and spoke with the ease of one who had explained the same story many times previously. "The Saudi's had a problem with one of the kids. My wife, Isobel was married before and has a boy from the first marriage. The Saudi's have insisted on a letter of authorization from the father. Isobel and her ex don't exactly get on so it's been a bit of a nightmare." He corrected himself, "Actually, not a bit, frankly it's been a total nightmare." His voice trailed off and he took another mouthful of the lamb and started chewing thoughtfully. Alex could see now that Karpolinski's earlier measured tones were more indicative of stoicism based on difficult firsthand experience rather than on his self-evident easy going nature. He resolved that he wouldn't let the same thing happen to him.

"You got any kids, Alex?" Pete asked, deftly changing the subject.

"Three boys."

"Sounds a handful, how old are they?"

"Three, six and seven." He suddenly felt a small pang of guilt. Christopher's birthday was in just over a month. He'd promised he'd be back in London for his eldest son's birthday. He needed this *Iquama* thing to be done and dusted by then. He resolved to get straight onto sorting it out as soon as lunch was over.

"How about you guys?"

"I've got two girls", said Pete.

Andy had finished his kebab and swallowed the last of his chips. "None", he wiped his mouth delicately with a paper napkin.

A thickset man, with brown hair in his mid forties was standing beside them. His pudgy red face sported a bristling moustache which gave him the air of a parade ground sergeant major.

"Hi there boys!" He tapped Pete on the back.

Pete turned around.

"Hi David, how are you doing?"

"Fine, mind if I join you guys?"

"No problem." The men squashed themselves together and let the man, who had rounded up a stray seat, take his place around the now crowded table.

"Another new boy then?" the sergeant major said with a blazing grin.

"Yes, this is Alex", volunteered Pete, "Alex, meet David Lee, he's from Audit."

"Hi" said Alex offering his hand.

The men shook hands and Lee settled himself and then picked up his cutlery. "I've got a bloke starting next week, ex-copper, from Sydney." He took a bite from his meal and quickly chewed it. "They're hiring in droves at the moment.

"Feels that way doesn't it", said Joe Karpolinski with a thoughtful look.

"So how's the trading going then fellows, made millions today?"

The men all broke into wide smiles at the question.

"Of course, bucket loads as usual." Pete replied with a sigh, whilst leaning back in his chair and arching to stretch out his back.

"Well, just keep hold of it", said the auditor with a grin.

Alex reopened the Bank's primer on getting settled in Saudi Arabia. Before arriving, Chris Barma had told him of the need to bring every piece of documentary proof that he possessed. Driving license, Birth certificates, not only his own but those of his wife and children, marriage certificate, exam and degree certificates, all the little paper markers of a life pursued with periodic dogged purpose. He needed to get all these documents translated into Arabic by an authorized notary.

"Pete, where did you go to get all this stuff done?"

Peter Koestler dug into one of his desk drawers and pulled out an envelope. Fishing around inside it, he eventually found a business card and gave it to Alex. "Try these guys, I found that they were quite good."

Alex read the little card which advertised legal and translation work. The address caught his eye, Palestine Street, Al-Balad. "Where is this place?"

"Just on Palestine Street it's very close to where we are here. It's the old centre of the city."

Alex thanked him and he walked back to his seat, phoned the number on the card and politely asked if anyone there could help him. The operator at the other end of the line, who spoke quite good English, reminded him that any photocopies had to be authenticated by the British consul before they could be used. The little primer had made no mention of this. Alex was just starting to walk towards the exit of the dealing room when Pete called after him.

"Are you off to the translators?"

"No. I'm off to the British Consul."

Koestler nodded sagely, "Don't pay too much attention to that guide, it's pretty useless."

"Well it does seem to be a bit out of date."

"It's worse than that, because they keep changing the procedures." He shook his head with resigned frustration. "The guide doesn't mention it but you'll need quite a few passport sized photographs too. There's a reasonable place you can get them done down on the parade between the bank and the hotel."

"Thanks Pete. So what should I do next then?"

"Get the medical stuff done first", he said picking up a phone line before answering "IAB Trading"

So this was the process that Alex found himself quickly inveigled in. The combination of misinformation and seemingly perverse working hours punctuated by Prayer times meant that each visit often required at the very minimum two trips. He became, as indeed all of the team did, an expert in morphing queues and how to remain calm in them. Not only was the process unnecessarily bureaucratic and absurd, but also invasive and demeaning. Back in January, in a drizzling Paris, he had undergone a full medical which the visa to visit Saudi Arabia had required. He had not really looked at the form, the time he had gone to get his results, as the doctor that the Bank had organized had efficiently filled it all out with a *"Tout est bien"* and a *"Bonne chance"*. Now in Jeddah, sitting in the waiting room he was reading through the medical form that was in both English and Arabic, waiting to undergo a chest X-ray, there listed in each section were the various tests; Tuberculosis, Malaria, urine samples, stool samples, Diabetes, Hepatitis B and HTLV III. He sat waiting and saw the doctor who had taken the blood sample from the Filipino nurse who had passed it to him in a little phial.

"Excuse me doctor?"

The genial looking man, about fifty, turned and answered him "Yes?" Alex saw the man's name on a little white tag, Dr. Ahmed El-Marak.

"HTLV three, what is this?" he pointed to the form.

The Arab doctor flashed a look at the paper Alex was holding and looked up as he spoke. "Human 'T' cell Lymphotropic virus, you know it as AIDS or HIV."

It was pretty much what he had guessed it was. Alex looked a bit alarmed and the kindly faced medic observed Alex's reaction. "Where and when did you have your first medical?"

"Paris. About six weeks ago."

The doctor smiled. "I wouldn't be too concerned. You've already been tested negative then" and he started to walk off down the corridor.

"Doctor El-Marak", the man halted. "How do you know that?"

"Because Mr." he paused and he examined the phial in his hand, "...Bell, you would not have got your visa to the Kingdom in the first place."

Alex silently fumed at this revelation, there being a multitude of contentious bones, many more than any X-ray could reveal. Firstly he was outraged at being tested for something unaware, not just once but twice. Secondly he was appalled at the hypocrisy of it. He wondered if religious pilgrims to Mecca were refused entry to Saudi Arabia if they were sick with AIDS. What a benevolent religion this Islam was. No, he was sure this could not be true. No. This was a condition levied solely upon foreign workers and it immediately made him feel cheap, like a piece of meat being stamped fit for consumption. That's all he was after all, nothing more or less, just another greedy or needy foreign worker. But in the end, what sickened him the most was his acquiescence, because despite the entire rancorous hullabaloo going on in his head, he remained primly seated, waiting in turn, for his chest X-ray.

The third night he had dinner with Jozef Karpolinski, who like him, was also on the fourth floor of the Red Sea Palace hotel. The dark wood panelled restaurant looked out over a man made lagoon and the two men sat and chatted easily, over a couple of thick New York Strip steaks. Joe's problems with his *Iquama* were the source of much of their initial conversation. Alex didn't wish to be callous and openly say it but he wanted to find out where the problems had been and thus try to avoid them for himself. So, his tolerant empathy, sympathetic ear and concerned demeanour were really just the creatures of his own selfish interests. After the heart string tugging of Sandrine over the last months that he had been in Paris, his emotional quotient was low so as the story unfolded that Joe's family situation was a little complicated, Alex found himself peering more and more over a wall of sceptical indifference. Joe had three children, a boy to whom he was step father and another boy and a girl. His wife was keen apparently to have a more. They had lived in the Middle-East before, Bahrain, not bad there, so he understood how things worked out here. Mind you, Saudi was quite different to Bahrain. Not the same, not the same at all. The eldest boy was dyslexic; it would be good to get him out of the school he was in, as his teacher was not a bit sympathetic. Bit of a battleaxe actually. The youngest had some food allergies so the medical was a bit tricky. Had Alex ever heard of 'Coeliac Disease'? Quite common really, bloody nuisance actually, gluten was in everything, he looked at the bread roll and prodded it with his fork. As far as the *Iquama* was concerned the problems they had were quite understandable, after all, his situation was not strictly conventional. How did Alex like France? Agreed entirely and what about those fantastic Hypermarket things? Nevertheless, quite frankly, he thought the Saudi's were rather arrogant and between Alex and him, Mum being the word and all that, he wasn't quite sure of that Ed Moore either. Weak handshake, never trust a man with one, his father had always told him so. Father had worked in the City, settled and now retired in Guildford. He had gone to school there too and then gone into the City straight away. Pretty good commute. Straight from school to work to become a Blue Button on the old Stock Exchange. Of course, now he wished he had gone to Uni, sounded good fun, but never really was his cup of tea. He asked Alex where he'd been to university and when he discovered this, remarked that he had always heard quite good things about Manchester. Good Red Brick apparently. Other chaps on the desk were all right. Andy was a bit odd though, bloody bright did Alex know, double first from Cambridge, frightening really. Alex listened to the even paced soliloquy and finished his main course well before the grandiloquent Karpolinski did. He nodded and ummed and arrhed at the requisite points. The men then finished up their meal, bid their goodnights and went off to their respective rooms. It was not quite ten.

Alex phoned his wife, Claire sounded exhausted on the phone. She had just managed to put the kids to bed. She,

Nessa Simmonds and Ellen Van Loos were going out that evening. She hoped the babysitter was not going to be late, that was all that she needed. They had booked a table at Daphne's on Draycott Avenue. She asked how things were going and Alex replied that everything was going just fine. He didn't tell her about the difficulties, she would only start fretting even more and needed little encouragement when it came to suggesting they'd be much better off back in England anyway. They said their goodbyes and he hung up the phone and after having a quick shower he flicked on the TV. He surfed through the channels. He started with CNN and kept pushing the button repeatedly, there was nothing on worth watching and sure enough he was back where he started. CNN was serving up its usual coverage of revolving news items, recycled on the hour, every hour. He turned off the sound with the mute button and dug through his suitcase to find his personal CD player which was hidden under some books he had brought. The case was now doubling as a sort of chaotic chest of drawers. He'd just impulsively bought a couple of new CD's in the departure lounge store and tore off the cellophane wrapping. Disconsolately he pressed play and listened to the first, it was, 'Everything but the Girl.' He lay back on the bed with the lights turned off, and sourly reminded himself that it was, actually, of his own making. He closed his eyes and listened to the album until the track, 'I don't want to talk about it', started to play. He opened his eyes and started to watch the reflected light of the television play across the ceiling of the hotel room until the misty eyed vision turned to silent tears which he unsuccessfully tried to blink back with harsh swallows.

"You look tired, Alex" said IAB's portly Head of Risk Management.

"Still finding it a little difficult to sleep at the moment, Omar, the air-conditioning seems to keep me awake at night."

Omar Al-Hamra gave him a benevolent smile. "Yes it is noisy", he agreed.

"How's the family?" Alex was getting used to this line of questioning. It was almost always the first thing that a Saudi would ask after "*Salaam Alicum.*"

"They're all fine thanks."

"Good, good." He gave Alex a kindly look and pitched his head a little to one side as he spoke. "Yes, it is always hard for the first month my friend." Al-Hamra looked glassy eyed for a moment in thought.

Omar Al-Hamra had many reasons for his interest in the new team that had arrived. Firstly, he was personally interested in these men and their activities. He was the bank's ears and eyes and his role was to ensure that they remained within their trading limits and not to blow the bank up on some huge risky trade. Secondly he had an interest because his nephew was one of the group of trainees that was to join the Prop team. It was one of the terms of their appointment that each of them was to be given a Saudi trainee. Sponsored by the bank and encouraged by national policy, 'Saudiazation', was the almost Orwellian term that was used for this process. Consequently he had an interest in finding out which of these men he would like his nephew Khalid to be assigned to.

Lastly there was the personal issue. As a young man he had studied and gained a doctorate in Statistics at Newcastle and had enjoyed his time there as a postgraduate student. It hadn't always been so, initially he was homesick and miserable and even wanted to quit his studies, he was 22, mad keen on football and desperately lonely. His tutor, a kindly man from Weardale, seeing his protégée's difficulties had introduced him to Newcastle United. Together they would go to St James Park as often as they could. The first game he had seen was the home win in 1971 against Liverpool and the young Malcolm Macdonald scored a magnificent hat-trick. He remembered how the Geordie fans around him had initially eyed him with suspicion, but the result and his own enthusiasm meant that his first game was accompanied by grins and friendly banter, most of which he did not understand through the thick fog of a Tyneside accent. It was the beginning of a love affair with Newcastle and a fondness for England or more specifically the North of England, so that now as he looked back, through his rose coloured spectacles, it had been a halcyon period for him. Consequently, he liked Andrew Whitman, the brusque Northerner and his no nonsense ways; he wasn't quite as sure about Jozef Karpolinski and as for this Alex fellow, well he seemed alright. He examined Alex Bell, he was looking like he wasn't sleeping that well. He felt a small stab of sympathy, he knew what it was like to be homesick and looking at this fellow Bell, he looked like he was suffering a little.

Alex was watching the Arab. It was true that the process was proving to be quite testing, but he felt he was up to it. Nonetheless he showed his appreciation for Omar's kindness with a half smile and a friendly shake of his head. Alex had noticed that, of all the Saudis there, Al-Hamra had been particularly open and friendly to the men in the Prop group. Actually, Omar Al-Hamra was part of an oversight function and could have been forgiven for keeping a more professional distance from them. In Alex's experience, the qualities that were required of their breed, were people with highly quantitative mathematical and analytical minds. PhD's were mandatory, as was an apparent love of rules and regulations. A lack of humour seemed to be an extra bonus. Al-Hamra was typical in the first respect, having a doctorate in Mathematics, but was atypical as he clearly possessed a ready and infectious sense of fun. There was only one thing that Alex found difficulty with Omar Al-Hamra and that was the subject of English soccer.

"So did you watch the game last night?"

"Were Newcastle playing?"

"Yes, a great game too", his face was a picture of boyish enthusiasm. He paused and looked at Alex this time with a more serious face. Alex expectantly waited for the thick waisted Arab to say something. He fidgeted with a pen and he appeared to be hankering after something.

"So have you seen the C.V.'s of the trainees you will be having?"

"No, we are still waiting for the last guy in the group to arrive before we do that, though I think that Chris has all of the details."

"Oh! So when is the last of your group supposed to arrive?"

"I think he's due in this weekend. He starts on Monday", replied Alex. He looked at Omar, the smattering of grey hair on his head sparkled as it was caught by the sharp daylight that flooded in from the glass wall behind. "Do you know anything about these recruits we are getting?"

159

Omar thought for a moment. "Well I know one, he is my nephew."

Alex took the information on board. "What's his name?"

Al-Hamra paused for a moment before answering "Khalid. He's my sister's eldest boy. Not a bad lad." This last comment could have been uttered from the stands of St James Park, the way it was said.

"Well I'll look out for him."

Omar shook his head emphatically, his jowls wobbled away. "No, no. I don't want any special treatment for the boy. Treat him like any of the others." He looked at Alex with his characteristic sideways pitch of his head and smiled a little sheepishly. "Really, I just thought I should let you know, you know to save any silly embarrassment in the future."

James Robson was the final member of Chris Barma's team to arrive. Barma gave his little introduction and Alex smiled and chuckled along with all the others except Andy who watched the familiar proceedings obliquely, whilst focused on his screens. Like all the others Robson was introduced to each of the members of the newly assembled group. Alex was sitting with three empty spaces between him and Ayman and had watched the new recruit walk the distance from the dealing room entrance across the room. Robson had a small moustache, was almost bald and was well built, about the same height as Alex. He walked along with a purposeful stride besides Barma who, like all the others in the team with the exception of Joe, towered over him. Like Barma, Robson was black.

When it came to Alex's turn the two men eyed each other and shook hands.

"Hi, Jim Robson, pleased to meet you." The accent was English, London but not cockney and his gaze was steady as Alex introduced himself. Jim had been working for a Swiss Bank in London. "How long have you been here?"

"Just over a fortnight" replied Alex. Barma smiled and handed the IAB welcome packet with its booklet on getting settled in the Kingdom to the newest and last of his recruits before raising his arms and signalling that he wanted everyone's attention.

"Just a quick announcement to make to you guys. Ed wants to speak to us a group at three this afternoon in his office, so please can you all be prompt. Thanks." He stepped off towards the exit.

"Jim, if you have any questions about that stuff, just ask me, OK?"

"Thanks Alex" and Jim Robson started quietly reading his primer.

At three o'clock sharp, Jim Robson could still feel the unpleasant feeling of his burger repeating itself within him. He sat with the other members of the Proprietary Trading Group around a large dark oval table. At the head of the table sat Ed Moore, peering at the assembled group, over the top of his half rimmed reading spectacles which sat insolently at the end of his nose. In his mid fifties, there was a certain weary doggedness to his round faced features and his wispy hair was stuck on his forehead in a cowslick. As he sat, his round shouldered body posture accentuated that he was quietly jogging to fat. There was something mildly comical about him which Alex couldn't quite place. He picked up a wreath of papers and handed out six sets of photocopies which were then passed silently, except for the ruffle of papers, around the assembled company.

"First, let me welcome you all to IAB. Some of you I already know, you've been here a couple of months, others", he looked at Jim Robson and smiled thinly, "have only just arrived, so a special hello you." He took a sip of his can of cola which was never far from his lips. "As you know, part of the reason for your being here is to help train Saudi nationals." He picked up the papers and studied the first page. "I've just handed out a number of C.V.'s of the men who have been selected to join your group. You can choose how you want to assign these trainees to each of you and of course you can arrange to rotate them or whatever you choose. However you do it, these guys are to be treated as part of your team though any P&L's generated will not be directly assigned to you individually or as a group. Chris is fully aware of the way this is going to be run and is happy with the set up, right Chris?"

"Absolutely Ed."

"I want you to know that the bank takes this very seriously, you're all highly skilled professionals and we expect you to be fully cooperative in this process. 'Saudiazation' is something that we are all committed to here in the bank, so we expect you to treat this as a significant part of your job. In return for your time and effort, the bank will reward you and Chris and I will make sure success is rewarded accordingly." Moore paused to let his words sink in. "OK well that's pretty much all I wanted to say, are there any questions?"

The men looked round the table at each other, Andy, Alex and Pete nodded their understanding. It was all a bit Boy-Scoutish. Alex's eye caught the framed photograph of the slightly younger round faced Moore with Secretary of State Shultz and suddenly was reminded of Charlie Brown. That was it. Ed was Charlie Brown 45 years on. All he needed was a jumper with a zigzag trim, a baseball hat and glove. Ayman who was sitting next to Chris signalled his understanding. Jim also smiled, though the face was one of contemplation rather than of any real enthusiasm.

Joe spoke, "Ed, just one thing, if one of these chaps doesn't work out, what is the procedure?"

Moore considered this a moment, obviously he had anticipated this question and his body language signalled that this was already taking more time than he had wanted it to take. "Well we'll have a monthly review process, to assess the trainees' progress and we'll make the appropriate decisions. Let's cross that bridge when we come to it, but the program is intended to last for a year." He looked at the men that were sat around his office, he felt a little annoyed by their smug faces and knowing looks. They were all professionals but hardly in the prime of their youth, all of them were young, but not that young, "We have many young men who could replace any of these guys, Saudi Arabia is a fountain of youth." Moore almost immediately regretted saying these words.

Alex was now finding it hard to stop the Charlie Brown imagery and a slight smile was playing across his features. Ed Moore was now looking at the men and re-gathered his momentary lapse. "Any more questions?"

Chris looked around his team and decided to speak for them all. "I think we've got the picture Ed. Shall we start?" The whole process took about 10 minutes and the men filed out.

"It looks like we'll be needing rubber gloves as midwifes

with this lot", said Pete under his breath as they traipsed into the dealing room in Indian file.

"Some of them are quite young aren't they?" said Joe folding the papers in half. "So, which Mohammed have they given you? Joe asked Robson.

"Jundi, I think that's how you say it" he answered.

"And you've got Khalid, Alex?"

"Yup, Al-Hamra's nephew", replied Alex

"Could be a bit tricky", said Joe flatly. Alex was beginning to find Karpolinski's ability to state the blindingly obvious just a little irksome.

"Fountain of Youth?" Andy was laughing now, "Well as long as they don't rain on my parade I don't give a fook."

Over the next few days Alex helped Jim Robson, who now sat next to him, as much as he could by giving him the benefit of his own recent experiences in getting his *Iquama*. For his own part Alex had been impressively single minded and through a mixture of determination and freak good fortune was now only a matter of a few days away from getting his own residency papers sorted out. He had been in Saudi for just over three weeks. Alex had visited a number of resident compounds and had, pretty early on, decided that he was going to be moving onto Sierra Village which was part of Arabian Homes, which is where Andy was living. Described in fawning terms by the almost

Albino Estate Manager, whose florid porcine faced features were framed with a pair of deeply unfashionable mirrored shades, as the most exclusive compound in Jeddah.

"Most of the larger multinationals locate their senior staff here you know?" he said with the seasoned ease of his profession, as they toured around the well tended streets of the western transplanted oasis.

Alex had already noted the impressive security measures at the entrance to the compound, but the sight of two uniformed US soldiers lazily walking over to a large white GM Suburban caught his eye.

"Are there many US military housed here?"

"Quite a few actually, so the security is pretty good as you can imagine." His sales patter was remorseless.

That much was elaborately true. The security was impressive, perhaps even slightly over the top. The car had been checked, bonnets opened and boots examined, wheels kicked, mirrors poked underneath and peered into various parts of the vehicle by four blue uniformed men at the gate. The gateway entrance itself was a series of tortuous turns around large concrete blocks. Alex wasn't sure if he was reassured or made even more concerned by this. He had been in Paris when a truck bomb had gone off the year before at the Al Khobar Towers complex, killing nineteen American servicemen and wounding many others. At the time it was just another incident in the Middle-East, now it was closer to home.

"Is all this security in response to the bomb that went off in Riyadh?"

The Estate Manager looked in the mirror before responding, "I think you mean Dhahran, Alex. No. They have always been quite security conscious ever since 'Desert Storm.'" The car came to a halt opposite a high cream coloured stone wall and they got out.

"That was in the Eastern Province; here in Jeddah it's much different." They walked the short distance to a high newly creosoted wooden gate strewn with pretty pink Bougainvillea that led through into a small whitewashed enclave of six identical villas arrayed around an aquamarine oval swimming pool. The heat was blasting off the smooth tiles around the poolside like an overused kitchen and Alex could feel his white cotton shirt starting to stick to his back. The day light was intense, even through sunglasses and the smell of freshly pruned vegetation filled the cloyingly humid air. To his left a small sweating Filipino man, wearing a dark blue hat like *Beau Geste*, was watering the thick flower beds. Apart from this activity, the only sound was the soft hum of the pool machinery and the occasional burr of air-conditioning units. They walked through two of these little groupings of houses via a series of spotless winding paved pathways. The place looked just like the photograph on the brochure, blue and white parasols, cream coloured villas with dark brown wooden doors and windows. Alex had spent money taking his family on holiday to identical places. It was like being in Val de Lobo or Quinta do Largo and fittingly this section of the compound was named Algarve.

The three bedroom villa he chose was slightly more than the bank's housing allowance, but he was happy to make up the difference. It was, he reasoned to himself, a small price to pay to ensure that Claire and the kids were going to be happy there, or at least happier. Ben, the Estate Manager gave him a sales pack, which showed the various décors that were available and dropped him off back at the bank. Alex told him he'd be back to him in a few days, but that he'd decided to take the villa.

The following Monday saw the opening of the "Fountain of Youth"" or "FOY" as they collectively were now known by the team. Each of the traders' had their own Saudi wet behind the ear understudy. For the first week Barma had organized a sort of induction program and had asked each member of the Prop team to give a quick talk to the small group.

Alex asked Jim what he was going to talk about.

"A bit of this, a bit of that." He replied with a broad grin in Mockney tones. In two weeks Jim and Alex were getting on in a way that only shared adversity can forge. Under the encouraging tutelage of Abdullah El-Khoury, both were now learning to scuba dive and had been out on a boat all day the previous Sunday doing the first part of their Professional Association of Diving Instructors or PADI course. They were becoming firm friends.

Jim looked thoughtful for a moment. "Honestly I'm not sure, I guess I'll do some basics on Macro Trading, Monetary Policy all that mumble, how about you?"

"I'm not sure either, maybe 'The Philosophy of Trading', or better, 'Trading the Nick Leeson Way'"

Just then Alex's internal phone line rang. For a short unpleasant instant he was overcome with the thought that it was Sandrine Giraud. He picked up the line. "IAB Trading." He let out a silent prayer of thanks; it was only that irritating broker from Dresdner Bank.

Two days later Alex was standing in a room in front of the six young Saudi's. He had spent a large part of the previous day trying to figure out exactly what he was going to say. It was hard to condense into a fifteen minute slot what it was that he did. He considered the philosophical oxymoron of trying to beat the market, the familiar arguments about the need to diversify, capital asset pricing models, modern portfolio theory, risk adjusted returns, the need for discipline yet the ability to avoid becoming married to an idea or position, game theory, zero sum games. He thought he would start with a quote that he had always liked before moving to the idea of the concept of the plausible fallacy and the scientific axiom of the null hypothesis, markets like science could only deal with proof of falsehood, never proof of truth.

He started by introducing himself and then reminded them to ask questions at any time. He continued, "gentlemen, we spend our time looking at prices, bond prices, stock prices, currencies, but remember, as Oscar Wilde said, 'a cynic is a man who knows the price of everything, and the value of nothing'". He paused to let the group take in what he had said. "A price is wholly arbitrary, it's negotiable, and it's totally transient. Never associate price with value. A trader's job, our job, is to find value."

A hand went up straight away. It was one of the two Mohammeds. "Alex, so are you saying price doesn't matter?"

"No of course not, price matters very much, we are slaves to the mark, but value is what we are looking for."

"Slaves to the D-Mark?" Mohammed knew the Bundesbank was very powerful.

"No. No. I mean, 'the mark to market.'" said Alex with alarm.

"Value, like water in a desert has value?" chirped another voice.

"Yes, but value is not arbitrary. You might pay a King's ransom in the middle of a desert, but the utility of the water remains the same."

"Like oil?"

"Yes a bit like oil..."

Khalid spoke next. "But Alex if they discover cold fusion, oil might become useless one day."

"Yes..."

"Well then its value will change too, wouldn't it?"

Alex hesitated before answering, "Well that's because its utility has changed..."

"What about the Saudi Riyal, this is linked to the price and value of oil isn't it?" said the other Mohammed.

"Oh dear", thought Alex and suddenly felt he was going around in circles. He steadied himself. "Look, bears make money, bulls make money, but sheep get slaughtered. Never follow the herd."

"That's what Jim said yesterday."

'Oh fuck', thought Alex.

8. Song of Saudi

He arrived back in London on British Airways BA132, for a week's holiday and was just in time for Christopher's birthday. He had never let Claire know just how touch and go it had all been. At one point, his efforts were nearly all undone by four days of holiday for *Eid Al-Adha* but he had charmed and wheedled his way through the labyrinthine workings of both the Saudi government's and also the bank's bureaucracies to at last finally get his *Iquama*. When he left for England both Joe and Jim were still in the Red Sea Palace, but Alex had just moved out, taking possession of the keys to his new home on Sierra Village the day of his departure to Heathrow and unknown to Alex, much to the chagrin of Sarita Shastaq.

It had been a difficult week. Claire and the kids were doing fine, though the demands of running a family without his being there were getting her down. After much soul searching he and Claire had decided that she and the kids would stay in England until the end of the summer term. The boys had just started school and were adapting well to their new environment and another switch so soon after moving from Paris was not really a very good idea. Only the youngest, David, was being particularly difficult at his new nursery school, the other two were doing fine.

Mummy didn't do the voices right for Thomas the Tank Engine. It was going to be difficult, but they'd manage. Claire organized an Australian au-pair, who only wanted to work for three months, which was all they needed, to help Claire out. Alex would be back in a month. The week itself, passed incredibly quickly and he got the plane from Heathrow, the Sunday afternoon flight, with a heart heavy as lead. He stepped out of the now familiar airport and walked over to the registered taxi rank and got a cab to Sierra Village for twenty riyals. He arrived at his new house and was filled with gloom, he missed them all tremendously.

Now that he was back in Jeddah, he looked at his watch for the third time in ten minutes, it was just half past seven and he was starting to feel a bit hungry. Outside, the dark of the evening had now closed in and he hadn't noticed this whilst he had flicked between a sports channel showing college gridiron, Buffy the Vampire Slayer and a movie on his satellite TV. He had seen them all the day before and it was not an edifying prospect. "Forty channels of shit" he said under his breath. He thought of calling home but with the time difference it was not an ideal moment for him to phone. Bored, he reached for the well thumbed, "Welcome Pack," left for him on the coffee table. He browsed through the glossy pages yet again, stopping at the picture of the supermarket on the compound. He hadn't been there yet he thought to himself. "Great" he said with a resigned sigh. Well, what else was there to do, and besides, he reasoned to himself, he needed some bread and some coffee. The compound supermarket was next to the restaurant so he'd go there and have a burger or something. Again. One week on the compound and each evening was the another déjà vu experience, he really needed to find something to while away the long evenings until Claire and the kids arrived. He made a mental note to go to the English bookstore the next day. He looked at his watch, the minute hand had moved slightly, 7:34pm. It was going to be another long evening.

The villa was absolutely spotless. It had been aggressively cleaned by the new maid he had found, or more correctly been found for him. On the second evening he had been moved in he had been disturbed by a knock on his front door. He had opened it to find a robust middle aged looking Filipina woman, quite heavily made up. She introduced herself without fuss, she was called Amelia. She was wearing a black *abeya* and was very businesslike. She wished him a good evening and did he need a maid, live in, live out she would organise it all. Many different maids were available. She had just the right one for a family man such as himself. When are they all arriving? That was very good but in the meantime he could have a daily. She could start whenever he wanted, tomorrow was fine, a couple of days a week. She flashed a smile and trudged off, business satisfactorily concluded. He met the daily, Christie, the next evening and gave her a key; he barely had any person possessions or anything valuable on him so he wasn't bothered that they would jointly burgle him or anything like that. Besides as everyone would tell you in Saudi Arabia, it was very safe, crime was virtually unknown there.

He got out of the armchair he was lounging on, dropped the remote, picked up his wallet and shoved it into the back pocket of his shorts along with his keys. Opening the door he noticed that some of the pool lights had been turned on and thought he heard laughter. In the darkness, the submerged lights shone invitingly through the shimmering water. The temperature was still really unbearable, even the tiles radiated heat up through his deck shoes and the heavy humidity caused his glasses to fog up with condensation. He fumbled with his keys as he checked that the door was properly closed behind him. The change from air conditioned villa to the outside was still quite a shock and he wondered if he'd ever get to acclimatize to the heat and the humidity. Slowly, as his eyes gradually adjusted to the darkness, he started to stroll down the path to the poolside and on out to the supermarket. He had only taken a few steps when he was interrupted.

"Would you like to join us?"

Alex turned and looked across the pool area to the threesome that was sitting around a white plastic table. They were sheltering under a huge blue and white ringed parasol, which was impaled through the table's middle.

He hesitated for a moment before adjusting his walk and slowly moving towards the group. The misty fog on his glasses was starting to clear and he quickly took in the little group, one woman, big and blonde and two men, one with a beard and rimless glasses, the other with a chubby jolly look about him. "Sure, that would be great", he replied with a slightly guarded tone.

The slim bearded man stood up and with a smile extended a handshake, "Hi I'm Dieter Werner".

"Alex Bell"

The jolly looking fellow pushed his chair back and also stood and shook Alex's hand, "Hullo. I'm Paul, Paul Abbot", he said with a slight shrug of his shoulders and a rather sheepish look. The handshake wasn't quite as forceful as the first.

The woman shifted forward across the table and also shook his hand enthusiastically, "Hi I'm Andrea, but most people call me Andy", she said with a huge grin, which revealed a row of big white teeth. "We live in number 47".

"Would you like a drink, we have beer or Sid?" said Dieter.

Alex looked down at the jugs filled with foaming beer.

"Sure, where did you get this?" he asked slightly incredulously.

"Well actually, we brew it ourselves", said Dieter with a wide grin. "It's really quite easy to make you know", he continued.

"I'll have a beer please", said Alex a little furtively as he lowered himself into the white plastic seat. "What was the other thing you mentioned?"

"*Sid*, that's short for *Siddiqui*, which means, 'my friend' in Arabic." Werner answered. "It's made from sugar and it's just about pure alcohol. It's used as a base to make other drinks."

Abbot raised his glass with a short flourish, "This is Sid 'n tonic" and turning to Dieter with a grin he swigged down the last of his drink, "Mine's a double thanks Dieter", and he plonked his empty glass back down on the table.

"Surely this must be pretty difficult to make here", Alex said as he picked up his drink.

"Well, we make the beer, which is pretty simple really. Sid is more difficult because you have to distil it, so we just buy it." Dieter replied.

Alex looked amazed. "You buy it?"

"Yes", replied the German with a smile.

"How much does it cost?"

177

"This was two hundred and fifty Riyals", said Dieter, peering at the one a half litre plastic bottle.

Alex raised an eyebrow. That was nearly seventy dollars and a great deal for something that might make you blind, "wow."

Alex took a swig of the beer Dieter had poured for him. So it tasted and smelt very strongly of yeast but... "Not bad, not bad at all." he pronounced with a slight disbelieving shake of his head, quickly followed with a happy smile of recognition.

"It's good isn't?" the tubby Abbot added. "See, there's another thing that you Germans do so well!"

Dieter and Andy both starting laughing, the same laugh Alex had heard when he was leaving his house a few moments earlier.

"Don't start that business all over again, he'll think we're all crazy", said Dieter Werner still shaking with merriment.

The laughter slowly subsided.

Abbot watched Alex as he took another deeper draught from his beer then he smiled a little mischievously as he remarked, "Yes it's good but has the drawback of making you fart like a trooper"

"Which is..." Andrea interrupted him with a huge grin and all three of them chorused,

"Another thing we Germans do so well" before again bursting into guffaws.

Alex smiled embarrassedly and tried to look in on the joke. Obviously they're all pissed, he silently mused to himself.

Paul picked up and tapped his empty glass on the plastic tabletop and began singing to the tune of, 'O Sole Mio'.

"Just one *Siddiqui*"

"Give it to me"

"Explosive mixture"

"Of Arabi"

It struck Alex that he had quite a good voice. Paul's reddening features as he held the last note like some diminutive Pavarotti give him a rather cherubic look.

"OK, OK, I surrender" said Dieter as he put his hands to cover his ears in feigned horror. "One *Sid* and Tonic, coming up!" he said with a flourish.

He then carefully poured out the clear liquid to about a finger's measure into two tumblers, then turned and rooted around in a large icebox behind him and dropped in a couple of huge ice cubes into each of the glasses. Next he lent back and pulled out two cans of tonic water left on a table behind him and opened then and filled the tumblers to the brim. It was all carried out with well practiced ease and with a cigarette gently smouldering between his lips.

He handed one of the glasses to Paul, eyes blinking rapidly from the pall of cigarette smoke that now wreathed him.

"*Prost*"

"Cheers my old bean" Paul replied, in mock Bertie Wooster tones.

Alex raised his glass and joined in the toast.

Paul took a swig from his drink.

"Ah, nectar…", still Woosterish

"So you don't make the *Siddiqui*, but you do make beer. Very good too." said Alex.

"Thanks. Well, beer is not too difficult. I'll give you my recipe if you like, but Sid is another thing altogether." As he spoke, Dieter stubbed out his cigarette into a half filled ashtray.

"Actually it's quite dangerous to make," Andy said with a broadening smile. "Dieter, tell him about that Dane in Sharbatly who blew up his kitchen."

Dieter wiped his hand across his mouth. "It wasn't his kitchen, it was a shed in his garden" said Dieter with a laugh. He turned to Alex and lit up a cigarette. "This house was like a mini factory, this guy I know, Steen, had two stills, one in each of his bedrooms. He and this other man, I think his friend's name was Ralf or Rolf, are quite big producers and they had this system where they stored the half fermented *Sid* in this shed." Dieter took a gulp of his drink as he warmed to his tale. "Anyway, Steen was away and told this Ralf or whatever his name was to keep the thing working with some instructions. Anyway, idiot Ralf had left this stuff bubbling away in the shed for too long and …"

"It blew up" Andy interrupted with a laugh.

Dieter gave his wife a reproachful look for having beaten him to his finale. "Yes, yes, let me finish. The shed had filled up with alcohol fumes, which they would normally have dealt with, but because Ralf and one of the gardeners had decided to have a quick smoke near this shed and…boom. Dieter's face had a huge grin strapped across it. "The shed was completely blown up, bits all over the place." He paused for effect.

"The gardener was quite shocked apparently and still doesn't know what happened." Dieter and Andy both started laughing.

"I… Still, don't believe it", said Paul with a wink. He was now chuckling along with the others. Alex smiled at the weak pun.

"Wait, I still have more to tell!" said Dieter who was now almost bent double with laughter.

"Good Evening."

With the exception of Dieter, who perhaps could see him, they all turned to look at the half hidden features of a tallish man standing around 5 meters behind them. Neatly camouflaged by a large Hibiscus that was growing on the trellising behind them, Alex could just about make out his features.

"Hi Willem, good evening to you" replied Dieter with a friendly wave. "Have you met our new neighbour from number 39?"

"No, I have not had the pleasure" he said stepping forward and walking purposefully into the little group's midst.

"Willem, may I introduce Alex Bell, newly arrived from…"

"England, via Paris" volunteered Alex.

"I'm Willem Schuster, very pleased to meet you." said the man with a friendly smile. Schuster stood rather formally as the others insisted he join then. "No, I'm afraid I can't, but thank you very much for the invitation." His speech, unlike Dieter or Andy's was very heavily accented. He was quite slim aged mid fifties with a trim beard and a rather stiff bearing. Unlike all the other men who were in shorts, he was wearing a suit and tie and carrying a briefcase.

"Another dinner to go to?" Andy enquired sympathetically.

"Yes I'm afraid so, perhaps another time." Schuster turned to Alex, "Nice to meet you Alex, if you need anything please don't hesitate to ask. I live in number 45."

"Thank you very much Willem."

Schuster turned and walked the short distance to his door and entered.

As the door closed behind him Dieter spoke. "Lovely man, always so busy, he's rarely here."

"Where's he from?"

"He's Swiss, he works for one of the big Jeddah families."

"Oh really", said Alex, not having a clue what this might mean.

"He's a big cheese here" said Paul with another of his cheeky grins. "A bloody big Swiss cheese."

Andy broke out into peals of laughter and even Alex was now starting to giggle. He picked up his beer, took another taste, yes, it did taste quite strong.

They all took a moment to sip their drinks and after a short while Dieter spoke with an attempt of seriousness. "So Alex, when did you get here?"

"I arrived about a month ago. I've been staying in the Red Sea Palace."

Their heads all nodded knowingly. The Red Sea Palace was not a place to be holed up for a month.

"So who do you work for?" enquired Paul.

"IAB"

"Did you work for them in London?"

"No I was with a French bank in Paris before coming here."

"Ah England via Paris, now I understand what you meant, for a moment I thought you were another of those bloody Frogs."

Andy laughed, "Paul is with the British Foreign Office."

Paul and Dieter both started laughing at this comment.

"I wish I bloody well was. Bunch of wasters..." Paul's face turned a little serious, for the first time. "Actually I work at the Military Hospital."

There was pause as they continued sipping their drinks. Alex felt the warmth of the alcohol filling him, turned and spoke in the direction of Dieter. "So how long have you been here then?"

"This is our fourth year here in Jeddah"

"You like it?"

Dieter thought for a moment and replied with a slight shrug, "You know, you get used to it..." His voice drifted off a little as he spoke.

"The kids love it". Andy's face was bright with enthusiasm.

"Jah! The kids love it" Dieter said, parroting his wife with a lopsided smile and a shake of his head.

"How many children have you?" Alex asked.

"We have two, Anna is eight and Jurgen is six", Andy's grin was now almost ear to ear as she spoke, "How about you?"

"I've three boys", Alex replied with a smile and he thought to himself that it would soon be OK to give them a call.

Alex finished his drink, "Well I was just going over to the restaurant to get some food.

"We're going to order in a curry, would you like to eat with us?"

Alex paused, flicked a glance at his watch, it was 8:30. It was a no brainer as far as he was concerned, "Sure, if you don't mind. I love a good curry."

"Here, have another beer" and Dieter was already pouring before Alex could answer.

"So how did you find living in Paris?" Andy asked and her big smile again took over her whole face. It was a question he had been asked many times both whilst living there and since having left. People never enquire of locals how they find living in a place as if the perceptions of visitors are more acute or pertinent.

"It was great really. I loved it." Rose was already seeping into his recollections.

Paul then spoke, gimlet eyed. "OK. So what was the best thing about it?"

Leaving, was his first but unsaid thought. Bell paused and memories came back of his apartment in the 16th. He thought of the warming Paris of a May evening and coming home to his kids all freshly scrubbed, soft skinned, damp haired. They would come running and leap up to meet him, hanging round his neck like a ludicrous set of beads. Paris was the smell of buttered toast in the morning, reading the papers on a Sunday morning to the sound of train noises. Paris was listening to music reading a novel. Paris was reading Thomas the Tank Engine in silly voices to his boys as they looked at him with expressions of wonder or grabbed the bed sheets to cover themselves at dramatic turns of the plot. Paris was kicking conkers around Parc Monceau. He suddenly missed them all with a sharp digging pain. Paris had been home.

"Well Paris has much to offer. It is a beautiful city, but I'd say it was the lifestyle that was best."

"Croissants and coffee with scribbling writers and all that kind of thing" said Paul earnestly.

"Yes exactly" said Alex with a puckered thoughtful look.

"Garrets and artists with bandages around their heads" Abbot was warming to his theme.

"Definitely" a smile was creeping across Alex's face.

"Lovers snogging by the Seine and toilets that are just holes in the ground." He was talking quite rapidly now.

"You sound like you've lived there a long time yourself," said Alex with a small glint in his eye.

"School trip 1970 only time I've been there, only Parlay Franglais."

Alex smiled and replied, "*très bon mon ami*."

"So what about the French *L'oiseaux* then eh?" he gave Alex a theatrical wink and then his eyebrows did a little dance to signal his playful innuendo.

"Oh, all of them were stunning of course, wall to wall drop dead gorgeous it was", he said adopting the school boy tone with a foolish grin.

Paul Abbot leant back in his seat with the thought of Bardot and Deneuve sashaying down the Champs Elysees. "Lovely", he murmured.

Of course Alex could not think of anything else apart from Sandrine at this point. Many times he had wondered how she was, had she flown into a blazing rage or had she just moved philosophically on. He reassured himself that she would be fine, she was, after all a very durable character. However on deeper reflection he figured that calm acceptance was not that likely given the type of person that she was. It was more hope on his part that she had found his sudden departure easier to deal with than she had feared. He just hoped that she was OK. He had no idea of when or how she would have found out, his French mobile was disconnected, the mail had been redirected for just a month. Every little detail had been carefully dealt with, he had planned and then executed it like clockwork and just disappeared from Paris like mist in the morning.

"Here it is." Alex roused himself from these sobering thoughts at Paul's announcement. He had seen the delivery man approaching. Their food had arrived.

It was nearly three in the morning when they eventually turned in to bed. Andy had left the men to their increasingly rambling conversations which had ranged from the sublime to the downright absurd as the rough alcohol took its toll on their senses. For the first time in a month, Alex woke up with a thudding hangover and gaseous bloated gut. He went to the bathroom and the porcelain bowl reverberated to his thunderous farting. Dull headed he showered and shaved and promised himself he wouldn't drink that lethal *Siddiqui* and tonic ever again. Still it had been a great evening, Germans with a sense of humour and alcohol, whatever next?

Back at the bank some of the trainee's were having a rough time. The arrangement that Ed Moore had alluded to in the meeting was that each of the young Saudi men was given a one hundred thousand dollar loss limit. Each mentor was then supposed to watch how the young traders got on and provide help and advice. Unfortunately two of the trainees had immediately gone quite deeply into the red on a series of poorly thought out trades, sweetly sold by silver tongued brokers in London. Their discomfort was a cautionary tale for the remaining four, but their precipitous rate of loss making had earned them the sobriquet of 'crash test dummies'.

The two unfortunate traders were Waleed and one of the Mohammeds. Joe was mentor to Waleed Ansari and Ayman was Mohammed's.

"Hang on a moment." Pete called out. Jim held the lift door open and waited for the South African to get in. He was carrying a red shoulder bag, "Shit, what a crap day. Nothing is going on at the moment."

Jim and Alex agreed. He pushed at the lift's button to encourage it to close the door.

"Did you see what was going on with that kid Waleed and Joe?"

"Not all of it. Why did something else happen?"

Pete's mouth turned down and he made a sour face, "A 'win-win' trade apparently. Can you believe it? He really is a total plank." Alex thought this was a little harsh on the youngster as the silver tongued salesman had talked the rookie into the trade. It was a common error and whilst admittedly quite expensive, not ruinously so. Waleed and his fellow Freshers would have learnt a useful lesson.

"Well it was bound to happen to one of them."

"Oh I know that and I don't really blame Waleed, but I do Joe, he's a right plank."

Over the near two months he had now been in IAB, Alex had come to understand that Pete's use of this term was reserved for particularly witless displays of behaviour or stupidity. Koestler had an interesting hierarchy of opprobrium, the lowest level was populated with Donuts, next came Muppets and Dipsticks, the whole lot was capped off by Planks. Unlike Willi Spethmen, Pete rarely swore. Another remarkable aspect of Koestler was his ability to speak languages and disparate ones at that. He spoke Afrikaans for obvious reasons but also Japanese, having worked in Tokyo for three years and as it stood right now, after nearly five months in Saudi, his Arabic was coming on remarkably well.

The lift doors opened, they were on the ground floor. "You know that he did ask Joe what he thought of it, but he was so wrapped up the success of getting his *Iquama* on Monday that he didn't even check the size the guy traded." Pete looked at the two other men to see if they understood what he was saying. "He's in cloud cuckoo land most of the time."

As they walked across the large atrium, the men's footsteps echoed out from the gleaming marble whilst in the background the now familiar sound of the call to prayer could just be heard starting up. First one voice and then all the others would start from the multitude of minarets at all points of the compass, the singular sonic eddies merged and rippled out into a constant wave of sound that flowed over the still sweltering city.

"Well, see you guys, thank God it's Thursday. Hey, is either of you going to the US consulate tonight?" They had all recently been 'put on the list' thanks to the efforts of Ed Moore.

"I sure am", said Jim.

Alex signalled his enthusiastic assent with a grin.

"By the way Alex, are you still renting a car?"

"Yup, I might buy one, but then again maybe not. Just drop it at the airport with the engine running and take BA 132 if needs dictate" he said with a short laugh.

Pete considered this for a moment. It wasn't such a dumb thing and he understood the sentiment behind it. "That's true. In a country where you have no rights, have no assets."

"Very profound. Captain" said Jim with a smile and an expressive eyebrow in the manner of Mr Spock.

"Its life Jim, but not as we know it!" said Pete with deadpan seriousness.

There were grins all round now. "OK. Well, see you this evening."

They stepped out and walked the short distance to the car park. Since Alex was only renting a car, he was not able to get a car parking space in the bank's lot because only owner registered cars were given permits. It wasn't a big deal, but it did mean having to cross some busy roads which always raised the survival stakes significantly. Alex now gave Jim a lift to work most days, Robson had moved to another compound, Lotus Four, further up the Medina road but fairly close to his own. Lotus like Sierra Village was considered one of the more prestigious compounds in Jeddah and where the theme on Sierra, was of Andalusian whimsy, that of Lotus was some sort of Provincial France. The compound's faux Gallic charm consisted of names like

Rue de Lyon and Rue de Paris. Alex had initially considered Lotus, but given where he'd actually just come from, thought this might well prove to be the straw to break Claire's back in the deserts of Arabia.

They drove up the Medina road; it was *Maghrib* Prayer time which was always a good part of the day to travel. The car, a small Toyota, was one of the cheapest models you could rent so the equipment was far from luxurious but it was all functional. Importantly the air conditioning worked well and Alex turned on the only English speaking radio the car could pick up, AFRTS. American Forces Radio and Television System served up a wholesome diet of middle of the road Americana, Sheryl Crow, Huey Lewis, Shania Twain and Jon Bon Jovi, into which were mixed public service type announcements and helpful hints on military life. "Remember boats and alcohol never mix", or more arcane, "Space 'A', You Got It?" It was OK for a short journey.

On the way they chatted intermittently about their own trainees. Alex was finding Khalid was starting to come out of himself a little more and whilst he was clearly the quietest of the new recruits, he was also one of the brightest. Jim thought that Mohammed Jundi was actually quite good despite being rather cocky at the outset. They reached Lotus IV and he dropped Jim off at his compound.

"Do you want to share a cab to the consulate?" asked Jim as he got out of the car.

"Sure, that would be great."

"OK, I'll be around yours at say, eight?"

Not long later Jim Robson was sitting in the lounge waiting for Alex to finish dressing. Alex came rushing down the stairs, "Sorry mate."

"It's no problem, I was a little early."

Alex thrust his wallet in his back pocket and checked he had his keys.

"What's this then, you thinking of converting or something?" Jim had picked up and was looking at a slim volume entitled 'Islam for Beginners' that had been lying on the coffee table.

Alex made the embarrassed little grunt of one whose activities had been unwittingly discovered.

"No, not at all, but I thought I'd try and learn a little bit about it though."

Picked up in a bookshop on *Tahlia* Street a few days earlier, Alex had learnt of the 'Five Pillars' of Islam which are considered the framework of a good Muslim's life. The first pillar is faith in God and acceptance of Mohammed as his messenger.

The second pillar is prayer, performed five times a day. *Fajr*, which was before sunrise, Sunrise itself, *Dhuhr* which was around lunchtime, *Asr* which was in the afternoon, *Maghrib*, which was as the sun set and finally *Isha*, which was in the early evening.

The third pillar is concern for the needy, given as a tithe estimated at two and a half percent per annum, called *Zakat*, a very precise a tax. Next was self-purification. Every year in the month of *Ramadan*, all able Muslims should fast from dawn till dusk, abstaining from food, drink and sex. Finally, the fifth and final pillar was that physically and financially able followers were expected to make an once-in-a-lifetime pilgrimage to Mecca. The last sees about two million Muslims accomplish the journey to Mecca each year and that was what all the towelling robed men on his flight from Paris, were about.

Jim flicked through the pages and noted each of the five sections, Faith, Prayer, Zakat, Fast and Pilgrimage.

Alex had bought the little book more out of frustration than almost anything else. Every activity in the kingdom seemed to be effectively pole-axed by the constant prayer times that punctuated the day. When standing in an office it might all suddenly come to a complete halt as workers would uniformly then turn and line up facing Mecca and then start praying. In IAB, whole swathes of workers would do this and there was no doubt in Alex's mind that considerable peer pressure existed on those that did not literally stop and start praying. Offices, shops, almost everywhere you could go, lights would dim and for fifteen minutes the murmur of men's voices, standing, kneeling, heads touching the floor up and down like a strange exercise video. This constant praying was something that personally Alex found had been very disruptive. You'd wait patiently in a queue and just as you were about to be dealt with, *"Allahu Akbar"* would start up and you were back to waiting until it all finished. It was apparently, what a good Muslim must do.

And what about this?" Jim was grinning, it was some pages from a research note from one of the large US Investment Banks, on the proposed structure of the new European Central Bank, "the Twin Pillars of the Euro?"

The irony was not lost on either of them and they exchanged good natured smirks. "Ed gave it to me a few days ago", said Alex by way of explanation with a shrug.

"C'mon let's get going, I can't wait for a proper beer", Jim said with a little disbelieving shake of his head.

They jumped into the cab and were swiftly taken to the US Consulate. The security was quite tight and they had had to pass through various checks and verifications performed by both embassy staff and US marines whose uniforms always bore name tags. They stood and waited, yes they were on the list, Gonzalez and Neimerman, the regulation green clad sentries, eyed the men as they passed through metal detectors and patted them down whilst they exchanged friendly banter with the expatriate visitors.

Once inside the large open space of the compound's interior they were delighted to take in two spiritually uplifting sights. The first was that of the well stocked bar which was packed to at least three deep with people clamouring for drinks. The second was the sight of uncovered female flesh. The scene was dominated by a large swimming pool which was surrounded on two sides by a large permanent looking corrugated awning structure. There must have been around four hundred or so people there. There was no doubting the 'Brass Eagle' as the happening venue was known, was the place to be in Jeddah that evening.

Alex immediately scanned the area for familiar faces amongst the mass of Western dressed people. Most of the men were wearing long trousers, jeans or chinos, though a few souls were dressed in Bermuda shorts and short sleeved shirts or T-shirts. The women were generally slightly more smartly dressed, high heels and well tended hair and make-up. They knew that most of the women there were married, but as they were to discover, there was a sprinkling air-crews and nursing staff amongst them. Enough around anyway to raise the interest of Jim, who immediately volunteered to get the first round:

"I'll get some drinks, what do you want?"

"Any beer will be fine mate."

Jim high-tailed it to the bar area and Alex saw Pete and a woman in a summery dress with a light scarf talking to Joe over by the pool side. Pete made a little waving gesture in Alex's direction so he wandered, checking faces as he went, over to them.

"Hi there, where's Jim?"

"He's at the bar."

Joe quickly finished the last of his drink. "I'll try and catch him with his order. Same again for everyone?"

Affirmative nods met him and Joe jerkily strode of to try and find Jim in the heaving bar area.

"Alex, let me introduce, my wife Helen."

"Hi Helen, nice to meet you."

Slightly waspish in her look, she was slim with dark shoulder length hair and examined Alex with a direct avian stare.

"Hello Alex, Pete has been telling me about all of you. You're the one from Paris aren't you?" She spoke in a soft West Country accent, but her manner remained quietly aquiline.

"Indeed. How are you finding Mura Bustan?" Alex was tired of talking about Paris.

"It's OK." She gave her husband a warm look, "on the Farm."

"It be mighty strange down on the old Funny Farm", said Pete in an over the top yokel accent. His wife laughed and gave him a friendly prod on the arm and a warm smile. They looked like a happy couple, the warmth of their relationship still palpable enough to keep strangers at bay.

Alex smiled a little embarrassedly, "So how are your daughters finding it?"

Helen Koestler's features darkened in thought for an instant before brightening up again. "I think they're both enjoying it now. Kids are very adaptable you know."

"They are, aren't they", he agreed. "How old are yours then?"

"Five and two, the eldest, Miriam has just started at Jeddah Prep." Alex had heard of the school, it was just one of the expatriate schools, each of which taught their own national curricula. There were American, French, German, Japanese an International and so on. Jeddah Prep was the British school.

At that moment Jim and Joe returned, Jim was carrying three foaming pint glasses of beer; Joe was carrying a couple of tall drinks with ices cubes still faintly crackling, colourless except for the come thither dance of a jaundiced finger of lemon. Alex recognized the familiar welcoming whiff of gin and tonic as Joe passed the two drinks to the Koestlers.

After the initial pleasantries and introductions, Jim sighed and pulled a wry expression. "Well at last some beer that won't go on fermenting in your stomach until morning." He took another sip and stood with a self satisfied look.

"I've got a recipe for beer now", volunteered Alex.

"What's it like?" asked Jim.

"Well I haven't yet made my own, but my German neighbour told me his and his was pretty good actually."

Joe was not especially impressed by this offering. "Well go on then Alex, spill the beans. Let's hear it how it's done then."

Jim flashed a questioning look at Alex, who then remembered that the German's instructions had been left unread in the kitchen somewhere. Dieter had even promised to come and help Alex with his first attempt. In any event he had not got the precise chronology or details for brewing the German's beer. "Can't actually remember", he admitted rather sheepishly.

Pete laughed, "well I've got one", and he quickly ran through the inventory of the process, twenty four cans of non alcoholic beer with a kilo of sugar added, mixed together, seeded with a little baking yeast that you got going in some warm sugary water, wait two weeks, bottle up the fermented beer. Wait two weeks, then pour into a jug and cut down by half by adding another equal part of non-alcoholic beer.

"Eh *Voila*. Open, drink, fall over."

"A kilo of sugar for each twenty four cans?" Joe was incredulous. "That seems like awful lot of sugar."

"So all ze sugar turns to alcohol", said Jim with a fine mimicry of a well known old beer advert.

"Did you know that Saudi Arabia is the largest per capita consumer of sugar in the world?" The men all turned towards Helen Koestler.

"How do you know that?" Joe's expression was disbelieving.

Helen broke into a grin. "Our neighbour works for a sugar importer. His wife told me. Apparently Saudi Arabia is a huge importer."

"Nonsense, surely…" Joe's eyes were widening.

Pete gave his wife a good natured wink. "Didn't you know that the Saudi's were such big tea drinkers Joe?"

"Yeah, right first thing that came to my mind", responded Joe with the beginnings of irritation in his voice.

While Joe was still smarting from the Koestlers teasing, Jim Robson's attention was drawn to a man in short sleeved shirt who had just waived at him, it was Ed Moore. Their boss was talking to a young, fit looking man in a fierce crew-cut. He appeared to be listening to every word the cigar smoking American was saying with reverential attention.

"Eh boys, looks like the boss has spotted us."

They all turned and could see Moore giving them another friendly wave. "Well s'pose we better go and see him since he got us in here."

The fit looking man, seeing the approaching group seemed to say a few words and then left just as they arrived.

"Glad to see you folks could make it." Moore was looking relaxed, wearing a striped short sleeved shirt and grey slacks; he looked at home in these surroundings.

"How are you Ed?" Joe was the first to speak.

"Fine thanks. I see you've found where the bar is."

"And a busy place too isn't?" said Jim just before finishing off the last of his drink.

"So Helen, how is Jeddah treating you?"

"Well we're settled in quite well now Ed. Though not being able to drive is still a real pain." Ed nodded sagely. "How does your wife manage?"

Ed Moore's eyes were always on the move, taking in everything around him. His face always seemed to have the makings of a smile but his eyes were rarely still or focused on the person he was speaking to. "Well she's an old hand here, you know. We've been here nearly ten years." He took a small sip of his drink. A slightly embarrassed silence followed and they all took little turns at their drinks, with Helen and Pete catching each other's eyes momentarily. Moore looked thoughtfully around the little party before speaking. He slowly blew out a cloud of bluish cigar smoke before speaking, "Alex?"

Moore had Alex's attention but he turned to Helen and spoke, "Sorry to bore you Helen, but I just remembered something."

"Alex, did you get a chance to read those research papers I left on your desk?"

Alex remembered the pile of research that Ed Moore's Filipino secretary George had dumped on his desk. "The one about the Euro?"

"Yup, that's the one." Moore was still looking at someone or something in the distance. "Good, we need someone to do some presentation stuff on this proposed new currency." He turned to look at him, "Chris suggested you." He rolled his glowing cigar around between his thumb and forefinger expertly.

"Really?"

"You know, what with you most recently coming from Europe an' all, we figured you're the most qualified" he smiled wanly and let the Englishman consider this. "Anyway think about it."

Alex shook his head to signify he'd consider it. "Sure. I will."

"Well look, nice seeing you guys here. Enjoy the party."
He stopped and scanned the group. "Where's Andy, is he
here too?"

"No, I haven't seen him" Joe answered.

Moore gave Karpolinski a quick glance, his lips pursed for
a moment. "How's your trainee shaping up?"

"Well he'll be OK I think."

Moore's eyes were once again roaming. "Good." He
looked at his empty glass. "I'll see you guys later", then
turning to Helen Koestler he smiled saying, "Enjoy your
evening too and don't let them bore you with talk about
work."

They watched Moore disappear into the crowd. "There
goes Charlie Brown", remarked Alex.

Pete looked at Alex askance. "Charlie Brown?"

"You know, isn't it all a bit Scout Masterish, our crash test
dummies? The Oh-and-ten, but still standing doggedness?
Saudiazation, the hair or rather the lack of it?"

Joe perked up, "You mean like Saint Jude, patron saint of
hopeless cases?"

"No not really." Alex was a little miffed that his humorous
and perceptive imagery was not being appreciated.

Jim who had already heard of the comparison earlier by
Alex spoke next. "Where do you come up with this stuff?"

Joe smiled enigmatically, the truth was, that he rather

enjoyed being unpredictable and off the wall. The rest of the team were becoming accustomed to his curious lateral thinking processes. Only Pete was less than impressed and had now labelled him as, 'The Weird Plank.'

"Polish Catholic, like the Pope" he said with a shrug.

"Jude eh?" said Pete. "I like that."

Jim looked at his empty glass examining it theatrically. "So do I have to pray to Saint Jude to get this filled with beer, since this seems a hopeless situation." He turned the glass upside down to emphasize his point, "or are you going to get your round in?"

"Sorry mate, I'm on my way. Same again for everyone?"

"Could I have a Beck's this time?"

Alex wandered off towards the bar. "I don't know about him being Charlie Brown, but do you think he might be gay?" Joe was looking quite serious.

"What Alex?" asked Pete with a short laugh.

"No, I mean Ed", insisted Joe a little frustrated.

"What makes you say that?" Jim was slightly incredulous.

"Well that weirdo he has for a secretary for starters, George whatever his name is. He's as bent as a butchers hook."

Pete now broke into a wide grin. "So you figure Moore is gay because he has an effeminate secretary?"

Joe took on an affronted look. "Well yes."

Pete shook his head in disbelief. "Look mate, most of the Filipino secretaries are gay in case you hadn't noticed." He turned and grinned at Helen, "Actually I quite fancy him myself."

Helen Koestler giggled and gave her husband another playful slap. "You two timer, you!"

By the time Alex came back, to his pleasant surprise their little group had been joined by one of the crash test dummies. It was Mohammed Jundi. The fact that there were no men in white *dishdashahs* or women in *abeyas* had made him think that the event was just for expatriates. Now he realised that the some of the guests must be Saudi and it was just that everyone was wearing Western style dress. Jundi was talking to his mentor Jim and was dressed casually in a polo shirt, a pair of denim jeans and leather sandals. Alex was part of a generation that looked at what used to be called 'Jesus Boots' with mild horror, now such footwear was associated by him with 2CV, *uber* Greenpeace types.

Pete, who had come to the bar to help him carry the drinks back, greeted Mohammed with a big smile. "*Salaam Alicum.*"

"*Walicum Salaam* Pete", replied Mohammed with a cheeky grin.

"I didn't know they let your lot in here", said Pete passing a drink to his wife and a beer to Joe.

Alex passed a bottle of beer to Jim. Mohammed, Mexican beer with a lime stuffed in the neck of the bottle, was good naturedly smiling at the cheek of Pete's comment. He took a short swig. "Well if we are good boys we can come in." he said in a mocking guttural Arabic accent complete with a Shakespearean touch of his forelock. Mohammed spoke perfect English with a pleasant East Coast accent; Hampton's not Harwich.

"Mohammed was just saying that he'd be happy to take us out on his boat", said Jim.

"Well only if you'd like to." He was looking at Alex as he spoke, "Don't expect great things. It's not a massive Gin-Palace that should be moored off Marbella you know."

"That sounds great." Alex took a draught of the cooling lager. This warm evening was proving to be quite entertaining.

"So you two are doing the diving course?" enquired Joe. Alex and Jim both nodded their agreement, like Tweedle Dum and Tweedle Dee.

"We finish our 'Open Water' course on Sunday." Alex said it as casually as he could manage but in truth he was rather pleased with himself.

"Isn't it dangerous?" Helen Koestler was looking a little concerned. Alex was pleased as punch at this question, an opportunity to show off his daring do.

"Oh not really." said Jim, beating him to the Alpha male punch line.

"Well, when you get qualified you can both come diving with me and my brother OK?" Mohammed said in his smooth American accent.

"Do you dive too?" Pete was intrigued.

"Not so much now, I do a fair amount of spear fishing, but the boat's equipped to do most things."

Pete brightened, "Is it good fun?"

Mohammed's face clouded for a brief moment. "Diving or Fishing?"

"Diving."

"Don't you get any ideas of doing it yourself, leaving me on the old Farm, I'd be worried sick", she rolled the word 'Farm' around her mouth like a marble then batted her eyelashes in the manner of a slim-line Friesian. Pete looked at her and she gave him another friendly dig.

Koestler responded with a deliberate hang dog look, "But Mum…" before breaking into a chuckle. "Nah, not my scene at all. Fish are only good with chips and vinegar."

"Feesh?" said Jim with a fair impression of the IAB chef and they all joined in the laughter.

"Thank God it's Friday tomorrow", Joe looked quite serious, "I couldn't face another IAB canteen meal."

"Hey, Fudruckers tomorrow boys?" Jim liked the restaurant and the men all nodded their agreement. It was not a bad burger place.

"So Mohammed, how are you finding this bunch that you work with, are they horrible to you?"

"Oh they're not as bad as they look."

"That's not saying much", Helen pulled a grimace and Mohammed looked at the little group with a playful glint.

"No really, they're OK."

"Hard to believe, next you'll be telling me they're useful."

"Oh, I wouldn't go that far" he said breaking into mischievous laughter.

As the evening wore on and started to cool down, the consulate guests were starting to drift away. Jim, Joe, Alex and Mohammed stayed, like quite a few, until the bar closed. Mohammed was telling Jim about the thrills of powerboat racing and Alex and Joe met a couple of off duty US servicemen who also lived on Sierra. They had regulation haircuts and were in their late twenties. Both were with the US military and were Advisors, or so they said. They seemed a bit young to be Advisors, in Alex's opinion, but they were easy going and friendly enough, a Nebraskan and a Californian. Like all off-duty military types their language was loaded with acronyms which they fired with bewildering salvoes.

"Yes Sir, we're TAFT guys with the USMTM here in Jeddah, directed by JAD and reporting directly to CENTCOM at MacDill." It seemed like complete drivel to Alex, or maybe it was just the copious amounts of beer that he had drunk.

"Daft guys?" Sometimes, all Alex wanted was for Joe to just shut up for a minute.

The taller one, Jerry was his name, smiled wanly and cleared up the confusion. "TAFT" he spelt out the word in a Midwestern accent. "Technical Assistance Field Teams."

"So you chaps are training the Saudi's?"

The two Americans were amused by the strange Limey's accent and periodically looked at each other with barely concealed humour. "Yes, Sir you could call it that." said Ernesto.

"Are you both flyers, like in 'Top Gun?'" Joe was persistent in his line of enquiry.

They both laughed at this. "That Tom Cruise sure has a lot to answer for", Ernesto swigged the remains of his beer. "No, we're support for the RSADF with field work and training of their Patriot missile systems."

Everyone knew what these were. Saddam's Scuds had been shot out the dark night skies by this flashy state-of-the-art anti-ballistic missile system during the Persian Gulf War of 1991. Alex even knew that its manufacturer was Raytheon, because it had a huge one company only compound slap bang next to Sierra Village. Single company compounds were a bit of a rarity these days, most like Sierra, now housed the global incorporated village. Just recently there had been some controversy over the Patriot Systems' claims to success and that its strike rate had been grossly inflated during the Desert Storm conflict. There was also some talk of its expense. "Patriot Missiles, Oh yes I remember the pictures on telly with all those bits of blown up Scud over Israel."

The American basked in the glow of the inferred praise. Alex thought about it, it had always seemed such a mismatch; even their names eloquently described the futility of the contest. Patriots were bold and sure footed, resolute and sharp eyed, what was a Scud? An odd little onomatopoeia for an aborted sneeze, how could something with so meagre and pathetic a name ever hope to be a threat? It was just silly.

Joe was also pensive. He was finding the Saudi trainee he had been given a little difficult to handle, not quite as explosive as the American's technology, but just as likely to blow up in his opinion. Waleed Ansari was a funny fellow and he and Joe were not, as he put it in his own words, really getting along. "Training Saudi's can be quite demanding", he said with an engaging smile. Perhaps he wasn't the only one experiencing problems with them.

Ernesto looked at Jerry and exchanged a knowing look. "Well we find they're darn efficient. Alpha Charlie Echo technically and all FUBAR"

"Fubar?" asked Joe. Alex noticed Jerry looked alarmed for an instant and he stared hard at Ernesto Sanchez.

"No, I said, 'super'", said Ernesto in a hugely over the top English accent, long vowels and sibilance vying for first place. Jerry laughed out loud at this and he slapped his mate on the shoulder with bearish bonhomie.

Joe's eyes flashed affront for a moment. Were these Yanks taking the piss out of him?

Jerry caught Alex's eye. "So you live on which part of Sierra Alex?"

"Algarve, it's quite Alpha Charlie Echo there too"

Jerry face cracked to reveal a perfect set of teeth. The thought quickly flitted through Alex's mind, that they must have good dentists in Nebraska. Jerry briefly bit his lower lip. He would have to have a word with Ernesto later.

"So how do you find Saudi?" He pronounced the name as many Americans did, as if they had missed the d in sordid.

"Tolerable, how about you?"

"Well Sierra's OK. Swimming pools, squash and tennis courts are my kinda stuff."

"You play squash?" Alex was suddenly interested.

"Sure, I prefer racquetball, but I play squash here", Allensen replied.

"Well maybe we could have a game sometime?"

"Sounds good to me", replied the Nebraskan swigging from his beer.

"So what else do you do on Sierra?"

"Well we have a party most Wednesdays somewhere on the compound. You're welcome to come along?"

"That sounds great", Alex was enthusiastic. Joe nodded too, but was more reserved, he was wondering if they were not being set up as some kind of amusement for this American's buddies.

"I'll let you know when we have the next one then", he said with a wink.

By now it was late and one of the consulate's green clad guards had wandered up to them. He looked tired, his shift was nearly up.

"OK fellows, its home time."

Fridays were generally quite easy days in IAB for the men in Chris Barma's Prop team. The bank was always almost entirely empty on a Friday. It was, after all the weekend in Saudi, the Sabbath more correctly. Only in Treasury, would a few souls be found. As for the Prop team, they would drift in around nine, dressed casually in jeans and T-shirts. On this occasion, thanks to the well stocked bar at the US diplomatic mission, several of them were looking the same colour as bottles of Becks beer, that they had so freely consumed the night before. Fridays in IAB for the Prop team had three big events. Firstly, more often than not, major US economic releases, which often set the tone in markets for the following week or even month if it was the Unemployment data, would flash across the screens of the world. Secondly was the weekly trip to get lunch at a restaurant 'Fudruckers', was the current favourite, since the delights of the canteen were closed due to it being the weekend. Lastly there was what the men called 'Chop-Chop'.

Whilst the IAB tower was itself a potent symbol of wealth and power, dominating the cityscape with its glass and steel, to the north just a short walk away at ground level was the real force within Saudi Arabia. Its power was far greater than anything that Mammon could offer and reached from the lowest levels right up to Allah himself. Execution Square. The Square itself was not clearly visible from the tower on account of the aspect of the building. The tower's triangular structure pointed directly at it so that it was on one of the building's three blind spots. Alex had thought that most likely this may well have been a design requirement since presumably the place of public executions had existed long before the IAB tower did.

Fridays were the day when those foolish or misfortunate enough to have trespassed the laws of the Kingdom made amends, according to Sharia. Public gatherings are strictly forbidden in the enlightened environment of Saudi Arabia. The last of the cinemas was closed in the seventies, so the only place where you will see a crowd, excepting the constant flood of pilgrims to and from Mecca who washed through Jeddah to perform the *Hajj* or attend Mosque, is perhaps at a road accident or more likely, a public execution.

During the first month he had been at the bank he had been asked if he wanted to go to see one.

"Would you like to come too?" asked one of the banks obese money market traders called Abdullah, as breezily as if it were to a country fair.

"Thanks but I think I'll pass."

Pete had already warned Alex about ever going. "They push the Westerners to the front so you can get a good look. I wouldn't advise it unless you've got a strong stomach."

Pete also had his own theory as to why they did thrust the Westerners to the fore. "I think they're saying, 'Look you, this is what'll happen to you, *Khawadger*, if you don't watch out'"

"*Khawadger*, what's that?"

"Foreigner."

"Have you ever been?"

His features darkened. "Yes. It was... awful."

"They say that they drug them before they do it."

Pete replied acidly. "Maybe, but the guy I saw looked pretty fucking aware of what was going on."

It was the first time Alex could think he had heard Pete swear.

This morning Joe was clearly looking bilious. His face was blotchy, he'd been less than clinical with the razor that morning and his eyes were still dull and bloodshot. As a rule, he was not a particularly big drinker, so he was decidedly the worse for wear after the previous night's bingeing. He had only recently moved onto Mura Bustan, much to the annoyance of Peter Koestler. The journey from the compound to the bank, which he was still not entirely familiar with, had not been easy with a thumping hangover, even with Koestler doing the driving and he was sure that the South African had quite deliberately driven through every pot hole from start to finish. He sat forlornly looking at his screen and tried to cheer himself up with the happy thought that his family would be with him by the next weekend. He looked back behind and around the dealing room. It was empty, barring his own team, three of their trainees and a couple of the Saudi money market traders who were over on the other side of the room. Both were large and very overweight, Ziad Al Makki and the

215

impossibly huge Abdullah Kitari. One of them, the larger of the pair, Abdullah, looked up from his screens and caught Joe's bleary eyed gaze. The Arab smiled, raised himself from his seat with a short grimace and started to toddle over to the Prop team's desk.

"Hi Joe, how are you?" said the obese Abdullah Kitari with a slight wheeze. Karpolinski guessed he must have been nineteen stones at least and was only five seven or eight in height. Kitari was hardly a picture of health, flat footed, he had a slight stigmatism and chain smoked Marlboro Reds. The Prop desk had christened him the 'Mobile Cardiac Arrest'.

"Hi Abdullah, fine thanks", he lied, "and how are you?"

"Fine, how is the family?" Joe blanched a little at this. He hadn't spoken to them yet that morning his painkillers still hadn't quite done the job. He cast a glance towards the clocks on the wall. London was 9:40 am. His wife Isobel would be wondering what he was doing, he normally called before the school run.

"They're all fine thanks Abdullah and yours?" he said a little guiltily.

"Fine thanks. We're going to the Square. Do you want to come?"

Alex and Jim who were sitting on the opposite side of the desk looked up at this enquiry. Kitari waved a friendly hullo in their direction. "You are welcome too" he said to them with a rheumy eyed look.

Joe stared at Alex and Jim. They looked a sorry pair, but they stuck together those two, annoyingly so. "Sure I'll come, what about you boys?" mischief flashed in his features for a moment.

Alex looked up from his screens and gave Joe a look of tired scorn. "No interest."

Jim shook his head to decline the offer.

Karpolinski was standing up now, feet astride and he had taken on a slightly jeering look. "Not up to it are we then boys?" It was said almost in the manner of a playground taunt and the trace of a leer was playing around the crease of his mouth.

Jim raised his gaze from the screens in front of him. He'd gone through a fair part of his school life hearing that sort of tone around him. It didn't bother him anymore, he hadn't anything to prove, opening the batting for Middlesex schoolboys and a first from Imperial had put paid to that. He gave Karpolinski a half cocked smile. "No I don't think so mate."

Alex just pulled a face and hit a speed dial to a broker in London.

Joe's features took on a slightly triumphant look. He surveyed the two and turned to see Pete studying him. He gave a little shrug before uttering in a ho-humming way.

"Oh well. When in Rome do as the Romans eh?" Andy stifled a laugh and a little grunt came in its place.

The tall Englishman turned and walked away, accompanied by the sound of the heavy wheezing of the obese Saudi. As they slowly made their way through the trading floor, the two men were joined by another of the Saudi money market traders. Turning the corner into the reception and now safely out of sight from the other men, steely eyed, he clenched his teeth with fierce determination. Those two might be all full of so called daring-do, he curdling thought, but they had no real sense of adventure of discovery. None of them did. He'd been in the Middle-East before and was much more a man of the world than those two, he would show them. He would show them all.

Alex watched Joe disappear from view and gave Jim a knowing look. Jim just gave a little incredulous shake of his head. Pete sensing the unspoken conversation on the other side of the desk stood up and looked over the screens towards them. Andy remained inscrutable, watching his screens with his arms folded across his chest like a prize fighter.

"What a Muppet!"

Clearly, according to the South African's unique pantheon, Joe was now at least half way to achieving some particularly foolish goal. At the same time the trainees were exchanging periodic discreet eye contact. Khalid, who sat to the left of Alex, leant back and spoke in Arabic to Mohammed Jundi who sat three places to his right. There was a quick exchange of words between the two.

"On the twenty second floor?" Pete had not caught everything, just the gist.

Mohammed looked up in surprise. Khalid turned and was looking at Alex as he confirmed Pete's words and spoke with a slightly apologetic tilt.

"Yes", he was looking directly at Alex and spoke very quietly. "Do you know that you can see the Square from the twentieth?"

Alex didn't know this, but he was not interested to know it either. He did not hold with Capital Punishment and believed that the death sentence was not something that could be considered in any case. He could understand that people might well deserve it, but that in his view, no authority, least of all the State, should have the right to take life. In an argument, his simplest defence was always that the risk of convicting an innocent man was sufficient alone to warrant its removal from the statute book. He found the idea of a public execution even more repugnant.

"Really?" Jim who had been bent listening carefully to the young Arab was curious. He turned to his right. Jundi was quite matter of fact about this piece of news.

"Yes there's a small balcony there. It's quite a distance away, but you can just about see what's going on" he said.

"C'mon let's go and see how Joe fares." Pete was already pushing his seat back under his desk. Jim hesitated.

"I'm not sure."

"Well you can always close your eyes." Pete said with a philosophical look.

"Are you coming?" Jim said sheepishly to Alex, he had pushed himself back from his desk, ready to get up.

"No way."

Inquisitiveness had got the better of Jim Robson. "Aren't you curious? It's the only place in the world where this still goes on. It's like..." he struggled to find the words, "like the Middle Ages or something."

"Really I don't want to go, it would be..." Alex's voice trailed off. What was it that he wanted to say? That to go and watch such a thing was condoning this barbarous spectacle? That it was the worst form of voyeurism? That it was a gruesome reminder of the savageness of the place, something that even a coma inducing bellyful of *Siddiqui* and Tonic could not obliterate? Surely better just to close your eyes. Or was it? Was it not just cowardice or worse, the refusal to see things for what they really were? So much evil is perpetrated through neglect or wilful ignorance. Doubt seeped into his mind. What was his objection based on? Nothing more than pretentious hurt feelings, like a whore's sour resentment for a trick's less than generous tip.

He looked at Jim at least Robson wasn't fooling himself with this self serving sentimentalism. Jim's guileless pragmatism shone through his eyes and he looked at Alex expectantly waiting for his decision.

Acquiescently, "Oh OK I'll come then."

The small balcony on the twentieth floor allowed an uninterrupted vista of the Square some two hundred meters away. They stood on the stiflingly hot white tiled stone flooring, upon which rested a gossamer veil of reddish dusty sand. The tiny particles, blown in from the Arabian Desert which stretched for thousands of miles on three points of the compass around them, were impossible to shift. Stuck in the grouting between the marble slabs, even the most energetic buffing and scrubbing of dozens of indentured Filipinos, whose livelihoods depended on the building's cleanliness, could not budge the gritty taint. Above them, the heat of the approaching high mid-day sun relentlessly pounded on the Westerners uncovered heads from the cloudless sky and the fierce intensity of the sunlight blazed almost directly above, the azimuth such that shadows were barely visible. The Square itself was large and featureless, except for the large blue dais which sat centrally near one edge of the square. The crowd, who numbered in the hundreds, were milling around and slowly coalescing into a large crescent centred about the dais and kept a respectful distance by several khaki clad policemen.

Below, Alex could see the figure of Joe sandwiched between the two rotund Saudi's, making painstakingly slow progress towards the square. Bizarrely the square was not solely a place where Saudi Justice was most visibly and perfunctorily dispensed. Its primary function for six out of seven days of the week was as a car park. Alex watched as the tall Englishman turned into the wide open space and passed under the black and yellow chevron barrier that restricted the height of vehicles so that large trucks or container loads could not use the parking lot. From the vantage point of the tower Joe could be clearly seen as he was one of the few there who was not wearing the universal uniform of a white *dishdashah*. The snowy sea was occasionally specked by a fair number of black *burqa* clad women. As far as Alex could make out, only the police and Joe were not dressed in traditional Arabic clothing.

"Look, there he is", said Pete, "this should be interesting."

All eyes on the balcony focused on him as he moved through the crowd, the white sea eddied around the tall Westerner and gently washed him through to the front row. Alex watched him closely, he was as visible and incongruous as a washed up bottle on a tropical white sand beach, and he wondered if Joe was not as unlikely to crack under the intense glare of the Jeddah skies.

A cortege of vehicles slowly approached and turned into the square. Led by the familiar sight of a blue Nissan Jeep favoured by Jeddah's police, there followed an ambulance, three large white vans and then to the rear another blue police jeep. The vehicles slowly moved to their places, the two police jeeps to the left of the dais, the three white vans drew up abreast of one another behind the two jeeps and the ambulance made for the other side and parked up forlornly, its lights flashing mutely for a moment before being extinguished as it came to a halt.

Joe like many there was wearing sunglasses. Before the arrival of the cavalcade, behind the welcome relief of his darkened lenses, he had observed that people had been chatting; ridiculous but it was almost like at a cricket match. Low murmurs, reserved, aware that some important thing was about to happen. Not yet, the star bowler was still warming up, no need to worry, nothing will happen yet. Joe started to feel a little faint. He breathed deeply; the thick unbreathable air seemed to boil in his lungs. He gritted his teeth, his jaw muscles were starting to ache. He was astonished to see some in the crowd had brought sandwiches and even more alarming, children were there too. With the arrival of the vehicles, the crowd became quietly transfixed by the unfolding events. All heads moved to watch as several policemen and bearded *Mutawwa'in*, the feared religious police, approached the rear of one of the vans and brought out the condemned. He stumbled, his hands were already bound behind his back and the dishevelled man, Asian, by the look of him was carefully led, blindfolded and made to kneel. His feet were then bound to his hands, thus hideously trussed, he awaited his maker. Joe looked closely, although wearing dark grey trousers the man appeared to have wet himself.

The executioner, dressed in white traditional Arab clothing, was unremarkable except for being bareheaded and wielding a large curved sword. Its vicious shape honed to gruesome perfection for the task literally in hand. The executioner raised his sword and looked over to his side. It was the condemned man's last chance.

In the case of an execution, the sentence may be commuted by the victim's family or estate at any time. Some cruelly, may grant the reprieve only once the sword has been raised, the executioner's look is the last opportunity to take the blood money and spare the life. The small bearded man representing the State was simply looking at his wristwatch. The State never commuted.

With a wringing cry of, *"Allahu akbar"*, the Executioner's blade came down. Joe closed his eyes.

Up in the IAB tower the little group had watched the events in heat induced hazy diminutive. The scene was far enough away to be conveniently abstract. Alex thought he saw the flash of the sword in the sunlight but the distance was such that he wasn't entirely sure. His view was somewhat hampered by the others anyway and he was relieved for that too. Nevertheless the gravity of the situation was palpable and the men descended the lift and trudged back to their desks in total silence.

Only Andy, who had stayed behind to watch the phones, was in reasonable spirits. "Entertaining was it?" The men looked sheepish. Andy shook his head.

"Only one this time", said Pete flatly. Jim and Alex looked at the South African in alarm, he shrugged. "I've seen them do three, just before Ramadan."

"Three? Holy fuck", Jim was incredulous.

"Oh yes. They pack them in then, because there are no executions held during the holy month." He raised his eyebrows in irony.

Andy called over to Alex. "By the way, some bloke called Jean-Marc called for you. He asked if you could call him back."

Alex thanked the Mancunian for the message but was unable to make the call right then. He sat and stared at the screen for some minutes deep in rumination. The digits of bonds and stocks danced their little daily matinee but he was not able to think of anything except the grotesque scene he had witnessed. He wondered how on earth Joe had managed. He shook himself out of this depressing line of thought and eventually forced himself to dial his old number in Paris. The line rang just once before he was greeted by the familiar tones of George Tatsakis. The Greek was in fine spirits and exchanged a few minutes of incidental banter with him. Alex found him as lewd and then as arcane as ever.

"Only camels to fuck out there then?"

"Personally I prefer Bactrians." Alex tried, but was not really in the mood for the conversation that George wanted.

"Nice apartment then?"

"It's not too bad."

"All nicely decorated then?"

"Absolutely" What was the guy on about thought Alex?

"George laughed out aloud. "You're priceless Alex. Here's Jean-Marc for you" and he was passed over to the Frenchman. The line was terrible as usual.

"Hi stranger, how are you then?"

"I'm fine thanks Jayem. A bit hung over but pretty good otherwise." Actually his hangover had passed some time ago but he was still reeling from the morning's grim spectacle.

"Sorry what did you say?" There was a strange clanking noise on the phone lines almost all the time.

"I said fine, but got a bit of a hangover."

"You've got a hangover in Saudi Arabia? I thought booze was banned there."

"Not on diplomatic territory matey." Alex looked up and saw Joe Karpolinski walk through the glass doors. He looked not just ashen faced, but almost broken, his eyes were even more bloodshot and his hair was plastered to his scalp, he looked as if someone had just emptied an entire bucket of water over him. He was drenched in sweat.

"You called me for something?" Alex enquired.

"What?"

"You called me earlier."

"Yes I did Alex. Look, some…" the lines were terrible today and Alex grimaced with effort to listen to the Frenchman's words. "What's your new address?" Alex didn't catch all that was said except the last.

He started to read out his new address from his business card, he would use the Bank's since the mail was notoriously inefficient, in fact it was considered even worse than the phone system.

"Alex I can't hear a thing."

"What?"

Just at that moment Joe Karpolinski got up, he looked simply dreadful, little rivulets of sweat coursed down each side of his head. He pulled a bitter face and appeared to be trying to swallow something unpleasant. Alex watched him closely; it was very clear what was going to happen next. He wretched with a sickening sound and then promptly threw up over his desk.

The South African made a sound of revulsion and was immediately on his feet. "Oh, for pity's sake."

"Do you want me to send it to…" the line was now full of static. All that oil money and one of the world's worst phone systems. It was beyond belief. Alex guessed Jean Marc said 'you' through the static.

"Yes sure. Look I've gotta go now. I'll call you later."

"No problem. Ciao." Jean-Marc hung up the phone. George Tatsakis was grinning like a fool, he loved a bit of scandal.

"Well, what did he say?"

"He said to send them to London."

"Really?" George looked thoughtful before adding. "Well it makes sense I guess.

 Claire and the kids will be with him. Right?"

"Right", said Jean-Marc, still deep in thought.

"Interior decoration eh?" George was chuckling away to himself as Jean Marc put the two letters into a large brown envelope addressed it to Alex's home in Fulham and then dropped it into the tray for the outgoing mail.

9. Big Brother

Talal pushed his brother back and lent over him to grab the TV remote control.

"I'm not watching this shit. We're going to watch the football."

Mohammed didn't respond to his brother's bullying choice, he just slouched deeper into the sofa with a slight scowl and cursed softly under his breath. Talal pushed the buttons of the remote dexterously and the TV responded back with the familiar blare of a soccer game.

"Not fucking Newcastle again", groaned Mohammed as he rolled his eyes upwards, "Allah please spare us"

Talal turned to his brother, "Well its better than watching repeats of Baywatch". The words tumbled out with hissing spite.

Mohammed visibly baulked at this last rebuff from his elder brother and he stared fixedly at the TV screen, his pride a little hurt by this last comment. The two young men sat for a few minutes in silence watching the flickering screen.

"Actually I hadn't seen that episode." he added with slight truculence. "Anyway I was watching the news before."

"That's crap Mo," Talal settled himself by rearranging the cushions of the sofa behind him, "Besides, Dad will be home soon and look we're winning 2-0."

The younger boy thought for a moment. That much was true, their father had only phoned a few minutes earlier to tell them he was on his way back.

"Wanna drink?" asked Mohammed, his tone conciliatory, as he got up.

"Yeah, but hurry up, you're gonna miss another goal." replied his brother.

"Yeah, sure." Mohammed's voice was heavy with sarcasm. He got up stiffly and walked over to the kitchen and then came back with their drinks. They sat watching for another five minutes in almost total silence, with only their noisy sipping of the cans of Pepsi breaking their quiet concentration. The game was nearing half time and the edge had drifted away from the contest. The listlessness of the match was now being transferred to the two brothers who were now slumped almost prone, in silent witness to the scenes that moved across the screen.

"Manchester United will win the championship again anyway, why don't you support them instead?" said Mohammed distractedly.

"You know why just as well as I do", Talal's answer was filled with ennui. The tracks of this conversational gambit were well worn.

"Well I think we should tell Dad that we want to support another team" insisted Mohammed.

Talal turned to his younger brother, "In Allah's name! You tell him if you like, but leave me out of it."

Mohammed was undeterred. "I don't see why we have to support them. Just because Father studied there we all have to support bloody Newcastle. It's stupid." Mohammed's voice trailed off slightly.

"Yeah, yeah." Talal's sarcastic response was barely audible as he was quietly focusing on the match.

Mohammed sighed with resignation, his head falling onto the back of the sofa and he stared at the ceiling. Just at that moment the commentator voice rose sharply and the silence was broken as Talal shook himself bolt upright on the sofa and shouted out, "Penalty!"

Sure enough the referee pointed to the spot and a few moments later the spot kick was taken.

"Yes, yes, praise be to God, what a well taken shot. That Beardsley is great!" he screamed, his face wreathed in smiles as he punched the air. Talal flopped down with a look of satisfaction on his face and poked his brother in the ribs. "See I told you they'd score again."

Mohammed looked at the TV screen his face still carried a slightly sour expression as he mumbled under his breath. "In God's name its only Coventry, I mean where the fuck is Coventry anyway? Now if it had been against Manchester

United that would have been a good goal." His eyes twinkled mischievously.

Talal sighed and got up. "I'm getting another drink, do you want one or are you going to tell Father that you want to support Manchester United?"

Mohammed looked up, his sheepishness returned, "I'll have a drink please", his voice now slightly plaintive.

"I thought so." Talal spoke with a dash of triumph and looked pleased with himself as the natural order had again been restored to the Al-Hamra household. Temporarily now that his senior sibling status had been wrestled back into place, he rose athletically and strode off towards the kitchen for another cold drink. When he returned and sat down on the sofa, Mohammed spoke softly under his breath his sourness still not yet dissolved.

"I wish Dad had studied in Madrid or Munich or Manchester" His thoughtful tone brightened for an instant, "any place beginning with M."

Talal considered this for a moment before smiling, "Or Marseille, they've been European champions as well."

"Milan or Monaco", countered Mohammed, suddenly sitting up with an enthusiastic grin.

Talal looked at his brother, "But Monaco haven't ever won a European title."

Mohammed looked at his elder brother and his features darkened for a moment, it was no good; pointless even. He knew his brother was an enormous mine of football trivia. He shook his head disconsolately and sighed with resignation and then sat back and watched the screen glumly.

A little while later the two brothers were back to their occasional but good natured banter, their Arabic pot-holed with English words, like "penalty", "off-side" and the occasional curse. However the match they were watching was not a classic in the sense of being any sort of edge of the seat spectacle. The boys watched the game with an increasingly soporific intensity since the result was no longer in doubt. Outside, they heard the familiar sound of their father's car, a dark blue, somewhat aged, but well cared for Mercedes, as it rolled to a stop on the gravel driveway below them. Talal searched for the remote control which had fallen down between the plush sofa cushions. His strong fingers delved between the heavily patterned and embossed folds of the material and found the chunky device. He pointed it in the direction of the large screen and lowered the sound of the television down to a soft background noise.

They steadied themselves as first the rising shuffle of weary gravel footsteps gave way to the gentle slap of leather on stone tiles, which then paused to the familiar click of the front door latch and the sound the door being opened and closed. A shuffle could be heard as he flipped off his sandals and put on a pair of soft leather *babouches*. Next there followed the familiar padding sound of their father's heavy gait, over the marble flooring. As he finally turned and emerged into the room his two sons were sitting primly for him seemingly concentrating on the match and sipping their drinks. After all, there was no need to antagonize the old man just yet.

"Good evening boys."

"Good evening father" the two young men chimed in response. It was a routine that they had employed for as many years as they could remember. Omar Al-Hamra was just a few years short of his fiftieth birthday, though he looked older, particularly after another energy sapping day at the bank. Shortish and piling on the pounds with the swiftly passing years, he had a pockmarked stub nose and kindly eyes that shone and twinkled just as mischievously as when he had been a boy, Al-Hamra sat himself down heavily into his favourite armchair.

"So what's the score?"

"Three nil to the Magpies" replied Talal.

Omar adjusted himself and blinkingly wiped his glasses with a handkerchief. He then carefully removed his *gutra* to reveal his slightly glistening forehead. He still had his thick head of hair, dark though thoroughly speckled with bristling grey, which he smoothed down with a well practised motion.

After a few more heavy breaths, having made himself comfortable in his seat he spoke. His voice was a little frayed. "So, where is your mother?" He half knew the answer, but it was all part of the normal evening routine.

"Shopping with Auntie."

Omar responded with a slight mumble and turned his attention to the football. After a few minutes Newcastle came close to scoring "We will win this one" he said with the usual tone of uncertainty that football fans have when watching their own team.

"Mother said she'll be back around seven", Talal replied.

Omar nodded knowingly. Presumably his wife would be back with more mysterious tales and tattle shared with her sister. Once together they were inveterate gossips. Undoubtedly he would have to listen to it all later on that evening. Outside the call to *Isha* prayers was starting up, he closed his eyes and relaxed into his comfy chair.

His pleasant reverie was disturbed by the raucous sound of the phone ringing, he stretched achingly and slowly reached across to pick it up, but was easily beaten to it by Mohammed who had rolled over to his side and expertly plucked the walkabout phone from its cradle.

"Yeah?" The electronic buzz of the voice sounded like a tinny mechanical mosquito.

"Huh…" he rolled back into position turned to his brother and handed him the phone. "It's for you."

Talal took the phone and wandered into the kitchen chatting discreetly all the way. Omar sighed, another 'friend'. His daughter, Seleema seemed to spend her whole time on the thing and his boys were not much better.

He took off his glasses, closed his eyes and gently massaged his eyelids with his thickset fingers. It had been another tiring day at the office. He peered at his younger son with his uncorrected blurry vision, they were good kids but still they worried him. He supposed he was no different to any father, even his own, though by his own assessment he himself had been a particularly dutiful son. Times change so, he thought. It was really so much more difficult these days. What would his own father have thought if he was alive today?

He got up slowly and went in to the kitchen. Their maid was busy making the evening meal. He spoke in English for her benefit. She had only been in the Kingdom for a year or so.

"Good evening Naila. That smells good." He eyed the pots that bubbled on the kitchen range. The Filipina maid, still having trouble with her Arabic, having only recently arrived in the Al-Hamra household, smiled and gave one of the bubbling vessels a quick stir of encouragement.

"It will be ready in half an hour, Sir" she answered in her now familiar staccato delivery.

Omar opened the fridge door and pulled out a can of soft drink and poured it into a glass. Talal was sitting at the kitchen table still busily talking on the phone to his friend, watchful of his father's movements around him. Omar had no idea who it was he was so animatedly in conversation with. He rarely did. He smiled wryly to himself as he slowly padded out of the unwelcome warmth of the kitchen and back into the cool of the lounge. The recorded televised game had finished and Mohammed had switched the television over to a blaring music channel and had cheekily turned up the sound. Omar Al-Hamra had elected the full range of satellite options so that his children would learn better English but the good intentions had been marred by the torrent of rubbish that was offered as programming. He looked at the images on the screen, salacious nonsense beamed directly into his home and bridled with annoyance.

"Isn't there something else on?"

The teenager shifted uneasily on the sofa, "Dad..." his voice was both plaintiff and at the same time resigned.

"Well at least turn it down." His son picked up the controller and begrudgingly complied.

"How was school today?"

"Fine." It was his son's offhand answer to almost everything. It had been since he was six years old.

"Haven't you got any homework?"

"Not much, I'll do it after dinner."

Omar took a sip from his drink and placed it on the small ornate table next to him. The empty phone cradle had a little red LED indicator which stubbornly flashed that Talal was still deep in conversation. Unusually, beside it sat one of his favourite photographs of his family, taken on a trip to Florida some three years back. It had been done in Disneyland, themed in the manner of the Old Wild West and was in sepia to enhance the effect. He was standing, comically dressed as a Sheriff, his wife Ameena stood beside him, smiling in a huge flowery hat and the three kids were sitting in front of their parents all in authentic looking cowboy garb, the boys all riding chaps and pistols, his daughter in creamy white flounced folds and holding a pretty parasol.

"Why is this photograph here?" It was normally on his bedside table.

"Naila still mixes them all up." Mohammed was engrossed on the screen.

Omar considered this for a moment. Normally there was a more formal and recent picture of his three children sitting primly on a park bench taken last winter dressed in more acceptable traditional attire. He shifted himself into a more comfortable position and sighed, he felt strangely inept and yet this was how he had wanted things to be. He had so wanted his children to be able to bestride both Western and

Arab worlds, but now he felt both cultures were letting him down.

He turned and desultorily observed the lurid images on the screen, it was a world that was becoming more and more alien to him and yet as a young man he had had nothing but admiration for the West and had felt quite at home within it. When he had been the same age as his sons were now, Occidental values were not so different to either, his own or even those of his father.

His father, who had the same name as him, had been a skilled artisan in a small goldsmiths business situated in the Old Gold Souk in Balad, the old centre of Jeddah. There were dozens of them all competing for the custom of the faithful, there still are. *Hajji* on their way home from Mecca would always try to get a little souvenir of their once in a lifetime pilgrimage before boarding the packed homeward bound ships from Jeddah to the far flung parts of the globe. It was hard but honourable work. His father would say how it was worthwhile just to see the happy faces of the pilgrims who would bargain and shop around to get the best deals they could and leave. As a boy he would go and visit his father after school had finished and watch the delighted tourists leaving the cramped workshop, marvelling at the detail of the craftsmanship and satisfied at the bargains they had struck. Often, some would leave so precipitously that they were almost running out the shop, afraid that the goldsmith might realise his mistake and ask for his goods back or for more money. It always made his father chuckle. Omar would watch them leaving and wonder what they did for a living as they went back to exotic places like Agra, Java, Marrakech, or Burma.

His own family had never been poor by local standards as such, but neither so comfortable, that ambition and desire for improvement were daily sapped by necessity or superfluity. Even before his father's eyesight started to fail he had been encouraged to improve himself and to learn; to become an engineer, a scientist or a doctor. Science, Technology and Medicine were the harbingers of all that was good and promised a better world. Better that than the back breaking, sight destructive work of the artisan goldsmith. Furthermore and importantly, they were the worthy pursuits of a good Muslim. He had struggled much for what he had achieved in life and had been greatly encouraged in this by his family but now he wondered what the end result of all this was. Had it been worth it?

He looked at his son Mohammed and his eyes softened with paternal concern. It was so different then he ruefully thought. American values were good, like American cars, refrigerators and chocolate bars. Hard work was valued and more importantly expected, opportunities could be grasped by all who really honestly sought them. Family values, respect for each other and God. Surely a society that has 'In God We Trust' printed on its currency couldn't be bad? He scowled at the television. A girl was dancing about on the screen singing some ear splittingly repetitive song. They all sounded the same to him now anyway, he peered at the image, she was strutting about absurdly dressed as a school girl, thrusting and gyrating suggestively.

"Who is this girl?" Omar asked with a mixture of confusion and distaste writ large across his puckered face.

Mohammed turned and looked at his father; he could give any answer he wanted to really. The old man wouldn't have a clue or probably even remember in five minutes anyway, he thought. "Britney Spears" he replied and turned back to continue watching the screen.

"Ridiculous."

He shook his head and his jowls wobbled like little stubbly blancmanges. It was hard to reconcile the differences that had taken place in a generation. It only seemed yesterday that he was watching movies at the open air theatre where the Red Sea Palace hotel, now stood. That was before it and all the others were all closed by the *Mutawwa'in* on the grounds of, 'perverting public morals.' It was different when he was a boy, the West was good, but America was best. Back then even their leaders had looked like film stars. He snorted under his breath, these days they were more as not likely to be so, he glumly conceded to himself.

His thoughts were broken by the sound of wheels coming to rest outside. He checked his watch it was just approaching seven fifteen. Omar picked up his glass and drained the remainder of his drink before rising with heavy limbs from his seat.

"That will be your Mother and Auntie Raha." Omar said it with the tinge of an admonition and it was taken as one by the teenager. Mohammed begrudgingly switched the channel to the local Saudi station.

The sound of several different footsteps shuffling across the gravel driveway gave way to the harsh cracking noise of sharp heels on the hard steps outside. The doorbell rang and Omar was already opening it, his friendly face, which was on the cusp of breaking into a warm smile, suddenly took on a more serious look. There standing before him was his Abdul-Rahman with his usual look of quiet menace, behind him were the three black clad women, his wife Ameena, his sister in law Raha and his daughter.

"Peace be with you."

"And with you too, Peace" replied Abdul-Rahman. The men kissed each other formally on the cheeks in the traditional manner of when Arabs meet. Omar could feel the steely grip of his relation as the men held each other's hands as they spoke. Abdul-Rahman was related by marriage, he was the elder brother of Raha's husband and in the tradition of extended Saudi families, he was known as uncle to the Al-Hamra's.

"What a pleasant surprise to see you my brother. How are you?" Abdul-Rahman put his arm possessively around his brother in laws' shoulder and was then politely encouraged to come in by the stiff limbed banker.

"Allah has indeed been kind to me. I'm here only for a short time." The two men entered and Omar just had time to give his wife Ameena, a puzzled reproachful look. In response, she in turn widened and rolled her eyes. Omar immediately understood; it was not the first time this had happened.

Inside the lounge Mohammed had heard the instantly recognizable voice of his uncle. He quickly turned off the television and stood up to greet him. He waited bolt upright and tight lipped, sentry like, for them to walk into the room. The first to enter was Abdul-Rahman.

"Ah, my young son, peace be with you." The visitor was looking him up and down with his usual coruscating glare.

"And with you too, Peace"

"You are strangely attired my boy." He stepped forward and kissed the boy on the cheeks before adding, "I hope you are not ailing?"

Dressed in a pair of blue denim jeans and a short sleeved T-shirt with, 'Polo' written across the left breast, Mohammed smiled embarrassedly and mumbled back barely audibly.

"No I'm fine thank you uncle"

"Good my son. I see you are no longer a boy", he stated with slight reproach before Abdul-Rahman released the young man from his embrace. He turned and gave Omar an enquiring look. The tubby father of three responded by pointing to his favourite chair and asking the visitor to take his place.

"Would you like to eat with us, dinner will be ready very soon?"

"Thank you very much my brother, nothing would give me more pleasure but sadly I must leave quite soon."

"Really it is no problem Abdul-Rahman. Please it would be an honour and a pleasure, though it is quite simple."

"You know my tastes my dear brother. Simple is best my friend, but you are too kind as unfortunately I have already accepted dinner with a friend." He paused before adding with a creepy look. "I just wanted to see you and your fine boys."

"Perhaps some tea or coffee at least" Omar was hopeful the man would decline and be on his way.

The dark featured man thought for a moment, "I don't want to disrupt your evening."

"No, no really" said Omar with rapidly diminishing hopes.

"Very well, you are very kind. Tea would be most welcome."

Having now accepted the offer Abdul-Rahman again thanked him and sat down; carefully arranging the folds of his slightly shortened white *dishdashah* around him. A nervous silence had descended on the little group. Whilst this had played out the women had dutifully followed the men into the room and had then unobtrusively moved on through to the kitchen. Just within earshot Omar could hear his wife and her sister talking in low rushed little tones and the sharp little click of her heels on the kitchen flooring tapped out frustration in a twitchy Morse code.

"How is the family?" Abdul-Rahman was surveying the room with a smile but the eyes had a stern look that missed nothing.

"Thanks be to God, very well", Omar replied with mounting unease, "… and how are you?"

Abdul-Rahman bin Hajez was a senior *Mutawwa*, the state controlled religious police force, and his eyes were now fiercely arrayed on the photograph on the little table beside him. Omar quickly realised what the man was looking at and his heart suddenly sank into an icy sea of angst. Even more perturbed by this realization, he rubbed his chin feverishly and became aware that he was starting to feel short of breath.

"I'm very well too", he was still looking at the photograph with undisguised contempt, "and where is Talal?" He raised his black eyes and smiled thinly at Omar.

"He is here." Al-Hamra replied weakly, he was feeling decidedly uncomfortable as he spoke and nervously added, "Mohammed, why don't you go and see where he is?"

"No, No, Please not on my account", said the *Mutawwa*, but the boy was already on his feet in a blur of panicky movement and indicating that it was not the least trouble at all.

"Really it's no problem, I'll fetch him immediately uncle." Omar smiled insipidly at his once removed brother in law, who sat calmly cross legged in front of him. He watched as the visitor slipped a hand into his pocket and brought out some well worn prayer beads and started to expertly finger his way through them. Abdul-Rahman closed his eyes, his lips were barely moving but just sufficiently, so as to seem conspicuously deep in devotional thought. Omar was used to this pious display but he knew better than to appear disrespectful of the man. This particular relation was a dangerous man to cross.

The silence was becoming claustrophobic and Omar could only hear the sound of his own breathing, which seemed to rasp more and more heavily, almost deafeningly in his own ears. Agitatedly and solely to break the oppressive tension mounting any further, he at last spoke. "How long are you to be here in Jeddah?"

The man paused, his features frozen in thought. He wore a long thick beard, almost entirely grey accept for a few stubborn streaks of black that ran through it. His face was thin and gaunt and his eyes were deep set with dark puffy bags under them. He looked like he needed some sleep.

"Just for a few days. God willing I'll be back in Riyadh for the start of the week."

Omar nodded sagely. Abdul-Rahman was not someone to question unnecessarily as he had a gift of being able to turn anything that was said into something embarrassing, or worse, some sort of guilty confession. Omar sat and waited for him to continue but the *Mutawwa* just sat and stared back at him with thinly veiled animosity. He took off his glasses, fished into his pocket to find a lens cloth, before breathing heavily on them and nervously rubbing the lenses translucent with his stubby fingers.

"How is business then my friend?"

Omar knew this was coming, it always did. The question was more loaded than a primed gun. For Abdul-Rahman, working for a bank was almost Apostasy, interest was anathema. Money was the root of all evil and nothing Omar could say would make things any better. It was the work of the Devil.

"Not so good." It was his standard answer. If he had said that, 'things were going well', then even more unwelcome questions would follow, the assumption would be that usury was underpinning the immoral earnings of the bank. Even an 'OK' would open up a similar line of reasoning. Only 'bad' would be sufficient to draw a line in the sand for this man from Riyadh.

This last piece of acquiescence pleased the religious policeman greatly. He knew it probably wasn't true, the house, the maid, the volumes of shopping that this man's wife had brought in with her, was positive proof of this, but he liked the fact that this supposedly educated man understood his position in life. His features cracked into an unfamiliar mask as an excuse for a smile broke across his face.

"That is Allah's will. As is written in the Koran, 'And know that your property and your children are a temptation, and that Allah is He with Whom there is a mighty reward.'" Omar nodded once more and wondered how it was that this man could always find a way of twisting the words of the Koran into something malign and threatening.

Abdul-Rahman sighed. "We live in a world that is full of evil my friend. Here in Jeddah I see much that concerns me."

Al-Hamra hoped it was something more than his family photograph that he was referring to. "Really, is it still much worse than in Riyadh?"

The *Mutawwa* pinched up his face and made a typical Arabic gesture, hand up turned and fingers rising together to form a little apex as if holding a tiny pea with the fingertips. "Only a little bit my brother, a little", he frowned.

Omar nodded his understanding. "So are you here on business or pleasure?" he asked with a self effacing look.

"Both, when I have a chance to see all the family," he said with what seemed to Omar something close to a leer as he scanned the doorway. Neither Mohammed nor Talal had appeared up to that point; Omar guessed what they were probably doing and chose to ignore the other man's words. They would be back soon enough and the less time his sons spent with this man was all the better as far as he was concerned.

"Business?" Omar would have liked to have laughed outright at this suggestion, the spheres of commerce and industry were another reprehensible world to this man, but laughter, however justified would have been more than unwise. There was nothing funny about Abdul-Rahman bin Hajez's business.

"Yes I'm here to check moral suitability and consistency for a new scholar", his features took on a more serious look.

"Oh really", replied Omar in a low murmur as noncommittally as he could.

"I will be interviewing and then listening to a new *Alim* who will be leading Friday Prayers at a new mosque in Al-Naeem. He closed his eyes and began rolling his prayer beads expertly between his fingers.

One thing that any citizen of Jeddah knew was that almost each week there was a new mosque being built in the city. Since the Ministry paid the salaries of the *Imams* and *Alim* who worked in the mosques it was necessary to provide direction to mosque orators and Imams regarding the content of their messages; in some instances, imams were banned from speaking. The State wanted to know exactly what was being said in the cool interiors of these new places of worship and Abdul-Rahman was just the man for this delicate job.

Their labouring conversation was interrupted by the arrival of the two Al-Hamra boys. Both had quickly changed into traditional white *dishdashah* and were followed by his wife who brought in the steaming hot sweet tea garnished with mint. She smiled and placed the tray on the small coffee table before retiring without saying a word as Abdul-

Rahman and Talal exchanged formal greetings. After these were completed the elder boy took his place beside his father and waited attentively for the visitor to speak. Abdul-Rahman continued fingering his beads as he asked. "So how are your studies my boy?"

"They are going well thank you Uncle."

"Very good" Abdul-Rahman took a sip from his small glass teacup. The sweetness was enervating and he could feel his tiredness evaporate as the warming liquid filled him. It had been a long day and the flight from Riyadh was always exhausting but he could feel himself quickly reviving. He pointedly stared at the silver framed photograph on the table beside him and then looked at the two boys in front of him. Omar saw this and felt another wave of unease breaking over himself.

The *Mutawwa* was looking directly at Talal as he next spoke. "I was telling your father that I will be meeting with a most interesting *Alim* tomorrow."

The boy's widening eyes took on an owlish look whilst Omar, with mounting concern, wondered where the conversation was going next.

"Interesting uncle?" asked the teenager with an open face.

"Yes indeed, he was recently in Pakistan where he was teaching but he is now, thanks be to God, back in the Kingdom and has had many interesting experiences to tell." He looked around the room before continuing. "Perhaps

251

you would like to come and listen to him?" He was now smiling at Talal but his eyes had a piercing intensity that left little room for resistance.

Seeing this, Omar immediately interrupted his son before the boy was able to reply. "That sounds very…" he groped for the words, his mind was racing ahead of his ability to speak, "interesting… but I think young Talal has quite a lot of homework to attend to. Haven't you my son?"

"Yes, I, I…" stammered Talal.

Abdul-Rahman raised his hand, "Omar, surely you don't expect your son to work all Friday?" His smile remained but the eyes now flashed momentary outrage. He was not used to being contradicted.

"Oh no of course not, my brother, but our mosque is much closer…" Omar's voice trailed off as he spoke, the *Mutawwa's* hand was still half raised.

"No, really it would be my pleasure to take him and to bring him back of course, that way he will still have time to do his study, but remember, 'As for those who disbelieve and turn away from Allah's way, He shall render their works ineffective.'"

His features had once again taken on a sombre piety as he recited these lines and Omar Al-Hamra felt his puny resistance beginning to crumble.

"That's very kind my brother but I'm sure it would put you out, you must be so very busy."

"Oh no, not at all. Really it would be a pleasure." Abdul-Rahman's eyes narrowed almost imperceptibly, as he continued, "perhaps Mohammed would like to come too?" He directed an encouraging look at the younger brother, who returned the man's attention with calm but inquisitive eyes.

Mohammed answered before his father could utter a word. "Oh yes Uncle, I would like that very much." He had been sitting and had eyed the way that his father and elder brother had been so easily out-manoeuvred by the wily cleric. Their insipid resistance had been embarrassing for him to witness, he hated weak and simpering behaviour. What were they so scared of anyway, he asked himself? He knew his Uncle was a serious man; perhaps even a dangerous one and frankly he quite admired him for it. Having given his answer, he now looked a little askance at his big brother and a trace of a smile played across his handsome features. Mohammed wasn't stupid, he had been acutely aware of the discomfort of both of them but he thought they were both mildly pathetic, so his enthusiastic response had been designed to put them in their place. It looked like it had worked. Besides it was an excellent opportunity for him to demonstrate that he was not afraid of his Uncle and that he was no longer someone they could push around as they wished.

Abdul-Rahman did well to hide his delight in the little scene that had just played out before him. "Praise be to God. Well that is settled then. I'll call for you both tomorrow at ten."

The brothers nodded and Omar, who was desperately trying to think of something to object to, was left mutely frustrated. Disconsolately he had to concede that it was useless, he had lost this particular encounter with his brother in law.

"Well I must be on my way. Thank you for the tea my dear brother." Despite his years, he was almost the same age as Omar, Abdul-Rahman was still a fit man and he got to his feet with swift feline ease.

"You are most welcome." Replied Omar with effort, trying to keep resignation out of his voice and noisily aware that again he seemed to be breathing like an overworked elephant.

In a few moments he had collected his brother's wife. Raha said her goodbyes hastily to the boys and before long they were on their way.

"See you tomorrow, God willing", said the *Mutawwa* as they descended the steps back down to the gravel driveway. "God willing" replied Omar with whitening lips.

In the car, Abdul-Rahman turned the ignition and gunned the car before pulling away.

"What was that, you said about tomorrow?" asked Raha a little hesitantly from the back seat of the car as they pulled onto the road. She felt herself blush hotly under her *burqa*; she rarely asked questions of her brother in law.

"I'm taking Mohammed and Talal to Friday Prayers" he said with firmness.

"Really? I…" her voice could not hide her anguish, but she was cut off before she could muster another word.

"What do you mean really?" The religious policeman's face had contorted into a picture of rancorous spite.

"Nothing…" she was virtually a bag of nerves now.

"If your sister and that fool of a husband of hers thinks she can turn your own son Khalid, into a tool of the infidels, then it pleases me that Allah should give me the chance to claim back two in return." He stared hard into the rear view mirror at her and she turned to look out of the side window to avoid the man's hectoring glare.

Inside the Al-Hamra household, things were almost as disharmonious. Omar was silently furious and could barely contain himself until Abdul-Rahman's car had pulled out of the driveway. He slammed the heavy front door and came wheeling into the lounge to confront his youngest son.

"Just what the devil are you playing at you little fool?"

Mohammed's former bravura had quickly given way to his more familiar hurt truculence. "What do you mean Father?"

"You know exactly what I mean", stormed his father. Mohammed turned hopefully towards his elder brother who was sitting just across the room from him and who returned his imploring gaze with a rueful face. Mohammed mustered himself; he could not expect any support from Talal.

"I don't see what the problem is. What's so wrong about going with uncle?"

Omar Al-Hamra shook his head vehemently on hearing this. "Nothing wrong, nothing wrong?" He parroted, his face becoming florid with anger. He started pacing up and down the room. "You know perfectly well what I think of your uncle's so called activities." Mohammed adopted a querulous tilt as his father continued his angry tirade. "He actively pushes for the strictest interpretation of Islam. He lauds intolerance and supports and uses violence against anyone who disagrees with his interpretation."

"He is just a traditionalist", countered Mohammed, amazed at this outburst.

"He is not a traditionalist, he is a crazy fundamentalist and…" Omar felt he was getting into his stride now, "he is a dangerous man. You say the wrong thing and he'll have you locked up."

"I'm not afraid of him."

"Well you should be." He paused and tried to calm himself down, realising this approach was getting him nowhere. Mohammed could be as stubborn as a mule. He took a deep breath and stopped his pacing around the room.

Mohammed was watching his father closely now. It was a battle of wills and this time he was not going to lose.

Omar turned directly towards his son with arms outstretched. "Can't you see what he's trying to do?" His tone of voice had adjusted to frustrated reasonableness.

Mohammed feigned resolute indifference and showed this by folding his arms across his chest while his father continued.

"You know he loathes everything I stand for, don't you?"

"Look father, I'm perfectly capable of making up my own mind. I'm not a kid anymore" said the teenager huffily and without the slightest irony.

Omar was about to deliver a sarcastic response to this when his daughter Seleema entered the room.

"Mum says dinner is ready." She looked around the room and quickly realised she had walked into an intense row. From the body language of both her father and Mohammed she could see where the conflict was centred. Talal was to his feet in a moment and was on his way to the dining room.

Omar bit down hard on his lower lip deep in thought, perhaps it would be better to discuss this once tempers had calmed slightly. "We'll talk about this later," but he already knew there was nothing to be said or done.

The meal was started in silence, each of the family in contemplative mood, with Ameena looking a little confused by the obvious edginess of her sons and husband. Omar took a few mouthfuls before he eventually broke it; he was looking directly at his wife as he spoke with deliberate restraint. "Please can you tell Naila that in future she is to make sure that she puts the photographs back exactly where she finds them rather than wherever the whim takes her?"

Ameena smiled and shook her head, "I've told her before, but she's always cleans all the silver frames at the same time and gets confused when she puts them back", she said pleasantly.

"Well it was a bit embarrassing with Abdul-Rahman."

Concern suddenly washed across his wife's face, "Why?"

"The picture of us in Florida was in the lounge."

Ameena was horrified and opened her mouth in shocked disbelief, "Oh No. Abdul-Rahman saw this?"

"I'm afraid, 'Oh yes' is very much the case."

"Oh what will he think?" She had covered her mouth with her hand and several bangles clinked together running down her wrist as she considered this. "Did he say anything?"

"No, nothing", said Omar flatly

"Oh dear, Oh God protect us."

A disturbing quiet filled the room. Both of them realised that it was entirely unnecessary for Abdul-Rahman to have said anything. They knew precisely what his words would have been had he spoken. He was, after all, a senior agent of the Mutawwa'in, whose mandate was to enforce the strict *Wahhabi* interpretation of Islam. Enshrined within the confusing national apparatus where religion and state are daily mixed and eventually personified in the Orwellian form of, 'The Committee to Prevent Vice and Promote Virtue', men like Abdul-Rahman enforced its rules; strict segregation of the sexes, an absolute prohibition of the sale and consumption of alcohol, the veiling of all women, the ban on women driving and many other social restrictions. Junior *Mutawwa* roamed the streets and shopping centres on the look-out for anyone breaking the rules, senior *Mutawwa* like Abdul-Rahman, would vet religious activity and perform interrogations on those errant souls misfortunate enough to be arrested for falling foul of the rules. One of these rules was that there should be no idolatry and perversely for this reason photography was disdained by the *Wahhabi*.

"Surely he can't say anything about it?" Seleema said with rising concern. "After all the privacy of a Muslim home is more important."

Omar knew this was true, the State tended to avoid entering a Saudi's home; it was one of the remaining taboos that the *Mutawwa'in* had been unable to change. Besides he was invited in as a guest and this was also a form of protection. He looked around the table and now regretted having raised the issue, it would have been better just to have spoken to Ameena alone.

"I'm sure that Abdul-Rahman will be fine, it was just embarrassing." He tried to smile reassuringly but inside he was in turmoil and fretfully took another mouthful of his dinner.

The phone began ringing and Omar's face darkened again. Before anything could be said Seleema was up and off to go and get the call. A few moments later she returned with the news that it was his nephew Khalid on the line and he wanted a quick word.

Ordinarily Omar would have insisted on finishing his meal before taking a phone call, but given the recent turn of events that had occurred that evening he was now keen to speak to him. His hopes raised for a moment as he took the phone from his daughter, perhaps Abdul-Rahman had been called away and tomorrows impromptu arrangements had needed to be cancelled.

"Hello Khalid?"

"Hi Uncle, how are you?"

"I'm fine thanks", he paused and waited for his nephew to speak. Since Khalid had been at the bank, conversations had centred around Omar's ability to offer advice and insight for his able and ambitious young nephew. His heart suddenly sank as he realised that this may well have been the reason for the young man's call.

"Uncle, I'm just speaking with Mohammed Jundi and he's invited me and two of the traders onto his boat for a dive trip on Sunday."

"Yes?" Omar was wondering what this had to do with him. He hated boats and his nephew knew this very well.

"It's just I was thinking, that since there's quite a lot of room on it perhaps Talal would like to come? Mohammed hasn't met him either and I thought Talal would like to meet the guys I'm working with…" Khalid hesitated a little before continuing, "its half term and everything..." his voice trailed off embarrassedly.

Omar gently interrupted him, he felt he knew exactly what Khalid was trying to do, he was aiming to be helpful, to give Talal some encouragement and to reciprocate in some small way, what Omar had in turn done for him.

"Which traders are going?"

"Alex Bell and Jim Robson, they've both just passed their diving qualifications."

Omar thought about this for a moment. "Well, that sounds fine to me." His mind was working quickly. "There is just one problem, as you know they are both on holiday and Mohammed was looking forward to being taken up to Taif for the day by Talal."

Omar's younger son perked up at the mention of his name and he watched his father's face for clues as to what he was talking about from his one sided perspective of the telephone conversation.

"Well I'm sure that Mohammed can come too." Khalid broke away for a brief moment and Omar could hear a quick muffled conversation take place before he continued, "I've just checked with Mohammed here and he says that would be great, there's plenty of room on the boat and he would be most welcome to come too."

"Well I'll speak to the boys but I'm sure they'd both enjoy it."

"Great." Khalid paused.

"Is there something else?" asked Omar gently.

Khalid stammered a little before replying. "No, nothing else."

Omar couldn't resist the temptation to find out if this invitation was not linked to the earlier debacle, he knew how his sister-in-law Raha worked. "Have you spoken to your Mother at all this evening?"

The answer was immediate and guileless, even over the phone line. "No why?"

"Oh no reason particularly, I was just wondering how she was."

"She is fine as far as I know." There was a faint questioning tone to his voice but it was quickly gone.

"Very good, I'll speak to you later then and thanks for that. I'm sure the boys will enjoy it."

"No problem, see you tomorrow at the bank Uncle. Bye."

"Bye Khalid"

Omar was very pleased with himself as he set down the handset upon the table. His sons looked expectantly at him, waiting for him to reveal what he had just arranged for them with their cousin. Omar grinned and basked in his newly gained status for a moment until Talal could not wait any longer and asked.

"Well aren't you going to tell us?"

"Ah yes of course. A colleague of Khalid at the bank has invited both of you onto his boat on Sunday."

"A fishing trip?" asked Mohammed with a tinge of disappointment.

"Perhaps that too, but I believe diving is their main activity."

The boys' eyes brightened at this prospect as they were both keen on the sport. Talal already had an advanced diver's qualification whilst his younger brother had his open water certificate.

"When?" Mohammed's earlier gloom had lifted entirely.

"This Sunday" answered Omar brightly.

Before anything more could be said the phone started ringing again though this time Omar was able to answer it first.

"Hello?"

"Peace be with you."

"And with you peace" replied Omar.

"Please can I speak to Seleema?" It sounded like a young man's voice.

"Who is speaking?" Omar did not recognise the voice.

"It's Farhan Al-Jibouri." Omar did not recognise the name.

"Who?" The furrowed brow and the tone of his voice were now not entirely friendly.

"Farhan Al-Jibouri", repeated the young voice a little hesitantly this time.

Omar made a small non-committal grunt and looked towards Seleema who now had the same look of wary expectation that her brothers' had moments before shown, written across her pretty feminised Al-Hamra features.

"It's someone called Farhan Al-Jibouri for you." He waved the telephone handset towards her in a determinately offhanded manner, silently hoping she would decline the invitation. He was out of luck; his daughter was once again lightly to her feet and took the receiver from him with a sweet smile before wandering out of the dining room whilst speaking into the mouthpiece in a restrained voice. Omar sighed as he watched her slip from view. He turned and peered at his wife, who returned his look with a slight smile and the most imperceptible of shrugs, before resuming the remainder of his evening meal.

They continued eating until eventually Omar found his wandering train of thought was brought to a halt by the clinking sounds of the Filipina maid, who was soon busying around and clearing the dining table of the place settings. A few moments later she brought out some freshly made coffee and set it down before him. This was the usual cue for the other members of the family to depart, since none of them were great lovers of the after dinner drink. He poured out the steaming liquid, which he cupped in his hands and sipped alone with his thoughts. For a moment he wondered if he would go and ask his daughter who this Farhan Al-Jibouri character was, but he would only get the same old answer from her as he got from his sons.

"Oh Dad, it's just a friend" and then they would be off into their rooms leaving him feeling foolish and inept. He could feel the fine grounds of coffee on his tongue as he mulled over the difficulties of parenthood. His thoughts drifted back to his own father and thought how easy things had been for him. He gave a little shudder, it was an absurd comparison, his father could never have understood.

Children, he thought to himself, who would have them? He took another sip of his cooling coffee and he remembered his own father and how he had spent the first few weeks after returning from finishing his doctoral studies in England. His father had been so proud and had organized a series of celebratory meals and visits to announce his son's safe return home, flushed with academic success. The young Omar had not minded as he was keen to keep busy and try not to think too much of the girlfriend he wrote to daily that he had recently left back in Newcastle. It was going to be difficult, but he had plans.

It had all changed the day when his father had called out to him and suggested visiting a particular friend's house. Uncomplainingly he had gone, as many times before, polite and formal but reasonably friendly. On this occasion he was perhaps a little surprised by the excessive formality of his father's friend. He remembered how they had all fallen silent as the two women of the house had suddenly appeared. Mother and daughter, both conservatively dressed with heads covered, had carefully offered and poured out the tea. He had just managed to catch the young girl's eyes as she poured the sweet mint drink and the coyest of smiles had flickered across her features. He remembered how the mother and daughter had then unusually taken a seat amongst the men and how surprised he was by the fact that the older woman had then spoken to him.

"Well, I expect that you are happy to be back home here in Jeddah and to settle down?" She had asked him.

"Perhaps, but maybe working in America could be interesting." He had replied, just slightly caught off guard by the implications behind the question the woman had asked. His thoughts had turned to those of his girlfriend from Tyneside.

"Really, I had no idea" she had immediately responded. Only her eyes were visible but wide open with curious enquiry. She turned to look at Omar's father.

"Oh, no he will be staying here, I'm quite sure", interjected his father, whilst at the same time giving his son a kindly but slightly reproachful look.

The older woman nodded her head and in a few moments both of the women had left the room and the men reconvened their intermittent, polite but obviously strained conversation. Omar had little in common with the men and their edgy talk meant that he couldn't wait to get away back to his letter writing. On the way home his father had been in fine spirits and had then spoken the words he would never forget. Omar remembered it all verbatim.

"So what did you think then?"

"Of what father?"

"Why of Ameena of course", he chimed and gazed at his son, eyes twinkling with a happy cheeky mischief that was magnified behind thick black rimmed glasses. "She will make a fine wife I'm sure."

And that was how he first met his wife. In a few weeks it had all been organized, a seemingly unstoppable express train of events rolled into life and before he knew what was happening he was, 'sorted out' as this mother said at the time, a married man.

He swallowed down the last of the lukewarm, bittersweet coffee. He had never dared to cross his father and it was the reason why he had raised his own children the way he had. His own youthful mute acquiescence still tasted bitter in his mouth and the daily grind of his existence since that fateful time had brewed a dark resolution that his own children would not be made to make the same mistakes.

10. Dive Groupers

A few days later, just as planned, Omar dropped off his two sons for the dive trip planned by Mohammed Jundi. The Risk Manager's blue Mercedes was just pulling up as Alex and Jim arrived.

"Hi Alex, you found us all right then?"

"Hi Khalid, it was no problem at all. We did all our dive training on Al-Nakheel beach which is just a little further up the coast."

Khalid and Mohammed nodded at this. Al-Nakheel was the most popular beach amongst the expatriates and next to impossible for a Saudi national to visit. In fact, Al-Nakheel was barred to all Muslims, so that unless you carried a foreign passport or held the tell tale brown coloured *Iquama*, which immediately identified its owner as a non-Muslim, entry was strictly prohibited. Foreign Muslims carried a green *Iquama*. During their diving instruction, Alex and Jim had become acutely aware that even the water was policed by the coastguard, who periodically dropped by, to ensure Saudi Arabia's strict *Wahhabi* rules were being observed on both land and sea.

In a few moments the two young Al-Hamra's had taken out their diving equipment in two big canvas bags, carried them over and put them into the rear of the Mohammed's Jeep.

Alex and Jim were both out of their car; still a little stiff legged from the trip. Jim lit up a cigarette.

"We'll drop them back home Uncle", said Khalid to Omar who by now had also got out of his car to say hello to the others. Since the arrival of the foreigners all conversation had been in English.

"Thank you Khalid, that's very good of you."

Omar smiled and greeted the two Englishmen with vigorous handshakes. "So you are both newly qualified then?"

"Yes, just a fortnight since we completed the course", replied Jim with a sly glance at Alex.

Omar's features darkened for an instant, he was about to issue a cautionary word but he checked himself before adding with an open smile, "Well have a good time then."

Mohammed Jundi gunned the big four litre engine of the Jeep and brought it up to the opening gates. The window slid down and he leant out of it towards the group. "You guys just follow me OK?" He looked at Alex's rental car and grinned. "I'm not sure that thing is going too far on the beach."

Alex shook his head in acknowledgement. Unlike the powerful Jeep, the Toyota was obviously not designed for off-road activity.

"When are you going to get yourself a decent set of wheels?"

"I'm thinking about it", lied Alex.

"Well you can park it just a way inside and then transfer your stuff into my car."

"Okey dokey", replied Alex.

In a few moments, both the Al-Hamra's had climbed into the back seat of the Jeep with Khalid in the front passenger seat and they waved goodbye to the slightly forlorn sight of Omar who watched the two cars pass through the high sided gates which then closed behind them.

Mohammed had arranged for the boat to be brought to the beach from the Marina at Obhur by his brother and it was already moored. Alex looked out to the sea, which was calm and a resplendent blue and searched the boats to look for activity. There were half a dozen lazily bobbing about on the water but no sign of life on any of them, though one clearly stood out from all the others since it was much larger and eye catching than anything else afloat and gleamed flashily like a supermodel at a school reunion.

"What type of boat have you got Mohammed?" asked Jim beating Alex to his next question.

"Well it's not mine, it's actually my uncle's" and he pointed vaguely out towards the sea. "It's that one, the Sunseeker."

This still didn't mean much to Alex, he was most definitely a land lubber but Jim seemed to know what his young trading protégé was talking about. Trips back to his relations in Jamaica had left their mark. Jim knew about rich men's playthings.

"The big blue and white one just there?" he was pointing directly at the largest of the boats.

"Yup" said Mohammed Jundi matter-of-factly.

"She's a beauty", said Jim in awe. He squinted at the lines of the boat before adding. "It must be over sixty five feet long."

Mohammed was busy pushing his diver's equipment into a big bag, "Closer to seventy but not a bad guess. He stood up a little out of breath from the effort, "Twenty one point one eight meters actually."

"A Sunseeker Predator sixty eight?"

"That's it exactly Jim. You know your boats."

Just then a little yellow inflatable outboard started to make its way from the rear of the boat towards the beach.

"C'mon let's get going, here comes Ammar with the tender", said Mohammed Jundi.

They made the trip to the water's edge, shifting the heavy kits bags and tanks, between the little beach cabin and the yellow inflatable in a couple of relays. As Jim and Alex made the last sortie towards the tender Jim spoke softly under his breath to Alex.

"That's several million quid of boat out there..."

Alex shifted his awkward bag over to his other shoulder as he considered this and replied conspiratorially, "Jundi's lot must be loaded."

Khalid and the two Al-Hamra brothers were already waiting topside on the boat as the remaining three men were ferried across in the inflatable dingy. Mohammed made the introductions, through the din of the whining outboard.

"Jim Robson, my new boss and Alex Bell, this is my brother Ammar."

"Nice to meet you", yelled Ammar Jundi over the noise and buffeting that the little tender was making and lending them a friendly salute with his hand.

"Ammar works for Procter and Gamble" said Mohammed by way of explanation, "So we call him Mr Soap" he added with a grin.

Both Alex and Jim smiled in response. Alex was watching the deserted beach as it gradually retreated into the distance. Chugging out over the gentle swell of the Red Sea, Alex could feel the sun's intensity more keenly now that they were on the water. In the humid air, the scent of diesel jostled for attention with the fresh salty aroma of the warming sea.

"My brother is half right as usual. Actually I'm in the 'disposable paper products division'." He said the later in the manner of a television commercial voice-over, before breaking into a good natured chuckle.

"OK not Mr Soap, Mr Diapers then", added Mohammed with a laugh and now all the men joined in the laughter.

"I've spent a small fortune on those bloody things", grinned Alex.

"Say Alex, how many kids have you got? Mohammed looked genuinely interested. Alex was becoming increasingly impressed by the natural charm of Jundi. Surely it was only politeness that he asked after things like kids. In his own experience, most twenty four year old men rarely showed interest in other people's children. Alex certainly never had.

"Three, but they're out of the nappies stage now", he replied cheerfully.

Approaching the larger boat, the pitch of the little outboard dropped down a few octaves as it slowed and then came to an idle. They were now aside the enormous blue and white Sunseeker powerboat and Alex turned around and took in the sight of the boat. Close up it was even more impressive looking with its name, 'Shazadi', emblazoned across its stern. He remembered the night at the US consulate when Mohammed had said not to expect great things and that it was no great 'Gin Palace'. He now only wondered what a real Gin Palace, according to Mohammed Jundi, would look like, perhaps Buckingham Palace on floats. He smiled to himself; of course in Saudi Arabia it could never be called a Gin Palace, but a *Sid* Palace.

Once they had loaded and carefully stowed their gear into place on the stern of the boat and the tender had been secured to the transom, they started on their way. The twin engines roared into life and the boat slowly rose out of the water and cut through the sea donning its natural trim and grace.

"Have you ever dived this wreck before?" Alex asked Khalid whilst Mohammed Jundi expertly handed out iced soft drinks, clearly used to the motion of the vessel.

"No I haven't, though Talal and I have done a couple, the Dallah wreck and Boiler wreck, haven't we Talal?"

Khalid's cousin nodded a little shyly. He and his brother had said little since the brief introductions at the gate to Blue Beach and Talal was sitting rather stiffly on one of the cream coloured leather seats on the luxurious, teak fitted sundeck. His stiffness was understandable; everything around them was in such immaculate condition, that it was quite threatening. Even the tabletops that their drinks sat on and the lockers around them were finished in a gorgeous rich cherry wood that looked like it had been crafted by

Chippendale. Talal's younger brother, perhaps feeling a little overawed by these surroundings was up with Ammar in the cockpit looking admiringly at the digital displays and analogue dials that reported a mass of different information. Everything from depth, speed and direction, through to air temperature, wind direction, radar images of other boats and hazards in the vicinity and the current compact disc that was playing on the boat's incredible hi-fi system were all dancing their digital displays.

Mohammed Al-Hamra had never before seen such an impressive sight in his short seventeen years of existence. Of course, he knew that there were some very rich families in Jeddah society, but this was a world that was as remote and different to him as another planet. He looked admiringly at all the wheelhouse gadgetry and he gingerly sat himself on the seat next to Ammar Jundi who was calmly steering the boat with one hand.

Ammar turned to the shy young man and spoke in Arabic.

"Would you like to steer for a bit?"

Mohammed hesitated for an instant feeling that his desire to take control of the boat might make him look childish to the others and was about to refuse when the other man made this hesitancy redundant.

"Here take this and keep this needle pointing on this bearing", Ammar said whilst getting up from his seat and indicating for Mohammed to take his place with an intelligent smile. "Would you like a drink?"

Mohammed looked wide eyed at the offer. He had heard of what the super rich could get. His mind was racing and he was full of trepidation.

"Pepsi, Apple Juice or Water?"

Relieved but slightly disappointed he replied. "Just some water would be great, thank you."

Arriving at the site of the Abu Farmish reef, they dropped the powerboat's anchor and readied themselves for the first of two planned dives, the first being to the wreck and the second then to the surrounding reef. They had organized themselves into three pairs of diving buddies, Khalid Abu Anzi and Mohammed Jundi, the Al-Hamra brothers and then Jim and Alex. Ammar was happy to stay with the boat whilst the others made their underwater discoveries.

Alex and Jim were first into the water and they took a few minutes messing around with their buoyancy control devices at the surface before they slowly withdrew into its clear warm depths. They could feel the water temperature gently drop as they made their descent and the wreck of the Ann-Ann was immediately visible and looked massive. As he swam down towards it, Alex figured that the sunken ship must have been nearly four hundred feet long. The sound of the rising bubbles from his scuba gear seemed to grow more intense in his ears and he became aware he was now breathing quite heavily. He realised too, that there was a heavy current which the two men were working hard against in order to reach the decaying wreck of the cargo ship below. After stopping to equalize a couple of times on the descent, they then first reached the bow section, which was thrust hard into the reef. Initially the two men swam gingerly around the precarious looking upper structure of the boat but gradually they gained confidence and familiarity with their surroundings. Soon they were examining the wreck quite closely.

The ship was gradually being reclaimed by the reef's dizzying colours and was now home to a huge range of spectacular looking fish. They passed closer to a darkened lair, on what looked like the remains of a windlass and Jim was first to point to a fierce looking moray eel which silently eyed the divers. Alex was enjoying himself immensely when a sixth sense and Jim's pointing finger made him aware of something very large right beside him. He turned his head and in the restricted and magnified vision of his dive mask, there right beside him was an absolutely colossal fish that now was practically touching his nose. The close proximity and surprise together hugely alarmed Alex and he immediately backed away from the beady eyed behemoth in a storm of hyperventilating bubbles. It took him a few heart stopping moments to realise that he was in no danger as the enormous Grouper placidly eyed the panicked Englishman. Alex felt a tap on his shoulder and turned to see the masked face of Jim with his hand up signalling if everything was OK and though he could still feel his heart pumping ten to the dozen Alex managed to signal that he was. The inquisitive Grouper, over five feet long and shaped like a barrel, was now slowly moving back towards the reef and Alex determinedly calmed himself as he watched the fish slowly depart. His instinctive reaction was chastening and reminded him that he was still only a novice despite all the study he had done. He paused for a moment collecting himself, it was no time for panicky reactions. He would be calm and collected after all, a wife and three children meant prudence was no luxury.

The two men swam slowly around the wreck devouring the huge visual feast until Jim showily checked his watch, air and depth gauges, and then indicated to Alex they would soon need to start their ascent. Taking advantage of their little time left, they swam out towards what remained of the stern of the boat, which was pitched at a sharp angle further into the depths. Moving further along, Alex could see some air bubbles rising from below, he swam forward and saw the two Al-Hamra brothers who were another five to ten meters deeper than he and Jim and who appeared to be investigating the edge of the reef shelf, which fell sharply away into dark blackness below. Alex saw one of the brothers; it looked like the one named Talal, waving at him. Alex instinctively made the divers hand signal to check all was well and the young Arab quickly responded by returning the sign with index finger and thumb that all was. Jim observed this and pointed to his watch so that Talal reacted by looking at his equipment and signalled they had a few more minutes. Jim and Alex then made their ascent by the anchor line that guided them to the surface and carried out a mandatory pause for five minutes at five metres depth to counter any decompression sickness. In the warmer water, nearer the surface, Alex turned the conch shell he had taken from the deck of the wreck over in his hands in quiet satisfaction before showing it to Jim and in a few minutes they were out the water and climbing the steps back onto the baking hot deck of the *Shazadi*.

Mohammed Jundi and Khalid were already aboard and helped the two men by holding the heavy tanks as they clumsily slipped out of them.

"The currents were quite strong, so visibility was not perfect", said Mohammed as he carefully set down the air tank onto the deck with a well disguised grunt of effort.

Alex nodded, "Thanks for that." The leaden tanks were a relief to get off. "Well it was certainly good enough for me."

"It sure was. That was just brilliant." Jim sat down beside Khalid who was unfastening his flippers.

They looked and saw the two heads of the Al-Hamra brothers break the water's surface. Talal waved and inflated his buoyancy control device and his younger brother followed him as they made for the *Shazadi* and the others helped the two young men back aboard.

"Did you see the shark then?" asked Khalid of his cousin.

"Yes he was around the back of the wreck" answered Talal a little breathlessly. His younger brother sat with his feet over the edge gently kicking his flippers in the warm water.

"There was a shark?" Alex tried to sound as cool as he could but his face registered altogether hotter sensations. His mind suddenly filled with images of swimmers being devoured in the movie, 'Jaws'.

Mohammed Jundi grinned at Alex, sensing his unease. "They're quite harmless. There aren't too many Great Whites in the Red Sea!" he laughed and gave Alex a friendly pat on the back. "But we do get them, mostly you'll see Whitetips."

Alex joined in with a sheepish look realising how foolish he was being.

"I didn't see you down there Mohammed", Jim said turning to Mohammed Jundi.

"Well we were there. I did some spear fishing, look!" He pointed to plastic bucket where a large tuna fish was, its naturally beautiful underwater colours already turning to familiar fishmongers fare. "Will sushi for lunch be OK", he added with some obvious pride.

"Couldn't you catch something bigger?" said Alex regaining his composure with a cheeky smirk.

"You must be kidding. It must be at least five kilograms, any bigger and I'd have been underwater skiing", Mohammed flashed back, still laughing.

"Hey, what's that there?" Jim had leapt excitedly to his feet and was pointing over Mohammed's shoulder.

The men all turned and marvelled at the sight. The water had become alive with movement and the graceful lines of several dolphins momentarily burst out the sea before disappearing and reappearing in a series of silvery flowing arcs.

"Shit, where's my camera?" Jim lunged forward and tried to find his kit bag which was lying, squashed beneath several other bags at the bottom of one of the voluminous lockers on the port side of the stern. "Shit, just my luck." Jim Robson started pulling out the bags and the elder Al-Hamra brother, seeing the difficulties of the frustrated photographer, scrambled over bits of dive equipment to help him out.

"You better hurry or you'll just get the shark fins", chuckled Mohammed Jundi.

"What, sharks as well?" Jim asked without looking up and still heaving away at a grey canvas bag with yellow stripes and Arabic script written on its side.

"The sharks always seem to follow the dolphins."

Talal grunted as he pulled out the offending striped canvas bag so that Jim could search more easily within the locker.

"Dolphins and sharks are so graceful", Alex intoned, captivated by the glorious scene.

"Where the hell is my camera when I want it?" groaned Jim as he fished around in the bottom of his kit bag before his eager fingers found the familiar feel of the camera case. He deftly slipped off the camera's case and stood up to see if there was anything to snap.

While all this excitement was going on, Ammar had come down from the wheel and was looking at his brother's catch. "Excuse me gentlemen, I'll have this I think" he said with a good humoured glint, whilst lithely working his way through the melee before adding, "Lunch will be up in fifteen minutes." He gave a parody of a bow and wandered back into the boat carrying the freshly caught tuna.

"Lunch too? You're quite the host" said Alex brightly, to which Mohammed Jundi responded by just raising an eyebrow and giving a self effacing shrug.

Mohammed Al-Hamra was feeling absolutely dreadful. Ever since he had ascended from the Ann-Ann wreck, he had not been feeling good. Initially he and his brother had watched the two foreigners flailing around on the surface and they had gone down before them. He had even had a chuckle at the way the two Westerners had trailed around the wreck like a pair of old women. The funniest scene of all was the way the one they called Alex had jumped, when the big Grouper had surprised him. He turned around and watched them through his rising nausea, the black one was still pulling at his bags like a demented man.

"What on earth was he looking for now?" he asked sourly himself under his breath before he again felt rising bile in his mouth and silently cursed. Strange, he thought, normally he never got sea sickness. The young Arab scratched his arms, they were itching badly too and he now he was feeling really dizzy. Perhaps he would feel better if he stood up. Rising to his feet, he turned and seeing the others all still chatting bent down and un-strapped his flippers. He stood up again quickly and this time suddenly he felt his sense of balance deserting him and a strange ringing in his ears. His mind was a fog and he staggered momentarily; suddenly feeling totally exhausted and fell backwards into the water.

The first mouthful of seawater brought him round from his dizziness immediately. His eyes opened and he could see the blue of the sky through the ripples of the water's surface above him. The shimmering overhead was broken with a small stream of rising bubbles of air, which he calmly realised was his own breath. Suddenly he wanted to scream but the panic that now gripped his mind had paralysed him and he felt his throat constrict as his larynx closed involuntarily, preventing both air and water from entering his lungs. Horror filled him as the realisation dawned that not only was he now underwater and but he was also sinking, he struggled to right himself kicking his feet but his weight belt was pulling him further down. He groped with the belts release mechanism but his fingers couldn't seem to respond, his arms felt heavier than the dull lead weights that were fastened around his waist. He pushed himself and kicked his feet but the burning in his lungs was now spreading throughout his body.
He needed to breathe, he had to breathe and he could feel the tearing hot sensation of his desperate aching lungs. He knew he was still sinking and his mind was now slowing, the terror that gripped his mind was dissipating, rising with

the little bubbles. Thoughts flashed through his mind like a slideshow and calmness descended upon him, his fraught thoughts now gone, replaced entirely by a cool assessment of his situation. Wait, what was that he could see? Yes, he could clearly see the face of his brother, who was swimming down to him. Talal was smiling and even waving, he was wearing a red shirt, a Manchester United shirt, where did he get that? He suddenly relaxed, he was all right, there was really nothing to worry about, he could even hear his brother's voice speaking to him and the clearing surface light, dappled above him was getting brighter all the time as he felt himself rising to meet it.

Aboard the *Shazadi*, they had not taken much notice of the splash as Mohammed Al-Hamra had dropped into the water. First the dolphins and then the prospect of the promised for sharks, had kept the men's attention and none of them thought much of it as the assumption had been that the youngster had decided to take a short cooling dip. It was after all, getting fiercely hot. A quick swim before lunch seemed like a good idea. It was Jim who was first to wonder what had happened to the young Arab.
"Where has he gone off to?" He asked Khalid, who was standing beside him. He pitched his head and pointed over the transom to where Mohammed Al-Hamra had been sitting lazily kicking his feet only a few moments before.

Khalid turned and examined the scene. The teenager's flippers and mask where all lying on the lower platform.

"Mohammed?" He called out as he slowly moved to the rear of the boat. He called out again, this time much louder, "Mohammed?"

On hearing his brother's name being called Talal looked around, a slight frown had creased his forehead, eyes just registering mild concern.

"Everything OK?" he asked in Arabic of his cousin who was now looking around the water all about the stern of the anchored boat.

"He's probably gone inside", volunteered Mohammed Jundi in English in a reassuring tone whilst moving towards the entrance to the spacious cabin. He leaned in and called out loudly and a little hoarsely into the plush cool interior.

"Only me in here", came the distant reply of Ammar Jundi, who was at the galley.

"Relax, the food's coming soon."

"No I'm sure I just saw him jump in." Jim said firmly.

Khalid and Talal were now looking seriously worried. There was still no sign of Mohammed anywhere as they searched and called his name with increasing anxiety. Talal looked at his cousin and suddenly the gravity of the situation hit him like an express, his features froze as the rising panic gripped him, his only movement was his hunted eyes which widened with disbelief. Alex could hear him talking faster and faster in Arabic, his voice breaking with emotion. All the while both Alex and Jim were scouring the surface for any clue as to where he had gone. The water was calm, disturbingly so. Jim turned to Alex and spoke quietly.

"Shark?" Jim's eyes were like saucers.

Alex shivered at the thought but didn't take his eyes off the water, "You heard him jump right? He probably…" Alex's mind had flown off ahead of him far faster than his ability to speak. He was about to say that any attack would have surely brought a cry of help or something, when it dawned on him that he may have just taken a severe cramp or had he been hit with the bends? Without thinking, he grabbed a mask, pulled it on and dived into the water, suddenly sure of what he was doing. From the boat everything was reflected glassy calm but now that he was underwater, he could see quite clearly in all directions. He rose to the surface, the others were looking at him expectantly, he turned and swam strongly ten or so meters with the prevailing current and took a large breath through the snorkel and dived down again. The visibility must have been at least forty meters and he spun around on his axis and suddenly caught sight of a dark object. He recoiled in horror; it was a shark, icy fear gripping his every sinew. Then he strained to see what it was that the predatory fish was swimming around. He squinted and saw what he first thought was the giant Grouper. He peered at the dark object and realised it was no Grouper, it was the poor Arab. He was perfectly stationary and not much more than twenty meters away, motionless, just a few meters below the water's surface. His body was gently rolling with the warm surface current heading towards the shallower part of the reef. Alex immediately surfaced and bellowed like an ox.

"Shark, Shark! He spat out sea water before screaming, "Here, I've found him, he's over here."

As soon as these words reached the ears of the others on the tense deck of the *Shazadi* they all went into complete panicky action. Talal simply leapt into the sea and started swimming, he spluttered at the surface as a mouthful of seawater caught him as he drew breath. He coughed and spluttered whilst he tried to recover himself. Alex who was already powering through the becalmed waters, his eyes focused through the glass of his mask on the lifeless teenager, forged through the water. His mouth felt parched dry, his heart was pounding and his whole body felt as tight as a steel hawser as he searched for the dark object that had been circling the still form of Mohammed but that was now even more worryingly out of sight. A few more strokes then he took one large breath, dived down and grabbed at the Arab, catching him by his thick black buoyancy vest which was partly inflated. Wrestling his hand under the

289

young man's chin he slung his arm around the limp head and brought him to the surface, kicking his legs furiously, his lungs bursting with effort. He hit the surface gasping for air and he looked back towards the *Shazadi*. Mohammed Jundi had already released the inflatable dingy and in moments was hurtling, with Jim aboard, through the calm waters towards Alex, who now bobbed with the lifeless form of Mohammed Al-Hamra.

As they passed by Talal, who stopped to unsteadily treading water as they approached him, Mohammed Jundi leant over and yelled at the young man to get back to the boat in a hail of vitriolic Arabic. The last thing anyone needed was another drowned Al-Hamra. Seeing the look of anger on Jundi's face, Talal paused and turned towards the Sunseeker, where from the rear of the boat Khalid was shouting similar instructions. Talal knew too that his strength seemed to be fading, suddenly he was feeling totally washed out. With a look of complete resigned misery he rolled over onto his back and started slowly swimming back to the *Shazadi*.

From the speeding dingy, Jim clearly saw two fins break the surface behind the two men in the water.

"Fuck me it's crawling with sharks", he gasped pointing at the tell tale trail.

Mohammed Jundi said nothing; just a look of grim determination was moulded to his features. "They won't attack" he said with equal force of will, only too aware that they could at any moment

For Alex, the next few seconds were by far the worse, seeing the dingy approach and Jim's pointing hand, he had turned and seen the two dark fins course through the water. To Alex, they were no longer graceful, they were the personification of death and he suddenly was conscious of slight warmth around him as his bladder involuntarily emptied. At last he truly knew the meaning of being scared shitless. Just one thought passed through his head. "Not like this, please God".

As the dingy pulled alongside, Alex desperately grabbed hold of the inflatable and Jim and Mohammed Jundi started to haul the young man aboard. Alex heaved from below with all his strength and it took every ounce of effort of the men to drag Al-Hamra's helpless flaccid form onto the inflatable. Still in the water, Alex turned and chillingly he saw the sharks fin approaching him. Forlornly he tried to pull himself up onto the edge of the dingy but his strength was almost entirely drained. Jim, seeing the look of complete exhaustion on Alex's face, grabbed him by the wrists and heaved him in with three huge energy sapping tugs, like a ridiculous prize catch. With his legs drawn clear of the water, the inquisitive shark passed beneath the boat, its progress unnoticed by the boat's bedraggled occupants. Whilst Alex lay slumped on the floor catching his breath, savouring the diesel tainted bilge of the little rescue boat, Jim immediately started on the seemingly impossible task of reviving the lifeless lad.

Alex slowly roused himself watching Jim as he breathed huge lungs full of air into the prone unresponsive shape of Mohammed.

"Is he…?" Alex couldn't bring himself to ask the question, it all seemed quite hopeless to him.

Between delivering each two breaths, Jim was pumping the young man's chest. Alex wondered where the hell Jim had learnt to do cardiopulmonary resuscitation.

"Come on, live you bastard, live" he pinched the man's nose and breathed more life giving oxygen into him before alternately placing one hand on the other and pumping his chest, massaging the man back to life. Jim Robson had never before done anything like this in his life, but now that he was faced with the prospect of failure his face had taken on a look abject desperation. They didn't warn you about this on the first aid course.

Seeing the Jim's face roused Alex from his momentary paralysis. Alex sat himself upright in the cramped space of the dingy. Wordlessly he bent over the Arab ready to perform the heart massage as Jim repeated the mouth to mouth.

It wasn't necessary. The first splutter of life from Mohammed Al-Hamra was something that none of the men on that boat would ever forget. Jim knew well enough that within three minutes of submersion most people are unconscious and that within five minutes the brain begins to suffer from lack of oxygen. As the young man came choking back to life, he wondered how long he had been starved of oxygen, what, if any, damage had the young man suffered?

"My God Jim you've done it." Alex was incredulous, he stared at Mohammed Al-Hamra who still had a strange bluish skin colouring but he was coughing back to life. Frothy pink sputum ejected from the man's mouth before he started his rapid short breathing.

Alex stared at Jim whose eyes were misty; his voice was almost breaking with emotion as he spoke. "Don't let me take on a responsibility like that ever, ever again" and he slumped back onto his haunches with his head hung forward and his eyes closed in silent thankful prayer.

As soon as the resurrected man had started breathing Mohammed Jundi gunned the idling outboard and raced the inflatable dingy back to the *Shazadi*. Within a few moments, his brother Ammar had raised the anchor and the muscular powerboat was planing at top speed back towards Obhur harbour. Ammar radioed ahead to the coastguard to inform them what had happened and that they would need an ambulance.

Meanwhile on the deck of the *Shazadi*, the men were arrayed all around the horizontal but fitfully conscious shape of Mohammed Al-Hamra. His brother, who was close to tears, sat beside him. His penitent expression, his nervous hand resting possessively on his younger sibling's shoulder, suggested he was aware that many questions awaited him once safely ashore. Initially thankful that the fatality had seemingly been narrowly avoided, Mohammed Jundi was now silently furious with Talal Al-Hamra. As they motored back it was clear that the two of them had gone too deep and ascended far too quickly. Jundi was sufficiently proficient a diver to recognise the symptoms of decompression sickness and a quick check of his namesake's equipment confirmed that the youngster had used a large amount of his air. What the hell had they been playing at? Despite the fierce rays above them, the slowly recovering teenager was still breathing in short little breaths and was starting to shiver.

"I'm cold."

"What did he say?" Jim was slowly recovering his composure.

"'He said he was cold'", translated Khalid who was looking awful.

Jim knew that under some circumstances of near-drowning a substantial increase or decrease in the volume of circulating blood can occur. This was probably what Mohammed Al-Hamra was suffering from.

"Have you got a blanket, he could be in shock and getting hypothermic?" Jim leant forward and listened to the man's chest. He was still breathing quick and shallow. "His heartbeat is very fast too."

Alex was watching all this happen in stunned silence. Perhaps because the adrenaline was still coursing around his body so, that he was as jumpy as the flying fish that periodically leapt out of the sea that streamed beside them, his own nervy excitement meant that he was entirely amazed at the sang-froid of his friend.

It seemed to take an eternity to get to the harbour but when at last they did the paramedics from the Ghassan N Pharaon Hospital took over. Jim and Alex stood around on the *Shazadi*, as the Jundi brothers answered the questions raised by some rotund gum chewing coastguards about the incident. He watched from the boat as Mohammed walked away still pushing his slightly slimmer wallet into his back pocket.   Talal and Khalid had gone ahead with the recovering Mohammed in the ambulance. The youngster had passed in and out of fitful lethargic consciousness a number of times on the fraught trip back, but his condition seemed to have stabilised once they were ashore. As Mohammed started up the twin engines of the huge powerboat, all he could say to the two Westerners was, "What a complete fucking nightmare."

The first half of the journey back in Alex's little car passed in almost total silence. Neither man felt particularly talkative as both of them travelled clothed in their own deep thought. Alex drove the journey back home much slower than the morning's manic outward leg. The men's senses were suddenly so much more keenly aware of everything, the preciousness of life still sparkling with novelty.

As they approached the city's outer limits, signalled by the slow creep skywards of ever higher walled homes, Alex switched on the radio. Tuned as it always was to the US servicemen's channel, AFRTS droned on its usual shiny buttoned up way.

"…and remember, boats and alcohol never mix", goaded the public service announcement, in its habitually condescending manner.

The preachy irony got the better of Jim. "Shit, the sanctimonious crap that we have to listen to."

Alex pulled a slight grimace as 'Hootie and the Blowfish', a particular favourite on the station's stultifying repetitive play list, started blaring out.

"You know Jim; what you did back there was amazing, you saved that young man's life." Now it was Jim's turn to pull a sour face.

"I was only able to because of your heroics."

"I'm not sure I could do that again."

"What, jump into shark infested waters?" he made a short little guffaw.

"Well I wasn't actually expecting to see any you know." Alex swallowed back a little wave of nausea, before adding "I think you probably saved mine too..."

Jim smiled and looked out the side window of the car. The passage of lush well tended gardens, seen sparingly though iron gates of the houses was in sharp contrast to the dusty brown wastes that lay between them. They looked as tranquil as he was feeling disturbed.

"And where the hell did you learn to do all that first aid stuff?"

"I did a course just before leaving England."

"Amazing", Alex shook his head, still trying to put the last few hours into some kind of perspective. "Do you think he'll be alright?"

"Dunno, depends on how long was he underwater."

Alex shook his head again. "I guess we'll find out tomorrow." It was a gloomy thought.

Alex put on a brave face. "Fancy a drink back at my place?" Both men still wanted to talk about what had happened that day but tiredness was overtaking them.

"Maybe not."

"It's my first attempt at homebrew. Dieter's recipe", Alex added coaxingly with a grin.

"Oh OK then. I guess I could use a beer after today's excitement."

Fifteen minutes later, in the gathering dusk, Jim Robson was relaxing in one of the white plastic chairs beside the swimming pool sipping Alex's first try at home made beer. They sipped the illicit drinks whilst the call to prayer echoed around them. The sound now was as familiar as church bells to them both, but had none of the appeal of reassurance. They toasted each other. By Jeddah standards, it wasn't too bad either thanks to the helpful influence of Alex's German neighbour, who as if on cue had just that moment returned from work. Sunday's still may well have been the weekend for the IAB traders, but for most others in Saudi, it was the first day of the working week.

"Fancy joining us?" Asked Alex of Dieter Werner, who eventually demurred if only to see how his handiwork had turned out. The men shook hands, by now Jim was a familiar face around Alex's pool.

"Not bad at all", was his considered opinion.

Within a few minutes, Jim and Alex were each recounting the story of the near drowning to the incredulous Frankfurter.

"He sounds a remarkably lucky young man."

"He is", agreed Alex and just then his mobile rang. It was Omar Al-Hamra.

"Hi Omar"

The other two men went silent as Alex listened to what the father had to say. Alex signalled a, thumbs up, to Jim whose features up to then had suddenly taken on great seriousness. Dieter looked inquisitively at Alex as Jim quietly explained to him who the caller was.

"No honestly it was nothing." Alex was feeling very good about himself. Jim could just hear the effusive nature of the Arab's thanks. "Thank you, thank you, you are very kind. Jim could see that Alex was looking more and more chuffed with himself.

"Actually he's here with me now. Would you like to speak to him?" Alex handed the phone to Robson who took it and was then also served up an equally loquacious auditory treat.

"So the man you saved is doing well?"

Alex took a swig of his warming beer and nodded with a smile. "Sitting up and should be fine, according to his father."

"That's good", replied the German.

Jim handed the phone back to Alex. "Well that's my good turn for the day done." He picked up his glass before adding with relief, "Thank God it all worked out."

"Don't you start", said Dieter with a wry smile, "This place is all about blaming God. He gets wheeled out for everything that doesn't work. *Inshallah* this, *Inshallah* that. It gets on my nerves."

"Tough day at the office then Dieter?" Alex was amused at the German's sudden outburst.

He nodded slowly, "You could say that." He took a small draught of his drink before continuing with the ease of someone on familiar territory. "The place is falling apart you know." He laughed. "Proof indeed of the existence of God, something I think particularly funny." He shook his bearded head side to side with grinning disbelief.

"I take from that, that you are not a believer in the Almighty then?" Jim asked bent forward.

"You can say that again. I'm a fundamental humanist", he replied without hesitation.

"You're an atheist Dieter?" asked Alex surprised a little by the man's sudden enthusiasm for the subject.

"Completely, I can't stand religion, any religion. Islam, Christianity, Judaism. All the 'ism's' Communism, Fascism, belief and dogma, it's, as you say, the root of all evil."

300

"Is that your own credo then?" said Jim with a wicked glint.

"Very funny, no but really, why does there have to be a God?"

Alex pondered this for a moment though Jim was quicker to respond. "Isn't the question more, why not?"

"Well, what proof is there?" The German was enjoying himself immensely. He lit up his second cigarette.

"What proof is there that there isn't?"

Dieter paused and took another draught of his beer. Alex picked up the jug and refilled all the glasses with more of the foaming drink. "So you believe in God?" Dieter seemed quite amused at this.

Jim paused, "Well yes. I do actually."

"And what about you Alex?"

"Well I'm not sure really. When things go badly I do pray. I certainly prayed today when I was in the water. So I suppose I must do."

"That doesn't seem a very logical position Alex. I would have thought you would have been clearer."

Now Jim laughed. "Not at all, in fact that's an extremely logical position. For if there is no God as you say Dieter, what does it matter whether you believe in Him or not? What harm can come from this belief? But, if there is a God, what danger do you run by refusing Him your belief."

The German considered this for a moment. Jim smiled before adding, I believe this is known as 'Pascal's Wager' after the Frenchman, Blaise Pascal, so I expect it's rigorously logical."

The German grinned widely at this. "Maybe so, but this place would be a lot easier without all this superstition, wouldn't it?"

"Dieter!"

"Oh shit."

The German's wife was standing beside the men. "Time to stop all your nonsense and come and deal with your kids."

"Oops, better go." He got up, a little heavy legged and then waved goodnight with his usual lopsided smile. "Thanks for the beer Alex."

"No problem and thank you for that as well as the excellent recipe."

Dieter chuckled and then wandered off following his wife and then disappeared into his house, Alex turned to Jim.

"You're on fire today mate, saving lives and waxing all philosophical like... like Plato, whatever next?"

"A refill would do nicely", he said laughingly. Alex poured the last of the jugs contents into the two men's glasses.

"So where did all that stuff about God and Pascal's wager come from?"

Jim leant back in his seat. "Well I did study more than just maths you know, though obviously I know him more from his probability and binomial theories."

Alex nodded, he had studied some statistics too, besides the fact that all the derivatives and options that he traded at the bank, were based on this branch of mathematics. "And so?"

Jim smiled tiredly, "It's one of the first examples of decision theory. You know, 'Prisoners dilemma' and all that guff?"

"I'd forgotten it all, remind me." Alex yawned, "You'll have to tell me."

Jim yawned too and glanced at his watch. "Another time... I had better be going." He stood up.

"Promise?" Alex was sleepy; the alcohol had done its job. He was feeling very relaxed and looking forward to speaking to Claire and the kids.

"I never promise", Jim stared straight at Alex. "As my old man used to say, 'a promise is a comfort to a fraud'".

"A comfort to a fraud?"

"Yes, whenever someone makes a promise", he smiled with genuine warmth, "think about it."

Alex frowned in thought before putting up his hand theatrically. "Hold that thought"

"Will do." The two men stood and spontaneously gave each other a hug before breaking into big handed back slapping.

"Thanks Jim, I thought I was a goner there you know."

"Don't worry about it."

"I not sure I'm ever going to forget today."

"Me neither."

Alex cleared off the table in a couple of trips, placing the empty beer glasses and jug into the sink in the kitchen for his daily Christie to clean. The house, thanks to the ever efficient Filipina was as usual, absolutely spotless and he sat down on the freshly plumped sofa and picked up the phone to call Claire. He was feeling great and was looking forward to retelling her the day's unbelievable course of events. After all, he reasoned, it's not every day that you get to do something heroic. He checked his watch. It was past six in the evening. Claire and the kids would be back from their weekend away with her friend Nessa Simmonds. He athletically got to his feet and bounced over to the phone, dialling his old number in Fulham with dextrous fingers. Life was good, not just good, great and he was a hero too. The phone rang just twice before it was picked up.

"Hello" Straight away he could tell something was not right. Claire sounded terrible.

"Hi darling it's me."

"I know." She sounded like she had a really bad cold.

"Darling, you won't believe what happened to me today."

"Actually Alex, you're quite right. I won't. I won't believe a word of anything you say." Alex felt the icy blast of her reply.

"What? What's wrong?"

Claire Bell paused, trying to find the right words and her almond shaped eyes were full of tears. She collected herself for a moment and Alex waited as she did. Claire had re-run what she was going to say in her mind a dozen times already, but she had forgotten it just when it mattered. Instead she just managed to blurt out, "Just who the fuck is Sandrine Giraud?" The name tasted bitter in her mouth like a burnt love letter.

"Sandrine Giraud? I…" he stammered, the two words had turned his mind to mush in a heartbeat. Alex felt as if his stomach was suddenly down by his knees and his knees.

"Well can you explain to me who this woman is?" Claire Bell was just managing to keep control of herself. At any moment she felt she was about to burst into tears, but for now the fury of her discovery was enough to keep her going. She knew she needed to keep that anger stoked.

"She's nobody, look I can explain, I… it was just a one off…"

"Nobody?" She laughed witheringly, "Alex, 'nobody', doesn't write you two letters proclaiming undying love. 'Nobody', doesn't write that they'll die, if you don't come back."

"Letters?" Alex was trying to figure out what was going on. Unwelcome new information was raining down upon him and his mouth was moving up and down like one of the fish he'd been watching earlier in the day. What had been written, how much damage had been done?

"Yes letters. Sent to your old office in Paris and forwarded by Jean-Marc here. The ice in her voice was already melting; the anger was thawing her out, turning her broken heart to slush.

"Darling I love you. I'm so sorry. I know I've been a complete idiot."

"Look I have to put the boys to bed. I'll call you later. We need to talk."

"I love you Claire."

Claire Bell hung up the phone and broke down in tears.

Alex Bell heard the phone line click into lifelessness for the second time that evening, the only sound being the ever present periodic clanking noise that always occurred on every phone line he had used in the Kingdom. Was someone listening to his conversations? It had bothered him before but right now he didn't care. His second phone call home that evening had gone a lot worse than the first. Claire had always been fiery, it had always been one of the things he had loved in her, but now her incandescent anger was just too hot to handle.

"Shit. What a colossal fuck up." He said out loud to himself. He stumbled stupidly towards the kitchen, making straight for one of the recently stocked cupboards and pulled out one of his freshly brewed bottles of yeasty beer. His mind was a mess. He clumsily opened the bottle and poured out its frothy contents into the jug that was still sitting in the sink. Mixing in some ice cold non-alcoholic beer, taken from the fridge, he had decided to drink himself drunk. At least here was something he could do well. It would dull the pain and even though he knew that there was nothing less attractive than a self-centred drunk, that was precisely what he was going to be. At least nobody could see him, he was safely alone. He roamed around the house, like a hunted animal, refilling his glass he walked past the kitchen window, the black night outside caused the glass to reflect his features darkly back at him. "You fucking idiot." But unsurprisingly, the reflection did not respond, it just looked dumbly back at him. In no time he had drunk the bottle dry and then went up to his bedroom and fitfully tried to fall asleep. Awake with only the drone of the air conditioning as his companion, he sourly thought how stupid and he now felt. A desperation brought on by the realization that even the woman he had chosen to cheat on his wife also now knew he was a worthless waste of time. Broken hearts and promises, Jim's father was right.

11. Cigars, Dens, Jail

"You both must be very proud of yourselves", said Chris Barma beaming at both Alex and Jim. "Quite a pair of heroes we have amongst us."

Alex looked askance at this. Right now there was nothing heroic about him at all, he was feeling simply awful. Not only was he nursing the remains of a hangover of biblical proportions, but the words of his wife were still resonating in his ears over and over again. "Complete bastard." He knew that the hangover was the least of his problems, it would pass, but the situation with his wife was far different. She was a long way from revising her opinion of him. Jim on the other hand was well rested and was happily basking in the glory of their recent exploits.

Discreetly, trying not to draw too much attention to himself Alex enquired, "Chris, I was wondering if I could have a word." Last night's second conversation with Claire had not been easy. He needed to get back to London quickly to try and fix things up.

"Can you give me half an hour?" Barma was clearly preoccupied, even perhaps agitated.

"Sure", Alex glanced at the clocks on the wall, "I'll swing by your office at say, nine thirty?"

"Yeah, no problem." Barma strode off, personnel stuff from his traders was something he really didn't need right now. The Deutschemark was already causing him enough grief.

When Omar Al-Hamra entered the dealing room he could barely contain himself. He rushed up to the two Englishmen and planted kisses on them like an over active politician at the stump, shaking their hands so vigorously that for a brief moment Alex thought that his arm might come off at the shoulder. His thanks were effusive and both the men even were a little embarrassed by all this attention.

Amongst the prop team, Pete and Andy were also generous with their praise but Joe Karpolinski was just highly entertained and thought the whole business sounded like a hilarious escapade.

"So let me get this right." He stood and paused so that the entire desk was listening to him. "Should we refer to you henceforth as Batman and Robin?" The two men grinned wanly at the humour.

"Well I'm genuinely impressed." Andy was always direct in his manner.

Seeing the seriousness of Andy and not wanting to appear ungracious Joe was immediately backtracking. "Oh I quite agree. I'm only joking you know." He turned towards Jim, "So what was it like, you know, giving someone the kiss of life?"

Jim looked at Joe, not quite sure where this line of questioning was going. His features clouded over in thought before he spoke. "Frankly it was nerve wracking. You don't know if it's working and for a short while I thought he was gone. That was the worst of it."

The men all thought about this, Joe's face was a picture of enquiry.

"But what I don't understand is why didn't he just sink?" It was clear to Alex that Joe was in one of his irritating terrier moods.

"Because his BCD was partly inflated", Alex answered.

"BCD?"

"Buoyancy Control Device. It's used to maintain neutral buoyancy underwater." Joe nodded his head sagely. "I see, tell me Alex have there been a shark attacks in the Red Sea?" He tone was just ever so mildly incredulous.

"Actually I've no idea."

"I think that you'll find there have been quite a few", interrupted Andy, looking quite serious. Joe was a little taken aback by tone of the man, there was no doubting that he found the brusque Northerner a little intimidating. Andy continued, "I know that there were at least three last year alone."

"Really?" Joe was genuinely surprised, as were most of the others on the desk who caught his words, his lengthened vowels and diction were not easy to miss.

"One, on a British diver and the other was on two fishermen." He raised his eyebrows and grinned over at Jim and Alex, "Apparently their boat was overturned by this bloody great shark, one badly injured but survived, for the other it was goodnight Vienna."

Alex gave a little shiver as his own extension started flashing on his phone board. He picked up the phone, "IAB Trading."

"Alex?" The voice sounded familiar, it was that damn salesman from Dresdner again.

"What have we got today?" asked Alex with tired relief, deciding that it would be good to have a temporary distraction from his worries.

"Leave early on holiday?" Chris Barma was not looking too pleased at Alex's request, "but you've only been away just a few weeks ago."

"There's been a bit of domestic trouble." Alex really didn't want to go into any more detail.

"What about your positions?" Alex had a couple options positions that were a bit lively at that moment.

"Well I can close them out pretty easily or get Jim to watch them for me." He hadn't asked Jim but he was sure he would do it for him. They had talked about it in principle a few weeks back.

Chris Barma shook his head, "So you need to go to London?"

"Yes"

"I don't know... all seems a bit..." Chris Barma was searching for the words.

"Well it's a bit of a delicate domestic problem."

"Like what, what's happened?" Irritation had crept into Chris Barma's voice. He really didn't need flakiness from his traders just now.

Alex hadn't really thought through what he was going to say when he had asked to see Chris earlier that morning. He just knew he needed to get back and tell Claire he was sorry, face to face. He knew too he would have to deal with her hurt and anger, try to put it all in perspective and try to move on. It wasn't irretrievable he was sure. There just was a violent emotional storm to be weathered.

"Do you mind if I don't really to go into it Chris, but I'd really appreciate it" Alex tried to look calm as he added; "It'll just be for a few days."

Chris Barma looked intrigued for a moment before taking on a pensive tilt. "Have you got your 'Exit Visa' sorted out?" His eyes danced back and forth from the computer screen that relayed flashing foreign exchange rates as the markets ground on in their relentless way.

Alex suddenly blanched as the full understanding hit home. What was he thinking? He couldn't just go and get on an airplane, he needed his passport which was held by personnel and he had to get the eponymous Exit Visa before he could leave.

"Not yet."

"Well you might find it a bit difficult." He paused before adding flatly, "speak to personnel, but it could be tricky." As he watched Alex turn and disappear from view he wondered what type of problem Alex had and hoped it wasn't going to be a serious one. He needed his traders to keep their focus; distractions like these were simply not acceptable. He looked at his computer screen. Family problems were one thing, but this was what really counted and he smiled as he saw the dollar had moved his way again.

According to Personnel it wasn't just going to be tricky, but quite impossible.

"Exit Visa, ten days minimum. Already we have request for one for you in two weeks", said the bearded man on the fourth floor looking at his desk. He raised his head and coolly eyed the expatriate with a steady gaze that brooked no compromise. "It's in the system."

Frustration was boiling up in Alex, with a monstrous effort he maintained his composure but his eyes were flashing with anger. "Look, surely there is a way to speed it up. It's very important for me to be able to get home for just a few days. It's an emergency."

This last statement from Alex seemed to trigger something in the man whose coolness appeared to drop below freezing.

"Emergency?" His thick accent unable to hide his attitude, he did not like Westerners.

"Yes, an emergency." What was it to this idiot anyway? Alex was fuming.

The clerk looked down at Alex's papers and scanned the pages. "What kind?" It was said with the same level of interest displayed by a youth serving in a failing fast food outlet.

"Does it matter?"

The man looked up at Alex; his features were unmoved, deliberately stony faced. "Matter, yes? Death or illness?" The man's menu offering was sickening.

"Neither."

"Then not emergency."

"It's my wife, she needs me to..."

The man was already shaking his head and had already closed Alex's file. "Papers are in system. Perhaps they come sooner. It's in God's hands. "

"What?"

"Inshallah Bokra Malesh"

Alex just managed to strangle a scream before birth, "Isn't there anything you can do?"

The man shrugged and gave a humourless smile before slowly shaking his head.

"No." The matter was closed.

Alex abruptly turned on his heel and stormed out of the fourth floor unaware that his passport was still sitting in the man's desk and that if the clerk had wanted to or been persuaded by a small *baksheesh*, he might have had it back in a day.

As he glowered in the lift, for Alex this was just another classic case of man against impossible system, IBM. He lit up a cigarette; he was smoking a lot these last two days. He shuddered, this was not good news to convey to Claire. He was stuck with the original schedule.

Claire Bell had barely slept that night. The arrival of the two letters she had read had taxed her hugely. She had not intended to open them; it was only that her youngest son, the three year old David, had torn open the large brown Manila envelope that Jean-Marc had sent. The two letters addressed to her husband were written in a distinctive handwriting and had sat over the weekend on the mantle-piece. When she had come back from a weekend away she had opened one of them, the one with the earlier postmark and had read it. Claire's French was not bad but neither was it sufficient to understand all of the letters contents, but very quickly she had gleaned the nature of it. Now as she lay fitfully in bed she tried to imagine what this other woman was like. Her thoughts ranged from the trivial to the murderous, what did she look like, how many times had they made love and where? She asked herself these horrible questions but she didn't really want to know the answers to them. Far better surely, to keep this woman at arm's length, that way she would always be a marriage wrecking monster. No, that was not the question that she asked herself the most. What she kept asking herself was why? Why had he betrayed her and how many lies had she been told? It was just like Alex to create a complete mess and then traipse out of it like that. It made her so angry she wanted to scream. She wanted to slap his face but he was three thousand miles away. Some of the lines she had managed to read sent shivers down her spine and kept repeating in her head. It was obvious what had happened, Alex had left Paris without telling this woman and Claire Bell took some small solace in knowing that he had obviously ended the affair. But several of the lines made little sense, either as they were written or in Claire's translation to English. Two lines stuck with her for different reasons, *'I was standing in the middle of the road but the car stopped. Life even death is not fair'* and *'I must try to live without you but I can't. I love you more than you can imagine and I will for the rest of my life.'* Even Claire could sense there was a kind of mild hysteria to the tone of

316

the letter. Her curiosity had got the better of her and she had opened the other with trembling fingers. This second letter was much shorter and much shriller sounding. Claire could not make out much, it seemed very confused and bitter, *'Life unequal and strange'* and *'viciously ape jealousy'* were some of the weird translations she had come up with. The two missives sat on the top of her bedroom dresser and she cast rancorous looks at them through bloodshot eyes from the emptiness of her bed.

She was busy feeding their youngest son David breakfast after the school run, when the phone call from Alex came. He had been waiting until both Jim and Khalid who sat either side of him had gone down to lunch, telling them that he would join them in a few moments. He dialled and as he waited for the line to be picked up he could feel his heart thumping in his chest.

"Hello."

"How are you?"

"How do you think I am Alex?"

Alex swallowed had and realised that this was not going to be an easy conversation. He immediately wished that he had thought more about what he was going to say.

"Look I've got some... well, some not so good news."

"Not so good?" The sarcasm in her voice was palpable and dripped into his ears like acid.

"Look Claire you've got to understand, this is a difficult place to get anything done quickly."

"Will you just cut the crap and tell me what is going on?"

"I can't get back any sooner than planned. I can't get an Exit Visa."

"What?"

"It takes ten days to process and mine is already in the system, whatever that's supposed to mean."

Alex waited for Claire to respond, the silence on the phone line was oppressive and Alex broke it after what had seemed like an eternity but was actually only five or six seconds.

"Claire, are you still there?"

"Of course I am Alex, I'm trying to think."

"You told them it was an emergency?"

"Yes I told them I had problems at home, but apparently only death or illness qualify."

"So this isn't a sufficient emergency for you Alex?"

"Darling it's not an emergency, it's..."

"It's not is it?" Her voice rising in hurt. "Well Alex, exactly what is it then? Can you tell me?"

Alex's scrambled mind searched for the words, "it's a crisis, we can work through it..."

"Crisis? Alex, don't start all your bullshit with me now."

"C'mon Claire we can get through this." Alex was desperately trying to calm things down. Claire had already demonstrated her furious temper and the second conversation last night was not one he wanted repeated.

"How long did this go on for?"

"Does it matter? It's over."

"Yes it does matter. I want to know how long you've been fucking this other woman."

"Claire this is not helping."

"Well you should have thought about that before, shouldn't you?"

"Claire I've told you already, it's over. I don't know why she's written to me."

"Well are you expecting more of them?" she said bitterly.

"Shit Claire, of course not." There was a trace of frustration creeping into Alex' voice. It was hard to hide, the damned letters might exist, but why did she have to open his mail anyway. It had been the first thing he had wanted to say when she mentioned them. Worse, he still had no idea what had been written. The not knowing was eating him up.

"What did they say?" He instantly regretted asking.

"So now you want to know? I don't know, they're in bloody French. Shall I keep then on a silver platter for you?" Her anger and hurt petulancy were rising. She knew too that she probably shouldn't have opened them either, but what was done was done. That had not been right, but she had uncovered a far greater wrong.

319

"No, it doesn't matter."

"Are you sure, there's an address, she's obviously moved, don't you want it?" The hurt and bitterness joined the sarcasm and fortified the vile mix that fed his blooming regrets.

"Claire please... look, just...just throw them away."

"Are you sure?"

"Yes I'm sure", he lied.

The following silence was only broken by the soft sound of their breathing and the ever present occasional far off clanking noise. If they were being eavesdropped it would make salacious gossip.

At last she spoke. "Alex do you still love me?"

"Yes of course I do darling." Alex could hear a muffled sound on the line.

"Look Claire, I'm so sorry."

"You are an idiot Alex."

"I know."

"Can you forgive me?"

"Perhaps, I just don't know." Claire's tone was much calmer now. She was feeling a little better. "I need to sleep on it. I'm exhausted by all of this."

Alex could only murmur his agreement. For the first time he felt that perhaps the situation was retrievable. At last, the scales had tipped, just a little in favour of hope over fear.

By the time Alex had descended to the canteen the others were already finishing up their deserts. He joined then after having taken just a couple of apples from the counter, stress having driven out hunger.

"You look a bit washed out mate." Jim was looking at Alex closely as he spoke.

Alex took a bite of the apple. It was sour and he pulled a matching face. "It's nothing, just a bit of hassle with personnel."

That evening Alex took a short stroll around the compound in surroundings that were now as familiar to him as his own features. Sierra Village was arranged as a series of blocks around a large central area. Alex' block, Algarve, was located to the west and was set up for larger families with its three and four bedroom villas, but there were many variants on the same basic design from slightly larger five bedroom villas through to one bedroom studios. Meandering on pathways through the perfumed evening air, he passed the carefully tended plants, busy floodlit tennis and basketball courts, was slowly overhauled by heavy footed joggers and forced a couple of times to sidestep as kids whizzed past on bikes. His circuit of Sierra Village was half complete; he was just by the singles apartments of Ronda when his dark ruminations were disturbed.

"Alex isn't it?"

He blinked in the severe light of the street lamp which cast the man opposite him as a large crew cut silhouette. Alex recognized the familiar colours of an on duty US soldier and immediately caught sight of the man's name written across his breast, it was Allensen.

Memories of his first evening at the 'Brass Eagle' always came flooding back whenever he saw Allensen. They played squash each week now. "Hi Jerry, how are you?"

"Doing great, all Alpha Charlie Echo, mate", he replied in his impossibly bad English accent.

Alex grinned back, that night of the acronyms and abbreviations had grown in retelling amongst the men of the IAB prop team.

"And how about you?"

"Oh you know, bit stiff and all FUBAR", replied Alex. Alex now used the American's expressions regularly during their intensely fought squash matches.

"Say, are your family over here yet?"

Alex shook his head, "Not yet, they're due end of August."

Jerry Allensen thought about this for a moment. "Well if you're at a loose end, you should come along to the den, we're throwing the usual tomorrow."

Alex brightened. "Thanks, I just might take you up on that."

"Sure, number fifty one, Ronda, from seven thirty. OK?" Allensen was already starting to walk off.

"Thanks, I'll be there."

Allensen had walked a few paces before he halted, turned and called back to Alex, who immediately stopped to listen to the young American. "Hey by the way, don't bother bringing any of that stuff you guys call beer OK?"

"OK" said Alex both a little surprised and relieved.

Jerry Allensen grinned and raised his hand to signify restraint, "No honestly, we've got loads of the real stuff." He grinned at Alex then suddenly looked thoughtful. "Say you can bring that other guy too, if you want."

"Do you mean Jim?"

The American looked thoughtful, "I thought his name was Joe?"

"There were two of them." Alex would rather have had Jim. Joe was unlikely to make it.

"Sure, no problem, ask both of them." With that he gave a good natured shrug and wandered off.

The next day Alex mentioned to both Jim and Joe the invite for the party on Sierra. Jim accepted a little cagily but Joe, as Alex had expected, was unable to make it.

"Thanks for the invite Alex, but Isobel and I are off to a party on the compound." He looked at Pete who had just come off the phone. "Are you going to that Sixties theme party tonight?"

"We might go, though I'm not sure, Eleanor is a bit unwell at the moment."

Joe looked concerned, "Oh dear, what's up with her?"

"You know, the usual stuff, Miriam was sick from school and now she's passed it on to her sister."

Joe shook his head resignedly, "I'll expect my lot will be down with it too then." It was a fair observation, coughs and colds flew around the compound kids like wildfire. His own three were as prone as anyone else's.

"Well you've got your hands full if your lot go down with anything." Andy added.

Chris Barma strode into the dealing room and sat himself down. He turned on his screens and sighed. "Say guys, what do you think of the dollar?"

Alex didn't really watch the FX market too closely but Jim was bitten by the currency bug. "I think we're going to see a bit of a dollar rally Chris."

Barma nodded. "Yeah, but it's getting quite overbought here isn't it?."

"Well I wouldn't short it here." Andy Whiteman said matter-of-factly. "It will come off but not yet, we could have a real spike over the summer."

Chris Barma suddenly looked worried. "Spike, what versus the D-Mark or the Yen?"

"Both potentially" Whiteman was looking very serious.

"Personally I think the dollar rally is over. Sell it", said Karpolinski with the pride of one who enjoys being the odd man out.

"Yeah", said Barma with a wide grin.

In the early afternoon Alex was making his way back to the dealing room and just passing the Treasurers' office when he heard Ed Moore call out his name.

The American was standing at his doorway. "Hi Alex, how's it going?"

Alex paused to think how should reply to the boss. "Well it's a tricky time."

"Seems that way", his face was creased into a smile. The look didn't entirely suit him.

Alex responded with a nod. "The currencies are on the move again, threats of more devalutions. Often it seems more about politics more than economics."

Moore looked at the Englishman and a sly look crept across the American's face. "Isn't it always?"

Alex shrugged, "I guess so."

Moore continued studying Alex's features before adding. "So you're off to a Den party tonight?"

Alex was quite taken aback by this sudden change in tack and looked completely confused. "Den?"

"That's what they call 'em, don't they?"

Realization flooded across Alex. "You're referring to the party on Sierra tonight?" Alex immediately wondered how Ed Moore knew all this.

The American could read Alex's thoughts. "Jeddah's a small place."

"Are you going?"

Moore shook his head. "As a rule I don't, but I know the unit's commander", he said with a thoughtful look now staring into the middle distance.

Alex was immediately intrigued. "How's that?"

Now it was Ed Moore's turn to chuckle, "We were both stationed in California."

"You were in the army in California?"

"No. Air Force, Monterey." Moore shook his head side to side and was smiling to himself.

"When was that?"

"A long time ago." Ed Moore's eyes narrowed, this Englishman was an inquisitive little fellow. "No, the reason I asked is that my old buddy has some cigars for me and I'll ask him to pass them to you, if you're gonna be there tonight."

Alex paused to think. He was feeling pretty tired after another sleepless night and the stresses of the day. He was thinking he would probably give it a pass, particularly since Jim was looking doubtful too, if he said yes he would now be compelled to go. Moore looked expectantly at him, his expression clearly trying to prompt Alex. It worked, "Yes, I'll probably be there."

"Is that OK with you, you don't mind?" Moore examined Alex.

"Sure that's no problem at all. What's your friend's name?"

"Oh he won't be there, but a guy named Lorenzo Evans will."

"Lorenzo Evans." Alex repeated with the merest trace of a smile.

"I'll tell him to find you." That would not be too difficult the American thought wryly.

As he had feared, Jim had decided against going to the party that evening, so Alex found himself making his way alone and a little hesitantly towards the tell tale noise of the party that was dully resonating from within the Ronda apartment block. He was timidly looking around the group, searching for a friendly face when he saw Jerry Allensen purposefully striding towards him.

"Good to see you could make it Alex", said the Nebraskan.

"Hi Jerry, how are you?"

"I'm doing great thanks." The military advisor was studying Alex and took a glance around, searching the assembled guests. "Say, are your buddies coming along?"

"Sorry, but they can't make it."

Jerry Allensen frowned for a second then brightened. "Hey, never mind. Let me introduce you to a few of the guys, but first what do you want to drink?"

"I'll have a beer, please."

"Follow me and I'll show you where you can get it."

Alex wandered behind the American and slowly made their way through the guests. The apartments the soldiers lived in were built in a similar style to the villa's where Alex was except they were much smaller, having just one bedroom. All around them were dotted about dark stairwells so that upper floor apartments could be reached. Unlike his part of the compound, there was no swimming pool, just a lush square of thick vegetation around which the apartments were seemingly densely arranged. Alex followed Jerry in the half light through a brightly lit door of one of them and suddenly had to work his way through a crush of bodies within. The first thing he noticed was the presence of a number of women, not many, but they were there though significantly outnumbered by the men. He had assumed that it would be almost entirely US servicemen and by the look of the men there, that looked to be the case, though there was not a uniform in sight. As Alex slowly wound his way through the dressed down crowd he could sense a slight edginess, eye contact was firm but wary. He was a stranger and the way that the fit looking crew cut men around him were coolly observing him suggested that this status was not about to relax.

Allensen pushed through to the far end of the cramped room, turned and passed an ice cold bottle of Michelob beer to Alex. This corner of the room had been converted into a small bar, complete with a high wooden counter, barstools and a rack of shelving full of drink. Behind the busy jump he could readily identify the usual suspects of various brands of liquor and watched the couple of servicemen in jeans and faded tee shirts who were busily serving. The bottles of beer filled two big dustbins packed with melting ice. It was all very well organised.

"Thanks Jerry. Is this your apartment?" Alex tone was measured he was trying to hide his incredulity as he was really quite taken aback. It seemed that Allensen was running a top class speakeasy.

The young American laughed. "Shit no." He took a swig from his beer and wiped his mouth the back of his hand before continuing in his deliberate sounding Nebraskan drawl. "Nobody actually lives in his apartment. It's just known as the 'Den'", he grinned.

Alex shifted on his feet, the crunchy state of the carpet replete with its cigarette burns suggested it was an established and popular venue. "So this place is open every night?" Alex was pretty sure it was not, he definitely would have heard from Dieter or another of his compound neighbours if this was the case.

Allensen laughed out aloud at this idea. "No way, it would be a real clusterfuck! Just Wednesday nights and sometimes on Thursdays too."

That made much more sense to Alex. "Thursday's being, 'Brass Eagle' night", the Englishman added with a knowing look.

"You're getting with the program." Jerry's laughter eased the slight tension Alex was feeling from the room, or perhaps it was the beer. Either way, it didn't seem quite as threatening as it had been on entering the crowded interior.

"So where are these women from?" Alex asked dropping his voice right down and tilting his head conspiratorially towards his companion so that his question was inaudible to anyone else.

Jerry Allensen matched Alex' sotto voce, "Mostly nurses, and some aircrew, we've got no Suzie's here..." He looked around before adding, "sometimes, though not tonight."

"Suzie's?"

"That's what we call the women in the service", he turned back to Alex, "but I wouldn't go using the term round here", he added under his breath.

"Hey guys what's all the covert activity?" Ernesto Sanchez was looking relaxed in a polo shirt and jeans. The short sleeves emphasised his muscularity and with his boyish haircut combined to give him the look of a young Latino prize-fighter. In the hard light of the bar, Alex could make out the old tell tale signs of a broken nose.

"Hey Ernie, you remember Alex?"

Ernesto Sanchez shook Alex' hand with much vigour and a winning smile, "Sure do. How're you going?"

"Good thanks Ernie."

The Californian let the diminutive pass, he hated being called Ernie but that's what he was christened by his fellow servicemen. They were creatures of habit and unfortunately next to impossible to change.

"So where's your buddy Joe tonight?"

"He's sorry but he couldn't make it. He's gone to a party on his compound with his wife." Alex pulled a face to indicate that matrimonial compulsion had been employed.

Sanchez grinned not quite sure of what the Englishman was rolling his eyes about. "Sounds good", he said before going on to consider the contents of his empting bottle of beer.

"So how is life in the Technical Assistance Field Teams these days?"

"Same as same as, still training the same guys." Though he was relaxed, Sanchez was still aware of the last time that he had met Alex. He would be more careful. Jerry had given him a short dressing down that night about needing to be more diplomatic. Allensen had told him he should be careful, offhand remarks could be misinterpreted. Sanchez had to take heed of Jerry Allensen as he was a senior rank being a Sergeant First Class to his own lesser status of Specialist.

A few minutes later Allensen was called away by another small group and Alex was left with Ernesto Sanchez who had quickly got a couple more beers for them. Once the NCO was out of earshot the Californian seemed to loosen a little more and was confessing to how much he was looking forward to some leave. The two men had wandered out into the cooler air of the surrounding gardens. Alex looked around dimly lit gloom and estimated that there were probably around forty or so at the party including the smattering of seven or eight women.

"So is everyone here with your unit?"

"Oh no, there are only a handful of us duck hunters stationed here."

"Duck hunters?"

"That's what they call us the Army Air Defence Artillery." Sanchez took a long draught of his beer and then continued.

"So what's it like working in a bank?"

"Pays the bills you know."

"Pretty nice job too, sit on your ass and dish out money to guys like me eh?" he laughed.

"Something like that", Alex smiled.

Ernesto Sanchez pondered for a moment. "Guess you got college degrees and all that coming out your ears?"

Alex broke into laughter. "Well I've got one degree, but it's not much use for what I do."

The Californian was about to say he wouldn't mind going back to college, when he saw the approach of Jerry and Lorenzo Evans. As far as he was concerned, Evans was a real pain in the ass. Despite their shared Hispanic heritage they were chalk and cheese. Lorenzo Evans was a West Point graduate and all round humourless asshole. "Fuck, here comes the Purple Suiter."

"The... what did you say?"

"One of the liaison guys, just be nice to him."

Jerry Allensen was now stiffly formal as he spoke, much as he was when they had first met. "Hey Alex, I've got someone who wants to meet you." He turned towards the other man, who seemed oddly familiar. Perhaps an inch or so taller than Alex, he had a very similar build to his own, though unlike the bank trader, his hair was cut fiercely short.

"Captain Lorenzo Evans, this is Alex Bell." The men shook hands and the previously serious looking Evans was immediately smiling charm personified. "Nice to meet you."

"You too."

333

"I believe these are for you", he said with a flashed smile and passed over a box of cigars. Alex took a quick look at the sealed case which was clearly marked as containing twenty five Romeo y Julieta cigars.

"Tell Mr Moore they are 'with thanks,'" the officer added.

"Cuban?" Alex was aware of the embargo to US citizens.

"Seems that way", Evans replied, his now watery warmth fast evaporating in the heat of the night.

"Very nice too."

"I wouldn't know, I've never smoked them." He was polite but firm in his manner. He shifted a little uneasily and seemed now to Alex to be a touch low on social small talk skills despite his initial manner. Noting this, Alex thought that he would try and coax something from the crew cut officer.

"So it seems that my boss was in the Air Force with yours?"

Evans smiled, "I doubt that."

Alex was immediately confused. "Sorry somehow I figured they were stationed together."

Lorenzo Evans nodded at the apparent confusion. "I think that they were at the same school actually."

"Monterey?"

The American's face hardly registered the question but his eyes suddenly became serious. "That's right." Alex studied the man's face and realised that though his features seemed fresh and clean cut, he had the eyes of someone much older.

He looked at his watch, "Nice meeting you, unfortunately I've got to go."

"And you."

Another handshake was again exchanged followed by a short wave to the confused looking Sanchez. Evans made a slight movement of his head towards Jerry Allensen who had been watching the two men talk and started to make his way off. The NCO immediately understood the rather blatant signal, made his excuses and inconspicuously accompanied his commanding officer as he strolled off into the humid darkness.

Sanchez was looking at Alex very closely now. "Pardon me, are they for you?" he asked in his West Coast accent which seemed to magnify his confusion as he pointed to the box of Havana cigars.

Alex shook his head, "No they're for my boss, Ed Moore. He smokes them."

The cloud of mystery that had fogged Ernesto Sanchez' mind since the arrival of Evans was slowly clearing. "OK", he replied in a long and rising note, like an opera singer warming up.

"You know him?"

"No, not if it's the guy I'm thinking of", answered the Californian rather cryptically.

Now it was Alex's turn to be confused. "I'm sorry?" His accent was equally unable to mask his own misunderstanding.

"Big guy with thinning hair, two hundred ten pounds, fifties I'd say?" It was a less than perfect description of Moore, but close enough.

"Wears half rim glasses?"

"Yeah. I don't know him, but I seen him talking to Evans." Alex suddenly remembered the first time that he had seen Lorenzo Evans. He had been talking to Ed Moore across in the distance the first night that he'd gone with Jim Robson to the 'Brass Eagle'. He couldn't swear to it but he was pretty certain it was the same man. Now the statement that Moore hadn't been in the Air Force made by Evans took on another meaning. Why would he have said that? Also, he never said anything about a school either. Alex had read enough John Le Carre and now his over active imagination was at work. He turned the box of cigars over examining it in his hands.

"So is there an Air Force base at Monterey?"

"Monterey?" Alex's question had come from wide left field as far as Sanchez was concerned.

Alex was more insistent now. "Yes, is there an Air Force base or school at Monterey?" Frustration was starting to rise within him, these Americans were starting to disturb him and he didn't like the idea of being their Patsy.

Sanchez' face puckered in thought for a moment. "I don't know, I don't think so."

He looked past Alex and waved to someone behind him. Allensen was already on his way back towards them. "Hey Jerry, is there an Air Force base or school in Monterey?"

The Nebraskan was carrying a fresh beer. "No, there's no Air Force base, but there's the Presidio."

"The Presidio?"

"Sure, the Army language school", he paused for a moment searching his memory for the correct name. "What did he say? That's it, the DLIFLC." The two other men waited for him to explain the new tongue twisting acronym. "The Defence Language Institute Foreign Language Center", he said with obvious satisfaction.

"So it's a language school for the military?" Alex was starting to feel a little more at ease.

"Sure is. I think that's where Captain Evans went too."

Alex gave Allensen another quizzical look.

Allensen now had quite a serious expression. "You know, he speaks Arabic, he's our liaison officer with the Saudis."

"I see." Alex was still a little perplexed.

Allensen continued. "Yeah he was just telling me that the CO and your boss were there in the late sixties or maybe early seventies, he's not exactly sure."

337

"Learning Arabic?" asked Alex incredulously. He had never heard Ed Moore speak a word of the language and certainly never heard anyone else mention that he did.

Allensen broke in to a wide smile. "Not back then. No, apparently they both were learning Vietnamese."

That made some sense. "So it's like a language school for all the services?"

Jerry Allensen nodded agreement. "That's it."

Ernie Sanchez suddenly struck up to the tune of Springsteen's 'Born in the USA'. "Sent me off to a foreign land, to go and kill the yellow man. Born in the U.S.A..."

In a few moments Sanchez was joined in the chorus by a couple of the other men nearby and they all sang rowdily through the familiar anthem. Alex watched a little sheepishly as the clannish behaviour of the brothers in arms went on in front of him.

Alex turned, beside him stood a tall, impressively built man. He quickly measured up the American with a sidelong glance; he looked like a hard case. He gave the man a brief smile.

"Duck Hunter?" said the Englishman breezily.

"Intelligence", he said with a slight sneer followed by a knowing look. Alex looked at the soldier, first impressions suggested this reply seemed an unlikely boast; he looked like the missing link.

"And you?" growled the anthropological specimen.

"I work in a bank", he said with a slight shrug.

"Nice," replied the man with total disinterest.

Alex looked at his watch. In the half light he could just about see that it was already fast approaching ten. He had a busy schedule the next day, ending with a flight back to London. The music playing in the background had changed, Sheryl Crow was singing, 'all I wanna do is have some fun' and the band of brothers were busily peeling their labels off their beers and singing along to the familiar chorus.

"Well I better get going."

The missing link gave him a nod and raised his beer bottle. Alex wandered off to find Jerry Allensen to thank him for the evening's invitation. He meandered back to the brightly illuminated 'Den' and saw in the harsh light that the Nebraskan was deep in conversation with a pugnacious looking man, whose aggressive finger stubbing manner was matched only by his diminutive size. He was still animatedly talking as Alex sidled up to the NCO and just caught the end of other man's rapid fire delivery. As he approached he could now make out more clearly the stream of obscenities that eddied around the listening Midwesterner. Alex had obviously just caught the rear end of a very unpleasant tale.

"So the M1 just wasted those mother fucking dessert niggers." The swarthy, short but heavy set man broke into laughter and swigged back his drink. He was dressed in shorts and a singlet tee shirt, which showed his ragged blued edged tattoos. If this wasn't fearsome enough, he was also remarkable for appearing to be wearing a necklace made of, what looked like to Alex, sharks teeth. Despite his height, there was something of Platoon's Sergeant Barnes about the man. Alex put his hand on Jerry Allensen's shoulder. It was definitely time to go.

"Hey Jerry, thanks very much for this evening. I think I'll be off now."

Allensen acknowledged the thanks with a nod, "I hope you enjoyed it. See you around buddy."

With that Alex trudged off into the night clutching his box of cigars.

Alex and Jim entered the reception of the Treasury together and Jim wandered on through to his desk. Alex halted and stepped slowly in the direction of Ed Moore's office.

"Saleem, where is Ed?"

"Sir, Mr Ed is going to be late today", said the little round featured man from Java.

Alex was standing by the door to Ed Moore's office but neither he nor his sunny faced secretary, George Harumba were anywhere to be seen.

Alex was still clutching the box of twenty five cigars he had been given for the American from the night before. It was a little unusual; Moore was an early riser and was, more often than not, in the office well before anyone else. "Can you let me know when he gets in please Saleem?"

Chris Barma's secretary gave his distinctive little acquiescent head movement. "As soon as he is in I will call you Mr Alex."

"Thanks Saleem." Despite any attempts over the last three months that Alex had made to put the little Indonesian more at ease, he remained implacably cowed in the presence of all around him in IAB. Alex gave the secretary his usual reassuring smile and pushed his way through the weighty glass doors onto the trading floor. As he walked through he could see Omar Al-Hamra was already in deep conversation with Jim Robson.

"Good morning Omar", Alex was in an excellent mood, he was flying back that evening on BA 133.

The Risk Manager gave Alex a big smile. "Just the man I was looking for."

"Oh dear, it's that bad?" he said with feigned horror and a slight guffaw.

Al-Hamra was chuckling now as well. "Not yet", he grinned before darkening with more seriousness. "I wanted to pick your brains."

Alex returned the grin and settled himself on his seat, "Should be a short exercise, fire away."

Omar and Alex stepped away from the desk and Jim looked on as the two men talked, in low indecipherable tones to each. As far as Jim could see the Arab looked quite animated.

"What was that all about then?" Jim's eyes were wide with enquiry.

Alex shrugged his shoulders. "I've no idea. FX options for sure, but he was being quite cagey. Complex Ratios."

"So it must be Ayman then?"

"Not Ayman, he made that much clear to me, maybe Controvolinski?" It was Joe's newest nickname on the desk. His latest moniker derived from his love of being controversial. His bearish view on the dollar was his current contrarian hobby horse.

Jim turned back to his monitor. "I don't think so. He never trades options, leave alone complex ratio options spreads."

"Strange."

"What about one of the crash test dummies?" Jim volunteered as an afterthought.

"Too complicated, no way they'd come up with something as sophisticated or big."

"Not Ayman?"

"Definitely not him... Chris?" suggested Alex.

They sat in silence thinking. In any case it was all just idle speculation. Alex shivered, it only needed one of the team to go rogue and blow the entire teams P&L or worse. Alex looked out of the large glass windows deep in reflection; Saudi Arabia was not the place to blow up a trading book. It might well end up with a short ride to Chop-Chop Square.

It was another hour before Alex picked up a flashing internal line and the wheedling tones of the secretary Saleem greeted him with the message that Ed Moore was now back in his office. Alex got up from his desk, picked up the box of Romeo y Julieta cigars and wandered through to the American's lair.

As his secretary George was still not there and the door was open, he wandered through into the Treasurer's office unannounced. At the opposite end of the room Moore was sitting hunched over his desk. He did not look himself.

"Hey Alex, how are you?"

"I'm fine thanks, how about you?" Alex scrutinized the American's face, it was a genuine enquiry. His normally fully fed and contented face had taken on an unhealthy grey pallor. He had bags under his eyes, and what was left of his hair was in complete disarray. He looked terrible.

Aware of the younger man's intense glare Ed Moore admitted a little sheepishly. "I'm a little tired actually. It was a late one last night."

"These are for you", Alex said brightly having deciding to change the subject as it seemed to be causing his boss

343

embarrassment. He passed the box of Havana cigars over to the American. Moore nodded his thanks, took it and read the label carefully through his half rimmed spectacles.

"Partargas number four's, very nice too." He said appreciatively as he opened the box. "You smoke cigars?"

"I do, now and then."

"Did the good captain have anything to say for himself?" Moore was smiling but he looked worn out.

Alex paused for a moment. "Not really, he just said 'thanks'".

The American momentarily pulled a thoughtful face before he slowly spun around on his chair and opened a large humidor he had sitting on the table behind him and carefully decanted the box's contents into it. He cautiously swivelled back around and was holding four cigars in his hand. "Here have these", he said whilst putting the four cigars back into the now unsealed box and handing it back to Alex. "Many thanks for getting them for me."

Alex took the box with its compliment of four Cuban cigars looking inside it. "Thanks Ed that's very generous of you. It was nothing."

The portly American pulled a smirk. "No problem."

There was a slightly embarrassed pause as the two men considered their own thoughts before Alex responded. "See you later then Ed."

"Sure." Ed Moore shook his head slowly with a fatigued look on his face. He watched the Englishman over his half rimmed glasses until he disappeared through the door before he scribbled a few lines on a post it pad. He was feeling really exhausted, the previous night had been a real pain in the ass as far as he was concerned. Why couldn't things be just a little less complex? He had been having business dinner with a couple of board directors and the head of one of the larger business families of Jeddah, when his mobile had rung. His source in the bank's Personnel department had relayed the message that one of his staff had been arrested. When he heard the name he knew he had to get down to the police station in Al-Nahdah where the man was being held. George Harumba had been arrested by the local police and though Ed Moore had no idea on what charge, he figured he had a pretty good idea. It would require speedy and efficient intervention on his part, though as with most things in the Kingdom, it depended on who was involved.

By the time he had managed to get down to the police station it was already nearly midnight, but then he discovered that George Harumba had already been transferred to another police station downtown. He drove on to the old jailhouse back down the Medina Road and then with the aid of tidy sums of baksheesh eventually got to see the Filipino detainee. As he followed the duty

345

officer, first through the dusty block and then down into the apparently labyrinthine bowels of the prison cells below, his hopes for the safety of his secretary slowly dimmed with each tired footstep. Moore was well aware of what went on in these kinds of haunts; they were not places to be found lingering in. When the heavy steel door was opened to the cell Harumba was in, he saw half a dozen or so men crushed into a cell that was designed for two at most. Ed Moore's eyes blinked in the harsh light that flooded out of the cell as he searched the gaunt hirsute faces of the men inside. He spotted his secretary, he was almost unrecognizable and sitting huddled in a filthy threadbare blanket against one wall, sandwiched between two heavily bearded faces. The stench of the room was overpowering, a mixture of stale sweat, urine and faeces rolled out of the sweltering airless room and made the American want to retch his expensive dinner up there and then.

"Harumba", barked the officer on duty. The Filipino on hearing his name was now looking at the doorway trying to make out the faces of the three men there. The right side of his face was terribly swollen and marked with a nasty looking cut which had the sticky crust of a brown clot forming over it; the eye was already nearly completely shut. Ed Moore instantly recognized the signs of a vicious beating. He turned to the policemen and was about to ask him how long he had been in the cell but realised the futility of it.

"Let's go George."

Hearing his boss' voice the Filipino suddenly blinked recognition and his almost unrecognizable features were immediately bathed in relief. He rose unsteadily to his bare feet, clutching the foul smelling blanket tightly around himself and stumbled over to the doorway accompanied by the low voiced jeering a one of the other prisoners, another of whom spate at him as he passed by them.

Ed Moore said nothing but put an arm out to help the man. At first Harumba almost collapsed into the arms of the American but managed to keep to his feet though he was still using his boss' corpulent shape as a much needed crutch. Moore struggled to hold the small man upright, wheezing heavily as they both climbed, heavy limbed, back up the stairs to ground level. A few more signatures and another discreetly managed pecuniary gift and they were on their way. As they were leaving the desk sergeant explained yet again to the Treasurer that the man had been found this way. They had questioned him but according to the Arab, the Filipino had made no sense at all. The *Mutawwa'in* had said they had found him like this when they had brought him to the station, he said shaking his head. He was very lucky, maybe next time he would not be so fortunate the policemen added with an ill disguised look of disgust.

Moore started the car's engine and slowly started to manoeuvre it out of the police station car park.

"George, what the hell happened?"

"We were stopped at a check point and then we were arrested by a *Muttawa*." He was still clutching the disgusting blanket around himself.

"Well I think we need to take you to hospital", Moore put his foot down and accelerated away from the police station gateway. He stole another couple of glances at his secretary as he drove.

"Oh no Sir, I'm fine. I just want to get home."

"That cut on your face looks nasty."

The Filipino shook his head vigorously. "Please Sir, I'm fine. I only want to go home."

"And shit that blanket stinks." He was pulling a face of disgust as he spoke.

"I'm sorry Sir, but..."

"But what George?"

The secretary looked out of the side window and tried to control himself. He was perilously close to breaking into tears.

"I'm sorry but I can't take it off until I get home."

"Did they take your clothes?" Ed Moore could see that the man was not wearing long trousers; his bare knees complimented his shoeless feet.

Harumba shook his head.

"George, are you OK?"

"I'll be fine Sir."

As far as Ed Moore could tell from the look of him, he did not seem fine at all. He stared hard through the windscreen deep in thought, the traffic was very light on the roads, but despite the open way ahead, Moore kept his speed strictly limited. He cast several looks at the cut and bruised features of the Filipino that periodically flared into sight, luridly illuminated by passing streetlights as they drove along the highway. "George, why were you stopped by the *Mutawwa'in?*"

Harumba swallowed, there was still the taste of blood in his mouth from the blow he had received and he could feel on one side of his jaw that several of his teeth felt loose. It was going to be difficult to explain.

"I was in a car with some friends on the way to a party."

Ed Moore murmured his understanding.

George hesitated, picking his words carefully. "Well there were four of us in the car."

"OK I'm with you." Moore was trying to be as coaxing as possible.

"The police pulled us over saying that they were checking for illegals and wanted to check our papers. We thought it was just the usual thing." Moore was intoning sympathetic little noises of understanding between each of the hesitant sentences that Harumba was saying.

"You had them? You had your *Iquama* right?" Despite his best efforts, slight incredulity had slipped into his speech. It was inconceivable that a Filipino in a good job like George would run the risk of being mistaken for just another illegal worker. He was far too fastidious a man for that to happen.

"Oh yes. I had it alright."

"And you weren't driving the car?"

"No it was my friend Martin who was driving." Ed Moore had met Martin once before. Now the story was starting to make some sense. George's friend was also part of the gay underworld of Jeddah, it was a little known but big enough scene that George and his friends happily and lucratively inhabited. The situation was now shaping up much more as he had expected when he had first got the phone call.

"Ok, so the Police stopped you to check for papers, so where did the *Mutawwa* come in."

"He was nearby just hanging around the check point." George Harumba fell silent in thought while Ed Moore silently waited for him to continue with increasingly impatience. He drew a deep breath to try and calm himself.

The silence remained unbroken until the American could hold back no longer.

"And?"

George was looking down and he clutched the blanket tighter around himself as he spoke. The car had stopped at some traffic lights and Moore just noticed the almost imperceptible rocking of Harumba in the seat beside him.

"This *Mutawwa* came over and saw us. He started shouting and saying we were not properly dressed. He kept saying it was *Haram*."

"Who was unsuitably dressed? What were you wearing?"

"All of us, but especially me and Harry."

"You and Harry, but why?"

"Because Harry and me were in the back wearing *Abeyas*."

Ed Moore shook his head slowly in dismay. George knew as well as anyone for a man to dress as a woman was forbidden. The religious policeman would have had a field day.

"What did they say?"

"One of them told us to get out of the car, but it was only me and Harry he wanted and then the other *Mutawwa* arrived." He swallowed again. "They put Harry and me in the back of a van."

"They did this to you?" Moore pointed to the secretary's bruised and battered face.

George nodded his head and looked out of the window. It was a shaming experience but he would have to live with it. He wondered what had happened to Harry, he had no idea. He screwed up his un-blackened eye and tried to shut out the images he had seen early that night, actually he had a very good idea but it was not something to dwell on.

They were approaching the Filipino's compound. Unlike the Westerners' compounds, it was basic, nothing more than a block of flats enclosed within a high walled perimeter.

"Thank you Ed very much for getting me." It wasn't the first time this had happened. Ed Moore shook his head sardonically before adding, "I won't always be here George, you know?" The Filipino looked sheepish and nodded his understanding. Ed Moore started to open the car door.

"It's OK I can do it", said the secretary weakly as he struggled ineffectually with the passenger door's mechanism. Ed Moore was soon around the passenger side and helping the dishevelled and bloodied man to his feet.

"George what the hell is this?" It was a rhetorical question. The vile smelling blanket he was using as a covering had briefly opened to reveal what the Filipino was wearing. He was dressed in what looked like a ballerina's Tutu.

"It was a fancy dress party."

The American was unfazed. "George, I don't want to know." He unsteadily carried the little man to the gated entrance.

"I'll be OK from here."

It was time to leave the man some dignity. "OK George. I'll see you in a couple of days, OK?"

The Filipino nodded. "Thank you, thank you Boss."

Ed Moore shook with head sadly as he watched his secretary disappear into his apartment block, safe from the prying eyes of the *Mutawwa'in* and anyone else. This was the third time that he had managed to deliver his secretary from the grips of the Saudi authorities. The parties that the Filipino went to were not just ordinary social affairs; he had access to some powerful men. It was this information that George periodically gave to Ed Moore which was useful. One day that information might not be so useful and he would not come and bail the Filipino out of the next jail he was found in, but right now it served the American's interests.

George Harumba let himself into his tiny one bedroom apartment. All he wanted was to clean himself, he felt filthy and depressed, shamed and humiliated. His face was a mess but he was hurting so much more inside his head. He started to run the bath; perhaps he could wash all the hurt away. He slowly undressed himself, his Tutu, made by the dextrous and skilled hands of a young seamstress who worked as a live in maid for a Saudi family, was torn and ruined. He dropped the flapping remains of what was left of it onto the bathroom floor. It had been a terrible night and he had only been saved from much worse as Ed Moore had got himself involved. George Harumba didn't know what Moore was doing in IAB, but he did know that Moore was CIA. He climbed slowly into the steaming hot water, closed his eyes and tried to shut out the memory being violently beaten and then systematically buggered by each of the foul mouthed *Mutawwa'in* in the back of the van.

12. Allah's Enemies

Abdul-Rahman bin Hajez dark eyes roamed the air conditioned interior and he sniffed discreetly. He slowly looked around the mosque, mentally sorting and filing the number of faithful, their ages and appearances, the congregation was growing with each week, the new *Alim* was doing a good job. This was the fourth time that he had been to this recently finished place of worship and the third time he had successfully managed to bring the two Al-Hamra boys. It was true, the Almighty had not made it entirely easy for him, their spineless father had been a continual problem, but the *Mutawwa's* persistence had paid off and Allah had rewarded him. He knew that the elder Al-Hamra brother, Talal was perhaps already too lost to the false promises of the infidels, but the younger one seemed an excellent prospect, this accident on the boat had changed the young man quite remarkably for the better. Mohammed Al-Hamra was showing all the promising signs of an excellent recruit to the righteous cause. He smiled inwardly at the mysterious way Allah's work was fulfilled; truly the Almighty was most wondrous. This last reflection caused the inward smile to become flesh for an instant as it played across his saturnine features. It was Allah's will.

These most recent prayers being answered, his mind followed step by step the prayers being led by the black haired *Alim*, who directed the assembled congregation to think of the poor and the needy and then inviting the faithful to make themselves comfortable upon the carpeted floor before starting his sermon from the wooden *minbar*, which stood slightly to the right of the *mihrab*, that pointed the faithful to Mecca. Abdul-Rahman had vetted and passed this cleric as suitable well over a month ago and many of the *Mutawwa*'s original concerns had slowly been shown to be unwarranted. Abdullah Bawani had shown himself to be an excellent and thought provoking *Alim*, though not without his well known controversial style. To a traditionalist like Abdul Rahman bin Hajez, Bawani's methods and arguments had initially proven very difficult to accept, but even he had to admit that the preacher's conclusions and principles were of the highest order. He cast a quick sideways look at his two charges, Talal was sitting, occasionally shifting a little here and there, obviously finding the hard stone flooring beneath the intricately woven carpet somewhat uncomfortable for his bony frame. On the other hand, his brother Mohammed was sitting motionless with a face of placid concentration. Abdul-Rahman adjusted himself on the floor, with his legs crossed beneath him and turned his attention to the words of the dark haired *Alim*. The man had just recited a *Hadith* and was now loquaciously slipping into his rhetorical stride.

"As you know my brothers, this cycle is mentioned in the Koran and it happens throughout history and will again. First Allah chose the Jews, the *Bani* Israel as he tells it in the holy Koran: 'O children of Israel! Call to mind My favour which I bestowed on you and that I preferred you to all other nations.' But my brothers, that duty Allah granted to the Jews was that they should carry the torch of the knowledge of Allah to the world. This was their duty and honour, to be Allah's torch bearers but, my brothers, they failed their mission, and so as even the Christians have known and recorded in their gospels, the kingdom of Allah was taken from the Jews and would be given to a nation bringing forth the fruits of His word." The *Alim* smiled before adding, "and that nation, we must, with joy in our hearts say, is the nation of Islam."

There was a murmur of approval around the assembled men. The preacher raised his hand to signify he had not finished, indeed he had barely started.

"So my brothers, amongst the Nation of Islam it was we Arabs who were given by Allah, *Salla allahu 'Alaihi Wa Sallam*, the great honour of being the torchbearers of light and learning to the rest of the world." The preacher raised his hands to his heart, "but we Arabs were too comfortable, this light was taken from us when the Turks and Mongols destroyed the Muslim empire and when they accepted Islam they in turn then became the torchbearers of light and learning to the world." The congregation started to stir at these words as the preacher shook his head. Abdul-Rahman watched the reaction of the faithful; the Turks were not well liked in the Arabian Peninsula. Abdul-Rahman's eyes took on a feral narrowness as he listened and waited to see where the *Alim* was heading with his sermon.

The preachers hand was now raised to silence the rising undertow of discontent and he continued, becoming more animated as he spoke. "My brothers do not fool yourselves, for the spirit of Islam is like water, it is not dependent on the shape of the glass container it comes in. My friends, do not look so agitated, the container I speak of is the Arab nation, our boundaries and the spirit of Islam is not dependent on our national or geographical limits. This then is what Allah shows us, first the Jews then us, the Arabs and when we became lax and weak he chose the Turks and when they in turn became weak yet another people and so on. The message is simple my brothers, if you will not be his vessel, then Allah will chose another. Is this what you want?"

At this there was another murmur of disagreement, as faces turned to look at each other. "No this is not what we want" said a voice from amongst the seated group.

The *Alim* slowly nodded his head, "Good that's what I want to hear. Brothers, you know that I'm a recent arrival here in Jeddah", he smiled mirthlessly, "and very nice it is too. A pretty place here by the pretty sea." He looked around the mosque before continuing. "But I can tell you the place I have come from is a model for all Muslims, a beautiful place. As some of you know, I've recently returned from this wonderful place." Abdullah Barwani looked theatrically around his audience. "And where is this place you ask? Well brothers, I can tell you, it is Afghanistan."

There was a low drone of approval amongst the gathering at this piece of news. The cleric continued, his dark eyes sparkled, as he spoke with increasing enthusiasm.

"I first journeyed to Afghanistan in the summer of 1413, just over five years ago. I was at a fine *madrassa*, in Pakistan, when a student friend of mine asked me if I would like to meet some friends of his who were fighting just across the border against the godless *Shuravi*." The cleric smiled as he added, "this is the Afghan word for the Russians." He cleared his throat. "It was a difficult time then, the *Shuravi* were sponsoring the Northern Alliance and other bandits all over the country and the *mujahedeen* were split into many factions. This was when I first met *Mullah* Mohammed Omar and what a fine man he is. Handsome, dignified, honourable and wise, I was impressed by him immediately. I will never forget the day when news of the calumny perpetrated by the godless *Shuravi* and their filthy lapdogs came to us. These vermin had defiled the local womenfolk at a checkpoint close to Kandahar. *Mullah* Omar was so angry, so furious, he could have torn a mountain to pieces with his bare hands, but he remained calm and said almost nothing. My friends, he was as solid and as implacable as the mountains that surrounded us, for Allah was with him. He showed no emotion other than saying we were to collect our equipment and follow him quietly. There were some thirty five of us, we walked for two days and then through the following night we ambushed the drunken bandits and rescued the women. Can you imagine this? A group of half trained students overrunning and capturing a platoon of Russians and their bandit friends, my brothers, surely this was Allah's will. The next morning *Mullah* Omar presided as judge and brothers. He was most fair in his judgement and listened to all the evidence. He considered all the arguments in strict accordance with *Sharia* law, pronounced sentence and hanged their commander. Not long after this all the local villages were asking for our assistance and that, my brothers, is how we, the *Taliban*, the Students for that is what *Taliban* means, first started."

The *Alim* paused for a moment to let his little anecdote work its way into the minds of his listeners. "So my brethren, if you are fortunate enough to visit this beautiful land, situated high in the roof of the world, you will find the most Islamic of nations quickly developing for there is no lack of new recruits to the *Jihad* in Afghanistan." A look of rapture spread across his face and he cocked his head to one side and beamed as he spoke. "You know that amongst the *Taliban* soldiers there was never any complaining. I saw one man have his leg amputated; no anaesthetic, no morphine or field dressing, nothing. Men only ever asked when it would be possible to rejoin battle. Allah was deep in their hearts and they knew there would be sacrifice. *Jihad* meant that throats must be slit and skulls must be shattered. This is the path to victory, to *shahada*."

He paused once again and looked around the squatting congregation to see the effect that his rhetoric had made. The sea of stares was temporarily becalmed, positioned in the eye of the storm of his captivating tale. There was no doubt that he had their complete attention, he took a deep breath and changed his intonation, now speaking with quiet seriousness.

"Every single man, woman and child in the villages that we freed from the hated *Shuravi* were so happy that we, the *Taliban*, were there and even if we were many, we only ever engaged the enemy on our own terms and when we did, we were swift and ruthless, but we were also like the mountain mists when the enemies of Allah searched for us, for we could disappear into the vastness of the mountains just as easily as those mists.

So you see my brothers, *Jihad* must remain a fixed aspect of the life of a Muslim, since we face perpetual aggression from of our enemies. God is Great."

At this point the slight murmur mutated into a low voiced chant as the assembled faithful joined together on a slowly rising tone, "*Allahu Akbar, Allahu Akbar.*" The cleric nodded and smiled before raising his hand to signal restraint, "Yes, yes indeed my brothers, God is Great, but who are these enemies of Allah that I am referring to? Do not think it is just the Godless *Shuravi*, whom we defeated and drove out from Afghanistan, no my brothers, it is the entire 'Camp of *Kufur*'. The two groups, the Jews and the Christians, together constitute this Godless alliance and will remain its two foundations until Allah allows their downfall and annihilation at the end of days and this day will surely come, thanks be to God. Thanks be to God."

"*Alhamdulilah*", chorused the congregation in response to the preacher.

"So my brother's I implore you to look into your own hearts, to look deep and to seek to do the work of the Almighty, listen to the voice of Allah for it is within us all here." Abdullah Barwani fell silent and looked at the men who returned his stare with open eyed faces. The preacher once again searched the congregation and caught the steady unblinking eye of Abdul-Rahman bin Hajez. The policeman returned his gaze with an enquiring tilt of the head. The *Mutawwa* was carefully listening to the cleric's words and was, for the moment anyway, happy with the sermon. He did not mind what he had said. As long as there was no incitement to civic disruption or seditious anti-government talk he was happy. It was a fine balance but it appeared to him that the preacher had well understood this.

"But my brothers, Afghanistan is a place where the infidel quake, whereas here in the comfort of this blessed land, even now the infidel are amongst us and yet we quake. You will remember that I said at the beginning how pretty Jeddah is, sitting beside the pretty sea. Do you know that this pretty sea is full of jellyfish? Of course you know this, but they are not only to be found in the sea. I am sad to say that this city too, is full of jellyfish. When I compare the young men of this land to the holy warriors of the *Taliban* and observe how they quake and do nothing against these enemies of Allah who every day defile our land with their Godless materialism, where I ask you, is the spirit of *Jihad*, where is the desire for *shahada?*"

"*Alim* we are here", was the spontaneous reply from one of the younger of the men squatting in the midst of the congregation.

"That honest cry from the heart warms mine, for it is the spirit of Allah that moves you my brother. May you too become the torchbearers and light of learning today to the Muslim world and be not afraid to say, 'death to Russia, death to Israel' or 'death to the Camp of *Kufur*'. So my dear brethren, I have taken much of your valuable time this holy day, all I ask is for you to remember to think what you can do and to join this noble *Jihad*."

With this, the men finished with prayers and afterwards slowly started to file their way out of the mosque. Abdul-Rahman blinked in the harsh light of the bright day and looked at his two young companions. He had been reassured and pleased, both by the sermon and also its stirring effect on those who had heard it. The *Alim* had said nothing that could be considered damaging to the ruling elite; that was his first concern, the Ministry would be quite content with the *Jummah* service in this mosque. That had been satisfying enough, but the pleasure he had experienced on hearing the outburst next to him of Mohammed Al-Hamra in the midst of the sermon had been quite unexpected.

"Peace be with you."

Abdul-Rahman turned towards the greeting and replied, "And to you be peace."

Abdullah Bawani embraced the *Mutawwa* and smiled. "Well I hope you found my humble opinions to your liking my friend."

"Admirable, it was a most excellent lesson and I'm sure my young companions agree with my sentiments." The *Mutawwa* turned and looked at the two Al-Hamra boys who were standing rooted to the ground and looking sheepishly at the *Alim*.

The cleric gave the two young men a quizzical look. "I do indeed hope that you did."

"Yes, very much so", volunteered Mohammed with enthusiasm whilst his elder brother simultaneously gave a less committal noise.

Abdullah Bawani broke into a nicotine stained smile, "These are the young men you were telling me about?"

"They are indeed", replied the uncle, "this is Talal and this is Mohammed."

The preacher cocked his head. "Your uncle speaks very highly of you both", he enthused as he shook their hands warmly. He turned to Mohammed, "So you are the one that Allah chose to return to us?"

Mohammed looked confused.

"I heard that you nearly drowned?" The cleric had a sharp eyed look about him.

Mohammed Al-Hamra took on a self deprecating look before mumbling, "Oh that."

365

The preacher was staring at the young man now. "Yes indeed that. I believe Allah must have some great designs for you." Mohammed Al-Hamra shifted a little uneasily and his cheeks glowed slightly with slight embarrassment from this last remark. "Perhaps one day you can tell me something about your experience?" he added.

Mohammed Al-Hamra nodded his head and blinked his silent agreement.

"I hear that you are looking to make a trip home?" Abdul-Rahman had received the preacher's request earlier that week.

"Well as you know, it is not really home for me, but yes I'm hoping to go to Cairo in the autumn, just for a few days."

"How many?"

"Not more than a week", replied the preacher, "I have some family business to attend to."

"That should not be a problem." The eyes of the *Mutawwa* narrowed. "As long as I have plenty of warning I can arrange temporary cover for you." He gave his usual thin smile.

During this last exchange another two young men had come and stood just beside the group and were looking expectantly at the *Alim*. Seeing the waiting worshipers at his side the cleric started to apologise. "You see that unfortunately I have others to minister to now. Please will you excuse me?"

"Brother of course. I'll see you at the usual time?" asked Abdul-Rahman

"I look forward to it." The preacher turned towards Mohammed and Talal. "It was a pleasure meeting you both. I look forward to seeing you next week?"

Mohammed looked serious before answering. "Definitely, I will be here Alim."

The men then formally said their goodbyes with kisses and handshakes and in a short while Abdul-Rahman was driving the two Al-Hamra's back to their home.

"So what did you think of the *Jummah* address?" Abdul-Rahman had directed the question to neither of two in particular but his eyes were watching Mohammed in the rear view mirror. Talal was seated beside him in the passenger seat.

"Does Abdullah Bawani know Osama bin Laden?"

Abdul-Rahman was taken aback by this sudden turn in events, he had been hoping for an entirely different line of conversation. He automatically shot a sidelong glance at Talal, who had just asked this thorny question before fixedly staring at the road ahead. He should have known that one of them would have raised it. Over the last few years Osama bin Laden had become a latter day local hero, particularly to the youth of Saudi Arabia.

367

"I'm not sure, I have never asked him", he lied.

"Do you think he does Uncle?" asked Mohammed from the back seat.

"I really don't know." The *Mutawwa* flashed a look at the younger Al-Hamra through the rear view mirror. "Perhaps you could ask him next week."

Mohammed slowly stroked his upper lip, deep in thought as he looked out of the passenger window before softly replying, "I will."

Silence fell upon the occupants of the car as the *Mutawwa* drove the nephews home. Abdul-Rahman bin Hajez pursed his lips deep in his own thoughts. It was a delicate and subtle issue. Obviously there was the official government line that he could have easily opted for, but that would have been entirely counterproductive. He knew as well as anyone that Osama bin Laden was someone that was universally admired by most of the youth of the country. It was perfectly understandable. A young man, hugely independently wealthy, some had estimated his own personal fortune to be in the region of over 300 million dollars, takes off to Afghanistan to fight for the oppressed people there against one of the mightiest military forces in the world. By 1984 he had established an organization named *Maktab al-Khadamat*, which funnelled arms and men from around the Muslim world into the Afghan war. His heroic status was confirmed when as a key *mujahedeen* leader he was closely associated with the failure and eventual capitulation of the Russian invasion of the country. His iconic status in the Kingdom had been cemented when the government made him an outlaw for his role in condemning the use of Saudi soil by America in the 1991 Gulf War. Osama bin Laden was the Robin Hood of Islam.

Abdul-Rahman bin Hajez sourly swallowed the slight indignation and frustration he felt back. It was too sensitive an issue to go into just now. The understanding of the fine line that existed and that he represented needed more husbanded minds than the young Al-Hamra's currently had. Fertile though their minds were, they were not yet ready.

"We shall see", he said softly under his breath.

Omar Al-Hamra sat and ate his meal in disconsolate silence. It was hard to eat anything with a mind filled with the all worries he had. He chewed his food slowly with no appetite and barely registering the bubbling chatter of his wife and daughter. Neither of the boys was talking, the sullen behaviour between the two was seemingly just short of open hostility. Ever since the diving accident the brothers' relationship had shown something had gone seriously awry. Of course, he had patiently asked each of them what was the matter but neither had told him anything, either separately or jointly. It was frustrating, he looked at his younger son through the thick lenses of his glasses and pulled a resigned face, there was no doubt that Mohammed was becoming more and more reclusive and closed. Omar had no idea if it was just the usual problems of teenagers growing up or something else, but whatever it was, he just could not get to the bottom of it. He put down his fork and looked at his meal which lay almost untouched in front of him. All of these problems concerned him mightily, but the worst of them all was the increasingly malevolent presence of that damned so called brother in law. Omar kept asking himself how the devil the *Mutawwa* had seemed to have inveigled his way into his family's life.

"So how were *Jummah* prayers?"

Talal cast his eyes downwards to avoid the enquiring gaze of his father, but Mohammed returned his father's look with quiet determination.

"Interesting", replied Mohammed.

"Interesting?" parroted the banker, with a sarcastic glint in his eyes and immediately folding his thick arms in a confrontational manner.

Mohammed responded to the challenge, "I like the *Alim* leading prayers there."

"What is it that you like about him?" asked Omar with quiet restraint.

Mohammed paused before replying on a note of rising defiance. "He speaks very directly, there is no confusion in his words."

"Oh really?" Omar's patience was wearing a little thin with the continual verbal fencing and parrying that he was encountering with his son. "Well perhaps I should come and listen to him myself?"

"You're welcome to but I don't think you'll like him."

"And why is that?"

"Father", Talal's tone was suddenly imploring.

"No Talal, your brother seems to have an idea of what I will and won't like about this *Alim* that you keep seeing with your uncle. Perhaps he can be kind enough to let me know what it is that I won't like." Omar's eyes were wide with anger though his tone was as coolly measured as he could manage.

"Please Dad." Talal was insistent.

Omar waved his elder son's intercession away. "Come on Mohammed, what is it that I won't like?"

Mohammed cut his father a withering look, "Most of it."

"And why is that?" his features had reddened as he spoke.

"Because he is a man of action and does what he says."

"A man of action, what are you talking about?" Omar scoffed.

"He's been to places, war zones and fought against the infidel."

"What places, which infidel, what foolishness has he been filling your empty head with?"

"That's always your answer isn't it? You call me stupid, when it's your ideas that are stupid." Mohammed stood up, "Stupid and weak."

"Mohammed!" Ameena Al-Hamra spoke with shrill shock in her voice, her younger son sent her a sharp wounded look, his gaunt jaw muscles flexed as he sought to control his anger.

With equal effort Omar also just managed to retain his own temper, "Son, I never said you were stupid."

Mohammed looked straight ahead and steadied himself. "Oh yes you did, after all it's what you mean isn't it?"

Omar's face darkened in the attempt of understanding. This angry exchange had been the most that they had shared in more than a week. He checked himself before continuing in a voice that was overdressed with reasonableness. "That's not what I meant at all. I just want to understand."

"Understand?" the teenager broke into a hollow laugh.

"Yes, understand. I want to know…"

Mohammed cut his father off before he could finish. "That's your problem. That's all you ever want to do, 'understand', but you don't because you can't know."

Omar looked flummoxed, "What are you talking about?"

"You claim you can't know anything for certain." Mohammed Al-Hamra raised his arms in a mocking imitation of one of his father's more recognizable mannerisms and spitefully mimicked his father's pattern of speech. "Nothing in life is certain except death and taxes."

"Mohammed you're deliberately twisting my words, I just mean that…"

"Oh I know what you mean alright. Well I can tell you I'm tired of all these excuses, 'understand this', 'think about that'. Some things don't need all your science and study."

"Like what?"

"Like the fact that Allah chose to save me in order that that I might serve him. I know this here." Mohammed brought his hand up to his heart and pounded his chest.

Omar's face took on a look of incredulity and he stared open mouthed at this announcement. "What are you saying that you want to become a cleric?" He could barely believe that there he was asking this question of his youngest son. Just a few months ago all he wanted to do was to play football and study in Europe, now apparently he wanted to join up with Abdul-Rahman and his lunatic fundamentalists. It was laughable. Omar steadied himself; it was simply a provocative gesture. His son was just being confrontational. He stared at his willowy framed son who was now looking with clear eyed determination straight back at him.

"That's right."

Omar looked down at the unappetizing sight of his cold dinner and shook his head in a showy demonstration of disbelief.

"Mohammed, you can't be serious." Almost as soon as he had spoken these words Omar regretted his reply. The young man gave his father a fierce look, turned on his heel and walked out of the dining room without saying another word. The silence that now descended on the Al-Hamra dining room was crushing. Omar looked up at his wife and as she returned his gaze he could see that her eyes were misty with emotion, Talal sat stiffly bolt upright and his daughter was now sitting slumped over the dining table, eyes shut closed with her head held between her hands.

"Well that was a great success", said Omar looking around the table but even this attempt of half hearted irony did nothing to salve the feelings of angst that had overtaken them all.

13. Special Sand

Having arrived only the night before, Claire Bell busied herself around the unfamiliar surroundings. She was carrying out an impromptu inventory of her new kitchen. Despite having been in Saudi Arabia for over three months, it was quite clear that her husband had spent most of the time ordering takeaways, there appeared to be practically no kitchen utensils, pots or pans but there were several menus for Indian and Chinese home deliveries.

She opened one of the many cupboards that covered the walls of the large open plan space. "I thought you said you'd got everything for the kitchen," she called out.

"I did, I picked up a whole load of stuff from IKEA and Habitat," her husband replied from the living room whilst playing with his youngest son David.

"IKEA? I had no idea they were here."

"This isn't quite the end of the earth you know."

"Well where is it all?" she asked opening yet another cavernous unit.

"I didn't quite get to unpacking it all", said Alex softly who was now standing at the doorway holding a piece of wooden train track. He walked over to the far end of the kitchen and opened a door to a small walk in store. Claire peered into it and saw a large bin from which emanated the sharp aroma of fermenting beer. Racked up on shelving there were some two dozen bottles with resealable stoppers. Beside this stood several large boxes which Alex proceeded to heave out one after the other. He opened the first of four large boxes and started to unpack its contents.

"So that's where you make your beer."

Alex nodded and gave her a winning smile.

"Darling isn't it a bit risky, I mean, what would happen if the police came?"

Alex laughed and continued unpacking the various smaller boxes containing every conceivable type of pot and pan that even the late Escoffier could have wished for. "Claire, everyone here makes their own beer, some even try wine but frankly all the stuff I've tried here's pretty vile." Alex looked up from his unpacking before adding as an afterthought, "Well except for Schuster in number 45 opposite, his is passable." He stopped and looked at a large saucepan studying it closely. "As for the police, there's an unwritten rule that they never would come onto this compound or indeed any Western compound. Honestly, it's not an issue."

Claire gave him a rueful look and picked up a large enamel casserole that David was attempting to use as a particularly heavy hat. Instead he picked up the box and started trying to put that on his head.

"By the way I didn't unpack it all as I thought you could decide where you wanted everything put or if you would want to change or return any of it", he added brightly.

Claire Bell smiled. There was no doubt her husband was doing his best to try to please her and while the issue of his affair in Paris had been the source of much hurt and several tearful and angry evenings on his return to England, nevertheless certain things had been resolved in the process. They had, for example agreed to try and spend more time together as a couple. A young family leaves little time for romance, let alone a sex life and it was obvious that this was leading to a decline in their relationship. Once they had agreed that they wanted to stay together they had organised a weekend away, without kids and that time spent together had gone a long way in restoring their relationship. The truth was also that the period spent apart had sharpened their senses to each other and in the end the love they shared for their children had provided sufficient glue for them to be happy to stick with what they had.

"Mum, can I have a drink please?" The eight year old Christopher had wandered barefoot and dripping water into the kitchen. The swimming pool had been an instant hit with the boys.

"Have you been in the swimming pool?" It was clearly a rhetorical question. "I thought I told you to wait until one of us is there with you?"

"Sorry Mum, I fell in."

Claire shook her head and frowned. "Christopher, please don't tell lies. Anyway it's not you so much, as David that I'm worried about. He's not a strong swimmer and I don't want any accidents. Where is Anthony?"

"He's sitting by the edge", replied the eldest boy.

Alex got to his feet. "I'll go."

Claire Bell turned and walked over to the enormous wardrobe sized fridge freezer and poured out another glass of apple juice which Christopher swallowed down in noisy thirst quenching slurps. Alex quickly stepped out of the kitchen, through the lounge and out into the pool area. Their middle son, Anthony, was sitting on the poolside happily kicking his feet in the water watching the ripples he was making run across the surface of the azure coloured pool. It was just approaching ten o'clock in the morning and the crushing heat of the Arabian day had already caused the tiled poolside to become uncomfortable to walk barefoot upon. Alex hastily made his way to the pool and dived head first into its clammy warmth. The August heat was such that it was like getting into a warm bath. Anthony Bell watched the underwater form of his father approaching him and broke into a huge grin as Alex emerged at the surface near his feet. The boy got to his feet and jumped into the pool with a squeal of delight. In a few minutes the other two boys had joined in and were hanging and jumping off Alex as he pretended to be a sea monster, pursuing them with loud roars and much face pulling, accompanied by their peels of excited laughter as they splashed about in the pool.

"C'mon Mum", shouted the excited Anthony on seeing his mother approaching the pool and who by now had also put on her swimsuit. She sauntered over, kicked off her sandals and using the broad tiered steps which gently sloped into the shallow end of the pool, carefully made her way into the water.

"Gosh, it's so warm."

Alex nodded his agreement and then smiled as he watched her slowly swanning towards them in a gentle breaststroke. After the birth of David and particularly whilst in Paris, Claire had struggled to keep her figure. Never exactly fat, she none the less had gained a few unwelcome pounds and appeared to Alex to be unconcerned about it at the time. In a way it had been fairly symptomatic of their relationship. They had both got into a rut. Things had certainly changed over the last few months, undoubtedly linked to the letters from Sandrine Giraud, thought Alex. Claire had obviously lost weight over the summer so that right now, as he looked admiringly at his wife, she was looking great. He invisibly winced as the thought struck him what on Earth he had been thinking back in Paris.

Seeing that his mother was now right beside him and noticing her dry hair and her sunglasses, Christopher immediately splashed some water towards her.

"Oh darling, don't do that. I'm trying to keep my hair dry", she responded.

Alex took on a mischievous grin as he spoke. "Oh no, let's not get Mummy's hair wet." The boys, instantly recognising this as an invitation to do precisely the reverse of what had been said, immediately started splashing their mother.

"Oh really, is that what you want eh?" she said laughingly, breaking into the good natured horseplay and in turn responding with some vigorous splashing of her own.

Alex swam up to his wife, took her in his arms and planted a big kiss on her. "I love you", he whispered into her ear.

"And I love you," she replied.

"Oh yuck, they're kissing", said Anthony, pulling a sour face and looking away.

Later that afternoon, Claire was introduced to Dieter and Andrea Werner. In no time at all their kids were quite happily playing in the swimming pool and running around the surrounding shared areas of the compound. When he had been visiting back in England, Alex had given Claire a few amusing cameos of the characters that he had met since arriving in the Kingdom. She was pleased to find out that his favourable assessment of the Werners had not been over embellished. She took to them quite as easily as Alex had, so that when they were lying in bed that evening, discussing what she had thought of her neighbours, Alex was relieved to find out that she was feeling a little bit more comfortable in her new surroundings.

"I always thought the Germans were OK, it's only when they're in large groups that they get a bit strange and start wanting to take over Poland", said Alex with a wink.

"Oh Alex, you are silly", said Claire as she snuggled up to him in bed.

The next morning David had awoken quite early, stirred by the sunrise shortly after six o'clock, so Alex took him downstairs to let Claire have a lie in. The previous day's activity and intense sun had tired them all out so the two elder boys were still asleep. David was content to play with his trains so Alex sat and flicked through his Euro currency presentation. He needed to refresh his memory as he was going to be presenting it again on Tuesday to some of IAB's larger corporate clients. As was now his custom, learnt from being on his own, he put on the television for some background images to keep him company, with the sound, turned down low. He barely registered the flashing images as he flicked through the channels and wondered about the week to come. Suddenly for some reason, he thought of Willi Spethmen and his girlfriend Svetlana Pavliva, he looked up at the television screen and there he saw the scene again. The picture showed a tunnel with a flashing light but beneath it his attention was now immediately drawn to the red bannered headline which reported the news that Princess Diana had been involved in a serious car crash in Paris and was in an intensive care unit. Astonishingly the scene he was looking at was the tunnel at Place d'Alma, precisely the place where his own narrow escape had occurred in Willi Spethmen's BMW that wintry night. The time on the television screen said it was 4.45 am and Alex automatically looked at his own wristwatch which confirmed that it was a quarter to seven in Jeddah. He grabbed the remote and turned up the sound to listen to the newscaster who now relayed the unfolding story and he watched spellbound as the details slowly emerged. Another fifteen minutes later and the headline confirmed that Diana had died.

"Isobel was in tears about it."
Alex looked at Joe Karpolinski and shook his head in slowly in agreement. "I know, Claire was quite upset about it too. She was on the phone to her mother and the whole business has made her quite homesick."

"They say it was the fault of the paparazzi chasing her all over Paris", said Jim as he poured over his position reports.

"Seems likely that the driver was drunk apparently", added Joe.

"Well he must have going like a bat out of hell, have you seen the state of the car?" replied Jim.

"I know," agreed Joe, "those S class Mercedes are built like tanks and that one was completely totalled."

"It was bound to happen to her. Poor woman", interrupted Khalid, who had been listening to the traders for some time in thoughtful silence.

Alex turned towards his young trainee, his forehead lined with an incredulous frown, "What are you talking about Khalid?"

"It's obvious isn't?" replied the young Saudi.

"I'm sorry but I haven't got a clue what you're on about."

"Well she has been a bit of an embarrassment for your Prince Charles for some time and she was about to marry Dodi Al-Fayed."

Alex laughed bitterly, "I think you'll find that she would have been unlikely to do that."

"Oh yes, I am sure. There is no way your Queen would want the heir to the English throne's mother married to an Arab."

Alex was watching Khalid and he could see Jim rolling his eyes and tapping the side of his head behind him.

Alex' eyes opened wide with disbelief. "Are you honestly suggesting that this was not an accident?"

"Of course it wasn't an accident. It was probably M.I.5 or Mossad, there is no way they would have allowed her to have the baby."

"Baby? Where on earth did you get that crazy idea?"

"Oh yes, she was pregnant." Khalid's expression was of complete seriousness. "Just imagine that, the next in line to the throne would have been a Muslim."

"Honestly Khalid, with all respect, I have never heard such crap in all my days."

Now it was Khalid's turn to look incredulous and he spoke with soft determination. "You believe what you wish my friend, but that is what they are saying here in the Arab world."

Jim laughed at this last statement. "Well Khalid, I think that sounds pretty farfetched, but as my old man used to say, 'that's my opinion and you're entitled to it.'"

Khalid Abu Anzi shook his head and made a half hearted smile that made no attempt to conceal the heavy sigh of resignation he emitted.

Chris Barma who had been talking in a hushed tone on the phone, hung up the call and stood up. "OK guys let's start" and so the morning meeting kicked off as usual.

Unlike the death of other famous people, where the market would be circulating ribald and tasteless jokes almost the moment their unfortunate souls had departed, the death of Diana was seemingly quite different. Perhaps it was just the physical distance but for Alex the response of some of his friends and business associates back in London was strangely difficult to come to terms with. There was no doubt that it was a very sad event, but the response on the nation seemed to be out of all proportion to what the woman really was. Even the most cynical of the bankers and brokers he dealt with was as silent and as baleful as the grave, not a note of irreverence, not a shred of wicked irony. It was an eerily strange Monday morning that slipped slowly by. Alex read some research reports and fiddled with his spreadsheets for most of it. The London markets were dead.

At around eleven this quiet activity was eventually interrupted. "Alex, line three for you," said Khalid who had picked up the phone.

"Who is it?" If it was that broker from Dresdner again he wanted to give him a miss. Alex had absolutely no interest in the trade he was touting.

Khalid asked who was on the line, he looked up, "Says he's returning your call, some guy called Willy or something…"

Alex picked up the line without hesitation. He had called the German earlier that morning, "Willi?"

"Hi Alex, long time no speak."

"You're telling me, hey how are you then?"

"Pretty good my friend, how about you?"

"Same as usual", replied Alex with a half snort. "So how's life treating you Willi?"

"I'm engaged. Svety and me are getting married in May."

"Hey that's great news Willi, congratulations.

The German's tone changed and dropped several notches lower in volume. "Say Alex, I know why you called me, what a fucking coincidence eh?"

"I know, it's quite weird isn't it."

"Unbelievable, it happened almost exactly where we had our lucky escape."

"I know."

Willi Spethmen dropped his voice right down low to a whisper. "Another thing Alex and I know I can tell you this, but the response here has been completely over the top. I mean, for fucks sake, she was hardly Mother Teresa. You Brits have completely lost the plot."

Alex dropped his voice right down. "Not me, but maybe it's because I'm miles away. It's not exactly stiff upper lip behaviour."

Willi laughed sardonically, "Stiff upper lip, don't make me laugh. Well it's the last time I listen to an Englishman telling me how reserved they are as a nation. It's like a national hysterical breakdown... scary."

Alex stiffened. "*Ein Volk, Ein Reich, Ein* Diana"

Willi fell silent for a moment. "Mob psychology is a fucking scary thing Alex."

Alex pondered the man's answer before speaking. He checked to his right hand side, Khalid was busily chatting on the phone to someone in Arabic. "It really is. Say you wouldn't believe the stuff the Arabs out here are saying about it."

"Like what?"

"Like it was organised by M.I.5 or Mossad and that she was assassinated."

Spethmen chuckled. "Really? That's amazing, the thing is, folks just want to feel there's a reason for bad things happening. Personally I only believe in the fuck up theory of life. Shit happens."

"You don't say."

"Well I've got to jump. All I can say is keep the last weekend in May free OK?"

"Wedding?"

"*Achtung* Stag Tommy!"

"Will do, cheers, Willi."

"Ciao."

The line clicked out and Alex slowly put the receiver down onto his desk deep in thought. The news of Willi's impending betrothal was not entirely surprising. He picked up the phone again and was just about to dial the number for Jean-Marc when the dealer board starting ringing. He automatically picked up the line. "IAB Trading."

"Alex, good to get you at last. I wanted to speak to you about the Italy Germany convergence trade."

It was the broker from Dresdner again. "Oh bollocks" thought Alex.

Over the following weeks Claire had speedily reorganised their home whilst Sierra Village had quickly adjusted back to normal life as the trickle of expatriate families turned into the full deluge as they all returned from their long summer breaks. The Werner's children soon became firm friends of the Bells' and it was not too long before it was Claire who was conducting the introductions. Alex would return from work to find various new faces of previously unknown parents of the kids' ever expanding circle of recently found friends, sitting and chatting around his poolside. It was hard to keep up with.

During the entire time that Alex had been there alone, he had only really met his immediate neighbours and some of the single men either through 'Brass Eagle' events or in the squash and tennis leagues which he now played in. In no time at all Claire and the kids had become the link to an entirely different social circle which earlier had been quite barred to him as a singleton on the compound. The only grating aspect of his working and family life balance there was the fact that he still operated on the normal Westerner's week, Monday through Friday. This had been fine when he had been on his own, but was now proving to be something of a major irritation for his family. The school week was Saturday to Wednesday and obviously most of the expatriates in the Kingdom worked the same five or five and a half day week. This issue quickly became a source of periodic domestic friction to Alex as his boys would invariably pose him the same awkward question.

On returning from work that Wednesday evening, he came into the cool villa to find his two eldest children were sitting watching a cartoon with the younger Werner child. He greeted his wife with an affectionate kiss and plonked his heavy case containing his ever present laptop down in the lounge, before collapsing into armchair.

"Hi kids"

"Hi Dad", chimed his sons whilst still glued to the hypnotically colourful images on the television.

Alex gave their young visitor a smile and the boy coyly returned it before once more refocusing on the television. 'Cartoon Network' was blaring away on the screen, unfair competition in the interest stakes when compared to a returning office worker and tired out looking father.

Alex slowly scanned the lounge. "Where's David?"

"He's upstairs with Anna", Christopher answered. The Werner's eight year old daughter enjoyed playing Teacher to the youngest Bell child.

The cartoon came to an end and Claire came into the lounge just on cue. "OK boys, that's enough telly. It's nearly time for tea."

"Mum, can Jurgen have tea with us?" Anthony asked.

"Of course, but perhaps he better check with his Mum", Claire remarked with a kindly look at the youngster.

"I'll go and ask now", said the boy flushing with excitement before he rushed out of the house without any further delay.

"Dad, why do you have to go to work tomorrow?" Claire gave her husband a sidelong look and started to make her way back to the kitchen where the smell of cooking food was wafting invitingly from. The working week arrangement was something she was not happy about either.

Alex sighed loudly, this time it was Anthony who had resurrected the difficult question of his office hours.

"Unfortunately I have to son."

"But none of the other Daddy's do."

"I know but I'll be back soon." Alex said with an optimistic look. Anthony's lower lip jutted out in truculent opposition. "It's not fair."

390

"Well on Friday I'll be home the whole day, OK?" Anthony just pulled an injured face and looked away.

"How was school then?" Alex asked brightly, trying rather clumsily to change the subject.

"Fine", Anthony's good humour was not about to be bought so cheaply.

He gave his son a warm hug. "Go on tell me what you did today"

"I can count to ten in Arabic, Anna taught me", said Anthony seeing his own opportunity to shine had just arrived.

"Oh that's pips", taunted his elder brother as they both then chorused the counting sequence to ten in a singsong manner.

"Wahid, Etnain, Talata, Arba, Hamsa, Sita, Saba, Thamina, Tisa, Ashara."

Four weeks in Saudi and the kids already knew almost as much Arabic as me, thought Alex ruefully. In the first three months he had learnt a little, but he had stalled completely whilst learning the cursive script which he had found difficult to come to terms with. His progress through 'How to Learn Arabic in Three Months', had halted at about the same point as his book on Decision Theory. A little knowledge is a dangerous thing he thought to himself and made a mental note to try and finish off both the tasks he had set himself. This line of self improving thought was broken by a knock on the open front door.

"Hi there."

Claire went to the open doorway. It was Andy Werner and a particularly miserable looking Jurgen. "Hi Andy, how are you?"

"Fine Claire, I've come to collect Anna", she smiled.

"She's upstairs teaching David the names of various 'Pokémon' characters", laughed Claire.

"Jurgen, can you go and get your sister please."

"Aw Mum, Please…" The little boy drew out his request on a long pleading note and gave his mother a baleful look.

"No Jurgen, I have already told you. Maybe next time", she gave him a reproachful look, "if you're good."

The boy broke into an expression of frustrated resignation, he could see there was no room for negotiation and slid past Claire to go up the stairs to fetch his sister.

Andrea Werner leaned against the doorway and smiled tiredly, "What a life. They'll be driving us mad", she said.

"I know."

Andy brightened. "Incidentally I was just speaking to Moira and Janet and we were wondering about going to the Intercontinental Beach on Friday. Would you and Alex like to come along too?"

"Well I'm not sure Alex is free but the rest of us are", she turned to look at her husband who had appeared just behind her shoulder.

"No that should be fine darling"

"There you go", replied Claire with a warm smile.

"Great, I'll give you a call later on to confirm the time but I think we'll go earlyish", said the German with a flash of her big boned smile.

"Who's going on this trip?" Alex asked his wife as the Bell family sat down to eat their evening meal.

"Andy's organised it all so I'm not sure, but I think the McDonalds and the Howards are coming too. There may be more."

Two days later and as promised Alex took off the day to join the family expedition to the beach. The Intercontinental beach sounded much grander than it was. The hotel itself was situated on the Corniche in the centre of the city; however the private beach of the same name was actually located another thirty minutes up the coastline, not far from Blue Beach, the name of which was to be forever engraved on the memories of both Alex and Jim Robson. Alex had told Claire of the diving accident on the *Shazadi* when he had got back to England and the story had come vividly to life once she had met Jim and heard his own account of it too. By now Robson was a frequent visitor around the Bell's villa, he had spent many evenings sitting drinking warming beer with the Bell's and their German neighbours and several other couples whose kids were now part of the children's social circle. Claire could see why Alex had taken to the Londoner; he was one of life's optimists and much like her husband. Furthermore, despite having no kids of his own, he was, nonetheless, something of a natural with them, so when Andy had confirmed the time of the trip and had asked Alex if Jim would like to come along too, Jim in turn, had readily accepted the invitation. For Jim Robson, his own compound, Lotus Four, was a fairly lonely place, filled with families who had little interest in socialising with the few single men who happened to lived there.

When they arrived at the beach the kids, who Claire had correctly predicted now numbered a total of eleven, all excitedly stripped off to their swimwear and dashed down to the swimming pool. Equally predictably and with the usual contrariness of children, they much preferred playing there, rather than by the beach waterfront. Meanwhile their parents found a suitable spot on the fast filling beach and decamped the volumes of coloured plastic, bags and boxes of kit to their chosen place. Errant sun-loungers and parasols were rounded up and corralled into position and it was not long before the parents were sitting or lying prone relaxing, chatting, sipping soft-drinks, whilst periodically hollering semi-ignored instructions to their offspring or energetically applying sun block to their tanning young bodies.

"Well at least the kids are enjoying themselves", huffed Moira McDonald as she thrust a bottle of sun-screen into a beach bag at her feet.

"They always do", replied her husband in his usual upbeat tone.

Moira McDonald finished adjusting her sun bed and lay back shielding her eyes from the blazing daylight with the highly effective combination of sunglasses and a paperback novel. She was about to reply caustically to her husband that everyone seemed to be enjoying themselves except her but resigned herself to another huffy sigh.

"Dad will you come and play with us." John McDonald's youngest boy, now smothered in factor thirty, who was around the same age as Alex's youngest, was pulling at his father's arm. Sensing an opportunity to call a truce to the contretemps between himself and his wife, the Scot uneasily got to his feet and wandered over to the swimming pool. On seeing this Alex also levered himself up and followed him.

"I'd better check that my lot are OK too."

Jim, seeing that everyone was still sorting out their children also got up. "I'm going for a little swim" and he wandered off down towards the shoreline holding the snorkel and flippers he had brought with him.

The other two men were mid way through inflating the inventory of floating plastic they had brought with them, with a foot pump. Several balls, a pink horse, a smiling crocodile and a large blue and yellow dingy were all morphing into shape around them. Dieter had beads of sweat forming and running off his face as he energetically pumped the inflatable toys up, all the while keeping an unlit cigarette gripped between his clenched teeth.

"We'll be with you in a mo." he said as Alex and John took off, though all he intended to do was to have a snooze.

The rest of the day passed pleasantly and for some at least, Bill, Dieter and Jim being the main beneficiaries, dozily by. The children never tired of playing around the swimming pool though they also spent periods around their lounging parents, foraging in ice boxes and ordering and eating copious amounts of ice-cream and fluorescent coloured ice-lollies. A brief attempt was made by some of the younger children to build sandcastles around their parent's little temporary enclave but the sand around them, being half way up the beach was far too hot, fine and dry to do this, so the task of constructing a mini Alhambra was made at the water's edge under the watchful aegis of John and Alex. Periodically the adults would go down and take a dip in the sea or the swimming pool but mostly Janet, Claire and Andy chatted away while Moira convincingly feigned sleep behind her dark glasses.

"How are you finding it?"

The three women turned shielding eyes or squinting in the direction of the speaker. It took a few moments to register from the man's pressed white shirt and badge that it was the Manager of the beach resort.

"Oh we're having a great time", replied Andy who, rolling her eyes expressively had now recognised the man's face. She was after all, a regular of the InterContinental's beach.

"Did you enjoy your meal?" The blonde haired man asked. The women nodded their assent, "The kids certainly did?" said Claire.

The manager looked pleased at this piece of news; the new Indian chef that he had recently employed was proving to be a fair choice. In his experience, chefs were always such ridiculous prima donnas, the last one had been a hysterical and highly strung fool. Firing him had been a pleasure.

"I'm very glad to hear that." Claire couldn't quite place the man's accent but it had the sing song tones of Scandinavia. She peered at the man's nametag and could now see he was called something Nielson.

Just at that moment, Anthony came roaring up the beach, his knees and lower legs covered in a film of wet sand.

The boy was breathless with excitement as his words came tumbling out, "Mum, Mum come quick. Come and look at the fort we made." The four year old started pulling at his mother's arm.

"In a moment, I'm talking."

Her son pulled an injured face, "You're always talking, come now", he added insistently.

The manager looked towards the waterline, "I can see you have made a very good castle."

The boy looked warily up as the blonde haired stranger and said nothing. Claire swung her legs over and put on her sandals, the sand was too hot to walk about on for any length of time. She stood up and peered down the beach and could now see her husband and John McDonald making their way back up towards them. As they neared she recognised the tell tale signs that they had both caught a bit too much of the sun. As she was doing this Andy was busily chatting away to the manager in German. Claire watched the two men approaching and passed a towel to her husband as David ferreted in an icebox in the search of more goodies.

"That's me done", said John McDonald sitting himself heavily down onto a sun-bed whilst making sure he was sufficiently shaded by a large parasol, "I'm feeling bushed."

"No, I don't believe you." Andy suddenly said in English to the Resort Manager.

"I promise you it is true", said the Swede earnestly.

"Go on tell these others then." Andy Werner said with a disbelieving shake of her head.

"Tell us what?" Janet looked up at the blonde haired man with enquiring eyes.

Andy laughed again before saying, "it's about the sand."

Jesper Nielson could not see what was so funny about what he had just told the blonde German woman and bit his lower lip in silent slightly wounded affront. Never mind, he thought to himself and he cocked his head a little as he prepared to speak, perhaps these other people would be more appreciative of what he had just told Andrea Werner. He stiffened a touch as he now formally addressed the little day tripping party.

"Actually I was informing Mrs Werner that the sand on the beach and particularly in the children's play area", he pointed a hairy blonde arm in the direction of the swimming pool, "has been specially prepared and is child friendly."

"Child friendly sand", Moira said with a developing smile then added sardonically.

"Is there any other type?"

Neilson gave a school masterly look at the Scotswoman, the kind delivered to a particularly dull pupil. "Why of

399

course there is, this is specially treated hypo-allergenic sand."

"Hyper-allergenic?" John McDonald chimed irreverently, while looking as if he had just bitten into something unpleasant.

"Hypo-allergenic" repeated the Manager with didactic precision, "imported from Belgium."

"You imported sand from Belgium." Dieter was now looking quite amazed and was sitting bolt upright at this snippet of information.

Jesper Neilson pitched his head to one side and nodded with satisfaction.

"You mean to say the sand here wasn't quite right?"

 The Swede was used to this line of questioning, it amazed him how little these people appreciated all the little things that were done to make their stay a pleasant one. "It was not ideal; it was too silty. This," he craned his head around the beach, "is biologically inert." Neilson remembered the salesman's compelling pitch almost verbatim.

Alex caught Dieter's twinkling eyes, he had a thoroughly mischievous look plastered over his face. "So this is biologically inert hypo allergenic sand. Amazing." The German was shaking his head and looking appropriately serious though Alex could easily see he was trying to stifle a guffaw. "Special sand", he added and then pinched his mouth together in order to abort his imminent laughter.

"Yes you could say that, special sand indeed", responded the Swede with absolute, po-faced seriousness. The Manager, now seeing he had obviously set the little group to thinking, considered it an opportune moment to retire and see how his other clients were faring. Customer surveys were all part of a Hotel Managers remit and he had quite a few to perform before the day was out. "Enjoy your stay and I look forward to seeing you all again."

"Thank you Jesper", responded Andy as the Swede turned on his heel and retreated back to his position. He was no sooner out of earshot than Dieter exploded into raucous laughter which soon had the whole group following his lead. As the laughter subsided the German wiped a tear away from his eye.

"Really that is priceless."

"Isn't it just?" responded John McDonald, still chortling away, to the German's statement.

"Have you ever heard such nonsense in all your life?" Dieter was looking around the group.

"I have to say I find that incredible, this country is ninety five percent desert, including the *Rub' Al Khali*, it's the biggest mass of sand on the planet", said Bill Howard with quiet authority.

"I tell you, I just wish I had that fucking salesman on my team", said John, "unbelievable, a man that successfully sold sand to the Arabs all the way from fucking Belgium."

401

Janet Howard gave the Scot a slightly reproachful look, she didn't really approve of such language, but the kids were not within range so she let it pass, "Well I wouldn't have believed it myself if I hadn't heard it firsthand." Her primness reminded the Scot he was in mixed company.

"This place is seriously screwed up", said Dieter. "My company has outstanding invoices of over two years or more for drugs and yet they have money to waste on buying sand." The German bent down and drew his fingers through the offending material at his feet. "It just makes no sense."

Bill Howard shook his head. "Oh c'mon you know what it's like here Dieter, everything has to have a fifty one percent ownership by a Saudi, we all have the same problem. Some stupid son of the owner wants special pink sand and presto special pink sand's what you get."

Dieter shook his head in sad understanding. He knew it all too well. It was just the way the place worked. Every corporate entity in the Kingdom had to have a majority holding by a Saudi National and these lucrative franchises were owned by a handful of inordinately rich families. Besides his own company's problem wasn't another company's failure to pay on time, it was the government or someone in the Ministry of Health. The only thing was that it was a persistent complaint from Head Office in Frankfurt that outstanding bills had to be paid; it was the bane of his professional life.

"Well I still think it's obscene." The men watched the German as he shook his head forlornly, "you know, in the end it's just all about money here isn't?"

The men remained silent and a thoughtful look descended on them as the German continued to vent his frustration.

"You scratch my *baksheesh*, I scratch your *baksheesh*; it's all about bloody *baksheesh.*"

The group of men nodded sagely.

"Aye it is", intoned John McDonald, "it's the way of the world my friend, especially here."

"Fancy a drink?" Bill Howard was delving into his icebox and brought out an alcohol free beer.

"Anything as long as it's not Pepsi", said the Scot with a grin.

"Nope, just toy beers I'm afraid", replied Bill as the others then gathered round the icebox.

"I didn't know that." Jim said, directing an enquiring look at Bill Howard.

Howard gave returned the enquiring look. "What didn't you know?"

"The bit about the law concerning majority Saudi ownership..."

Howard gave a shrug. "Yes, it can be a bit of a problem sometimes." Howard also knew first hand of the some of the problems associated with corporate life in the Kingdom. He was one of the senior managers for Proctor and Gamble. "It's just the way things work out here. Actually our lot are quite good," he replied diplomatically. "Better than you derivatives Investment Bankers and all that, 'eye ripping', you get up to", he added breaking into a cheeky grin.

"Eye ripping?" Alex looked blank for a moment, he had been reflecting on what Dieter had been saying and had only been half listening but he snapped back to reality at Howard's comment. Both the bank traders immediately knew exactly what he was cheekily alluding to. "Hey, I never worked at Bankers Trust", replied Alex with a grin, but I don't know about that fellow Jim."

14. Back Stage Seen

"Did you see this?" Jim pointed to the newspaper; his furrowed and pained expression conveyed the grimness of the news.

Alex glanced down at the newspaper. The 'Arab News' was the English Language newspaper of Saudi Arabia, vetted, scrubbed and sanitised to the satisfaction of the authorities. The front page headlines were all about the massacre of fifty eight tourists in Egypt at the Temple of Hatshepsut in Luxor. As ever, political extremism was the reason according to the paper, probably sponsored by the Iranians. For the men in the IAB Treasury, any Middle-East attack, but particularly those directed against Westerners was always unnerving for them.

"Horrific, what are these people thinking?" said Alex.

"God only knows, some bunch of lunatics called, *Al-Gama'a al-Islamiyya*, 'The Islamic Group' apparently."

"Fucking madmen, what the fuck do they think they'll achieve?" Alex said with disgust.

"Well I guess we'll never know, seems that all the suspects were killed by the Egyptian security forces", said Jim as he folded the paper away.

"It was probably Mossad", said a voice to Alex' side.

Alex turned to look at his trainee Khalid. "Mossad?"

The Saudi gave a look that suggested it was the most elementary piece of information known to man.

"Or the CIA", he volunteered with a shrug.

Alex shook his head in frustration. He was now more than used to the basic premise of most of Saudis concept of global geopolitical events. Simply stated, many young Saudi's like Khalid Abu Anzi believed that the US was ultimately pulling the strings, frequently using the hated State of Israel as its tool. Nothing was ever simple or straightforward or random, it was the mirror image of the principle of, 'Keep It Simple, Stupid'. Alex had long since given up trying to argue otherwise. "If you say so Khalid."

The young Arab took on a slightly hurt look. He, like most of his fellow trainees, liked and even respected these particular Westerners with whom he worked, but he was frequently amazed by the naïveté of some of them.

"Ask yourself, who benefits from such an act?" Khalid reasoned.

"Please don't tell me it was part of some grand strategy of the US."

Khalid simply raised his eyebrows which had the effect of eloquently conveying his thoughts.

Alex pulled a sour grimace, "Oh, c'mon Khalid."

"It's simply the new world order isn't it?" replied the Arab.

Alex sighed; they were back to the same old story. According to the world view of many in the Arab world and Khalid actively considered himself one of these, it was simply a case of if you can't beat them, join them. To men like Khalid, the West was basically corrupt and bordering on evil, you just had to live with it, as you would with a bullying antisocial neighbour. When you were rich enough you could eventually build a big enough wall to keep him out or pay the stupid fellow off. Well that is what he intended to do, if given half a chance. It was simply a pragmatic view, nothing more or less.

"OK guys, let's start the morning meeting", said Chris Barma tiredly

"I think Barma has lost the plot" Andy Whiteman said as he put down his fork at lunch that day.

"It's a bit worrying you know", agreed Joe.

"A bit?" Pete almost shouted, Karpolinski's trite statements of the obvious were becoming. "Well all I can say from the FX balances I'm seeing is that he must be running some big and I mean big, positions.

"We'll just have to have it out with him tomorrow." Whiteman had folded his arms across his chest.

"That's going to be tricky." Jim had a deep furrow etched across his forehead.

Alex nodded, "What can we do? We're just guessing what his positions could be."

"We just need someone to have a quiet word with Omar," said Pete.

"What about Jim or Alex", replied Joe wiping his mouth with the back of his hand. Karpolinski's eyes moved over the two men, "After all, he loves you two after what you did for his son."

Jim's features clouded over, "I'm not sure about Omar. The poor bloke doesn't seem to be himself these days. I think he's been having problems." Khalid Abu Anzi had already discreetly informed both Jim and Alex that apparently Omar was having some difficulties with his youngest son.

Alex showed his agreement with this last statement, besides he did not feel fully at ease with the course of action that was being proposed. "I agree with Andy. We should just have it out with him on Friday at the weekly strategy meeting."

Pete pulled a sour face. "He better fess up and explain what he's doing. I'm not spending the rest of my days rotting in a Saudi jail. He just never says what the hell he's doing and he's getting so weird and secretive."

"Look the way things are going and if he's long the dollar he should be making a bundle." Joe took a swig of his drink.

"I've already told you Joe, his positions indicate he was long but is now getting short and shorter with each move up." Koestler's exasperation was barely hidden.

Alex spoke quietly. "Look I'll try to have a discreet word with Omar, but I'm not going to push it OK?"

Periodically Omar Al-Hamra could be found sitting in the small room, just off the trading floor, that operated as his office. Like many Risk Managers, he also had a position out in the dealing room, kept in order to better to sense the goings on amongst the traders, but Alex figured he didn't want to have any delicate conversations overheard, so waited for an opportunity to catch him in the privacy of his office.

"Hi Alex, what brings you to my door?"

"Nothing much, just passing by. How's the family?" For the first time Alex found the usual Saudi conversational opener useful.

Omar looked down at his desk, he had been finding the last few weeks particularly difficult. His young son Mohammed had now become a completely closed book to him. "Fine", he sighed unconvincingly.

"How are your boys?" Alex automatically asked, having other things on his mind he had not really noticed the man's downcast demeanour. He had not seen them since the visit to Omar's house with Jim some months back, where grateful thanks and polite conversation had been the pleasant but dominant theme. The near drowning accident on the *Shazadi* already seemed like ancient history.

Omar looked at the Englishman with a resigned tilt and ran his hand through his thick wiry hair. "It's not easy my friend. Not easy at all."

Alex stepped a little hesitantly into the man's office and now recognized how tired out the portly Arab was looking. "What's up Omar?"

"I don't know, kids these days are so hard to understand." Alex waited for the man to elaborate and gave the Risk Manager a sympathetic smile. "My youngest boy was never the most easy to understand but..." his voice trailed off as he spoke, "he's not a boy anymore. They grow up so quickly you know?"

"Don't they just." Alex agreed, still attempting some light heartedness, all the while closely studying the Saudi.

Omar bit his lower lip, "Education is such an important thing these days."

Alex wondered where the Arab was going, he seemed almost in a trance as he spoke. Omar shook his head, seeming to snap himself out of his torpor. "Do you know how many foreign workers there are in the Kingdom?"

Alex had not really thought about it and pulled a face to indicate he was unaware of the number.

"Six million…" he feverishly rubbed his forehead as if they were all untidily packed within his skull, "six million out of an entire population of twenty five million." He stared directly at Alex, "that's more than thirty five percent of the working population."

Alex felt a little uneasy at this observation. After all, he was one of the six million that was causing the Arab such apparent consternation. Omar immediately recognised the signs of confusion and embarrassment in the Englishman's face. "No Alex, I don't mean you specifically. You're a specialist in a small…" Omar paused before asking, "What is the word you use?"

Alex puckered in thought, "niche?" he replied hopefully.

"Yes that's it, that's the one 'niche.'" He stared at the wall for a moment, seeming to be considering the word before continuing. "No, what I'm talking about are the jobs that are done by foreigners, which our young Saudi men should be doing."

Alex smiled a little uneasily, "I see."

"This place is full of Syrians, Egyptians, Somalis, Indians, Pakistanis, Filipinos", the Arab counted them of on his hand. "They do everything", he added with resignation.

As if on cue there was a knock on the open door, "Sorry to interrupt Omar, but I need to put a new network card into your pc. When would be good for you?" It was Eric, the trading floor IT engineer.

411

Omar peered at the man thoughtfully, "Lunchtime, would be good Eric."

"OK boss", and the tubby Filipino was gone as quickly as he had come.

Alex shrugged and gave Omar a sardonic little smile.

"You see what I mean? It really is a problem, my son has given up on trying to work for a living. It is just too difficult. He no longer wants to get qualifications and instead he's going to become..." Omar paused before summoning the strength to say it, "a cleric."

"Really..." For some peculiar reason visions of country vicarages and genial parsons came to Alex' mind. "Is that so bad?"

Omar presented Alex with a stare of deadly seriousness and slowly shook his heavy jowls. It would be too difficult to explain to this recently arrived Englishman what the reservations he had were and indeed why. The Arab's dark eyes momentarily softened and he sighed. "Well I'm not sure", he lied.

In fact Omar was very sure. He was desperately concerned, not only about his son's vocational choice and where it was likely to lead him, but also on the malign influence of his brother in law Abdul-Rahman. The religious policeman was now, sickeningly for Omar, almost a permanent feature of the Al-Hamra household. The presence of the *Mutawwa* was crushing and felt like an unending black night that forever postponed Omar's dawning hopes for his son.

Alex watched the Arab as he fidgeted; suddenly questions about positions in foreign exchange markets seemed hopelessly unobtainable. Clearly this was not the right time.

Omar once again snapped out of his brooding. "Anyway, enough of that. What can I do for you?"

"Oh nothing specific", Alex stammered, before recovering. "Just hadn't seen you in the dealing room for a while."

Omar's eyes narrowed imperceptibly, "Thank you, as you see my friend, I'm fine. Troubles, but otherwise fine."

"Is everything OK?"

Alex turned to the familiar sounding voice. Ed Moore was standing across the doorway.

"Yes all fine I think", replied Omar

Moore nodded, "Omar could I have a word with you?"

Alex gave a quick nod to the Arab and seeing his opportunity had completely disappeared, excused himself from the room with a brief smile as he passed by the American.

The following morning Alex sat tensely with one eye reading the news wires and one eye on the trading floor entrance. The men had decided they were going to have it out with Chris Barma at their weekly meeting anyway.

413

They just had too. Alex watched as yet another one of the trainees drifted in.

"Morning", chimed Nabeel breezily as he sat down a little stiffly next to Andy.

"*Salaam alicum* matey," responded Andy with warmth.

"Did you get home OK?" asked Nabeel.

"I certainly did and thanks again", said Andy

"Anytime my friend."

The men checked watches, there was no sign of Chris Barma.

"Did Chris say he was going to be late today?" Joe asked of no one in particular.

Heads shook to indicate nobody knew anything of the sort.

The men watched the doorway and the clocks and waited.

"He's still not answering his phone", said Pete putting down his handset.

"I hate Fridays", said Alex.

Another hour passed and all of the Saudis started to get up from their desks and gathered by the trading floor exit. Alex and Jim exchanged a brief look and then watched the assembled group troop off to Friday Prayers. The men waited until they had all departed.

"You know, I've got to say it still always amazes me when they all go off like that to the mosque", said Joe

Pete nodded. "Intense peer pressure."

Andrew Whiteman was not so easily sidetracked. "Where the bloody hell is Barma?"

"Probably praying in the mosque", said Joe with a glint.

Out of Joe's sight, Pete rolled his eyes and then cast them down to his wrist watch. It was another hour before the restaurants would re-open for lunch. "Well that's that. Its Fudruckers then, in an hour."

Andy shook his head. "Shit."

As the men made their way to their regular Friday restaurant, outside and seventeen floors down in the square below, the cleaners were washing away the freshly drying evidence of that week's demonstration of *Sharia* justice. None of the crowd stayed back to watch the last of the bloody evidence drain away into the arid ground but had by now almost entirely melted away under the harsh Arabian sun. The spectacle over, the faithful were then coaxed into the cooling interiors of the surrounding mosques as the city resonated to the call of the *Muezzin* from a competing cacophony of minarets. Unknown to the men on the trading floor, with their carefully orchestrated panorama of Jeddah, over in the North-west of the city, men were slowly shuffling into the mosque of Abdullah Bawani, preparing to listen to the fiery cleric's inflammatory rhetoric. As usual, Abdul-Rahman bin Hajez was already there accompanied by the young Al-Hamra brothers. The *Mutawwa* gave the

Alim an enquiring look, which was returned with a knowing smile.

"I will return to you shortly, but I must speak to our brother Abdullah Bawani", the religious policeman explained to the Al-Hamra siblings before working his way through the filling congregation and stepping into a small room where the cleric was making his last preparations for the coming *Jummah*   address.

The Saudi shut the door and cut immediately to the chase, there was little time for formalities. "Are you quite sure that you have left no unfinished business?

"I assure you Abdul-Rahman there is nothing to link me at all. The chain is short and secure."

The *Mutawwa* was a bristling image of contained anger. "I hope for your sake that you are right."

"What are you saying? The operation was a success." The cleric turned and picked up a copy of the Koran and opened it to where a bookmark had been placed.

"Success?" Abdul-Rahman spat back under his breath. "The Americans are squeezing us everywhere and the whole Egyptian operation has now been totally compromised. Your friends' tactics have now caused us many problems."

"That is not possible, the entire unit was martyred, the command structure is quite secure and there is no link to me or any of the family."

"That's as may be, but there were itineraries, visa requests, and your name came up on the Interior Ministry database again."

"Coincidences my friend," replied Abdullah Bawani with the most emaciated of smiles.

"You know very well that there are no such things as coincidences in matters such as this, there is no room for them." Despite his attempt at firmness, a slight trace of nervousness had edged into the voice of the *Mutawwa*.

Abdullah Bawani smiled humourlessly, revealing a thin yellowing gash of rickety teeth in a deliberate display of sangfroid.

Frustrated at the man's lack of response Abdul-Rahman continued with a sneer, "So I suppose that you think it's just a joke then, when two separate leads point to you?" Abdullah Bawani showed not the slightest concern on hearing this information. "One of which referred to you as, 'The Pyro-technician'?" The *Mutawwa* emitted a hollow laugh then stopped and stared at the preacher with a vicious scowl.

Abdullah Bawani did not even blink as his nom de guerre was spoken out aloud; he was examining his fingernails as he softly responded, "Just childish nonsense."

Disbelief flooded across the features of the *Mutawwa*, "Nonsense? I had to use considerable means to quash that line of enquiry."

The *Alim* closed his eyes, brought his hand up to his mouth and slowly rubbed his bearded face before replying with calculated coldness. "Well done. So why don't you just stick to what you are best at and leave me to what the great Almighty has granted that I am best at?" The Egyptian smoothed his hair before continuing. "The operation was a success, it has passed. We can now proceed as planned." He turned and drilled the *Mutawwa* with a steely glare. "Now if you would just let me pass, I have a sermon to minister."

The grey streaked bearded *Mutawwa* bit his lip in frustration and stood aside to let the *Alim* pass by. There was little to be done. It was true, the matter had by now largely passed, but the pressure immediately after attack had been enormous. Requests had come from the Americans and the Egyptians, even the British, all the intelligence services had been viciously prodded into life. The reaction, particularly that of the Egyptians, had not been expected. Abdul-Rahman followed the cleric out and took his place in the congregation who were quietly sitting on their haunches waiting for the *Alim* to lead their prayers. As he sat himself amongst them, Abdul-Rahman tried to put thoughts of his problems out of his mind. As soon as the attack on the infidel tourists to the Temple of Hatshepsut in Luxor had occurred back in mid November, there had been the usual stirrings in the Interior Ministry. Requests for information, details of recent arrivals and departures to Egyptian destinations, particularly of Egyptian nationals, everything was sought, cross referenced and filed. Of course, Abdul-Rahman knew that Abdullah Bawani was in contact with *Al-Gama'a al-Islamiyya*, though he was not sure to what degree. He did not need to, operationally they were entirely autonomous and their activities were directed by their own command structure. Even so, he knew that complications were to be avoided, so his ability to clandestinely exclude Abdullah Bawani's name from any of the circulated lists was more than a little useful.

The prayers began and Abdul-Rahman, seeing the quiet intensity of the young Mohammed Al-Hamra beside him, closed his eyes and banished these concerns from his mind. The Almighty would find a way, he always did.

Once the initial prayers were done with the *Alim* gave another of his rousing and increasingly popular sermons. Abdul-Rahman noted on how the mosque was now filled to capacity. The young men, for they were mostly so, listened and when the cleric had finished, they filed out of the mosque, edgy and brooding. Many, like Mohammed Al-Hamra stepped out into the bright afternoon with their hearts afire and minds filled with burning ambitions, their frustrations and the inequality of their existences were the tinder that the preacher's fiery oratory had so easily ignited. Through this preacher's words, Mohammed felt that there was some reason to his own seemingly pointless existence. The *Alim* understood how the world worked and was prepared to stand up and look it squarely in the eye. The *Alim* was not afraid and he trusted to the Almighty and that was how Mohammed wanted to be too.

While the faithful spilled out of the mosques filling the previously empty squares and streets, the IAB prop team was just arriving in two cars at their weekly Friday lunchtime restaurant. 'Fudruckers', with its shiny chrome décor, pin ball machines and Americana welcomed them in. They jauntily filed in, still wearing sunglasses and glad to be out from the sapping heat. Even in late November, the midday sun was still intense, but accompanied as it was, with the ever present humidity from the Red Sea, it was a combination that hurried them into the air conditioned comfort of the restaurant. On the walls all around them, the now familiar iconic posters of James Dean, Elvis Presley and Marlon Brando vied for attention with faux US State number tags and million selling, presentation encased forty-fives. With its soda fountains and burger menus it was like a set from Happy Days, which of course it was meant to be. The men took their usual place in the popular restaurant which was already starting to fill. The five Westerners, along with Mohammed Jundi, fitted comfortably into one of the large burgundy coloured banquettes and gave their orders to the friendly Filipino waiters. While waiting for their food to arrive they would go off in twos and threes and play pin ball, Jim was winning as usual, a sure sign of a misspent youth was Alex' tongue in cheek accusation and simultaneous defence for his own poor pinball wizardry. Alex got up and wandered over to where Andy was standing and joined him as they watched Jim rack up another insurmountable lead.

Andy spoke under his breath. "Well that wasn't much use."

"You know that this deaf, dumb, blind kid is just too good for us", Alex said with a sardonic laugh. Andy turned his head and gave a little frustrated look at Alex, the Mancunian was a touch annoyed by this false levity.

"You know what I mean, Barma's definitely up to something and where the hell is he?"

Alex nodded his acknowledgement. It was no good trying to pretend that the whole business was not hugely concerning. "We do need some proof", he added a little plaintively.

Andrew Whiteman gave a little frustrated sigh before replying, "I know."

"Shit", said Jim as he banged the side of the flashing pin ball machine as the shiny chrome ball disappeared into its entrails. "Your go mate", he added with a smile at Alex.

"So what are we to do if we do get the proof anyway?" posed Jim.

"Go to Ed with it obviously", Andy replied with a furrowed look.

Jim nodded his head, "You think that would be the best idea?" His tone clearly indicated that he considered it might not be so.

Andy's furrowed look had taken on a deeper look of concern and his eyes narrowed. "What are you suggesting we should do?"

"Well it might be more appropriate for one of the risk managers to be the ones to bring it to Moore's attention." Jim took a swig of his alcohol free beer.

Whiteman scowled at this. "Look I really don't see the point in going round the houses in this."

Alex was already on his third and last ball. He let the plunger go and the metal ball shot into the labyrinthine workings of the machine which immediately responded with yet more mechanical yelping as it flashed and clanged away. "Isn't this all a bit academic, we still have nothing to back up this accusation?"

"I'll find it," said Andy with steely determination, "and when I do I'm going straight to Moore and Internal Audit with it."

Alex flashed a look at Jim who simply raised an eyebrow, Alex looked back down only to see his last ball trundling into the bowels of the pinball machine and the noise of his final paltry score racked up on the noisy machine, "Bloody game", he muttered. He turned and saw the welcome sight of their lunch orders arriving and so they all sat down to eat. "Ah food at last, I'm starving."

Initially there was little talk as the men hungrily began to eat. Their immediate hunger satiated, the conversation soon started up through half eaten meals.

"So what were you thanking Nabeel about then?" asked Joe with a slight leer.

Andy broke into a smile and slowly shook his head, "You're not going to believe this" he said in reply to Joe but he was looking around the table. The other men all stared at him fixedly waiting for him to continue, seeing that he had gained all their attention he continued. "We went out into the dessert and Nabeel took me to meet his family." He laughed, "Oh and he showed me how an Arab rides and shoots."

"What?" Jim was the first to respond.

"I'm not kidding you."

"Rides and shoots?" Alex was incredulous; Nabeel always looked half wrecked most of the time and this piece of news indicated altogether different reasons for his frequent dishevelled appearance.

Andy broke into a big grin. "I'm telling you, he only leapt onto this bloody horse and rode it bareback, hared off into the distance and then came charging back like Omar bloody Sharif." He chuckled at this, "honestly, it was like something from out of a film." Andy looked around the little wide eyed group gathered around him. "He's a 'full blooded Bedouin'" he said, attempting to impersonate the Saudi's guttural diction while thumping his chest and then breaking into a large grin.

"And what was the shooting bit about then?" asked Joe, wide eyed.

"That was even more bloody amazing", replied the Northerner with genuine excitement in his voice. "They all lined up and starting blasting the shit out of these oil drums they'd brought with them for targets with pistols, automatic rifles and then machine guns."

"No way", interjected a dismayed Pete.

"Way, flaming Kalashnikovs, Heckler & Koch's, fucking Uzis, you name it, they had the lot. Nabeel was showing them all to me and explaining how good they all were."

"Our Nabeel?" Jim echoed, opened mouthed in amazement.

"Yes, our quiet little Nabeel," responded Andy with dumbfound. "Apparently his family are involved in the security service. His uncle runs the secret service for the Hejaz region."

"The Hejaz Region, that's more than just Jeddah right?"

"You bet, Mecca, Medina, Yanbu, Taif" said Pete with a disbelieving frown.

Andy slowly shook his head as he spoke. "Well I tell you, you wouldn't want to fuck with his lot. They are armed to the teeth." There was a general sense of shock as the men exchanged looks with each other around the table.

"So how the hell did you get involved in all this?" insisted Jim.

Andy let out another stifled laugh. "Bugger me if I know. He asked me if I wanted to go on a desert trip with his brothers, but it turned into this big..." he paused, trying to think of the right word before continuing. "Well, it was practically a tribal gathering. We all arrived in these four by fours, the tents were already up and then the horse riding started and next came the gun displays. It was just incredible." He looked around the table and then took a big bite from his burger.

The men fell silent pondering this latest piece of colourful gossip about one of their trainees. In many ways it was not altogether surprising. Nabeel clearly was not the sharpest of the intake and privately both Jim and Alex had wondered what had been the criteria used for getting some of them onto the bank's 'graduate intake program.' In the case of Nabeel bin Ahmad, this was now slightly clearer.

"Sounds like you had quite an evening", said Jim.

Andy Whiteman pitched his head thoughtfully before responding a little distantly, "It sure was, cardamom flavoured coffee and Kalashnikovs."

Once the men had finished eating, a few more rounds of pinball were then played. Jim, Alex and Andy were once again all gathered around the flashing raucous machine and discreetly reconvened their unfinished conversation on Chris Barma's trading positions.

"Are you sure that going straight to Ed Moore is the right thing to do Andy?" asked Jim.

"Yup" he replied."

"We'll all be fucked if you do that Andy", said Alex as his last ball disappeared to a chorus of clanging and his pitiful score totted up on the machine.

Andrew Whiteman gave Alex a rueful look before adding simply. "I think we already are mate."

A few days later little more had come to light despite Andrew Whiteman's best attempts to get to the bottom of the story of Chris Barma's trading positions. The trail seemingly had run cold, though it remained an unspoken hot topic for all of the trading team and simmered away, unwanted and uncomfortable in their minds. The presence of this concern meant that the peculiar irony of their tenuous existence in the Kingdom had been given even sharper focus in their thoughts. For both Jim and Alex, it had increasingly become a source of much dark gallows humour during their shared journey to and from work each day. Their sense of unease and alienation was only made greater by the sharp paradoxes of daily life in Jeddah. At one level, the increasingly frequent images of burning US flags and angry demonstrators beamed from the West Bank or Lebanon onto the news channels and plastered over the front pages of the newspapers was disturbing enough. To this could be added the huge and vocal popular support, candidly expressed by almost all of their Arab colleagues, for the Palestinians' cause. This was qualified and underscored of course, by the constant reminder of a brewing anti Western sentiment which was most resolutely focused on the US and its citizens. It would have taken a particularly thick skinned individual not to feel doubly unnerved by witnessing all of this within the totemic trappings of a bank; almost the personification of the rotten heart of the new market driven world order so sanguinely described and accepted by Khalid Abu Anzi. Nevertheless, the real irony as far as Jim and Alex were concerned, remained the way that, despite this open hostility to the US and its citizenry, there remained paradoxically, such a

427

slavish desire for all the outward trappings of middle-America. The roads of Saudi Arabia were filled with huge General Motors and Chrysler SUV's which aimlessly drove from American style diners and fast food outlets to shiny marble clad shopping malls filled with Ralph Lauren, Donna Karan and Calvin Klein. Whilst Saudi men were always attired in their traditional white and the women were covered, head to toe in their uniform black *burqa,* the children of affluent Saudis were dressed as facsimiles of their Western counterparts. If imitation is the finest form of flattery then it seemed to Alex, that many in Saudi Arabia must be deeply and disturbingly conflicted.

As they made their way back from work, the car radio tuned to the ever present AFRTS was playing the Spice Girls' 'Wannabe' which was now the recognizable anthem for every preteen girl on Sierra compound. Alex quite liked it for there was something deliciously subversive about the concept of 'Girl Power' in an aggressively intolerant place like Saudi Arabia. Sadly he could not help feeling that the inane lyrics had a peculiar and unwelcome resonance as they coursed down the filling roads towards their compounds. The truth was that whatever the concerns that the traders had, they too were 'wannabes'. They too knew what they, 'really, really' wanted. They really wanted their bonuses and disturbing as Saudi Arabia was or was not, they were not about to quit whilst the large pay cheque due them was still in the offing. Disturbingly it begged the question of who was really being schizophrenic. Jim broke the silence. "Shit I hate this stupid song."

Alex stifled a guffaw, "It is pretty crap. This station drives me crazy."

Jim dug into his pocket, searching for his keys. "I'm really looking forward to going home for Christmas", he said with a low sigh. They were into the first week of December and familiar thoughts of the festive season were taking on much more significance to him. He could not help feeling a bit miserable as he only had yet another lonely evening on Lotus to look forward to. Thoughts of Christmas were making him homesick.

"Me too", agreed Alex while just managing to avoid the crushed remains of more yet more road-kill; strays were not an obvious problem in Jeddah, the roads were littered with their mangy carcasses.

"Yup, I just can't wait to get on flight BA 132 and high tail it out of this place for a bit."

"I know mate, only a few weeks to go" Alex replied. All the traders were booked on the same Thursday night flight out of Jeddah, a week just before Christmas. The men planned to have quite a party on the flight back to London.

Alex, as usual, dropped Jim at his compound before making his way back to Sierra Village as the evening light began to fade. Over the last few days security at the main gates to the compound had been stepped up yet again. A few more twists and turns and sleeping policemen had been added to the main entrance driveway. Alex slowly negotiated this freshly laid obstacle course, cut the engine and waited his turn. He managed to coax himself into a tired smile for the benefit of the now familiar faces of the security guards as they performed their checks in the failing light. One man searched under the car with a mirror whilst another opened the bonnet and examined the engine and the boot with a flashlight. Satisfied all was in order, they then signalled him on with a friendly wave. As he pulled away he cast a wary eye in the rear view mirror and realised that the increased security measures only served to raise yet further concern in him.

He drove slowly toward his section of the compound. Passing the central block he was struck by a peculiar sensation that the place now increasingly seemed to evoke. Despite the outward show of normality, he felt that a creeping siege like mentality was slowly forming within the compound walls. It was not just the heightened security, there was something else, but he just could not put his finger on it. Perhaps it was his imagination or more likely it was just that he needed a break from the place, but nevertheless a dawning sense of vulnerability was rising within him. Everyone knew that outside the compound walls, Westerners were expected to be respectful of their host's sensibilities. Western men and women were to cover themselves and to dress conservatively, not to draw too much attention to themselves. For the most part, the expatriates followed these rules very closely. It was foolhardy not to, the religious policemen, who roamed the streets and shopping malls, were on the lookout for signs of what they perceived as moral laxity or religious subversion. Arrests and beatings were the most likely outcomes for those unfortunate enough to fall foul of this unwritten code. When Alex had first arrived in Jeddah, he had found it all faintly ridiculous, even comical. His secular and rationalist armour had made him immune to these impositions, furthermore, and he was the first to acknowledge this, he reasoned that while he was a guest in this country, he should abide by its rules. Besides, life on the compound was supposed to be excluded from all of this, safe within its high walls, a Westerners' privacy and lifestyle was permitted, but that was before. Right now, Alex could not help feeling that it all seemed to be under attack.

He pulled up, got out the car and made his way through the now familiar dark pathways that were lit by a pearly array of glowing lamps around which moths and other unrecognizable flying insects were just starting to gather. Deep in thought, he strolled along the pathway, accompanied by the ever present low drone of air conditioning units and emerged into the poolside area beside his villa to find an equally familiar scene. His wife and some of her friends were still sitting around one of the tables beside the pool's edge. As he approached, he could now recognize the talkative group, their neighbour Andy Werner as well as Claire's other friends, Moira McDonald and Janet Howard were engrossed in their conversation, the sound of which easily vanquished the dull evening hum around them. He sidled up to them, unnoticed until his last few steps on the stone paving gave him away, Andy stopped talking.

"Hiya Alex!" said the German, who was first to see him.

"Hi there" said Alex a little more brightly than he had intended.

He was met with smiles and waves from each of the little group. Spilled around the women were the last damp remains of an afternoon spent by the pool. There was no immediate sign of any of the children, though the evidence of them being close by was strewn all around them in the form of multicoloured plastic debris and half drying towels.

"How was your day?" Claire looked like she had caught a bit of sun.

"OK and how was yours?" replied Alex looking around the table.

Moira McDonald broke into a laugh, "Just another day in paradise, right girls?"

This comment evoked some light laughter amongst the women and Alex broke into a nervous smile. His slight unease was unnoticed as just at that moment, three children came hurtling out of the Werner's villa and ran barefoot, raucously shouting behind each other across the pool area.

"Slow down you lot," Andy shouted out as they disappeared through the open door into the Bells' house.

"Well the kids are obviously having fun", he paused and turned on his heel, "I'll go and get changed, I've got a league game in fifteen minutes."

"OK darling", responded Claire with a warm smile as he started toward his door.

The women briefly watched Alex as he slowly strolled off. As he walked around the pools edge he recognised one of his sons sodden T-shirts, stooped down and picked it up. In the near distance, the excited tones of the conversation that he had interrupted, once more began.

Alex recognised the imploring voice and rolling diction of the Scot. "C'mon Andy, so don't stop there, tell us what happened next?"

"That's all I saw", replied the German.

"You actually saw them both coming out of the stationery cupboard?"

"Yes. I promise you I did, you know, the one behind the auditorium."

Alex wandered off; undoubtedly Claire would give him the low down on the most recent Sierra Village gossip later on that evening anyway.

Two hours later Alex was sitting at his dining table tapping away on his laptop. He frowned at the text on the screen. Freshly showered and dressed in dark blue shorts and a clean white T-shirt , he was still glowing with the after effects of a punishing squash match.

"Are you ready to eat yet?" Claire called out from the kitchen.

"Yup. I'm feeling pretty hungry now actually."

A few moments later Claire came through carrying a big bowl of spaghetti bolognaise and Alex moved around to the other end of the table which had been set for their meal. She delved deep in to the meat sauce and spooned out a large serving for her husband. "So are those cigars over there for Ed Moore again?" She was referring to the clear plastic bag containing a box of Montecristo cigars that was sitting the coffee table.

"Yes, Jerry gave them to me after the game."

Claire shook her head and frowned. "The guy must smoke like a trooper."

Alex gave a half cocked smile; Claire was not keen on his occasional habit of lighting one up himself. "Well he has an office where he can puff away to his heart's content."

Claire gave him a reproachful look. "You know smoking is not allowed in the dealing room," he added a touch defensively.

"I suppose he'll give you a couple again."

Alex shrugged his shoulders and returned her gaze with an open faced look, "Hey want can I do?" He hungrily forked the pasta and then gave an appreciative noise before adding. "This is good"

Claire smiled and chewed her own meal thoughtfully. Suddenly her face darkened and she gave him a serious look.

"Alex, you won't believe what I've just heard."

"What's that?"

"You know Andy has been working as a teacher's assistant at the school for the last few months?"

Alex remembered well enough, "Of course, she started at half term didn't she?"

"Yes that's right. Well, you'll never guess what she witnessed happening yesterday afternoon at the school." Claire's tone had slipped into a conspiratorial whisper.

Even though he was feeling exhausted, he was visibly tired after his exertions on the squash court; Alex just managed to muster a sufficiently inquisitive look. Despite this, the thought flashed through his mind that there was no way he could remotely guess what Andy had seen and he was not particularly interested to do so either. "What was it then?"

"Well she only saw these two teachers coming out of a stationery cupboard, can you believe it?"

"Stationery cupboard?" he said with a slightly perturbed squint.

Claire looked at her husband who appeared to be a little nonplussed by this latest piece of information, wide eyed she continued, "Oh c'mon, you know what I mean, they were doing it in there!" Her salacious emphasis on the verb at the end of the sentence left little to the imagination.

Alex raised his eyebrows in a questioning manner. Her expression indicated that the couple concerned definitely should not have been engaged in this type of extra-curricular activity. He let out a slight snort; it was just the kind of gossip that fuelled the idle poolside conversations of Sierra Village so well. However despite not knowing who the protagonists were, where there had been just tiredness, there was now a slight feeling of unease in him. Discomfort was percolating into his thoughts, his own recently exposed infidelity selectively filtering the information and exposing the stains of his remorse. He swallowed guiltily before he replied as evenly as he could, "Really?"

Claire gave him a long look. "Yes, apparently the woman has only been there since the beginning of term."

"I see..."

"Well, you might know her husband. Apparently he works at the bank, he's Australian.

Alex suddenly felt sorry for the big man from Wagga Wagga, "What's her name?"

"Maggie... Maggie Heaver."

Alex slowly shook his head.

The next day, Andy, Jim, Joe and Alex were huddled around the table, still waiting for the arrival of Pete. The Zimbabwean eventually arrived carrying a tray with his lunch, strolled over to them and sat himself down. The four men gave him a moment to settle himself before Joe broke the silence.

"Well, c'mon tell us then?"

Pete shook his head and gave a resigned little sigh. "It's come through alright, about two hundred and fifty million."

"What?" Joe was a picture of astonishment.

"That was the size of the second option position. It's just hit up on the FX account, booked in the wrong account apparently." Pete let out a sarcastic short grunt that posed as a laugh.

Andy shook his head with incredulity, "Shit, he'll never get away with it."

"I think he has nobody seems to have spotted it", replied Pete simply.

Joe rubbed his chin, "Fuck me, he was lucky."

"Don't you mean 'we'" corrected Jim.

Andrew Whiteman stood up. "Well that's just not right."

"What do you mean?" asked Joe.

"You know perfectly well what I mean. We let this go and we're all part of it."

"Oh come on Andy."

The Northerner gave Karpolinski a withering look. "You might think its OK, but I'm going to speak to Moore."

"Perhaps we all should," said Alex.

Joe looked alarmed. "You can count me out of it. Until you get something tangible this is still all just speculation."

"Well as I said before. I'll get the evidence." Andy then turned on his heel and then walked smartly out of the cafeteria.

The men fell silent watching the Mancunian disappear from view.

"Room for a couple of small ones?" David Lee and his Australian colleague, Bill Heaver, stood hopefully beside them.

"Jeez, what's up with you guys, somebody died?" asked the Australian.

"Not yet," said Pete dryly.

"Looking forward to Christmas then?" asked the red faced David Lee.

Jim perked up at this. "Sure am."

"On tonight's flight then?"

"Yup we all are," responded Jim.

"Good for yous," said the Australian.

Karpolinski finished of his drink, "How about you Bill?"

"We're off to Dubai. I got a great deal for a week at the Jumeira Beach Resort."

"That sounds good," said Alex with a smile.

"Yeah, the missus doesn't want to go back to Oz for Xmas, so we figured we'd do a bit of the Gulf instead."

"How is Miss Heaver enjoying it here?" asked Joe with a grin. Alex suddenly felt a slight unease creeping over him. Heaver looked a little taken aback by this. "Seems to like it I guess."

"Well Christian certainly likes his new teacher. At home it's nothing but, Miss Heaver says this and Miss Heaver says that."

Recognition suddenly flooded over his bushy browed features. "Ah yeah of course, your boy's in her class."

Joe rolled his eyes apologetically and continued smiling, "Yes the middle boy, he's quite a handful."

Heaver nodded before returning to enthusiastically tucking into his lunch.

"What does she teach?" asked Alex.

"She specialised in Drama," replied Heaver in a matter of fact way.

"Ah, that explains it," said Joe thoughtfully, before brightening. "Has she joined the Jeddah Players then?"

The expatriate amateur dramatics group was also based at the school.

The Australian chewed more slowly now and seemed deep in thought. His wife certainly spent a lot of time late at the school these days, marking school work or rehearsals, whatever it was she was invariably busy. A couple of times he had gone to pick her up and had found she had already gone to rehearse some part at someone's house or was hidden away somewhere doing 'back stage organization', as she called it.

"What play are they working on at the moment?"

Heaver rolled his eyes, "You'd like it I'd expect." His tone implied he certainly didn't.

Joe gave him a quizzical look.

"Bloody 'Blithe Spirit,'" he snorted derisively.

15. On the Inside

Alex's eyes swept around the airport terminal looking for the familiar faces of his workmates as he walked in the direction of the gate where his flight was scheduled to leave. He was not in a particularly good mood when he set out to the airport, now he definitely was not. The announcement that the flight was delayed by an hour and a half had been especially galling. Scanning the faces in the near distance, the departure lounge was not that busy, he caught the unmistakable hunched shape of Jim perched, on a stool by the bar. Alex wandered through the area that had been themed into an 'English Pub', its walls covered with kitsch mirrors, faux horse brasses and the lingering mixed aroma of stale beer and disinfectant.

He placed a friendly hand on the man's shoulder, "Hi there matey."

Jim, nursing a Guinness and a smouldering cigarette, was reading the Sunday Times. He turned and broke into a big smile and the two men shook hands warmly. "Hi there and a Happy New Year to you."

"You too" said Alex dropping his hand luggage down.

"Seen anyone else?"

"Yeah, Pete is over at the newsagents getting something to read on the flight." He nodded in the direction of an empty stool where an almost full pint of ice cold lager was sitting collecting condensation.

Ninety minutes later and several rounds of lager and Guinness to the good, the three men wandered merrily over to the departure gate. Unlike other passengers flying to less restrictive destinations with a duty free allowance, the men from Jeddah had to carry theirs inside them. They had made a fair effort to do so too, their last chance saloon for a final legal drink had not passed them by. While they stood awaiting their turn, Jim caught sight of a familiar face and suddenly called out in an deliberately over the top south London accent, "Oi Andy, all right there mate!"

Andrew Whiteman, who had been sitting quietly reading a book, looked up on hearing his name and turned, as did several other waiting passengers, to see his three colleagues waving at him. He raised his arm in acknowledgement and after passing the final check point, Jim made a beeline straight for him. Robson dropped his voluminous canvas bag with 'Red Sea Divers' scrawled in huge lettering along its length onto the floor with a heavy thump and slumped into the seat next to the Mancunian.

"How are you then?" Jim had a wide smile plastered across his features.

"OK, where were you guys then?" asked Whiteman half rhetorically. It was pretty clear where they had been.

"The old 'Rub a Dub'," replied Jim falling back again into his Mockney accent.

"How was your Christmas then?"

Andy rolled his eyes.

"Don't tell me, it was a slice, right?" said Jim using the Northerner's pet parting phrase.

"Yeah, it's been a slice," replied Andy with a tired look.

Whiteman gave Pete a smile as the blonde haired man sat himself down opposite him.

The Zimbabwean gave a nod and a polite smile. "Hi there, how are you Annie?"

"Very well thanks Pete," replied the woman.

Jim leant forward to look past Whiteman and pulled an anguished expression. "Oh hell, I'm so sorry Annie, I didn't see you there."

Annie Whiteman smiled and shook her head self deprecatingly. "That's alright." She was in a good mood most the time these days, pregnancy suited her.

Last to sit himself down was Alex, who sauntered through, four pints heavier and sat himself next to Pete. He gave the Whitemans a sheepish grin, "Hi there, Happy New Year to you two."

"Thanks very much Alex and a successful one for you too," replied Andy a little stiffly.

Alex looked up and saw the familiar features of his fellow compound dweller from Sierra village, John McDonald.

The Scot responded with a smile, got up and wandered towards the little group and then exchanged friendly greetings with the little gathering. McDonald sat himself down next to Alex.

"I should have got a later connecting flight from Glasgow," he said wryly.

"Don't worry about it. I'm on the wrong flight," replied Alex with a wicked grin.

"One way ticket to Palookaville," countered the Scot.

"Tell me about it," said Pete.

They sat there for a moment in silence before Jim spoke, this time in a voice that could have come straight off the American Forces radio station, irksome sounds that the men would soon be listening to.

"Well folks, here we are and it's, 'Space A, yes we've got it!'"

There were smiles all around at this, though Annie Whiteman looked a trifle confused. "What is it with that 'Space A' thing on the radio?"

"Space available my friend, get your cheap flights to the worlds hottest holiday destinations and I really do mean hottest folks!" Jim's rising intonation and sharp suited voice was just like the perma-tanned, blow-dried sounds you find on day time television quiz shows. This last comic turn brought all the men to open laughter.

Alex thought for a moment before joining in with his own imitation, "Yes indeed folks, you lucky winners can fly in a Hercules C4 for nothing to the middle of nowhere, strapped in beside a three hundred pound gorilla called Mike and a consignment of fruit flavoured condoms courtesy of Uncle Sam."

"What type of bomb would Sir prefer, smart or dumb?" simpered Jim as effeminately as he could manage, to much raucous guffawing from both Alex and Pete.

Their laughter subsided and Alex, wiping a nascent tear away from his eye turned to catch the disapproving look of another passenger. He looked away, a sense of déjà vu suddenly overcoming his previous alcohol fuelled light heartedness. He turned back to look at the man again, mid thirties, bespectacled and wearing a heavy business suit, with his overcoat primly folded on his lap. He was unremarkable except for his slightly superior expression. In a flash the dark thought crossed his mind, that was exactly how he must have appeared to those 'workers' when he had gone off for his interview the previous year. For a short instant Alex thought about getting up and giving the man a tip about the cab ride into town but thought better of it when his smile was met with a look frostier than the January weather outside.

445

Ramadan, the ninth and holiest month of the Islamic year was always a difficult time for Omar; he just seemed to pile on so much weight during the holy month. This year it was worse than usual. The abstention from food during the day was not the problem, he could maintain the fast fairly easily, but the huge hunger it invoked always drove him to over eat once the nightly *Iftar* feast was on offer. It was a time when relations and close friends would always be around the house in the evenings and then the eating and chatting would go on late into the night. This year's though, had been even more difficult for Omar. Rather than the usual polite easy going conversations of the past few years, the almost permanent presence of his brother in-law, Abdul-Rahman bin Hajez during the month, had become the source of much stress to him. In Omar's case, this discomfort also led to overeating and as he looked at himself in the mirror that morning, before setting off for work, he could clearly see the unwelcome signs of yet another developing chin. He stepped back and squinted at the mirror, the steam from his shower and his poor eyesight ensured that his expanding girth was, mercifully, not quite so apparent. Turning sideway on, he took a big breath in and pulling in his stomach myopically examined himself. He relaxed and let out a heavy sigh, who was he fooling? It was not good and he resolved to lose some weight as soon as *Ramadan* was over, which he consoled himself, was not too long.

Hastily dressing himself, he quickly made his way into the dark gloom of the kitchen before helping himself to some fruit and then downing two large glasses of water. The gloom lifted as the dawning light of the day started to break through the blinds and he stared at the empty tumbler in his hand before then diverting his gaze out of the window and wondered what his father would have said if he had seen him just then. The old fellow would not have approved of his haste. "You just made it my son, but it was not well done", those would most likely have been his words. To his father drinking water in a standing position was lacking in proper respect for the precious commodity and he would always say so. His own father was strange like that, he would invariably insist on sitting down before drinking any water and most times and particularly in the presence of guests, there was a very precise form of behaviour. Firstly he would grip the glass with the force of a strangler, before saying, "In the name of Allah, the Compassionate, the Merciful", then he would let the water touch his lips and then swallow it all in big throaty gulps before uttering a satisfied grunt, thumping the glass back down on the table and saying, "Praise be to Allah." If there was someone else with him, they would then politely respond, "Pleasurable and health", to which his father would then reply, "May

Allah make it pleasant to thee." Omar stood pondering this and then placed his own empty glass back on the table just as his son entered the kitchen.

"Good morning, my son."

Mohammed gave his father a stern look, day light was flooding into the kitchen and he immediately felt contempt, it was clear to him that his father had again failed to maintain the *Ramadan* fast properly. He stared at the glass tumbler and then replied with barely concealed scorn, "Morning."

Omar's own eyes fell to the empty tumbler before he flashed a look of wounded anger back at the young man.

"Back from the mosque?" he asked with considerable restraint.

Mohammed Al-Hamra nodded, "Yes father," before picking up some books and papers and purposefully walking towards the kitchen doorway.

"School work?" asked Omar hopefully, but his son had already gone.

Mohammed strode on back to his room. He carefully placed the books on his bedside table and then lay back on his bed, he would study them later, now was not the time. He closed his eyes against the frustration that had suddenly welled up within him. He knew that he was being difficult with his father but he felt he had every right to be and in his own mind, there was simply no other way. After all, had not he just turned eighteen and was it not about time that his father understood that he could not be like him, even if he had wanted it? No, he would be his own man and good God fearing Muslim, nothing more and nothing less. He opened his eyes and stared at the ceiling still deep thought, remembering the words of Abdullah Bawani. The Preacher was right, the world that his father believed in, simply just did not exist. His father's world was a ridiculous, childish place where it all was for the best. The truth was that this world was cruel, evil and unfair; there was nothing but injustice and as he was quickly learning, there was only one way to deal with it and that was head on just as the *Alim* was always saying. Mohammed sighed, the *Alim* had said the path to righteousness was a hard one and as usual he was not wrong, his legs ached and his head felt so heavy, he closed his eyes as the fatigue of his sleepless night started to overcome him. It had been the first of several long nights to come and he had been awake for all of it, praying at the mosque with several other men throughout that night. As the *Alim* had instructed them, the last ten days of *Ramadan* are a time of special spiritual power as everyone tries to come closer to God. The night that the Koran was revealed to the Prophet, known as the, 'Night of Power', when most ordinary Muslims would pray all night, was still a week away, but the *Alim* had implored them that they should treat all of the last ten days as just as important.

449

"You must purify your heart before Allah," had been his words and Mohammed intended to follow the *Alim's* instructions to the last letter.

Exhausted, he turned and checked that his alarm clock was properly set, he would have a couple of hours sleep, school started at ten during the holy month, so he had a chance to recover. He would sleep again in the afternoon if he needed too. In the background he heard the familiar sound of his father's car starting up and rolling over the gravel of the driveway. "One down and nine to go", he whispered to himself before letting out a long slow breath and falling soundly to sleep.

For the men of the IAB proprietary trading team, *Ramadan* was a tedious time. Whilst prayers times, the closing of shops and restaurants and the call of the *Muezzin* were a constant oblique reminder of the nature of the country they were living in and the significant part that religion played in it throughout the year, *Ramadan* was quite different. As far as Alex and his colleagues were concerned, during *Ramadan* in Saudi Arabia, the country all but closed down during day light hours. Admittedly it then went into dizzy life as soon as the sun had been chased from the skies, but this dizziness, as Jim Robson had once wickedly remarked, was induced by hypoglycaemia, with streets full of marauding families looking for the nearest sugar rush. As far as they were concerned, it was certainly no Mardi Gras and more saliently, there was no escaping it.

In IAB itself, the mandatory fast meant that the canteen was closed for the whole of *Ramadan* and since all the restaurants were also firmly shut, the men were compelled to go elsewhere if they wanted lunch. Fortunately, the Italian Consulate, complete with its own restaurant and located only a very short drive from the Bank, was available to them. Jim, Andy, Pete and Alex would troop out each lunchtime and return an hour and a half later, bellies filled with Italian fare. Sometimes they would get rancorous looks from their Arab colleagues as they departed or returned; sometimes little half smiles and looks that conveyed that those they left behind wished they too could go.

"Off to lunch then gentlemen?" Omar, just entering the floor, had opened the heavy glass door to the trading room and waited there holding it open for them to pass through.

"Yup," replied Jim for the men, "You're welcome to come." He gave the rotund Arab a cheeky wink.

Omar grinned at this, "I do like Italian food, but unfortunately, not today."

Jim paused and gave the kindly Arab a warm smile. "After *Ramadan* then, OK?"

"Most certainly," replied Omar with a good natured nod.

The men passed by and Alex who was last to go through thanked him for holding the door open.

"Enjoy your lunch," said Omar and he walked off towards his seat.

The men had been back in the Kingdom for the best part of a month and their return journey was already a distant memory. The men's families had only just recently arrived for the start of Jeddah Prep's spring term. Claire had been loath to leave England and had arrived with the kids the day before school started. Any slight novelty of living in the Middle East had worn off long ago and all she was looking forward to was returning to England for Easter. She hated it, but as she said almost every day to herself, at least Alex was due a good bonus.

As the men made their way into the restaurant and were shown to their now habitual table, the chatter amongst them was increasingly centred on the forthcoming bonus announcements, due at the end of the month. The only concern that they had was that they still had not seen the final year end numbers for their group as a whole. Given all the worries they had back in December, this was more than a minor irritant. This unease was further fuelled by the continued absence of Chris Barma, who was still on holiday.

"I really need to get a break from this place." Karpolinski said with emphasis once the conversation had fallen silent. .

"Are you planning to get away then?" asked Pete.

"I'd go tomorrow but the kids have school and everything. God knows when." His voice tailed off gloomily and he looked glumly out of the open doors that looked onto a pretty courtyard.

"*Alhamdulilah.* My friend, *Ramadan* is nearly over," Jim said with an attempt at brightening the mood of the little group.

"Not for another week at least." Joe was not about to be cheered up that cheaply. "Bloody fanatics, the lot of them."

The men looked around the table at each other.

"Oh c'mon they're not that bad," Jim replied with a half smile.

"Oh you think so do you?"

Jim gave Joe a querulous tilt, "Not really."

"I think you just need a break from here," said Alex trying to lighten the darkening mood.

"I need a break alright, but I'm telling you this place is totally fucked and Islam is the cause of it all."

Alex cast a furtive eye around the room, fortunately there was no one else around so this last comment had gone unheard except for those around the table.

"Oh come on, all religions are the same," said Pete, his voice was deliberately measured.

"Oh no, they're not, just look around you, Islam is a religion on the rise. Its winning converts among the poor and the needy, from Africa to Indonesia. Do you know that it's the fastest growing religion in America, particularly in American   jails?"

"Is it really?" questioned Pete with what seemed to Alex more like sarcasm than irony.

Joe sighed and looked with resignation out of the window.

Jim raised an eyebrow and he spoke with studied evenness, "You mean amongst blacks then?"

Joe shook his head, "It's not a race thing Jim. It's the politics of the underdog and the marginalised. It's becoming the socialism of our time, with an ethic that appeals to the oppressed and we..." Karpolinski thrust his finger at Jim, "people like you and me are its number one enemy."

"Oh come on Joe," said Pete as he signalled for the bill.

Joe shrugged his shoulders. "Well you can believe what you want Pete, but I'm telling you this place is fermenting religious fundamentalism and one day it's all going to blow up."

Pete turned to face Joe, his voice was betraying his frustration. "Mate, this place will never blow up as long as the Americans are running it."

The men fell silent as the bill was brought to the table and they searched trouser pockets for wallets.

Alex put down his espresso. "When is Chris due back?" It was the first time the boss' name had been mentioned that day, though he was not far from the men's minds, December's events had left their mark.

"As far as I know, he's not back until the middle of next week," replied Pete.

"I can't believe he managed to take off practically the whole of *Ramadan*." Joe gave a little movement of disbelief before continuing. "He didn't mention he was going for that long to me, mind you that's not so surprising, he barely spoke a word to anyone."

"Maybe he's done a runner." Jim said half seriously.

A sardonic chuckle broke out amongst the little group at this last remark, only Andy, whose face featured the merest shadow of a smile, remained silent.

"No, he'll be back," said the Mancunian with a quiet authority that immediately grabbed the other men's attention.

Joe wiped his mouth with a napkin and gave Whiteman a piercing look. "What makes you so sure?"

The other men all turned to look at Andy, who at first responded with a slightly belligerent pose before shrugging his shoulders. "Just call it a hunch."

Poker faced smiles and a telling silence fell upon the men as they considered this last remark. The restaurant, half empty anyway and now with their own conversation silenced, seemed as mute as the grave.

Jim leant forward, "Did you speak to Ed then?" It was the question that had been uppermost in their minds for weeks since their return. Jim and Alex had discussed this very issue on their shared daily commute many times already, though none of them had dared to ask it before this moment.

"No" replied Andy simply.

Later on that afternoon, Alex was sitting alone at his desk reading another research report when he was disturbed by a familiar voice.

"The only problem I find is that it's so difficult to concentrate properly in the afternoon."

Alex turned to his left where the unmistakeable tones of Omar Al-Hamra had come from.

"I'm sorry Omar, what did you say?"

"*Ramadan*," he pointed to some papers he was holding in his hand, "makes it difficult in the afternoon to read this stuff." He shook his head like a drying dog and broke into a huge grin.

Alex grinned back, "Omar, I'd say that stuff is difficult to read anytime."

The Risk Manager rolled his eyes and nodded agreement vigorously. Seeing the seat next to Alex was free, the Arab took his place and presented Alex with his query regarding a trading position that Alex had just recently put on. The conversation they had was brief as it was a simple problem to resolve and the Risk Manager tiredly put down his pen onto the pile of computer reports he had been leafing through.

"How are you anyway?"

"Not too bad Omar and you?"

"Hungry," he smiled.

"Well, *Ramadan* is nearly over isn't it?"

Omar showed agreement at this before adding, "It's good for the soul, you know, what will you be giving up for Lent?"

"Lent?" Alex was slightly taken aback; he had long since considered himself as having lapsed into secularism but strangely found himself hesitating before answering, for at that moment he felt a sudden pang of guilt. "Chocolate perhaps," he added unconvincingly. He wondered for an instant if all the enforced piety around him was not just ever so slightly infectious.

Omar gazed at Alex and reflected on this for a moment, "So you are not a practising Christian?"

Alex heaved an apologetic sigh, "Not really a regular churchgoer as such." He smiled as images of the midnight

Carol Service he had gone to just a few weeks ago, came vividly back to him. He and Claire had laughed when their middle son had asked why the congregation had not all gone prostrate to their knees, when the vicar had asked them to pray. "Well, except for Christmas and maybe Easter," he added.

Omar smiled, he had his own recollection of a Christmas carol service. More than twenty years previous, he had gone along with several other students and had quite enjoyed the funny singing they did and then afterwards he had drunk mulled wine at a party in a student house. However the reason he remembered it so particularly was because that was when he had first met the young woman who was to become his girlfriend and subsequently, to his devoted astonishment, his lover.

Alex studied the thoughtful looking Arab, who seemed a million miles away at that moment. Omar suddenly came back to animated life. "Come Ye Faithful" he said brightly, recalling one of the hymns that had been sung all those years ago.

Initially Alex could barely conceal a look of perplexed surprise before giving Omar an acknowledging nod. "Yes, that's the kind of thing."

Omar returned Alex' confused look with his own lopsided smile and let out a short little sigh, he was still thinking of his old girlfriend Nicola and wondered for an instant what she might be doing. Married with kids like him most likely, life was funny, he thought, without the slightest trace of humour.

Alex imagined that Omar had probably seen some film with carol singers in it, something with Jimmy Stewart or Bing Crosby, all full of fir trees and the feel good factor. "I didn't have you down as a carol singer Omar," said Alex, eyes narrowing mischievously.

Omar recalled the smell of damp clothes and the dank mustiness that greeted him that drizzly December day in the little church in Newcastle over two decades previously. "Not exactly, but I have been into a church, as well as some of your cathedrals," he said with obvious satisfaction before momentarily pausing to remember their names. "York Minister, Westminster Abbey, Canterbury Cathedral" there was a touch of pride in his features as he counted off the names.

"York Minster and Westminster Abbey," corrected Alex, simultaneously touched and impressed by this latest revelation. He was now starting to feel a little guilty of his presumptuousness. Omar was not some crazy fundamentalist and yet Alex had found himself slipping into the worst form of prejudice, Karpolinski's lunchtime rant was still ringing in his ears.

Omar gave Alex a slightly reproachful look. "There is much more in common between our faiths than there are differences, you know Alex?"

"I suppose so," said the banker without much conviction.

"Whoever kills an innocent soul, it is as if he killed the whole of mankind.'" That's what it says in the Koran. Just like the Bible, it is about how to live well together, no?"

"I suppose so."

"Of course so my friend, Christians and Muslims are like two wheels of a bicycle. Together we are bound by a single chain of monotheistic belief, a common philosophy and shared values. It is the same with the Jews, for it is the same God that we all believe in."

Alex threw a look of astonishment at this. "Jews as well?" he had thought that all Muslims and particularly Arabs, loathed Jews. As far as he could see, it seemed to be the only thing that united them.

"I'm not talking about Israel," replied Omar. "That is another matter, but we are all people of the same book, we are all the sons of Abraham."

"All the sons of Abraham?" Alex shook his head slowly and thought about this last comment. "I suppose we are," he said at last.

"Indeed we are," said Omar, radiating bonhomie as he collected together his papers, got to his feet and shuffled off towards his office.

460

Ed Moore set down his drink, picked up and drew another large mouthful from the cigar he had been smoking. He slowly blew out a large blue tinged plume, "Seven and a half million you say?"

The crew cut Lorenzo Evans puckered his lips and cocked his head. "Yup, that's what Langley should expect to see come through the usual channel."

Moore briefly scribbled some letters and numbers on a piece of paper beside him. "OK, I'll look out for it."

Evans took a sip from the glass of whisky that Moore had poured out for him. It had been a long day and these weekly briefings with him were always somewhat stressful even though they had now become pretty much routine over the last year or so. Their first meeting had been edgy and business like and Evans had assumed that the man would eventually loosen up. At that first meeting, when Moore had offered him a drink he had assumed the tubby Treasurer would open up a bit, but that was not the case at all. Moore always offered a drink but never came close to finishing his own. In fact it seemed to Evans that the man barely ever touched it. Evans had been warned the banker was a major tight ass and so it had proved to be. Despite this, Evans was periodically still not immune to trying to make conversation.

"How're things down on the ranch?"

Moore looked bored, "You know Lorenzo, the same as usual."

Evans took on a thoughtful expression and briefly reflected that he had no real idea what the, 'same as usual' actually meant with Moore, "Right," he acknowledged with dull resignation.

Ed Moore blew out another blue ring of Cuban smoke and looked at his chunky watch, a heavy set Rolex and one of his few ostentatious belongings, paradoxical since anything less would have drawn attention to the Banker in the rarefied world of high finance in the Arabian Peninsula. "Is there anything else?" It was his usual expression to signal that their meeting was at an end.

Evans swallowed down the remainder of his drink, the ice had barely melted and chimed away as he set the tumbler back down on the table beside him and started to get to his feet. "No, that's all, Sir," he croaked as the burning sensation of the bourbon ran through the back of his throat.

Moore raised his eyebrows and gave him a questioning look.

Evans pulled an apologetic expression, "Sorry."

Moore put down his cigar and got to his feet. "Well, have a good evening Lorenzo."

"You too… Ed."

In the darkness of the chilling evening, Ed Moore waited and watched Captain Lorenzo Evans' car pass through the villa's high gates, which then automatically closed behind the disappearing tail lights of the car. Moore pondered for a moment before retracing his steps, Evans might not be a bad military officer, but he was a less than perfect intelligence liaison operative. He stuck out like a sore thumb. Not only did his stiff bearing and forgetful insistence on calling Moore 'Sir', make Evans less than ideal for the job, but he was also prone to discussing previous assignments and missions. Perhaps it was just that the younger man was trying to impress him, but such talk was always a risk. In Moore's experience, the past was always worth forgetting. Live in the now and just maybe you would see tomorrow, that had become his own bedtime mantra and to date, it had served him well enough.

Returning to his chair, Moore sat down and took a long draft from his still smouldering cigar. He closed his eyes in thought, mentally filing away the information Evans had just given him before slowly reopening them, satisfied that everything was now carefully ordered in his own mind. It was not a great effort for him because he was accustomed to it. It had been a long time since it had been anything other than this way, in fact, it was hard to remember anything other, though it had been a strange genesis.

Ed Moore was not actually a CIA employee, but he may as well have been so. A single child, at school he had always excelled at languages and with the help of one of his teachers he had successfully managed to get a deferment from the Vietnam draft despite being poor. He went on to college, where he had studied French and Spanish and graduated top of his class. His success, like most of his early life was unnoticed by his alcoholic mother, who never even made it to his graduation ceremony. In the summer of 1968 immediately after graduation, the draft letter arrived and after a quick assessment, he was on his way to the cross service Defence Language Institute at Monterey in California. Parting with his smart East Coast girlfriend had been difficult, but worse were her later accusations that he was now bombing babies in Hanoi. His aptitude at languages was again proven when having taken and completed the initial course in Vietnamese, he was then put on an accelerated program and within eighteen months he was teaching soldiers and airmen basic Vietnamese. The prospect of being part of the next Tet Offensive was a powerful motivating force and all he had to teach was, 'What is your name?', 'Hands up or I'll shoot' and 'Name, rank and serial number.' In the end he had, largely thanks to good fortune, managed to avoid any active combat role which ultimately, had always been his prime intention for despite his somewhat combative pug faced appearance, Ed Moore was not a violent man. He recalled how the other men in his section at the Presidio had good-naturedly taunted him that he was 'getting short', and how he had literally counted off the days to the end of his two year long conscription. He could barely wait for his enforced tour of duty to end, for California on the cusp of the seventies was not the place to hang out with an unflattering regulation haircut. There were the pointless verbal confrontations with Vietnam protestors and the disapproving looks in bars to contend with and it was all but impossible to get a date. Just a few weeks before he was due to finish his conscription his mother had died, killed in a drunken car crash. The funeral back in Missouri was attended just by him and his mother's sister. When he did eventually get out, he immediately signed up with the Peace Corps and started to grow his hair. Characteristically for Moore, it was not just some case of misplaced altruism or rebellion but it was also because he wanted to learn another language and that after the Peace Corps, graduate school was a real option thanks to their bursary scheme. The Peace Corps gave him an intensive three month course in Arabic, resurrected his French and then sent him to a school just outside Marrakesh, teaching English to dark eyed teenagers. It was during this time that he polished up both his Arabic and more impetuously, married his first wife. She was half French half Moroccan and the middle daughter of the headmaster of the school where he was teaching.

465

He finished his MBA at Northwestern and within three more years he had embarked upon his now long standing career in the Middle East. He had been in Tehran, a vibrant cosmopolitan city and living the high life, working for Citibank for over two years, when Ayatollah Khomeini breezed in from Paris and put an end to the partying.

The revolution that he witnessed firsthand was already well underway by the time that the banished cleric had returned in early 1979. By the time that the massed demonstrations of the early autumn occurred with cries of, "Death to the Shah," his employers quickly managed to arrange for his wife and two small children to be flown back to the States. He stayed to hear the new demands, "Khomeini is our leader" and "We want an Islamic Republic." It was the first time that he had heard the last one and thanks to his excellent Farsi, he was able to keep a very low profile while the tottering Shah's regime broke around him.

The declaration of martial law was the end game, he became indistinguishable from anyone else, as he let his beard grow and dyed his hair black.

Over the next few months the country gradually ground to a complete halt. The oil refineries shut down, as did everything else, right down to the bazaars. Throughout it all Ed Moore remained, discreetly making his way into the office, dressed as unobtrusively as possible and ensuring that payments to correspondent banks were being made.

By then Moore was already a familiar face at the embassy, where communications were secure and information was sparingly available and this was when his first exposure to the intelligence community occurred. In particular, a man simply known as 'Ollie,', who described himself as an advisor, wanted to know about the transfers that were being made from the Iranian Central Bank into the international banking system. At the third meeting with Ollie, the advisor had taken a couple of photographs of him, 'for good orders' sake' and then gave him a phone number to call if he was ever in serious trouble. At the time Moore had thought it was all faintly ludicrous, but he kept the number all the same. By the end of December he had personally seen over two billion dollars being transferred out of the country. Anyone who was anyone in the US sponsored regime was liquidating everything they had and the ubiquitous greenback balances were flying out of the country at a truly staggering rate. Everyone from the Shah down was salting away everything they possessed.

Oil was crucial and business is business. Ed Moore and most of Washington felt no long term damage was likely to occur. After all there have been worse regimes than Islamic theocracies that the US has managed to work with. It would all blow over.

Every day there were fresh diplomatic and business feelers being put out by US, but Ed Moore saw first-hand how they were all wrecked by a colossal act of foolishness; the unintended consequences of an act of kindness. The hated Shah, who was now diagnosed with terminal cancer, was absurdly admitted to the US for medical treatment in October. It was then that things turned very sour, very quickly. The fledgling Islamic Republic, bristling with indignation at this further provocation was finally tipped over the edge.

"Send him back to answer to the People of Iran, who demand Justice", Moore had listened on the radio as the spitting rhetoric of the newly appointed 'Supreme Leader' of the revolution spoke. With rising intonation, the aged cleric virulently exhorted his people to demonstrate against the United States, the so called 'Great Satan' and 'Enemy of Islam'. The septuagenarian Ayatollah and 'Time Magazine Man of the Year' was not about to be disappointed.

By the time that Moore noticed the menacing mood of the throng of people that had gathered around the US embassy for his weekly briefing with Ollie, a crowd of hundreds had already gathered. He couldn't even make it to the gates.

As it turned out that was an unbelievable stroke of good fortune for him, for the mood of the mob was already turning horribly ugly. That day he shouted, 'Death to American', 'Death to Israel' in his perfect Farsi as loudly as anyone else and made good his escape.

Later that evening he called the number given to him by Ollie, he was told to go to the Hilton the next day. That very next morning in the foyer of the hotel, he was handed a battered looking Canadian passport, a press pass and five hundred dollars. Ollie and his friends had organized it all. Within forty eight hours he was back in New York. Journalists, God bless them.

At the same time the Soviets were just into the first few months of their ill fated and costly invasion of Afghanistan. Like the US in Vietnam, it would take them ten years and four heads of state to eventually pull out, or at least, that is what the Americans sincerely hoped at the time. And just to help them along, they sent men like Ed Moore, a dependable cog in the necessary machine.

CIA money needed to flow to support both the resistance fighters in Afghanistan and the Iraqis in their war against the still stubborn Iranians. Naturally, the funds were sent to America's closest ally in the Middle East via its insomniac banking system. Ed Moore was at the heart of this murky process, discreet, trustworthy, the ideal banker.

Additionally the support of wealthy Saudi's was eagerly welcomed. As far as Washington was concerned, it was a case of the more the merrier. The claim by the Russians, that they were fighting a pre-emptive war against Islamist terrorists was met with derision and then by barely concealed glee.

By the mid Eighties it was time to really stick it to the 'Ruskies' and sending cash to the blood thirsty *Mujahedeen* to take back Kabul and Kandahar from the Kremlin was a good use of hard pressed US tax payers' money. If that financial burden on American citizens could be reduced, by no strings attached donations from the Arabian Peninsula, then so much the better. Amersaud was the necessary, legitimate and welcome conduit for all of this.

By the end of the decade, the closeness of interests between the Washington and Riyadh was indistinguishable, sophisticated arms and business deals consummated the two together. That is, until the Russians pulled out of Afghanistan, followed only months later by the systematic collapse of Communism, symbolised by the fall of the Berlin Wall that very same year. None of this had been predicted by anyone, including Ed Moore. Even his contacts at CIA headquarters in Langley had not anticipated the incredible speed of the Velvet Revolution, as the Wall came tumbling down like some latter day Jericho, releasing a clutch of dazed former Soviet satellites into the bright light of a new World Order.

This was bad news for Ed Moore. No longer needed, his bosses, forever changing as the bank merged, acquired and grew ever larger, suggested a year's sabbatical to start in September of that year, which he duly took. On his return, he was told he was no longer needed. Things had changed; it was a difficult time, they offered him generous terms and best wishes for the future. He sat at home watching Saddam Hussein's forces rolled unopposed into Kuwait and argued with his estranged wife.

Two months later, he was in the last stages of the divorce, when the call from the head-hunter came through. The bank, one of the biggest in the Middle-East suddenly needed a Treasurer. It had been no surprise for him since his contacts in the CIA had told him to expect as much. Within a month he was briefly and politely interviewed, though it was pretty much a foregone conclusion. In the wake of Dessert Storm, IAB's wealthy Saudi owners were left in no doubt that if henceforward they were to operate in the world's financial system then they needed to tow the line. The owners were "colourful" according to his CIA contacts, "but on our side". Irrespective of their hue, they were politely advised that they needed to appoint suitable competent senior management; the US authorities wanted someone they could trust on the inside. No fuss, they were just to do it. When the owners asked who might be an acceptable choice they were referred to the head-hunter, the shortlist was just that, one name, Ed Moore's.

Ed Moore took the merest sip from his still full glass of bourbon. He rarely drank alcohol, it did nothing for him

471

and he despised drunkenness, having seen enough of its effects as a boy on his mother. The bottle had been given to him as a gift by one of the many fabulously wealthy Saudi's that he knew and he allowed the alcohol to evaporate on his tongue as he mulled over the latest piece of intelligence that Lorenzo Evans had just given him. It was all standard operating procedure, money needed to be wired through IAB to pay for inventory that the CIA backed Panamanian company had purchased. Ed Moore did not ask too many questions, he pretty much knew exactly what the phantom inventories actually were; you did not need the brains of Abraham Lincoln to figure it out. Arms one way, drugs the other. He was now part of America's war on drugs, Afghanistan being the world's largest producer of opium seed, with over 30,000 hectares of poppy fields and the country was littered with makeshift narcotics processing laboratories.

Ed Moore looked at the scribbled piece of paper again before putting it into the heavy glass ashtray beside him and lighting a match. He watched the dancing yellow flames as they quickly licked up around the crumpled paper and turned his mind to his other pressing issue. While periodically his function may well have been to watch and report on the laundering of money into the banking system, he also had the actual day to day job of being a Treasurer and just recently things had gone irritatingly awry. As far as he could see, one of his hot shot traders, the one with the funny accent, had claimed that Chris Barma had been, according to the trader, 'economical with the truth.' Obviously alarmed by this accusation, Moore had discreetly asked Omar Al-Hamra to look into the allegations and the tubby risk manager had eventually unearthed the well hidden deception. Moore had initially been furious, one thing he did not need was a rogue trader and particularly the Head of his proprietary trading team. All he had wanted was for the trading group to quietly tick over and leave him to do his real work. This was now a problem and right then he had no real idea of how he was going to deal with it. Whilst his first response had been that he should confront Barma with the facts and then to fire him, it was not quite as simple as that. The yearend accounts had already been signed off by him and an internal investigation might end up with all sorts of new unforeseen problems. His job was to put out fires, not to light them. Besides, he like all the others was due his annual bonus, and an ongoing investigation would surely put paid to that. No, that would simply not do, he needed the money as much as he needed to try and sort out this mess as quietly as possible. Ed Moore stared disconsolately at the charred piece of paper deep in rumination and hoped that the solution he had been working on was going to work.

16. Hopeless Conspiracies

Alex was still chuckling as he hung up the line to Thomas Spethmen, the German sounded just like his brother, only without all the usual Willi profanities.

"What are you up to then?" Jim Robson asked with a slight glint in his eye.

Alex, still half smiling, turned and offered an apologetic shrug. "I was speaking to the brother of an old friend of mine who's getting married in June. The brother's organizing the stag in London."

"Sounds good."

"I'm sure it'll be great, but I don't think I'll be able to make it."

Jim's features clouded for an instant. "Why's that?"

"I'm not sure that I can leave Claire and the kids here while I go gallivanting around London for a long boozy weekend."

"Gallivanting eh?"

It was not a term that Alex would have normally used and he offered another apologetic shrug. "Well I could just imagine what Claire would say."

Jim smiled and responded with a resigned nod, "You have a point."

Alex gave a weak smile and looked around the trading room. It was practically deserted, save for the Westerners on the trading desk. "Is *Ramadan* ever going to finish?" he asked with tired frustration, changing the subject. The end of *Ramadan* meant that bonuses would soon be on their way.

Jim shrugged his shoulders and pulled a face that indicated that he knew as much as Alex. "I guess we'll know when Chris deigns to return."

Joe, who had been doing a crossword in the paper, perked up. "He'll be back in three days, I should think."

"Is that so?" said Pete with a slight note of irritation. The merest utterance from Karpolinski now seemed to annoy the Zimbabwean.

"I'd say so," responded Joe distractedly, while entering a few letters into his crossword. "Last night was the *Lailat ul-Qadr*, so *Ramadan* is almost over."

"The what, did you say?" asked Jim.

Joe was still focused on his crossword as he spoke, "The *Lailat ul-Qadr*, it means the 'Night of Power' and happens on the 27th night of *Ramadan*. It's supposed to be better than a thousand months." At last he looked up from his puzzle and grinned, turning his eyes around the room. "This lot will have been up all the night praying, reciting all 77,934 words of the Koran or whatever it is they do."

Even Pete smiled at this observation, before adding, "Last year the Mobile Cardiac Arrest wrote off his car, fell asleep on his way in to work apparently."

"I didn't think they made cars big enough for Kitari", volunteered Jim with a sly grin.

"Bloody great GM Suburban," replied Pete with a short laugh.

"That's the only car he'd be able to fit his bulk into," said Jim laughing.

"Him and his six kids," added Pete with disbelief.

Karpolinski's features had darkened. "They were in the car when he crashed it?"

"Of course not you Donut," Pete had pulled a sour face as he spoke. "I just meant that was the size of car he needed with such a massive brood."

Joe, who had taken the rebuff with his usual insouciance, nodded understanding before adding. "Just another average sized Saudi family then."

A brief pause fell upon them as they thought about this latest image.

"Did you know that the population in Saudi is growing at close to five percent each year?" Jim had spoken in a voice like Michael Caine and looked around the desk for a response to this observation.

"I'm not surprised in the least, you just have to look around this place." said Alex flatly, still glum about the missed stag party.

Joe had again returned to his crossword and spoke offhandedly. "That would mean that the population is doubling every fifteen years or so."

Jim was looking at his screen and blew a low whistle. The flashing digits showed that crude oil was getting sold again. "Shit, fifty odd million Saudis and oil at ten dollars, this place would fall apart."

Alex shook his head, "Well there's no way the State would keep funding them like this."

"Too bloody right, don't forget the number of princes that just keeps on rising, there's thousands on the royal payroll," said Joe with a sigh, finally giving up on the puzzle.

"Well oil had better pick up soon or this place is toast."

Joe shook his head in agreement with Jim. "Oh don't worry about that, it will. There'll be another war or something and it will be back to thirty dollars."

Pete bridled at this last comment. "And who exactly will be in this war then Joe?"

Karpolinski shrugged. "I dunno, does it really matter?"

"Well let's just hope it doesn't start while we're here eh?" Koestler looked at his watch in frustration, seemingly prompted by the thought of an imminent outbreak of hostilities. It was still an age before lunch and he looked around the deserted trading room. "I can't bear *Ramadan*, this place is like death when it's on. Worse than last year and that was bad enough."

"Pete, were you here through all of *Ramadan* last year then?" asked Alex.

"Yeah, worst luck. It started later last year," he replied with a slow shake of his bushy blond head.

"Really?"

Now it was Pete's turn to shrug. "Yup, the Islamic calendar is eleven or twelve days shorter than ours so it's always moving forward. I think that last year it started on the 11th of January so that's why this year it started on the 31st of December."

The men briefly fell silent while they considered this. Jim looked around the desk. "Anyone know where Andy is this morning?"

His question was met with blank stares.

A few days later, just as Joe had told them, the trading room was back to normal. "*Eid Mubarak*," said Alex' trainee with a huge smile while shaking the Englishman's hand warmly.

"And *Eid Mubarak* to you too Khalid," replied Alex, having watched the Saudis as they greeted each other. 'Happy *Eid* ,' indeed thought Alex with some relief, *Ramadan* was finally over. It had been the same with all the Saudis as they had returned to work, happy faces and warm embraces for their friends and colleagues. Most, like Khalid Abu Anzi and his family, had celebrated *Eid ul Fitr* with the ritual slaughter of a lamb, part of which was then donated to the poor. This last deed, the performance of an act of charity, being the fulfilment of the responsibility of *Zakat;* one of the Five Pillars of Islam and another important part of a good Muslim's life.

Pete was sitting, looking relaxed and chatting with his trainee, Rashid Abdel-Aziz. Alex watched with no little envy as the FX trader freely conversed in Arabic with the young Saudi. It was an impressive display made all the more so by the flashed smile and discreet wink that Pete cast him as Alex looked on. Unsurprisingly, Koestler was easily the most popular expatriate amongst the little group of Westerners and neither Alex, nor any of his colleagues, could begrudge him that this was a fair return on his investment in time and effort. Alex' own attempt to learn Arabic was lying, language tapes still pristinely shrink wrapped, in a corner of his lounge. That morning Alex scanned each of the faces of the men as they entered the trading room, looking for the appearance of Chris Barma. Sure enough, the oversized man came ambling into the dealing room with big smiles and handshakes interspersed with '*Eid Mubaraks*' and 'Welcome Backs.' Whilst the stock of the head of trading might have fallen with his own team, commensurately it had risen with the rest of the trading room. It was understood that the Prop team had done well and this in turn had only reflected well on him.

Barma, his face momentarily creasing with a slightly sardonic smile, gave his team a raised hand of acknowledgement and took his place at the trading desk. Easing himself into his chair, he turned on his desk monitors and started the protracted process of logging onto various systems. While waiting for them to come on line he cast his eye around the desk before fixing his stare on the empty position of Andrew Whiteman. Neither he, nor his trainee Nabeel bin Ahmad, were present. Barma turned to his side and spoke in his deep voiced, authoritative way to Joe. "Is Andy in today?"

Joe shook his head affirmatively, "Yes Chris, he's been off for the last week or so, but I saw him this morning. I think he's with Ed."

"Ed?" Chris Barma raised an eyebrow. Across the desk Jim and Alex exchanged equally questioning looks. Barma nodded his head sagely for a few moments before continuing, "…and Nabeel?"

Karpolinski made a short half laugh, "That I have no idea. You know Nabeel."

Chris Barma pulled a resigned face, like all the other men he did indeed know Nabeel. The Saudi was as likely to drift in late, looking half dead, as he was to not turn up at all. Nabeel bin Ahmad operated on his own terms and few

481

people who knew him were likely to cross him. Barma had been briefed by Ed Moore when the trainees had first arrived, Nabeel was a special case. In Saudi Arabia, you did not set yourself against a person like him, particularly one so closely linked, through direct family, to the feared security apparatus of the country.

"Ok, well we'll shelve the morning meeting for today then," said Barma as he returned his attention to his computer screen. "I've got a pile of emails to deal with anyway."

Later that morning, as Alex was walking back from the bathroom he caught the eye of Ziad Al-Makki, one of the money market traders. The Saudi gave him a curious look and broke into a warm smile, so Alex wandered up to the him. "*Eid Mubarak* Ziad."

The overweight money market trader huffily got to his feet and vigorously shook Alex' hand. "Thank you Alex and a Happy *Eid* to you too. How are you?"

"I'm fine thanks Ziad", Alex knew what was coming next.

"Very good, and how are the family?"

Alex smiled, these Saudi's were such a predictable bunch; the conversation gambits were always the same. "They're well thank you and how is yours?"

"Very well thank you Alex."

The Englishman nodded and was about to continue on his way back to his desk, when the Saudi gave Alex an odd look. He dropped his voice, "Alex?"

"Yes."

The Saudi stood up and put his arm around the Westerner guiding him away from earshot of the other Saudi's on the desk. He gave a furtive look around. "I have something that might interest you."

Alex immediately thought the Saudi may have some information about Chris Barma, "really what?"

Ziad dropped his voice to a whisper. "Do you like whisky?"

Alex gave the man a quizzical look "whisky?"

"Yes, Johnny Walker, Black Label?"

Alex shrugged, "it's OK I suppose."

The Saudi broke into a big grin. "Good, good, I thought so."

"Why?"

The Saudi bent forward and whispered in his ear, "I have some, would you like a bottle or two?"

Alex gave the man a wary look. "I might do." Ziad Al-Makki relaxed and looked very pleased with himself. Alex' gaze narrowed. "How much do you want?"

The Saudi gave him a wink, "Honestly Alex, I give you very best price...Six hundred fifty Riyals."

Alex restrained a snort. Over one hundred quid for a bottle of whisky, he would have to be mad.

"Six hundred and fifty?" Alex shook his head in dismay.

The Saudi suddenly looked very concerned. "You'll not get a better price." Alex looked unconvinced, but the fat Saudi was holding his arm, "Look, come with me, I'll show you."

Partly shocked, partly thoroughly intrigued, Alex duly followed the insistent Saudi out of the dealing room. They got into the lift and descended in silence down to the ground floor.

"Where is your car?"

"In its usual place" replied Alex.

"Excellent, very good", Ziad wandered over to his car and opened the boot. "See?"

Alex looked inside, there sitting in plain view was a case of Johnny Walker's finest. Alex counted nine bottles.

"How many do you want?"

Alex gave the Saudi an amazed look. "Err...I'll have one then."

The Saudi looked disappointed, "only one?"

Alex nodded. At a hundred quid a bottle, he was not that desperate. "Yes, just one thanks."

The fat money market trader shrugged. "OK, my friend" and he picked up one bottle, wrapped it in a plastic bag and gave it to Alex. Alex held it in his hand and suddenly felt very nervous. He scanned the car park for people, it was empty. The Saudi shut the boot, turned and gave Alex another big winning grin. "Any time, just ask me, OK?"

Alex nodded and walked uneasily over to his own car, opened the boot and locked the illicit alcohol in it. The Saudi gave the Englishman an expectant expression. Alex responded by delving into his pocket and pulling out his wallet. He handed over the money which the Saudi shoved into the pocket of his brilliant white *dishdashah*.

"Excellent, very good" said the Saudi as the two men walked back into the cool interior of the bank. He still had quite a lot to get through, he had over ordered for *Eid*, but, *Inshallah*, he should clear the inventory fairly soon.

"Well I'm, sorry to see you go." Ed Moore was as skilled a liar as ever.

Andy Whiteman got up and offered his hand, relieved it had been so straightforward. "Nice knowing you Ed and thanks."

"No problem. I hope it all works out for you. Keep in touch," replied Moore quickly releasing the Englishman's handshake.

Andrew Whiteman stepped out of the Treasurer's office with a light step, relieved it was done and started to walk towards the dealing room. The last three weeks had been an amazing whirl of activity and he still could barely

485

believe his good fortune. First was the unexpected phone call from Nabeel about needing to see him. The young Saudi had driven round to his house and picked him up, saying he had an uncle who wanted to meet him for lunch. They drove for about half an hour while Nabeel explained that his uncle needed some advice and that the man had heard many good things about him. Now this uncle wanted to meet Whiteman in person and Nabeel was pleased about his role in the introduction. As they drove, Whiteman imagined the man, probably some rheumy eyed, gun toting sixty year old Bedouin, looking for tips on stocks and shares. He figured he should just go with the flow, after all, he liked Nabeel.

Andy Whiteman was not easily impressed, but when the gates closed behind him and they finished the trip up the short driveway to the main villa on the private compound, he was mightily so. The huge Hacienda style villa, surrounded by beautifully manicured lawns spread before him and he was greeted by a white coated servant who immediately asked him if they would like anything; tea, coffee, a cold drink or something else perhaps? Nabeel had immediately asked for a whisky with lots of ice. They were shown into a large opulent room and seated with their drinks when the 'uncle' arrived. He looked not much older than Nabeel and was dressed in cream coloured chinos and a beautifully pressed, salmon pink, long sleeved open necked shirt. Clean shaven, with jet black hair and aquiline features, he looked like something out of a glossy magazine, the type that Andrew Whiteman had only seen in smart private dental waiting rooms.

"Sorry not to have been here to greet you, please forgive me, rather crass I know," he said with a winning smile. The clipped accent was very moneyed and very English. He introduced himself simply as Yasser and smiled warmly again, revealing a much less common English feature, perfect dentition. After ordering his own gin and tonic and a short conversation, he suggested they have lunch. Sitting by the poolside, Whiteman carefully listened to the urbane Arab as they ate salmon parcels and drank chilled Chablis. He discovered they had both been to Cambridge, missing each other only by a few years, his father was sick, currently being treated for liver cancer in Geneva, unfortunately incurable and consequently only on palliative medication. He gave a self deprecating shrug as he explained that he was now the acting head of the family and he needed someone to oversee his family's financial portfolio. He thought the private bankers they had in Switzerland were a bunch of 'gnomic thieves' and wanted a more hands on and directly accountable approach. Nabeel had given a glowing account of him as had others in the bank. It was a two billion dollar fortune and he needed someone to oversee it from within Saudi Arabia, someone just like Andrew Whiteman. The Mancunian, aware of where the conversation was headed almost choked on his fiddly dessert. Sure, he could have as much time as he wanted to think over it; that was quite understandable, it was a big decision. He said Nabeel had informed him of his wife's condition, congratulating him and hoped she was well. He recommended a private clinic in London and assured him that if he was to take the job then that would be arranged straight away. As he was leaving Yasser gave him his card with his mobile phone number and said he very much hoped to hear from him soon.

He had discussed it long into the night with his wife and after a bit of background checking he got back to Yasser Al-Dahrani. The second time they met, the discussions were much more detailed. He himself had discovered that the Al-Dahrani family had huge interests in everything from shipping to shopping malls, but it did not end there. The family fortune was worth many billions more than just the financial investments that Yasser had first alluded to. The financial package on offer alone was just too good to pass up, but there were a wealth of perks included, travel medical, housing. He could hardly believe it; in salary alone he had been offered precisely double what he was being paid at IAB with a very attractive bonus structure. Given the fallout from Chris Barma's phantom trading that he expected to see at IAB, it was an easy choice.

He had then gone to see Ed Moore shortly afterwards to get an update on the situation back at the bank and unsurprisingly his worst fears had been confirmed. Moore seemed to suggest that an internal investigation was now on the cards and that it was very likely the unit was going to be wound up. He said that as the whistle blower, Whiteman could expect to be treated well but that nevertheless, it was clearly not a good situation for anybody. When Andy Whiteman indicated that he was considering resigning, Ed Moore had looked a little pale but said that he could understand the trader's decision and that obviously he would do anything to help. Whiteman had asked if that was a serious offer and Moore had assured him it was. That was when Whiteman asked if he knew of the Al-Dahrani family. Ed Moore looked surprised, of course, he replied, everyone knew the Al-Dahrani Group, the family was closely linked to the Royal family and they were reputed to be one of the richest in the country. Moore's round face then had suddenly become slightly hawkish and he had asked in a faintly disbelieving tone why Whiteman was asking him this. Andy Whiteman in turn, gave the American a thoughtful look and admitted that he was considering an offer from them to act as their financial advisor. On hearing this, Ed Moore emitted a slight snort and a sceptical expression crept across he

489

features; the combined effect of which communicated that he thought such a claim to be highly unlikely.

"Well, if that's the case you'll hardly be needing any help from me," Moore had said with what Whiteman took to be the merest trace of affront.

The Englishman responded with an enigmatic smile before speaking. "I'll need a reference. You know how it works here Ed."

Moore paused and gave Whiteman a direct look before he replied, "That will be no problem."

Whiteman responded with an equally direct stare, "I don't want any Ed."

"I can assure you there won't be. I'll see to it personally."

A couple of days later everything had been signed and sealed. Andrew Whiteman was employed by Yasser Al-Dahrani and his wife was organizing her stay to the Wellington Clinic and a holiday to Sandy Lane in the Caribbean. That morning's meeting with Ed was the last he would have. He had gone in with the sole intention of formally tending his resignation to the middle aged American. Even Andy had to concede that Moore had been as good as his word and had smoothed the whole process for him.

Initially it had been one of his main concerns, but Ed Moore had, as promised, done all the necessary paperwork.

It had not been without its complications. Headhunting of key expatriate personnel between companies in Saudi was almost impossible. Work permits and visas could only be sponsored by companies and they were rarely accommodative in such cases. Normally an employee would have to resign, leave the country and go through the whole process afresh. Amazingly, Moore had managed to completely circumvent this process. As far as the Bank was concerned, Andrew Whiteman was a valuable employee who would be much missed and only wished him success in his future career, wherever that may lead him.

Whiteman walked the short distance across the dealing room and stood at his desk. He cocked his head and gave a rueful smile as he cast his eyes around the desk. Having been on leave for the last week or so while the last few details were being sorted out, his colleagues all returned his half smile with slightly quizzical looks. Alex, like all the others, watched him as he quickly riffled through his desk draw and then picked up his 'Manchester United, League Champions' mug. He took a last look at the desk and spoke in a low voice. "Well boys, it's been a slice" and with nothing more than that, he turned on his heel and walked straight out of the dealing room.

Alex turned towards Jim whose astonished features were already facing him. Alex let out an incredulous snort, "Did you just see that?" Jim just nodded, open mouthed with silent alarm.

Chris Barma, almost entirely unaware of what was going on around him, picked up his line which had just started ringing. It was Ed and he wanted to see him immediately. Barma got to his feet and walked slowly in the direction of the Treasurer's office.

"Sit down Chris, I've got something to tell you." Moore's face was impassive but his face was flushed and deadly serious.

The tone was not missed on Barma and he took the proffered seat the other side of the American's impressive desk and obligingly sank into its enveloping folds; even his immense bulk was overwhelmed by the cloying grip of the chair. Despite the supremely efficient air conditioning in Moore's office, Barma could feel small beads of sweat starting to break out on his forehead. He had a bad feeling in the pit of his stomach.

"Two things, first Andrew Whiteman has just given me his resignation, which I have accepted." Moore paused and minutely studied the features of the man sitting opposite him. "Secondly is there anything you'd like to say to me in the way of explanation?"

"Explanation?" Barma stammered.

Moore cocked his head though he remained resolutely silent and simply observed the reaction of the Head Trader. Only the American's facial expression changed, moving to a coruscating glare that Barma felt was practically impaling him into his seat.

"I don't know, was he unhappy or something?"

Ed Moore remained impassive, his face simply registering mild surprise at this latest obfuscation.

Clearly flustered Barma added, "Honestly, I can't imagine why he would have wanted to resign just before he was due to be paid his bonus."

The American's expression darkened at this latest offering, he slowly shook his head and maintained his intense stare on the man, silent, waiting for Barma to explain himself.

Barma finally shrugged, "Look Ed, I haven't got a clue why he would have wanted to resign."

"Are you trying to be funny?" Moore had the expression of an undertaker.

Barma just blinked and rubbed his sweating upper lip, his mind was racing ahead of him and he felt nauseous, as if he were suddenly being sucked down into an abyss. His bonus, his contract, his whole career; all were suddenly plunging into the sickening darkness of his fast rising despair. "Why, did he tell you?" he at last blurted.

Ed Moore paused before answering, looked down at the papers on his desk and slowly donned his half rim glasses. "Yes, as a matter of fact, he did."

"So what did he say was the reason?" Chris Barma sucked in the air like a drowning man and just managed to defray the panic and alarm in his voice with a supreme effort of will.

Moore's seeing the obvious discomfort on Barma's face relaxed; this was going to be easier than he had thought. "He claimed that there had been irregularities."

Chris Barma pulled a furrowed questioning look. "Irregularities, what kind of irregularities?" he suddenly seemed to revive on the slightly absurd sound of the word and Moore instantly regretted his choice in using it.

Ed Moore nodded, it was time to go for the kill. "Fraud."

Chris Barma froze for an instant. He had known all along that at some point he might have to face this very situation. Now that it was here, he felt grossly unprepared, yet he had played out his responses endlessly in his head for the last month or so. As time had passed he had become increasingly convinced that he had managed to get away with his clandestine actions and so he was quite amazed to be facing them now. The monthly accounts had been signed off well before the end of December; in fact, he had specifically stayed in the office over the last few weeks to ensure that nothing unpleasant was unearthed. In the end, nothing was, he had even managed to get the Back Office manager, Ali Bakra, to issue a written warning to one of his staff for failing to do his job properly over the phantom trades. When no money is lost, investigations are unnecessary, the trader's word was law; that was why this latest disastrous turn was so wholly unexpected.

Ed Moore had not intended to pussyfoot around, but he needed Barma to make the first move. To start with he needed the man to accept his guilt; it would then be a foregone conclusion that he should offer his resignation. Once this was done Moore could organise things. The Treasurer took off his reading glasses and sat, Solomon like, ready to pass judgement. If things went as planned, he expected Barma to be out of the building within hours and the country within days. Moore leant forward expectantly, waiting for the inevitable confession to tumble from the man's lips.

Barma sat, silent and still, almost bent double in the increasingly sickening embrace of the hideous armchair. He blew a long low sigh under his breath and his eyes narrowed in thought. Slowly he got to his feet and now stared back at Moore who was hunched over his desk, absolutely still, waiting for the trader to admit his actions and fall on his sword.

"So Whiteman has gone without his bonus?" Barma's muttered question was just barely audible.

Ed Moore chose to ignore this slightly incomprehensible enquiry. He was focused on hearing just one thing, the trader's admission of guilt.

Chris Barma cocked his head, a slim ray of hope had just flashed across his mind, temporarily holding back his ever darkening thoughts.

"You paid Andy Whiteman?" Barma almost added the word 'off' but did not and it hung unspoken between the men, like an imminent declaration of war.

The American's ice cool demeanour was suddenly under intense pressure and he almost crackled as a steaming rush of blood flushed his face to a hot crimson. "Whatever happened to Andy Whiteman is totally irrelevant, this is about you."

The earlier flash of hope that had raced through Barma's mind was swiftly changing into a dawning realisation. If Moore had chosen to hush Whiteman, then he might be prepared to hush him too. Then it struck Barma like a hammer blow, Moore might have as much to lose as he did if things turned nasty in an internal investigation; maybe even more.

Chris Barma suddenly stood tall and began to bristle with rising indignation. If Moore had uncovered his fictitious trades then why hadn't he come out and said so instead of talking of 'irregularities'. It was a high stakes game, his whole future was on the line and he was not going to throw his hand in without at least forcing Moore to play his own. Chris Barma screwed up his courage and his features as he spoke. "About me? I don't think so Ed."

Moore sucked in a sharp little breath at this and eyed the trader with undisguised rancour. The man was as brazen as any he had met and in his fifty odd years, Ed Moore had known some truly stubborn fools. He could see now that this was going to go down to the wire. "I don't think you understand what I am saying, your position has become untenable."

Chris Barma had spent most of his life with his back against some type of wall; dealing with untenable positions or indeed any other type of them was his stock in trade. "I don't see what is so untenable about making the budget. If you want me to go you'll have to pay me."

The American swallowed, this was not going to plan, not at all. He closed his eyes momentarily before once more fixing them on Barma, he would have to settle with plan B. "Sit down Chris."

On the desk there was eerie sense of unease. Initially there had been an instant buzz of worried speculation around the drinks machines located just outside the dealing room, about what was happening, almost as soon as Barma had left the desk. None of the men could figure out exactly what was going on. All agreed it was not good and that was over an hour ago. For the last half an hour phone lines were being quickly dealt with as the dealers went about their business with schizoid effort. The events unfolding about them meant that concentrations were almost entirely focused on what unknown things were going on just across the green carpeted dealing room in Ed Moore's office. Alex hung up his phone and tapped away at his keyboard, typing out a brief email.

While the Westerners were like cats on a hot tin roof, their Arab understudies seemed blissfully unaware of what was unfolding around them. "So what do you think of the Clinton stuff?" Khalid asked breezily, seeing that Alex was now off the telephone.

News of the Monica Lewinsky Affair had just broken, the wires were alive with jokes about Cuban cigars and the images of an uneasy President were filling all the television screens.

Alex turned to see Khalid, who was grinning from ear to ear, a copy of Newsweek, with a picture of the eponymous Beverley Hills Intern plastered over the cover, sat grinning on his desk.

Alex, thankful of the diversion offered by this, thought for a moment before replying. "I don't know, it's hardly surprising, he seems a bit of a ladies' man."

"Lady?" Khalid made a short laugh before then attempting to mimic the man's southern drawl. "'I did not have sexual relations', what a joke."

On hearing the Arab's fair attempt to sound like the President, Jim who had been listening to the two men, joined in. "I don't know about not having 'sexual relations', the way things look he won't have any relations," he said with a wolfish grin.

Alex shrugged, "Well it at looks like a bit of a set up, the tapes and all that stuff."

Khalid smiled with little humour, "What else can you expect from such an American President?"

Alex realised in an instant he had inadvertently fallen into the swirling world of conspiracies and doublespeak that Khalid so fervently believed in. He gave a rueful look before continuing. "Don't tell me you think it's another anti-Arab plot."

Khalid responded to this with another cheeky, taunting look, "Lewinsky, is that an Irish name?"

Even Jim guffawed at this, "Ah, c'mon Khalid, you're being ridiculous."

Khalid sighed, "My friends, you are so innocent."

Alex bridled at this patronising line, "Look, whatever you may think of him, at least his foreign policy has been good."

Khalid shook his head, "What American foreign policy?" he asked disbelievingly.

Alex hesitated before answering, like many Europeans, he liked Bill Clinton; the former Rhodes Scholar seemed more cultured and approachable than his predecessors. At least he did not come across as a scary nuke wielding redneck. "Well he's been instrumental in bringing peace to Northern Ireland and then there's Bosnia." Alex racked his brains for another example.

"…and there's the Oslo thing too," added Jim who had bent forward across the desk in order to take part in the conversation, also happy for the distraction.

The Arab watched Alex closely as the two men compiled the list and slowly shook his head, clearly unconvinced by their efforts. "Well I don't know about Ireland, but you can't be serious about Bosnia or Palestine?"

"He's stopped most of the killing and the horrific ethnic cleansing that was going on in the Balkans."

"Meddling and then only after practically all of the Muslims had been slaughtered," Khalid bristled.

"I think you'll find both sides managed to slaughter each other with equal brutality," stated Jim with an open faced expression.

Khalid Abu Anzi pulled a sour look and spoke with real bitterness in his voice. "Thousands died and nobody lifted a finger."

Alex was about to reply when his eyes caught the unmistakeable sight of Chris Barma walking across the dealing room floor. Alex studied the man's face as he approached for any clues as to what had been happening; from the look of him all was far from well. The big man came to a halt beside his seat, threw back his shoulders and stood there with a totemic expression, waiting for all the men's attention. Pete was the only one on a phone and he quickly hung up once the realization of what was going on around him had dawned upon him.

Barma started to speak; his deep mid Atlantic tones suddenly back in order. "I have a brief announcement to make." He shot a quick look around the desk, satisfied that he had all of their undivided attentions and thrust his chin out like a prize fighter before he continued. "Andy Whiteman has resigned for personal reasons." He looked around the desk again, only this time his eyes blazed with confrontation before he added menacingly, "I'll be looking for a replacement shortly."

The news was greeted with a telling silence as Barma slowly took to his seat. Each of the men fell into their own private thoughts, all that is, except Joe, who rubbed his chin and asked the question that all the traders had on the tips of their tongues.

"So, when are we going to know about bonuses Chris?" asked Joe with disarming simplicity.

Barma turned to his left and looked at the pockmarked Englishman, schoolboy acne had left its mark and Chris Barma examined him closely, almost as if expecting a fresh breakout. "You'll all know tomorrow."

As soon as they sat down to eat, the traders' low voiced conversation in the canteen that gloomy lunchtime was all about what had happened to Andy Whiteman.

"And he didn't say anything to you either?" Joe Karpolinski was still incredulous that Pete was as mournfully uninformed as everyone else. "I mean, you and he are pretty good mates aren't you?"

Peter Koestler closed his eyes and shook his head. In ordinary circumstances, Joe's persistence would have riled the Zimbabwean immensely, but in this new, intense and deeply unsettling environment that they now found themselves in, even Pete's nascent hostility to Karpolinski had waned substantially. "Joe, you know as well as I do that Andy kept himself pretty much to himself."

"I called his mobile, but he's not answering," added Jim.

"It just doesn't add up. Why would he quit before getting his bonus?" asked Karpolinski in the same insistent tone.

Jim rubbed his face with both his hands and shook his head, before answering Joe's virtually rhetorical question on behalf of the group. "God only knows."

"Maybe he found out that there are no bonuses being paid and just quit?"

"That just doesn't make sense either Joe. For fucks sake, I mean, surely he would have said as much when he left, wouldn't he?" Alex responded angrily.

Murmurs of agreement followed this before another oppressive silence descended on the men. Joe leant forward and holding his head in both hands, prescient as ever, spoke out aloud the thought that all the others were grimly coming to terms with. "Shit, I just know we're totally fucked."

Claire Bell could barely believe her ears. After all that the last year had thrown at her, this was the last straw. "I still don't understand. How can they do this?" Her eyes were blazing with frustrated anger.

"Darling, you know as well as I do they can and they bloody well have."

Claire shook her head with disbelief, "And why didn't you tell me about all this before?"

Alex looked humbled at this last accusation. "I didn't want you to worry, besides it was just a ..."

"Worry?" Claire broke into a hollow guffaw. "Don't make me laugh Alex," she said, glowering at him with narrowing eyes. "I know the real bloody reason."

These last words pierced Alex like a shard of glass, forcing him to bite his lip as he winced at the pain of the unspoken accusation. It did not need saying. It was not worry that caused him to say nothing about Chris Barma's wayward trading. It was fear; fear and cowardice to be precise. He knew his wife only too well. After all the disappointment and heartbreak of the last year he understood exactly what would have happened if he had told her of his concerns back in December. Claire would never have set foot outside England. Bringing Jim back with him and discussing it into the small hours had only delayed this inevitable confrontation. Claire was furious.

"This is the second time this has happened. At least in Paris I had a life." Claire's earlier accusatory tone had turned to angry bitterness.

"Look Claire, I'll make it up to you."

"And just how the bloody hell, are you going to do that Alex?"

Alex was keenly aware that this was not a rhetorical question. In the confusion that had descended upon him since the meeting with Chris Barma that morning, his mind was still foolishly trying to find something positive from the shockingly disappointing news. Exhausted and clueless as to how he was to make good his claim, he looked down at the ground, his shoulders hanging forlornly, like last year's decorations. His wife watched this display with rising indignation waiting for him to say the only thing she thought that he possibly could. To her it was obvious; they should all be on the first plane back to England that they could get, end of story. It had been a disaster, just exactly as she had told him it would be. She waited, frustrated with her husband's stubborn refusal to accept the facts.

"That's it. I'm taking the kids back to England. You can stay in this godforsaken hellhole as long as you want, but I've had enough of it."

"What?"

Claire gave her husband a withering look. "You expect me to follow you around to the ends of the bloody earth. You cart me and the kids to this, this..." Her anger still on the rise, she was genuinely, momentarily speechless with rage.

"Darling I..." Alex stepped towards her.

Claire Bell put out her arm, her palm raised like a traffic cop halting Alex in his tracks. She closed her eyes, both to calm herself and to avoid directly looking at him. "Don't fucking, 'darling' me Alex. I've simply had it."

Alex tried to adopt a reasoning tone, "Look Claire, we're both tired. Let's sleep on it and talk about it again tomorrow."

Claire shook her head slowly before she replied, "It already is tomorrow Alex."

17. Brothers in Arms

Less than a year ago and Omar would have laughed out loud at the suggestion, now there was nothing remotely funny about it. Foolishly, he had thought to himself, that he had experienced most things that a normal middle aged family man could reasonably expect to see out of life, but no, he was wrong, so very wrong. This latest turn of events had thrown him entirely and his senses seemed completely at sea. Frustratingly, all he found himself doing was rubbing his bushy eyebrows in fevered thought, having already polished his heavy spectacles to a translucent shining excess.

"But Abdul-Rahman, I've told him already that I… " Omar was running out of both energy and coherent arguments.

The voice on the phone remained as cold as the wintry wind of a desert night. "Brother, I know what you said to him, but he is a man now and we must respect his decisions."

Omar gave a derisive laugh. "But how is he to live? I…I won't support him you know." Al-Hamra was being far more direct with his brother in law than he had ever dared to be in the past.

Abdul-Rahman coolly examined his nails, as he spoke into the receiver. "My brother, I can assure you he will not need any help. Allah is most bountiful and young Mohammed will be fine here."

Omar slumped even lower onto the dining room table; the receiver still clasped to his ear and shook his head despairingly. He swallowed, emotion filling his words, "Abdul-Rahman, can you just put my son on the line again for me please?"

Abdul-Rahman covered the phone and turned to the young man and pulled a resigned expression. "He says he will not support you. You are to go home."

Mohammed bit his lip and looked down at the ground. Rising anger was filling within the young man; his father was just being ridiculously pathetic if he thought such stupid threats would work. "Tell him I don't need his support," he said without looking up, his eyes still defiantly fixed on the ground.

"But he demands to speak to you…"

Mohammed shot a look of anger towards the *Mutawwa,* who was watching the young man's every move.

"You can tell him I've got nothing more to say."

"Forgive me my young brother, but he is insisting." Abdul-Rahman's tone was precisely pitched to bridle the young man and the mocking open eyed look he gave him was a perfectly executed challenge. The *Mutawwa* held out the receiver like a school yard taunt and watched as growing indignation flushed across the young man's features.

"I repeat. I have absolutely nothing more to say to him." The words tumbled spitefully out of him and just as Abdul-Rahman Bin Hajez had hoped and planned, they were the only words that Omar heard on the line from Riyadh.

"Mohammed, Mohammed my son, please." Omar's desperate imploring was only heard by the *Mutawwa*, who gave the young man a quiet approving nod.

"I'm sorry my brother, you have heard him. I promise you, he will be fine."

"But Abdul-Rahman you must see, he's just a boy, he's …."

The religious policemen cut the banker short. "Omar, I will speak to him, but please try to understand."

"My brother, please I beg of you."

The *Mutawwa* was once again examining his nails. "I will call you in a few days. Goodbye my brother, peace be with you."

Omar Al-Hamra closed his eyes and hung on, listening to the metallic drone of the disconnected phone line, as tears started to roll down his heavyset cheeks. Momentarily, his anguish had totally overcome him and he drew in heavy breaths, now painfully aware of his own surroundings. He wiped his eyes and sniffed before putting on his glasses. Having steeled himself, he raised his head and took in the anguished face of his wife. "I'm going to Riyadh," he said with a blinking eyed quiet determination as Ameena once again broke into uncontrollable sobbing.

Omar swallowed back his own upset, stood up and walked, leaden limbed around to his wife, putting a heavy arm around her shoulder. "Calm yourself my darling, we will have Mohammed back with us very soon."

Ameena Al-Hamra lifted her head balefully and attempted a weak smile of acknowledgement before once again covering her face with her hands.

The next day Omar boarded the plane for the hour long flight from Jeddah to Riyadh. As the aircraft taxied to take off, the usual prayers were said over the passenger address system and Omar joined in, silently mouthing the words, whilst his thoughts still remained fixed upon his youngest son. He sat the duration of the short flight, declining offers of food or drink, deep in thought. Even he was not entirely sure of what he was actually trying to achieve with this desperate dash to the capital. All he did know was that he wanted to see his son with his own eyes and to hear first hand that this was really his son's own choice. Omar refused to believe that it was nothing more than the malign influence of his idiotic brother-in-law, Abdul-Rahman. If he could only just have a short time alone with his son, he was sure he could get him to see sense. After all, he reasoned to himself, surely he knew his own son better than anyone else.

Landing at King Khalid International, Omar made straight for the taxi ranks and ordered the driver to take him to the address of the house where Mohammed was now living. Being a native of Jeddah he had only been to the capital a handful of times, but even to Omar it seemed an altogether different and unfriendly place. Unlike sultry Jeddah, with its ancient port and where the old and new parts of the city rubbed humid but happy shoulders together, Riyadh was so very different. As far as Omar was concerned, the capital of the Kingdom was stiff and hostile, arid and aloof. As the cab made its way towards the city with its jagged, half finished skyline, littered with towering cranes, it struck him that everything in Riyadh was too big, too aggressive and even faintly malign. The cab passed by huge building sites, like the half finished Al Faisaliah Center and Tower, which was intended to be the tallest building in the Arab world. All around him, the newly created city seemed to have been mapped out to some grand and threatening design, its monotonous geometric grids sprawling out like some vast choking net. His cab ride took him right past the muscular heart of this rigid city network. At the very centre he gave the strange enormous concrete flying saucer that housed the Interior Ministry, where Abdul-Rahman and thousands others had their offices, a furtive glance. The menacing building sat hunched over the city like a predatory beast, seemingly ready to spring into savage action at any moment.

The driver now continued westwards and before long they came to a stop outside an anonymous looking six story block. The apartment building appeared to be a little less well kept than those that surrounded it, with its paint brittle and peeling under the ever present, unforgiving sun. Omar first confirmed the address with the driver and then paid him before clumsily getting out of the cab, his movement made difficult due to his ponderous overnight bag. He had never been to Abdul-Rahman's home before but the address was now burned into his mind. He looked through the list of names that appeared above the buttons, searching for Abdul-Rahman bin Hajez's. At last he found it; the cursive lettering was faded and barely legible. He pushed the button which buzzed with a low drone. He waited for what seemed like an eternity and pushed again, holding down the grubby button with mounting impatience.

"Yes", the long rasped tone was immediately disturbing. Omar had been expecting to hear Mohammed's or even Abdul-Rahman's voice. It didn't sound like either.

"Peace be with you. Abdul-Rahman is that you?" Omar's questioning tone was already rhetorical; he knew his brother-in-law's voice.

"And with you be peace. No, he's not here." The reply was as wary as it was curt.

"I'm sorry to disturb you, but I am looking for my son, Mohammed Al-Hamra. I am Omar Al-Hamra."

Omar stared at the entry-phone as the momentary silence that followed was broken by a muffled sound of what obviously was talking. The banker screwed up his face in concentration as he listened but he was unable to decipher anything from the blur of noise he heard.

"Hello?"

"I'm sorry, but he is not here either."

Confusion swirled around Omar for a moment as he took in this latest piece of unexpected information. "So when do you expect him back?"

"I don't know."

"Can you tell me where he is then? Are you a friend of Abdul-Rahman?" Suddenly Omar was filled with a hundred questions. Who was this evasive, rude man he was speaking to anyway?

"I'm sorry I have to go, please call back later when Abdul-Rahman is here." The intercom clicked out.

Omar pushed on the buzzer repeatedly. "Hello? Hello?" Silence.

Angry and frustrated be shoved on the door to the apartment block but it was locked solid. He banged on the glass of the door hoping someone would hear him, but if anyone did, they did not answer. He pressed his nose against the door and peered through its darkened glass, but the dingy looking residential block seemed utterly deserted. Crestfallen he dialled his brother-in law's mobile, which infuriatingly switched straight through to answering mode. After listening to the *Mutawwa*'s brief message and with immense effort he just managed to maintain a polite restrained tone. "Peace be with you, Abdul-Rahman. This is Omar, I'm in Riyadh. Can you call me back as soon as possible? Thank you."

Omar leant against the wall of the drab looking apartment block trying desperately to collect his thoughts. Sourly he realised that it was almost entirely pointless to just stand there waiting, it could be some time before Abdul-Rahman or more importantly his son returned. He cast a forlorn look down the dusty, litter strewn street before suddenly letting out a curse, for he was now utterly furious with himself. The element of surprise he had so carefully planned had now been stupidly wasted. What on God's good Earth was he doing? He shook his head ruefully, suddenly filled with bitter remorse that he had been so foolish as to leave a voicemail message on Abdul-Rahman's mobile phone. He cursed again and scowled at his watch. It was already nearly midday; very soon the call to *Dhuhr* prayers would be ringing out from the city's mosques, he had to make a plan. He squinted into the deep

513

blue, cloudless sky above him. The spring sun, high overhead, joined forces with everything else that seemed to be conspiring to make his life difficult and beat down upon him with increasing savage intensity. He could feel his sweat quickly starting to prickle uncomfortably under his white *gutra* and he responded by taking off his headdress for a moment. He quickly wiped his beaded forehead with his handkerchief, before swiftly and expertly repositioning it back in place whilst all the while staring with unseeing eyes down the deserted street.

Aware for the first time since leaving Jeddah of his own aching limbs, he felt suddenly tired and uncomfortable. He regretted too that he not had eaten or drunk anything at all on the plane trip. He let out a lengthy sigh; events were not going as he had planned and stepped out onto the street, casting a last embittered look up at the building before walking off with heavy slapping footsteps, in the direction he thought he had come from. As he walked he quickly scrolled through the numbers in his mobile searching for the IAB office number in Riyadh. It would be better to wait there until he heard from Abdul-Rahman or go back to the apartment later that evening. Until then, he resolved to himself, that he would go to the main Riyadh office of IAB and wait to hear from the *Mutawwa* there.

Back in his own cool, quiet, air conditioned office, Abdul-Rahman put down his mobile and pawed at his grey streaked beard, deep in thought. The arrival of Omar Al-Hamra, whilst not a complete surprise, was nevertheless, an unwanted, though quite natural complication. He sat for a moment quietly ruminating and collecting his thoughts. Obviously in more ordinary circumstances it was far easier, but this was not an ordinary case at all. He was dealing, for the first time, with someone who knew him personally, so consequently the situation was not as straightforward as he was used to. Omar could turn out to be more than an irritant; he would have to be careful. The religious policeman knew from past experience, that this was a very critical time.

The *Mutawwa*'s mobile began to ring, for a moment breaking his line of thought. He checked the incoming caller's number before he answered; it was his voicemail. He listened to the tense voiced message twice with pursed lips and a furrowed brow. No surprises, it was Omar, just as Abdullah Bawani had already informed him from his apartment a few minutes earlier. Abdul-Rahman briefly lent back in his chair and stretched himself. This just meant that he would have to put his plan into effect more quickly than he had wanted, it should be fine. He took out a cigarette and lit it, blowing the smoke calmly out while again considering the options. He puffed out another plume of smoke and a small smile broke out on his narrowed eyed face. No, it would be fine, everything was under control and he had a plan. He took another drag and then extinguished his cigarette before carefully dialling his brother-in-law's number.

"Peace be with you, Omar, what a pleasant surprise."

"How much do you want for it then?" Joe was studying the photograph of the Isuzu Trooper four wheel drive SUV, very closely.

"A hundred and ten thousand Riyals, mate," replied Bill Heaver adopting an even more arid tone than was usual, even for the bushy browed ex-copper.

Karpolinski frowned and handed back the handwritten advertisement that Bill Heaver was about to put up in the internal notice boards on the trading floor. "And how many miles have you done in it?"

"Twenty two thousand clicks or so." He pinned the picture of the car, with its brief, carefully handwritten, sales pitch; nearly new, one careful owner, to the board and stood back. He let out a low slightly satisfied sigh and briefly admired his handiwork.

"Seems a bit steep, don't you think?"

The Australian turned and gave the Englishman a withering look, before sarcastically responding, "Yeah, well we'll see then won't we, right?"

516

Joe Karpolinski shrugged his shoulders and watched as the fraud expert turned and strode huffily away.

"You really do love to wind that bloke up don't you?" said Jim with a shake. He and Alex had sidled up unnoticed to the man from Surrey and had been quietly observing the little scene unfold before them with barely concealed conspiratorial grins.

"What do you mean?" countered Joe, surprised as much by the sudden arrival of the other two men as by Jim's statement. He pulled a slightly wounded look.

"Oh c'mon, you know what we mean", added Alex distractedly whilst still watching the departing Heaver as he passed the along the other side of the vast glass wall of the dealing floor. He was wondering if the man's wife from Wagga was still causing tongues to do the same at Jeddah Prep.

"Look, I just said it was a bit expensive that's all," he said with widening eyes. Alex and Jim looked totally unconvinced as Karpolinski followed with a frown, "Anyway, why's he always so flaming touchy?"

"No idea mate" Jim snorted back, sounding like Crocodile Dundee and just managing to restrain a laugh.

Joe ignored Jim's response and adopted a reasoning tone, "look it beats me." Karpolinski nodded in the direction of the notice board, "besides I am actually looking for a car, you know?" he added earnestly.

"Really, what's wrong with the one you've got?"

"Costs a bloody fortune to service and is constantly on the blink…Isobel hates it." Joe rolled his eyes around expressively like an overactive silent movie star.

Jim laughed adopting a slightly Blimpish tone, "Well if you must 'buy British.'" Joe gave self effacing shrug of acknowledgement as Jim continued, dropping back to his more normal tone of voice. "Anyway, Isobel doesn't even drive it, does she?"

"The fact that she isn't allowed to drive it doesn't change the fact," replied Karpolinski a little mechanically, repeating almost verbatim, his wife's own frequently stated position on the matter.

Jim Robson smiled, "How's she and the nipper doing?"

Joe paused before replying. "Well I guess she's recovered well enough, you know, all things considered…" His voice drifted off and his features momentarily seemed to darken in a mist of deep contemplation.

Jim still watching the man closely; cocked his head sideways and spoke. "What do you mean?" His interested tone, now much gentler, was softly encouraging.

Joe gave the South Londoner a long stare, weighing up his response. "Let's just say it wasn't exactly an easy birth." Both Jim and Alex responded to this latest statement with open enquiring faces. Joe's eyes roved quickly across the two men before he gave a little resigned shake of the head.

"Look, I'll tell you about it sometime," he added and then gave a short stubby sigh. With this last dismissive noise, Joe pivoted purposively on his heel and started to make his way to his place on the trading desk. Alex and Jim followed closely behind the taller lolloping gait of Karpolinski who turned back towards the two other. "Anyway, how are things with you guys?"

"Hey, just peachy, Joe", replied Jim with a mirthless snort.

Karpolinski paused and wheeled his seat out from under the desk. "And how about you Alex?"

Now it was Alex's turn to give his own slightly forlorn shake of the head. "Doing just fine," he replied with scant conviction to which Joe just gravely nodded.

Within a short space of time the trading floor quickly filled to capacity, humming with its noisy multilingual chatter. Across the room the salesmen launched into their morning calls with gusto, their speech, as ever, fractured with the curious periodic littering of technical English words or names. The strange bilingual concatenations frequently brought smiles to the Westerners' faces, as the harsh guttural but flowing sounds of Arabic conversation would suddenly be punctuated by phrases like; 'Discount Rate', 'Federal Reserve' or 'Alan Greenspan.'

Alex, like the other traders on the desk, first checked his personal email, something he had been doing, ever more frantically, since the day that his disappointing bonus had been announced. Yet again there was nothing worth considering, nothing at all to raise his flagging spirits. The phone calls to head-hunters and former colleagues back in London had yielded painfully little to date; his job search was taking much longer than he had expected. Myopically the fact that he was based in the Arabian Peninsula, whilst looking for a position back in London, had not seemed to him to be too great a handicap. Already that simplistic and overconfident view was being sharply revised. In fact, it now seemed quite ridiculous to him that he had ever thought this in the first place. The truth, as he now ruefully understood, was it would not be easy getting an even half way decent job back in London.

For the third time in fifteen minutes Alex checked his watch; it was not quite half past eight, which meant that it was not even half past five in the morning back in London. It was still far too early to call anyone back home. He cast a gloomy turn around the dealing room and tried to settle down to work. Alex was far from being the only one on the desk to find this a tough task. The oppressive atmosphere that now surrounded the men on the Proprietary Desk was unbearably stultifying; Chris Barma's presence pressed heavier upon them than ever it did before. The head of the Prop team had exacted a heavy toll on his subordinates for what he perceived as the insolence and disloyal behaviour of his team. Awarding himself the lion's share of the bonus pool had been his first act of retribution, but his next and more satisfying act was to impress his control over them. A new regime was in place; more onerous reporting, more questions about the traders' positions, no weekly meetings, even and more crucially for the traders, their requests for holidays were now mulled and deliberated over. The critical Exit Re-Entry Visa was granted at his behest and he would make them grovel for one each time they needed one. From now on these men were on a tight leash and they were meant to know it.

The morning dragged on and Alex impatiently waited until it was time for him to call home.

"Hi my darling, how are you?"

The longish pause on the line before the reply was uncomfortable and worrying. "We're fine Alex. How are you?"

"I'm fine, how are the kids darling?"

"They're missing you. Do you want to speak to Christopher?" Claire sounded tired.

"Sure, is everything alright?" but Alex's question went unanswered. All he heard was a muffled noise over the line whilst the receiver was being passed on to his eldest son.

"Hi Daddy, when are you coming back?"

Alex swallowed hard. "Not long now son. How is school going?" he enquired with as upbeat a tone as he could manage, trying to change the subject.

"Fine, I miss you Daddy."

"I miss you too Christopher. Are you looking after Mummy and your brothers like I asked you to?"

There was a brief pause before the boy answered a touch coyly, perhaps fearing some reproach might be coming down the line, "Yes."

Alex grimaced, forcing himself with great effort to keep the positive tone in his voice up to scratch. "I know you have my son... you're such a good boy Christopher. How is the football going sonny?"

"Daddy I'm in the team for our next match."

Alex's gloom was entirely lifted by the boy's cheery response. "That's great son."

"Will you be back to watch me Daddy?"

Alex was forced to swallow hard yet again. "I'm so sorry son, but I won't be able to just this time."

"Oh Daddy please, why can't you?" His son's long imploring tone shot through his heart and he immediately felt his strength of will seeping out of him through the same wound.

"Look Christopher I promise I'll be back really soon. I'll try and be there for the next one, OK?"

"There might not be one," came back the hurt sounding response.

"Son, of course there will."

Alex squinted in concentration as yet more muffled words of conversation between his wife and his eldest son filtered dully down the telephone line.

"Mum says I've got to go. Bye Daddy."

"Goodbye son."

Claire picked up the receiver and spoke. "Alex I have to go, we're going to be late for school. Call me later OK?"

"OK darling I'll call back. Is ten o'clock OK with you?" asked Alex into the phone as it clicked out of life.

Alex put the handset down onto his desk and stared into his computer screens with a tired vacant look.

"You OK mate?" asked Jim who had been watching Alex and who was fully aware of what was happened to his friend.

Alex turned toward the kindly face of his friend and gave him a brave smile. "I'm fine Jim, thanks."

Jim Robson gave Alex a sympathetic nod and turned back to stare at his own flickering screens. He was worried about his friend. He knew Alex was not happy about Claire's sudden departure with his kids, but things could be worse, at least Alex had a family.

Back in Riyadh Omar was finding it difficult to sit still. His mouth felt dry despite the copious amounts of tea he had drunk and his unease seemed to increase with each thin lipped smile his brother-in-law gave him.

"He will be here soon I'm sure." Abdul-Rahman repeated with yet another insipid curl of the mouth, masquerading as a smile whilst returning his mobile phone back into his pocket. "Would you like some more tea Omar?"

"No thank you." Omar looked at his watch yet again. It was getting on for eight o'clock and he had now been waiting for over two hours. He had arrived shortly after the *Maghrib* prayer time, expecting Mohammed to be there, just as Abdul-Rahman had instructed him. Then the *Isha* prayer time had also come and gone and still there was no sign of his son.

"Where is he?"

Abdul-Rahman gave a slight shrug. "You know how these young men are Omar. He says he is with his friends, but he said he will be back soon."

"And you didn't tell him I was here?"

Abdul-Rahman bin Hajez gave a nod. "I said nothing."

"I just don't understand it", muttered Omar barely audible and with a sad shake of his head.

"Omar my friend, I have followed your instructions just as you asked me to. I made no mention of your arrival here in Riyadh. Is that not what you asked me to do?"

524

Omar nodded agreement and took off his glasses, rubbing his tired eyes. So far the trip to Riyadh had been a complete disaster. He had not seen his son and now he was not sure at all that he would. He gave the senior *Mutawwa* another piercing look, trying to hide his mounting distaste. He was sure Abdul-Rahman was not telling him the truth, but there was no way of proving his suspicions other than waiting there for Mohammed to arrive. He would wait, but it was not pleasant sitting with this loathsome cold man.

"So my Brother, how long do you intend to stay in Riyadh?" Abdul-Rahman enquired with an anaemic smile. The question jolted Omar from his dark brooding.

"I had only planned to stay for the day, just to see Mohammed."

Abdul-Rahman shook his head sadly, "Of course, but you should have called me before you left and all of this misunderstanding could have been avoided."

Omar paused for a moment. "So it would seem."

"Well you are most welcome to stay here."

Omar just managed to raise a smile. The thought of spending a moment longer than was utterly necessary with his brother-in-law chilled him to his well covered bones. "Thank you, but I will have to go. My flight is at ten."

Abdul-Rahman lifted his arm and looked at his wristwatch. "Really, that is such a shame."

Omar drummed his fingers softly on the armrest of the threadbare sofa he was sitting on. The apartment could barely be described as furnished, the oppressive blank walls and faint scent of disinfectant combined to heighten discomfort. It was bleak. He imagined that this was how a prison must feel and wondered how his son could possibly tolerate such a place.

"Will you not have some food?"

Omar raised his hand, "No really Abdul-Rahman, I would rather not" his appetite had deserted him. All he hungered for was to see his estranged son.

"Well perhaps the next time I am in Jeddah I will try to bring Mohammed with me."

Omar gave a startled look. "But he is coming here now isn't he?"

"God willing, but if he is delayed for some reason, then..."

"Delayed? Why would he be delayed, he doesn't even know I'm here does he?" Omar's hope was quickly draining out him and being replaced with angry frustration.

"He has no idea that you are here my brother." The *Mutawwa* narrowed his gaze, "you heard me on the phone, no?"

Omar nodded as Abdul-Rahman kept his eyes fixed on Omar and continued with rising firmness, "He said he is on his way, he will be here soon, God willing."

Omar let out a deflating sigh, "God willing."

Abdul-Rahman fingered through his ever present rosary beads, his voice now back to its usual slightly menacing tone, "God willing I will bring Mohammed with me next time. Besides, as the Director of the Committee to Promote Virtue and Prevent Vice told me only today, much work still needs to be done in Jeddah, so I will be there more often than I am here." The *Mutawwa* paused and steadied his gaze upon Omar before continuing. "There is still much evil doing there, is there not?"

Omar restrained a shiver and wondered how this man always managed to twist everything into a threat, how he turned everything into an interrogation. "Not that I know of", he replied warily.

The *Mutawwa* pursed his lips. "Come my brother you, know very well. Young Mohammed has told of much that concerns me."

Omar was completely taken aback. "Mohammed? What exactly has Mohammed said?"

"My brother, there are evil and dangerous lies being spread every day. The people need our protection and guidance. You can't ignore the fact that in Jeddah sin is openly tolerated." Abdul-Rahman's eyes glowered as he spoke. "There is debauchery, drunkenness, idolatry, sexual deviancy. This is God's own country Omar, yet we permit the Kaffirs and infidel to walk openly amongst us, defiling everything we hold sacred with impunity."

Omar gave a bewildered look, "Who exactly are you speaking of?"

The religious policeman paused and eyed Omar very carefully; he would not be drawn so easily. Collecting himself, his intonation dropped back to its usual rasping delivery. "My brother, open your eyes and look and around you. The army of the Devil is here, encamped in the very heart of Islam."

"You mean the foreigners, the Americans?"

Abdul-Rahman just nodded agreement with a sour expression before replying. "And others too, we must always be vigilant."

"But the Americans are our allies. Did not the King request their help when Iraq invaded Kuwait?" asked Omar hopefully.

Abdul-Rahman clapped his hands together in satisfaction. "There, you see my brother, precisely the kind of filthy lies that I am talking of. We were tricked into having them here. Saddam, the unholy Kaffir has gone, but are not the Armies of the infidel still all around us? Brother, we do not need them here and it is one of the greatest sins tolerated in Islam today that they are here now. It is forbidden, forbidden, utterly forbidden."

Omar looked suitably shaken by this last declaration and watched the *Mutawwa* closely as he spat out the word, "*Haram*", several times under his breath.

"I see, but if it is forbidden, why does the King tolerate it?" Omar had cleverly adopted a face of complete naiveté.

Abdul-Rahman's eyes narrowed for an instant as he considered his response. "I tell you, the King, Custodian of the Two Holy Mosques and Prime Minister has never supported this. Have you ever heard him utter a word of support on this matter?"

Omar slowly shook his head. "No but surely…"

"No my brother, no such heinous words were ever said by our King, but others within the government have been bribed and corrupted into allowing this filthy travesty."

"Who?" asked Omar wide eyed.

Abdul-Rahman shook his head slowly. "I am sorry but I am not at liberty to tell you my brother, but what I can tell you is that we in the Interior Ministry know who is to blame. It is not something that will be tolerated and I can assure you Omar, we have the means to right this evil."

Omar looked chastened and was about to push for more information when the sound of a key being turned in the door of the apartment stopped him in his tracks. Omar was onto his feet in a heartbeat, his anxiety switched in the same time to joy at the arrival of his son. Stunned for an instant, he was greeted by the sight of a man he did not recognise at all. Omar's expectant expression fell for a moment until his son emerged from behind the unknown man.

"Peace be with you father", said his son who stepped forward and then stood motionless.

"Why do they do that?" said Jim as Alex braked heavily to avoid yet another collision with a taxi which pulled, punch drunkenly, into his lane on the Medina highway.

Alex gave a quick disbelieving shake of his head before growling back through gritted teeth, "bloody nutters."

"You'd think some sort of Darwinian force should be at work, wouldn't you?"

"What, like the survival of the fittest or something?" Alex asked with a hollow chortle as he accelerated and started to overtake the offending, battered taxi which was still crawling along in the central lane.

Jim turned and stared angrily as they passed the driver, who grinned obliviously back at him. "Look at that fucking idiot, he hasn't a clue."

"He isn't the only one", Alex said with a resigned snort.

Jim turned and stared unseeingly down the packed highway deep in thought. The men sat in silence for a few moments as they continued their familiar homeward trip. "Are you playing squash this evening?" asked Jim.

"Nope, not tonight." Alex turned and gave his friend a quick half knowing look. "What are you up to then?"

Now it was Jim's chance to snort, "the usual."

Alex turned towards his friend and gave him a sly smile. "Fancy a jar?"

Jim broke into a huge grin. "I thought you'd never ask."

"I'm askin'", said Alex with a laugh.

"Then I'm dancin'" replied Jim.

Two hours later and the men were sitting in their usual places outside Alex's villa on Sierra compound. Their third jug of homebrewed beer was close to being finished and their conversation which had started on the ever present subject of Andy Whiteman and his complete disappearance, nobody had a clue where he had gone, had now shifted to the malign presence of Chris Barma, now frequently referred to with gallows humour as Lord Baldemort, a name first coined by Joe.

"The man is a fucking nightmare, in fact this whole situation is a fucking nightmare." Alex's words tumbled out with real venom.

"It's unbelievable that he was never actually on the trading desk at Morgan Stanley and only briefly as a junior at Goldman's. He was a temp in the fucking back office." Jim swallowed down the last of his beer.

Alex shook his head in tired disbelief. "I know, I know Jim, I just never assumed…"

Jim cut Alex short, "look mate, none of us did. As far as the bank was concerned, they were hiring some big shot from London. Now we find out Chris Barma is just a massive con artist."

"Well he certainly fucking fooled me," said Alex tipping back the last of his own drink and then plonking his empty beer glass back down on the table with a thump.

"Well that wily son of a bitch has fooled lot of folk", said Jim. He lent forward and poured out two more foaming drinks and emptied the jug. "But then again maybe we made it too easy for him."

"Easy?"

"Sure, we were blinded by our own greed." Jim Robson gave Alex a long look. "Each of us is here for the same reason, right?"

"I guess so", conceded Alex.

"There's no guessing in it Alex."

Alex nodded his agreement. "I know, but I still can't believe it, I mean…"

"What?"

Alex gave a sheepish look and then steeled himself. "Well I mean…" Alex stammered for a moment. "I suppose I thought that because he was black, that he had to be good. I figured he'd have to be, you know?"

"Have to be?" Jim was taken aback.

"The City and banks aren't exactly bastions of liberal thought. I just assumed it would have been more difficult for him than your average white male."

Jim gave Alex a sad looking smile. "Look I know what you mean, but that's just another form of racism Alex."

Alex looked contrite and gave another affirmative shake of his head. "I know, I understand that now… I'm sorry."

"Honestly Alex, you disappoint me, I had thought more of you."

"Sorry."

Jim shook his head and looked deadly serious. "Look the only way you'll make it up to me is to get me another beer", said the handsome black man suddenly breaking into a wicked laugh.

"Done," said Alex with a hugely relieved grin and getting to his feet in a flash.

Jim wiped his mouth and then looked thoughtfully at Alex. "So Alex, was it really just the money that brought you here?"

Alex stopped in his tracks and gave his friend another coy look. He thought for a moment as images of a bouncing naked Sandrine flashed across his mind. "I guess so", he lied, imagining Jim would now think even worse of him if he mentioned his affair back in Paris. Jim shook his head sadly whilst rubbing his chin and Alex, noticing his friend's faraway look, was now suddenly curious. "Why, wasn't it for you?"

"Sort of..."

"What do you mean?"

Jim hesitated before replying. "Well, I had just broken up with my fiancée."

"Helen?" Jim had mentioned her name a couple of times before, but had never conveyed that the relationship had been particularly serious at all.

"No, she was just someone on the rebound."

Alex was intrigued. "Really, you were engaged?"

"Yup," Jim nodded.

"What was her name?"

"Patsy, or Patricia Mary Jennings to be precise," he said with a fixed smile.

"What was she like?"

"She was lovely." Alex gave his friend an understanding smile and for an instant a sad look swept across Jim's face before he announced, "it was love", with a grin, brimful of bravura. "Anyway, where's my beer?"

In a few minutes Alex returned with another jug of homebrew. He had dashed back and had spilt some of the still bubbling liquid onto the poolside tiles.

"Watch your step", said Jim with a grin.

"You never said anything about being engaged before," said Alex, entirely ignoring Jim's last remark.

The banker gave Alex a steady eyed look. "There's not much to say, she dumped me." His tone was entirely matter of fact.

Alex tempered his own tone, suddenly aware that he might be intruding into something better left alone. "Sorry, I didn't mean…"

Jim waved the half finished apology away. "Forget it. It's ancient history anyway."

Alex took a long draught of his beer as the men sat silent for a moment with only the ever present noise of the air conditioning droning on in the background.

Jim put down his glass. "She was more into her career than me."

Alex gave a slow movement of acknowledgment, waiting for Jim to continue.

"I wanted kids, she didn't."

"I see. And what did she do?"

"She worked at Goldmans."

"Worked like a lunatic I suppose?"

"Yup, they work 'em hard there. In the end that's all she ever did. Money, she sort of became obsessed with it." Jim gave a shrug. "...still...glasshouses I guess."

Alex gave a snort of appreciation, the irony was inescapable. The men sat silently in thought for a few moments, with only the ever present hum of air conditioning in the background.

"So did she know Chris Barma?"

Jim gave an empty laugh. "I've no fucking idea. I haven't spoken to her for eighteen months."

"It's a small world."

"Isn't it just", replied Jim thoughtfully, before taking another sip of his drink. He put down his glass and leant back in his chair. "Talk about out of the frying pan into the fire."

Alex gave a quizzical look.

"You know, here we are for whatever reasons, but essentially it's to make money, right?"

Alex nodded his agreement as Jim continued. "In a way I came here to make a shed load, almost only just to justify it to myself. I needed to prove that I could do it and to show other people that I could."

"Any people in particular?" said Alex with a glint.

"OK, so perhaps I wanted to impress her, make her rue her choice. And yet, money is just a... is just a fucking instrument. In of itself it is not a value, but we need values as well as instruments. We need ends as well as means."

Alex pulled a long face. "That's pretty profound stuff."

"Maybe, anyway it's what Umberto Eco says and I have to fucking agree."

"I've heard of him, wasn't he at Goldman's too?"

Jim broke into laughter at this. "Very funny, c'mon I'm trying to be serious here."

"I know, I know. Look I agree with you, but we're only saying that now because we've been turned over by that cunt Barma. If we had both been rolling in it we'd be laughing all the way back home by now."

"Maybe, but that still doesn't make what I'm saying wrong." Jim picked up his beer and slugged back the remainder of his drink.

"So what else does this Eco bloke say?" asked Alex with an increasingly alcohol fuelled grin.

"His point was that the biggest problem faced by human beings is finding a way to accept the nasty fact that each of us is eventually going to die."

"Jesus."

"Precisely."

Alex' stomach groaned loudly and he looked at his watch. "I'm starving, fancy something to eat?"

"Sure, just not a curry this time, I'll be farting like a busted zeppelin on this stuff anyway."

Alex broke into a belly laugh at this. "A busted zeppelin, where on earth did that come from?"

"From my ex-fiancée, she had these great tits", said Jim now also breaking into laughter, though not as enthusiastic as Alex's.

"Really?"

Jim's features saddened for a moment. "Yeah, she really was something."

Two more jugs of beer and a couple of pizzas later Jim eventually got a little shakily to his feet. The taxi he had ordered to take him back to his own compound had just arrived and was now waiting for him.

"Well that put the world to rights."

"Sure did, but we still have no idea of what those bastards Barma and Moore cooked up between them", said Alex with a forced grin as he got to his feet.

"You know Joe's wife, Isobel saw Annie Whiteman in the supermarket? Apparently she completely blanked her. She's as big as a house too."

Alex gave a sad shake of his head. "Pregnant isn't she. So Andy is still in Jeddah?"

"Seems so."

Alex continued with a slow shake of disbelief, "Weird, totally fucking weird."

"That Moore is a wily old fucker", said Jim with a sad snort.

Alex bent shakily and picked up the empty jug and beer glasses, turned and carefully took the steps up towards his villa. The open doorway was brightly lit and he deftly made his way up. As he took the last step he heard a dull thud and then Jim swearing like a trooper. Alex turned to see his friend bent double holding his foot.

"Fuck, what happened?"

Jim was rocking back and forth and was gripping his ankle tightly. "I slipped on spilt beer I think. I've twisted my fucking ankle, shit"

Alex quickly dumped the things he was carrying and went back down to his friend's aid.

"This poolside is lethal when it gets wet. Are you OK?"

Jim winced, "I'll be fine." He slowly got to his feet with Alex' assistance and still leaning on his friend he tried to put some weight on the injured foot. The banker winced and swore again.

"Do you think you need to go to hospital?"

"No I'll be fine."

"Sure?"

"No it's not too bad. It's wearing off a bit. Ouch. C'mon my taxi's here."

Alex half carried Jim to the waiting taxi, the driver gave the two men a curious look as they appeared arm in arm with Jim draped over Alex's shoulder.

"I'll pick you up the usual time then?"

"Yup" Jim eased himself gingerly into the back seat of the cab. Alex closed the door for his friend and Jim then rolled down the window with a pained smile. "See you tomorrow then."

"See you" and Alex watched the taxi drive off slowly into the cool night.

"I'll tell you when we get there." said Omar to his taxi driver. The driver acknowledged his instructions, gunned the engine and started the drive into Jeddah from the airport. Omar sighed and looked disconsolately out of the window. The trip to Riyadh had not just been a complete waste of time and money, it had been an unmitigated disaster. He had achieved nothing. A sad bitterness filled him as he realised that he had lost the battle to save his son from his manipulative brother-in-law. Even worse was that his son's past life was being systematically erased by these men and there was nothing he could do about it. Omar was still shocked by the way that his son had displayed such loud and belligerent behaviour in Abdul-Rahman's apartment. He had never seen his son like that and all that nonsense about, 'helping his brothers in Palestine' and 'continuing the struggle'. It was absurd and he had told him so too. He had reminded his son that he personally knew lots of Palestinians and they were doctors and lawyers in America and far from struggling. Whatever he said, it did not help and he left the *Mutawwa*'s apartment shortly afterwards empty handed. Omar sighed and looked out of the window, thrusting his hand into his *dishdashah* pocket and pulled out the unused ticket he had bought for his son. He looked at it forlornly and swallowed bitterly attempting to staunch the tears now welling in his eyes. What was he going to tell his wife? Suddenly he lurched forward, the taxi he was in had pulled up abruptly at a set of lights, shaken for an instant he scowled at the driver and angrily set himself back into his seat. "What are you trying to do, kill us all? Slow down you fool", snapped Omar in frustration.

"Sorry Sir" said the Pakistani taxi driver a little nonplussed by the man's sudden outburst. He had not been going that fast. He gave the man a quick glance in the rear view mirror. All the Saudi's were the same, he thought.

Omar scowled out of the passenger window at the offending traffic lights. Just opposite another cab was already waiting for the lights to change and the two cab drivers, knowing each other by sight, gave a friendly wave as they passed. In the rear of the other cab, Jim Robson sat nursing his swollen ankle and an aching heart. He too was looking out of his own window, deep in his own painful world. The two men passed by each other, oblivious to each other's existence, wrapped deep in their own distressing worlds all the while travelling the same road in opposite directions. In pain since departure, they passed like ships in the night, with neither assigning much hope of relief at their arrival.

18. Arms and the Man

Alex fastened his seatbelt and quickly sifted through the clutch of the glossy Investment Bank research reports be had brought with him. None of them looked particularly appetizing but nevertheless he grumpily picked out what seemed to him as the most promising of them and tried to make himself comfortable for the flight ahead. He had not been happy when he stepped onto the plane, but his sense of humour had entirely deserted him when he had seen the state of the passenger he was going to be sitting next to for the next seven hours. Beside him, the tubby red faced man, who had briefly grumbled something both profane and unintelligible when forced to get up and allow Alex to take his allotted window seat, had already fallen back to wheezing sleep. Slumbering noisily and looking like he had been in his clothes for a week or more, the man seeped the strong stale scent of alcohol and cigarettes and was taking up much more than his fair share of space. Alex sat stiff and uncomfortable, feeling particularly cramped and invaded by the man slumped and wheezing next to him. Annoyed, he grumpily forced himself into his reading, aware that he really needed to get through as much of the dry, matter of fact material as he possibly could. After a short delay, the plane at last started to rumble and move and with this as his cue, Alex turned and peered out through the window and stared at the heat haze that shimmered on the baking asphalt outside whilst the aircraft slowly shuddered and taxied for takeoff. He turned his attention back to his shiny backed strategy paper entitled, "Oil and Politics Don't Mix" and settled back in his seat. The plane briefly braked as the pilot straightened up at the top of the runway and the engines began their familiar rising crescendo as the plane then accelerated down the tarmac and took to the air with a brief stomach churning jolt. Alex dropped the glossy report onto his lap, shut his eyes and closed yet another deal with God. These days he was beginning to loathe flying.

"The majority of plane crashes occur on approach or landing you know?"

The banker turned to his right and looked at the puffy eyed man with slightly raised alarm; with his florid features, Alex put him at about sixty years of age, maybe a little more. His fellow traveler was no longer slumped and wheezing in his seat but was now blankly staring at Alex with his baggy eyed, lived in face. "One in fifty-two point six million actually and only seventeen percent on takeoff", he added flatly, as if he was talking about the weather. Alex looked a little nonplussed at the man, whose grey bloodshot eyes he was now peering into. "You a nervous flyer?" asked the man with a noticeable drunken slur.

Alex gave him a wary look before responding, but now mildly affronted at the accusation. "Not particularly so", he replied, sounding more defensive than he intended and then self consciously easing his cast iron grip from his seat armrests.

The man gave an understanding nod. "Me neither, well at least not with this lot."

Alex briefly eyed the man before responding noncommittally, "I guess so."

The rubicund featured man gave Alex a short unfocused stare and broke into a half smile. "They're alright, better than the locals anyway."

Alex thought he detected a slight West Country burr in the man's intoxicated speech. He smiled his agreement politely back at the man before turning and again peering out of the window next to him. Unseen he momentarily pulled a sour face and cursed silently to himself, it was just his luck to be sat next to this old soak. He checked his wristwatch, with the dawning realization that it was going to be a very long flight if this oddball beside him was going to spout plane crash statistics all the way along. Just then the plane started to bank steeply and Alex consciously pushed such uncomfortable thoughts aside as he gazed down on the vanishing world below. Outside, clear blue skies were now all around, save for a few adolescent strips of cloud that loitered with little intent. These little puffs, scattered here and there, failed to hide the unhindered expanse of sea that was still clearly visible far down below. The plane continued its ascent and leveled off, its cruising altitude being silently announced by the switching off of the overhead seat belt lights. Alex took a deep breath, eased his seat back and closed his eyes thinking that he should perhaps try to sleep, he was pretty sure he was going to need it once back on the ground.

"There's not a cloud in sight is there?" said the man.

Alex reopened his eyes and turned towards the talkative man, he now much preferred the earlier silent, slumped version. The man was leaning over Alex and squinting at the glare from the window. Uncomfortable at the sudden unwanted proximity of the man, Alex shot him an intense look of irritation, but the puffy, bloodshot eyes of the businessman registered none of his annoyance. Alex was determined that he was not going to be drawn into an inane conversation with this drunken stranger. "No, there seems not to be," he replied with polite but patient finality, as if he was talking to a child. Irritated, Alex pointedly looked away and huffily started to read through his research paper, insulating himself with a furious concentration.

For the next twenty minutes Alex was left undisturbed and he successfully finished his reading material. Now he felt a little happier, as he felt that he had at least managed to learn something useful from the report and as an added bonus, the slurring man beside him had been silent the whole time. He put down the paper; its conclusion was that oil was apparently much too expensive and would sell off before long. Satisfied he had finished with it, he thrust it forcefully into the seat pocket in front of him.

"Been in Bahrain long?"

Alex turned sideways towards the persistent man next to him with the sad realization that it was indeed going to be a very long flight. "No, just passing through", he answered politely, though still cool enough he expected, to freeze out further conversation. Frustrated and without really thinking he picked up the airline's in-flight magazine, it would make a change from the oil swaps market.

Beside him the man shook his head knowingly at this anodyne answer as if Alex had passed him some particularly important information. "I see, so where have you come from?" he asked, still clearly radiating alcohol fuelled bonhomie.

"Saudi", Alex sighed, eyes still firmly down on his copy of 'High Life.'

"Whereabouts", came back the immediate reply, "Eastern Province?"

Alex turned and gave the man a shake of the head. "No, Jeddah."

The man suddenly looked a little disappointed by this last piece of information and a little frown fell across his puffy unkempt features. This disappointment was short lived as the sound of the clanking drinks trolley had just announced itself. Pushed at one end by a largish woman and pulled at the other by a slim hipped man.

"A large G&T please madam", asked the man entirely unprompted whilst dropping his stowed table into position with the practiced ease of a frequent flyer. The stewardess quickly handed out the man's drinks with matching mechanical efficiency.

"Anything to drink for you Sir?" asked the heavily built stewardess with her professional, glazed smile.

"I'll have a beer thanks", replied Alex.

The flight attendant handed Alex his drink and dropped a small packet of something onto his tray. The banker picked up the packet and briefly scanned the ingredients, packed with E numbers and monstrous amounts of monosodium glutamate, it looked inedible. Alex turned to watch the mechanical Dolittlean creature trundle on to the next row of seats.

The man bit into the corner of his own little packet and took out a few bits of its unappetizing contents before shoveling then into his mouth with undisguised relish. Head down, Alex studiedly focused his attention on the magazine he was holding, quietly hoping that the man next to him would again fall back to sleep.

The businessman took an enthusiastic slurp from his drink. "Just stopping over in Jeddah then?"

Alex crushingly realized that his monosyllabic replies were just not getting him anywhere; it was futile. "Actually I live there at the moment."

The man pulled a long face and nodded as he put down his drink and then forced his tubby fingers into the little packet searching for more to eat. The packet crackled irritatingly as he eventually managed to get another morsel out with ham fisted difficulty. For a moment he studied the crispy snack with slight disappointment before popping it into his mouth. "Really? I've been there a handful of times over the years myself, always so bloody humid isn't?" he said rhetorically through his continued bovine crunching. He swallowed before only partially restraining a belch. "Personally I much prefer the Eastern Province anyway."

Alex took a sip of his beer. "Really?" he responded with disinterest.

The man wiped his mouth, "It's alright, seen a lot of changes in twenty two years", he said a touch wistfully.

"I can imagine", replied Alex still polite and distant.

The man gave a short pinched look at him as if that was something that he could not quite believe. "Yup, a lot of changes", he repeated to himself picking up his drink and taking a long draught from it. He put it down to the sound of the rattling ice, quite empty of any liquid. Fortified, he pushed the button on his seat to hail the stewardess. "Need another sharpener", he said with a conspiratorial wink. "So what brings you to the Middle East?"

"I work in banking."

The man gave Alex a sidelong glance, his brow suddenly slightly furrowed, "who with?"

"IAB"

"Can I help you?" the businessman's brief frown was interrupted by the broad hipped stewardess. She had been rolling her ponderous trolley backwards down the aisle and now had briefly stopped beside them. She learnt over and pushed the hostess call button to 'off' in the man's seat.

"Another G&T please", replied the old businessman heartily as he handed his empty glass back to the tight lipped woman. The stewardess duly obliged, expertly twisting off the tops of the bottles and placing them and a fresh glass filled with ice on the man's table.

"Thank you madam", said the talkative man with what seemed to Alex to be the trace of a leer. The stewardess broke into another polite and professional smile and wearily restarted her backwards journey.

"Any chance of some more of those savory thingies?" enquired the man with a hopeful grin.

The woman paused whilst her thin-waisted colleague delved into a drawer of the slightly battered drinks trolley. "I'm so sorry Sir, we seem to have completely run out",

549

replied the immaculately dressed steward with a wounded pout, "I'll check with the next cabin, I'm sure they'll have some."

"You can have mine if you like", said Alex offering his own unopened packet to the man.

"You don't want yours?" asked the red faced man brightly.

"Not at all", Alex replied as he offered it to the man.

"Thanks very much, don't mind if I do", he added with a cheeky grin. Alex continued with his magazine as the man noisily opened the packet and once again began his enthusiastic crunching. "IAB eh... Been with them long then?"

Alex closed his magazine and turned to face his persistent inquisitor. "Just over a year", he replied whilst barely managing to restrain a sigh and now acutely aware that the seven hour flight to Heathrow was going to be a very long one indeed.

"All still quite new then?"

"I guess so", replied Alex a little wearily.

The heavyset man gave an understanding nod, took another sip from his drink and then tipped the last remains of the packet directly into his mouth. "That's better, I was famished", he said as he wiped his mouth with the back of his hand and once again pulled a faintly pained expression as he restrained yet another belch. He pressed his seat button, levered it back as far as it would go and then stared blankly into the seat in front of him as unseen, Alex turned and gave him another annoyed look.

"I did some business with IAB a couple of times…a long time back." His tone was once again longing and wistful and it struck Alex that it might only be measured on a geological timescale, the Cretaceous or Jurassic perhaps.

"Really, with IAB?" replied Alex, now with an embryonic interest.

"The usual stuff you bankers do, you know, LC's, gad…"

Alex vaguely remembered letters of credit in his first year of training but he had never heard of the latter. "Gad?" he questioned, his attention raised a little more.

The red faced man shook his head, "No, I said C.A.D.", he replied, spelling out the last three letters. "You know, cash against documents?"

Alex gave a nod of understanding, though it still meant little to him. Trade Finance was not his thing at all. "I see and what type of business are you in then?"

"Oh this and that, you know, import export, that kind of thing, nothing too spectacular these days." The podgy fellow gave a smile which displayed a set of formidably crooked teeth.

Alex nodded sagely at this and wondered what this actually meant. Shorthand for dodgy dealing most likely, he thought. Saudi Arabia imported just about everything and had only one export and that was solely owned and controlled by the Saudi Royal family. He took another sip from his beer and thought for a moment. "So where are you based in Eastern Province, Dhahran?"

"Dhahran?" the man replied with obvious incredulity and then emitted a short mirthless laugh. "Oh no, I'm not there anymore thank God. No, I'm based in Bahrain these days", he added with a note of satisfaction in his answer.

"Right", responded Alex slowly, with slight confusion starting across his features.

Catching the doubtful tone that had crept into the banker's reply, the portly businessman continued with a knowing smile. "No, but I used to be based there. Well, Damman to be absolutely precise."

Alex again ignored the slightly slurred sibilance that accompanied the man's last words and let out a brief affirmative noise.

The businessman cleared his throat and then added with self mocking seriousness, "British Aerospace, man and boy."

"I see."

He made an apologetic little shake of his head. "Joined them after my seven hundred and twenty eight days for Queen and country…"

Alex' eyes narrowed at this slightly cryptic reply, "seven hundred and twenty eight days?"

"You know, my two years of National Service", he said with a short proud snort.

"Oh yes, of course", Alex replied suddenly feeling a bit foolish.

The man picked up his empty glass and peered at it with a frown. "They should bloody well bring it back too, if you ask me.

Alex made a noncommittal noise.

"Of course they won't, will they, especially this so called New Labour lot, eh?"

Alex stoked his upper lip as if in deep thought. "No I suppose not, not likely at all", he agreed, keenly aware of where this conversational line was most probably going to end. Bring back the birch and hanging would undoubtedly be too good for them.

"Well, not quite yet anyway." He gave a wry smile. "You ever been in the services?"

Alex shook his head. "No."

The puffy faced man gave Alex a knowing look and let out a slightly disappointed sigh. He leant forward, fiddling with his seat armrest looking for the hostess call button which was trapped under the folds of his crumpled jacket. Breathing heavily, at last he located it and gave it an impatient shove. The little light above them turned on and it was followed shortly after by the arrival of the matronly stewardess.

553

"Can I help you?" she said, her tone now tinged with impatience as she turned off the button.

"Would you mind if I asked for another one please?"

The woman gave the man another vapid mechanical smile. "Of course not", she replied as she noisily cleared the man's table of the empty miniatures and snack packets.

The businessman watched the woman walk back down the aisle towards the galley, sat back and gave Alex a quick smile. "I think she likes me", he added with a wink.

Unlikely, thought Alex as he briefly acknowledged the man's cheeky grin, before turning away and closing his eyes. He figured that he had talked quite enough to the wheezing drunken man and now he wanted to get some sleep.

The banker's thoughts immediately turned to his next few days ahead. First there was the weekend with his family and then there was his interview. Planned for the following Monday, it had come right out of the blue. Initially he had thought that he had somehow blown the long telephone interview because he had heard nothing back for five days after it. He was thrilled to be proved wrong when the call came through that he had made it onto the short list. However that was just the start of his problems as he was to discover, they wanted to see him in London within a week. It had not been easy, but Alex was learning. Dieter's bitter words on the beach that day had left a mark on him. You scratch my *baksheesh*, I scratch your *baksheesh* and Alex had adopted this approach. Amazingly, as far as he was concerned, it had worked. Discreetly, a couple of two hundred riyal bribes to the bank's sour faced visa clerks had converted them into models of smiling efficiency, that and the sudden death of a distant fictitious relative had done the job. To his utter astonishment his passport, complete with its troublesome Exit Re-Entry Visa was back in his hand the very next day.

Even when he had discovered that all the flights to London from Jeddah were full up he was still undeterred. Unfazed, he systematically tried connections through Riyadh, Dubai, Dhahran and finally Bahrain. As far as he was concerned, from now on, getting out of Saudi Arabia would never be a major problem again. Whereas in the past he had to worry about getting Claire and the kids out with him, now it was far easier. It was just him and as he had discovered the hard way, all he needed to do was lie a tiny bit and throw a little money at the problem. He did not like doing it, but there was simply no alternative.

He was just starting to doze off when he received a light tap on his shoulder. Irritated he turned with the beginnings of a scowl breaking across his features. What did that drunken fool next to him think he was up to waking him up like this?

"Would you like the chicken or the lamb Sir?"

Alex sighed and relaxed; it was the pouting steward. "I'll have the lamb thanks"

The steward deftly slipped the latch of Alex' seat table and carefully placed his meal onto it, "Red or White wine?"

"I'll have the Red thanks", he replied automatically.

The steward gave Alex a perfunctory smile and then straightened, now adopting a slightly po-faced expression and spoke to the man next to Alex, "and for your Sir?"

"I'll have exactly the same, thank you", replied the red faced man with sudden prim precision in his voice.

The steward speedily served the man as directed and then moved quickly on. The import export man waited a moment before starting to unwrap his cellophane entombed meal. Frustrated at his clumsy efforts to liberate his lunch, he paused, turned and cast a quick backwards glance to check that the steward was out of earshot. Satisfied that he was, the businessman leant over towards Alex. The hungry banker, suddenly aware of the closeness of the talkative stranger next to him, immediately felt uncomfortable and halted his previously enthusiastic chewing.

"Bloody funny types they have serving on this route eh? Seems to attract them", said the man in a conspiratorial whisper that was carried on wheezing alcoholic breath.

Alex gave the man next to him another noncommittal grunt and waited. The unpleasant proximity of the speaker, right by his ear, was totally off-putting and he felt his hunger extinguish under the man's dyspeptic breath. Fortunately and to Alex' enormous relief the man then eased himself back into his own seat and restarted the task of trying to free his lunch. Through the side of his eye, Alex watched as the businessman continued his absurd struggle. After several failed attempts the import export man eventually managed at last to bite through the stubborn packaging to free up his cutlery. He clutched his knife with a stubby grip and triumphantly stabbed it through the top of the offending cellophane barrier with an annoyed snort. As he pulled the last remains of the cellophane wrapping off, he muttered something inaudible to himself before adding in obvious frustration. "I don't know what the place is coming to."

Alex said nothing, not entirely sure what he was referring to, but dimly aware that he probably wouldn't have agreed with him anyway.

The two men continued the remainder of the meal in silence. Alex's thoughts had once again turned to his family and what they would be doing; right now Clare was probably just finishing the school run. Alex wondered how the boys were getting on at their new schools and whether Christopher was in the school football team this week. It would be fun to watch his son from the sidelines and cheer him on. Maybe they could do a barbecue on Sunday too.

Beside him the man drained the last of his wine and placed the empty glass back onto his tray with a satisfied grunt. "So are you on leave then?"

Alex looked at his inquisitor for a moment, all thoughts of home suddenly driven away. He reflected for a moment before replying warily, "sort of."

"Sort of?" parroted the man with the merest hint of a taunt.

Alex immediately regretted his ambiguity. Even though he had no desire to tell the man about his interview there was nonetheless within him, the faint warm glow of pride on his recent coup. Despite his best effort to downplay it, he was desperately excited about the opportunity of getting back to London. He missed his family hugely. "You know, a bit of business but mostly pleasure", he added with determined offhandedness.

"Ah" said the red faced man whilst theatrically tapping his nose, "Mums the word eh?"

"Quite", said Alex now distinctly annoyed with himself.

"Oh yes" said the man with another yellow toothed drunken grin, "I know how you banker types work, all very hush-hush eh?"

Alex was again irritated at the man's absurd, conspiratorial tone. He was not sure either, but it seemed that a slight taunting note had crept into the businessman' inebriated speech. Alex shook his head, "No, not really."

The red faced man raised his hand suddenly apologetic and cut Alex short. "No, no I quite understand. I know the form, no names, no pack-drill eh?" He gave Alex another chummy wink as if they were now sharing some intimate secret. In return and now slightly bemused, Alex gave the man an intense stare, still trying to work out the strange man sitting beside him. As he did so the businessman suppressed another intoxicated belch and met Alex' stare with his own bloodshot gaze. "We know how this place ticks eh?"

"We do indeed", replied Alex now much more relaxed; the fellow was simply an inebriated oaf, nothing more.

The man gave Alex a sharp look. "Most folk haven't a bloody clue", he said with a dismissive sniff to which Alex just nodded his apparent understanding as the fellow continued. "The truth is they don't want to know eh, not really."

Alex pulled a thoughtful face. The businessman dropped his voice to a low whisper. "'Still much better that way I suppose, especially since the Yanks are back in again and trying to balls it up for us, eh?"

Now Alex was intrigued. "Again, how's that then?" he said, deciding it would be fun to play along with the man.

The man leant back and briefly attempted to stretch himself before continuing. He took on a serious expression. "Well they're always changing their minds aren't they? Too bloody big for their boots that's their problem…comes from always trying to be too clever by half if you ask me."

"Sorry I don't quite follow you."

The red faced man gave Alex a disappointed shake of his head; in his experience most of these young pups like the one next to him now could often be a bit slow on the uptake, that, or just plain naïve. As far as he could make out, this one looked like he was probably both. Sharp suits and laptops, most of them were utterly clueless. He cleared his throat, "look, it's pretty simple really, when good old Maggie was around, she knew what was what. Did a bloody good job too with the Saudi's, especially once she'd sealed the Al-Yamamah deal for us in '86. The country made a packet, the biggest deal ever done by a UK company. Did you know that?"

Alex shook his head, "No."

"Well most people don't, but it was, I can tell you for nothing. Biggest contract ever, fantastic it was. Straightforward too, planes, ships, practically every piece of kit we had on offer, the whole nine yards." For the first time on the flight, the man sounded utterly and brutally sober.

"Good for the country, surely you mean just British Aerospace plc?" suggested Alex with a slightly hollow laugh, his curiosity rising.

"Are you joking? Of course the country, it's a strategic bloody industry isn't?" the man countered with astonishment suddenly flushing his perennially red face to crimson. He paused for a moment and collected himself before continuing, now with obvious restraint. "I'm not saying it was not good for the company, of course it was, but you've got to see that it was much more than just that, much more. We're talking jobs in our factories back home and all the rest of it you know. Lots of jobs…and jobs my friend, equals grateful voters." The businessman gave Alex a hard searching look before adding sternly, "These are big deals you know…bloody big."

"Yes I know that, BAe employ a lot of people back in England", said Alex now trying to sound a little less flippant in the face of this sudden onslaught of unexpected seriousness.

The man gave Alex a grave look. "Not just back home, though ninety thousand jobs is nothing to be sneezed at… here too. They've over four thousand working in Saudi you know? We've got contracts to keep all this kit working too, you know, for years to come. But it wasn't always so, I can tell you for nothing." The businessman fixed Alex with a steady glare and then shook his head almost sadly, though his tone was still reproachful. "Not easy, not at all you know. We've had our work cut out… had to cozy up to all sorts I can tell you." Now it was the businessman's turn to give a short hollow laugh before fixing Alex with a thoughtful gaze. "Difficult as I'm sure you can appreciate, right?"

Alex nodded his understanding.

The older man's features darkened. "And that's despite all the usual tricks our cousins over the pond could come up with."

"I can imagine", agreed Alex now thoroughly intrigued and completely clueless as to what types of tricks the man was referring to.

"Mind you the Yanks are forced into it I suppose. It's because they're constantly changing their minds over what they can and can't sell to the Saudis. Bloody nonsense of course and *entre nous* never been a problem that we've ever had." The man gave Alex a quick wink and flashed a wicked smile. "Anyway, that's always been our strength as far as our clients are concerned and its served us well, very well indeed" The man followed this last statement with a proud, almost aggressive grin that once again revealed his startling crooked, yellow teeth.

"I see," said Alex thoughtfully, "well that's the Americans for you", he added, now attempting to seem knowledgeable, but ending up sounding strangely enigmatic.

"What's that?" Now it was the businessman's turn to sound confused.

Alex was slightly startled by the man's sudden furrowed brow. "Well I mean the Americans have a lot on their plate, haven't they... a global strategy and trying to calm things down in unpleasant places, no?" he stuttered hopefully."

The businessman gave a derisive snort. "If you say so, but frankly they're welcome to it." He paused for a moment, beetle browed. "Well, whatever they might go around saying we've been beating them hands down for years in this place fair and square." He prodded his stubby finger into the air for emphasis, "from '73 right up to now we've sold more kit to the Saudis than the Yanks have, each and every year without fail."

"Are you sure?"

"Absolutely, no word of a lie" he replied full of pride, before picking up his drink and emptying the remainder down his throat with what looked very much like a flourish. Alex suddenly thought of Jerry Allensen and Ernesto Sanchez. The American soldiers with their Patriot missiles and the huge Raytheon compound that was situated right next to Sierra Village and wondered if they also knew that Britain was making more money than America selling arms to the Saudis. In any case, it certainly was news to him.

"Bigger even than Raytheon?" Alex was still slightly disbelieving.

"Raytheon? Don't make me laugh, we're bigger than all of them put together and anyway that Patriot thing doesn't even work, despite whatever CNN may tell you", replied the import export man. He shook his head with disbelief. "Anyway ever since Desert Storm the Yanks have been up to their tricks all over again. Right royal pains in the backside, that's what they are." He leant over towards Alex and dropped his voice to his now familiar conspiratorial whisper. "Mind you, not as much as the bloody locals eh?"

Alex gave a shrug, still unsure of what the red faced man was actually on about whilst he once again eased back into his seat. The businessman sucked in a long wheezing breath before letting out an equally sized resigned sigh. "Turned over like an apple pie I was, still, that's life I suppose. We live and learn eh?"

There was a brief pause as Alex considered this latest anecdote. "We do indeed", he agreed in a soft drifting voice, mulling over the man's earlier statements. Alex turned to gaze out of the window, there was nothing to see except the blue skies outside. Once again his thoughts returned to home and he now wondered if Claire would be meeting him at the airport. In the last phone call he had made, she had said that she would try to; he was to call when he got to the baggage reclaim.

The man sniffed noisily; unaware of his traveling companion's wandering thoughts and shook his own head slowly still deeply wrapped up in his own. "Yup, we live and learn."

Another silence fell upon the two men and Alex took this opportunity to get some rest. He pushed his seat as fully far back as it would go and attempted sleep. Eyes shut firmly closed, he heard the man next to him asking for several large glasses of, 'fizzy water'. Even he had obviously had enough 'sharpeners', thought Alex sourly. He tried sleep and managed some, but racing, disturbed thoughts chased any real possibility of rest away. In his fitful mind, perplexing images of Claire, then of his forthcoming interview continued to unnerve him. These and the constant crackling of pretzel packets, followed by the noisy folding and unfolding of newspapers from the seat next to him, meant that proper sleep remained a dreamy ambition. After more than an hour and a half of fretful attempts at sleep, Alex finally gave it up. Besides, it was impossible to sleep on a day flight, he reasoned grumpily to himself as he righted his seat.

"Eve's tomb is there isn't it?"

Alex was still quite drowsy, "sorry, what was that you said?"

Responding to Alex' question the man repeated. "Eve, you know, Adam's wife, she was supposed to be buried in Jeddah you know?"

Alex had never heard this and pulled an expression that succinctly communicated both his ignorance and his lack of interest in the matter. Frankly it did not trouble him for he had come to understand that life as an expatriate in Saudi Arabia did not encourage too much curiosity anyway. As far as the official line went in the Kingdom, history started in September 1932 and you incurred hostility if you ever questioned this. "Is that so?" he replied flatly.

The businessman pulled a sour expression, just barely restraining another effervescently fuelled hiccup. "Yup, great big thing it was, you couldn't miss it, saw it back in the seventies, funny really", he added without a trace of humour.

"In Jeddah?" Alex had seen most of the old town, no such edifice existed.

The man pulled a slightly disappointed face and seemed to ponder this for a moment. "Just outside the city it was. Of course it was probably just a load of old codswallop and she'd have to have been forty foot tall to fit into it. Anyway, but it's not on any of the maps these days." He paused for a second before producing a mischievous grin. "They concreted it up, you know?"

Alex stymied a guffaw; he had not heard anyone use the term codswallop for years. The last time it was uttered was in reference to particularly hopeless history essay he had handed in at school, he had been twelve at the time. "Why was that then?"

"Well it's all part and parcel of the same thing, doesn't fit in with today's version of events, does it? For centuries pilgrims to Mecca used to visit it, but the *Mutawwa* didn't like that at all, un-Islamic you see, idolatry or something or other. Probably didn't like them praying to a woman, most likely", he added with a laugh."

Alex shook his head and smiled in agreement, "yes I bet that would be a problem with the *Mutawwa*." "Anyway, it's just another example of history getting wiped out because it doesn't suit those hardliner *Wahhabi* nutters." Barton gave a little ironic snort before continuing, "makes me laugh, it does."

Alex gave a slow baffled nod of agreement.

"They do that a lot you know?"

"What's that?"

"Concrete over the past", continued the businessman. "'Re-inventing yourself', that's what we call it", he added with another empty laugh.

Alex gave another slightly nonplused shrug.

The businessman drew in a sharp intake of breath and leant over, "You know I'm very sorry, but I seem to have

567

forgotten your name", he said with an apologetic shake of his head.

Alex gave a short chuckle. "Actually I don't think I told you, I'm Alex Bell."

The red faced man broke into another of his now trademark crooked smiles. "Alex eh? Funny that, we've been chatting away all this time and I've never thought to ask you your name. Must be getting old…well nice to meet you Alex. I'm Gary, Gary Barton."

The men exchanged belated smiles of acknowledgement at this. Alex snatched a look at his wristwatch. Not long to go, he thought and they would be landing.

"So are you planning to stay for a while in the Kingdom then?" Alex noted that the slurred speech had completely gone. It seemed that the businessman had sobered up a great deal over the journey, which was miraculous given the amount that he had drunk earlier and the state he appeared to be when he had boarded.

Alex shook his head firmly, "Nope, not at all."

Barton nodded gravely, "I don't blame you either. It's a strange old place and it's not going to get any easier, not with oil so weak and the old King on his last legs", he added with another of his frequent snorts.

Alex pondered this for a minute. It was well known that King Fahd was likely to die at any moment. A severe stroke some three years before had rendered him almost entirely crippled and unfit for his role as absolute monarch of the Kingdom and so consequently his role was being fulfilled by his half brother, Crown Prince Abdullah. Ever since this stroke of misfortune, rumours had been constantly circulating about the King's imminent death, but still the old man hung grimly on to life; contemptuously echoing Mark Twain's retort that reports of his death were greatly exaggerated. As for Barton's statement on oil, well that was what most of Wall Street and the City thought too. As the turgid research paper he had just read noted; the proposed cuts to production by OPEC would never happen as none of the oil producers were willing to cut their own output. OPEC was a busted flush, ten dollar oil was here to stay and what with the enormous potential of the newly privatized Russian oil companies, it was likely to go lower, or so all the experts were saying.

"Honestly, I can't see it changing much when the King dies", Alex countered.

Barton gave another grave shake of his red faced head. "No obviously not that much once Abdullah takes over, whenever that does actually happen. But the man is now in his seventies and going forward the real question is this. Who will succeed him? I tell you, there's going to be real fireworks when that eventually occurs."

Alex gave a shrug; frankly the question of the succession of the rulers in the Kingdom of Saudi Arabia was not one that he had thought worth much asking. Who outside the country could possibly care, what possible ramifications could there be? "Why's that? Surely it doesn't matter that much?"

Gary Barton's grey, though still slightly bloodshot, eyes narrowed under a slightly arched eyebrow. "Personally I think it may count for quite a lot in the future you know. This place ticks along just fine as long as oil keeps up." The businessman paused suddenly deep in thought. "Still neither of us will be around when that happens." Barton cleared his throat and gave another yellowing smile. "Anyway, so what do you think of IAB then, interesting bunch aren't they?"

"They're alright", replied Alex offhandedly.

"Is Ed Moore still there?"

Alex was completely taken aback by this unexpected turn in the conversation and turned to give Gary Barton a closer look, "yes, he is. Do you know him?"

Barton nodded and gave a tight lipped smile before adding. "Thought so, he's quite a character isn't he?"

Alex was suddenly unsure how to respond to this statement. "He's the Treasurer there", he added redundantly but now very guarded.

Gary Barton shook his head side to side knowingly, a thin smile still played across his red, veined features. "Indeed he is. He's a wily one for sure. Still watching the higher ups then eh?"

Instantly this last question made Alex feel distinctly uncomfortable and he felt himself flush red, now feeling both embarrassed and defensive. He understood well enough that he knew next to nothing of what Ed Moore might or might not be and yet this strange wheezing man beside him seemingly knew all about him. Alex stared at his traveling companion, glassy eyed in thought as his mind raced off far ahead, suddenly aware that he might have misjudged the man beside him. That Ed Moore could be described as wily was plainly obvious. In fact it was the very same word that both he and Jim had used to describe the American the night that his friend had slipped and nearly broken his ankle. Alex inwardly restrained a wince as he recalled that 'wily' had probably been the most complimentary term that they had used that drunken night. The trader's mind whirled in an unwelcome litany of unanswered questions, provoked and stirred up by the man sitting beside him. For a moment Alex hesitated, caught between his fear of disloyalty and his keen hunger to know more. His hunger won hands down.

"Higher ups?" coaxed Alex.

Gary Barton now flashed a brief frown. "You know, the Bin Bafaz family"

Alex stymied a look of disbelief, "the Bin Bafaz'?"

The businessman's features darkened and he gave Alex an intense look, "you've heard the rumours about them haven't you?"

Alex' open faced expression succinctly conveyed his transparent ignorance.

Gary Barton sucked in a short breath of air before emitting a low sounding murmur as he continued to stare at the banker. This young fellow really was shockingly naïve; about the same age as his son he imagined. "Well, let's just say that your owners are firmly on the Kingdom's naughty boy list."

Alex felt both affronted and increasingly confused. "I'm sorry but I don't quite understand what you a getting at?" he stammered. All of this was completely new to him, nobody in IAB had ever mentioned anything like this to him and he was feeling stunned and shocked by this latest revelation. Alex wondered what on earth Barton was driving at now.

Gary Barton dropped his voice down to a near whisper and leant over towards Alex. "It's because the Bin Bafaz family have some interesting friends and relations. You could say they're a bit 'persona non grata' in Saudi."

Alex stared back at the grey eyed man, still taking stock of all of this new and disturbing information, and waited for the businessman to continue. Barton, obviously enjoying this moment paused as he noisily cleared his throat before continuing on in his low pitched West Country burr. "Well for a start Khalid Bin Bafaz' sister is married to Osama bin Laden."

"Osama bin Laden?" The name meant little to Alex. Of course he had heard of the Bin Laden's, who in Saudi Arabia had not? They were the largest construction firm in the Middle-East, everyone knew that. Initially the family's fortunes had been secured by the huge commissions they had earned for the lavish reconstruction and development of Mecca under King Faisal. Since then most of the shiny new highways that now criss-crossed the country and a good deal of the largest and most lucrative construction projects had been theirs for the asking, courtesy of their very close links to the royal family. It was just an impression, but as far as Alex could see, practically every new building in the Kingdom seemed to have been built by the Bin Laden group. That was not surprising, after all, the Bin Laden Group was headquartered in Jeddah.

"Yup" replied Barton, momentarily relieved that the man he was speaking to had at last grasped what he was saying.

"Osama bin Laden, which one is he then?" enquired Alex, trying to make light of his lack of knowledge.

573

Gary Barton shook his head again. "He's only perhaps the highest profile dissident in the Kingdom." This time Barton leant right over towards Alex and added in a hushed conspiratorial voice, "He wants to get shot of the entire royal family for starters."

"I see", said Alex uncertainly before edging back in to his seat and away from the uncomfortable proximity of the other man.

Gary Barton studied Alex with a long sad look before once again shifting back into his seat. "Yup, the man most feared and loathed by the Al-Sauds is your owner's brother-in-law." Barton gave a short sardonic, almost taunting chuckle, "I'm surprised you didn't know that."

Alex gave another uneasy shrug, still trying to adjust to the heavy burden of his ignorance. "I've never heard of him."

"Well you won't find anything about him in the jolly old Arab News, if that's what you're after." Barton replied as he broke out into yet another short mirthless snort.

Alex bit his lip at this latest rebuke, feeling chastened and foolish he rubbed his chin thoughtfully. It was all very disturbing. This type of speculation was not the kind he was used to at all. "So how do you know Ed Moore then?"

Barton paused and sucked on his teeth before he answered. "It's a small place, this part of the world, particularly when you've been here as long as I have. I've run into him a couple of times over the years, way back when he was based in Riyadh."

At last Alex heard something that he was already aware of. Moore had made no secret of his long history in the Kingdom and that he had worked for Citibank's subsidiary in the capital. "Yes, he was with Amersaud Bank in Riyadh," he said brightening, glad at last to be seen as not be entirely ignorant.

Barton briefly nodded agreement, "Yup that's the one...purely social of course."

Alex gave the man a doubtful look, suddenly seeing everything much more clearly. The man next to him was in the business of selling arms. Ed Moore seemed to know loads of military types and had worked for a joint US Saudi bank. Barton was a fair bit older than Moore but they probably knew each quite well and might well have done huge amounts of business together for all Alex might know. "Oh, of course, I understand", Alex replied with a sly look.

Unconvinced and even less concerned by Alex's reply, Barton responded with a knowing yellow flash of a smile. The businessman then turned and mumbled something about the seat and shifted uneasily within its leg numbing confines, trying vainly to make himself a little more comfortable. He followed this with a half hearted attempt at stretching himself out before slumping back into his former round shouldered position and puffing out another low, resigned breath. He glanced down at his wristwatch, expensive and Swiss, "not much longer to go now", he added before yawning and closing his eyes.

Behind the shuttered eyelids Barton's thoughts briefly returned to Ed Moore. The truth, despite whatever this fellow next to him was currently dreaming up, was that he had never had any direct dealings with the Moore or any American for that matter. After all, they were their main competitors, them and to a lesser degree the French. Barton casually searched back in his memory to recall when his last meeting with Moore had been. It was something Barton prided himself on; he never forgot a face or a name. Yes, it was certainly in Riyadh, back in the mid eighties, last time was at some embassy function. If he remembered correctly and he was sure he did, Moore was very likely CIA or something of the sort back then, today with IAB he almost certainly was. Funny chap, he recalled that Moore was practically teetotal. Gary Barton never trusted a man that would not have a drink.

It was not long before the plane was making its final approach into Heathrow. Alex had long given up on his reading matter and was still trying to put unwelcome and confused thoughts away. He stared out of the window to see snatched and disorientated views of the rooftops of

London below, which peeped occasionally out from the thick folds of cloud that cloaked the city. Beside him, Barton was still slumbering away and Alex was now thoroughly frustrated with himself that he had not plugged the mysterious man next to him more effectively for information. The opportunity had seemingly passed as Barton had been sound asleep for the remainder of the journey. As the plane bumped along the runway Barton roused from his open mouthed, dead to the world sleep and wiped his red wine stained and cracked lips. Alex catching the man's movement turned and gave the old man a smile and a friendly nod.

Barton stretched, "Terra firma, at last."

"Yup, on time too", replied Alex.

Barton checked his watch, "so we are."

"So how many planes crash on landing then?" said Alex with a cheeky grin as they stood up to leave the aircraft. As he did so he pulled out his mobile phone, he had forgotten to turn it off and the battery was now dead. This was not good.

"Fifty one percent, but I wasn't going to tell you until we'd landed", replied Barton with his crooked smile.

19. Misguided Patriots

Pete Koestler had not noticed it until he was practically out of the door. At first the Zimbabwean thought of just leaving it there, after all he was already late for work and it was most probably for his wife Helen anyway. Most likely yet another invitation to join the needlepoint club or some other Funny Farm event, he thought to himself. Even so, there was something odd about the envelope, it was bulky looking and a bit dog eared, so he knelt down and picked it up. Turning it over, he saw that it was addressed to him, though he didn't recognize the neat handwriting. He opened the letter, inside was a short note and a set of keys, it was from Bill Heaver.

Koestler read it and his face creased into disbelief.

"Helen" he called out loudly.

"Yes darling?"

"Take a look at this." Koestler walked back towards the kitchen to be met in the doorway by his wife. Hair in a mess, she was giving their two young daughters breakfast. Koestler handed the short note to his wife.

"Whatever you like?" she repeated, "what on earth does he mean?"

"Not a clue…and look he's given me these keys.

Helen briefly examined them. "Those are keys to his house aren't they?

Koestler nodded, "Sure looks that way."

Alarm flashed across Helen Koestler's thin face. "Oh my God, you don't think he's killed himself or something, do you?"

Koestler's confused expression turned to astonishment, "Bill Heaver?" He shook his head with disbelief, "no way…"

Helen Koestler looked imploringly into her husband's eyes, concern written deep across her pretty features.

Pete was suddenly hesitant, "No…surely not?"

"You better get round there Pete. God only knows what this all means."

"F…" said Pete, cutting himself short.

"He's done what?" Jim Robson's questioning expression was mirrored on the faces of all the men on the trading desk.

"He's cleared out, disappeared, there's no trace of him at all", said Koestler.

"Show me that," said Joe with unnecessary force as he pointed to the envelope that Pete was holding.

Pete gave Joe Karpolinski a stern look before he passed Heaver's note over to him. Joe scanned it and shook his

579

head. The short letter seemed to have the same effect on anyone that read it.

"What does it say?" asked Alex.

Joe looked at the piece of paper and read it out aloud. "'Mate, I've had enough of all of this. I'm off to patch things up. There's some beer under the stairs. Take whatever you like....Bill Heaver'"

"Take whatever you like, what the hell is that supposed to mean?"

"Not a lot, there wasn't much to take. His place was practically empty", replied Pete with a shrug.

"I know his wife left more than a month ago and hasn't returned yet. She was Christian's teacher, he quite liked her." added Joe in a thoughtful tone.

"Have you spoken to Lee?" suggested Jim helpfully, ignoring Joe's typically arcane anecdote.

Pete shook his head slowly to indicate he had not, "not yet Jim, you know those audit guys, they're never in before nine thirty. Maybe he knows what's going on."

"Weird, I should have guessed really," said Joe, still pensive.

The men all looked at Joe. "Why's that Joe?" asked Jim from across the desk.

Joe pulled a serious expression. "Because I bought his car and he threw in a whole load of stuff for free. I didn't really think much about it at the time."

"I didn't know you bought his car. You gave him such a hard time about it, said how it was too expensive and all that", replied Jim with a slight look of incredulity.

"Well, when he called me up a couple of days ago, he just said that he wanted a quick sale and that he was prepared to take an offer", Joe answered a touch defensively.

"How much did you offer this *Khawadger*?" asked Waleed, who like all the other trainees, had been listening to this latest news with rapt attention.

"That's my business", snapped back Joe Karpolinski to his trainee with obvious annoyance.

Sitting next to Joe, but slightly behind the Englishman who was still pouring over the note, Waleed Ansari pulled a knowing look, seen by all except by Joe. Now everyone was staring at Karpolinski.

"What? Why are you all looking at me like that?" An expectant silence fell over the trading desk as Joe Karpolinski rubbed his chin suddenly deep in thought. "Look, I gave him eighty five for it, OK? It was a fair price given he wanted it all in cash …" he added in a voice that trailed away.

"Eighty five thousand riyals, the guy must have been mad", muttered Waleed with a shocked expression. The young trainee had only spoken out aloud what all the others around the desk were also now thinking.

"What are you suggesting?" spat back Karpolinski, now very defensive.

"I'm not suggesting anything. I'm just saying he must have been pretty desperate to sell at that price." The young Arab gave Karpolinski a thin rictus smile before adding with obvious insincerity, "good for you." As ever, there was never much love lost between Karpolinski and his trainee.

Conspicuously chastened by this, Karpolinski quickly handed the letter back to Koestler and sat himself down without further fuss.

Pete Koestler, took the paper, refolded and slipped it back into its shabby envelope. The blond haired man relaxed a little, for it now occurred to him that selling a car was not the action of a man who was going to kill himself. Indeed, far from it. It increasingly looked as if the Australian auditor had simply just done a runner. After all, it was not unheard of in the Kingdom by any means.

"Well I guess he's on his way back to Sydney or wherever it was he came from", he said with a growing sense of relief spreading through him. Koestler sank back into his seat as the tension that had gripped him since early that morning, melted away.

Any chance of the gossipy meeting continuing was quickly terminated by the arrival, in the dealing room, of the brooding presence of Chris Barma. Quietly he took his place, in his now accustomed manner, which meant he made no attempt to acknowledge the existence of anybody else on the trading desk.

Feeling less pressurized, Peter Koestler held back his phone call until he figured that David Lee would be at his desk. As far as he knew the audit department, like most of the others in IAB, seemed to work to pretty relaxed hours, so it was closer to ten o'clock before he chose to ring the man from Birmingham.

"David?"

"Yes", came the uncertain reply.

"Hi, it's me, Pete…from downstairs."

Recognition suddenly filled the phone line. "Ah Pete, how can I help you?"

Koestler was not quite sure how he was going to proceed and now felt a bit foolish. "Err…I was wondering if Bill was around at all?"

"Bill?" replied David Lee with surprise.

"Yes Bill, it's just that I got this rather odd message from him."

"From Bill?"

"Yes from Bill", replied Koestler with an edge of irritation creeping into his voice.

David Lee did not seem in the least concerned. "Well, he's on leave, he flew out last night. He'll be back in two weeks."

"I see, well perhaps in that case I think you might want to see this."

Pete Koester waited by the lifts for the arrival of the burly auditor. He didn't have to hang around for long and he watched as Heaver's note took its usual effect on the reader.

Lee looked utterly shocked. "When did you get this?" he stammered.

"This morning, it was posted through my front door, probably late last night, with these." Pete displayed the set of keys to Lee.

"Are those his keys?"

"Yup, I went around to his place, it was practically empty."

" ... I don't understand, he never said..." David Lee's eyes opened up wide in disbelief. "I just don't..." Literally speechless, the auditor read through the note once again. The auditor stared at the paper as Koestler waited for him to speak. Then without a word he carefully folded it up and slid it back into the battered looking envelope and handed it back to Koestler.

He gave Pete a piercing look. "This does not look good", he said flatly. He turned and pushed the button for the lift.

Pete Koestler stared at the stout man from the Midlands as he waited for the lift to arrive. "So what do you think we should do?"

"We?" said David Lee suddenly flushing crimson, little beads of sweat were starting to break out across his pudgy face. "'We' as you put it, are not going to do anything. Have you shown this note to anyone else?"

Confusion spread across Pete Koestler's features, "no, just the guys on the desk."

"Well if I was you, I'd suggest you didn't mention this to anyone else and I'd tell the others the same."

Koestler ran a hand through his long floppy mass of hair and scratched his head in bewilderment. "What do you mean?"

The doors opened and David Lee lurched into the waiting lift. Once inside he quickly pushed the button for his own floor and then turned to face Koestler before breathlessly managing just two words. "Lose it."

"What?"

Lee swallowed hard. "You heard me", he turned and pushed the button again with heated impatience. "This does not look good..." he repeated, as the doors of the lift silently closed on him and whisked the scarlet faced, barrel-chested, auditor away.

Pete Koestler stared vacantly at the steel grey lift doors, desperately trying to order things in his own mind. His sense of relief had been cruelly short lived and had once again been replaced by worried unease, only this time it was not for the safety of Bill Heaver, it was for himself.

Back at the desk, Joe had been waiting for the arrival of Pete Koestler. Impatient for the return of the man from Zimbabwe, he then had to wait until Barma had stepped away from the desk. As soon as this happened, Karpolinski sidled round to him and spoke to him in a whisper. "So, what did Lee have to say about it?"

"Nothing", hissed back Pete his eyes were emotionless, fixed unflinchingly on the screen in front of him.

"Nothing?" Joe repeated with astonishment. "He must have said something?"

Pete bit his lip in frustration; Karpolinski really was a complete plank. He turned to face Joe and replied in a low growl. "Look, he just said I should forget about it." He gave Joe Karpolinski a stare as hard as granite, "…and not mention it to anyone."

Across the desk, the other men watched this inaudible conversation take place, their eyes then following him as he slunk back to his position. Alex like the others, briefly peered over the monitors to look at Karpolinski, who was now sitting, feverously rubbing his forehead, his features crumpled in concern.

"Hey look at that", Joe's trainee was excitedly pointing at the screen.

Joe turned to face his prickly charge. "What now?"

"See, the Russians have just raised their rates again. They are now up to one hundred and fifty percent, *Alhamdulilah.*"

Joe looked shocked and immediately turned to his own screen for confirmation, just as all the others did except Alex, suddenly spurred into life by Waleed's outburst.

"Shit", shouted Joe as he scrambled to pick up his phone.

Alex suddenly aware of the commotion around him scanned his screen. He covered his handset speaker and turned to his own trainee sitting beside him. "What's happened Khalid?"

"The Russian Central Bank has raised rates", he said without emotion.

Alex pulled a face, suddenly trying to figure out what knock on effects there could be to his own positions. The dollar would sure rally further on this, but what about US rates? His thoughts were suddenly halted by the insistent voice in his telephone earpiece.

"Alex? Alex, are you still there?"

He uncovered the mouthpiece, "Yes I'm here darling, sorry."

"Alex I asked you a question, are you going to answer me?"

"Sorry darling, I couldn't hear you, there is a lot of noise here. What did you say?"

"Oh for Christ's sake Alex, it's like talking to a bloody brick wall." The line clicked.

"Claire, Claire?"

Ed Moore only looked up from his desk once he had heard the welcome sound of the door closing on the departing Chris Barma. Slowly he rubbed his tired eyes and carefully put on his half rimmed reading glasses. It was on days like these that he was really beginning to feel his years, he thought ruefully to himself. One thing was for certain, his life was not getting any easier and it was definitely not being helped by the troublesome Barma. The Head Trader was becoming an ever increasing burden to manage and consequently a continual and unwanted diversion from his real work. What the hell were they doing owning Russian Bonds anyway?

Ed Moore took a sip from his coffee, which had already grown cold and was about to start working through the pile of papers on his desk, when his phone began to ring. He picked the handset up whilst partly restraining a fatigued yawn, "yes George."

"Sir, I have a call from Mr. Leary, shall I put it through.

Ed Moore was immediately fully alert. "Sure, put it through thanks. Hey and George, can you get me some coffee?"

"Yes of course I will Sir", responded the ever efficient secretary.

Ed Moore waited a moment for the line to click through, "Hi Pat, what's happening?"

"Hi Ed, well you know…the same as usual."

"Everything OK?" It was entirely normal to get a call from Leary, but this one was three days early. Pat Leary normally called on Thursdays; it meant something was up.

"Sure we're just fine here. Say Ed, we've got something out of Meade that we'd like you to follow up on."

"OK."

"Suggest you check with your account manager."

"Will do", replied Moore.

"Yeah that'd be good, tonight would be best, if that suits you?"

"No problem Pat."

"We'll organize that. Oh and Ed…" There was an awkward lull as Ed Moore waited for the man to finish his sentence, "could you check your account statement?"

"Sure, will do."

"Bye Ed."

"Thanks Pat."

Ed Moore clicked the line out and paused for thought. Whatever it was that the National Security Agency at Fort Meade had come up with, it must be pretty important. The global listening station, filled with the military's sharpest analysts and cryptologists, sifted, collated and assessed intelligence from around the world. He turned to his computer and logged on the webmail account Langley had set up for him. It only took a few minutes to download the message from a fictitious cousin in New York and copy the encrypted file attachment to a floppy disk.

Just as the disk stopped its whirring, there was a knock on his door.

"Come in"

Ed Moore's secretary opened the door and walked slowly into the room, carefully nursing a piping hot cup of Arabica. George Harumba gently placed the Treasurer's drink onto the desk, replacing the stone cold one, with the steaming, freshly brewed one. Ed Moore gave his secretary a fleeting smile. Harumba was still very thin these days, though the red eyes had now gone.

"Thank you George."

The Filipino gave a warm smile and walked slowly back towards the door under the watchful eye of the portly American. George Harumba still carried the limp and the scars of his beating by the *Mutawwa'in* from the night that Ed Moore had rescued him. He always would.

Ed Moore watched his secretary close the door and raised himself unsteadily out of his seat. With its conference table, his desk and the screened off recessed area behind him, Moore's office was both large and private when needed. Hurriedly he padded around into the recessed part of it and quickly sat himself down at the small desk in the corner. Safe from prying eyes, he opened a case which contained a computer and a slim book of jokes. He put the book to one side and brought out the small laptop which he then turned on. After typing in various passwords and starting up various programs he inserted the floppy disk that had the encrypted file on it. A few mouse clicks and keystrokes later he was reading the decrypted email from the CIA's headquarters.

While Ed Moore was busily reading his covert emails, George Harumba was limping over to the kitchen by the lifts, still clutching the cold coffee cup. These days he couldn't get back quickly enough to his workplace in order to eavesdrop on Ed Moore's conversations. Anyway, he didn't mind that his boss was a secretive man; for George Harumba understood that he owed the American a great deal. Above all, he knew, despite the scars and the pain, that he was still very fortunate. Harry had been far less so. Harry, his friend and lover, had been found dead by the roadside two days after the beatings; the victim of a hit and run, or so the Saudi authorities had claimed. George knew better, George kept the cutting from the Arab News, that, and a picture of Harry by his bedside.

Abdul-Rahman bin Hajez stepped into the cool dark interior of the cramped little building. He was glad to get out of the insufferable dusty heat of the Riyadh summer.

Initially he walked quite slowly along the bare and cracked walls of the corridor that led him on. The walls were occasionally punctuated with doors, behind from which, low voiced murmured chants could just be made out as he passed by. His progress remained slow until his eyes had fully adjusted to the darkness around him, which was a sharp contrast to the harsh glare of the bright day he had just left outside. At last, he came to the door to the classroom he was looking for. From inside he could again hear the muffled chant of a single voice and the *Mutawwa* paused briefly to smooth out and straighten his clothing, whilst he listened to the words. Wiping his wet brow with the back of his hand to dry himself, he then quickly ran his fingers through his long grey streaked beard, knocked on the door and opened it.

Inside the room, eight young men were sitting on mats in front of an *Alim* who was still talking. The man stopped and turned to see who had entered the room.

The sprightly old *Alim*, rose to his feet with vigour and embraced the *Mutawwa*. "Peace be with you"

"And with you Peace", responded Abdul-Rahman. The Mutawwa turned to the assembled men and greeted the group, which in turn responded with a chorused deferential reply.

"Thank you my young brothers. I wonder if I might interrupt you in order speak to our dear *Alim* for just one moment?"

"With God's Blessing", the men chimed in reply.

Abdul-Rahman carefully guided the older man out of the classroom. He closed the door and turned towards the old white haired man. One of the longest serving *Alim's* in the small school, he had seen much over the years. His judgment of suitable candidates for *Jihad* was considered second to none.

"So Abu Bassam, how have our young men been progressing so far?" Abdul-Rahman towered over the shorter, older *Alim*.

"Thanks be to God, progress has been excellent Abdul-Rahman, excellent."

"Ah yes, the religious instruction has been first class, Abu Bassam, I know."

"Thanks be to God, I do my best and thank you Abdul-Rahman."

The *Mutawwa* smiled. "Yes as ever, you are doing a fine job Abu Bassam. So tell me, which of our students is showing the greatest promise?"

The religious scholar and former soldier looked a little confused. "Greatest promise? They all show great promise Abdul-Rahman, in the right hands and guided by God."

"Indeed Abu Bassim, but you know what I mean, which of them shows the most appetite?"

The *Alim* shook his head slowly, "well Bashir and Yasser both have excellent minds…"

Abdul-Rahman's darkened with disappointed. "Abu Bassim, I know that the ink of the scholar and the blood of a martyr are of equal value in heaven."

"Yes, yes you do indeed", replied the *Alim* with a knowing smile, "but you know that good memories, means they forget not what they have learnt. More importantly they have fully embraced Islam and have completely rejected the entirety of their past lives. They are ready for *Jihad*."

"What about Mohammed?"

"Al-Hamra?"

"Yes."

The old *Alim* slowly nodded his head in agreement. "Ah yes Mohammed… generally excellent. Fiery certainly, very good English too, so I hear, but still, I have my reservations."

Abdul-Rahman gave the old man an intense stare, "what are they?"

"I fear a weakness remains, a certain softness, perhaps he needs more time. It has not been long."

Abdul-Rahman nodded his understanding. "Well, let us proceed as planned and let God be our guide."

The old *Alim* gave a sly smile, "Thanks be to God."

The two men reopened the classroom door. Inside, the men who had broken out into a low pitched chatter, whilst the two clerics had been out, immediately fell into a respectful silence. Abdul-Rahman and the *Alim* sat down in front of the group. Abu Bassim cleared his throat noisily. "My young brothers, the time has come for us to choose which paths you must lead."

A loud cheer and wide smiles broke out amongst all the men. This was the moment they had all been waiting for and it had been a long time coming. These eight men had studied, prayed, eaten and slept together under the careful watchful eyes of Abu Bassim and two other Alim for an unbroken three months. Ninety days of intensive round the clock indoctrination, had fired them to the giddiest heights of martyrdom.

The *Alim* smiled and raised his hand to silence the men. "Yes, yes I know you are all ready to do your duty by Allah. *Jihad* against the occupiers is a must and we all know that it is not only our legitimate right, but our absolute religious duty to do so." The smiles evaporated and the men nodded their impassioned agreement with deadly serious expressions.

The Alim slowly ran his eyes over the group, examining the faces of each of the men with a steady gaze before continuing. "Now with the help of Allah, Abdul-Rahman and I will speak to each of you privately, in turn and with

God's grace, we will be guided in our decisions. My brethren, the righteous path is thin and hard to follow and each of you will have your own distinct path to tread. It is hard, perilous and trying and by tomorrow morning you will have already left this place and set upon it. May God bless you my brothers."

The two men then got to their feet and asked the group to wait outside. The men duly filed out and then waited impatiently in a huddle outside the classroom awaiting their turn. Inside, the two men again sat cross legged on the floor, discussing the group of individuals for the last time before finally making their minds up. Then the exiting interviews started.

Once they were interviewed each of the men was instructed to go immediately to one of two rooms and to wait there. As each of them left the two men told them they were not to speak to each other until the entire process was complete.

Mohammed Al-Hamra stood and waited for his name to be called out. Just like all the others in the small fervent band, he so dearly wanted the chance to prove himself worthy of his calling. Over the course of the last three months he had spent much time thinking of what he was being told and his heart was enflamed to bursting with the desire for *Jihad*. He watched the first man enter the classroom and his thoughts turned to what he had been taught.

Before, politics had never much interested Mohammed, until now that was. Today he understood that his situation was far from unique, that a global community, the *Ummah* really existed and felt exactly the same as he did. He was not unique or alone, he was simply at the vanguard of it. He and the close knit band that he had been with, every minute, night and day, over the last three months, had all learnt this important truth. These men around him were now his closest friends and they all fed of each other's freshly fired enthusiasm.

Above all, he now understood that the problems of the world today, were due to the arrogance and moral weakness of the West and in particular, the hated pariah, the US. He had listened intently to the words of the *Alim* when he spoke of the weaknesses and wickedness of the godless West. Greedy, imperialistic, corrupt, there was nothing sacred in their empty world.

When he really thought about it, just about everything of his previous life had been proved to be utterly worthless. What was the purpose of living in such circumstances? To live by scraping by, barely existing and only surviving by means of a hand to mouth existence, granted at the whim of some corrupt government, corporation, or some unprincipled godless individual. To live by their supposed rules, was willingly to accept a lifetime of slavery. Only through Islam, could this evil ever be vanquished and these immoral forces turned back forever.

He had listened with rapt attention and enormous pride as the *Alim* had frequently recounted how the cowardly Westerners had quaked in their boots when confronted with the fearless forces of God's Army. They were afraid of death, but to Mohammed and his friends, death was simply the last step to paradise. Throughout history, he had been shown how the forces of his religion were always stronger than any other politics. The great Satan, America, had chosen to wage war upon Islam and this, whilst inevitable, was a war that simply had to be fought. The West's actions were corrupt and only ever self-interested, they were never about values and ideals, just about influence and money. In the past it simply sickened and enraged him every time he thought about it, now it fuelled his every step.

Mohammed Al-Hamra watched as one by one, all seven of his new friends were called before him. Each of them was carrying a brown Manila envelope and a serious expression when they left the room. When at last his name was called, he stepped into the room boldly though his nervousness clearly showed through.

"Please be seated my brother" said the *Alim*.

Mohammed sat down cross legged in front of the two men. Abdul-Rahman gave his protégé his habitual thin smile. So far, in his own mind at least, Mohammed Al-Hamra was turning out to be an inspired choice for recruitment to God's Army. As far as he could see, the several months of intensive work that had been invested in the youngest Al-Hamra looked liked time well spent. He gave the young man a friendly but penetrating stare.

"So Mohammed, do you think you really will be able to benefit properly from this next step? It is just the first of many you know?"

"Oh yes Abdul-Rahman, God willing I know I can and I know it is an honour to do so. Thank you."

"My brother, you do understand that this will not be easy?"

"Praise be to God, I do." Mohammed still had no idea of what they had in store for him.

"And it is my duty to inform you that there are many others who would gladly go before you. This must solely be your decision. The struggle is not for boys or weaklings."

"Praise be to God, I do know this, Abdul-Rahman"

The *Alim* watched the young man closely as he answered the *Mutawwa's* questions.

"We think you would benefit from further training in Pakistan."

The young man's face fell as soon as he heard the words of Abu Bassim. He had been hoping to be sent out to one of the places that needed immediate help, the Sudan, Egypt, the West Bank or best of all to Afghanistan, where Osama bin Laden was rumoured to be.

599

"Pakistan?"

The *Alim* nodded, "Yes my brother, there is opportunity for further technical training we would like you to undertake."

"You think I need more training?" asked the young man uncertainly.

Abu Bassim gave a quick sidelong glance to Abdul-Rahman before turning to face the young man. "We both think you would benefit from more specific training Mohammed. We are engaged in a war that requires technical knowledge and we want you to utilize all of your talents."

"I see", replied Mohammed disappointed and with little conviction.

"Mohammed, my young brother, this is not a race you know. We have to work carefully, to marshal our strengths, to think before we act. We are simply the tools of God's will."

"I understand."

Abdul-Rahman gave the young man a stern look. "Before anything can happen we will need to tie up some loose ends."

Mohammed's expression registered confusion, "loose ends?"

The Mutawwa nodded, his features darkened over. "Firstly, you will need a new identity. Nothing of your former existence must remain. Nothing whatsoever, is that clear? Anything that can be traced back to here, to us, or your family must be eliminated. Do you understand?"

"I understand."

The Alim reached into a folder beside him and pulled out an envelope. "From now on this is your new name." He passed the envelope to Mohammed. "You may open it once you have left here and you are in room 105."

Mohammed looked blankly at the envelope.

"Have you any questions my brother?"

"Will I be able to see my family again?"

Abdul-Rahman sifted uneasily and the *Alim* cast another sidelong glance towards the *Mutawwa*. The old man turned back and gave Mohammed a thin smile before speaking. "You will have the opportunity to… if you must, but it would be better, much better for them, if you didn't."

"I see", replied Mohammed, suddenly aware of his mistake. Abu Bassim gave the young man an intense look. "The road is hard and solitary Mohammed, are you sure you can do this?"

"Of course *Alim*, I'm sorry to have troubled you, it is not important."

"Don't worry my brother, we will keep them well informed, that is how things work best."

Abdul-Rahman looked at his protégé sternly and broke into a thin smile. "Then I will make the arrangements, may God protect you."

601

Thursday evening was as busy and hectic as ever at the bar of the US consulate, the perennial summer exodus of the hot summer months, was still to come. The milling crowd was made up of most of the great and the good that Jeddah had amongst its large overseas contingent. Alex and Jim had, as was now usual, arrived early and together in a taxi and had already managed to down several beers by the time that Joe Karpolinski and his wife, Isobel unexpectedly loomed into view.

"Fancy a top up then?" asked Joe.

"I'm fine thanks Joe", said Alex with a grin.

"Me too", replied Jim, raising his practically full glass as proof.

"White wine Isobel?"

"Yes darling that would be lovely, thank you", answered his wife.

Joe Karpolinski disappeared off towards the crowded bar, leaving his wife with the two men. On the trading desk Karpolinski's wife had a reputation of being a bit of a combative nightmare. As far as they could see she definitely wore the trousers in their relationship. Whilst at work Joe always seemed to revel in confrontation and controversy, but in the presence of his wife, Joe became an entirely different and unrecognizable sort of animal.

"So how are you two bachelors getting on then?" she asked brightly.

"So, so", replied Jim.

"How about you Alex?"

" OK, I suppose", he replied offhandedly, wondering what Isobel was implying. He wasn't a bachelor yet at least, as far as he knew.

" Missing Claire, and the boys I'd imagine," she added with a smile.

Alex pulled a sour face for an instant, "yes you could say that."

"When are you next going to see them?"

"Hopefully in a couple of weeks", replied Alex.

"I hear the weather has been awful back in England, nothing but rain, rain, rain…oh and grey skies of course", she added with apparent glee.

"Is that right?" said Alex with a bored expression and now reminded that the lack of seasons was another thing he missed. The unrelenting sameness of the weather in Saudi was now getting at him, mind you he thought to himself, not as much as Isobel Karpolinski. Her unrelenting brightness could be just as exhausting as the July Jeddah sun.

"Yes, apparently so. Thank God, we're here eh? I just love the sun."

"What, even in July and August?" asked Jim with the beginnings of astonishment.

"Oh yes, of course, I don't mind that, not one bit."

Jim and Alex briefly passed a knowing look, but Isobel Karpolinski oblivious to her listeners, carried on regardless.

"Of course it's more humid here than in Bahrain, but you quickly get used to it, don't you?"

The men nodded.

Isobel's face clouded over. "Though I loved Bahrain and must say I never wanted to leave it. It was just a wonderful place." Alex thought for a moment of leaving Jim to the delights of Bahrain. He had repeatedly heard about the wonders of the little Island whenever he had seen Karpolinski's wife.

Isobel Karpolinski, leant forward and dropped her voice to a whisper, her eyes wide open with repressed delight. "So then you two, what you think of the Heavers? Quite extraordinary, don't you think?"

It had been several days since the news of Bill Heaver's curious disappearance and by now the men on the trading desk had grown tired of speculating on the reasons for the Australian's hasty departure. Obviously Alex clearly remembered the conversation he had with Claire about the not so mysterious happenings in the school stationery cupboard, but thought it better not to mention any of this to his colleagues. He just felt sorry for Bill Heaver and acutely aware that he was in no position to judge other people's relationships.

"Stranger than fiction," said Jim.

"Oh Jim, it was hardly that mysterious was it? Well I blame her entirely."

Jim frowned, "who, Heavers wife?"

Isobel Karpolinski gave Jim a shocked look as if he had uttered some vile profanity, "Of course his wife, surely you know?"

Alex restrained another sour expression, while Jim cocked his head and asked with a curious, slightly disbelieving smile, "What about his wife?"

Isobel Karpolinski's expression said it all before she even spoke a word. "She was a right tart."

Alex winced. Whilst Joe Karpolinski's accent was distinctly plumy and Home Counties, every now and then his wife's similar sounding accent would crack, exposing beneath it a raw, proper Cockney twang.

Jim's restrained a laugh. "I'm sorry Isobel, what are you saying?"

Isobel was just about to explain, when her husband appeared on the scene.

"One chilled white wine. A lovely little number", he said with a winning smile and presenting a glass that was already gathering humidity on its chilled glass surface.

"Cheers", he added and took a long draught from his own glass.

"I was just telling Jim and Alex about Maggie Heaver", said Isobel as she took a sip from her glass.

Joe suddenly looked sheepish. "Oh that…"

"So why was she such a tart then?" asked Jim with sudden interest.

"You really don't know?" she replied wide eyed. She turned to her husband, "you haven't told them Joe?"

Joe suddenly looked very ill at ease, "Well not really darling, there didn't seem much point..."

Isobel pulled a quizzical frown and then turned to the two other men. "She'd been carrying on with another member of staff. They'd been seeing each other after school; caught red handed by the wife of the man she'd been shagging." Isobel seemed to be enjoying herself immensely.

"I see", said Jim with a shake of the head. He turned to Alex, "well that explains quite a lot doesn't it?"

Alex just nodded.

"So how long have you known all this?" asked Jim with his ever present frown of curiosity

Isobel turned towards her husband. "Oh I don't know. How long would you say, darling? Four or five months at least."

Jim stared at Joe Karpolinski open mouthed and Joe's eyes dropped to the ground. "Err, I wouldn't like to say really…a while."

Jim gave Karpolinski a sad look before a wicked glint flashed across his features. "So how is the new car running Joe?"

"Oh it's so much better than the old one," said Isobel with a mile wide smile, "isn't it darling?"

"Yes dear."

"I bet it is", said Jim with a slow shake of the head and another crooked smile. He took a long draught of his drink, deliberately draining his. "Looks like I need a refill", he added, showing his empty glass.

"Me too, I'll go get them", added Alex in a flash.

Jim gave Alex another knowing look. The Londoner was not about to let Alex leave him with these two. "I'll come with you…fancy stretching my legs." Jim turned to Joe and Isobel with a friendly smile, "see you later" and the two men made a speedy exit.

As the two friends picked their way through the milling mass of smart, but casually uniformed expats towards the bar itself, Alex just spotted Ed Moore in the far corner talking to Lorenzo Evans. He had been to the Brass Eagle at least two dozen times since his first visit. This was the first time he had seen them together since that first time.

Back then they had disparagingly referred to Moore as 'Charlie Brown', not any more. In that moment a dozen questions came bubbling to the surface of Alex' mind, he stopped in his tracks. "Hey Jim, I'll be back in a sec', I just want to have a quick word with Ed."

Jim gave Alex an odd look, "what about?"

"Ah nothing serious, just something that's been bugging me."

Alex turned and started to work his way through the melee towards the two Americans. He was not half way across the crowd, when he felt a firm tap on his shoulder.

"Hey buddy, how are you doing?"

Alex turned to see the familiar crew cut face of Jerry Allensen.

"Oh hi Jerry, how are you?"

"Pretty good", he said, patting his flat stomach.

Alex gave him a good natured grin. "Feeling fit are we?"

Jerry gave Alex a good natured slap on the shoulder. "You bet and I'm gonna whip your ass boy."

"Fat chance" said Alex still grinning ear to ear. "What was the score last time?"

The Nebraskan gave a knowing grin. "Yeah, yeah, you were lucky."

"Yeah sure I was" agreed Alex with good natured sarcasm.

"Hey Alex, you not drinking or something?"

"Nope, just water for me, I'm in training", said Alex suddenly with a hugely serious expression.

The Nebraskan pulled a face of disbelief, "training?" He looked the Englishman up and down, he did look pretty fit.

"Yup, I'm on a strict diet and a punishing fitness regime and intend to win the squash competition. No pain, no gain, right?" Allensen's confused expression was a picture. Alex couldn't keep a straight face any longer and broke into laughter; the American soldier was always so easy to wind up. "No, of course I'm not. Jim's getting me one in now."

Allensen broke into his trademark grin, once again displaying the formidable talents of Nebraskan orthodontics. "Right", he said in a long drawl as the penny dropped.

"Look I've got to hop, I'll speak to you later" and Alex turned to go.

"You still on for Saturday?"

Alex paused for a moment, "sure, I'll see you at the court at seven."

The banker peered through the crowd and saw that Moore and Evans were still deep in conversation. He pushed his way through the last few close knit bodies of the crowd. Evans caught Alex' approach and visibly stiffened for an instant, he continued talking to Moore who turned and gave the Englishman a welcoming smile. Alex made the last few yards, watched by them both.

"Hi Alex, how are you?"

"Fine thanks Ed, and you?"

Moore stared into the mid distance. "Good thanks. I think you two already know each other, right?"

"Sure we do", volunteered Lorenzo Evans as he offered his hand and the two men exchanged a firm handshake.

An embarrassed silence fell upon the small group of men, as they stood motionless in the turgid evening air. Moore drew a long breath on his ever present cigar.

"It's a real crush here tonight isn't it?" Alex remarked.

"Yup it sure is", agreed Moore as he blew his smoke out in a slow long breath.

Another silence fell on them and Alex immediately regretted not having a drink in his hand to distract himself. He desperately trawled his mind for a conversational icebreaker. "You've got an interesting name haven't you?" Alex was looking at Evans and he could not believe what he had just come out with.

The off duty intelligence officer gave him the briefest of smiles. "You think so?"

Alex reddened, "well Evans is a Welsh name."

Lorenzo Evans smiled. "My grandparents emigrated from Argentina."

"Oh really?"

The American nodded and Alex responded with a slightly embarrassed grin.

"So Alex, how is your family doing?"

"They're fine thanks, Ed." He had not actually told anyone that Claire had decided to return back to England. Obviously his colleagues all knew, but Chris Barma and the rest of IAB had no knowledge of it.

"Is Claire here tonight?"

"Err no Ed, she's back in England." Alex reddened again.

Moore nodded sagely, he already knew that Alex' family had left long ago. The Treasurer kept a full record of all the Entry and Exit Visa requests of everyone that worked for him. Alex' family had left months before. He nonchalantly blew out another plume of blue tinged cigar smoke. It didn't surprise him in the least that this man's wife had decided to leave. Moore knew the type of wives that could tolerate conditions in Saudi Arabia. He had met Claire Bell; she was the type that could not.

Alex gave another nervous smile, he wanted to ask Moore about Gary Barton and his years in Riyadh, but suddenly, he felt unsure if he should. If he did, he would also need to explain why he had left the Kingdom for a long weekend, at short notice and more importantly, without proper approval. Chris Barma was still entirely ignorant of Alex' last dash out to London and back again, as far as Barma was aware, Alex had been off sick.

Alex decided to tweak the truth a little. "I met someone who knows you and who sent you his regards."

Ed Moore eyed Alex warily for an instant, "who was that then?"

"A chap I met recently called Gary Barton."

Ed Moore blew out another slow puff of smoke, "I'm not sure I remember anyone by that name." The tubby American was staring out into the mid distance.

Alex watched his boss closely as he spoke. "He said that he had met you in Riyadh, back in the eighties."

Moore shook his head slowly, "Nope, doesn't ring a bell I'm afraid."

Alex looked disappointed, "Oh"

"Met a lot of people over the years Alex, when did you see this guy?" Moore was looking directly at the trader.

"At the British Consulate, a while back."

"Is that right, the British Consulate here in Jeddah eh?" Moore stymied his incredulity at this last statement. It was highly unlikely that Gary "the bagman" Barton was in Jeddah. Still he had to give the Englishman his due; he had lied without batting an eyelid.

Alex felt pretty uneasy after this latest exchange and decided that he needed to change the subject, quickly. "So I hope Lorenzo here is keeping your supply of Cubans topped up."

Ed Moore broke into a laugh, "Hey easy Tiger, are you trying to get me and Lorenzo kicked out of here?"

He turned to Lorenzo Evans still chuckling, "A man can't even indulge in a small vice without it getting him into big problems eh Lorenzo?" The West Point graduate suddenly straightened and looked at Ed Moore as if he'd given him an order. Moore turned to Alex and dropped his voice to a low whisper. "Hey Alex, Cuban cigars are strictly off limits for guys like us, embargoed by Uncle Sam, savvy?" The treasurer gave Alex a wink. "That's why I asked Lorenzo here to ask you to bring them to me. It's our little secret, right?"

Alex felt an idiot. "Right, I see."

Ed Moore gave Alex another warm smile and a wink. "C'mon, indulge an old man eh?"

Alex felt he was just about to drop himself further right in it when he was saved by the welcome arrival of his much needed friend Jim. "I was looking for you mate, here, this is yours", he pressed a schooner of beer onto Alex.

"Cheers", replied Alex with relief and gratefully taking the drink from the South Londoner.

"How are things going with you Jim?" Moore asked.

"Not so bad Ed."

"No nasty Russian paper in your book then?"

Jim took a swig of his beer before answering, "Nope, not my choice of poison."

Moore nodded appreciatively, "that's good to hear. How is Joe doing?" Joe was the only one on the desk with substantial and direct exposure to the Russian market.

"I think he's cut back on some of his position", replied Alex, "but I guess you'll have to ask him or Chris for the precise picture."

Moore gave another podgy appreciative nod and glanced at his heavy Rolex. He stifled a yawn and whilst doing so briefly caught Evans eye. The ever attentive captain showily checked his own chunky wristwatch, "Is that the time? I've got to make a move now." said the intelligence officer suddenly.

"Early start?" asked Alex hopefully, still trying to get something out of the oppressively taciturn captain.

"Something like that", he replied. He cast his eyes around the little group, "goodnight"

"See you", said Alex as the crew cut American strode off into the crowd.

"Nice meeting you", added Jim pointedly having barely exchanged a word with the American officer.

Ed Moore said nothing, simply watching the man depart, whilst taking yet another long draw on his only vice. His only acknowledgement of his compatriot's leaving, being a gentle, unseen wave of the smoldering Havana.

"Well I guess I should be off too, it's getting late", said the Treasurer.

As soon as Moore had stepped away Jim turned to Alex. "So what was that all about?"

"Ah nothing really", replied Alex with a forlorn shrug.

Jim looked unconvinced. "Ah c'mon Alex, what was bugging you so much?"

Alex shook his head, "Nothing mate, I was just putting two and two together and coming up with eight."

Later on the two men were standing outside the consulate, queued up, like quite a few of the departing guests, waiting for a taxi. They stood waiting patiently for their turn, the normally long line of taxis strangely depleted that night.

"My driver is here, can I offer you a lift?"

Alex turned to see Willem Schuster, the big Swiss cheese, standing right next to him. Beside the elegant Swiss was his familiar red headed friend, John McNeil. Dwarfed by the larger man, the little Scotsman looked like a ventriloquist's dummy perched beside him.

"Hi Willem, that's very kind of you." Alex had hardly ever spoken to his neighbor from across the pool. As usual the Swiss looked terribly formal, his starched white shirt still crisp despite the humidity and sporting a pair of dark trousers with shiny black shoes.

He turned quickly to Jim. "Suit you?"

"Sure" replied Jim in flash. There were no taxis here, it would be much easier to get one from Sierra.

"Willem, is there any room for my friend here?"

"Auch, there's plenty of room", piped the diminutive Scot whilst Schuster gave a quick affirmative nod.

The two traders stepped out of the line and followed the other two men past the front of the queue and around the corner and stepped into the waiting car. Schuster got in the front next to his driver, while the other three men sat in the back of the large Mercedes.

"Thanks for the ride Willem. I'm not sure where all the taxis are tonight", said Alex.

"Yes, tonight there is not so many", replied Willem in his strongly accented English.

Next to him, the Swiss' driver muttered something to his boss. Schuster's head slowly bobbed as he listened to the driver's words.

"Ah, Abdul tells me there was an accident on the Medina road."

"Should have guessed as much", interjected the Scot with told you so tones.

Alex sighed with tired relief. It was lucky for him the Swiss was still about. Unusual too, as he and his equally tall wife, normally left quite early from the Thursday consulate nights.

"So where is Lily tonight?" asked Alex, suddenly wondering, for the first time, where Mrs Schuster had got to.

"She is, for the summer, back home", replied Schuster with a tired voice.

For the remainder of the journey conversation was fairly negligible amongst the tired group. The car slowed to a crawl as it worked its way through the heavily guarded entrance of Sierra Village with its convoluted concrete labyrinth.

As they passed through the tight lanes of the compound, an empty taxi waited for the Mercedes to pass.

"Oh great, a cab, can you drop me off here?" exclaimed Jim excitedly.

"Sure", replied Schuster.

The driver flashed his headlights at the taxi and halted the Mercedes. Jim quickly got out, "thanks very much Willem. He flashed a smile at Alex, see you tomorrow."

Alex waved goodbye as Jim slammed the door shut and ran over to the stationery cab. The confused looking cab drivers face quickly changed to a big smile as he realised he had fortuitously just picked up another fare. Alex gave his friend another wave as the Mercedes passed by.

The car came to a halt outside the larger villas of Algarve and Alex and McNeil got out of the car whilst Schuster briefly continued to speak to his driver. The two men waited for the Swiss businessman to come out of the car. Eventually the tall, neat Swiss stepped out. "I see you after next week Abdul", he said as he then slammed shut the heavy car door and turned to face the two other men.

"You driving yourself around these days Willem?" asked the Scot with cheeky grin.

Alex turned to look at the Swiss, with his neatly clipped beard and noticed that Schuster suddenly looked very tired.

"No, I'm flying to Riyadh tomorrow."

"Tomorrow...but it's the weekend?"

"I know", Schuster answered with resignation.

"How long are you there for?" enquired the Scot.

"One week."

McNeil shook his head, "poor you. You work too hard Willem."

The Big Swiss Cheese gave a fatigued smile, "I know."

"Well I'll wish you goodnight gentlemen", said the Scot, suddenly all formality and primness,

Schuster gave his friend a brief wave. "Goodnight John."

"See you", said Alex and the two men left the Scot as they made their way through the winding pathways towards their villas on Algarve. The twisting, familiar path, opened out onto the pool that separated the two men's homes.

"Thanks very much for that Willem"

"A pleasure Alex" replied the Swiss with his habitual stiff formality.

Alex smiled and gave a friendly parting wave. "Have a safe trip."

618

Schuster returned this action with a tired one of his own as the two parted whilst around them the humid night air hummed with the ever present monotony of the untiring air-con units.

Safely back in his own rarefied world, Ed Moore sat in his favourite chair, brow furrowed, mulling over perturbing thoughts yet again. It had been a difficult week, not only had he been forced to meet with Evans twice that week, he had also got some extremely unwelcome news. The meetings with Evans, the first one at the request of his CIA handler Pat Leary, the second that very same evening in the foetid grounds of the US consulate, were troublesome enough, but still that was now the least of his problems. The encrypted email had informed him of two things. The first was that the listening station at Fort Meade in Maryland had picked up some disturbing chatter in Kenya and Tanzania. At this stage, nothing specific, but Langley wanted to know immediately of any sizeable transfers from any accounts from IAB to either country. That was fine; it was second thing that was much more disturbing. It appeared that the Feds were sniffing around; this was very bad news indeed and was the reason for Leary's pre-emptive call. The intelligence services did not like the FBI one bit and Ed Moore had no reason to do so either. They were a menace. The Feds were just glorified cops with bad suits and worse attitudes. In his opinion, they were not just stupid, clumsy oafs; they could be totally destructive. They could take a perfectly good man down simply because their priorities were unsophisticated, unquestioned shibboleths, like Truth and the Rule of Law.

He would never forget the day when his friend Ollie, the man who had quietly saved him from the baying mobs of Tehran had been forced to stand in front of the circus of the Iran Contra congressional hearings. It was the first time he had seen the man's face since Tehran. The iconic image of the Marine officer having to endure the vitriol of tub thumping politicians, drunk on their own rhetoric as they implicitly accused him of every crime on the statute book, lived with Moore to that day. Ed Moore shook his head in sad bewilderment; Ollie North had only been doing what they had asked him to do for the furtherance of democracy, just as he was now. Moore had no desire to be exposed and exploited as some misguided patriot.

Back in Riyadh Abdul-Rahman bin Hajez surveyed the four young men sitting before him as they sat waiting for him to speak. The four had now been with their own *Alim* for a week in this small nondescript flat in the outskirts of Riyadh. It was the first time Abdul Rahman had seen any of them since the day they were given their final interviews, that was now over a week ago.

"So my young brothers, you have each been given new people to become, can you each tell me about yourselves?" He had a piece of paper which he looked down and quickly read. Looking up, he turned first to Mohammed Al Hamra. "You, my young friend, what is your name?"

Mohammed swallowed nervously before speaking, "my name is Saeed Al-Ghamdi."

"And where do you come from?"

"Originally I am from al Bahah province, but now I am in Abha."

"I see," said Abdul-Rahman with a nod of approval. "Tell me, what are you doing in Abha?"

"I am a student. I am studying catering at Prince Sultan College for Hotel Management."

"Do you like Abha?"

"Yes." Mohammed suddenly looked confused, the pressure to get things right was just immense, for a horrible moment his mind had just gone completely blank.

Abdul-Rahman's face clouded over, he repeated the question. "Do you like Abha?"

Mohammed reddened for an instant before the words tumbled out of him in a sudden torrent. "Yes, I like Abha very much, the mountains are quite beautiful and the city is very clean..."

Abdul-Rahman gave a frown and turned to the man next to Mohammed.

"My brother, what is your name?"

"My name is Ahmed Al-Ghamdi."

Abdul-Rahman broke into a thin smile, "So do you have brothers?"

The man responded with a genuine smile. "Yes, I have."

"What are their names?" Abdul-Rahman enquired still smiling.

"Saeed and Hamza."

Alex wiped the dripping sweat from his eyes, drew upon all his concentration and served the ball high into the backhand corner of the court. Jerry Allensen stretched and struck a powerful back hand volley back down the wall and the two men were once more engaged in another fiercely contested rally. Alex moved around the court gradually feeling his thighs starting to burn and ache, more and more as the two men fought for each point as if their lives had depended on it. Alex watched in delight as a ball he struck arced high across the court, hit the nick and died, leaving Allensen with nothing to return. The American swore under his breath at his misfortune and his opponents luck. Alex sportingly raised his hand for a moment to acknowledge this good fortune, but it was only half meant, he was aiming for the nick between floor and wall most the time and it was about time he got another. Alex turned and eyed his opponent; Allensen was dripping with sweat and looked utterly exhausted. In a deliberate effort to further undermine his opponent, Alex bounced into the service box, feigning endless energy and gave Allensen a smile. Inside Alex, with this latest felt like collapsing on the floor, but this was all part of the game. Both men knew that squash, like most racquet sports, was an intensely psychological one. Show your opponent weakness and you were finished, lose your temper and you were finished, rue the last mistake and you were finished.

"Eight five," said Alex as he readied to serve. He didn't need to; both of the exhausted men knew it was match-point.

Alex served and Jerry Allensen, still smarting from the previous lost point, hit the ball hard and low desperately looking for a winner, only to see it smash noisily into the tin.

Alex turned to his opponent and the two men exchanged an exhausted sweaty handshake.

"Thanks Alex."

"That was a tight one", Alex replied with a huge grin.

Jerry Allensen gave a tired nod, "Too good for me today."

The two men stepped off the court and made their way to the water cooler where they both helped themselves to several desperately needed beakers of water and sat themselves down on a bench. The two men were still breathing hard but just starting to recover from their exertions.

"So your family are staying in England?"

Alex nodded and rubbed his red, sweat covered face with the front of his sodden t-shirt.

"That's tough. You must miss 'em", the Nebraskan said with an understanding shake, his features equally covered in perspiration.

Alex pulled a sad face. "Yeah, the house feels pretty big and empty." He gave the American a crooked smile, "nothing much to do except play squash."

Allensen responded with a grin. "Yeah, it shows."

"So how are things with you?"

Allensen gave a nod. "It's all pretty sweet."

"SNAFU?"

" That's the one", said Allensen wryly.

"Well I better be off", said Alex taking a look at his watch, "I've got some work to do."

Just then the door opened and Hashimoto, one of the keener Japanese players stepped through the doorway.

"Good game?" asked the Japanese engineer.

Allensen gave a shake, "Same result as last time."

Hashimoto gave a grin and walked through onto the vacated court.

The two men got up and made their tired way out of the super cooled courts into the ever present warmth of the outside evening air.

"See you Monday then" said Alex as the men parted.

"Yeah, see you Alex".

Allensen wondered what kind of work the banker was doing on a Saturday night and figured that whatever it was, it must be making plenty of money for him to stay in a place like this without his family. Money, it was something that these guys seem to have falling out of the pockets. Not like him, he thought sourly, he had nothing but a pile of shit to deal with, especially now. Situation normal, all fucked up, was right for sure. Alex did not know the half of it.

Yet again he was being asked to, 'do over', his latest technical report. His unit, like all the other Technical Assistance Field Teams, was currently involved in presenting Patriot Missile performance statistics. There was a problem though. The radar guidance system was regularly failing; the missiles were going all over the place. The American had to retender his report, dropping out some of the less favourable data. Though he did not know it, Allensen like Ed Moore, was dealing with his own, equally troublesome, misguided Patriots.

Joe Karpolinski had thought that his day could not get any worse. The continued collapse of the Russian debt market, despite the brutally usurious interest rate of one hundred and fifty percent, had been hugely expensive for him. Yet even now he had been lucky, because since he had bailed out of his position, the rouble denominated bonds had tumbled even further. The rot had briefly halted as the IMF had agreed to bail them out with 4.8 Billion dollars. All the same, as Karpolinski had quite reasonably argued, the Russians could either devalue or default. They would not default as this would be a first; no sovereign had ever defaulted in their own currency. The Russian Government would likely devalue, like all the others before. The contagion that had started in Asia was now spreading around the world, but unlike the collapse of the Asian Tigers' debt markets which were denominated in US dollars; this was in the Russian Rouble. It made no sense, for the Russians could print as many Roubles as they wanted and whilst this currency may not have been worth much, that was another issue altogether. That would be insane. However, as Joe was to discover, that was not the only madness around him at the moment.

"I'm sorry I don't understand what you are saying." Joe had now raised his voice so that all the others on the trading desk were now listening to his conversation.

"Stolen? Of course it is not bloody stolen, I bought it from him."

"What?" Joe shouted as a look of utter dismay spread across his pock marked features. His mouth hung open as he listened to the voice on the telephone.

Suddenly sapped of any energy Karpolinski hung up the phone, the line had gone dead on him. Everyone was now watching him as he rubbed his eyes and his face gradually switched from shock to utter outrage. "Fucking, fucking bastard."

"What?" asked Jim, "what's happened?"

Joe smashed his desk with his clenched fist in angry frustration.

"That fucking bastard sold me a car he didn't even fucking own."

"Didn't own?" asked Waleed with mischief dancing in his eyes.

Joe shook his head. "It was on HP, the fucker hadn't even paid for it."

"Hire purchase?" repeated Waleed, "but didn't you ask him for the cars papers?"

"Of course I fucking did. The bastard said he was going to bring them round the next day." He shook his head in furious disbelief.

"Think of it as tax"

Joe gave the Saudi a withering look, "What did you say?"

Waleed gave Joe a sly look. "Just think of it as tax, after all, you don't pay any do you?"

Joe ruefully closed his eyes, he felt utterly exhausted. "Just shut up will you."

Bill Heaver did not pay taxes, in fact he made sure he paid for next to nothing. As the men were soon to find out; the departure of Bill Heaver was accompanied with quite a few other unpaid reminders, just as David Lee had very quickly realized. He had used his IAB credit card on a spending spree all the way and then around Australia and masterfully had taken it right up to its limit. Then there were the outstanding unpaid loans to IAB and assorted hire purchase agreements too. It was one of the advantages of being a specialist in bank frauds; you knew exactly how to do them.

20. Blow Ups

"That's such bad luck, Alex."

"Tell me about it."

Jim gave his friend an incredulous look. "And they never came back to you?"

"Nothing, not a word."

Jim knew all about Alex's trip to London for his interview, but he had just assumed things had not worked out for his friend and he did not want to pry. When he had first got back, Jim had straight away asked Alex how it had all gone, but all Alex would admit, was that it not been good. At the time, Alex' expression had eloquently conveyed it all and Jim had simply left it at that. He glanced at his friend. He was wearing the same expression now.

"So you never even met the bloke?"

Alex shook his head emphatically. "Nope. This other guy just told me his mother had died over the weekend and that he was on emergency leave. That was it."

"What a pain."

Alex gave another rueful shake of his head. "Stroke or something, whatever it was, the bloke was not there, so I couldn't meet him."

It was not something that anyone could have anticipated, but as Alex now fully understood, a sudden bereavement had unintended and pretty dire consequences if you were on a flying visit from Saudi Arabia. By the time the man he was supposed to be meeting for the interview had returned to work, Alex was already back in the Kingdom and the short list of candidates was shortened by one more name, his.

Jim cast a sympathetic eye over his friend. "So it was a completely wasted trip?"

Alex nodded. In fact it had been more than a wasted trip; it had been a complete disaster, right from the moment he had landed. Claire had gone to meet him at the airport, but Alex's mobile had gone dead, so he never got her message. He had eventually got through to her, once he had arrived home and then immediately called her on her mobile. She was not pleased. She was still at the airport and he was a complete idiot for not having called her as previously agreed in the baggage reclaim. What on earth was he thinking? If he had known now what was to happen then, he would have just got on the next plane back.

"You could say that", Alex winced as he recalled his last trip home. He had tried to put the whole depressing thing out of his mind and so far this tactic had partly succeeded. Only now with Jim's gentle prodding was it all, painfully, coming back to him. First to mind was the accident, on Saturday morning. His youngest son, whom he was foolishly horsing about with, slipped whilst being chased by Alex, fell and hit his head on their solid wooden coffee table. That bloody incident resulted in a trip to Chelsea and Westminster's A&E unit and four stitches in his son's eyebrow. Then as a direct result of this, he was left sitting in the waiting room of the hospital with the tearful David, when he was supposed to be watching his eldest son Christopher playing football. Even now he still felt the painful sting of his eldest boy's tearful accusation. "But Dad you promised." Alex took his eyes off the road, being a Friday, the normally chaotic highway was all but deserted and glanced at his friend beside him. Jim's father's words, came back to him. 'A promise is a comfort to a fraud', the man was so right.

Jim had caught Alex' movement and was roused from his own sad musings on Patricia Jennings. He almost always thought about his lost fiancée, Patsy, on his way into work, for whatever else he may have said to himself, in reality, he knew in his heart, that it was the only true reason he was making the daily trip. Jim turned to Alex. "So what did Claire think?"

Alex let out a snort that was filled with tired exasperation. He honestly did not know where to start to describe her response, leave alone explain it. Angry, betrayed, cranky, depressed, he could have trawled his way through the whole lexicon of misery. "She was not happy."

"I can imagine", replied Jim softly.

Alex paused as his mind replayed the heated arguments he and Claire had had. "Things are not good between us." Understatement was something he was getting used to.

Jim made an understanding noise and waited for Alex to continue.

"Well to be brutally honest Jim, terrible actually."

This was hardly a shock to his friend. The evidence was writ large across Alex' features, this and every day since his return. "I'm sorry to hear that. It's got to be difficult?"

Alex blew out a long, low, exhausted sigh, "it sure is."

The men continued their journey into work in a pensive silence whilst the car radio served up the usual American Forces diet of Sheryl, Shania, Huey and Jon, made complete with its side-orders of hectoring, cautionary announcements.

By now, it was early August the markets were getting more and more stretched by the tensions that were everyday mounting, US Bonds, the global repository of risk free money were gaining value bit by bit every day. Alex had bought call spreads that were all the time slowly rising in value as the market sought desperately to reduce exposure to any other type of risk.

Jim scanned through his overnight P&L report and checked his screens; he was doing pretty well, in fact very well indeed. He turned to look at Alex. He was probably doing even better given his friend's positions in US Treasury options. "Hey Alex...looking good Billy Ray."

It had been a while since either of them had used this old joke. Like anyone who worked in a trading room, the one-liners from movies like Wall Street, Bonfire of the Vanities and Trading Places were meat and drink to them, the latter being a particular favourite. Alex immediately turned towards Jim and gave him a big open smile. It was the first Jim had seen for a while. "Feeling good Louis."

Jim returned to his flashing monitors and thought how, whilst they both might be unlucky in love, they were lucky in, if not exactly cards, another game of chance and probability.

As ever, the morning was passing quickly, Friday with its late start, casual dress and promise of pinball and cheeseburgers to come always went fastest. Despite the gnawing tension in the markets, the atmosphere on the desk this day was very good, in fact even better than that, as Chris Barma was not around.

Then at around eleven the first reports started to flash across the screens of another attack on US interests in the world. The newswires and television screens were all suddenly screaming the same shocking story.

Huge truck bombs had blown up the US embassies in Nairobi and Dar-es-Salaam. East Africa did not seem like a long way away from the coastal city of Jeddah and truth

633

was it was not. Alex peered across the desk, studying his colleagues faces and realised from their expressions that he was far from the only one there who was watching and wondering if Jeddah's 'Brass Eagle' might not be hit at any moment too.

Being a Friday, Ed Moore was at home when news of the virtually simultaneous strikes on the embassies in Kenya and Tanzania were being beamed into his villa via satellite television. Frustration rose in him as he realized that the intelligence from Fort Meade, whilst prescient, was still too nebulous to have been of any practical use. It had been a week since he had, as instructed by Pat Leary, gathered and sifted through IAB's records to see if any substantial transfers of money had recently occurred. As far as he could see, there had been none. No names, no leads, nada and that was exactly what he reported. He had, to use a tired cliché, which he had unfortunately employed, gone through the usual suspects, but there really was nothing report. Now after such a major disaster, there would be an equally major steward's enquiry. This was the first attack on the US since the Khobar Towers explosions back in 1996 and furthermore it looked much worse. He distinctly remembered the hiatus that one had caused.

However, as Ed Moore had quickly assessed, this was very different. Co-ordinated strikes like this meant impressive organization, manpower and considerable financial means. The stakes had suddenly risen quite dramatically. Grimly he sat, with one eye watching the television, the other on his computer screen. As the scenes of carnage were spread by the rubbernecking circus of the world's media, he awaited the inevitable email from Langley. It did not take long. Once unencrypted, Pat Leary's email was short and entirely lacking sweetness. *'Repeat exercise, Egypt, Sudan, Somalia, Tanzania, Kenya, 2K threshold. Immediate.'* Ed Moore knew it was going to be a long day.

By the time that Alex was knocking off from the dealing room with all the other Westerners, the casualties from the bombs were already numbered in the hundreds. Alex was not the only one to notice their boss was at his desk as the men passed Moore's office on the way to the lifts. His normally open door was firmly shut; the ubiquitous unspoken signal that the American did not wish to be disturbed. Moore would often pop into the office even on his only full day off, like today, so his appearance, bent practically double, deep in concentration whilst pawing over papers on his desk, raised no eyebrows amongst the trading team as they departed.

Jim pushed the button for the lift. "I bet the security will be fierce at the consulate next Thursday"

"Can you imagine?" agreed Alex.

Pete gave a wry look. "It would have been a disaster. Just think...no booze on a Thursday night and we'd be forced to go to the one at the British consulate."

Pete's observation brought disbelieving shakes and sarcastic groans from all the others.

"Now that really would be a disaster", said Joe with a loud guffaw.

"I'd rather be teetotal", added Alex remembering the last occasion he had been there. He had been twice and he was unlikely to go a third time. Unlike the quite cosmopolitan make up of the 'Brass Eagle's' guest list, the British Consulate's, so called 'pub night', held on Mondays, was solely reserved for ageing Brits, or at least that's what it felt like. It was an utterly depressing place.

"Well I've known worse places", said Jim with a smile.

Joe shook his head. "Hard to imagine, it's like some dingy, Northern working man's club, stained and filthy carpets and what's that stupid dart board about, I ask you?."

"You been to many workingmen's clubs then Joe?" enquired Pete with a feigned look of innocence.

Joe's face darkened, "no obviously I haven't, but you know what I mean. It's so cramped and dirty, why can't they brighten the place up a bit?"

"I guess they just want to keep it low key", replied Jim as they climbed into the lift.

While the men were making their way back home through the light *Yom Al-Jummah* traffic, Ed Moore was still running the computer program he had been given by his CIA bosses. Loaded onto his own terminal of IAB's secure network, the program was searching through the bank's internal databases, only now, with the additional criteria that were set in the email sent by Pat Leary. Ed Moore was no computer programmer, but he had to admire what those smart techie kids in Langley had come up with. All he had done was to send a half a dozen screen dumps and told them which software provider had developed the bank's internal accounting programs and presto, they had sent him this. He waited while it whirred away, passing the time reading over some internal memos. It only took a few hours and the program had done its job. He looked at the report on the screen, raised his eyebrows, hit the print screen key and saved the file to the floppy disk that also held the whizz kids' program.

Within another fifteen minutes he had transferred his typed response into his laptop which then encrypted it along with the screen shot and merged it to a graphic file that he had chosen, just another scenic photo of Jeddah's fast changing skyline. He stepped back to his desk, attached the photo to an email that consisted of a pretty humourless joke and sent it on its way to his non-existent cousin in New York.

That evening Alex arrived home to find his German neighbours had obviously decided on an impromptu gathering. It was not quite the usual crowd around the pool. Most of the families had already departed the heat of the summer or were about to. Both the McDonalds and the Howards had done so with their children in tow, shortly after Jeddah Prep had broken up, but their husbands were still around. As Alex walked towards his villa he could see Andy Werner with two other women, Maureen Abbot the young trophy wife of Paul and hiding under a sun hat, he just managed to recognize the highly strung American, Kate Stratton. In the pool, four children were laughing and messing about with various floating toys, trying to capture and retain them from each other whilst they bobbed and splashed unsteadily on top of them. Alex stared wistfully at the children's faces and wondered how his three were doing.

"Hey Alex, do you want to join us?" shouted Andy, her face red with all the sun she had caught. By the time he had crossed over to the assembled group, Dieter had already poured out a glass of *Siddiqui* and tonic for him.

"Here have one of these", said his good natured neighbour from Frankfurt with a wide beam. Alex gave him a thankful smile and took the tumbler with mumbled thanks.

"You folks had a good day then?" he asked, as he pulled up a seat.

"Not bad was it?" The buxom blonde German gave a big toothsome grin as she looked around the little group for confirmation of this.

"Not bad at all", agreed Maureen Abbot as the others smiled in agreement; all except Kate Stratton, but that was not unusual.

Alex speedily cast an eye around the group and turned to face Maureen Abbot. "Paul's not about then?"

"You've just missed him. He literally just left a minute ago", replied the dark the haired Mrs Abbot with a friendly smile.

"At least he was here", interjected Kate Stratton in her instantly recognizable west Coast drawl before taking a large mouthful from her drink. The slim, blonde, whilst being a few years older than the other women, was still a head turner, but her good looks were not on display right now. She did not look happy at all. "God knows where he's now...always working." The two other women lent their American friend sympathetic expressions, as she disconsolately waved her hand, spilling part of her drink as she spoke. Kate Stratton did not like 'Sawdee' as she pronounced it and made no secret of it either, in fact, she hated the place. When she had been there, Claire and Kate had got on well.

A knowing look momentarily flashed between the two other women whilst the thoughtful silence that had descended upon the gathering, lingered and changed into a slightly embarrassed silence.

Despite her frequent awkwardness, most of the other women on the compound liked having Kate around, for she was a desperately needed reminder that their own lives were not all that bad. However much they may be struggling with their own existences in misogynistic Saudi Arabia, they were not struggling half as much as the Californian blonde. The wives liked her because, like some emotional lightening rod, Kate Stratton unwittingly conducted and transformed the other women's frustrations, which if kept untreated would have left each of them far too dangerously overcharged. Instead, their own misapprehensions of life in the Kingdom were made to feel less acute and less significant, converted through her into a palliative distraction of concern and sympathy. It was a process that may have worked for the others, but it exacted a heavy toll on Stratton, paid for with excessive alcohol and copious amounts of prescription drugs.

"So Alex...how was work today?" asked John McDonald, keen to terminate the uneasy stillness that was hanging over them.

"OK thanks John. It was quite busy today."

"Stock market crash?" asked the Scot with a quizzical look.

Alex responded with a tired shake. "No, sadly nothing like that."

"Was it those bombs?"

Alex nodded. "You heard about them?" Alex assumed that the day's excursion to the coast meant the others would not have heard the news yet.

"Yes, just heard on the radio on the way back from the beach. Shocking isn't?"

"Yup it is."

"We're gonna be next", Kate said slowly in her unmistakable drawl. The others all turned towards her. Stratton gave a little shiver and Alex now noticed how weary she looked. He had not properly caught sight of her face until then as she was still mostly hidden under the big brimmed straw sun hat she was wearing. Unlike the sun worshipping Europeans around her, Stratton had carefully avoided the days' hot intensity and so was not red and sun burnt like the others. The Californian, raised in Laguna Beach, had seen what the sun could do a woman's face over time.

Andy Werner shook her head vigorously, "Oh c'mon Kate", she replied with a theatrical puckered brow barely disguising her ever present smile, "this place is as safe as anywhere, isn't it?" The blonde German, once again looked around the gathering for agreement. "I mean... look at all the security we have here." This time the faces that greeted her looked a good deal more hesitant than before but before anyone could respond, the Werner's youngest boy ran up to his mother's side.

"Mum, I'm thirsty."

Andy gave her son an indulgent smile, "Ok, but no more fizzy drink, or you'll pop"

The young boy gave his mother a pleading look, "Aw Mum..."

"Go on, you heard me."

The seven year old boy gave his mother a hurt frown and started to trudge off in the direction of the Werner's front door. As if on cue, Maureen Abbot's daughter then came skipping across the tiles, streaming water, towards he mother. "Mum, can I have a drink too?"

Maureen Abbot grabbed a towel and started to dab it on her daughters' glistening shoulders before wrapping it around her. "Yes, follow Jurgen, he's getting one now." The slim limbed little girl turned and skipped off. "And no more Pepsi, you've all had enough", she called out over her shoulder.

"Not Pepsi!" exclaimed McDonald with mock horror. He waited for the girl to fall out of earshot and then the Scot leant forward, a wicked grin plastered across his face, "but they can have a Coke."

This last stage whispered comment brought smiles to the small group. John worked for Coca Cola; his mission was to try to reign in the huge market share of Pepsi that dominated the Middle East. Like a handful of other American corporations, Coca-Cola had been singled out by the Arab League as supporting Israel and had been boycotted since the mid seventies in Saudi. Only recently had they been allowed back in the Kingdom and it was an uphill struggle, as John McDonald could readily vouch. As he often said, nobody concedes a monopoly easily.

"When are you off John?" enquired Dieter.

"End of this week, I'm in Dubai until Tuesday and then I'm back home."

"I never asked you how Moira was getting on?" Maureen enquired.

"She's doing fine, she staying with her parents at the moment."

"She's so lucky, I just can't wait to get out of here", these last words tumbled out of her with real feeling and all eyes again turned towards the American.

"Well it's not long now is it?" said Andy in a kindly voice, radiating her usual warmth.

Stratton shook her head slowly, "Still way too long for me honey, I feel like I'm flipping out here." Stratton took another gulp of her drink finishing the remainder of her *Sid* and tonic. She leant forward unsteadily and put her glass back on the table. "Hey Dieter, you got another one of those for me?"

The German cast an uneasy look at his wife, "well of course I have Kate" and he began to fix her another drink. It only took him a few moments, Dieter, being typically German, was noted for his efficiency in all things and particularly in making *Sid* and tonics.

She took the drink, "thanks honey." Stratton sat back into her seat and then raised her head so that she could see from under the wide brim of her hat. "Say Alex, so how is Claire doing?"

Alex stared back at Kate Stratton who was holding him with a heavy lidded gaze. Alex could see that the *Siddiqui* was already taking its effect on her. "She's OK thanks." He really did not want to go into details.

"When are you off then?"

Alex gave a crooked smile, he was thinking of his boys. The thought always made him smile. "I leave in a fortnight, how about you?"

"Two days honey and we're off."

Dieter turned to the Scot next to him, who had just finished his drink. "Fancy a refill John?"

The Scot shook his head, "No thanks Dieter, one of those is enough for me thanks."

"Mum... mum", Andy's son was running towards the group of sitting adults. Racing up to them, he came to a noisy halt beside his mother, his sun tanned face was even more flushed, was on the verge of breaking into tears.

"What is it darling?"

"Mum, Emily says I smell and our house smells."

Andrea Werner gave her son a furrowed look of concern.

Maureen Abbot immediately looked in the direction of the Werner's villa. Her daughter was standing in the doorway. "Emily? Emily will you come here, please", her tone indicated it was not a request. The little girl stood rooted to the spot, she knew she was in trouble.

"Darling of course you don't smell." Andy gave her son an encouraging smile and a hug.

Maureen Abbot called out her daughter's name again and the little girl started to edge her way towards her mother, head bowed in anticipation of the scolding to come.

"Emily, come here, why are you being so nasty to Jurgen?" The little girl, head still bowed carried a wounded pout and was also on the cusp of breaking into tears. "I'm sorry Mummy, but there is a nasty smell."

Maureen Abbot felt embarrassed by her daughter's accusation and shook her head, "Stop this Emily and don't be so silly."

"But Mummy it does", insisted the child in a trembling voice that could just barely be heard.

"Actually I smelt it too Mummy", said the boy to his mother in a quiet voice.

Andy reddened, "Don't be ridiculous. What did you smell?"

"I don't know, but it was in the kitchen. It was horrid", said the boy. Vindicated, the girl looked up for the first time and nodded her own agreement.

Andrea Werner got to her feet. "I'll go and look" and she stepped off in the direction of her house.

Dieter took a sip from his drink. "Did you leave the cheese out?" and gave a short guffaw.

A few minutes later Andy returned, she had a bottle of water and some plastic cups.

"So did you find the source of the problem?" her husband asked.

Andy looked untroubled, "Well I did smell something but it was very faint. I think it's coming from next door."

Alex peered across the pool area towards number 45 where Schuster lived. He had not seen him since the night that the man from Switzerland had given him a lift back from the US consulate.

"He's probably left something out and it's gone off. Is he back from Riyadh yet?"

Dieter shook his head, "I don't know. I haven't seen him since he left Saturday. He was supposed to be there all week, maybe it dragged on."

"Doesn't he have a maid?" asked Kate Stratton.

"Yes, but I think she tends to skip her duties when Lily is not around."

"Oh yeah her", replied Kate, "she's a bundle of laughs." They all knew Lily Schuster. She was, as Kate Stratton had sarcastically implied, not exactly a laugh a minute kind of person. She and her husband were well suited.

"Looks like he left his lights on", said Alex, staring at the glow behind the curtains that could now be seen in the gathering dusk.

Andy beamed another big, toothy grin, "he's hopeless when his wife isn't around."

"Aren't we all", replied Dieter giving his wife an affectionate smile.

Alex immediately thought of Claire and glanced at his watch. Approaching six, the light was already fading fast, but with the time difference it was still too early to call home. He took another sip from his drink.

"C'mon, let's be getting you home", said Maureen to her daughter. She got to her feet and called her other daughter who was still playing with the Werner's eldest child Anna, in the swimming pool. Gathering her belongings and her children, Maureen Abbot then bade the others a good evening and tramped off into the evening gloom.

Kate Stratton watched the Abbots until they fell out of sight and sighed. She looked at her watch, it was late, her husband was late, in fact, everything was late, way too late. Leaning forward, she planted her drink heavily on the table and tiredly took her straw hat off, dropping it on the seat

647

that Maureen Abbot had just vacated. The American leant back in her seat and ran her fingers through her blonde hair. Only two more days to go she thought as she picked up her drink and drained its contents in one.

Claire ran her fingers through her dark brown chestnut hair and replaced the receiver back on its cradle and pulled up the covers tight around her. She closed her blue grey and slightly bloodshot eyes and tried to find a reason why her husband always had to get so drunk? Perhaps in his alcoholic haze, his confusion of thoughts resolved into something rational, but whatever it was, she was getting to the point of past caring. What was he playing at? It had to be two in the morning over there and he was making less and less sense the longer he stayed in that godforsaken hole. According to him, everything was always going to get better, but her faith in his judgement had just worn too thin. He was deluded. Her husband's thoughts were a feast of woolly abstractions that only ever led to a famine of actions. She could no longer believe his words when he said that things were going well at work. Why should she? He traded interest rates and currencies but his words had lost their value, inflated to worthlessness by his preening ego.

Claire turned and looked at the photograph of them on their wedding day which sat on a bedside table. They looked happy, she in her wedding dress, he in a dark morning suit. They were a good looking couple and seemed to have everything. Now, it seemed like a million years ago. Claire turned and looked away from the picture feeling the tears welling up in her eyes and closed them ever tighter, fighting back the bitter sadness. There really was no pain as acute and rapaciously keen as a broken heart. Once again she swallowed back the tears and once again tried to think. It was just so hard. She knew so well that she should not allow this hurt to skewer her very being, she needed to pick herself up, to try to maintain some sort of pride and sense of self worth and yet deep within her, she only felt the yawning chasm of her broken self esteem. He had betrayed her.

Claire Bell spent the whole of the night tossing and turning, unable to find rest, her mind filled with terrible images of her husband with this faceless woman. This was not even the worst of it, for deeper inside her there was yet another anxiety, that she somehow had brought this upon herself, she had been a fool and remained one as long as she allowed herself to be treated like this. Anger and emptiness was all she could feel. Exhausted from lack of sleep, she was still awake when the angry alarm sounded. She had forgotten to turn it off before she went to sleep, it was a Saturday. She rolled over and turned the unwelcome noise off and automatically got out of the big lonely bed. She had tried to sleep, it was hopeless. Claire glanced in the mirror and withheld a look of self loathing before walking across to the window. Outside, she could see that a light mist was still hanging in the air. She rubbed her red eyes and walked slowly through to the bathroom. In a little over five minutes she had showered and was drying her hair and once again looking out of the bedroom window. She watched as the last of the thin mist vanished to nothing, driven off by the brightening summer daylight and realized that her love for Alex had gone with the mist.

Alex was asleep in bed, when he was awoken by a loud bang and sound of screaming from outside. He opened his eyes and tried to focus, his head still thick from the alcohol he had consumed the night before and his mouth was still filled with the sour taste of *Siddiqui*.

This time he clearly heard the word "Help." He quickly struggled to his feet and looked through the window. Down below by the poolside he could see a woman, a Filipina screaming at the houses. He also saw a gardener was running away from her. Naked, he frantically grabbed a pair of shorts, pulled them on and went flying out of the bedroom and down the stairs. He ran out of the door and his first thoughts were that the woman had been attacked or that someone might have fallen into the pool, a child or one of the workers that filled Sierra, a gardener or a maid. As

650

he ran round the edge of the water to the woman he scanned the pool, but there was nothing there and by the time that he reached the woman, another gardener and all the Werners had reached the woman. Unlike Alex, Dieter was fully dressed.

"What's happened?" Alex blurted out breathlessly, the gardener was talking to the woman who was violently shaking and sobbing. Alex turned to Dieter who had a strange, worried looking expression on his face, one that Alex had never seen on his friend before.

Andy stepped up to the inconsolable woman. "Rosa, what is the matter?" The woman was gulping down breaths of air between uncontrollable sobs. Dieter turned and started to wander over to Willem Schuster's villa. The door was closed.

Andy Werner leant forward and put a friendly arm around the Filipina maid, "Rosa, what is wrong?"

"Mr. Schuster…" the woman broke down and again began to wail.

Arm still around the tiny maid, Andy leant closer, trying to calm the hysterical woman. "What about Mr. Schuster?"

The maid swallowed and took a deep breath before trying to speak. She looked like she was going to be sick. "Mr. Schuster, he dead."

Andy's face switched from concern to one of utter shock, "Rosa, did you say dead?"

The maid covered her mouth with both hands and nodded.

Andy turned ashen faced and shouted something out in German to her husband. Dieter pushed on the door, it was locked.

"*Hat sie den Schlüssel erhalten?*" He called to his wife.

"Rosa have you got the key?"

The maid nodded and passed the key to the German. Andy passed it to Alex who started to walk towards Dieter.

"No, you two stay here", she said as her curious children started to follow Alex.

The trader walked quickly around to where Dieter was standing waiting by the door to Schuster's villa.

Alex handed over the key to his neighbour, suddenly wishing that he was not there. He had never seen a dead body before and he was scared. Dieter gave Alex a nervous look and put the key in the door. As soon as the door opened the men were hit with a revolting stench of decay.

"*Mein Gott*", said Dieter as he covered his nose.

Alex immediately regretted being there. The cloying smell was utterly repugnant. The Englishman covered his nose and mouth, hesitating at the doorway. "Dieter, don't you think we should call someone?"

Dieter gave his neighbor a thoughtful frown, "Yes, of course, good idea." He turned and called out loudly to his wife. "*Andy, Nehmen Sie die Kinder nach innen und rufen*

Sie den Sicherheit Schutz an." He turned back to face Alex, "OK, let's find out what's going on."

Tentatively Alex followed Dieter into Schuster's villa. Apart from the horrific stench, everything else seemed quite normal. The room was tidy and quite chilly, thanks to the over active air-conditioning, otherwise, nothing looked out of place. It was quiet; the only sound was that of the air-conditioning which struck Alex as being unusually loud. Dieter walked towards the kitchen with Alex following right behind him. The door was ajar and the stench was now becoming almost overpowering. Dieter pushed the door open with one hand, the other firmly across his nose and the two men peering fearfully inside. There, lying on the kitchen floor was the bloated and blackened corpse of Willem Schuster and the loud sound was not the air-conditioning, it was the sound of the mass of flies that filled the air. Alex managed one last look before another wave of nausea overtook him and he ran back out of the house, followed immediately by Dieter. The German slammed the door shut behind them and the two men walked quickly away from the house and back to where Andy was sitting. Taking shade from a parasol, Dieter's wife was sitting and talking in a soft low voice to the distraught Filipina maid, who was still shaking uncontrollably.

"Horrible, the poor man", said Dieter as he sat down next to his wife. He had gone white as a sheet. Alex was still too shocked to say anything, he also felt physically sick. For a moment he thought he was going to vomit, but he managed to control himself and sat himself down next to the maid. At that moment all he could see was the image of the rotting corpse.

Dieter took of his glasses and rubbed them feverously, "my God, how long has he lain there?"

Andy put her arm around her husband's shoulders and spoke to him softly in their native tongue, stroking the back of his head as she comforted her husband. She turned and gave Alex a kindly look. "Are you OK?"

Alex nodded.

Dieter spoke quickly in German to his wife and she replied, her voice soft and reasoning. Alex looked dumbly on at the two as they conversed away. Catching Alex' slightly lost expression Andy shook her head sadly, "Rosa says she has not been in the house for a week."

Alex looked at the Filipina maid, who had now stopped her wailing and was quite motionless. Still clearly in shock, she sat staring blankly at a chair.

"I should have known", said Dieter rubbing his glasses again and putting them back on.

"I know. I feel the same. It's just terrible thinking how long he has been there." Andy ran her hands through her hair and then sat with her head bent forward held in her hands.

"He's been there since last Thursday night", said Alex in a flat monotone.

"What?" Dieter looked aghast. Andy moved her hands to her mouth in shocked disgust.

"How do you know that?" spluttered Dieter

Alex gave his friend a sad look "I recognized the clothes, that's how he was dressed at the Brass Eagle. He gave me a lift back."

"*Mein Gott*", said the atheist.

If there was little anyone could do for Willem Schuster in life there was even less in death, as Alex found out. Whilst living in Saudi Arabia might be difficult, dying was an altogether more unpleasant process, for a host of unexpected reasons. After a cursory examination, Schuster's body was taken to a morgue where it sat for a week whilst his 'Final Exit' papers were processed. The cause of death was a 'cerebral haemorrhage' according to the post mortem, which Dieter after a huge amount of effort found out. As he remarked to Alex, the staff at the mortuary could not have cared less or been less helpful if they tried. Fortunately for Schuster, working for one of the more powerful families in Jeddah had its compensations; they handled the paperwork which required eight different government departments' authorizations and the family also paid the three thousand dollars needed to transport the man's body. Alex and Dieter watched as the casket was loaded onto the plane, only identified by the airline industry's 'HUM' code in the cargo-description box of the manifest. The men watched through fencing from a distance and were appalled as one of the handlers pushed the casket with his foot. It was as undignified a departure as could be imagined.

Dieter shook his head, "Did you see that?"

"Yes, bastards."

Later that day Dieter phoned the cargo handlers to complain about the way they had behaved. It was a pointless exercise. The man on the phone informed him that he could not control what had happened at the airport and was even surprised at getting the call. He informed Dieter that it had all gone through most efficiently and that Schuster was lucky. If he had been a migrant worker from Asia or Africa, he would still be in the morgue and would have later been interred in an unmarked grave. He reminded the German that only Muslim's were entitled to a burial. After all, if they allowed the non-Muslims to be buried there, this would be followed by the practicing of their religion.

"Prophet Muhammed, peace be upon him, said it himself, that there should be no other religion except Islam on the Arabian Peninsula." Dieter hung up the phone.

A few days after what was left of Schuster had been flown back to Switzerland, Alex and Jim were stuck behind a slow moving jalopy on the Corniche Highway. Alex was now much more cautious and even more defensive in his driving. He really did not want to end up being kicked about in a casket like poor old Schuster. Like any young man, the fear of death was not something that he particularly suffered from, however the ghastly and callous way that Schuster had been dealt with had left a mark on him. Dying in Saudi Arabia was not an option.

For the first time in a while the subject of Schuster did not come up. Today, events were once again dominated by the subject of terrorism, being in the Middle-East meant it was never far from the men's thoughts. Jim had printed out the full story from the Web and was reading from it. "Two hundred injured and twenty nine killed."

"Honestly Jim, these people are just animals." Alex said with real anger.

Jim nodded sadly. "I know, but what can anyone do about it? It seems like it will never change."

Alex shook his head, "why do you think they did it? What can they possibly gain from it?"

"God only knows. It only takes one madman, just one nutter."

"I don't know about it being a nutter Jim. This was a deliberate act of sabotage intended to cause the maximum amount of outrage and to derail the peace process."

"I know that Alex, but the hardliners have no interest in peace and they are the ones that set the agenda if the average person lets them. The more outraged people get, the less likely a compromise will ever be reached. That's when terrorists win."

"You ever been there?"

"No, how about you?" said Jim.

"Well I've not been to Omagh but I've been to Ireland a few times."

Jim looked at the paper and folded it in half, "bloody madness."

By the time that Alex was on the plane home for two weeks holiday there had been a great deal of changes that hot summer month. The 'Brass Eagle' gatherings on Thursday nights at the US consulate had been suspended, as part of the tightening of security, in the wake of the US embassy bombings. Despite his earlier reservations, it looked like he might have to go to a 'pub night' at the British diplomatic mission, after all. He would see how he felt about it when he got back. As he sat in his seat on BA 132 sipping a beer he wondered how Joe was fairing. Unbelievably the Russians had actually defaulted, in their own currency and Joe had, as a result, lost a small fortune. Worse, the man from Guildford had blown his loss limits and was now very likely to get sacked. Alex felt very sorry for him. He wondered what Isobel Karpolinski was likely to do and gave a little shiver, poor Joe. He wondered who would be the one to pull the trigger and sack Karpolinski, Chris Barma, or Ed Moore. Probably the former, he looked like he could not wait to do it. Alex expected that as soon as things calmed down a bit more, they would probably do it.

He was glad to be on the plane. The markets were all over the place, LTCM; the goliath hedge fund was in the last stages of its catastrophic collapse. At that time it was not clear it would happen, but the phone lines were abuzz with its much unexpected demise. People likened the hedge fund's strategy as to picking up dimes in front of a steamroller and a lot of big peoples reputations were about to be flattened. LTCM, the biggest hedge fund in the world, was staffed by some of the top names on the Street, with even a couple of Nobel Prize winners thrown in for good measure. Quite a few folk were quietly relishing their misfortune.

In the end, Alex was wrong that Chris Barma would be the one to do the sacking. Barma had his own problems as Ed Moore was fast discovering, so it was the American who called Karpolinski into his office and gave him the unfortunate though hardly unexpected news. As he said at the time, he was sorry, but there really was nothing that the Treasurer could do for him. He gave him a month to sort out his affairs and to move his family. It was brutal, but unfortunately that was how it went, it was nothing personal. "Sorry, and good luck Joe", was all he said and the Englishman made his way out. Moore shook his head in sadness and once again started to read the news item that had caught his eye. The screens reported that Scott Ritter had just resigned from UNSCOM, after vociferously criticizing both the Clinton administration and the U.N. Security Council for not being vigorous enough in insisting that Iraq's weapons of mass destruction be destroyed. Moore shook his head in frustration. Well at least he knew he was doing his bit even if Ritter did have a point.

Ed Moore's emailed information along with other CIA intelligence had gone up the chain of command and action had been taken, despite whatever this grandstanding guy was saying. Moore turned back to the neatly folded newspaper that was sitting on the corner of his desk. He picked it up and unfolded it, and again felt a little surge of pride. There under the caption of "Double Strike" was the report of President Clinton's authorization of Cruise Missiles strikes on Sudan and Afghanistan in direct response to the East African embassy bombings.

21. Dangerous Liaisons

It was late afternoon when Mohammed Al Hamra got off the plane and quickly passed through the domestic arrivals terminal building at Abdul Aziz Airport. He, like his three newly named brothers in arms, Ahmed, Hamza and Wail, had their papers briefly examined on departure by the bored looking security staff at Riyadh airport. Initially concerned, the men stood nervously in line, waiting to pass through the security checks. They did not need to worry. They all passed through, completely unremarked as their papers were cursorily looked over. In a country where the population is growing as fast as Saudi Arabia, families with four or five siblings were the norm, not an exception. Furthermore as their passports showed, harkening from the remote and undeveloped province of Al Bahah meant that the brothers need not even be blood relatives. Four brothers travelling together was commonplace, four men with the same tribal surname from an area like Al-Bahah did not even pass muster. Abdul Rahman Bin Hajez' source at the passport issuing section of the sprawling Interior Ministry had ensured that all the documents were absolutely authentic. When asked, they were on their way to Mecca.

Abdul Rahman watched as the four young men eventually came through the arrival gates and felt a glow of pride in his chest. They were four fine young men and already between himself and Abdullah Bawani, the fiery Egyptian preacher and explosives expert, they had much planned for these committed *Jihadi*.

Each of the four men warmly greeted the *Mutawwa* in turn, holding the greying bearded man's hand and kissing him several times on the cheeks, in the traditional manner of the Gulf.

"Peace be with you and welcome to Jeddah"

Of the four, only Mohammed, who was also the youngest, actually came from Jeddah. The slim, bespectacled Ahmed also knew Jeddah but was originally from Yanbu. The industrial city of Yanbu' al Bahr, also located on the Red Sea coast, is nearly four hundred kilometres to the north of Jeddah. Ahmed was the son of a chemical engineer who worked at the huge refinery there. Bright, he had been studying aeronautical engineering at King Abdul Aziz University before dropping out and adopting his new identity. The remaining two Al-Ghamdis, formerly known as Bashir and Yasser and regarded by the white haired *Alim,* Abu Bassam as the most prepared for *Jihad,* were from Ha'il. Unlike the coastal cities, Ha'il was located to the north of the country, deep within the interior of the Arabian Peninsula. As cousins and descendants of the Al-Rashidis, there was no love lost between them and the House of Saud. Their hostility to the present dynastic rulers of the Kingdom was based on centuries of formidable enmity. Originally their family and many others like them, had been forced to leave Ha'il and settle in Riyadh, after Ibn Saud captured the mountain oasis and put an end to Rashidi rule in 1921. Over fifty years later, when rumours of Rashidi involvement in the assassination of King Faisal gripped the country in 1975, their uncle had been arrested and murdered by the paranoid autocracy. In their early twenties, they were both newly qualified school teachers.

"Come my brothers, let us not waste time, we will be just in time for *Maghrib* prayers and I have someone who is looking forward to meeting you all." The group of men walked out into the late afternoon towards the *Mutawwa's* car. Abdul-Rahman turned and gave Mohammed his customary emaciated smile. "How was the journey Saeed?"

"It was very good, thanks be to God"

The *Mutawwa* nodded appreciatively, "Unfortunately not all your journeys will be so comfortable."

A few hours later and having eaten their fill, the four young men sat around a table and were talking to the black haired Abdullah Bawani. Unlike before, where he spoke in generalizations, the 'Pyro-technician' was no longer so limited. He was amongst friends and there was no need to preach to the converted.

"So you have met Sheikh Osama?" asked Ahmed

Bawani nodded and blew out a plume of cigarette smoke. "Indeed I have, I have fought beside him and on three occasions I have spoken to him."

"Tell us about him" implored Saeed.

"My brothers, he is a man of many talents, truly he is." Abdul-Rahman felt a ripple of jealousy as the young men's eyes, spellbound, focused on the Egyptian as he leant back in his seat.

"The first time I saw him was in Afghanistan many years ago. I met him when he was fighting the Godless *Shuravi*. Like many others, I had travelled the road from Peshawar to Jalalabad and into Eastern Afghanistan. Once we were in Afghanistan, we could only travel at night as the *Shuravi* would bomb anything they saw on the roads during the day. My friends, you should see Afghanistan in the cold moonlight when the mists have cleared. The mountains are so beautiful." Abdul-Rahman scanned the rapt faces of the men around the table and gave them a wan smile. He had heard Bawani's tales many times before and he only wished that he too could tell them first hand. Automatically he began to finger his prayer beads as he studied the men's reaction to the *Alim's* words.

Abdullah Bawani cast a look around the faces of his audience as he spoke. "We trekked out of Jalalabad for another three days. Our guide was an Algerian who knew the mountains as if he had lived his entire life there. He had only one arm, but I tell you my young friends, he had legs like a mountain goat, incredible. Anyway, on the third night our guide took us to this deep ravine and we climbed up it for several hours and there cut into the side of the mountain was a vast dark hole. Imagine my friends, it was huge, perhaps six meters high and it was entirely man made by Osama bin Laden and his men. And do you know what it was?"

The men gave looks of questioning wonder and shook their heads.

My brothers, it was a hospital for *Mujahedin* wounded and it was here that I first saw him."

"What did he say?" asked Ahmed, his eyes sparkled with enthusiasm.

"Say?" Abdullah Bawani laughed. "I said nothing. You don't just go up to someone like Sheikh Osama and speak to them. Praise be to God no, for I had just arrived. Oh no, it was not until more than a year later that I actually spoke with him."

"So what did he say to you?" asked the enraptured Ahmed.

The dark haired Egyptian paused before once more breaking into another, nicotine stained grin, "he congratulated me."

"For what *Alim*?" asked Saeed.

"For blowing up three Russian tanks", replied the preacher, who was unable to hide his obvious pride.

The young men all quickly exchanged looks of admiration for the Egyptian mujahedin.

"What else did he say?" insisted Saeed.

Abdullah Bawani gave a wry smile. "Not much else, he asked me where I came from."

The young men's faces clouded over, slightly disappointed by the ending of the Egyptian's tale. The young man, formerly a teacher and now known as Hamza Al-Ghamdi leant forward. "What about the second time?"

The Alim nodded, "that was more recently, in Sudan a few years ago."

"Was that before the Americans tried to assassinate him?" asked Hamza with a flash of anger.

The Egyptian nodded and smiled. "Yes, that was before the Khartoum attack, he remembered me from our time in Afghanistan."

"A filthy cowardly attack sponsored by the CIA" said Hamza with real venom in his voice.

Abdullah Bawani raised his hand to silence the enraged young man. "Indeed my young brother, but I can tell you

666

that Sheikh Osama is protected by Allah himself. You know, I was with him once when a Russian mortar shell landed just about there." The *Alim* pointed to where Abdul-Rahman was sitting, "but it did not explode." He broke into another yellow grin. "My brothers, I would not be telling you this if I had not been standing right beside him, by the Grace of God Almighty."

Seeing Bawani's smiling face, the young men followed suit and also broke into huge smiles, "God is Great" they all spontaneously chorused.

The Egyptian still smiling took a sip of his tea whilst the men waited for him to continue. "I last saw him in Sudan, that was when he was again constructing roads. This time when I met him he asked me what I thought of the road he was building. He even joked to me that at least this time the *Shuravi* weren't destroying his new highways."

"I heard about that highway that he built", said Ahmed in a tone of reverence.

Bawani nodded, "Exactly eight hundred kilometres from Khartoum all the way to Port Sudan." The Egyptian was still grinning. "He had brought the equipment over from Afghanistan. The very same equipment that built the hospitals and tunnels that we used in Pakhtia."

The *Alim's* face darkened. "However my brothers, what I can tell you is that he was not entirely pleased with our efforts here in the Kingdom, in fact to be blunt, not happy at all."

The group of young men responded immediately to this last statement. The grinning faces switching in an instant to sombre expressions. Bawani paused and stared across the room, slowly his unblinking dark eyes narrowed. "Sheikh Osama is deeply concerned that, as yet, we have done next to nothing to rid ourselves of the vile American presence. Every day that the infidel's armies are encamped here in the heart of Islam, is a day that shames every true Muslim to the core."

The four men sat silent and still, their heads bowed and stony faced, whilst their eyes flashed with anger.

Alex stepped on the squash court for the final of the Arabian Homes competition. Above him the umpire asked them to choose heads or tails. Alex lost the toss and took himself to the rear left hand corner, ready to receive the first service. Jerry Allensen gave his opponent a quick smile and served.

As usual, right from the first point, the battle between the two men was intense and hard fought, but Alex felt confident. He had beaten the American the last four outings and expected to do so again. Initially the small crowd that was watching the match from the gallery clapped appreciatively when either of the players struck a winner. However as the match progressed, the spectators quickly divided along the fault line of national loyalties. The process was instigated by Allensen's persistent, highly partisan and increasingly vocal support, in the form of a dozen or more US servicemen from Ronda. Alex's own support, initially restrained, formed in direct response to the Americans' overactive band of brothers. By the end of the first game, the noisy American barracking had convinced anyone who was not from the fifty States of the Union to come out for the Englishman. Alex was the favourite to win and he still fully expected to beat Allensen despite his poor preparation. After an hour of gruelling play, as was always the case between the two men, the match was in the fifth and final game. The only surprise was that this time it was Alex who was unexpectedly facing defeat. The trader, dripping sweat, his leg muscles burning with lactic acid, committed every ounce of his strength to winning the next few points.

"Seven five", called out the Umpire

"U.S.A, U.S.A chanted the Americans."

Alex waited, feeling only the thump of his heart pounding away in his chest. He wiped the palm of his hand on the wall to dry it; his shirt was too sodden do the job. Allensen served the ball high into the right hand court. Alex stretched and volleyed the ball straight back down the forehand wall. In a fraction of a second the small black ball ran the entire length and came close to hitting the nick at the back of the court. Allensen had moved to the right just in time, stretched and barely managed to retrieve the ball. His desperate swinging shot, just clipped the ball so that it spun wickedly to the front of the court, striking the wall just above the tin and ricocheting into a lucky winner. The American supporters in the packed gallery whooped with delight and high fived as Alex cursed his luck under his breath.

"U.S.A, U.S.A" chorused the US soldiers with gusto.

"Come on Alex", Alex gave a tired look up to the gallery. Amongst the crowd of faces he recognized Hashimoto, Bill and the Werners all urging him on, like the United Nations on speed.

"Eight five, match ball", called out the Umpire.

Alex moved to the left hand side of the court as Allensen bounded in to the service box. He gave Alex an intense look and served. Utterly exhausted, Alex went for the winner and drove the ball straight into the tin with a loud bang.

The Americans in the gallery behind him erupted into a cacophony of "All rights" and "You're da man Jerry."

Alex bowed his head and trudged, leaden footed up to the American, offering the victor his hand. The Nebraskan clearly elated, had a huge grin plastered across his profusely sweaty features.

"Played Jerry."

The American took the trader's hand and gave him a firm handshake, "thanks Alex." The Englishman sent a rueful look at the grinning Allensen as he turned and punched the air and gave a final wave to his rowdy enclave of supporters.

Shortly afterwards and much to Alex' chagrin there was a presentation ceremony. The trader wanted to get away as soon as possible and was still smarting from the defeat but had to wait until Ben Williams, the Arabian Homes Manager, had done his bit. It seemed to take ages. Ben had supplied a huge pile of T-Shirts with 'Arabian Homes Squash Tournament 1998' emblazoned across the back, which he was energetically handing out to anyone that would have one. For once he was not wearing his sunglasses, though his ever present mirrored shades were perched on his chest. The blond headed man was enjoying himself and never missed a chance at promotion of the Arabian Homes name.

At last, as far as Alex was concerned, the tiresome process began. Williams was standing in front of the group of people that numbered around thirty to forty. He cleared his throat, "our runner up, Alex Bell." The group gave a quick round of applause.

Alex quickly stepped forward and was given a handshake and an envelope that held an 'Al Jazeera Book Shop' gift token for a two hundred Riyals. "Well played", said the red faced Manager.

"Cheers" replied Alex. He smiled, the winner's prize would have been much better. The enormous Al Jazeera bookshop was well known for its huge selection of books and compact disks.

"And now for our winner. The Arabian Homes Squash Champion 1998, Jerry Allensen.", announced the Estate Manager grandly. The group lent another round of applause. Alex gave his friend a warm smile. Williams handed a small cup and an envelope with a four hundred Riyal gift token over to the Nebraskan. Allensen beamed his wide perfect smile as he stood with his trophy while one of his compatriots took his photograph.

The soldier scanned the group looking for his vanquished opponent. "Hey Alex, let's have one with you in it too."

Alex shook his head with a tired smile and then stepped up next to the tall American whilst Ernesto Sanchez snapped away.

As the group started to break up, Hashimoto came up to Alex. "Very funny, I thought you would win."

Alex gave the Japanese a shrug

"What happened?" asked the fit man with terrible teeth.

"I don't know", replied Alex, but he did and very well too. There was no point in making excuses, but the fact that he had hardly slept the previous night and quite a few before was not worth saying. He was exhausted before he started the match. Claire's words still rung in his head every sleepless night and had done so since his return from holiday.

"Maybe next year," said Hashimoto.

Alex nodded. "Maybe", but he knew there would be no next year for him.

Across the street from his home the former Mohammed Al-Hamra watched his house, he was trembling he was so nervous. He knew he was taking a real risk but he had a plan if he was discovered. The middle class house looked deserted, neither his mother's little car or his father's dark blue Mercedes were to be seen. He stepped out into the quiet street and rang the bell. With any luck there would be no answer, Naila the maid, who he had not seen, normally had the Tuesday afternoon off. He waited and rang again, there was still no answer. His only concern was that his elder brother Talal might still be in. He put his key into the gate and opened it. With one quick look behind him to check no one had seen him he slipped in and ran across the gravel driveway. In a few moments he had swiftly opened the front door and was inside his old home.

The first thing he recognized was the familiar scent of the house. He took a deep breath and quickly surveyed the scene. It was all exactly as he remembered it. He stood absolutely still listening for any sounds and breathed a sigh of relief. The house, as he had hoped, was deserted. He walked into the lounge, suddenly drinking in the familiarity of his surroundings. Quickly he strode into his old bedroom and stopped in his tracks, everything was exactly as he had left it. Even the poster of his father's beloved Newcastle United was still on his wall. He walked over to his desk and opened the drawer. It was still there. Urgently he picked up the book and opened it. He flicked through the pages of photographs of him with his family. Holidays, birthdays and family gatherings, the everyday and the exceptional, that were all stored for perpetuity in his little photo album. Turning the pages he stopped to stare at one. It was a copy of the one of them that was normally in the lounge that had been taken in Disneyland with the whole family dressed as cowboys. Ridiculous, he peeled the clear plastic back, took the photo out and stuffed it in his pocket. Quickly he looked through a cupboard and grabbed some clothing. He opened another cupboard looking for a bag, in the rush he had forgotten to bring one with him. Thinking for a moment, he searched the bottom of one of the wardrobes and pulled a canvas bag. It would have to do. He fumbled as he shoved the clothes into the bag and slung it over his shoulder. Closing all the cupboard doors so as to leave it undisturbed he gave his room one last look and then quickly left, running down the street and away, with the words 'Red Sea Divers' on the canvas bag bouncing on his back as he spoke breathlessly into his mobile phone.

Back in Abdullah Barwani's small stoic apartment, the *Alim* studied the photographs he had been given by his young recruits. Over the last fortnight the developing group of *Jihadi* had been given the task of watching the to-ing and fro-ing of American servicemen from the Sierra Compound. The big GM Suburbans that daily ferried the members of the United States Military Training Mission had been identified and he and Abdul-Rahman would ensure that Sheikh Osama's opinion that nothing was being done by anyone in the Kingdom, would soon be changed. The August bombings in East Africa had led to a marked increase in visible security at both the American bases and the US Consulate, so a direct strike on them was not an option. Besides his resources were not that great, however as the Egyptian, who had blown many Russian tanks to pieces knew well, there were still many opportunities. The key was to identify the target and establish a pattern. He was pleased to see that one was emerging.

Barwani looked at his watch, the recruits were late. He frowned with slight annoyance; his young band should be here by now. Not one to waste time, the *Alim* picked up one of the photographs, taken from quite a distance and scanned the grainy image of four Americans. Uniformed and with close cropped regulation haircuts, they were as indistinguishable to his eye as the godless *Shuravi* he sent to hell on the road to Kabul.

Twenty minutes later and then at last, came the much awaited sound of the agreed signal on his door. Two knocks, a pause and then three more. He got up and looked through the little security spy hole in the middle of the door. The fisheye lens filled with the image of the four men. He opened the door.

As each of the men filed past Abdullah Bawani and he greeted each of them warmly but formally. "Peace be with you."

"And with you peace" as each in turn replied when they entered.

The men sat down around the table, Abdullah offered them each a hot cup of tea. "What happened to you? You were supposed to be here at five."

All the men's eyes dropped down except Mohammed. "I'm sorry my *Alim*, it is my fault."

The Egyptian's eyes narrowed, "Why whatever happened?"

"I'm sorry but I thought I saw a relation and had to hide in a mosque." It was the first time he had lied to the *Alim* and Saeed reddened.

Bawani's intense stare never for an instant even waivered from the youngster, "were you seen?"

676

The young Saudi nodded that he had not and the Egyptian continued to watch him like a hawk, "are you sure Saeed?"

"Absolutely *Alim*", he was positive his trip to his former home had been unobserved by anyone.

Abdullah Bawani let out a sigh. It was nothing serious, thank God. "Did you see this relation Ahmed?"

The bespectacled *Jihadi* shook his head, "No *Alim*, I had to go to the bathroom."

"Bathroom?" he spat out. He was not used to dealing with such boys. He had seen men walking into field hospitals holding their intestines in. He turned on the man from Yanbu. "My lad, next time you need to go to the bathroom, you either hold your water or piss on the street." The former student of aeronautical engineering looked shamefaced down at the table. "Do you understand?"

"Yes *Alim*", replied the chastened Ahmed in a soft voice.

The Alim smashed the table with his hand. "I can't hear you. I said do you understand."

Ahmed looked up and stared the *Alim* in the eye. "Yes *Alim*, I understand."

The Egyptian blew out a heavy breath and eyed the four men. "This is not a game my brothers. You work in pairs for a reason. If you get separated, you know the drill. If one of you is injured, incapacitated, arrested or killed you know the drill. If anything happens you know the drill." Bawani smashed the table again with his hand.

677

"What is the drill?"

"Contact, failed contact, go to rendezvous", chimed the men in unison.

"So?" he turned on Saeed.

"My phone had no signal in the mosque *Alim*. I called as soon as I got out." Saeed had thought of everything. There was absolutely no trace of a mobile phone signal in the mosque.

The Egyptian turned on Ahmed again. "What about you?"

"I just thought I'd wait, we weren't actually on a task and then I heard from Saeed so I thought it was alright."

"Fool" shouted Bawani, "everything we do is a task. Every action we make is part of the greater mission. Do you understand?"

"Yes *Alim*."

The Egyptian wiped his hand across his forehead in frustration and stared at the men. He had already told Abdul-Rahman of his doubts of using Saeed in Jeddah, but the fool was so insistent. They had been lucky. He would have to speak to the *Mutawwa* about this as soon as he saw him. The cleric took a deep breath and gave a thin smile.

"Right, let this just be a lesson. Always observe the drill."

"Yes *Alim*" the men replied.

"Right, let's get to work my brothers. Today we are going to learn how to strap an explosive charge to the bottom of a vehicle, but first a prayer."

The departure of Joe Karpolinski was quite unlike that of Andy Whiteman, in fact the polar opposite. Whilst Andy's exit had been announced with his succinct, even meagre, personal catchphrase, 'It's been a slice' and a simple wave as he walked out the bank, never to be seen again, Joe's was an indigestible gateau of goodbyes. There had already been two parties on Mura Bustan, a couple of lunches at the Italian Consulate and now, as the men had now just found out, a last minute trip to the British consulate, for the 'Monday Pub Night'. The American consulate's 'Brass Eagle' nights, sadly, remained suspended.

"Why doesn't the Muppet just bugger off", said Pete on being reminded of the next Karpolinski caper.

"I think Isobel has been the driving force behind it all to be honest" said Jim.

"So are you going to it?" asked Alex looking across to Koester.

"I don't know. I'll see what I can do, I don't like leaving Helen and the girls."

"Oh go on Pete, they'll be fine", said Jim with an encouraging expression, "and it'll be a laugh, I bet."

Pete looked unconvinced, "yeah sure"

Jim shrugged his shoulders. "It least it will be a change from all this". Jim turned to Mohammed Jundi, "How about you Mohammed?"

Mohammed shook his head. "Sorry, no Ayerabs", responded the Saudi in his smooth East Coast accent.

"What?" said Jim with a look of obvious annoyance and frustration across his features.

Alex nodded his head, "Oh shit, I'd forgotten about that."

"No Blacks, no Irish, no dogs" said Jim in a low voice to himself.

"What's that?" said Alex, not quite properly hearing his friend.

"Nothing mate", said Jim, "just a weak non joke."

Later on that evening, the IAB men were sitting at two small tables in the cramped smoke filled bar of the British Consulate. In the end Jim had managed to convince Pete to come along too. As it turned out, the Zimbabwean's wife had been invited to a separate soiree with Isobel's friends on Mura Bustan. Jim was pleased that he had persuaded Pete to come along, as it was a pretty dismal place not made better by Alex who seemed in a pretty miserable mood that evening.

Joe had also brought along two friends from his compound, a friendship centred more on his wife's social circle than on him. The two men talked animatedly and in sleep inducing detail to each other about some recent camping expedition that their families had been on. Stuck on the wrong table between his colleagues and the two men from Joe's compound, Alex listened politely but with zero interest. He had forgotten the men's names almost as soon as he had been briefly introduced.

Pete took a sip from his beer. "So this was Isobel's idea then was it?"

Joe gave a brief half smile, "pretty much so". He looked around the bar area and studied the carpet. "Well I won't be missing this place, that's for sure."

Pete also looked around and then gave Jim a wry look, "low key eh?"

Jim features clouded for a moment before he gave a smile, "yup that's the one."

"So what are your plans?" Pete was staring at Joe, his expression was benevolent. Joe's situation was not something he would have wished on anyone.

"Well nothing's fixed in stone, but I think I'm heading back to the UK for good", Joe replied.

"How does Isobel feel about that?"

Joe hesitated before he answered and his shoulders drooped as he paused to think. "Well, you know, she's coming round to the idea." He let out a sigh, "it's all been a bit of a shock to be honest."

The two men nodded, Joe's circumstances certainly warranted sympathy.

"How about your kids?" Jim enquired with a look of concern.

Joe pursed his mouth, "that's still an issue. Haven't found places for all of them yet, they're on waiting lists."

A brief silence fell on the men as they then sipped their drinks. Joe aware of the depressing mood gave a brave smile, seeking to change the conversation. "How is Lord Baldemort getting on?"

Jim gave a sad shake. "No idea mate, he didn't even come in today."

While the three others talked about Chris Barma, Alex was still stuck with the two happy campers and supping his pint slowly looked around the place. Dotted around the stuffy room there were other disparate groups of similar sizes that were also conversing quietly amongst themselves. Alex recognized most of the faces. Only one collection of expatriates stood out, it was slightly larger and louder than the others and from their profane and strident conversation it was clear they were all workers down from the refinery up the coast in Yanbu. The trader looked around the room, it was a grim spectre and he sourly contemplated that low key did not do it justice. He quickly finished the remainder of his drink and got to his feet. "I'll get the next lot in, same again for everybody?"

There were yeses and nods of agreement from the others. "I'll give you a hand", said Jim getting to his feet. The two men wandered over to the cramped bar and stood awaiting their turn.

Alex turned to his friend. "This place isn't low key, its double bass"

Jim grinned, "Ah so we're brightening up a bit then, are we?"

Alex made a rueful face, "Trying to." Beside him he felt a push, as a burly man tried to get to the bar.

"Poor old Joe, things are pretty bad."

"I know, it's not good..." said Alex.

"Who's next then?" said the barman looking in the direction of Alex.

Both Alex and the man next to him both replied at the same time.

"Two bitters and three lagers please," said Alex

"Seven pints of lager and seven vodka chasers, mate" insisted the burly man from the group from Yanbu standing next to him.

"Actually I think we were here first", said Jim

The barman, an off duty diplomat looked thoroughly confused as his eyes quickly moved between the men in front of him. He had only just served the rowdy group an identical round, he didn't want any trouble. He gave Alex a brief nod, "One moment please gentlemen. So two lagers and three bitters is it?" The diplomat's accent was clipped and precise, very Home counties.

"No, the other way around, two bitters and three lagers, thanks very much", said Alex.

The man next to him let out a frustrated snort and swore as another scrawny man then spoke up. "Oi mate we was here first, what's going on?"

"I'll be with you in a minute," replied the barman.

Alex heard another snort and ignored it feeling the man's angry gaze turn upon him.

"Fucking typical", said the man to his friend.

"Yeah" said the other man and he whispered something into the other's ear to which the burly man once more snorted derisively. As the order started to arrive, the thickset man next to Alex continued to stare but this time his anger was directed at Jim as he carried the drinks back to their table.

Alex sat down and took a draught of his drink.

"What a pair of arseholes", said Alex

Jim just raised his eyebrows, shook his head and took a gulp from his drink.

The men had another two more rounds before Alex had decided that he had spent enough time in the depressing place. Now it was almost empty except for them, a few of the staff from the consulate and the noisy refinery workers. After all, it was a Monday night and whilst Joe might not have to get into work, the others still had a full day ahead of them, besides he was getting annoyed by the group of oil workers who periodically kept on looking in their direction.

Their ire still clearly evident and more vodka fuelled than before.

"You ready to go Jim?" He was driving and one of the campers had volunteered for the men from Mura Bustan.

"Yeah, let's make a move."

As the two traders got to their feet the scrawny man with an armful of tattoos from the Yanbu group suddenly broke into song. "In the jungle the mighty jungle the lion sleeps tonight."

The burly man, his face flushed red under his shaved head, broke into loud monkey noises and several of the others then started to laugh.

Alex still didn't know what was going on but Jim had long before guessed exactly what was happening. He had seen it in the men's eyes from the first moment they had met; hostile, ignorant, racist. You did not see them as much back in England these days, perhaps this was where they had all gone. "C'mon Alex, let's get out of here."

They had to pass the baying group on their way to the door, the ape like noises continued ever louder. "Want a banana?"

Alex stopped and stared at the shaven headed man. He was slightly taller than the banker.

"C'mon Alex just ignore them", said Jim under his breath.

"What's your problem?" said Alex. Suddenly everything was in a rage within him, his fucking marriage, his fucking job, this fucking place, even the stupid fucking squash game. He was a walking time bomb just waiting to go off.

"I'm not talking to you. I'm talking to the spa..."

Before the man had even finished his abusive sentence Alex had stepped forward and sent his right fist smashing into the jaw of the burly red face. The man's eyes instantly rolled skyward as he went out like a light, his legs crumpling like a paper bag beneath him and he hit the deck with a clattering of tables and a smashing glass. A couple more ineffectual swings came through on top of Alex from another man who leapt forward in defence of his prostrate mate, but in the crush of bodies no serious blows were landed and in the next few moments Alex was being held back by Pete and Jim whilst the diplomats held back the other man.

"You're barred", said the barman to Alex as he was escorted from the consulate.

"Good", replied Alex.

As they drove home that night the adrenalin was still coursing through Alex' veins and his hands continued to tremble as he held the wheel. The man's jaw was hard and his knuckles were red and sore.

"What the hell came over you Alex?"

The banker shook his head, "I dunno Jim, just a lot of things."

Jim laughed, "Well I have to say, that was one hell of a punch."

Alex turned and gave his friend a smile, his own lip was fat and swelling from one of the punches he received. "It wasn't bad was it?"

"You're a funny bloke Alex. Do you always fly off the handle like that?" said Jim with a curious look in his eye.

Alex kept his eyes on the dark road ahead. "I don't know, maybe it's just this place, but..."

Jim's face turned serious "Well in future let me handle my own fights Alex. You can't just go around punching people out whenever they say something offensive mate."

Alex gave a shrug. "I guess so."

Jim broke into a laugh "I mean, I'd still be stuck in jail if I behaved like you."

They drove along the last bit of the ramshackle road to Jim's compound, Alex drove at a crawl to navigate the voluminous pot holes that led up to the gates. Eventually he slowed and halted for Jim to get out.

"Lotus Four."

"Thanks mate", said Jim.

"See you tomorrow", Alex revved the engine.

"Oh and Alex"

"Yeah?"

"Back there, you know that was appreciated mate, unnecessary", he gave his friend a warm smile, "but appreciated." Jim closed the door and Alex reversed and then drove off down the potholed road, suddenly feeling utterly exhausted as the last of the adrenalin ebbed from him, back to Sierra.

Jerry Allensen had just lost to Alex and was mopping his brow of sweat whilst sitting breathing hard and slowly recovering on the bench.

"So have you used your Al-Jazeera voucher yet?"

Alex shook his head. "No, I haven't had a chance to get there."

"Me neither, hey why don't we go there tonight? You could drive me there" said the American.

"I would if I had a car", replied Alex zipping up his squash racket in its cover.

"Why what's happened to it?"

"I fucked it a couple of nights ago, drove it into a pothole and damaged the suspension."

"Shit luck buddy", he gave the Englishman a slap on the back. "You can afford it. Say never mind, I'll give you a ride with me and the guys tonight."

"Tonight?"

"Sure why not tonight? We normally do a Pizza run before Den nights anyway. The bookshop is right on the way, no problemo."

"OK"

"I'll see you in fifteen, then?"

"Sure in fifteen minutes, outside Ronda."

Alex got up to go. "Say Alex, just one thing. I know this sounds a bit kinda dumb but Ernesto fucking screwed up the photographs from the squash tournament."

Alex gave the American a shake of his head and a big grin. "Oh no Jerry, I'm not doing that again."

"Aw c'mon buddy, give a guy a break."

"OK, so what is it you want exactly?"

"Well if you could do another photo with me that would be great"

Alex gave the man from Nebraska a nod, "OK."

"Say Alex, it would be real cool if you could wear that T-Shirt that jerk was giving out for free" The trader looked at the American with slight incredulity. "Aw c'mon, it's for my folks you know, not for me. I sorta told 'em about it ya know, winning an' everything."

Alex shook his head, "Sure Jerry. Somehow I feel you had this all planned."

"You're a real sport, old chap", said the American making a real mess of his supposedly English accent.

Saeed Al-Ghamdi watched as the dark blue GM Suburban pulled into its familiar spot outside the Pizza parlour and the doors spewed out its contents of American GI's. He looked at the faces and counted the usual four men, one of

689

whom was wearing a white T-Shirt with something he could not read clearly scrawled across his back. He looked again. Strangely there was a fifth man who was also in a white T-Shirt. Saeed Al-Ghamdi saw the face suddenly felt his blood run cold. Surely he was mistaken. He blinked as he scanned the second man in the white T-Shirt. No, he just had to be wrong, he must be wrong. He watched as the two men in white separated from the three others and walked towards the Al-Jazeera bookshop. The other three men walked into the Pizza parlour.

"Give me those", he grabbed the binoculars from Ahmed who was also sitting in the back seat of the car.

"What is happening? Why have they separated like that?" hissed Barwani who was sitting in the driver's seat of the innocuous white Toyota parked across the street. "This is not normal."

To the left Wail moved into view, he was pushing a hand drawn cart with a large sheet of plywood that was designed to block the view of the car from the men inside. Hamza Al-Ghamdi stood waiting for the cart to pass across the Pizza parlour's window before he made his move. As soon as it did he ran and swooped down beside the servicemen's car. As they had practiced a hundred times before, he quickly stuck the explosive charge to the underside of the car and pushed the timer. As he was trained, he stood up and then walked quickly away, crossing the street and

690

walking past the white Toyota without so much as a glance at the men inside. As Hamza passed by the men in the car Wail had already cleared the windows of the Pizza parlour, he continued pushing his cart, only this time much more quickly. Saeed watched as the cart passed by the windows of the bookshop. The Saudi again scanned the interior of the shop and caught sight of the face again. This time there was absolutely no doubt in his mind. It was one of the men that had saved him from drowning.

Saeed Al-Ghamdi looked at his watch. The bomb was timed to go off in exactly fifteen minutes. How long had it been? How many minutes were left, nine, eight? He had no idea. His mind was a panicked whirr of confusion.

Saeed rubbed his mouth and forehead with his hand. His face was covered in sweat. What could he do and why was the stupid Englishman there at all? Oh God above what should he do? God had used this man to save him. Surely it was not God's will that he should be the one that took his life? He scanned the shop window again. Maybe the Englishman Bell would stay and the Americans would drive off without him. He scanned to his left and peered through the binoculars at the Pizza parlour, the other three men were still waiting for their order to arrive. Rivulets of sweat started to break out across his head and his heart was thumping in his chest.

691

He watched as Wail abandoned the cart around a corner, crossed the road and began his own walk in the same direction as Hamza had gone.

"Excellent", said the *Alim* and he put the key in the ignition. He would wait until he had seen the infidel get into the car before he drove off. It still was not right. Abdullah Bawani narrowed his eyes. "Why have the others gone in the bookshop?" he asked aloud. If the other Americans joined them then the bomb might go off without them being in the car. "Get in the car, get in the car", he hissed through clenched teeth, willing the soldiers into the trap. Bawani turned and looked at the two men in the back. "Who is this fifth one?"

"He is new *Alim*. There have only ever been four, every Wednesday like clockwork. They get pizza and then go", said Ahmed

Another minute ticked by and then another. The cleric blew out a sigh of relief. "At last, thanks be to God". The three Americans were carrying a dozen large pizzas and had climbed into the Suburban.

Bawani's attention turned on the other two men. "Why won't the others get in the car?"

Saeed Al-Ghamdi could take it no longer, he had to do something. Surely he would be cursed by God for eternity if he did not? In one movement he opened the door and was out of the car.

692

Abdullah Bawani could not believe his eyes. "Saeed? Saeed, what are you doing? Come back you fool."

The Saudi ran across the street into the bookshop. He stopped at the doorway and feverishly scoured the store to find the Englishman. His heart was pounding in his chest like a hammer. He strode over to where Alex was standing. "Mr Bell, Mr Bell?"

Alex turned and saw the young Mohammed Al-Hamra standing before him. It was the first time he had seen him in a lot more than a year. "Mohammed?" He was taken aback by the arrival of the young Saudi.

Jerry Allensen was standing at the checkout, he had already spent his token and had a pile of cd's and books in his arms. "C'mon Alex, let's get going. The pizzas will go cold, c'mon buddy hup hup", he added with a grin.

Mohammed still had no idea what he was going to do. His mind raced ahead to find a reason to get the Englishman out of the shop. "Mr Bell I need to speak to you, you must come with me." He was tugging at the Englishman's arm.

"Mohammed, what are you on about?" Alex pulled away from the young man. "What is wrong?"

"Please Alex, I need to speak with you, urgently." The insistent young man grabbed at Alex and forcefully pulled him around a corner pillar.

Allensen had opened the door and was just about halfway out of the shop. "C'mon Al..."

Jerry Allensen never finished his sentence as the blinding flash of the explosion immediate preceded an enormous blast that hurtled the American back and blew half the shop to pieces. The next thing Alex knew he was somehow picking himself up, choking back the plumes of masonry dust that filled his lungs and blinded his eyes. Around him small fires were burning and he stumbled out through the wreckage of what was left of the huge double fronted bookshop, his face blackened, his clothing ripped and torn to shreds hung limply from him. Somehow he struggled out of the smoke filled debris strewn bookshop and saw the burning wreckage of what was left of the Suburban before he stumbled to his knees and passed out.

22. The Unquiet Americans

Ed Moore got news of the car bomb from two different sources within a few hours of its happening, which was later on that same Wednesday evening.

The first call came from Lorenzo Evans. "Ed, bad news, just got confirmation, that we've had a car bomb here in Jeddah. TAFT indicated three dead on the scene, one critical and they're not sure he'll pull through."

Moore bit his lip, things really were going from bad to worse, "where in Jeddah?"

"Just off Tahlia, right outside the Pizza joint there. I don't know if you know it."

"Shit, yeah I know the one." Things were getting out of hand. "Got any intel on the explosive?"

"Not yet, but guys on the scene say it looks like Semtex, they'll have more once the bomb guys go over it."

"Anything else?"

"No, but if I hear anything I'll let you know."

"Do that, thanks."

"Bye."

Ed Moore hung up the line and immediately started checking his inbox for the next couple of hours. Sure enough before long he had a message from Pat Leary. He downloaded and quickly decrypted the message onto his laptop and read it. It was much worse than he had originally feared. *'Today approx 20:05 local time car bomb on USMTM in Jeddah, 4 casualties, 3confirmed dead, forensics pending. Other casualties reported but all information embargoed per previous agreement. In light of East African actions and this latest one on US personnel, effective immediate FBI sanctioned investigation now underway, James (Jim) O'Neill to head. Expect contact from them soonest after regional diplomatic rounds, exercise caution, zero tolerance. FBI propose to put Al-Qaeda onto TMWL.'*

He reread the email and turned the laptop off in disgust. He knew that unless he was extremely cautious, he was just a few dangerous steps from being hung out to dry. However his situation was not like Ollie North's at all for he would not even have a uniform to wear. "Shit."

Ed Moore collapsed into his favourite armchair, suddenly feeling exhausted and sick to his stomach. Things were going to get really heated if that message meant anything at all. Certainly this time everything was going to be very different to anything that he had experienced before. If the FBI was thinking of putting Osama bin Laden on their top ten most wanted list, then their mandate had changed fundamentally. *'Zero Tolerance'*, what the hell was he supposed to do? It was all well and good for Pat Leary and everyone else at Langley to sit there on their fat fannies and instruct him to offer zero help to the FBI when they came knocking on his door, but they would not be the ones facing criminal charges. It was his neck that was on the line and that was the real unwritten text of the message. As he sat disconsolately in his armchair he still just could barely believe it. Never had he thought that he would see the day the CIA was losing control, perhaps this is what was really meant by the end of the Cold War.

Ed Moore spent the rest of the night deep in thought as to what he should do. It was not hugely productive but the American knew from previous experience that if you did not think about things, you would make big mistakes. Right now he needed to think a great deal. By the time that he was drinking his sixth cup of black coffee it was already sunrise and he still had not come up with a solution, less a course of action. He stretched himself and ran his eyes over the papers he had been scribbling on throughout the night. So far, despite all this ink, he had drawn a complete blank. He checked his watch, he needed more time. He picked up the phone and called his office.

"Mr Moore's office" said George Harumba in his usual perky little answering mode.

"Hey George, it's me."

"Hello Sir."

"Say George, I'll be working from home today Okay. Let the others know and can you rearrange any diary appointments I have?"

"Of course Sir", replied the punctilious secretary.

As Ed Moore put the phone back down a thought crossed his mind. Given the magnitude of the event the previous night he wondered why he had not heard from his usual source in the local police force. That was strange.

Alex blinked and tried to focus as he heard the voice again. He squinted and turned his head away from the light, it was so intense it hurt. He was lying on his back, he realised he was in a bed looking at what must be a ceiling. In one ear there was still a constant ringing from the blast.

"How much did they pay you?"

His mind was haywire, everything was confusion, where was he, what was this voice?

"Mr Bell...that is your name, is it not?"

Alex nodded.

"Mr Alex Bell, you work for IAB yes?" The accent was slight, but the words were said with very clear diction and at a perfectly modulated tone as if speaking to a child.

Alex tried to move his arms but they were pinned to his sides. He turned back towards the voice but the bright light was still shinning in his face. He licked his lips, they were cracked and dry. His mouth felt so dry and his face and skin felt like it was burning over his entire body.

"Please open your eyes Mr Bell."

Alex blinked and tried to focus, he could see a dark oval. It wasn't quite a face but it was shaped like one. He tried to speak, "where am I, what's happened?", but the words just would not come. He closed his eyes. His last clear memory was of the burning car. No, he remembered more, voices, yes that was it, voices. The sounds of Arabic and then flashing lights, blue and red lights and faces, many faces, then white walls. He remembered the smell of a hospital. That was it; yes he must be in a hospital.

"Please open your eyes Mr Bell, we are here to help."

"Where am I?"

"What, what did you say?" asked the voice.

"I need some water", Alex could barely speak.

The oval above him shouted something out in Arabic. "Alex, please understand me, you are in a very serious situation. *Yanni* I want to help you *habibi*."

Alex felt so thirsty, "water, please."

The oval came right up to his face. "What?"

"Water please"

"You want water?"

He nodded and passed out again.

That same morning, Jim was outside Arabian Homes patiently waiting for Alex to step through the gate at any moment. Alex' car was still at the garage being repaired so the two men had organized it such that Jim would get a taxi first and then come and pick Alex up at his compound. The Londoner checked his watch for a third time with mounting annoyance. He needed to get into work on time today. Alex was now getting to be really late and that was unusual for him because his friend was pretty reliable when it came to timekeeping. With great difficulty in the cramped back seat of the cab, the trader took his mobile out of his trouser pocket and scrolled through his phonebook and finding Alex, rang his friend's mobile. It rang for a couple of seconds and then went straight through to his answer phone. Jim left a quick message. He then rang Alex' villa, it was frustratingly the same story. Annoyed he told the driver to wait and stepped out of the cab and approached one of the security men that stood about by the gate.

"Have you seen Alex?"

The Pakistani guard looked blankly at the Londoner, "who Sir?"

"You know the bloke I normally get a lift with, Alex, Alex Bell." The guard looked completely clueless as to what Jim was asking for. "Can I go in and get him?"

"Yes of course Sir", he pointed to a little booth where another man was stationed.

Jim asked the second man as the taxi hooted behind him.

"I ring please, what number apartment?"

"39 Algarve, Alex Bell."

The guard rang and listened to the phone line. There was no reply. "Sorry Sir, no answer."

"Can I just nip through and see if he's there?" After the hideous death of Schuster, Alex and Jim had agreed that they would always check on each other if only to verify that a dose of Alka Seltza was all that was needed.

The guard gave a weak smile and signalled it was not possible. "Sorry Sir, must have invitation to enter. Security yes?"

Jim thought for a moment, "Can you try Dieter Werner for me please."

The guard rang the Werner's number. There was also no reply there either. In the background the taxi hooted again. Jim checked his watch, he really needed to get into work; the markets were torrid at the moment. With slight prick of annoyance at his friend, Jim disconsolately walked back to the cab and made his way into the office. Maybe Alex just has a hangover or something after a big night at one of those Den nights he thought with a rueful shake of his head.

The next time he came around he was shocked to find himself tied to a chair. He looked up, this time he could just about see. It was not clear, he needed his glasses. He felt strange, light headed as if he was floating.

"Hello Alex." It was the same voice as before.

Alex blinked and tried to focus, he tried to move but his hands were bound to the chair palms upwards, his legs were tied together and there was a restraint across his chest. He had a drip in his arm. He looked around unsteadily, utterly disorientated as two faces gradually came into focus.

"Alex, we have been very patient, now we want you to help us."

"Where am I, who are you and what is the meaning of this?"

The man made a tutting noise. "My friend, you were in a hospital, now you are here with us. I am called Saleh."

"What's happened, there was an explosion."

"Yes there was, was there not? A very big explosion, tell me about it."

Alex' eyes closed trying to remember what had happened. "I don't remember much, I was standing in the bookshop and..." Alex suddenly remembered the blinding flash and searing heat of the blast. "What's happened to Jerry and the others?"

"The others are dead, exactly as you planned no?"

Alex blinked in astonishment, his eyes suddenly flashed anger. "Planned? What the fuck do you mean planned?"

The man nodded and Alex screamed in agony as suddenly he felt a sharp burst of pain across the palms of his hands.

The man's voice did not waiver, the tone exactly as before. "Do not speak to me like that Alex. Do not raise your voice to me. I don't like it, do you understand?" Alex stared uncomprehendingly at his interrogator. The uniformed man nodded again and Alex cried out in agony as once more he felt the intense searing pain on his outstretched hands. "Do you understand?" Alex nodded. His interrogator smiled and gave a slow sad shake of his head, he nodded again and Alex screamed in anguish as the burning pain ripped through him. "I can't hear you Alex. Do you understand?" The man was still smiling.

"Yes, yes, I understand", cried out Alex through tears of pain.

Jim's concern for his friend was heightened as the day progressed and was crystallized by the news that there had apparently been a car bomb in the city the previous night. News reports were scanty other than the information that all the casualties were US servicemen. There had been fatalities, but no names were going to be released until relatives and loved ones had been informed. By one o'clock he had already called Alex's villa or mobile at least a half dozen times. If he did not get through he would definitely call round Sierra Village that evening. Those ridiculous guards would have to physically restrain him. By three thirty even Pete was starting to look worried.

At just past four Alex's line again rang. As throughout the day he picked it up hoping it was Alex calling in to explain his absence. It could be his wife though that was less likely these days. Jim had noticed that Alex was normally the one that made the calls and that it was no longer a daily thing. No, it was probably just another broker. Jim picked up the insistent flashing line, "IAB." There was a long pause on the line. "Hello, IAB trading", said Jim.

"Err...is that you Jim?"

Jim couldn't quite place the voice on the line, "yes?"

"Jim, it's me, Dieter. Is Alex OK?"

"Dieter I have no idea. Nobody has seen him since yesterday." There was a very long silence on the phone. "Dieter, are you still there?"

"Oh shit, I just hope he has left then. Fuck"

Now Jim could not believe what he was hearing. "What's going on?" Surely Alex had not done a Bill Heaver, it made no sense. His friend was making a fortune in his trading.

"Jim, the police were here, they were searching his house."

"What?" This really was extraordinary. The Saudi authorities almost never dared to enter the Westerners' compounds. It was unheard of for two reasons. Firstly because there was almost never occasion to do so. Crime, as the Saudi Authorities would tell you and official statistics showed, did not exist in the Kingdom, thanks to *Sharia* law, though the security on the compounds might have something to do with that as well as the potential draconian response. Matters were dealt with internally. Secondly and perhaps much more importantly, the sanctity of a Muslim's home was never to be violated. In Saudi Arabia as in most Islamic countries, what went on behind closed doors in a man's home was not for others people's eyes. A man and his family's privacy would always be respected. It was cultural, it was *Haram*.

"Nobody seems to know anything", said Dieter.

It was early evening now and Ed Moore wondered why his expensive informant in the police had still not called him. He was annoyed because he paid him enough and he expected at least something from the greedy fool in return. He picked up the phone and called him.

"Yes."

"Why haven't you called me?" asked Moore in his direct but excellent Arabic.

"What?"

"You know exactly what I mean. What happened to our understanding?"

"I'm sorry, but there is nothing to say."

"Nothing, don't be absurd? A bomb goes off right here in Jeddah and you have nothing, do you think I was born yesterday?"

"This is very different Ed. This is high profile, much too high profile. It's not in our hands at all. The Interior Ministry have taken complete control of this one"

"I don't care what profile it is, or who's in charge, I don't pay you for silence. How many people were involved? Casualties, suspects, what have you got?" Moore knew that strict censorship in Saudi Arabia meant any official releases were a web of fiction. Normally the authorities would never acknowledge any Saudi casualties, only foreign ones unless somehow cornered into doing so. As for the possibility of Saudi nationals being responsible, well as far as the powers that be were concerned, that was simply out of the question.

"I don't know for sure, some foreign workers in the Pizzeria and the bookshop, a few shoppers perhaps."

"Perhaps?" replied Moore dripping sarcasm. "Find out."

"But..."

"Don't give me any crap, or you'll be explaining exactly how you bought that new car to your boss."

"OK, OK, I'll try again."

"You be a good boy and do that, right now." Moore slammed the phone down.

That night Jim Robson thought long and hard about what he should do next. Despite huge reservations he decided to call the police first thing the next morning. Infuriatingly it being a Friday, the office was practically deserted, his Saudi trainee Mohammed Jundi was not in the office so he turned to the quietly spoken Khalid.

"Police, why do you want to call the police?"

"Well Alex might have been in an accident."

"Accident?" Khalid looked unsure, "But why should they help, don't you mean a hospital?"

"I just want a number."

"OK, of course if you want it" and in a brief moment he had found and given the Londoner a phone number.

Jim dialled the number. "I'm looking for someone, a foreigner, British, called Alex Bell. I'm afraid he might have been in an accident."

"Britisher?"

"Yes, Alex Bell"

"Alex?"

"Alex Bell."

"Who are you?" asked the voice on the line in a thick accent.

Jim spoke carefully and clearly. "I'm a friend. I wanted to know if Alex Bell has been involved in an accident."

"Why, what is your name?"

"I just want to know if he has been involved in an accident."

"Are you a relation?"

"No. I work with him," replied Jim

The voice now seemed completely unbothered. "Nobody name like that here."

"What?"

"Officer in charge, not here, *Inshallah bokra*."

Jim bridled, "look I just want to know if my friend is OK."

"Call the mortuary" and Jim listened as the line went dead.

"Fuck this place", said Jim with angry frustration.

Khalid gave the Londoner a look of concern. "What did they say Jim?"

"He said to call the mortuary."

Khalid gave a look of disbelief, "here, let me call them." The young Saudi picked up the phone and called the same number. He spoke quickly and animatedly into the phone, all Jim could pick up was Alex' name in the terse guttural conversation. Khalid put down the phone.

"Well, what did he say?" asked Jim.

Khalid gave a sad look, "He says there's nobody of that name there. He says have we tried the hospital?"

Jim shook his head, "but there are dozens in the city."

Khalid nodded agreement and picked up the phone. "I will call my uncle, we will need more help."

He was right. They were going to need more help. Jim dialled Mohammed Jundi's mobile.

"Saeed, just what in the name of Allah were you trying to do?" Jim Robson and Ed Moore were not the only people that day whose frustration had crossed the line into anger.

Mohammed Al-Hamra was lying on his back, his body covered with cuts and bruises from the blast of the bomb that his colleagues had so successfully planted. He opened his eyes and surveyed the small room, his thoughts were scrambled and it took him a moment to realise it was his room, the one he shared with Ahmed.

"I just wanted to ensure..." he trailed off and closed his eyes.

Abdullah Bawani stared at the young man intensely, "to ensure what?"

"... mission..." and he mumbled something unintelligible.

Still angry the black haired Egyptian leant closer to prostrate young man's form and tried to listen to his feeble utterances. The *Alim* shook his head, barely able to make out what the *Jihadi* was saying. The youngster was quite injured, but the Egyptian knew he would live. Bawani had plenty of experience of death and knew its face well enough to be absolutely sure of that.

"Ensure the mission?" the Alim replied with anger, "you nearly jeopardized everything."

"... man in the bookshop...couldn't...American"

The *Alim* only hearing a few broken words from the young man shook his head sadly and gave him a look of sympathy. "My brother, you cannot expect everything to work to plan every time. There are always unexpected complications. God willing there will be many more chances to come for martyrdom."

Mohammed Al-Hamra gave a tired shake and again fell asleep.

Bawani got to his feet still annoyed at the young man, but his displeasure was passing. There was no doubting Saeed's enthusiasm for Jihad and martyrdom. He recalled how as soon as the explosion went off, he and Ahmed rushed into what was left of the bookshop to find a disorientated young Saeed holding one of the Americans and trying to carry him to where the bomb had just gone off. The young fool nearly killed himself and despite his attempts to kill more of the infidel he had inadvertently saved the cursed man life as shortly afterwards the building had caught fire and collapsed.

"Look I know nothing about any alcohol" and Alex received another agonizing reminder for this latest outburst. Despite everything he did to try to keep himself strong and focused he found himself whimpering like a baby. The bearded man with the stick snorted loudly and spat.

"Alex *Habibi*, when are you going to realise what has happened? This is not a game. No one is coming for you." said his interrogator in his horrible monotone. He gave an insipid little laugh, "do you think perhaps that you can escape and run away?"

Alex' swallowed. How he hated the man in front of him. The Englishman's face was now freshly bruised, but the interrogation techniques the Saudi's used were totally state of the art. They had learned them from the best that money could buy. How to interrogate and torture a man without leaving a mark was something they were gradually becoming adept at. Of course normally in the Kingdom it was not a consideration at all, in this case it just might be.

"Alex, I don't think you understand your situation. Let me enlighten you." The Saudi known as Saleh pulled up a chair. "Four Americans have been killed. You were with the Americans and yet remarkably you are the only survivor."

"But I was only..."

The interrogator nodded and Alex felt another wicked blow rip into the soles of his feet sending paroxysms of burning pain right through him. "Alex, I'm speaking, please don't interrupt me. It is very rude is it not?"

"Yes" whimpered the Englishman.

He smiled and raised both hands in mock supplication. "Remarkably you, Alex, are the only survivor." "Now let me explain your situation, so there is no confusion." Tied to the chair but on his back, Alex's head dropped sideways and he stared at the floor in despair. The Saudi nodded and yet another agonizing blow fell upon his feet. "Alex, look at me Alex. Alex... I don't want you to look at the floor or the ceiling or anywhere else. I want you to look at me, just as I am looking at you." Still whimpering with the pain, Alex turned his head towards his tormentor and stared at the man's eyes, wishing with every drop of what was left of his being that if he could just have one moment with this man alone, unbound, he would kill the scrawny bastard without a second thought.

The whole time the Saudi's voice never showed the slightest emotion. He spoke at the same speed and the same sickening, reasoning tone throughout. He smiled; it seemed the arsehole never stopped smiling. "Good, I have your attention. Now listen carefully to what I am about to say to you. You are already dead Alex Bell, nobody knows you survived that explosion, nobody is looking for you. I could have you executed this minute by my friend here and send you to the morgue. I only have to give him the signal." His interrogator broke into another fresh smile, "it is not a nod, in case you were wondering." The Saudi stared at Alex as if he expected him to join in the joke and start laughing, Alex just tried to breathe. "Do you understand me? You no longer exist."

"How long have I been here?" The Saudi nodded and Alex gritted his teeth, knowing what was coming next. He screamed again, writhing as the pain shot through his body convulsing him once more.

"Alex *habibi*, I hope you believe me when I say we have much experience in dealing with difficult people here." The interrogator smiled thinly and looked around the dark stinking cell, "Really, we have everything at hand here that we need to bring light and co-operation from our guests."

Alex's eyes dimmed as the man continued to speak in his mechanical lifeless tone. "Did you know your chair, it conducts electricity very well."

Another bilious wave of terror overtook him, "No, please...."

The interrogator nodded and Alex felt another vicious blow fall upon him that made him scream in agony.

"Alex, I believe you are an intelligent man, but really, *habibi*, is this necessary? I think not. Now I am going out for some tea and my friend here is going to give you a pen and some paper and all I want is for you to write down your confession." The Saudi got to his feet and walked towards the door behind Alex.

"What do you want me to say?" said Alex, his voice barely audible.

"Well, exactly what you did, that you planted the bomb and that you killed the Americans over a deal that went bad."

713

"What deal?"

"Alex please, you are being tiresome, we have already discussed this, the whisky, five cases that we found in your house." Saleh turned off the light, plunging the filthy cell into darkness and then switching it on again, filing the little piece of hell Alex that was now in with the intense and harsh light. The interrogator repeated it again. "You'll find it conducts electricity very well Alex." The man broke into a stream of Arabic and then left the room followed by the bearded man who snorted and spat again, but this time quite precisely on Alex's anguished face.

Behind him two men then entered his cell and lifted Alex into an upright position. They dropped a ballpoint pen and some paper on a table and unbound him.

Alex heard the sound of the door slamming shut behind him. It sounded heavy and the noise of the door seemed to set off more ringing in his right ear. Alex looked at his arms, they were covered in lacerations from the blast and he could feel his face was tight with clotted blood. If his face looked anything like his arms and legs he must look a mess. He closed his eyes and felt his will to continue slowly ebbing away. He was on the way to the point of past caring, they could do anything they wanted, say anything they wanted; he was absolutely powerless. He tried to move in the seat but even the slightest movement brought pain everywhere, the effects of the blast were all over his body but the soles of his feet and the palms of his hands now just constantly ached thanks to the merciless beatings he had received since the explosion.

Inside the tiny cell there was nothing but the stale smell of urine and his fear. Despite the heavy door he could hear every footstep beyond echoing down the corridor outside. He made an effort to stand, his feet were so sore they were barely able to take his weight. He edged forward dragging the chair with him towards the table. The door made a sharp clacking noise as a latch moved and a beady eye watched every inch of his painful progress.

They had arrested him, trumped up and planted evidence on him, starved him and beaten him almost continuously since the moment of the blast. He still had absolutely no idea how long he had been there, but it already felt like an eternity and he knew that what little resistance he had was already starting to evaporate from him. Now every time he tried to sleep they woke him up. He was completely exhausted, but every time he closed his eyes and started to fall asleep, the door would open and he would get a sharp kick from his jailers. All he knew was that unless someone knew of his existence it really was utterly hopeless.

By the time that Jim Robson walked into Ed Moore's office the tubby American had more or less guessed what the trader was going to tell him. All Ed Moore knew was that he did not expect this conversation to be easy as the two men were obviously good friends. The previous night Lorenzo Evans had called and he had news. According to the medics the one American that had survived the blast was actually going to make it. The man was incredibly lucky to be alive, but Evans had some even more disturbing news. There had been a fifth man with them. Alex Bell. It seems Bell was simply in the wrong place at the wrong time, what was left of him was probably incinerated in the subsequent inferno that consumed the remains of the bookshop. It was not good or pleasant, but for Ed Moore at least it meant there were no difficult untied ends to deal with. He knew how things could so easily get twisted in events like this. The American eyed the Londoner as Jim informed him that he had some bad news about Alex. As he did so Ed Moore wondered how he would break the news of Bell's death to his friend.

"Apparently the police were all over his place yesterday." Moore gave a concerned look, trying to give the impression that this was the first time he had heard the news. "The police?"

Jim nodded, "yes. Now I called the police."

"You did?"

Jim shook his head, "Yup, but they were less than helpful, so I went down to the city mortuary." Ed Moore studied Jim Robson with an unblinking gaze. Maybe the Londoner was going to save him a bit of time. Moore maintained his look of concern. Jim had a deadly serious expression; there was little point on going over the pact that he and Alex had forged in the aftermath of the ghastly Schuster affair.

Moore's eyes narrowed. "You went to a mortuary?"

"Yes, there's one dedicated just for immigrants, but there was no record of any Westerner being brought in at all. We checked."

Moore's hawk like expression never erred, "We?" The American had not expected this at all and he had to give Robson some credit, the fellow was pretty persistent.

"Yes, quite a few of us have been looking for him. Pete, Mohammed and Khalid have been helping me."

"I see", Moore also knew that Mohammed Jundi's family was both well connected and powerful.

"So we visited a number of hospitals." Moore's remained motionless. "Alex was admitted to the GNP Hospital."

"What?" Moore was shocked by this piece of news.

"I know" said Jim with a disbelieving shake, "and he discharged himself."

Astonishment flushed the American's face. "Did you say discharged?"

"Yup, I saw the release form. The hospital knew all about him, he was obviously injured in that bomb. I had thought as much. I think he was with those Americans." Jim gave the red faced Treasurer a worried look. "But Ed, what is

717

really strange is that it was not his signature on the form and no one has seen or heard from him since."

Ed Moore's earlier uneasy sense of control completely evaporated. "Have you told anyone else this?"

"No not yet, but I thought I'd tell you first to see if there is anything you can do. You know some of the American forces, maybe he's in a hospital with them? I can't think what else to do."

Moore was staring into the middle distance, his mind was working overtime.

"Ed?"

"Yeah, you should call the British Consulate, OK? Do that and I'll see what I can do."

Jim turned to leave and realised there was one thing he needed to do and had been putting off. Phoning Claire Bell was not going to be easy, he had the number, it was one of Alex' speed dials, but how on earth was he going to tell her? He wandered out of the American's office as Moore angrily picked up the phone to call his errant Saudi informant.

The Saudi named Saleh, dropped the blank piece of paper back on the table and shook his head. "Alex, I'm a patient man, but even I have my limits." He looked at the Englishman with a thoughtful expression. "In your country you say life is cheap do you not?"

For a moment Alex looked at the Saudi with uncomprehending eyes before a hideous sense of foreboding filled his every sense.

"Well you are wrong, for it is not life, but death that is cheap, my friend, as you will see."

Beside him the other man menacingly wielded the stick that had introduced Alex to a world of pain that he could not have imagined in his worst nightmares. He heard the man snort and spit inches from his face, primed once more for his merciless task.

His unflappable interrogator gave Alex another sad shake of his head. "Well *Habibi* I have done my best to help you Alex." He gave another nod and Alex waited for another agonizing blow to arrive. It did not, instead from behind him he heard the heavy door swing open and two men entered the cell and picked up the Englishman, one under each arm and started to drag him out of the cell.

"Good bye Alex" said the Saudi in his hideous emotionless monotone.

"What?" screamed Alex, "what are you going to do to me?"

The two men practically pulled the banker along the corridor, Alex screamed and tried to resist but it was pointless, his strength had almost entirely deserted him. Desperately he tried to slow his progress as they held him upright but so exhausted and in such pain from his bruised feet, he was unable even to keep up with them, leave alone resist their combined forward momentum. They dragged him still whimpering into another room. Despite his colossal fear, Alex immediately took in his new sickening surroundings. Above him on the ceiling was a vicious looking hook and Alex felt another stomach churning wave of terror rise within him, what were they going to do to him here? The guards dropped him onto the floor and he fell forward onto his knees and took a breath, resting only a little of his weight on the sore palms of his hands.

The man responsible for his beatings followed Alex into the cell and slowly walked across the room. In front of him he noisily unlocked a cupboard door and opened it. Alex watched in absolute terror as the man brought out a huge sword, his eyes transfixed by its hideous glint. The man turned and gave Alex a look of utter contempt, snorted and spat.

"No please, I confess. I'll do anything you want right now. Please, please I don't want to die."

Behind him he heard the voice of his interrogator. "I'm sorry Alex, but we are beyond confessions. Sit up it will be much better for you."

"Please I'm begging you..." Alex's next words were muffled as a filthy, stinking hood was roughly pulled over his head and his hands were bound behind his back.

He heard the footsteps of his executioner move towards him.

"Say your prayers", said the interrogator.

Alex continued to plead for his life but his words were muffled in the hideous choking confines of the hood.

"I said say your prayers Alex."

Utterly broken Alex began to recite the Lord's Prayer in a voice that was barely audible. Suddenly his fatigued mind was operating at blinding speed, images of his wife, his children, his entire world flashed before his closed eyes as the words tumbled out of him.

He felt a sharp prod in the small of his back and then a dull heavy blow across the base of his neck that sent him sprawling forward across the room. As he lay whimpering on the floor all he could hear was the laughter of the men above him.

Claire Bell had spent most of the Friday afternoon and a good deal of the following Saturday on the telephone. It had been incredibly frustrating. At the time she had wondered why she had not heard anything from her estranged husband since the previous Tuesday night. Initially she had put it down to their last barked conversation, but even if the two of them were barely on speaking terms, he at least always wanted to talk to their children. Now she knew that he had been caught up in some sort of explosion directed against American soldiers though Jim had reassured her that Alex was alright. The news had shocked and angered her and she was still quite dismayed as to how her idiotic husband had managed to get himself into such a situation.

Thinking back she had briefly heard about it on the radio, but a small car bomb going off in the Middle East is hardly newsworthy and since it only mentioned American servicemen she did not give it a second thought. Only after Jim Robson's phone call had it all fallen into place. Since then she had been in contact with the Saudi Embassy and the Foreign Office. The former had been completely useless, that latter not much better, though eventually she had managed to get through to speak to someone. The official's voice on the line informed her that locating a missing person in a foreign country was not easy. After a few questions Claire Bell immediately regretted admitting that she and her absentee husband were not on good speaking terms. The official's tone had changed completely after hearing this admission and the voice had even suggested she might want to contact Relate and the Child Support Agency for advice too. This last suggestion completely infuriated her, she knew her husband had many faults, but he was not the type to run out on his kids. She called back several times, this time simply saying her husband had been involved in the blast and that he was missing.

Peter Wheeler, the consular official hung up the phone, his normally quiet existence had been disturbed by the two phone calls in quick succession. It was nearly three o'clock in the afternoon and normally this would signal that the end of day was at hand. This Sunday it was different. The first call was from a colleague, who had informed him that they had earlier received information on a British subject that had been caught in the blast near Tahlia Street. The man had discharged himself from hospital but apparently he was now missing and police had been seen around the man's house according to this friend.

The second call was from the Foreign and Commonwealth Office back in London. It seemed that some persistent woman had been phoning the diplomats headquarters in London and anyone else that would take her calls over the last couple of days. His boss in London did not need to remind him that it was an unnecessary nuisance. British interests would not be being served if the man was somehow mixed up in this matter. In both cases the same British national's name had come up. He looked at the name he had scrawled on a piece of paper in pencil, rubbed his upper lip in thought and picked up the telephone.

Perhaps this posting might be more interesting than Oman after all.

Alex stared into the bright light with an exhausted expression.

"Alex, we will need to do that bit again."

The trader gave a tired nod.

"Would you like some more tea?"

Alex shook his head. "No I am fine."

His interrogator gave a thin smile. "Good, then let us start again."

"Where from?" asked Alex with eyes that looked devoid of life. He knew that every contrived word he uttered was signing his own execution warrant, but there was nothing he could do. Maybe if he confessed the UK authorities could somehow get him extradited. Saleh had said it was his only hope, extremely remote, but it did, nevertheless, exist. At least the beatings had stopped and Saleh had promised him he would have access to someone from the UK consulate once he had confessed.

The man simply known as Saleh, rewound the video tape and watched the image on the monitor beside him and listened to Alex's confession. He stopped and turned to Alex. "From 'under the passenger seat', you started to nod your head in a strange way. Please keep perfectly still and just point to the diagram beside you exactly as I showed you."

Alex continued with his staged confession as the video camera recorded his every self incriminating word. He pointed at the diagram beside him. "I planted the bomb under the passenger seat, here..."

Ed Moore's unease had turned to near panic. His source in the police had managed to find out exactly where Alex Bell was now incarcerated and Moore knew, only too well, what the circumstances were that the young trader was likely to be enduring. For Ed Moore this development was wholly and heartily unwanted. Not only was there a clear and unambiguous link to him, he could not even be sure what Bell may be made to confess to. Given where he was checked in, he would likely admit to just about anything the Saudi authorities wanted him to. In any event, discovery of any link back to Moore or even IAB was completely unacceptable. If CIA headquarters at Langley were to discover this then God only knew where this might lead, worse still, if the FBI were to be involved then all hell could break loose. He would be on his own. Ed Moore held his head despairingly. He needed to figure out a way of getting Alex out of the clutches of the Interior Ministry and he needed it fast. Fortunately for both him and Alex, his mind worked even faster. The American had plan A and also a back-up, plan B. He picked up the phone.

"Jim, could you come in here a moment?"

The British consular official looked at Alex Bell from across the table. "Well I don't know how you have got mixed up in all this." Peter Wheeler looked down at the charge sheet, written in Arabic. "Trafficking in alcohol, extortion, blackmail, possession of explosives, planning and executing explosions, destruction of property, murder, is there anything else you want to admit to?"

"I told you what happened."

"Mr Bell, I have seen the videotaped confession, what exactly am I to think?"

"For God's sake have you any idea of what I have been through?"

Peter Wheeler had been with the Foreign Office since graduation from Oxford. A gifted linguist, this was his second foreign posting, he was twenty three. The young official gave Alex an odd look. "What exactly have you been through then Mr Bell?"

"They've been beating me since I got here, they even staged an execution. You have no fucking idea what I've been through." Alex showed him his hands, the bruises were still evident.

The young diplomat studied the bruises, they did indeed look nasty. He averted his gaze and then examined the wreath of official papers lying in front of him, picking out one. "The Saudi's say you were caught in the blast due to your own incompetence. That all these injuries are in effect self-inflicted." His translation was excellent.

Alex could barely contain himself. "For God's sake, do you honestly believe them?"

Wheeler gave the banker a wary look. "Mr Bell, I have to stress that I am not a lawyer, as things stand you will be appointed one in due course, but with this confession of yours, this makes things very tricky, very tricky indeed."

Alex looked at the callow faced diplomat with slack jawed incredulity. "Look, I've been bloody tortured here and you sit here quoting their bullshit like it's all true. It's a complete pack of lies. Everything was made up by them, can't you see that?"

The diplomat let out a long low sigh. "Mr Bell, I am only here thanks to a phone call from a friend of yours. How he found out where you were I really don't know, because we have been looking for you for a while now. But even so, now that we've found you, I have to stress to you that the situation is extremely delicate. Thanks to your confession, things have been made very difficult. Of course Her Majesty's Government seeks to protect her citizens, but there are protocols and procedures that must be carried out.

We have to honour their evidence gathering, judicial process and legal system and to act accordingly in the interests of all parties concerned. "

Alex looked at the official with almost as much anger as he had for the man who had systematically beaten him for the last four days. "What the fuck are you on about? I need you to get me out of here."

"I'm afraid that is impossible at the moment, but let me assure you..."

"Assure me? Assure me what for fucks sake?"

"Well frankly speaking, given the severity of the charges and your confession, I have been instructed to tell you that we have a limited set of options, but we can hope to commute the death penalty, though that is not within our powers to guarantee."

Alex looked at the young diplomat with utter desperation. "My God, you can't be serious?" This was not what his torturer had told him, he had said that if his government resisted his execution then it would be waivered. It was his only hope.

The diplomat gave a grave shake. "Mr Bell. I'm sorry to say I'm being deadly serious."

Alex gave the diplomat a long stare. The diplomat unblinkingly stared back at Alex, seeing only a haggard face with an expression of utter wretchedness. "So what can I expect to happen to me?"

"Well at the moment, the evidence is being collected and your confession and knowledge of the victims has all been documented."

Alex bridled. "You keep talking about this fucking confession. It was beaten out of me by these bastards, can't you see, that?"

The diplomat shook his head. "I'm sorry to have to tell you this but that is now of little consequence here. In Saudi Arabia a confession is an admittance of guilt. It's as simple as that."

"Please can't you do something? You must see it's just so..." Alex's voiced trailed off

"As things are at the moment you will be appointed a Sharia lawyer and will stand trial in the not too distant future."

Alex could not have looked more devastated, "not too distant?"

The official shook his head. "I know it's difficult, we'll see what we can do, eh?"

"What about my family?"

"They will be contacted by someone. You should be able to write to them, but obviously all mail is strictly censored." The young official gave Alex a reassuring smile. "Look, keep your head and do not sign anything or make any other statements without a lawyer being present, OK?"

Alex nodded and the young linguist got to his feet, he offered his hand, "I'll be in touch shortly."

Peter Wheeler knocked on the door and left the small interview room and Alex broke down in tears.

Ed Moore listened to Jim Robson's account of the diplomat's meeting with Alex.

"I see", said the American with a frustrated snort.

"It doesn't look good at all Ed", said the Londoner.

"It sure doesn't" replied the American.

"I'll keep you posted on developments."

"You do that." Moore watched Jim Robson as he walked back out of his office. The man from Missouri had to give the British their due. They really were a mercenary lot. As a student of French literature he was well aware that Napoleon had referred to the English as a nation of shopkeepers. The little Corsican was absolutely right, as their callow faced attempt to free Alex had demonstrated. They would sell their own grandmothers given half a chance. The fawning relationship between Britain and oil rich Saudi Arabia meant that citizens like Alex were entirely expendable to narrow market interests. The Brits could not give a shit, but on the other hand, multi billion pound contracts for armaments were exceedingly powerful laxatives for politicians, businessmen and diplomats alike. Moore however, had his own more personal reasons for actually giving a shit. He picked up the phone to Lorenzo Evans. He would have to resort to plan B, in his heart he always thought he would have to anyway, it was much the better one.

"Lorenzo, you know that matter we discussed yesterday?"

"Yup"

"Well I need you to execute it right now. We have no other option."

"You know this is calling in a heluva lotta favours Ed."

"I know. Can you do your side of it now?"

"Think so, we'll only have one shot at this you know?"

Ed Moore stared at his computer screen. "Yeah, I know, but I think it'll be enough. Langley is right on board for the bigger picture."

"Have you got some kind photo or ID we can use?"

Ed Moore gave a wry smile. He loved it when a plan really came together and worked. "Sure I'll sort that out right away. See you at eight sharp."

"Will do", replied Evans and he hung up the phone.

Back in England Claire Bell heard her door bell ring and quickly tidied her hair before opening the dark, heavy wooden door. Her face was unmade and her eyes were still slightly red. She had not been sleeping well these past few days.

"Mrs Bell?"

731

Claire gave the couple a quick once over before answering. "Yes?"

"My name is Edward Williams and this is Vanessa Thorpe", Claire's features pinched in concern, the tone was official like that of a policemen. She steadied herself for some dreadful news. "We're from the Foreign Office, may we come in?"

"Foreign Office?"

"Yes, we've come about your husband."

Claire Bell held back her shock and quickly invited them into the house. She brought them straight into to living room where the two officials sat uneasily on the edge of a sofa.

The man spoke first. "Mrs Bell, as you may know your husband is currently under arrest."

Claire nodded, that was exactly what Jim Robson had told her.

"Well it seems there is a large amount of adverse evidence in your husband's case."

"What are you talking about? He was the victim of an exploding bomb for God's sake. He was with his American friends when it happened."

The woman gave a reassuring smile. "Mrs Bell we know this is difficult"

Claire Bell restrained a shriek, "difficult? You have no bloody idea how difficult it is."

The man spoke again, his voice forcedly calm. "Mrs Bell, your husband is in a dreadful position. He has admitted his responsibility to the explosion that killed three American soldiers."

Claire Bell was outraged by this statement. "Alex? Are you out of your minds? He's a bloody derivatives trader, not a terrorist for God's sake."

"Mrs Bell, we know that, but as we're sure you are aware, Saudi Arabia is not England. Things are different there."

"Different?" She gave an empty laugh, "you can say that again. Have you ever been there?"

The two foreign office workers looked sheepish. "Mrs Bell, that is beside the point. Your husband is there right now and under Sharia law he is facing the likelihood of the death penalty for his part in this incident."

"Incident, I can't believe you actually think he is involved in this at all. It's utterly absurd, ridiculous, it would be laughable if it wasn't so..." Claire Bell buried her head in her hands unable to finish her sentence.

The woman spoke, her tone softer and full of sympathy. "Mrs Bell, we're here to reassure you that we are doing all we can for your husband. But..."

Claire moved her hands away from her face, "But what?"

The man sifted uneasily. "Well we just want you to know that everything that can be done is being done for him."

"Which is what exactly? When are you going to get him out of that hell hole?"

"We are confident we can eventually come to some arrangement with the Saudi Government."

"Eventually...arrangement?" Claire Bell couldn't believe her ears.

The two officials exchanged a quick look amongst themselves. The man cleared his throat. "The thing is this Mrs Bell. We need to be as discreet as possible in this matter."

"What do you mean discreet? He's locked up in jail on a trumped up charge and you say we need to be discreet?"

"Well it's just that we don't want to aggravate things. The Saudi's are very sensitive to criticism and it would only make matters worse."

Claire exploded with anger. "Worse? How can they be any worse? Do you think that bringing up three children with no money and a husband in some black hole or executed, that things can get any worse?"

The woman edged forward. "Please calm yourself Mrs Bell, this really is not helping matters at all. The thing is, to be honest, Mrs Bell, that your husband's interests...well...they would be best served if we kept all this under wraps. Our little secret, if you understand what I mean."

"What?"

"No newspapers, publicity or anything like that."

The man nodded his head in agreement with the woman's words. "Vanessa is quite right. It really would be in nobody's interest if this was to get out, least of all your husband's."

Claire Bell's voice was filled with acidic sarcasm. "So you're saying I should just leave it to you and everything will work out?"

"That's exactly what we're suggesting", responded the man with an uneasy smile.

Claire looked at the two officials, "so that's it?"

The man nodded whilst the woman gave another reassuring smile.

"Well I've never heard such rubbish in my life. He's facing execution for a crime he did not commit and you tell me to just sit here and do nothing. I just won't do it. How long do you think he will languish in jail then, months, years...how long exactly?"

The man's features darkened. "He won't languish in jail at all as long as you co-operate."

"And co-operation is silence, is it? That would be in my interest right?"

The man straightened himself. There was no point in beating round the bush any longer. "Mrs Bell, anything that reflects badly on the Saudi Government or the Saudi

Royal family, for that matter, will be paid for by your husband."

"What do you mean paid for?"

"Let me speak frankly. Your husband is in a Saudi jail. We have absolutely no control over the way he might or might not be treated. If the Saudi authorities feel that they are being unfairly treated by us or the British press they will not like it. They will exact a heavy toll on your husband. Am I making myself clear?"

Claire's pretty features flushed crimson with complete outrage. "This is nothing but blackmail. This is fucking blackmail." Claire Bell got to her feet, she was in a seething rage at everyone, but most of all at the two fawning officials in front of her. "Get out of my house, get out this minute."

The two officials got to their feet. The man cleared his throat, "Mrs Bell, if you want to see your husband alive again, then we suggest you follow our instructions. If you decide to act differently, then that is your prerogative, but let me assure you of this. Your husband will suffer immeasurably more if you choose to ignore us. He will likely be flogged mercilessly, have all of any meagre privileges he might have removed and be allowed absolutely no access to the outside world. You will be administering his death sentence. You need to be fully aware of this. It's your choice, goodbye."

Claire Bell slammed the door shut behind the two Foreign Office officials, speechless with impotent rage. Once more she buried her face in her hands, her fingers damp with her frustrated tears, unsure of who was worse; the sadistic Saudi government, or the spineless, mealy mouthed, complicity of her own.

At precisely two o'clock in the morning, Lorenzo Evans stepped out of the big desert camouflaged Humvee into the midst of the band of men who were all fully armed with an array of deadly weaponry. He swallowed hard; this was not going to be easy. "Ok men, are you ready for this?"
"Sir, yes sir" replied the platoon.
 Evans brazenly marched up to the prison building leading his small but heavily armed platoon.
The intelligence officer banged on the door, presented a piece of paper and barked an order to the guard, who terrified by this unexpected arrival, automatically opened the door to allow the group of military men in. They walked into the prison and almost immediately came to another much more impressive gate.
"I want to see the prisoner Bell, A, responsible for the bombing and murder of three US military personnel immediately," snapped Evans in his impeccable Arabic.

The dishevelled looking guards behind the first set of iron gates, who had been half asleep, looked at the American officer bleary eyed.

One prison guard with a thin moustache stepped forward. "On what authority do you come?"

"I come here with the combined authorities of the Interior Ministry, Prince Sultan, the Custodian of the Two Holy Mosques and the United States Government, Military Mission to Saudi Arabia. Evans briefly shoved the piece of paper in the face of the guard and bristled with authority.

The guard looked unsure. "This is not the time for interrogation of prisoners. I have received no such request. This is not authorized."

"Open this door right now or face the consequences. I have orders to interrogate the prisoner Bell A right now. Three dead Americans are lying in the mortuary and I have orders to interrogate the suspect immediately. "

"I must check with headquarters", said the guard.

Evans took out his revolver and pointed it at the head of the guard. Simultaneously, from behind the captain, the entire platoon raised and cocked their weapons and pointed them at the two other guards. "You, my friend, are acting in violation of chapter 47, UCMJ, subsection two, point eight, one, one article eleven, cease and desist or face the consequences. I have my orders." The guard did not move. Evans was not in the mood for games, the American cocked his standard issue revolver; the barrel was pointed square in the face of the guard. Lorenzo Evans was aware he was playing an extremely dangerous game. If he even blinked or let on for one moment, his bluff would surely be called and then it would get messy.

The guard stared hard at Evans and quickly realised the American was deadly serious. He gave a nervous smile and opened the heavy iron gates.

Evans clicked the safety on his revolver and re-holstered his firearm. "Take me to terrorist prisoner Bell Alex."

Two soldiers stayed at the gate and the rest of the platoon followed the West Point graduate. They all trailed the guard who requested passage past another four more locked doors and gates. Evans never even flinched as he heard the doors lock behind him.

Inside his dark cell, Alex was awoken by the approaching loud sound of heavy footsteps from down his corridor. Since his confession his new cell was luxurious in comparison to the one that he had first been incarcerated and tortured in. In this one he even had a bed. However on hearing the heavy footstep he once again suddenly felt fear gripping and twisting his insides. He listened and prayed that the footsteps might pass by but they halted ominously right outside his door. The key grated in the lock, the door swung open and light flooded into his darkened cell. The first to enter his terrible dark little world was the

739

unmistakeable sight of a Saudi guard. Alex flinched, was he about to get another beating? The Englishman immediately recognized the dark form as a guard from the tell tale black silhouette that stood in the doorway. Alex heard a dull thump and watched as the man appeared to stumble and then slowly sink to the floor. Suddenly the light switched on and there was the guard lying prone on the floor with Lorenzo Evans standing above him holding the barrel of his revolver.

"Time's up Alex." If anyone else had uttered that phrase on entering his cell Alex might well have just expired there and then. As it was, they turned out to be the best words he had ever heard in his life.

Three hours later and Alex Bell was experiencing, 'Space A', for the first and he guessed, probably last time of his life. He still could not believe what had happened. Everything had occurred at such dizzying and confusing speed. All he knew for sure was that he would never be returning to Saudi Arabia. That was impossible and Lorenzo Evans had already left him in no doubt of that.

The military intelligence officer sat beside him on the plane to Bahrain and gave the Englishman another tired but friendly nod. "You're a mighty lucky guy Alex." said the American.

Alex looked into the mid distance still completely confused as to the course of events.

"So Jerry is OK?"

Evans gave a nod. "He'll pull through. He's already back home. He told us what happened."

Alex gave the American a questioning look. "I don't understand, why did you do this for me?"

Evans snorted and gave half a smile, this English guy really was a sap. "I'm sorry to disappoint you, but it wasn't about you at all."

Alex gave the American a wary look. "It wasn't?"

A cold expression flashed over Evans' features that communicated to Alex that he was deeply mistaken if he thought the American had done this or anything else for him. Evans looked away and closed his eyes for a moment. Fatigue was starting to overtake him. The operation had been a success, but even so it had been hugely draining. "No, we're just not impressed with that bullshit 'confession' story. It was unnecessary and definitely not helpful."

"What?"

"We found out what that they were going to release some videotape stating American forces were being killed for selling alcohol or some such shit." Evans wiped his brow, "Nobody back home liked that line."

The mist cleared as Alex started to see a reason for his miraculous escape from his Saudi jailers. Able to think clearly for the first time, he realised his 'confession' had sullied and tainted the murdered American servicemen.

"We're not going to have men loose lives for shit like that. We were targeted, plain and simple and we're gonna get the fucks that did this and drive them off the face of the earth."

Alex suddenly realised it really was not about him at all. It was about something far more important. How could he be so naive? Uncle Sam was a global protector and defender of freedom, not a profiteering bootlegger.

Evans leant forward and delved into a canvas bag sitting between his feet. "We know who's behind this, it's just the Saudis won't accept it." He sat back up and handed Alex a Manila envelope. "Here, you'll need this."

Alex opened the envelope and pulled out a flight ticket and a passport.

"Compliments of Uncle Sam."

Alex looked at the cover, it was an Irish passport, he flicked it open and there was the familiar picture of him staring smiling back at him. He instantly recognized the image. It was the one that IAB had taken of him for his security pass at the bank. His profession was stated as journalist

"Irish?"

Lorenzo Evans nodded and briefly checked his watch. "The next flight to London leaves in four hours, you're booked on it. You should make it, no problem."

Alex studied the airline ticket. He was flying BA back to Heathrow. "How did you manage all this?"

Evans yawned before he spoke. He both sounded and looked tired. "We have our ways, but if you ever see Ed Moore again, you should remember to thank him."

Alex nodded his head.

"Oh and just in case you're wondering, you realise that none of this ever occurred. You were never held by the Saudi's and this little escapade never, ever happened. Do you understand?"

Alex looked uncertain, "Nothing?"

"Absolutely nada, we'll be informing your government as you arrive. I imagine they'll have a similar thing to say to you."

Tired but unbelievably elated and even more unbelievably relieved, Alex peered out through the window. Down far below he could just manage to see the lights of cars driving on the highway below. Alex turned back again and flicked through the passport.

"Journalist?"

"We find that works best"

More than twenty five thousand feet down from him Alex was unaware that one of those cars that was driving the lonely highway northwards that night contained the four Al-Ghamdis, the men that Lorenzo Evans and his compatriots were so intent on finding and razing from the face of the earth. They too were also on their way to pick up a flight, but unlike Alex they were not taking a scheduled flight from Bahrain to London. All four young men had been driving across the fierce desert terrain towards the less policed northern borders of the Kingdom with the UAE. Comprised of seven Emirates, of which Dubai and Abu Dhabi were the best known, it was to the smaller Emirate of Sharjah that the men were now heading. Long ago, during the days of the British Empire, the little Emirate of Sharjah was accorded, 'three gun status', the lowest that could be awarded, by their erstwhile mercantile rulers. Located on a piece of coastline on the Arabian Gulf, that was formerly known to the world as the Pirate Coast, it was fitting therefore that the men, like thousands before them from the Arabian Peninsula were making their departure from that same remote and lawless coast, in order to ply their timeless, unregulated trade. The men's later flight, on the decrepit and barely airworthy Arianna 727 from the subjugated Three Gun State was to take them to the never subjugated Thirty One Gun state of Afghanistan. Saeed Al Ghamdi, like Alex, was leaving the Arabian

Peninsula clandestinely and incognito, also fully aware that he would never return.

23. London, Paris, New York

Within days of Alex's impromptu and clandestine departure Chris Barma had managed to get badly caught up once again on the wrong side of some huge and wickedly volatile US dollar moves. This time there was no reprieve for the big man and his towering ego. His own, heroic demise was caused by the final death throes of the Leviathan hedge fund LTCM. So great was the market turmoil and subsequent financial carnage that the US Federal Reserve was called in to play, forced twice into lowering interest rates. The hue and cry of the whole of Wall Street's finest, so it was rumoured, was heeded for they were, so they said, all on the point of collapse. The heads of the world's largest banks were arrayed around a table in a room in New York City arguing over who was going to foot the bill. Unsurprisingly, none of them wanted to and in the end, it was the US taxpayers, who once again stumped up their full faith and credit in order to protect the banks from a wholesale systemic crash.

To an outside observer it was curious that the sum lost by LTCM and the banking system amounted to almost the exact same sum that the IMF loaned to Russia, but as the bankers subsequently pointed out, after the deal was agreed, that was merely serendipitous coincidence.

In any case, it had been Alex's and his former colleagues' opinions, that it was only a question of when, rather than why, Chris Barma's wild market bets would eventually blow the whole of IAB's considerable risk capital away. For Ed Moore this event merely offered him the welcome opportunity of shutting down the whole failing proprietary trading experiment. So far, two traders had blown up and another had been blown up, a novel twist on a familiar theme. In Moore's view, it was all getting unnecessarily complicated and he wanted to have a clear out. Paradoxically he explained his decision to the Board of the bank by saying that it was just too risky a business. He, he said, preferred more manageable risks. The Chairman of IAB, Khalid Bin Bafaz merely nodded at this latest announcement, the brother in law of Osama bin Laden already had much more pressing concerns.

So by the beginning of October, both Jim Robson and Pete Koestler were, like Alex all back in London. Joe, who had been back longer than the others, organised a re-union of the team. He had an announcement to make and all of them wanted to know what had actually happened to Alex. Consequently it was not until late November that the former colleagues did all eventually meet up. The venue was a bar near Liverpool Street, in the heart of the City

Alex had declined meeting up on several occasions, making various excuses, but he was eventually coaxed and persuaded to join them all by Jim. In all, it had only been four days that he had been incarcerated in the Saudi jail, but he was still deeply traumatised by his experience. Over the last few months Alex had found that the best way to deal with this was to shut it away and soak it in alcohol. It was simple and effective.

Joe was very pleased with things and had proudly announced that he was now working for an IT company. He was helping to build applications for trading the embryonic but fast developing credit markets. Despite their own recent experiences, both Pete and Jim were still pretty upbeat about their future prospects, Jim already had a second interview lined up.

It was only Alex, who remained stubbornly though understandably both taciturn and withdrawn. His friends, only vaguely aware of what had befallen him, waited until an opportune moment on which to press him further about his own extraordinary experiences. At the time of his hasty departure, Ed Moore had explained to them all that Alex had left the country under something of a cloud, but that essentially all was well with him. As far as they were aware he was fine, though Moore pointedly advised them that they should wait to hear from him, rather than seeking to contact their friend for themselves. It was better that way, the American had reassured them. As Alex distractedly listened to the men's now almost meaningless banter, he found himself vividly reliving his horrific past. The physical scars from the explosive event and his incarceration had already healed. It was the mental ones that were still red raw and open though he did his best to bandage them up with a mix of vodka, and the thin tissue of bravado that he had left.

It had been Alex's intention to contact both Ed Moore and Jim Robson almost as soon as he was able to. However this enthusiasm to reach them had been severely curtailed by a deeply unpleasant meeting with government officials that were impatiently waiting for him on his arrival at Heathrow. The meeting went on for several hours and left him with few choices and no doubts. There were the papers that he had to, and then was made to sign. The 'major problem and 'embarrassment' of his so called confession and then the 'unfortunate things' that would happen, should he divulge anything of what occurred to him to anyone else. Then, he would find himself being transported back to Saudi, they assured him. Really, it was best for everyone that this whole, 'unfortunate diplomatic issue', should be left well alone. All he needed was some rest they assured him. He was instructed that contact with his former colleagues back in the Kingdom should not be considered. It was not in his interest, and it was most certainly not in theirs. In the end Alex was simply too exhausted and relieved to have survived, to care anymore. All he wanted to do was to forget about the whole sordid, nightmarish business. He was then taken for a check up and then released after another 48 hours.

However here in the bustling noisy bar, his former colleagues were not quite so ready to be persuaded to consign the recent events they had lived through to their personal psychological scrapbooks, as Alex was.

As usual and predictably it was Joe, who waded in, waist deep, with his oversized footwear.

"So c'mon Alex, dish the dirt, tell us what happened to you?"

Alex paused; he simply did not know even where to start. He had spoken to nobody, it was all just buried away deep within him. "There's not much to say really."

"Well you were there right, weren't you? Where those Americans were killed?"

Alex nodded.

"So what happened, what did you see?"

Alex quickly became aware that all three sets of eyes were now unerringly turned upon him. His voice became hesitant. "...I don't remember much from the explosion.

You see, I was inside the bookshop when the bomb went off. But..."

"But what?" Joe's eyes were bright with eager interest. He was sure he would have something juicy to tell Isobel and their friends.

Alex caught the man's salacious hunger and suddenly felt a momentary flash of anger, what was the point in bringing it all back anyway? "Oh nothing much, I don't remember anything really."

Joe's face immediately registered his disappointment.

Jim leant forward over the table. "But Alex, what the fuck happened when you came out of the hospital?"

Alex gave his friend a long thoughtful look and spoke in a soft voice, "'a promise is a comfort to a fraud', eh Jim?"

Jim responded to this with a quizzical frown, "What?"

Alex recalled the absurd promise that he had been forced to make by the officials on his return home. Fuck them, what did it matter? "I was held by the Saudis and made to confess to having planted the bomb."

"What?" responded Pete with utter astonishment, Jim, for his part, just rocked silently back in his seat and was completely speechless. Joe started to shake his head side to side and then broke into a warped disbelieving grin.

Alex looked as serious as a cardiac arrest, "That's what they told me. I had to confess to the bombing."

"My God", said Jim now rubbing his face, "what a nightmare."

Joe started to laugh, "...a bomber, you? No way. What an absolute hoot...unbelievable."

Pete turned on Joe in a sudden fury, at last breaking every one of his self imposed rules. Now he did not work with the man he was no longer impelled to suffer in frustrating silence. "Will you shut up you fucking moron?"

Joe took on a look of affronted alarm. "Christ, what's wrong with you?"

Jim, sitting between them, ignored the other two squabbling men. "Confess?"

Alex again slowly nodded, "they made me." He was ashamed. He did not want the others to know to what state he had been reduced and so quickly.

Jim understood immediately, before this he had wanted to ask a hundred questions, now just one came blurting out of him. "How Alex, how did they make you confess?"

Alex swallowed hard, he suddenly felt like bursting into tears. He closed his eyes and saw the face of his Saudi interrogator, the face that now woke him screaming almost every night since his return. On hearing Jim's laser like question, Pete and Joe had stopped their arguing and were now watching Alex very closely.

Alex swallowed again, trying to compose and steel himself, the men waited, motionless for him to speak. As he did, he stared at the table top as he recounted his story, the banker's voice never above a whisper. "For days I was tied to an iron chair and they beat me every day on my hands and on my feet. Each time I gave a wrong answer or was silent, they hit me. If I gave them a strange look they hit me, if I didn't look at them, they'd hit me. They would not let me sleep. If I ever fell asleep they would come in and kick me awake." In a barely audible voice he then described his mock execution to the men. When he had finished he looked up at the others, his face was expressionless. In front of him, his friends sat in utter shocked silence.

After what seemed like an eternity, Joe broke the silence. "But surely they just can't do that, what can we do... what about evidence?"

Alex gave a tired wan smile; strangely he was feeling much better, even relieved to have spoken about what had happened. "They came up with everything they needed."

"Like what?" asked Pete.

"Well they said I was selling whisky, so they made me handle all these bottles so that my finger prints were on them."

"Whisky?" Jim's face was a picture of incomprehension

"That was their idea of a motive. I was supposed to be buying the stuff from the Americans and then selling it on.

According to them, they had double crossed me and I had decided to get my own back on them."

Pete looked astounded. "By blowing them up, but that's absurd...surely?"

Alex bridled slightly, "Don't think I didn't try, but it was hopeless. I just had to go along with everything they came up with. If I so much as questioned a single fucking word of their version of events, I was punished and I swear they took fucking pleasure in it...the bastards." Alex's sudden anger and stridency immediately released the men from their own nervous silence and embarrassment at his terrifying experience.

Joe was first to grab this lifeline of sanctimonious outrage. "Well that's just despicable, what a fucking disgrace, what about lawyers, evidence, your civil rights?"

Now it was Pete's turn to break into laughter, "Hey I thought you were supposed to be the old Middle-East hand Joe?"

"Why, what do you mean?"

"Oh c'mon, you can't be serious? You know damn well that such niceties as individual's rights and due process don't exist in places like Saudi. Why do you think we got paid so much?"

Joe was not about to be so easily contradicted. "That's not the point and anyway we weren't paid that much more than here anyway, it's just that we paid no tax."

The man from Zimbabwe gave a look of derision. "Well it comes to the same thing. You pays your money and you takes your choice, or in this case, you don't, because we never did."

Joe was emphatic. "Crap. I'm sorry, but I simply don't accept that. Are you saying that only taxpayers should be exempt from wrongful arrest and imprisonment? I bet lots of people paid their taxes under Hitler and Stalin."

Jim turned to face Joe, "I think the point that Pete is making is that we knew what the place was like, it's just we never ever had to deal with the reality of it." Jim shook his head sadly. "With hindsight maybe we should have been paid a lot more, but in the end it was our choice, wasn't it?"

Joe remained adamant, "I still don't see how that changes anything." He turned and stared at Alex, "But what about our government, surely they should do something? There must be international laws against this kind of outrageous behaviour." Joe added with arched indignation.

"What the hell are you talking about Joe? If you're referring to the Geneva fucking Convention, then just forget it OK? You're talking bollocks." Now Jim was losing his patience too.

Alex shook his head, exhausted by their pious outrage. "Honestly, they couldn't care less. In prison they told me it was entirely up to the Saudis. They said there was nothing they could do..."

"They said that?" Astonishment flushed Joe's pock marked features crimson. His earlier certainty was getting a beating comparable to the physical one that Alex had endured at the hands of his former captors.

Alex stared straight at the Surrey man. "Yes, that is exactly what they said", he replied with deliberate and intended finality.

There was a moment of silence as this sunk in. "Then how the fuck did you get out Alex?" asked Pete.

"The Americans", responded Alex simply.

Now it was Pete's turn to look astonished. "The Yanks? How the hell did they get involved?"

Alex recalled the words of Lorenzo Evans and the long, humid night of his flight to Bahrain. It was all still incredibly vivid in his mind, it still seemed like it was only yesterday that it had all happened. He decided he would stick to the bare facts; it was the least he could do to repay them. "They just came in and got me out. It was as simple as that."

Joe imparted a derisive snort, "What, charging in like the Seventh Cavalry or something?"

He nodded, "something like that."

Jim gave his friend a piercing look, "and they flew you out?"

"Fucking Space A", said Alex with an ironic laugh.

Joe Karpolinski took a long draught from his drink and set it down, Alex had barely touched his. He gave a slow shake of his head. "Well all I can say is thank God we are here. That place is a fucking nightmare. I mean, can you ever imagine anything like that ever happening here?"

Pete shook his head vigorously and Jim gave a nod of agreement, Alex just blinked, still thinking, as he almost always was, of his escape from the unaccountable Saudi authorities and thinking that now, simply nothing seemed as black and white as the man from Guildford was suggesting. Joe picked up his drink, "No, of course not. I mean, we have laws and human rights, don't we? We're civilised, freedom of speech, habeas corpus and all that mumble." He gave a winning smile to the others. "Not like that fucking place." He raised his glass, "to England, where things like that, just don't happen."

Alex stood up. "Sorry guys, I've got to make a move."

"What's up Alex, c'mon we've only just started?" complained Joe with a half grin. "I'll get the next round in."

"No really, I've got to go. I'll see you around." Alex had nowhere to go, except to his lonely flat, but he was not able to continue listening to this.

Jim immediately got to his feet, "are you alright mate?"

"I'm fine, but really I have to go. Silly but I'm double booked this evening." Alex quickly offered his palm and shook his former colleagues by the hand and made to go. Jim gave the two others a quick worried look and then followed him a few steps behind. Jim's words were hushed and filled with concern. "Wait a minute Alex. Alex, are you sure you're OK?"

Alex dropped his head, still taking stock of what had been said, it made him feel sick but above all there was still one thing that from the very first moment he had come round from the bomb blast that had all along had plagued and disturbed him. "Jim, have you got a sec?"

"Sure, of course I have."

The two men left the bar and stood just outside in the cool dark November night huddled under the eaves. Jim lit up a cigarette, whilst around them a very slight, but persistent drizzle was falling. Alex, still not acclimatised to the cold, briefly shivered and turned towards to his friend. "Jim, do you remember Mohammed, Omar Al-Hamra's youngest boy?"

Jim's face suddenly contorted into confused questioning, "Mohammed? Yeah of course I do, why?"

Alex gave his friend an intense stare, "he was there."

"Where?"

"At the bookshop, when the blast went off."

Jim was once again shocked, but this time he was seriously starting to question his friend's mental state. Alex seemed a mess and was making little sense. He was nothing like the man he previously knew. For the first time he immediately questioned what Alex was saying. The Londoner figured that perhaps some kind of post traumatic stress disorder had led to imaginings and confusion which might have over taken his friend's mind? Both Ed Moore and the British consular officials had warned him of just such a thing happening. "The bookshop, are you quite sure?"

"Absolutely Jim, I'm one hundred percent sure. He wanted to speak to me."

"Mohammed Al-Hamra was in the bookshop when the bomb went off." It was not a question. Jim did not mean to sound incredulous but Alex could not fail to hear the note of disbelief in his friends tone. He was not mistaken, for as far as Jim was concerned, this was just not possible.

"Alex I just find that difficult to believe, you must be mistaken."

Frustrated confusion swept over Alex' features as he stared at Jim open mouthed. "Why do you say that?"

Jim gave his friend an intense but sympathetic gaze. "Because we were all looking for you mate, including Khalid and even Omar Al-Hamra. At no stage did they say Mohammed was missing or hurt or anything like that. In fact I know for definite that he was in Riyadh when the bomb went off, Omar told me so."

"But...honestly, I saw him, I swear it Jim."

759

"Alex, mate, you've been through a lot. The mind can play tricks you know when you've been through something like you've been through." Jim's voice was the personification of good sense and reason.

For the first time in a while Alex did think he was about to lose his mind, "tricks?"

Jim shivered, it was not like Saudi, the temperature was dropping faster than the intermittent drizzle that they were dismally failing to shield themselves from. "PTSD, apparently it does this to you."

Alex knew exactly what post traumatic stress disorder was. He just did not expect it to be used as an accusation from Jim Robson. "What are you talking about? Jim I know what I saw and it was real." Alex could feel his anger rising.

Jim gave his friend another understanding smile. "Look Alex, they said..."

Alex bridled. "'They said', who's they?"

Jim's skin colour and the cold night hid his sudden flush of embarrassment, but his halting speech did not. "The blokes...the officials from the consulate I saw, they said that you'd been badly treated and..."

Alex raised a hand; he could see the writing on the wall of incredulity that was steadily being built higher around him. Apparently he was now delusional.

"They saw you?"

"Yes, of course they did. I mean..."

"OK Jim, just forget it." Alex shook his head. "Prisoners dilemma", and then gave an empty laugh.

"What?" Alex was making no sense whatsoever.

"You know Jim. After all, you're the one that told me about it, 'Prisoners Dilemma', 'Decision Theory', all that stuff, right?"

Jim's face clouded, "yeah but..."

"The problem with that is it assumes that the prisoners' interrogators are actually looking for the truth. What if they simply don't care, then what?"

"Alex?" Jim watched as his friend turned and walked off into the cold, wintery darkness.

Afghanistan's leaders, unlike other sovereign leaders from places like France or the United States, were not just accorded the Royal Salute of twenty one guns by the British Empire, but thirty one. This was because, unlike the rest of the huge Indian sub continent, which had eventually yielded to the pernicious but effective strategy of *divide et impera*, Afghanistan remained resolutely unshackled, ungovernable and beyond any Empire's ambitions. The British discovered this painful reality, with the annihilation of an entire army in the ignominious retreat from Kabul under Major General Elphinstone, a man who had served with brave distinction under the Anglo Irish

Duke of Wellington at Waterloo. The sole survivor of this hubristic, over reaching foray, was assistant surgeon William Brydon, who managed at last to reach Jalalabad on his broken and dying mount, the stylized image of which was captured by Elizabeth Butler for Victorian Britain and now hangs forgotten in the Tate Gallery in London. Undeterred by this catastrophic defeat, the like of which was not suffered by this Empire that the sun would never set upon until exactly a hundred years later, at the fall of Singapore, policy makers in Whitehall and Calcutta driven by the 'forward school' thinkers of the Great Game, waged yet another war on the Afghans another forty years later on. In the end, this Second Afghan War achieved even less for Britain than the First, though there were some lasting ramifications for the British. The first effect was obvious; from now on the Empire's reach in that part of the world most certainly did not include the Pashtu lands and several years later the Durand Line, the boundary of where British India ended and Afghanistan began was formally drawn up. The cartographic euphemism, 'Northwest Frontier', did little to hide the indomitable intransigence of the Afghan tribesmen that lived either side of this arbitrary thin red line, though, of course, it looked conveniently neat and tidy when drawn on an atlas with a Mercator perspective. The second effect, as so often is the case in such matters, was an unintended consequence. Courtesy of Prime Minister,

Benjamin Disraeli's private desire to clear Central Asia of Muscovites and to drive them back into the Caspian Sea, he oversaw his own brand of nineteenth century Shock and Awe by despatching another utterly fearless Anglo Irishman to settle the restless Afghans. General Frederick Roberts' keen desire to right the wrongs of the massacre of the British diplomatic mission of Cavagnari in Kabul, led the General to set about a particularly brutal retribution on the Afghans that he came across. Once Roberts had advanced into Kabul, he immediately began to punish local Afghans with a series of public hangings. According to the British, the indeterminate and shadowy nature of their foes, the Afghans were not organised as a formal force, justified treating them not as captured prisoners of war, but as criminals. Unfortunately the General's over enthusiastic use of force and the lack of the exercise of due process of law were to cause considerable embarrassment to both him and the Conservative government back in Britain. For the then British Prime Minister, the suave, urbane, populist Disraeli, this unpleasant episode led to a collapse in support for the war and was to be a major contributory factor to the fall of his government just a few months later.

Even so despite whatever profligacy the forward planners from Whitehall would have in sending, the sons of India, Ireland, Scotland and Wales to the farthest flung corners of their wobbly Empire, the air of British Invincibility so carefully nurtured after Waterloo was to be regularly questioned by Arabs in Khartoum to Zulus at Rorkes Drift. This delusion, popularized, romanticised and stoked by politicians and poets, the Disrealis Palmerstons, Tennysons and Kiplings of Victorian Britain would help inspire spectacular, mad, bravery and unbelievable waste. Pro Patria Mori and Jerusalem would be the hallmarks of the sons of this Empire, the last words on the dying lips of the Pals from the smallest hamlets to the greatest cities of the Sceptred Isle and all its possessions, until the utter waste and pitiless carnage of the Somme, Passchendaele, Gallipoli, brought cathartic introspection.

It was to be another hundred years before yet another Empire would once again deign to try its hand at taming the Afghan peoples. However the Forward School of thinkers from Whitehall and the British Raj were very wrong that it would be the forces of an aggressive Muscovy with designs upon the British Empire's Jewel in the Crown, for that prize possession had long been lost. However unlike the British Empire with its essentially mercantile *modus vivendi*, the Empire of the USSR had only ideological aspirations for regime change in Afghanistan. It was only to be a brief encounter, so the Politburo said, but the legacy of the bloody, near ten year war was to be felt long after the collapse and implosion of Soviet communism. The

Russians to their dwindling credit, it being considerably less than that of the profligate British at the height of their Empire, managed to lose only 14,000 Russian soldiers over this entire period, which was just about the size of Ephinstone's disappeared army. Also unlike the British, this time they were opposed not only by bands of fearless Afghans but also by Muslims recruited from all around the globe and led with conspicuous bravery, by one Osama bin Laden, who was that time at least, officially sponsored by America's own breed of forward thinkers in the White House and the CIA. Preserve us from Godless Communism, cried the forward thinkers and the Muslim Diaspora had dutifully obliged.

So it was not that very different to Dr Brydon, in the manner that Saeed Al-Ghamdi and his fellow *Jihadi* made their perilous way into Jalalabad on their own almost broken down Ariana Afghan Airlines steed . On the bumpy flight, only a few of the passengers were female, their presences marked out by their head to toe covering in thick black *burqas*, the four sat in silence. Otherwise all the faces that the young Saeed saw were bearded, including the fearsome looking cabin crew. The young Saudi closed his eyes as the plane lurched and the pilot banked steeply, bringing the decrepit, barely airworthy plane to a juddering halt on the former Soviet military airstrip. The plane stood

765

for a moment, just narrowly short of the rusting and broken Russian military hardware that was piled up at the end of the pot holed and patched up tarmac and started to taxi.

"Thanks be to God, Jalalabad", said Ahmed. He gave his friend a prod. "Are you OK Saeed?"

Saeed opened his eyes once more and looked at his friend, giving him a warm smile. His face still carried the fresh scars of the blast in Jeddah, though he was, by now, almost fully recovered. "I'm fine thanks, my brother."

Ahmed grinned back and then turned to his other side, still grinning with excitement. "We're here at last."

From across the aisle, both Hamza and Wail responded with wide smiles.

It was only many months later, feeling slightly better and now back again working for another American bank that Alex met up with his old German friend, Willi Spethmen from his dim and distant days in Paris. It was an eye opening experience on two counts. The first he should have guessed, if he had not been so stupid or so close to the problem, the second too, if he had not been so distant.

He quickly learnt why he had received the treatment he did from UK officials on his return to London. The tall blond German was still with Enron and busy trading the burgeoning energy markets. By now he was as well informed on what was going on in them as anyone.

Unfortunately at the precise time that Alex was involved in the Tahlia Street bombing, the United Kingdom Government was heavily involved in negotiating huge gas projects with the Saudi Kingdom. The officials were doing everything they could to keep the Saudis sweet. Alex and his little mistimed adventure could turn out to be a huge problem. As Willi said to him with a good natured slap, "it was just bad timing Tommy."

Since his return Alex was slowly beginning to understand, that, whatever he may be feeling, the world moves on and he had to learn to do so too. Willi was a case in point and he certainly had. In the three years that he had been with Enron, the irascible German had learnt everything there was to about trading the newly pumped up, energy markets. As he kept on repeating; it was just a monster market. New markets like Russia and all the myriad Asiatic republics were simply black goldmines. Enron was making an absolute killing and so was he. When Alex asked after Svetlana, Willi was once again wreathed in smiles. "We're expecting now."

Alex smiled, "that's great news Willi."

"How about you, how are Claire and your boys doing?"

Alex put on a brave face. "Well actually, Claire and I have separated now."

Willi nodded and pulled a sympathetic expression, "I'm sorry to hear that Alex."

"It was mutual, we're still on good terms…you know…"

Willi nodded again and took a draught from his drink.

"Sure, sure, that's good to know", he looked at his watch.

Alex sensed the man's unease and decided to change the subject. "Say, have you seen Jean-Marc?"

"Jayem? Why sure I have. He came to my wedding."

"Oh yeah, I'm sorry I missed that."

Willi gave Alex a wry smile, "Yeah, that was a shame, we missed you."

"How is he doing?"

Willi shook his head. "Haven't you heard?"

Alex gave a questioning look. "Heard what?"

"He's running the whole shooting match there now, Head Honcho."

"You're kidding me…Jean-Marc?"

Willi took another draught and sighed. "Nein my friend, he took over from Altenburg."

"Altenburg left?"

Willi gave Alex a look of disbelief. "Boy you have been out of it. Altenburg died a year ago. He was killed in a car crash. Fuck me Alex, where have you been?"

Like Alex, Saeed Al-Ghamdi also needed to move on, but in a far more literal sense. The young Saudi was learning that being a foot soldier in the war against the infidel was both exhausting and at times mind numbingly boring.

Afghanistan was not at all what he had been expecting. The Russians had long ago departed and the *Taliban* now ran the country but, though unknown to him, he would have benefited much more from Willi Spethmen's knowledge of the country, its new masters and their plans and a lot less from foot slogging around the mountainous Hindu Kush.

The four Saudis had only just recently returned from Chechnya, it had embarrassingly been a completely wasted trip. All they had wanted to do was to fight against the Russians, but the Chechen fighters were simply turning away anyone who was not properly trained. They were not. So Saeed and his brothers ended up back in *Al-Qaeda* camps in Afghanistan to learn their trade. At the moment the four of them were based at the Al-Farouq training camp.

It was, he had by now discovered first hand, a land of great contrasts, imposing high mountains that would descend with breathtaking views into languid and deep tropical valleys. It could be insufferably hot or bone crackingly, bitterly cold, luxuriantly beautiful or bleaker and more hostile than anything he had ever imagined. The Afghans claimed it was God's own country, he was inclined to agree.

Just like his fellow *Jihadi*, Saeed fervently wished he could meet Osama bin Laden first hand, to hear with his own ears what the great man thought, but as he quickly leant, that was unlikely to ever occur. Indeed, practically impossible whilst he led this transient daily existence, marching from here to there across this testing terrain with no enemy to fight, training, training, and more training. It was endless. Still, as they were always being told, it was vital preparation. Their time would come.

As Saeed was now increasingly coming to appreciate, whilst Islam might be used as a means of recruiting and seeking aid, the *Jihadi* around him had very sharply differing ideas of what could and should be done. It was not surprising. They came from all around the world, why should they all agree on the details and specifics of their calling? That was not necessary at all. Only that they shared the same vision; the goal, the global *Ummah* and the divine right of their cause. Allah moved in mysterious ways, that was something they all agreed on and in the end, was that not the most important thing of all, their unshakeable faith in Him?

The evenings were now always lively and unlike the schools in Saudi or the *madrassa* he had briefly stayed at, first in Jalalabad and then in Kandahar, the discussions were unimpeded by the *Alim* and their finer religious points. In truth, he had never been that interested in the intellectual interpretations of any particular *Sura* or *Hadith* other than as a means of purifying himself by the rigours of focusing his mind, emptying it entirely of worldly baggage and opening it to Allah. Like the others, he loved his prayers, each recitation clearing out the doubt that Satan sought to plant in his mind with every arduous step he took. Here, beneath the stars, as he sat amongst his fellow brothers, discussions, thankfully, were of practicalities, freewheeling and quite often fiery and confrontational. This evening was no different, the four men from Saudi had been joined by another four men, a Palestinian, a Syrian a Kashmiri and a man, Pakistani or Indian, Saeed was not sure which, who spoke very poor Arabic and even worse Pashtu, but who apparently came from somewhere called Blackburn. Saeed knew of the place, but never said so, Alan Shearer, his father's Newcastle hero had played for a team called Blackburn Rovers. That, like everything else, did not matter anymore.

Saeed liked it when the Palestinian got excited, it was always interesting. The former teacher, now named Hamza was naturally the leader of the four new recruits, being both the eldest and most assured of the men from Saudi, but Saeed enjoyed it when Hamza had this assumed authority tested. After all, in Islam, all men are created equal; none are masters, only the Almighty. Even great men are humble, look at Sheikh Osama.

Over the last few weeks it was clear that Hamza Al-Ghamdi and the Palestinian did not always see eye to eye. Saeed slowly sipped his milky sweet coffee and watched as the Gaza man spoke; his excited spittle every now and then caught by the flickering campfire. "Arafat has always been in league with the Zionists, he sold us out at Oslo for his business interests and for keeping his little West Bank Principality, he preferred running protection, it made good money. I should know." He spat into the fire. "May he rot in hell."

Hamza nodded, "yes, Arafat has been completely corrupted by the forces of Satan. I'm sure there is not an *Alim* in the entire *Ummah* who has not said the same from the lowest to the highest *minbar*. But why do you not fight back with everything you have? After all, everyone is with you."

The Palestinian snorted. "Everyone? Don't make me laugh, not everyone is like you my brother. Of course we fight, what do you think the *intifada* is? But we need to do more than just shake the Jews. I have already told you about my home, Jabaliya, where every day the Israelis abuse and kill us. We fight, but we fight with stones and they have these." The Palestinian thrust his Kalashnikov into the air. "And even these are not enough against tanks and their cursed missiles. And anyway, even if none of us is afraid of dying, it is just that our leaders are not."

"Maybe you could try to lead them", said Hamza with a mischievous look.

"Oh yes, you can afford to joke. You are fortunate, you rich Saudis, you can afford humour too eh? But I am here because I have to be. I am hunted in my own land, but you with your oil and your houses, why are you not helping us more?"

Saeed suddenly spoke out. "Because, brother, our leaders are as corrupt as yours, you know that, as well as we do."

The man from the huge refugee camp of Jabaliya nodded. "Yes, yes I know, everywhere it's the same." He shivered and wrapped his clothing tighter around himself. "Do you know what I heard recently?"

"What?" Hamza drew closer.

"I hear that even here in Afghanistan, there is corruption." The Palestinian's piercing black eyes danced in the firelight. "In Kandahar itself"

"Never."

"Some in the *Taliban* are already speaking to the Americans."

Saeed was utterly outraged, "impossible."

"I don't believe it." The normally quiet Ahmed spat into the fire.

The thickset Palestinian turned to the thin man beside him. "Go on Yasser, you tell them what you heard."

The Kashmiri, tall with light blue grey eyes, the colour of Lake Dal on a winter morning nodded. "It's true, they say the Americans want to build a pipeline, natural gas through from Turkmenistan. People are saying it will all happen when Clinton has gone."

"Unbelievable" said Hamza shaking his head.

Saeed cursed and then looked at the man, a native from the roof of the world and then shivered. The temperature was still dropping as precipitously as the mountain sides around them. The Kashmiri, who was in his late twenties, gave a sad shrug and pulled his own warming shawl around himself before giving the Saudi an equally warm smile. They all sat in silence for a moment watching the flames of the fire, deep in thought.

The Kashmiri looked into the fire. "We need a bomb."

"Semtex is best" said Hamza suddenly feeling sure of himself.

"No bigger, I mean a proper bomb, like India or Pakistan, like America", said Yasser with a shake.

Hamza's eye lit up, "you mean nuclear?"

The Kashmiri nodded. "I once felt the ground shake from a test."

Saeed looked impressed, "really?"

Yasser was still staring at the jumping flames of the fire. He looked as if he was almost in a trance. "Now I am become death, the destroyer of worlds."

Hamza looked confused. "What?"

"That's what they said."

Saeed was more and more intrigued by the man from Lake Dal. "What did you do before you came here?"

"I studied physics."

Saeed shivered and gave the blue grey eyed man an envious look. "You never get cold, do you Yasser?"

"I would, but not with this."

"What is it?"

"Goat."

The Palestinian laughed and turned to Hamza. "So, my friend, knowing this, tell me, who is a goat and why do you come here?"

"Trying to get some business out of you Jayem...me?" replied Alex with a mock look of horror.

Jean-Marc gave Alex another warm smile; he hadn't changed, well not so much. "Well you are aren't you?"

"I guess so, but frankly I just wanted an excuse to catch up."

"Well it was a real pleasure seeing you again my friend." As Alex stood up, the Frenchman eyed him up again. His old friend looked so much thinner than he remembered. The head of Banque Paris' capital markets division also got to his feet, sourly reminded that his own girth had grown dramatically since his promotion, now weighed down by more than just his expectations. "Don't make it so long next time eh?"

Alex nodded, suddenly uncomfortable with himself. "No I won't"

Are you taking the train back?"

The intercom rang again. "Your two thirty is still waiting for you, Monsieur Sevres"

Alex checked his watch, "Sorry, I'll be off."

"Well let's do dinner when I'm next over, OK?" They shook hands and Alex started, slightly hesitantly, for the door. "Oh and Alex?"

"Yeah?"

"I'm really sorry about...you know...I didn't..."

Alex stopped and gave his old friend a half smile. "Forget it mate, really. It was my fault."

He stepped out into the suddenly familiar scene and quickly walked across the trading floor. He walked to the elevator, passing the three chirruping receptionists who were still alternately screening and preening. They gave him a perfunctory smile as he passed by, did they remember him? Probably not and he sighed and stepped leaden footed out into the street. He turned and looked back at the chattering threesome, they were like the three Fates, Clotho, Lachesis and Atropos, all chicly draped with Hermes. For a very brief instant he almost wanted to ask them if they could tell him his future before a wave of anger and self loathing once again began to overtake him. He stood absolutely rigid as his mind raced ahead; replaying the lunch he just had with his recently promoted friend. They had talked of the letter, it was never intended but it was unavoidable, it had all just come out. The letter, his failed marriage, everything, but Alex found that he was only asking more and more questions of himself. What had he done, what exactly was he doing now? Still playing all that squash and running around, that is what Jean-Marc had asked him. Running, but running from what?

He pulled out his mobile and dialled. Ever the trader, he never forgot numbers.

It rang a couple of times before a woman's voice answered. "Yes"

"Sandrine, is that you?"

There was a pause on the line, "Sandrine?"

"Is that you Sandrine? It's Alex. Look I'm sorry for calling. I just wanted to say..."

"Who is this?" Alex squinted as he listened intently to the voice. Now he was sure, it was not her.

"Sorry, is Sandrine Giraud there?"

Silence.

Alex' French was creaking and rusty and he had to think for a moment. "Hello can you tell me if Sandrine Giraud still lives there."

The woman's voice was suddenly very hesitant. "I'm sorry, but she has...passed..."

"She's passed?"

The voice ignored his question and called out. He instantly recognized the name the woman used. It was the name of the policeman. Alex heard a muffled noise as the woman spoke and he heard her say his own name. Suddenly a bark came down the line. "Who is this?"

Alex hesitated, "I'm an old friend. I'm..."

"Ah yes, I know exactly who you are, you son of a bitch."

"I'm sorry I just..."

"Well I hope you're happy, what kept you, you fucking asshole?"

Alex was stunned, he had not expected this. "I'm sorry I just"

"Save your breath. Here's something for you, you English cunt, you fucking killed her. Do you know that?"

"What? I..."

"She may have killed herself, but it was thanks to you. Stupid bitch and good riddance, you did me a favour."

"Killed herself?"

"What are you deaf as well as fucking stupid? Don't you understand me? M.O. R. T."

Alex crumpled, "but?"

"Under a train, messy, now fuck off before I call my mates", and the policeman slammed the phone down.

Ed Moore got up as the two men entered his office and walked around to meet them. They were exactly on time, just as he had feared. This was not going to be easy. The two clean cut men, both carrying briefcases and perspiring in their heavy suits, took the seats that Moore offered them and looked around his office. They introduced themselves, as agents Elroy and Andrews.

"So, how can I help you gentlemen?"

The older man spoke first. He had a pair of dark glasses perched on his barrel like chest. "Well first let us thank you for seeing us Mr Moore, we appreciate you're a busy man."

"Well anything to help the FBI is fine by me."

The older man, named Elroy, in his mid thirties, gave the Treasurer a quick smile and a nod. "I'm pleased to hear that. We're just trying to cover all the bases, I'm sure you know the rap."

Moore stared back at the man. "Sure I understand."

"We're investigating a couple of lines of enquiry concerning the attack on the USS Cole."

Moore nodded, "So your colleague said on the phone."

The FBI man opened his case, "Does the name Mohammed Jamal Khalifa, mean anything to you?"

Moore did not blink. "I'm not sure. I could check."

The cop passed a grainy image over to the banker. "He's one of our key suspects. He was also implicated in the hostage situation in December of '98 also in Yemen."

"My, that's quite a long way back."

"It's not even two years." These were the first words spoken Agent Andrews, he was staring directly, unerringly at Moore.

779

Agent Elroy pushed another photograph across. "Well we want to be thorough. It was the same organization, the so called, Islamic Army of Aden."

The man called Andrews lent forward. "Are you aware of a Yemeni company called Al-Sharif Import?"

Moore blinked. "I think I may have heard of that one. Yeah, I think it might have a sister company here in Jeddah."

Andrews was staring right at Ed Moore. "Is that right?"

Elroy pushed a piece of paper across to Ed Moore, "Mohammed Jamal Khalifa is a director of both these companies."

"Mr Moore, did you authorise the transfer from Mazurro Trading a Panama based company of two hundred thousand dollars to Al-Sharif Import here in Jeddah?"

"Yes. I've got all the paperwork."

Andrews gave an ironic shake of his head. "I'm sure you have Mr Moore."

Elroy was still looking down at the papers he had spread out on the low table in front of him. "Are you aware that Mohammed Jamal Khalifa is a brother in law of Osama bin Laden?"

Ed Moore swallowed.

Agent Elroy looked up, fixing Moore with a questioning stare. "Are you also aware that Khalid bin Bafaz the chairman of this... bank, is another brother in law of Osama bin Laden?"

Ed Moore nodded. "Sure I know that. The bin Laden's are a big deal over here. Osama is the black sheep of the family. What do you guys want?"

"Mr Moore ever since June of last year the Saudi Arabian, Osama bin Laden, has been on our most wanted list in connection with the East African embassy bombings and now the attack on the USS Cole."

Ed Moore nodded his understanding.

Agent Elway pulled a stern face. "You are aware that the FBI have a much larger remit than ever before in the light of these horrific events? We're gonna get to the bottom of this. This comes right from the top. Do you understand what I mean?"

"Sure, and I hope you do."

Andrews gave the banker a withering look. "Mr Moore is there anything you want to tell us?"

The American stared back at his interrogators, his mouth clamped shut, silently rueing again that he did not even have a uniform.

Saeed spat the dusty red earth out of his mouth. "In the name of Allah, where did that thing come from?"

Hamza picked himself up from the dirt, his face blackened and torn from the satellite guided explosion. "These infidel

Americans have eyes in the sky everywhere. Allah curse them, the black devils."

Wail, still on his knees, turned and looked back at what was left of the camp they had been in. "Filthy bastard cowards, why can they not fight like men?"

Saeed turned, towards his right, Ahmed was lying motionless, still unconscious from the vicious blast. "Ahmed, Ahmed my brother, are you alright?"

Across in the distance the Kashmiri, Yasser, was now running towards the still prostrate group. "In the name of God, what has happened?" he screamed as the athletic man from the mountains quickly bounded and covered the rocky distance to reach the Saudis. For a moment he briefly paused, surveying the burning wreckage of what was left of the camp that had been their base for the last few days. Deftly the Kashmiri got out his water bottle, knelt and gave it to Saeed who gratefully took a mouthful. Yasser then moved over towards the other injured man and poured some more of the precious elixir onto the blackened and bloodied face of the still lifeless Ahmed. The thin gaunt Saudi responded by slowly opened his eyes.

"Saeed?"

Saeed moved across and was looking down at his friend. "I'm here my brother, Thank Allah, are you OK?"

"My glasses?"

The Kashmiri's eyes searched the broken ground around the prone Ahmed and caught the glint of a lens in the morning light. He leant over, scraped and pulled out the cracked spectacles. "Here, I think you'll need new ones."

Ahmed looked at the two faces above him. "What happened?"

Bloodied and bedraggled the little group made their painful way back to the burning camp. As they approached the carnage of their camp, the cries of dying souls and broken bodies greeted them. They tried to help as much as they could, but it was futile. The dead were already in Paradise, the dying were mercifully on their way. Like many others, the young man from Blackburn had been vaporized.

"In God's name we will avenge this." The group turned, it was the Palestinian, his black eyes blazing with fury.

"Where in the name of Allah have you been?" Hamza's voice was almost accusatory.

"I had gone for a walk, by the grace of Allah" he replied coolly before he pushed past the five men and carried on in the direction of where he had been encamped. He turned, "quickly, pick up whatever is worth taking. The Americans will strike again within the hour."

Within five minutes, they had all done as he had instructed and the six were making their way across the rocky terrain in a tramping single file column. Forty minutes later the air was split by another supersonic crack and in the far distance they heard the sickening boom of a distant explosion. The man from Jabaliya had been absolutely right.

That night the men sat around a small fire but their conversation was smaller than the frightened little fire that they had lit, terrified of being seen by unsleeping eyes from outer space.

Saeed was still fuming with anger. "How did they find the encampment?"

The Palestinian gave the Saudi a sad look. "They have powerful technology my brother, you must always remember that."

Wail shook his head. "Women, children, anyone, they don't care. Infidel monsters."

Hamza turned to the Kashmiri, "You are so right, we need a bomb, the biggest ever and to drop it into the rotten heart of the Devil America."

The Palestinian eyed the Kashmiri and the Saudi, "Just hold on to the fire, remember this. They cannot bomb Allah out of our hearts. They can turn us into feral monsters if they wish, but they will never win, that is why they fight us like this."

Ahmed had tears in his eyes. "I don't understand. The others they died for nothing."

The Palestinian shook his head, "no my brother not for nothing. Every one of us counts in this battle. That is what the Americans don't understand. They have their technology and we are just numbers to them, dots on their devilish computers, blinking targets like their stupid arcade games. But we are not, we are men and every one of us is inspired by the other and by God. We know our cause is just, they know nothing, they believe nothing. They are empty vessels that only fill with the filth of their material world. They are frightened of us."

"Frightened?" Hamza laughed with sour bitterness. "You think these Americans are frightened by us? How can they be? They have everything, missiles, bombs, tanks..."

The Palestinian raised his hand and Saeed wondered how the two men could still be arguing after what they had been through. "No, they are afraid, that is why they don't come and fight us like men."

"But Abbas"

"No, not 'but' my friend, just when? That is the question. Sheikh Osama himself has said. Why will they not fight us? We have tried so hard, we bomb their embassies, we kill their soldiers, we blow up their stinking ships, but still nothing. We need them to come to us, to here in Afghanistan or anywhere in the Islamic world, then we will fight and then they will surely lose as night follows day."

Saeed had tears of frustration rolling down his cheeks. "What in the name of Allah can we do?"

"We will find a way to wake the Devil America, we must. Time is running out for us here in Afghanistan. Did you know that as we speak, the *Taliban* and the Americans are even now in negotiations on this cursed pipeline? They want to pass it through Afghanistan then through Pakistan and even into India. Anywhere, but not through Iran or Russia, they can't buy them, they're too expensive, even for the Americans." The Palestinian spat into the fire. "As we speak the oil executives of America are pouring millions of dollars into corrupt men in Kabul and Kandahar."

"Allah help us", said Saeed with bitter sadness.

"Fear not my brother. We will find a way. We just must." The Palestinian pulled his woollen blanket closer around himself. "Anyway we must get some sleep. Tomorrow we rise early."

The next morning Saeed was awoken by a shove, he licked his dry lips and stared at the orange sky, above him he saw the Palestinian. He was already fully dressed.

"Come on my brother, we need to go."

Saeed raised himself up on his elbows and blinked in the brightening light, his body still ached from the previous days horrors. Slowly he got up. He looked around at the mountainous terrain and then bent down and opened his water bottle, taking a long draft from it. He still felt tired and breathed in the morning air, steeling himself for the day ahead and watching as the three other Saudis also slowly roused themselves.

Yasser was still motionless, he walked over towards the sleeping man. He looked again, his mouth was wide open and a huge gash was slashed across his throat from ear to ear. Saeed swallowed back his horror and revulsion, the earth around the Kashmiri was dark with the blue grey eyed man's spilt blood.

"In the name of God, please no..."

The Palestinian tucked the Kashmiri's shawl around himself. "Don't waste your words. He was a filthy spy. I found this in his bag." He showed Saeed a satellite phone. "He was the one that called the American strike in."

"What?"

"I never trusted him, all that useless talk about bombs and stupid words. I followed him two days ago and then again yesterday. I saw him call, burn in hell, American filth."

Hamza gingerly walked over and stood over the lifeless body of the man from Lake Dal. He raised his eyes and gave the man they called Abbas an unsteady, nervous look. "Don't look so worried my brother, much better to be a goat than a snake."

Alex sat in the busy dealing room utterly transfixed and horrified by the images that flashed before his eyes. The television played the tape of the 'confessions' of the men accused for having blown each other up released by the Saudi Authorities. He saw the expressionless face of the poor wretch, forced to utter the absurd self destructive words. The man's movements were mechanical, his frozen, dead eyed, features almost dreamlike, a marionette caught up in the strings of other men games. Alex swallowed hard, every ghastly memory suddenly vivid in his head. As he stared the woman opposite him watched him and then turned to the screen.

"Why do they say that? They face the death penalty over there don't they?" Alex turned to see the woman who had spoken these words. The American, blonde with a New York investment banker's dentition, stood with her hand on her shapely hip. "I mean...come on, are these guys for real?"

"I don't think they have much of a choice," said Alex in a flat monotone.

The woman turned and gave Alex a look of incredulity. She knew all about choice, Harrods or Bloomingdales, Holland Park or the Hamptons, life was all about making the right ones. "Choice? Perleeese. Honey, believe me, they just need better lawyers."

Alex just nodded, "Yeah that would do it", he muttered under his breath.

"I mean, I just don't understand how they can be so dumb. Weren't you there for a while?"

Alex nodded.

She gave a disbelieving shake of her well coiffured head. "They were trading in...what was it again? Alcohol? Gimme a break."

Alex sighed, what was the point of explaining? That the charges were undoubtedly ridiculous and trumped up? That the trade in alcohol was savagely guarded and jealously controlled by powerful members of the Saudi establishment and that if they had really been involved, that these men would have been dead long ago, buried alive in the hot sands of Arabia. That a single container load, freighted through Dubai, was worth over one and a half million dollars in cold cash, that prohibition had simply raised the level of 'tax' on these goods. Was it worth stating that the price of cocaine that investment bankers snorted, in noisy bars, through hundred dollar bills and fifty pound notes, that the New Yorker frequented, was driven by precisely the same economic forces? Alex looked at her and wondered what kind of break did she think she needed? An arm or a leg, or that recently fixed up nose? Maybe he could tell her that men like his old interrogator Saleh, would provide that service for no extra charge, the pleasure would have been entirely theirs?

She flashed a look at her expensive clunky watch, "anyway, I'm off to lunch." She peered over Alex' head at the view outside, it looked a bit grey and cold, London chilly, not New York chilly. She picked up a shawl and wrapped it warmly around herself.

Alex eyed her for a moment, explaining, he did not even know where to start and anyway she was not even remotely interested. It was a world away and despite whatever he may have thought and felt, nobody cared. It all meant absolutely nothing to anyone. It was utterly irrelevant.

"Nice scarf" said Alex of the flaming fushia coloured wrap. "Isn't it gorgeous? I just love it. I got four last week, aren't they're just divine?" She preened and tucked it around her well toned and expensively clad torso, its softness caressing her perfumed neck. She smiled, ear to ear. "It's called a Pashmina, they're from Kashmir, have fun", and she bustled out for her lunch appointment with her four hundred pound goat hair shawl.

Alex picked up the phone and dialled. "Jim? Hi, how are you   doing?

"I'm fine Alex. I guess you're watching the TV.?"

The same clip had been played at least a half dozen times, caught in the treadmill of a News channel's one track mind, until the next breaking event. "Yeah, have you seen the way those guys look that are accused of blowing up bombs in Riyadh?"

"Yeah", Jim waited nervously for Alex to continue but his silent friend was still tramping the same mental rut.

"I guess it brings back some nasty memories for you?" said Jim his voice sympathetic.

"Maybe there's a big arms deal or a gas contract for grabs?"

"What? Alex, for God's sake, whatever happened to keeping it simple?"

Ed Moore was sick of waiting. He needed some kind of action from his bosses in Langley. The heat was on and no amount soothing words from Pat Leary telling him to stay cool were helping. For the last two years, since the Embassy bombings, his activities had been centred on acting as a small part of the machine that sought to infiltrate and nullify *Al-Qaeda*. The CIA had always been responsible for counter espionage and yet even now, despite all the promises from Virginia that things would soon be back to normal, they were not. Not by a long way. For Ed Moore and his bosses it was unforgiveable that the FBI were still ludicrously involved, attempting to use law and order to counter men who had adopted war like tactics. From the moment that the new President, the son of a former Director of the Agency, had taken office, they had been mouthing the same excuses. The new President's role was to play the goat, and even Moore had to agree that the Texan frat boy did it flawlessly, but was it going to be enough? He looked at the phone, at any moment he might be getting another call from puffed up cops like Andrews and Elroy. Deputy Director Jim O'Neill, their boss, was the FBI's top Al-Qaeda expert and chief bin Laden hunter. He had been responsible for investigations into the bin Laden-connected bombings of the World Trade Center in 1993, the destruction of an American troop barracks in Al-Khobar in 1996, the African embassy bombings in 1998, and now the attack upon the U.S.S. Cole in 2000. He was a menace, connecting the dots and for Moore and the CIA, it was not a pretty picture that was emerging.

The phone rang. Moore's heart was pounding in his chest.

"Yes George?"

"It's Pat Leary"

"Thanks George, can you put him through please?"

"Would you like a coffee Sir?" The perceptive Filipino knew what was good for him.

"That would be great."

The secretary put the call through, hung up his phone and made his slow limping way off to the machine.

"Pat?"

"Some good news for you Ed."

"I'm all ears", replied the man from the land of Lincoln, Kennedy, Roosevelt.

"We're in the clear, we've got O'Neill, sideways and out. He's gone."

Moore could not believe this, it was fantastic news. "What about the rest of the team?"

"Everything, totally decommissioned and redeployed. The nightmare's over."

"I don't know what to say." The banker almost felt like crying, the pressure had been intolerable.

"C'mon Ed you always knew we'd pull through."

Moore sighed and he felt his calm recovering. "Did you?"

The CIA man was silent for a moment. "Oh and we've been able to tidy up a few loose ends too, the Yemen thing for one."

"You have?"

"Yup, we've not been idle. It's still a mess, but we're cleaning it up. I'll update you in the normal way."

Ed Moore was intrigued. "So what's happened to O'Neill then?"

"You can forget about him, he's quit to become head of security at the WTC."

Moore gave a short mirthless laugh. "Thanks Pat."

Later that evening Ed Moore was reading his decrypted brief, the crowd of acronyms that his eyes fell upon informing him that all was restored in the garden. The cell they had covertly nursed, the so called assets, in CIA parlance had been neutralised. Unmanned satellite guided planes, armed with laser missiles had been sent to erase the last remnants of desperate men hiding in hovels in far corners of the world. Moore pulled a wry half smile, unmanned, that was a joke, each hi-tech sortie involved fifty five highly trained personnel; pilots, navigators, metrologists, engineers, programmers, linguists, technicians, logisticians, tacticians, strategists. All they had needed was a text message and Mohammed Jamal Khalifa was atomized as effectively and as routinely as half a dozen other targets around the globe. Pat Leary was as good as his word. They had been far from idle.

Unable to sleep, Saeed stopped picking at his teeth with his *mishwak* and silently began to pack his small collection of belongings into the canvas bag. Faded and threadbare, incredibly it had been with him all these years, his uncomplaining companion since he had carried it off from his home in far off Jeddah. Along its battered side the lettering had almost entirely faded but if he held it at the right angle to the light he could still just about read it, 'Red Sea Divers.' In the lining of the side pocket he pushed a hand in, felt about and brought out a tatty folded envelope. He opened it and pulled out the frayed photograph. He rarely looked at the image, as it always had the same effect on him despite the passage of years; sadness. He stared at the faces, his parents, his brother and sister and that of his own smiling, prepubescent features. Like Ed Moore he also flashed a wry ironic smile to himself, for the scene was comic, ridiculous, a little dark eyed Arab boy dressed as a cowboy. To this day he still did not know what had motivated him to take that particular photograph. Initially it had been something like embarrassment, but over the years he had never found it within himself to ever destroy the foolish image. He kept it, partially as a reminder of how far he had come, but also because deep within him and no matter how he tried, there was still, the smouldering embers of a loving remembrance. Even so, in his mind it was now absolutely, crystal clear. Yes it was sad, for they had done this to him, but they only had themselves to blame. In the end, Allah would be his sole judge, not his infidel enemies. He checked his watch, gave the photograph one last look and carefully returned it to where he had kept it. He washed, said his prayers and made his way to the airport and on to Paradise.

When in 1914, Gavrilo Princip fired his revolver in Sarajevo he could not have imagined that his actions would forever change the entire world and millions would die. However the men that flew the hijacked planes on September eleventh were never under such an illusion. Emphatically not, their actions were wholly intended to provoke, shock, outrage and revolt. They were not to be disappointed. Up to that day, all Alex knew of 9/11 was that it was the model of Porsche Willi Spethmen drove; that was all going to change. He and the rest of the world watched in horror as the images of the tragedy unfolded. On that terrible day, everyone became a New Yorker. Like many on the world's financial trading floors, Alex' initial response was to react, that was after all, what he was paid to do. He like many London based traders, thanks to their experience of terrorism first hand, reacted by buying Government bonds and selling everything else, it was easy money but even this hideous avarice halted as the sickening images filled screens and senses. In the end there was just numbness.

The appalling nature of the event was not lost on anyone, least of all Arab leaders. Nobody wanted to be tarred with this desperate mark of Cain. It was condemned by everyone. When after some days the story finally started to emerge that seventeen of the nineteen suicide bombers had come from Saudi Arabia, there were many that breathed a huge sigh of relief. Paradoxically, overnight, the moral high ground had been wrestled from the iniquities of the West Bank to the ash covered brownstones of Manhattan. New York, never shy, picked itself up and stepped forward, transformed into a secular, muscular, Mecca. Shock turned to fury in the land of the mighty dollar and someone was going to pay.

As the days passed by, the names and faces of the Saudis responsible for the outrage flashed around the globe. Alex picked up the newspaper and looked at the photographs of the faces that stared from the pages in front of him. One caught his eye and he suddenly felt physically sick. It could not be so. He read the caption under the face. No, he must, just had to be mistaken, besides the name was entirely wrong. He sat for a while, blankly staring at the plethora of screens in front of him, the flickering beacons of his daily existence, which had always guided him, through turbulent and perilous markets, to his daily bread. He tried to focus on the flashing digits but the thought just would not go away.

He picked up his phone and called his friend. "Jim?"

"Hi Alex, how are you?"

Alex ignored the question. "Jim, have you seen the pictures of them, the...?" Alex did not know how to describe them, hijackers, murderers, monsters, Saudis? They were all these things and as he suddenly horribly, realised, so much more.

"Of what?"

"The men, the photographs of the men responsible for 9/11?"

"Sure I've seen them, why?"

"Have you looked at them closely?"

"Not particularly." Jim was wondering where this was all going.

"Have you got the pictures there now?"

"Of course I have Alex. They're in every single paper."

"Just have another look, tell me what you see."

Jim's face creased up with incomprehension. "What now?"

"Yes, I'll hang on while you do it."

Jim Robson picked up the paper and gazed at the faces. "Do you mind telling me what I'm supposed to be looking for?"

"Have you seen him yet?"

Frustration tinged Jim's voice. "Who am I looking for Alex?"

"Mohammed Al Hamra"

"What? For Christ sake Alex, are you serious?"

"I'm telling you Jim it's him. Look at the face of the one named Saeed Al Ghamdi."

Jim scanned the paper, there was a bunch of Al Ghamdis. He searched through the names and peered at the face. He studied it carefully.

"Well?"

"I don't know. OK, there's a resemblance, but I couldn't swear to it. Anyway, the name tells you it's not him."

"Oh c'mon Jim, it's him, look at the eyes."

"Look Alex, I've got to hop. I'll speak to you later OK?"

Alex had to know. He immediately called the main number for IAB in Jeddah. "Can I speak to Omar Al-Hamra."

The voice was hesitant, "I'm afraid he is no longer with us."

Alex recognized it. "George?"

"Yes, who is this?"

"It's me, Alex Bell."

"Hi Alex, how are you?"

"I'm fine thanks. Omar has gone?"

"I'm afraid so, he had a heart attack about six months ago."

"Shit, Is Khalid Abu Anzi there?" Alex was in a hurry.

"Sure, I'll put you through. Take care Alex."

"Thanks George."

"Well this isn't a surprise Alex. And how are you?" said Khalid.

Alex ignored the prickly sarcasm. "I'm fine thanks Khalid and how are you?"

"Well all things considered, I guess I can say OK, but that would be about it. Anyway it's been a long time since your name came up round here, how can I help you?" His old trainee did not sound happy and suddenly Alex didn't know quite what to say.

"Is everything all right Khalid?"

"Well if you think being called a murdering bastard by so called professional people is OK, then I guess I'm having, as you used to say, a slice."

"Shit I'm sorry about that."

"Well I'm glad at least to hear that from you. I tell you Alex, it's been a nightmare. Why the fuck did they have to come from here? People here just can't believe it you know?"

"I can imagine."

"Those people they say are responsible, they're all aliases. God knows where they're really from. One father was on telly last night saying that the picture was not his son, it was nothing like him. People here say Mossad are behind it or the CIA."

"Come on Khalid."

"Anyway, I'm sorry about my earlier comments. For a second then I thought you might be about to do the same."

Alex was silent, suddenly guiltily aware that this was not going to be easy. Saudi Arabia needed people like Khalid, in fact right now, not just Saudi Arabia, the whole world did. At least he could try to be tactful. "I heard about Omar, how is he?"

Khalid spoke in his careful, soft way. "Not good Alex, Do you know his hair went white overnight?"

"My God, poor man."

"I'm sorry to say that we're prepared for the worst."

"I see. I'm really very sorry to hear that." Alex suddenly felt awful.

"I'll pass on your regards."

He still needed to know. "Yes please do. Say, how are your cousins, Talal and Mohammed?"

Khalid sighed. "Talal's fine, still crazy about football, but nobody has heard from Mohammed for years. He disappeared in Riyadh. To be honest with you I think it's the reason why Omar is so sick."

"Right well..."

Khalid sounded strange, more distant than ever. "Do you remember the boat accident Alex?"

"Of course I do."

"Hard to forget eh?" he gave a sad empty little laugh. "You know, sometimes I think it would have been..."

Alex felt like crying.

"Goodbye Khalid."

"Goodbye Alex."

Alex tramped the dark streets to his simple one bedroom flat in the run down area that was now his home. His neighbour was just leaving as he put the key in the latch. The tall black man briefly stared at him. Bald, he reminded Alex of Chris Barma and Alex gave him a brief smile. His neighbour in turn gave a nod of recognition and passed on. Alex opened the door and turned on the lights. He stepped over to the window and stared at the dark reflection of himself, older, thinner, sadder, suddenly remembering his long ago interview with Barma. What was it that Barma had asked him? That was it. What one word would describe him today as he stared back at himself? Foolish, preening, thoughtless, greedy, selfish, broken, lonely, just one, it had to be...changed.

The world too had also changed, for the law of unintended consequences did not just apply to Alex. Armed with its moral authority America dispatched battle groups; Lincoln, Kennedy and Roosevelt to the Arabian Gulf, dropped Daisy Cutters and fired missiles galore. It was to be awe inspiring and biblical in its response, an eye for an eye until blind fury was its only guide. They tore up Tora Bora and the Geneva Convention, brought back torture and the Guantanamo Gulag. Put up the Patriot Act, muzzled and cowed the FBI, chucked out habeas corpus and trial by jury. At home the police were acting like an occupying army and soldiers were sent off abroad to do policing in lawless, ungovernable places. As far as Alex could see, now the West was much more like Saudi Arabia, than ever before, which would have pleased the confused Arab boy in the cowboy hat no end. The only difference being that its secular religion is materialism and the penitent purchase carbon credits, like latter day indulgences, to ease their path to the sales.

Printed in Great Britain
by Amazon

27429909R00443